# ARCHETYPAL

## JOSEPH TRAVERS MACKINNON

Guy Faux Book Company Ltd.
Toronto, Canada

For my parents. Thank you for your wisdom, support, and love.

"The mind is its own place, and in itself can make a Heav'n of Hell, a Hell of Heav'n."

Milton, *Paradise Lost*

# ARCHETYPAL

JOSEPH TRAVERS MACKINNON

# PROLOGUE

Five months ago, Los Angeles was turned upside down by a series of strategic attacks on the Outland Corporation and its data-storage facilities. The rationale was not political but rather personal, spurred by a decade-old tragedy. The individual linking the blood lost then and coagulating now: borderline-psychotic Outland Noosphere Department head, Dr. Paul Sheffield.

Sheffield, along with his assistant Dr. Oni Matsui, his partner Dr. Shouta Katajima, and Oasis-systems engineer Allen Scheele, together developed a virtual space called the CLOUD wherein time could be dilated and users could instantaneously assimilate one another's experiences. The CLOUD was lauded by then-Outland-CEO Niles Winchester III as a tool to prevent war, witness impossible arts, regain lost memories, and communally redesign society. It would become Outland's gift to the old world and the catalyst for the new.

Driving Sheffield's interest in the technology was his fear that the neurological defect plighting his youngest daughter, Pythia, would be her ruin. Dead set on curing her and convinced the CLOUD was the way, Sheffield rushed its development and began human trials, ignoring protest from Outland's Board of Directors as well as from Drs. Matsui and Katajima.

Allen Scheele was the first human inductee into Sheffield's CLOUD prototype. This feat was possible only as a result of the synchronization of his neural implant, Sheffield's CLOUD servers, and Outland's data-storage towers (i.e. "cypulchres"). Within seconds of entry, Scheele amassed an encyclopaedic breadth of knowledge too great for both his organic brain and the storage-unit assigned to support it.

Scheele's colleagues celebrated his flawless introduction to the virtual space, but their excitement quickly turned to terror. Given the limited means of data-storage they had at their disposal and the rapid growth of Scheele's virtual brain, there was no way they could reunite him with his body before incompatibility set in.

Pythia's cure eluded Sheffield and in its pursuit he had killed a friend.

While Scheele's body rotted away, Sheffield was brought before the Outland Board of Directors. Upon clear demonstration of guilt, he was handed over to local law enforcement. Although Sheffield had pre-emptively destroyed his recollection of what was tantamount to

1

manslaughter—effectually lobotomizing himself and further undermining his sanity—CCTV footage and Dr. Katajima's testimony were sufficient evidence for a conviction. Coinciding with his conviction, Sheffield was also fired, divorced from his wife, and exiled.

While Sheffield slowly lost his mind in isolation in the Californian desert, Outland continued to develop the CLOUD with plans for a wide public release. To both the technology and Sheffield's credit, the CLOUD's first official use was in the brokerage of the peace accord that ended the Unholy War. After this high-profile proof of concept, Outland's CLOUD tech went to market and instantly became massively popular.

Frequent CLOUD-use led to dependence, and dependence strengthened Outland's technological dominance in and over Los Angeles. Cypulchres popped up across California and Jefferson, ensuring constant synchronization. Body modifications enabling physical maintenance also proliferated, sustaining users' CLOUD-highs and transforming Outland's affiliate BiAnima into a federally-recognized utility company. In the ten years Paul spent cursing Outland, it had quadrupled in size.

Dr. Katajima, who replaced Sheffield as head of the Noosphere Department, broke protocol and contacted Sheffield to inform him of the official pronouncement of Allen Scheele's death. (The CLOUD prototype to which Scheele's mind had been assigned was thoroughly wiped in a humanitarian sweep.) However, Katajima's was more than a courtesy call. He wanted to use Scheele's funeral as an excuse for Paul to re-enter the city of Los Angeles—the idea being that Sheffield might be able to help him troubleshoot a data-anomaly wreaking havoc inside the CLOUD and assimilating user-data at an alarming rate.

Dr. Katajima's plea came at a particularly odd time for Sheffield. Sheffield's paranoia was off the charts. He had just received a cryptic message from an Outland server within hours of learning that his daughter had been implanted and permitted use of the CLOUD. Mindful that his daughter Pythia was potentially threatened along with the millions of other Americans who regularly used the CLOUD, Sheffield agreed to help Dr. Katajima.

Sheffield determined that the data anomaly was an extinctive event for CLOUD users. Unfortunately, his warnings, parroted to Winchester by Katajima, were disregarded. Winchester was either apathetic or being manipulated by misinformed or malicious counsel.

Necessity forced Katajima to use his position within the Outland Corporation to secure for his unlikely partner tools with which he could troubleshoot and eliminate the anomaly. Katajima's subversion did not go unnoticed.

While readying his personal computer at his desert compound for Sheffield to remotely access the CLOUD, Katajima's BiAnima implant was hacked. The hacker took control of Katajima's body and tore it to shreds. Implicated in the murder, Sheffield was forced to flee the compound, taking with him Katajima's personal computer.

Deemed a high-priority target by local and state authorities, Sheffield went into hiding and sought the help of a few unlikely allies to bring down the CLOUD. Dr. Oni Matsui, who left Outland in protest of its CLOUD-tech soon after Scheele's death and Sheffield's dismissal, agreed to lend Sheffield a hand. At her field clinic where she administered help to CLOUD addicts and to those who had lost memories after being unable to pay for Outland's data-storage services, Matsui revealed to Sheffield that she too was monitoring the data anomaly. They agreed that the anomaly was not only a threat to CLOUD users, but to humanity as a whole.

Along with Matsui's band of humanitarian renegades—Father Edmund Barros and Booker Gibson—she and Sheffield determined that the only way they could stop the alleged anomaly and protect all of the minds unwittingly threatened inside and by the CLOUD would be to finish Sheffield's program called the Empty Thought.

The Empty Thought was a program Sheffield worked on at Outland, analogous to a black hole: no data could escape it. Sheffield and Matsui speculated that by implanting the Empty Thought directly into the cypulchre housed within the Outland Citadel, they might have a chance of destroying the anomaly. To avoid destroying the minds also in the CLOUD, they would have to "rain them out" using either Katajima's personal computer or Winchester's personal kill-switch, located in his Citadel office.

Concerned for the safety of CLOUD users and his company, Winchester sent two Sentinel squads to assassinate Sheffield and Matsui, as well as to capture Katajima's personal computer. In the ensuing firefight, Matsui's Rift-side clinic, Camp MUD, was ravaged and her staff abducted.

Sheffield followed the hostage-takers to the PIT in hopes of freeing Matsui's staff and recovering Katajima's personal computer. He was unsuccessful in rescuing either, and returned empty-handed to witness Father Edmund die of wounds sustained in the melee.

Sheffield, Matsui, and Booker Gibson agreed, shortly after the failed assassinations, that they now had no other option than to break into the Citadel, knowing full-well such an incursion would be their last.

They distracted Outland Security Forces by organizing attacks on a number of Outland outposts and cypulchres, and proceeded to hijack an Outland cargo jet destined for the Citadel. On arrival, Sheffield and Matsui killed over fifteen service personnel and a small army of droids, while Gibson supervised their progress from Camp MUD.

Matsui snuck into the Citadel cypulchre to upload an encrypted version of the Empty Thought to Sheffield's off-board memory server.

Sheffield went straight up to Winchester's office where he determined to either convince Winchester to rain out the CLOUD or throw the kill-switch himself. By the time Sheffield made his way into Winchester's office, the security mechs accompanying the CEO had already been hacked by the anomaly. The result was bloody.

Winchester was eviscerated and Sheffield mortally wounded. Despite his injuries, however, Sheffield still managed to flip the kill switch and rain out all of the CLOUD subscribers. He then rigged an explosive device and synchronized with the CLOUD.

When Sheffield's explosive device went off, his body was obliterated. In the event of a user's death, the CLOUD automatically assimilates all of his off-board data. In this case, the CLOUD decrypted Sheffield's off-board memory as well as the Empty Thought stored inside it. The program was fast to act. It destroyed all CLOUD data, including Sheffield and the anomaly he sought after.

Outland Security tracked Dr. Matsui down and pursued her to the rooftop of the Citadel, where she hijacked Winchester's personal Dragonfly jet. Neither jet nor pilot have been seen since.

# CHECK

Three floors shy of Winchester's blown-up office, a tall woman in a black-and-white collared splice-dress and a Patton-esque US Marine stand crewed together overlooking midnight Los Angeles. The Outland Corporation's Citadel offers the most definitive and the most biased view of the city. On a night like this, with few clouds except those grouping like tumors over the ocean, you can see the blue rings of plasma jets keeping colonial frigates airborne over Seal Beach. Even further south—nothing more than a faint orange tinge on the horizon—you can almost make out the rebel fires in San Clemente. Even without daylight casting the Citadel's shadow over the RIM or the PIT, this is undeniably a triumphant view. *Up here, you feel like a god.*

Waving away the General's cigar smoke, Interim Outland CEO Celeste Charming topples the first domino in her argument. "They aren't afraid of death." Leaning over the baluster, she continues: "They are one in many. They are archetypals. Each and every one of them is contained in the Omnitype, and the Omnitype is, at least in part, contained in each of them. Find the Omnitype, General, and you will find your peace. Kill it and the archetypals will die confused like royal guards without a monarch. Control it, and you will be more powerful than anyone in the history of the world."

General McCabe is no stranger to power. He has levelled mountains, moved borders, and dethroned desert kings. He knows its corruptive quality and resists the Caesarian drive to take more than what he has been given by the Republic. Making his disgust known with those muscles left unsevered under his thick skin, McCabe glowers. "I highly doubt that."

"Doubt without evidence is belief, and belief is vulnerability. The archetypals are not like you or I. They have lived outside of their humanity. They have touched the darkness and stolen its secrets… Forget about their evolved communal intellect and telekinetic abilities—think about what a group unconcerned with individual aspirations can accomplish."

"Ms. Charming," says McCabe dryly, puffing his chest and slimming his scarred neck with a stretch. "I know exactly what such a group is capable of." He flakes burnt corojo onto the deck. "I call mine *the United States Marines*. Difference is my boys have had three hundred years of practice."

"One practices what he wishes to be, General. The archetypals need no practice. They simply *are*. Nothing—no one—can stop them if they are unified." Celeste looks past the General to the Outland transports tracing chalk outlines over the somber sky. "Not without the support of the Outland Corporation."

McCabe grinds his teeth so hard it sounds like he is popping corn. "*Is that right?* Well forget the Corporation. Your predecessor's recklessness is the very reason these mutants exist. Never mind the fact that you threw the CLOUD up in the first place. Recklessness I can abide. But weakness? *You* let it fall!"

"*Niles Winchester* let it fall."

"Same difference."

"Oh no, General. I disagree. If it were up to me, the Anarchist and his friends would have died long before they starting blowing holes into humanity's future. The CLOUD was never the problem; it is human frailty—an inability to embrace what the future has left on our doorstep."

McCabe turns to face the city he is charged to protect from tyranny, including the kind schemed in twenty-thousand-dollar dresses. "I wasn't born yesterday, Ms. Charming. I know all about Paul Sheffield and Allen Scheele. Outland has risked the lives and minds of countless Americans before. It won't do it again."

"The CLOUD saved innumerable American lives by ending the Unholy War through complete understanding."

"I'd say we arrived at complete understanding after we evidenced the efficacy of the Shadow Bomb…You will see to it that your company cooperates. I have full oversight and no time for shuttered windows. All secrets out in the light. And, *Ms. Charming*, if Outland stands in the way, the way *will* be cleared."

"Well of course, General." Celeste nods to the point of bowing.

The General drops his cigar and stamps it out with the toe of his boot. He horks over the railing and starts inside, finished with the conversation and having set his conditions; he's made the Republic's will known.

"Please permit me a minute more…That is, if you want to protect *your men*."

The General stops in his tracks. A youthful look breaks the pillory of wrinkles and scars set about his eyes. It is a look he has not worn in a long time. Old men of rank usually have come to grey because of their excellence and luck, but also and more frequently than not, because somewhere along the way they managed to take hatred out of their emotional sequencing. Hatred, after all, clouds judgment, sours the will, and makes good men bad. Until this very moment, McCabe had control of his hatred. However, with two words said just right—an appeal to his love for his men—Celeste has elicited love's darkly-reflected twin, knowing full well she can direct it, mold it, and set it to complement her agenda. "The hell did you just say?" he spits, restraining what his long-allayed emotion bids him do.

"Your troops..." Celeste clasps her hands at her waist. "You must inoculate them against the archetypals' powers."

Turning to face Celeste, McCabe responds: "The archetypals are a bunch of malnourished rainouts. Once *the culling* is approved, it'll take me an afternoon, if that...*My men* can handle themselves. "

"The archetypals' intellects grew by an order of magnitude in the CLOUD...They can mentally crush an aggressor in more than one way."

"And you know this how?" McCabe asks, balling his fists.

"I have teams running tests."

"Tests!?" McCabe roars. He steps within reach of Celeste—close enough for her to smell his rotting gums. "Are you telling me Outland has abducted American citizens on American soil?"

To her credit, Celeste is no slouch. She looks McCabe dead in the eyes and answers back with a machine-gun lilt: "The same Americans you wish to kill on American soil. After the attack, we had innumerable employees and Outland contractors exhibiting bizarre behaviour. Outland tried to help its own, but they proved to be beyond saving. Plighted with psychoses and cultish delusion. Some were exercising mental powers we didn't think possible."

"Are they contagious?" McCabe shakes his fist, not so much at Celeste but more so at her suggestions. "Should I be expanding the quarantine zone?"

"A quarantine isn't necessary. These anomalies are bound to others like them, which will make it easier to bury them with broad strokes. Once they're eliminated, *that's it.*"

"So what is inoculation going to accomplish?"

"Your forces will be shielded from mental attacks."

McCabe lowers his arm and adjusts his jacket. Looking dolefully to his base on Seal Beach, he nods. "I presume Outland can help in this regard."

7

"Absolutely."

"And the favour?"

"I suppose less a favour and more tit for tat. I'll see to it that your forces are equipped to handle the archetypals if you'll permit my Sentinels to assist in the hunt and elimination of certain high-priority targets."

"That is out of the question."

"Consider it a coalition of the willing. You might even save Uncle Sam some money and blood."

McCabe grinds his teeth and nods. "Alright Ms. Charming, I will let you join your link to my chain. If it bends, I will personally take it to the anvil."

# NOSEDIVE

Metal on metal screeches riff on the *ruh-re-re* bass line blaring from an incoming jet's exhaust nozzles. This destructive refrain is neither normal nor desired; the norm would be a low, pulsating hum, and even the most confident pilot would desire total silence. Signalled by a pop, there is a crescendo in the brutal score. The doomed jet bleeds smoke and flame over the partitioned city of Los Angeles like a meteor gravitationally hugged to death.

The commotion overhead drowns out the sound of the medical tent's quavering and finds Dr. Oni Matsui, dazed. She has blood on her hands and a mangled body on the medical gurney before her. She does not recognize the patient. She does not remember scrubbing-in, trying to stitch the pieces together, giving death another victory, or much else for that matter. *It's alright*, she tells herself. *You're at Camp MUD, your home away from a home away on the RIM's eastern border, a canyon away from the walled-off PIT.*

A thunderous burst seizes Oni's attention and pulls her into the scene and out of the tent. The jet—an Outland *meat transport*, full of subversive subscribers, unconscious hackers, and enemies of the Outland Corporation—is on a crash course with the easternmost edge of the RIM, the Rift: a deep secondary fault line halving Los Angeles that marks the RIM-PIT border.

The jet—designed with the presumption of perpetual thrust—does not have the aerodynamics necessary to keep it up let alone permit it glide gracefully to some RIM airstrip. Three out of its six engines are ablaze. The other three are groaning, attempting to compensate. The attempt is no good, though; the massive black-and-white-striped transport rolls Oni's way, glinting in the dying evening light. Although it might be a fatal progress, any Outland pilot would take a RIM-side death and a Rift-basin burial over a PIT-side landing.

Oni quickly surveys her surroundings. In addition to the braindead RIM jocks pointing unloaded rifles at the corporate comet and a few patients walking about on their own volition half-naked, there are several nurses tending to the infirm. Among them and leading by example: Emily and Constance. Of all the people in her woeful life—barring Father Edmund Barros and her exiled mentor, Dr. Paul Sheffield—these two women are the closest Oni has to friends and the most knowledgeable about Camp MUD's security protocols.

"Emily!" Oni screams, directing her voice to the leathered

nurse with the saffron-coloured hair. "Throw up the concussion shield, double-time! I'll try to reboot the cannon."

Emily does not register the order. In fact, she does not react at all. Her fingers are linked, vaulted, and shaking. The rest of her body is eerily still as if set in marble by epic disappointment.

The meat transport sags in the direction of Camp MUD.

*Tarnation.* With an intended Pygmalion effect, Oni screams sense into the statuesque nurse: "Em! Come on! Get the shield up! Then get everyone you can gather into the compound, yourself included. Do not open it for anybody."

Emily turns a vacant stare Oni's way, revealing a grotesque aberration: her nose is crushed and her mouth is sealed without any evidence of so much as a crease having ever been there. A sympathetic cry forms on Oni's lips, but she stops, noticing the iconoclastic vision of Emily begin to flicker. The terrible state her friend finds herself in is not plausible, Oni decides. She silently diagnoses herself with *sleep deprivation* to account for this unprecedented hallucination. The alternative—instability of the variety suffered by her mentor, Paul Sheffield—is loathesome: *seeing things; forgetting things...Can insanity be transmitted mind to mind virtually?* Returning to real time and faced with a monster and a falling star, Oni concludes: *The most dangerous of all diseases: one that targets reality and dismantles it, brick by brick, byte by byte.* "Em, just do it," Oni yells, re-committing to her self-diagnosis. She points with an authoritarian firmness. "Damn the cannon. I'll get the shield. Just get these people out of here."

Oni races to the security tent. The balls of her feet barely touch the ground. It feels like her mind is lifting her body—as if will alone dictates her course. An implant-scarred patient, dragging his IV along like a blind man his dead dog on a leash, stumbles into her way, just feet shy of the security tent. Oni miraculously makes no contact with the skeletal CLOUD-addict despite traipsing right through his immediate path. Untouched, she drives into the tent, compulsively muttering, "Sleep deprivation," under her breath.

The rainfly chaperons her inside a dim theatre. Dust lends shape to the inconstant glow of a stack of monitors and holofields whose pale light blasts a pair of greasy chairs, a few utility crates, and some ammo boxes on the other side of the tent. Camp MUD pulsates on the screens, divided into conceptual and literal feeds; some drone-mounted and others composites of granular-sensor readings. The words, "INCOMING PROJECTILE" strobe in bold red across the spider-eyed array.

Oni slaps in her biometrics and activates the concussion shield. The shield will absorb one-third of the impact's energy, which it will repurpose to deflect smaller fragments and slightly reduce the larger projectile's speed. That is the idea, anyway. It is not in the same league as a plasmic shield, but the best MUD can muster.

The Outland meat shuttle's roaring engines now sound more human than machine; their message to the hapless and helpless voyeurs below: that this peril is mutually felt and personal. Oni refuses to be wowed by the noise. She doublechecks her digital request as well as the shield's stats. A readout on the top-right screen suggests a success rate of seventy-five percent. The passing B-grade and the meaningless glyphs cycling behind it restore Oni's confidence in this first- and last-ditch effort. It is enough to tinge her cheeks rose.

Additional alerts overlap the previous warnings: "PROJECTILE FRAGMENTATION POSSIBLE." In tandem with the bad news, seventy-five drops to thirty-eight percent, and on that dire note, the spider eye of screens blinks and—with a punctuated flash—fades to glossy black.

Oni jolts forward, tapping furiously on her control tablet. "What the hell?"

A stream of two-dimensional symbols runs down the spider eye diagonally, lighting screens en route to bottom-right. Another message appears, defying and finding space in the chaos: "Oni, are you there? We have to get out. Can't keep doing this. They are coming for you."

The spider eye goes dark again. This time, the CPU pops, sending gizmos hissing every which way. A spark arcs from the smoldering sphere to Oni's hand. Pain climbs up her arm, and realizes its full, agonizing potential in her shoulder. Stifling a cry, she reminds herself that *pain subsides, death abides,* and dashes out of the tent to face the Icarian menace plaguing her cripple castle.

Stepping into the shadow of the jet, Oni clasps her hands behind her head and sighs. The screaming engines dub the sound of her shock as the jet penetrates Camp MUD's air space. Surveying the prospective collateral damage, she notices that the camp is empty. *Good job, Emily. That's my girl.*

Oni jerks forward in advance of the collision, feeling a chill push through her core. Ghostly outlines swarm her and disappear into the bullet-riddled compound west of the clinic. They wail and moan as they cut through, by, and around Oni, leaving imprints of their motion in the air behind them like smokescreen Polaroid's. Righting herself, Oni zeroes-in on the jet. *Whatever is causing these visions, sleep deprivation or not, can likely be cured by a ninety ton weigh-in.*

There is another crack and a massive boom.

The ship's other three engines erupt into flame two-hundred-yards out. Whatever push was orienting the meat shuttle RIM-side and towards Camp MUD disappears, and the zebra monstrosity rolls east towards the Rift. Debris from the jet is splashed away from the clinic by MUD's shield.

Although she lacks both her former mentor's faith and her parents' superstition, Oni silently expresses her gratitude. To who or to what, she is not sure. Luck? A blessing? Divine intervention? Her prayer transforms into admiration. *Dependable engineering and, for lack of a sword, sturdy shielding.*

Gone is the threat, but so too the threatened: the ghosts that frenzied about the camp before are nowhere to be seen. In fact, Oni's team and the few patients who were mobile—hell, even the ones strapped down to gurneys clogging the tent alley—have vanished. Under the concussion-shield's protective dome, Oni Matsui stands alone.

A dull thud announces the Outland meat shuttle's destructive end. Absent some secondary bang or explosion, Oni is imbued with a sense of hope and urgency: to rescue the slaves and enemies of the Outland Corporation, and salvage some life-saving technology from the crashed jet for her clinic.

Head on a swivel for stragglers, Oni returns to the security tent. Inside, the screens are still offline and the processor sphere is damaged beyond repair. In the darkness opposite the defunct stack, Oni seeks out her shotgun. After rummaging through three empty crates, she cracks open a fourth containing a variety pack of brutal implements, including her shotgun and a BFG on-loan. Right arm paralyzed with inexplicable pain, she reaches in for the chrome tri-barrel with her left. As she grips it and her index finger finds its groove, myriad voices start on her like an all-consuming static. The pleas and attention-grabs cancel out one another's meaning, becoming nothing more than an incoherent scream. This scream is short-lived, however; one voice humbles the rest: "We going to go through the motions again? Alright then. After you."

This auditory hallucination is as convincing as the surrounding reality, jeopardizing Oni's relationship with it. That being said, the shotgun in her hands feels awfully genuine. She opens it and examines the action, deliberating on her next.

*Something's seriously off.* "Monocle," she says, feeding the shotgun shells, barrel by barrel. Her subdermal implant projects an overlay one millimetre in front of her eye. "Schedule a full self-diagnostic. Doublecheck connectivity between prefrontal cortex and substantia nigra. Submit all observations to Father Ed for review…Block all chat and mute all incoming comms."

Satisfied that she has at the very least officiated her intention to tackle her s*leep deprivation*, Oni recommits to finding and making the most out of the crash site, *Outland be damned.* She activates a live-holographic map of the area and pinpoints the crash via Monocle. The makeshift bridges and piping hanging out over the Rift have prevented the wreckage from falling to the bottom. Wet, septic overflow from the eastern walled city slicked the ship's touch-down so it did not explode into a million unsalvageable pieces.

At the head of the Rift trail, a worn American flag struggles to flap, but has folded in on itself. An accidental knot in the halyard has caught higher up the pole, hiding at least twenty of the fifty-five stars. Beneath Old Glory waves the RIM's defiant bear and its Kingsnake necklace with the motto: "N'ne more ready. N'ne more free." Passing the colours, Oni grimaces. She cannot identify with this place let alone with the thoughts in her head. Who or what deserves her loyalty, she wonders. *My friends? No. Perhaps the cause*: destroying the Outland Corporation *for my friends.* That is if one can be loyal to such a cause— loyal to a proposed absence. *Paul would call me satanic.* She thumbs back two of the gun's three hammers and smirks. "Fitting," she says aloud for only her benefit, "that I should be headed for the PIT."

It would take the uninitiated hours to find a safe way across the Rift where it widens to a proper canyon near Camp MUD, especially at twilight, but the acrobatic routine takes Oni no time at all. Swinging from an old power line to a cantilever bridge, one rainfall away from slipping into the marsh far below, she completes the cross. Monkeying over to the PIT-side has left her right arm throbbing. She takes a moment and a painkiller, and zooms in on her objective, dwarfed both by the cliffs and the Partition wall above—sealing PIT rats in and keeping the prying eyes of the world out.

The crashed ship's black and white armor has buckled back, accordioning to about midway down the fuselage, revealing a white-hot honeycomb girding the cabin walls. Pronged flames pitch out of the cockpit, which is half-buried in the canyon's yellow side. Thick smoke pours out the tail-end hatch, which opened automatically on impact. Fortunately for Oni, other scavengers have yet to descend on this Blue Zone prize.

Panicked and muffled hollers inside the wreckage advertise impending doom. An explosion jettisons a section of armor from the rear of the jet with a shockwave and teases the Rift with a flash of light. The deafening report reverberates throughout the canyon, quaking the ground and shaking shopping carts, skeletons, and other antiques free of their museum molds in the walls.

Tumbling rocks from the cliffs above slam into the soft refuse surrounding Oni. One boulder nearly decapitates her as it passes overhead and chews off the nearest ledge. Although she does not vocalize her relief, something else does. A squeaking, tumor-laden rat emerges from the muck. It presses the metal leaves strewn about the surface aside and brazenly crosses Oni's path, dragging behind it another rat. Oni mimes a trigger pull, annoyed by the rat's presumption of pardon, and then presses onward, keen on dodging the next avalanche.

The smoke pouring out of the rear hatch is thick enough to lean on. One foul breath is all it takes to convince Oni to don a medical respirator. She tightens its straps so she is as snug as a Martian miner, and takes a clean breath despite the wooly aerosol barraging her face.

Fogging her vision with excited breaths, Oni starts inside, however something blocks the hatchway. A fire-branded Sentinel stumbles forward, trying desperately to feel his way out with charred hands. His moaning and flailing chases Oni back out into the twilight.

He passes Oni—too blind to notice her or too pained to care— and wades through the barbarian sludge. "Tower, do you copy?" he mumbles into his comm. The heavplast components of his suit sizzle. "Tower, MAT Trans 107 is down." Tapping his temple, he tries to hail his imperial betters. He misses a step and somersaults into a rocky cleft that catches him before an otherwise fatal fall. Resting his head back on one of the two rocks pinching him, he finds dialogue over the comm:

"Yes! Most of the stasis pods are intact...Coordinates?"

*Can't risk the unwanted company.* Oni targets the Sentinel. She pulls the trigger and corrupts his brain with one-hundred-or-so electrically-charged pellets. *He didn't see it coming,* Oni thinks to herself. *It's better that way.* More humane to have him with hope on his palette just before the taste of iron floods the place.

Celebratory squeaks indicate the body will not go to waste.

Having made certain she will not have to rush on account of an Outland retrieval team, Oni enters the wreck, finger on the trigger. The smoke immediately forces her onto her hands and knees even with the respirator working overtime. Crawling deeper into the wreck, she spots a neon-green flame. *The ship's batteries are going to explode.*

A squad of Sentinels lie paralyzed near the batteries, blanched and contorted like plaster Pompeiians. They are still alive, but their cybernetics and exosuits are toast on account of electronic distortion from the misfiring engines and weapons systems. They silently beseech Oni to save them. She couldn't even if she wanted to, and she doesn't.

An ambient voice finds her in the inferno: "A fiery womb and a clean slate..."

*Sleep deprivation,* Oni reminds herself, trying her best to ignore the voice.

She examines the stasis pods immediately past the Sentinels. They are filled with nothing more than organic rust and humanoid pastes, all definitively dead. Growing more and more restless with each fleeting autopsy, she finds one with some promise. Red mountains and valleys track across the heart monitor on the corresponding pod panel—it has a living occupant.

On reaching the stasis pod, she checks to make sure the hatch is still unobstructed. Seeing that her exit is assured, she checks the pod's embedded tablet, which provides her intended rescue with a name: "BOOKER TALIAFERRO GIBSON."

No longer fighting her déjà vu, Oni blurts out: "I've gotta save Booky." *Booky?* Suppressed enthusiasm breaks its fetters and claws Oni's insides. *Booker...*

Her Monocle synchronizes with the pod's interface and runs through pod-code combinations to unlatch the lid. Waiting for a match with the ship caving-in around her, Oni reads file fragments concerning the pod's occupant: "Booker Gibson: six feet five; African-American; A-positive blood; two hundred and forty-five pounds; assassin;

remotely convicted under the Calgary Accord for terrorism..."

*My macho merc*...Oni palm-wipes the glass to get a glimpse of the occupant advertised as Booker Gibson. There is too much smoke; she can't see much of anything.

Her Monocle has found the right combination. The latch on the stasis pod fires back, and the door jaws open. Oni frantically looks in—

On the verge of exploding, the batteries feed the neon-green flame and throw it the width of the fuselage. The flames coat the bodies of the Sentinels pre-emptively sent to Hell and reveal the contents of Booker Gibson's pod: a raven-haired Japanese woman with ribs exposed over a mulched stomach, a boney residual of a right arm, and metal fragments embedded in her skin from head to toe. Even under all the gore, there is no mistaking the woman's identity: Oni Matsui.

Oni falls back, overcome with bodily horror and pain at the sight of this false likeness spoiled by violence and sin. "No...It can't be." The first of the battery packs explode, throwing sparks overhead and showing Oni her double reflection in the glass of the pod's concave lid. "What the hell is going on?" *Definitely not sleep deprivation.*

Panicked, Oni hurries back to the hatch. The batteries explode behind her, licking her feet with corrosive tongues. She pulls herself out of the crash just as a fireball squelches the dreamers unwittingly entombed by and for Outland.

Metal and plastic pelt the cliff side, peppering Oni's head and back. Wheezing, she slithers across the warm muck, pulling herself forward with one hand and avoiding a roll off the ledge with the anchorage of her shotgun.

Monocle begins feeding Oni images mentally, bypassing her retina and transforming the data directly into light impulses. Her former lab at the Outland Corporation materializes along with her mentor, Paul Sheffield. He spins in a desk chair at the centre of their old lab, impressed with a large smile. Sensing Oni's gaze, he stops spinning and stands up, wobbling until his dizziness passes. Paul, eyes clear of the insanity that had once darkened and recessed them, opens his mouth as if to speak, but nothing comes out. He tries desperately to convey some sort of meaning, which looks more like gagging than anything else.

A sonorous voice—certainly not Paul's—falls down on Oni,

interrupting Monocle's specious feed and reintroducing Oni to the Rift, to the crash site: "He was a good man, all things considered."

"What? He *was* a good man?" Oni asks blindly, muck now creeping up her sleeves.

There is a tug on her shotgun. Nearly asphyxiated, she has only the energy to point at her weapon, lifted from her by a knot of leather digits. Giant boots shoring up two massive legs background the weapon's ascent.

Although the fire bleeding out of the meat shuttle into the borderland sky illuminates the stranger's armour and hefty limbs, it fails to reveal his face. "We have to finish what he started—what we started. Otherwise we're all damned and he goes down as the devil of our time."

Oni drags her knees through the muck to her chest and leans back on her heels. "I don't understand."

The stranger loses solidity and transmogrifies into an elaborate wire structure. "The path will find you," vows the scaffold of a man. "It's treacherous as Hell, but all doors made by angels can be opened by one. And besides—I am here if you need me. Now, *wake up.*"

## ASSEMBLY REQUIRED

*There is the ache and then there is the cold.*

Oni arches forward, coughing out froth and fluid. She cannot manage to clear her airway. Convulsing, she throws her hands into the surrounding darkness in a vain attempt to summon help. If she found it, she would not know how to put it to work in this all-consuming, unfocused panic.

Whatever was choking her is now inching up her windpipe and into her mouth and nostrils. She snaps her mouth open wide, and digs a numb, unfeeling finger to the back of her throat to coax the mysterious matter out before it has an opportunity to suffocate her again. It coats her finger.

*Monocle...* Oni manages to internally turn on her neural implant. Before the interface has a chance to project, introject, and then welcome her to version 32.4, Oni triggers its night-vision feature. Shades of green attack the darkness, claiming edges for the visible world.

Palms up and fingers back like an upended tarantula, Oni confirms her materiality. With this most rudimentary and necessary form of sentient reflection attended to, she brings the crawling substance closer for inspection. A squadron of surgical drones—so-called mechrophages—compensates for her finger's turn and marches across her wrists, headed back either to their origin or to the trash. Spitting, she liberates the rest of the tiny army. Wherever they land, they quickly find others like them and together head towards the far corner of the room, marking their progress with a rhythmic dinning.

"Hello?" Oni rasps. Her throat is dry and sore. The sound barely scrapes by, and when it does, it comes out as nothing more than a pained meow.

The little surgical aphids pause, as if struggling to determine if Oni had addressed them.

There are no soft and familiar edges among those Monocle has discovered. No Emily. No Constance. No Ed...No Booker Gibson. No one hellos back. With the mechrophages paralyzed by curiosity, the only thing left to hear is *the hum*; that throbbing low-frequency pattern whose very perception is the standard of quiet.

Taking *the hum*, uninterrupted, as a cue, the tiny bots continue their crawl.

Oni massages her throat and leans over to regain coverage of the mechrophages' lousy exodus, however something else steals her attention. Below, rowed and numbered: white boxes with transparent covers, all full of some kind of red and black hodgepodge.

*Where the hell am I?*

A quick survey of the room prompts more questions. She is sitting upright in a half-pipe—a cryo-tube sans shielding—that has been converted into a medical bed, lined with foam and sullied surgical linens. A curtain of chains dangle overhead, each with a fishless hook at its end. X-Rays of some mangled cyborg are plastered over a closed door, which looks like a splintery transplant from an old maritime-captain's quarters. In the far corner, a Z-series android sits hunched over its amputated legs. Its back is opened up like a chrysanthemum with all its synthetic tissue curled outward around the haphazard incision. The android will not play marionette or puppeteer again.

Queasy and disoriented, Oni counts down over shallow breaths, giving her heartbeat a chance to stabilize. She drops one leg over the edge, and shifts in the bed until the other falls over on its own.

Any recollection of how she came to be here, *wherever here is*, fails her, stuck in traffic behind a parade of trauma. Like horrid Mardi Gras floats, cartoonish images pass through this intersection of *then* and *now*. Faces, names, and a mishmash of pain felt and remembered, barrage her senses. *Winchester. The Citadel. Allen Scheele. The CLOUD.* It is too much to handle.

She wretches, but nothing comes up, except for some spit that singes the scrapes left by her "Hello."

Training focus on activating reference- and localization-display, Oni manages the compulsory minimum: her Monocle's interface scales over her iris and doubles with a direct broadcast of data to her cerebral cortex. The feed is uneven and glitchy. Minimalist graphics strobe over the constant orange and black eyetop. Several warning indicators and a "Fatal error" message blink at its bottom right. Oni turns the opacity up on the display, fading out the eerily-dark room in her peripherals.

LOG: BGIBSON_INCOMING_TRANSMISSIONS

Transmission 1:28:15—"Oni, watch your back. I think Winchester knows…"

A flood of similar messages start piling into her inbox, all dated the day of the Citadel incursion, apparently five months ago—almost all from Oni's good friend Booker Gibson. His voice is strained and anxious. Weak, too, on account of his temporary paralysis. (He had given Paul Sheffield his PILOT device who had crashed all the same.)

*Watch my back?* Oni stares blankly both at the virtual and at the real. Messages are not the only things flooding her head. As if freshly impressed, the memory of her abolitionist attack on the Citadel returns to her.

*Winchester knew alright;* now he is as unfeeling and unthinking as the red mulch in the containers under Oni's bed.

Transmission 2:33:31—"Outland has massacred the diversionary forces at the Partition Gate 14. Six private fighter jets just bounced, Citadel-bound. Looks like they are now turning all of their attention your way. Do you copy? Oni?"

The Citadel's jammers prevented Oni from receiving Gibson's warning. In the end, it would not have changed much, but she would at least have known to save her countermeasures.

Transmission 3:45:53—"The explosion is all over the G-Feed. Outland, the LAPD…even the Marines. They're all running containment. Red alert across the state. Where are you?…I've secured transit for you, Paul, and I, to San Diego. We'll go underground in the Coronado Wastes. Call me when you're out. I'll wait for you."

Several more messages and media transmissions pulsate ready in the queue, but the interface glitches and dissolves, leaving Oni once again with the darkness and the cold.

"Booker…" Oni whispers, stirred by loving and disjointed memories.

Shuffling feet preface a metallic clang on the other side of the door. Not so much a knock as the sound of a pocket full of change being turned inside-out over a snare drum.

Oni slides off of the medical bed, unintentionally sending the white containers stowed under the gurney spinning across the room. Before the chill from the floor has a chance to quill Oni's senses, her legs fail her. Like a paper mâché figurine caught in a rainstorm, she collapses onto her side, breaking one of the containers open. Bone and puréed flesh spill out, wetting her medical gown.

The doorknob shakes. A click-crank sound. Finally, the right key cuts into place. The door swings inward followed by a flood of unnatural light.

Oni desperately pulls herself through the slick biomatter and under the medical bed. It is a futile attempt at self-preservation, but *you ought to gamble all of your hope if survival means a short life without any.*

"Hello? Dr. Matsui?" The inflection and the timber of the voice hint at the speaker's familiarity and age. Limping in, barely lifting his feet so that they scuff and squeak, he paws at the wall and catches a light switch.

Strobing low-blue light accompanies the prefatory hum of the fluorescent bulbs. With a click, two lights pre-flash and then brighten, painting the room in drab colours that Oni's Monocle failed to interpret in the darkness. Despite her best effort at hiding, the stranger sees her right away. A horseshoe-shaped bloodstain on the floor ends in a shivering and pale, 30-something Japanese-American.

The old man's mole- and skin-tag-beset face wrinkles around a kind smirk. "Dr. Matsui! Whatever are you doing?"

Sure that she is seeing things, Oni presses as deep into the space beneath the bed as she can. "W-where am I?" she stammers, staring through the bed's undercarriage.

"On the floor. Now, let me help you get up before you catch a cold or damage my handywork." Frustrated by Oni's defiance, he raises his voice: "Please! We are running out of time." He runs a sleeve across his forehead, catching his spent concern. "I wanted you to be up days ago, but had to repair one more internal tear."

Oni's eyes report a hopeful vision that her brain has trouble accepting. "No."

"It would make a world of difference," he says, hurrying through his delivery in order to sneeze. Wiping his nose on his sleeve, he smiles. "Dr. Matsui? *Watashitachiha jikan ga arimasen...*"

And with that bilingual shuffle, Oni recognizes the speaker. Time has neither let him age gracefully nor let him part with his unique manner of speaking. "Dr. Kobayashi?"

"Jin. Call me Jin."


Jin's prune-like fingers feel like fibreglass against Oni's back. As his digits track closer to her spine, she senses them less and less until her only rearward awareness of his clinical curiosity is the little prods shifting her forward on the bed.

Oni exhales heavily.

"I'm sorry. Does this hurt?"

"No, Dr. Kobayashi. Not at all."

A thud and a nearby crackle rattle the room, nearly toppling Jin. He resets his hands and continues his examination. "Don't be so

21

formal," he says, trying simultaneously to ignore the seismic phenomena drawing nearer and nearer the clinic. "This is the PIT, after all. A snooty title will get me killed or worse: those savages will come to depend on me."

"Jin…"

"No pain? Are you sure?"

"Yeah. I feel nothing, actually."

"Ah, yes. Hmm. That is just the Longdream…Should be wearing off." He screws something into place, and leans over to pilfer his toolbox for the next piece to Oni's spinal puzzle. "Remind me to give you something for the pain."

"It's fine. Really."

"Now it is, sure. Comas are tricky like that."

"Coma?"

Jin funnels a sigh through his nostrils, which flare as if they were free of any cartilage or definition. "An hour from now, my little additions here are going to feel out of place, and everything in-place is going to ache a great deal."

Oni attempts to make a fist, first with her left hand—which barely knots—and then with her right—which closes with ease and a hydraulic whine. *Feels stronger.* "How long?"

"Pardon?" Kobayashi's voice goes shrill on the second syllable.

"How long have I been out of commission?"

Jin adopts a hardened look of resolve and shakes an index-pronged fist at Oni, which she can only partially discern out of the corner of her eye. "Questions later, when you're ready and once we're somewhere safer." Sensing he has said too much or too little, Jin chews his words. "You were in a coma for just over five months…To ensure your mind did not rot away while you were out, I plugged you into my *kurokumo*—a local-network VR loop. Modeled after your OASIS Construct, as a matter of fact."

The realization parts Oni's dry lips: "That wasn't a dream after all…"

Oni had developed the OASIS Construct with Paul Sheffield. It was little more than a proof of concept for what later became the CLOUD—a virtual reality with heavy-handed time and mental-motion constraints. For a time, it was also the purgatory to which Allen Scheele's mind had been assigned when his body was destroyed. In fairness to Scheele, a purgatory without heaven is no better than a personal hell, and like Lucifer, he did his best to escape perdition.

"Your implant is fried," Jin says matter-of-factly, "So I had to bypass it and create my own little neural link. It was only good the one time; should dissolve overnight." He grips the sides of Oni's head and tilts it into the florescent glow. "Technically it was a simulation, but since it was under your subconscious control, it functioned like a dream. I just hope it was a pleasant experience. Would have been a better sim if your implant was functional."

"It was more of a distorted memory than a dream or a sim. I just watched the Outland meat transport I found Booker in crash a second time. Felt so real. My friends—Emily and Constance's faces…" Oni perseverates on a key detail Jin tried to gloss over. "Oh my god… Five months?" The loss she hadn't the time to register before her attack on the Citadel now hits her hard.

Jin nods, sympathizing with his patient's frustration, and places his hands on Oni's shoulders. "First we make sure you have a future, and then we will deal with your past. *Hai?*"

Resorting to the language her parents utilized only in their domestic spats, Oni concedes: "Hai…" *Bad news deferred.* Bedside manner is not something Oni has been taught or will ever pick up. Android nurses are kinder in their disregard for feelings. Just the truth, no matter how bitter or provocative. "Do you have something for the taste?" Oni asks, rolling her tongue around a dry and flaky mouth.

Jin's lapse in sheepishness has thrown him off kilter. He takes a step back and a short pause before registering Oni's question. "Taste?" His eyebrows flutter as if they have taken off on a breeze the rest of his face is too heavy for.

"It tastes like my mouth's been washed out with mercury."

"Ah, yes." Jin quickly turns to his instruments. "Again, that's the Longdream. I will see what I can do…" He fumbles around in his pockets and presents without second consideration two containers: one, a transparent mint container full of little red pills, and the other, a pack of cigarettes.

Crooking a smile, Oni shakes her head. "I'll be fine. Will just have to brush my teeth when we're done here." She tries to run a Monocle search, but *it's still on the fritz.* "Jin, do you have anything I can run a Minerva search on? I need to track down a friend."

Minerva is a *proper* AI—a user-specific access guide to and guardian of the digital universe. On face: a three-in-one CLOUD guide, sorting function, and search engine that has the keys and coordinates to all real- and virtual-world coordinates to corresponding CLOUD tech and implants. Under the skin, it is a virtual demiurge charged with optimizing and policing the CLOUD—improving interconnectivity, security, network classifications, match-making, and the overall user-experience. Without being prompted or supervised, it ensures simulations are true to their source materials. It can, for example, crunch all of the data on a sunset in order to simulate all facets of witnessing it while synchronized, from its warmth to the worms one gets under one's eyelids after looking at it for too long, to the deep-rooted sense of animal panic over the coming dark. All data passes through Minerva's channel, regardless of encryption or privacy settings, and serves to enlighten it, and by extension, enlighten the whole system. It is another one of Paul Sheffield's footprints in the Californian sand. Thankfully, neither Paul's insanity nor Allen Scheele's ambitions have leached into the primordial bytes or influenced Minerva; both would prove to be catastrophic.

Jin, preoccupied with tweaking whatever implants he saw fit to equip Oni with, warms her back with his muffled voice. "No Minerva. When the CLOUD went down, Minerva did too. Makes sense, though." He pauses to avoid competing with the sound of his drill. Drill powered-down, he returns to his thought: "No point searching for CLOUD data or subscribers... No point having a library catalog if the entire library has been burned down."

Although Booker Gibson is at first blush off-the-grid, he uploaded memories to the CLOUD. All of his intentionally vague, boring, and innocuous shared memories contain an anachronistic addition: a cat-themed fridge calendar. Red-markered circles around the numbers on the calendar provide Booker's coordinates in real time. With Minerva's help, Oni would be able to find the calendar, and with the calendar in mind, eventually find Booker. *Damn.*

Oni sighs and looks around the room. Feeling a slight pinch, she investigates the bandage around her right wrist. Her heart stops. Underneath the top layer is a grid of stitches loosely holding together a carmine mess. Something glints under the fluorescent bulbs. *Chrome?* She squeezes the graft and stretches the stitches, revealing a rivet. "Tarnation!" Oni extends her arm and winces in the opposite direction.

Jin chuckles. "Still fond of that term, I see." He murmurs "Tarnation" to himself, and then its meaning, "Damnation." He shakes his head, oblivious to Oni's terror. "Won't get anywhere in this city talking about the banned theology…"

"Stop and tell me!"

Taking a step back, Jin crooks his neck. "Tell you what?"

"What have you done to me?" Oni swallows, closes her eyes, and takes a deep breath. "What have you done, Jin?"

The little surgeon puts down his utensils, and circumnavigates the bench and the gore on the ground to address Oni directly. "Please be calm." He gently grips the controversial arm, and lowers it. "A great deal has happened in a very short period of time. Changes that will take some getting used to. But know: all that I have done, I have done to help you. To repay you…"

"*What* did you do?"

Jin slides his goggles over his brow, leaving them to rest just below his sparse hairline. He cautiously cups Oni's right hand and pauses to allow for trust to follow. He turns it slowly, and nods to her wrist. "You fled the Citadel in Winchester's special jet."

"His prized Dragonfly…" The ship looked like headless caribou antlers. Oni can't remember what the inside looked like, apart from red warning-lights and sparks.

"You were shot down, and in the crash, your arm was shattered and…I would list the muscles that were torn to the point of unrecognizability, but it would be easier to name the original tissue you still have. Normally, I would have amputated above the shoulder, but I had to do everything I could, knowing full well that you, Ed, and Mr. Gibson gave me back everything I have."

"The chrome? Is it a brace?"

Jin averts his eyes. "Dr. Matsui…a brace is for support. What you have there is braced by what remains of your arm."

Oni pulls her hand away from Jin's gentle grip. It is heavy and prickly. She stifles tears and a look of shock. "It's not mine…"

"It *is* yours. You could not tell until just now that it wasn't the one you were born with. That is how it will always be. Your skin will bind around it and heal. Your strength will return to you. *In fact*, this arm is ten-times stronger than its predecessor. It is immune to most electromagnetic interference, corrosion, and—" Jin pauses to sneeze and wipe his nose on his sleeve. "—disease." Studying his handywork, Jin caresses the stitches. "It is fused to your humerus and bracketed at the joint to reduce tension around your shoulder and neck. As is the case with BiAnima prostheses, your brain will suffer no delay transmitting intentions…"

Oni grunts. "Alright." She kicks her legs back into the bed's undercarriage, as if trying to launch herself off. Jin raises his hands to catch her. The sudden motion breaks all of the tears glued to Oni's face. She releases another shaky sigh. "This is a lot to process. Do you mind giving me a minute?"

"You do not have a minute. If you intend on getting out of here before those bombs become something more than an annoyance, I must finish calibrating your back."

Oni clasps the bandage back around the alien bone and steel, and leans forward. Her feet swing above the glassy floor, ready to bear her disheveled form a second time.

"Stop!" Jin places one hand on her sternum, and the other on her left arm. "Stop and listen. I know what you are going through. I have been where you are now. And I can tell you, you are in a much better place than I was—in a better place than most who have suffered to the extent of what you have suffered."

"You have no idea—" Oni says, her lips curling away from bars of acidic spit.

Jin nods compulsively and steps back. He pulls the front of his bloody smock to the side, revealing a matte-black prosthetic leg fitted into a harness. The other leg, far skinnier in his pant leg, shivers subtly beside its fraternal heavplast twin.

"I'm sorry," says Oni, folding forward.

Jin places his hand on Oni's shoulder. "Don't be. I'm not. After you saved me—after I left MUD—I turned my life around. Tried to make all my stolen experience worth something…I surrendered part of my old self to become my current self, and so far, it has been worth it."

The walls shudder, and the fluorescent tubes flicker above them. A demo reel of pops and crackles plays on repeat with screams serving as percussion.

"Dr. Matsui…"

Stretching and leaning her head back, Oni smiles up at the ceiling tiles hemorrhaging mineral fibers. "Oni," she says, bringing her eyes level with his. "No snooty titles, right?" The slow back-and-forth motion has unsettled her. Her lips purse so that all but the outline of their pink is gone, and the corresponding smile vanishes like a chalk drawing angrily palmed into oblivion. She caves like she is about to throw up, but strives to ensconce her pain. "I'd almost forgotten we brought you back to Camp MUD with us—Booker's idea, of course…We thought you were a goner."

"I was. Rather, I would have been without your help. A goner or something much worse."

Another nearby explosion unsettles a few of the containers slotted alphabetically on the shelf behind Jin. Brain fragments and mysterious giblets swish about in their respective brines. The aftershock reorganizes the 'H' section—a colourful palette of implants and tissue samples—and sends shards of soda-lime glass flying.

"I bet that took some getting used to," says Oni, indicating the broken glass on the floor.

"This is actually quite unusual. Smoke and flame frequently pass over and around this part of the PIT, but never rise from it."

Jin helps Oni down off the bed and leads her out of the room into the greater clinic. The clinic is a cross between an army barracks and a pre-Downturn office space. Several cots and gurneys line the sides. An aisle bisects the two rows all the way to the front door, which is covered with more padlocks than Paris' Pont des Arts. Adjacent to the backroom Oni woke up in, there is another door—likely to a bathroom or an office.

Seating Oni at another table with a carpentry set sprawled across one side, Jin lets out a sigh of relief. Before he can refill his chest, there is another boom. Oni would recognize it anywhere. *What's a rail gun doing going off in the PIT?*

Concrete and rebar shred several of the clinic's walls, puncturing them with rebar like broken ribs kicked through intestine. Slowing after a mile of infernal damage, the gun's molten projectile fans a bloom of particulate into the back room where they were just standing. Smoke furls over the decimated captain's door, and into the clinic. *That was close.*

"Chikushō!" Jin cries, grasping the table for support. Upper-cutting Oni with a forlorn look, Jin seizes her hands. "Oni, you must leave this place." His hands are cold and, with the exception to the mucous cysts bulging about his knuckles, nearly fleshless. "Outland and the Military are hunting 'terrorists'." Realization purples his eyelids. "The only reason for them to come this way is if they found the remains of Winchester's Dragonfly…Yes. Someone must have told them you were moved. No loyalty anymore," Jin says, taking laboured breaths full of sooty air. "Whatever the reason for the ruckus, it is sufficient cause for you to lay low at my conapt until the smoke clears. Dr. Matsui, I must stress this next point: you can trust no one. Not your old friends. No bright-eyed children or glass-eyed rojin. No one. Word of your survival has spread like fire. It does not help your case that the rebels blow the flame, hoping for a leader to show herself—to finish what she has started." Silt from the ceiling dulls the sheen on Jin's forehead. He takes his goggles off and cleans the lenses.

Stung by the notion that Paul posthumously passed his Midas touch onto her—whereby everything and everybody touched or loved dies or turns to shit—Oni grabs the sleeve of Jin's coat and addresses him earnestly: "You're not safe with me here, and you won't be safe with me at your place, and…"

Anticipating Oni's conclusion, Jin interrupts very cooly, mollified by her touch: "Safety, Dr. Matsui, is an illusion favoured by the unchallenged." He opens a small gate on his artificial thigh. Three syringes, fastened together around a small cylinder by a fine metal wire, slide out. He removes one from the cylinder, full of a dry, tarry substance, and shoves the other two back into his personal compartment. Flicking the syringe, and in doing so awakening a thousand-or-so micro-mechrophages, Jin offers Oni a sympathetic shrug. "To maximize neural connectivity." He plunges the syringe into Oni's shoulder without warning. "They will evacuate by morning, so you needn't worry about being bio-hacked."

Oni closes her eyes. "Doctor knows best." Seeking to distract herself from the needle, the end of which has to be at least three millimetres in diameter, she poses the question: "How did you find me?"

"Providence." Jin throws the empty syringe to the side, which settles amidst all the other medical equipment strewn about the place. He silently instructs Oni to step down from the table. "Salvagers set up an on-site auction, at the crash site that is. *Please turn.*" Jin quickly fastens one last piece to Oni's exposed exo-spine. "You were dying offstage. Antonio, a butcher from San Marino who deals in *parts*, picked you up for next to nothing. The wreckage was sold to a mandroid named Akbashi—no, that's not right. Ak—"

"*Akbari*," Oni murmurs.

Jin looks troubled, mulling over the name.

A memory insulates Oni and warms her: Booker Gibson is

loading gear into a rusted van. Bahram Akbari, the eldest son of Hex Akbari—the PIT's unofficial overlord—lights a pipe, making no effort to help whatsoever. Bahram is impressed with a smile, which he maintains even when drawing from his Cohiba, and for good reason: Oni and Gibson saved the life of his younger brother, Kadin.

Kadin had overloaded his pirated memex after spending entire weeks synchronized to the CLOUD. When Kadin's implant overloaded, it shocked and irreparably charred his brain. Although his mind and memories were intact in a virtual form, his meat was consequently unsalvageable. Without recourse to Outland or to a Blue Zone hospital, Hex appealed to two black-market redeemers for help and shuttled them over to his PIT-side fortress. There waiting for Oni and Gibson: Hex's eldest son Bahram and a cybernetic duplicate of Kadin. Oni obliged, and skillfully managed to transfer Kadin's sentience to the OASIS Construct, and then over to the mandroid. The mental transmigration would have failed if it were not for the AI she introduced to the duplicate to help with the transition. As thanks for saving his son, Hex Akbari paid for Camp MUD's emergency bunker, sparing no expense.

"Hex Akbari?"

"Hmmm. 'Hex' doesn't ring a bell, but yes, it was certainly an Akbari. He paid millions…" Jin says, crooking his head back and wincing to perfect vision along his nose. He makes another adjustment to Oni's arm. "That is my understanding."

*Akbari hates Outland and the government. If he purchased Winchester's Dragonfly, it would have been to give me a head start or to procure leverage against his institutional nemeses. But that doesn't answer my question.* "If Antonio the butcher found me, how did you find him?"

Jin smiles, forgetting the bullies outside rattling his cage. "With limited access and virtually no official channels to tap, I resorted long ago to piecing together patients with whatever I could get my hands on. Printed parts, android parts, pig parts, human parts…Sometimes those parts belong to a Sentinel who got caught in a spider's web. Other times, those parts belong to a spider that cast too wide a net and drew too much attention to himself." He procures two solid tabs of Longdream, plots them in Oni's hand, and molds her hand closed. "Five months ago, some parts came in attached to an injured friend in a real bad way. Lucky for you and *this new arm,*" Jin gestures to Oni's arm as he ushers her to a door adjacent to the smoking room the railgun found, "One of my scroungers was looking for a healthy heart. His instructions were to leave it in place. Didn't want to corrupt the veins or arteries. Found you on a heap tagged DOA. You came to me by fate, fortune, a scrounger, and..." Jin showcases his yellow picket fence of a grin. "Antonio, the butcher from San Marino. Very lucky!"

Oni scratches at a phantom itch and leans against the doorframe. "I hope whatever luck brought me here stays with you." Through the crack in the door, Oni glimpses silver salt smiles halving the faces of several intubated, bald children. Jin's office is something of a portrait gallery. All of his files and paperwork crowd his writing desk at the centre, making room for the patient photos that begin at the floor. Even the wardrobe squeezed into the corner wears a dozen framed photographs. "I am going to take off—get out of your hair." Looking to Jin's remaining plugs of hair, wet and thatched, she regrets her phrasing. "You just keep on helping people."

"You will leave as soon as I am finished with my calibrations. A job worth doing is a job worth doing well. If we manage through the night without interruption, I can find you someplace safe to rehabilitate. In the PIT, of course."

Another explosion unsettles the remaining jars, vials, and canisters from their respective slots on the surrounding shelves in the clinic. Surveying the damage, something catches Oni's eye in the smoking backroom—something extra to the fire and embers, moving about on its own volition. Oni retreats into the doorframe of Jin's office, and howls: "Tarnation!"

"What is it?" Jin yells, interest apparently piqued only by the most blood-curdling cry.

Oni is too engrossed by the pitiful sight to respond. The legless android pulls itself out of the backroom, whipping its spine about like a scorpion tail. The fiery disturbance must have awoken some facet of its brain that Jin failed to cannibalize—some facet that wants to survive despite its vessel's melting skin and scorched features. In a horrendous attempt to communicate or maybe as a result of a forgivable malfunction, the android begins to chomp its exposed jaw in Oni's direction.

"Jin..."

Oni pushes back into the office and in so doing shoves the door open wide enough for Jin to make out the monstrosity. He barrels past Oni, spraying her with geriatric sweat, and frames the gnashing teeth with his gait. Permitting himself and the android a moment of ethical consideration, Jin lets the teeth come close enough to bite. "I'm sorry," he says, with a sincerity that challenges Oni's perception of what she is witnessing. Jin caves in the android's head with a bionic stomp.

A panicked giggle escapes Oni's raspberry lips. "I'm glad you were more patient with me…"

Jin gestures to Oni's arm. "Please try not to move." He strides back into his office. "I have to secure the recent additions. Perhaps you can manage the fine-tuning."

"With ease," Oni fires back. She bites her lip, fearful that her comment, intended to reassure Jin, came across as smug. However, judging by the golden glean on the old man's forehead, now is probably the best time to demonstrate a little bit of confidence.

Jin meets Oni in the doorframe with another syringe. "For the pain," he says, jabbing her scarred shoulder with a small injection of Pethidine.

"What pain?"

Dropping the spent syringe, Jin smiles tenderly and turns Oni with a tailor's touch. He produces his wrench and tightens another loose piece on her back.

Oni groans. "Jin, I need to sit."

"The wooziness will pass. We need to get you some clothes."

Oni looks down at the bloodied fringes of her medical gown, and signals her agreement.

"For whatever reason, hospital dresses have gone out of fashion." He guides her from his office back into the greater clinic. "Sit here," he orders, setting her down on a wooden bench. He holds a thumb out to guesstimate Oni's size, nods, and hurries over to the wardrobe in his office.

Beside Oni on the bench are several oncological antiques, including a half-filled bag marked "Mytoycin." She is clearly not the first person sent here to die.

Jin shuffles out holding some less-than-choice fabrics. He hands the articles to Oni, item by item. T-shirt. Leather jacket. Long johns and a pair of leggings with heavplast padding. The padding was probably intended for a mosh pit and is now destined for a PIT war.

"Leave the top till last," Jin says pointing at the t-shirt. "I still have some adjustments to make…"

31

Oni wriggles into the corrugated, grey long johns, and forces the leggings overtop. The combo may be tight and lumpy, but it reinforces her weary legs. Jin helps her pull the medical gown up over her head, revealing a topographic map of scars. She tries not to focus on her broken skin. Instead, she calms herself with some focused breathing.

The bench beneath her grinds against the floor as Jin finesses her prosthetic and her spine as if she were a race car and he its mechanic. In addition to the ambiance of war, she can hear Jin turning something into place. It sounds horrific but it is virtually painless. "I meant to ask—" Oni starts, but is interrupted by a high-pitched wail.

A red light embedded in the ceiling foam begins pulsing. Accompanied by a feminine Japanese note of caution, an eye-level security holographic appears, depicting two armed figures dragging a third through the lobby beyond the clinic's front door. Zooming in, an infographic overlay identifies the intruders as "PIT rebels."

Jin jerks the wrench, and pulls Oni close. "Oni, I do not mean to be curt, but see over there by that box?"

"The dialysis machine?"

"Yes. See the brown doors? That's an old cremator we had installed before it became customary to dump bodies out in the open."

"I know I might be a risk but…"

"Oni," Jin yells, now exasperated and sweating himself to the point of dehydration. "It is a secret tunnel leading to Saint's Corner. You need to go. Now!"

Staring at the figures in the holographic struggling under the weight of their wounded comrade, Oni's eyes widen. "Don't you help these kinds of people for a living? I mean, I might be the least of their concern."

"From time to time. But never before have I had the nation's most-wanted felon keeping me company. And who knows? Maybe they *are* here just for you."

Oni pulls the t-shirt on with great difficulty, and then tries slipping on the leather jacket. Noticing her drug-hampered coordination, Jin helps guide Oni's prosthetic through the sleeve.

"These guys and I might share a few things in common," Oni says, cheeks bulging over a hopeful smile. "In fact, they might be fans of my handwork back at the Citadel."

Jin makes his disagreement with Oni's positive outlook known with a zealous glower and shake. "A twenty-nine-million-dollar bounty is enough to override any sense of comradery or admiration."

Surprised and flattered, Oni leans forward. "Twenty?"

"Twenty-nine."

"Tarnation. You could help a lot more people than just one old friend with that kind of money. In fact, I am tempted to turn my own self in..." With an *unmph*, Oni stands.

"Oh heavens!" Jin cries, focusing on Oni's feet. "What size are you?"

"Huh?"

"Shoes. You're going to need shoes if you don't want to become a pincushion."

"Seven-and-a-half..."

Jin hurries back into his office. "Would have stocked up on military fatigues in the bazaar had I known you'd become a warrior."

Examining her reinforced knuckles, Oni makes a fist. "You'd be amazed what a few months of war sims can do for the reflexes."

In his cuss-directed rummaging efforts, Jin manages to break at least several heavy-sounding glasses.

"Remind me: why haven't you?" Oni yells.

A saline bag flies out of the back room and splatters against the floor. Jin glides out with a pair of calf-high combat boots in hand, nearly spinning on the saline solution. He tugs on the shoelaces until they become loose, and sets the boots down on either side of Oni's feet. "I'm not sure I caught all of your question..."

Oni puts on the boots and challenges herself with the task of lace-tying without muscle memory. Mystified, she looks up at Jin. "Why haven't you turned me in?"

Jin turns to his security holographic. Staring at the figures readying to storm the front door, he wets his wrinkled lips. "A person enriched by betrayal is devil-owned. Besides, if you are worth twenty-nine million to the groups that fertilize their money trees with the flesh of slaves, you're worth at least twice as much to this city free. *Get to the tunnel.*"

Oni, recognizing that Jin had made up his mind long before she awoke, considers life outside of this room. "What about my back?"

Jin leers into the clinic. "You broke it," he declares. Recognizing the haste and bluntness with which he offered this insight, he checks himself. "I mean: it was broken in the crash. Would have been lethal were it not for your spidersilk implants. I have doubly reinforced it. The only cybernetic vertebrae I could find in all of this godforsaken hellhole was an *Outland special.*" He gestures to another android, this one headless, strapped to a chair, and splayed out like a gutted deer.

"Tarnation, Jin!" Her mouth, tight with anger but unfixed to either a scowl or a grimace, forms a surprised 'o.' "Forget the arm. You could have led with that little insight!"

Jin ignores her outburst. "A word of warning: be careful when interfacing with your Monocle. Your neural implant is still inoperable so your thoughts are private. However, those things, *those* ..." Jin flounders, searching for the word, and makes a fist upon finding it: "*Technopaths* will still be able to scan or co-opt your Monocle feed. I am not entirely sure if they can influence or tamper with the component making your Outland Special spine truly special."

"Technopaths? What component?"

"You take the good with the bad, right?"

"Jin..."

"There's an exocortex buried between your T3 and T4. Belonged to Blemyah, here." Jin indicates the android. "Blemyah was supposed to house a Blue Zone geriatric whose body had finally failed him...If your implant still worked, you could virtually store and synch your mind in and with it. Going one step further, had you a beacon, you could remotely project yourself into any dark CLOUD you'd fancy.

"You're telling me I'm walking data-storage? A self-contained cypulchre?"

Jin grinds his teeth. "On the right side of the cherry blossoms. The exocortex is not active. It has also been cleared. There is no need to worry."

There is a fizzing sound in the lobby and a bright light on the security feed, followed by a meaty bang. A uniform puff of dust advances under the clinic's front door, leaving behind a thin grey line.

"Time to try out your new frame and put it to good use."

Jin and Oni freeze. Two rebels dressed in dragon-tooth armour help a third, tattered rebel into the room. Leaving his comrade to carry the gimp, the second rebel bolts the mangled front door closed behind him. Why he is bolting a door he just destroyed is beyond comprehension, but shellshock certainly has something to do with it. The door falls again.

"Old man, get over here. Going to need you to work your magic."

"Just one moment," shouts Jin, frazzled and just about out of sweat.

"Hey doc! Our guy dies, you die," yells the other shrapnel-raked Luddite.

Jin nods to the impatient men swirling around their bloody mess of a friend, and whispers to Oni: "Fortunate is the man whose evil dies with him and whose good outlives him." He ushers her over to the cremator gate, and spins towards the rebels, costumed in an expression and disposition Oni is unfamiliar with. "How's your friend injured?" he yells.

"Badly..." says one of the men bearing the wounded man onto the nearest examining table.

Jin grabs a clutch of first aid supplies, and whisks it over to the rebels. Scrutinizing the fleshy flowers budding over the patient's chest, he forcefully demands answers: "*What* did it?"

"What the hell does it matter *what* hurt him? Just fix it, you butterhead!" The skin about the rebel's neck is saggy and contorted; telltale signs of long departures to the CLOUD without a proper PILOT device. *Rainouts...*

Oni looks around for a weapon. Sadly, all of the blades are rowed on blue cloth beside the soldiers, and she cannot get to the carpentry set near Jin's office without making a show of it.

Standing his ground and maintaining an assertive, clinical tone, Jin points at the wounded rebel. "*What* is very important, young man. If I treat a bullet wound the way I would treat a laser wound, he will die."

The wounded man, reeling on the table in pain, blurts out: "Monarch drone! Therm-therm, ugh..."

His racist comrade fills in the gaps: "A thermobaric pincer!"

Jin straightens the wounded rebel on his back, and pushes the other rebels aside. "Give me some room." Looking over to Oni, he gestures to the cremator. "Nurse! Stop gawking about and prep the scanner for our friends here."

"Mind my mate and shut up, old man," spews the rebel lurking by the door. He looks to Oni. "And you..."

Explosions, this time closer than ever, shake the clinic and pelt the façade with debris—sounds like the inside of a tent during a sandstorm.

"Unless you want your friend here to die," Jin says, wrapping a stethoscope around his neck. "I advise you to let my assistant proceed without interruption or heckling."

The dough-faced rebel hovering over his wounded comrade mimes shooting Jin.

"Layton, let her do what needs doing." Throwing a dagger of a glance Oni's way, the blurry-eyed rebel spits words of caution: "If you try anything, there's gonna to be more than one open belly the old man's going to need to suture."

As the wounded rebel squeals with his guts tied around Jin's able fingers, Oni looks at her own digits, worried they will not be able to lift the cremator gate. She manages with ease, although a few of the stitches in her wrist eject, letting the lip of her wound pout.

Before an audience of anxious rebels, Jin yells over to Oni. "Check to make sure the rear scanner is operational."

Realizing her departure is as good as a death sentence for Jin, Oni whispers "No," to the cremator.

Out of the corner of his eye, Jin spots Oni where he expected nothing but a closed door. "Nurse! Do not make me ask you one more time."

The rebel called Layton pulls his sidearm and points it in Oni's direction. "You're distracting the doc, you little bitch." His face wrinkles-up. He takes a step forward. "Wait...I *know you.*" Layton jitters as if buffering while trying to make connections in his truncated mind. "Where the hell I know you from? Hey, Tank!" he yells to the man hovering over their wounded ally. "You recognize this broad?"

Tank is preoccupied, watching Jin's nimble fingers pluck and prod through scorched intestine. "Nah."

"I think it's the Jap from the news," Layton says, greed creasing his eyes. He cocks the hammer back on his revolver. "That rogue doc!" Taking another step forward, just into Jin's peripheral vision, he orders Oni: "C'mon over, we're going to take you to see some friends we share in common..."

"LT, don't cut us off a bigger problem when we can barely put a dent in the one we've got," Tank reasons to the back of his comrade's head. Glimpsing something ominous in Oni's eyes, his voice rises. "Focus on the mission. She's not worth the trouble."

"Thirty-something million," Layton says, with a gross, skeletal smile further deforming his face. "Screw the PIT, man. That's enough for us to live like Bee-Zee kings!"

"What?" says Tank, ejecting enough spit to lubricate several more dumb questions.

"That's what the talking heads on *NewsLink* were saying. Forty-million bucks." Half-turning to Tank, with his gun still trained on Oni, he prattles through the side of his mouth: "Nuts to the revolution, man. Nuts to the PIT. With fifty million, we turn-coat, get the guilt wiped from our exos, and retire someplace that's never seen a wall."

Oni shifts uneasily, scrutinizing the cremator gate. Around it: a tapestry of wires painted-over to camouflage the piss-poor concrete. No indication of a tunnel other than Jin's word, which is as good as her standing.

"Don't move!" Layton roars. "Do as you're told or—"

As if his friend's dripping intestines behind him had vanished from mind and memory, Tank scrambles to Layton's side. His face is transformed; no longer smooth, its imperfections are highlighted along with the hulking veins in his forehead.

"Or what?" says the old doctor. A good man is hard to find, they say. And yet, here he stands before a pair one pulse away from becoming a firing squad. *Jin Kobayashi.* Navy medic; two tours. Lost a battle to greed, but is about to win the war for the light.

The frenzied clinic seems to coagulate into an indistinct picture—another hideous Mardi Gras float. Oni shakes her head, seeing Jin's determined expression turn into a confident smile, his belief in her and whatever mission she is on worthy of his sacrifice. She tenses, wishing to stop time and talk Jin out of it. *Surely there's another way!* Not all PIT rats are rapists and murderers...Silver flashes in Oni's eyes.

Layton seems to notice the silver flash and tries to orient himself to the source of Oni's alarm, but is too late. The scalpel Jin would have saved Layton's comrade with is the same tool now driving through the rebel's frontal lobe. Jin's last decision means taking one away from Oni, but perhaps giving her one thousand more.

Layton's gun drops, and discharges, sending a ricochet clanging somewhere in the back of the clinic. He staggers forwards, and with jaundiced eyes rolled back into his head, gropes at the scalpel dug deep into the root of all his bad decisions. His wounded compatriot convulses, while Tank panics behind his machine gun. Jin closes his eyes as Tank spears him with a single shot, which throws open the front of his lab jacket like red and white confetti, and sends him crashing to the floor.

This scene, now and forever impressed on Oni's optic plate, gets louder and more wet-sounding as she plunges into the cremator. She pulls the gate closed behind her.

Tank bulldozes through the carnage, and claws at the cremator's rainbow-coloured glass. "You bitch!" he screams. "Screw the reward! My brothers' blood is on *your* hands. I'll pull sixty million out of you in screams!"

Oni kicks away from the gate, and scoots back into the rear of the coffin-sized box. She smacks the walls frenetically, hoping for some unseen door to yield or peel away. Nothing gives.

Past Tank's fiery-red eyes, striped by bloodlust and shot with fury, Oni glimpses Jin. Sliding around on all fours, no doubt blind from blood-loss, he grapples for something tangible—something to help himself up. A fuzzy apparition appears above his head. A security holographic indicates more unwanted guests barging through the lobby to Jin's unplanned party.

Tank tries to shoot his way into the cremator. Its window crinkles; web-like fractures spread out in all directions like rebellious white weeds. Apparently Tank has neither the strength nor the sense to open it up as Oni had.

With her Monocle acting up, night vision is not an option. She cannot tell whether her new arm has found the lever, for she has no feeling in her fingers. *"Irreparable nerve damage," according to Jin.* Using her good hand, she scrapes against the ceiling, and finds three switches. Desperately, she flips all three simultaneously. With a whiz and a click, the wall behind her begins to slide back.

Tank offs another barrage, this time splitting the glass. Crooked metal jacket peppers the near-exit divots, claiming shattered reflections of Oni over their outward bulge.

Oni hears a deep and muffled voice over the sound of the escape hatch opening: "Put the gun down and turn around slowly."

Funhouse-mirror versions of Tank turn in unison to the voice. "You! *I know you.* You can eat me, Outland trash!"

A thunderous blast punctuates Tank's sentiment, and sprays the remainder across the cremator glass. His grey matter slides down in blobs, casting a fuchsia tint on Oni.

Behind Oni, the hatch has widened enough for her to get out. She orients herself forward, and fires her legs backwards, just in case there is a drop. Hearing Jin speak, however, freezes her, as if he had cast a loyalty spell over her new parts. "This is a clinic, not an executioner's row!" the old doctor declares.

The muffled voice addresses Jin now that Tank is no longer holding up his end of the conversation. "Harboring enemies of the state, Mister...?"

"Dr. Kobayashi," Jin answers back defiantly.

"Well, *Mr.* Kobayashi..."

The unmistakeable smack of metal on tile, quickly followed by *a click-shluck*, announces a successful rifle-reload. After several respirator-assisted breaths, the muffled voice continues: "I tell you what: on account of your injuries sustained while no doubt fending off these enemies of Outland and the State of California, I absolve you of your sins."

"No guns. Outland not welcome here...Get out."

Laughter, low and high. *The man with the muffled voice has an audience.*

"Well, Mr. Kobayashi, I think I'll be holding onto my gun. One condition of your absolution is that you tell me what is behind that door the savage was so keen on opening. No doubt something worth hiding."

Running on fumes, Jin gargles Japanese curses, and then asks: "What door?"

"The door I just covered with that PIT-rat's CLOUD-eaten brain."

"Cremator."

"Mr. Kobayashi, please cooperate."

"Crawl in, *gunslinger*. I will show you how it works." Despite having spent his entire adult life in Los Angeles, Jin's fury and indignation erode his tonality and assumed accent.

"Skyr, perhaps Dr. Kobayashi has caught us an archetypal," suggests the feminine third party.

*I know that voice. Late nights working on the CLOUD with Paul at Outland—I heard it then.*

"Perhaps. I will take a look, if he doesn't mind."

Jin growls. There is an umph and a clang.

"You disappoint me, *Mr. Kobayashi.*"

A gunshot rings out.

Oni prays the gunshot was intended to intimidate Jin, but the soft thud that follows sears that last raw and sympathetic nerve carrying her hope for his well-being. Sensing footsteps approaching the gate, and noticing Tank's fuchsia tint darken, Oni—Dr. Jin Koybashi's final masterpiece—slips into the tunnel.

# EXCUSES

*There's no excuse*, Lyle decides; *no excuse whatsoever for letting oneself go like that.* The man in question—sitting on the other side of the aisle in a seat that would scream if it could—looks more like a deli counter than a human being. On his head sits a ball cap, which does a poor job of damming back the putrefied sweat shining his temples. He is a poor advertisement for the defunct team whose avian symbol it evokes. Knotted together over his heaving belly are nine blotchy sausage fingers, the absent tenth a likely victim of diabetes. *Someone who can't avoid mutilation on account of an illness now as preventable as polio doesn't care about himself, and someone who doesn't care about himself is a danger to everyone around them.*

Lyle convinces himself he can smell the man unwittingly awaiting his extrajudicial verdict. Now, it is all he can smell. Rotten meat, skunky body odour, and a faint touch of mint. *Why bother with the mint? Funereal incense?* No excuse. *I'd help him with his problem if I wasn't already running late.*

Disgusted to the point of anger, Lyle gets up, gathers his belongings from the overhead bins, and shuffles down the aisle of the train wallpapered with colonial propaganda. He looks down in anger as he passes the inexcusable mass, telepathically summoning a change. No result, of course.

The door to the next car is blasted by outside light, mediated by the blue-tinted emergency-hatch window. At this speed, Seattle is nothing more than a rainbow blur framed by red letters: "DO NOT PULL IF POD IS IN MOTION." Lyle grins, pleased to have escaped the Emerald City's jurisdiction un-cuffed and unblemished. *Would be even easier without these goddamn headaches.* Enticing though it may be, Lyle elects not to spice things up by releasing the hatch while averaging 850 miles an hour. The inexcusable mass would no doubt shed some weight. The act, although in clear violation of the red letters, would produce a net gain for humanity. But then Lyle Badegger would also be dead, spread like bacon grease over the South Cascades. Marius Tyndale or some other wet-nosed junior partner would take his law practice and his clients, and Dorota, his confidant and muse, would realize her true potential and escape. He would have surrendered to impulse at his penultimate peak, when godliness was just within reach.

Lyle motions to the door to the next car. It is locked, access contingent on digitally-accredited sociability. He runs his wrist over the scanner, and in so doing makes a farce out of *their precious system* with a fake ID.

"Welcome back, Mr. Rinsler," sounds a box embedded in the wall above the scanner. The AI mimicking these human sounds and meanings is the same system that runs life support and archives on Titan—a neutered version of the CLOUD's search AI, Minerva. *Talk about picking the short stick. To have such an exceptional mind trapped in a box, greeting mortal meat as it waddles from compartment to compartment...Shame, shame, shame.* Lyle smiles, and whispers to the scanner: "Better you than me."

The door to the dining car opens up. Warm air sullied by the smell of minty waste rushes past Lyle, quick and forceful as if the unwelcome spirit of the human luggage behind was exorcised and appointed a new host yonder.

"Have a good day!" chirps the wall-mounted tragedy.

Lyle looks askew at the speaker and mutters: "Don't tell me what do to."

As soon as Lyle is through the threshold, the door whooshes shut. If he had a tail, it would have been clipped off, and left to coil and bleed in the other car to the tune of the ferryman's "Hellos" and "Good days." *"Good day, Mr. Rinsler's severed tail! I envy your ability to die! Good day!"*

A few eyes dart up, scrutinizing the new inductee into this car stocked with prefabricated and vacuum-sealed lunch items. Lyle tries to smile, but gives up before hooking both cheeks. *Fuck-em; these valueless non-entities' opinions, desires, wants, and needs, ought all be recycled with their hosts back to helium and hydrogen, and put to work lighting the fringes of space.*

Intuiting a throwaway sum into his swipe, Lyle purchases a sponge-like confection with a frill of brown along the inner-seam—so-called "Real roasted beef." *Real* as in not imaginary, *beef* as in vaguely resembling brown, salty meat.

With his excuse for riding in the dining car tucked under his arm, Lyle looks for a vacant seat. There are two: one between two children, undoubtedly related judging by their unfortunate commonalities. Their blotchy skin and massive foreheads gives their zonage away: *RIM ticks.* Any responsible Blue Zone parent would have given them the advantage of prenatal gene therapy. The other vacant seat is on the far side of the car, just around the corner from taped-off and defunct CLOUD-synchronization stations.

Lyle mopes over to the far side, out of earshot of the little brats. He sits and sets down his sandwich, turning it to find its best face. Pleased with the glint he has managed to give the maroon rind, he clicks on his projector pad. *Better eat this with my eyes closed.* His Monocle picks up the otherwise invisible projection—a subdued prism to the naked eye—and he reflexively switches to his personalized newsfeed.

A villain's photo album of gruesome thumbnails soars into view. Los Angelian scandals feature prominently: "'Archetypals siphon power from nuclear plant, then destroy it...', 'Non-violent rainouts being arrested en mass...', 'Minerva, the world's most-trusted search engine, remains down for the twentieth week after CLOUD crash...', 'BiAnima stocks continue to plummet...', 'Post-trauma memory wipes face federal ban...', 'Citadel bomber, Oni Matsui still at large'..." Among the options, one piques Lyle's interest: Saturn, pale yellow and potbellied, rotates with "TRAGEDY" written in a crisp Serif bolded in the foreground. Monocle registers Lyle's intention to tune in to the extra-terrestrial drama, fades out his vision, and throws him into a shiny, minimalistic news studio. Infographics and 3D models of Outland's Olympus Outpost on Saturn's most profitable moon, Titan, monopolize the wings of the stage.

Two men sit at centre stage, surrounded by 3D-capture units. A projected nametag identifies the man trembling beside the show's host as Serge Demidov. The host is, of course, *NewsLink's* Tom Tinrod.

"Mr. Demidov," says Tinrod, trying to connect with the disheveled figure on his left, "Would you please tell our viewers what it is you saw on that *fateful day*?"

Serge looks out at the immaterial audience, a field of ambivalent avatars gaping at him, keen to hear the details of his personal misfortune. His skin and muscle droop. Earth's atmosphere is crushing him. Very slowly, he answers: "Days."

"Sorry?" says Tinrod.

"Fateful days...It was bad for a while before it ended. They are calling it 'space madness'..."

The audience murmurs.

"Outland, I mean; Outland is calling it *space madness*...But I think we were poisoned."

Two-million-thousand virtual knees jerk. Everywhere gasps are digitally archived. A torrent of indignant texts and telegraphed comms sent in by doubting viewers roll down either side of the stage. None of them is censored. Half of them are self-promotional. The other half advocate for Serge to face a dark-CLOUD interrogation at the hands of the government or the Outland Corporation.

Smiling, the jaunty host—his hair striped black and silver liked magnesium—grips Serge's hand reassuringly, pretending to be something more than a parasite attempting to extort ratings. "Poisoned, Mr. Demidov?"

"Everything was going well," answers Serge with watery eyes, trying his best not to 'vah' when pronouncing his 'w's,' "Both in Olympus and in the greater colonies. We did not have an accident in months. Just about everybody was working their fingers to the bone and then camping out in the CLOUD the rest of the time. "

The host sneaks a knowing look to the audience. Lyle can see through Tinrod's flash-paper exterior. He has immaturity wrapped around his eyes. There are still some men—this host included—who have avoided the wrinkles and nightmares borne by those not exempted from either the War of the Americas or the so-called Unholy War. They either have a knack for it or a privilege to it. Like growth rings on a tree stump—detailing age and the climate in which it rose— the eyes tell all. Tinrod's thinly-barked bachelor eyes speak of nothing but fair weather. His face's resultant brightness and tightness inspire relaxation: a trap for those without the knack or the privilege. While he is hoisted above the wreckage, his confiders lay tangled in rebar twist ties beneath mountains of cinders or, in the case of this interview, defamed and damned on the great American stage.

Tom Tinrod silently bids Serge continue with a slight turn of his hand.

Serge catches the host's returning wink, and grimaces. The man is no fool, unless the social awareness hinted at by his facial expressions should be an extra-mental phenomenon. Before an amphitheatre of soulless, virtual eyes, it must be clear to Serge that he has already been judged and that his fate is predetermined. After all, the law is silent when the drums beat, and the drums are beating—one-million viewers banging their keyboards and tablets like mad apes. When found guilty by the emotional and Netted mob, you better hope you have a lawyer like Lyle Badegger defending you, otherwise you are finished. Even with Lyle on your side, if you have been appointed the Company's scapegoat, you best bleat your way onto the altar.

"We received our monthly Terran shipment from Outland…"

Tinrod addresses the disembodied audience. "For the sake of our subscribers just joining us now, let me catch you up. I'm sitting with one of seven survivors of last year's Olympus massacre who returned to us via the Hermes."

Tinrod's interruption forces Serge to bow his head and pre-chew his reply. Following an impotent point, Serge continues: "It was actually the Hermes that brought over our EFeed, vapor resupply, and energy cells. It had made a stopover on the Orpheus settlement on Hyperion first, then came over with the essentials plus extra cargo—*a body*. Docket said he was an Orphean miner. There were specific instructions to run an open-air autopsy on him. Thing is, I know the entire Orpheus crew, and this body was nobody—nobody I knew, anyway. Mr. Tinrod, I do not know why they did it, but I know that they did do it. Outland sent us a booby-trapped corpse…It is the only thing I can think of…"

An infographic watermarked with a question mark soars across the stage, simulating an astronaut choking. *They've gotten awfully efficient at generating these damned animations off the cuff.*

"I find it difficult to believe, as I'm sure our audience does, that Outland—who financed the majority of this operation from EME—would sabotage Olympus, pay postage on corpses, or attack their own employees with what I presume you're insinuating was a biological weapon. Never mind that they'd have nothing to gain; corporate masochism at the level and of the degree you're suggesting would jeopardize both the Company and its holdings. Forgive my skepticism Mr. Demidov, but I don't think you returned to Earth with all your senses intact, and to be quite honest, I think these kinds of conspiracy theories do those less fortunate than you a second disservice."

The comment feed lights up with vindictive messages.

Crimson fires into Serge's sweaty, pale cheeks. Staring up at Tinrod through his barbwire eyebrows, he offs a barrage: "I never said it was a biological weapon."

More gasps from the bodiless crowd.

"No, the body was charged. The Chief Medical Examiner performed an autopsy. Body exploded. Lights clicked, and—"

Spreading his legs and drooping in his seat, Tinrod focuses on the chattering in his ear. He parrots his producer's feed: "Huh…Mr. Demidov, the Chief Examiner reported nothing unusual in his declassified report. The body's torso ruptured because of 'Saturnian

45

gravitational stress and space-accelerated tissue decay'. There is no mention anywhere of him having found any explosive material."

"Nonsense! He's lying! There was a magnetic disturbance—and the CLOUD shut down!"

"The CLOUD shut down everywhere, I'm afraid," Tinrod jabs back. He claps his knees together and stretches his fingers out overtop of them.

"Months before the CLOUD crashed on Earth," Serge quickly rejoinds. "Olympus had a private cypulchre and server bank. We couldn't connect with Outland's Terran Network on account of cosmic rays and the like. They were totally separate. It took me a year to get home, and the Olympus crash is what sent me."

"I hate to have to keep recapping, but there is just too much sense here for me to confuse…Outland sent a body full of invisible magnets to crash Titan's CLOUD all in order to accomplish what?" Tinrod's eyes are aglow with updates on his viewership.

Demidov looks just about ready to murder Tinrod. "If not Outland, than who or what? What made fathers cut up their own children? Huh!? What made blood run down the commons like a river? All these people—my friends, my family—they were all cleared by BiAnima's quacks. How do good people turn into animals overnight?"

"Mr. Demidov…"

"They don't!" Serge looks like he is going to have an aneurism. Tomato red and shaking, he continues: "We built them a base and when they didn't need us anymore, they experimented on us. They wanted to see what would happen if their CLOUD moneymaker stopped working…The timing was perfect too! Saturn wasn't going to keep protecting us from solar flares, so they used us to test a theory while still covered by their insurers."

"Mr. Demidov?"

Noticing more and more viewers entering the viewing introjection field, Serge tries to restrain himself. He takes a deep breath and firms up.

Tinrod leans in, mind on the viewer traffic and face a druxy dressed in false sympathy. "Could you tell us a little bit more about fathers cutting up their children?"

Olympus is last quarter's accident, but unfortunately for Serge, it is today's news. And Serge missed his opportunity to carry the Company flag into branded legend. If he will not be their hero, he will be their villain.

Without the CLOUD, he cannot show the world the truth by shoving his memories up their spines and into their minds. That means Serge will have to evidence his victimization with scars or wounds, neither of which he has on the outside. *He is royally screwed.*

Images of blood-smeared hallways with sparking outlets and flickering lights emerge behind Serge and Tom Tinrod. Serge glimpses the images, and turns to Tinrod, furious. "Screw you." With an angry point, Serge demands: "Take them down. Take them down right this instant."

Lyle gropes blindly for his sandwich, and fiddles with the wrapper, nominally entertained by the colonist's angst.

Tinrod, secreting his bright teeth between stiff lips, taps his chin and nods, listening to a report wired straight to his Monocle. "The official report just came in..." Tinrod taps Serge on the knee, and repeats the report to the audience. "Upon post-mortem psychological review of a large cross-section of sentience files belonging to the two-thousand Olympian dead, it is now believed that Kalnychuk Syndrome, better known as space madness, was in fact the cause of death in every case, either directly or indirectly. Autopsies corroborate this theory, with reports of 'meningitis-like symptoms', glandular swelling, and spikes in the subjects' adrenal levels."

Serge stares daggers into Tinrod. Lyle covets his passion, his anger, his frustration. *Throttle the son of a bitch.*

Reorienting his attention to Serge, Tinrod puffs his chest and tries to evince deliberation with a wince. "It strikes me as strange that you weren't affected by the illness, Mr. Demidov. Good fortune, perhaps. Or perhaps there is something to your poison theory."

The insinuation catches Serge off guard. He shakes his memory into focus. "I was present when they opened the body. I repaired the sensors after the magnetic disturbance. But..." Despite having had a year in a non-newtonian fluid sac on his way back to Earth to play detective, Demidov has apparently waited until now to solve the mystery. "Most of the time I was with my team—a small team, six men including myself—on a terraform station. We dosed instead of using the CLOUD...They survived—we survived. Whatever was in that body targeted the CLOUD and those using it..."

A 3D image of a mushroom-like atmosphere-generator twirls in the foreground, with indecipherable statistics streaming below it.

"Where are they now? Your team, that is."

Stuttering, Serge folds his hands and grinds his thumbs together. "I—I don't know."

"How convenient!" shrieks the host, turning to the audience like an inquisitor set to bait the foaming mob. The mild-mannered interrogation is over. The kangaroo court is now in session.

Serge goes on the aggressive: he pounds his fist into the desk, toppling Tinrod's mug, apparently full of nothing. "What the hell are you implying, you mudak? I had nothing to do with whatever Outland did to the CLOUD that messed everyone up…They were my friends, god-damn-it."

"Perhaps, Mr. Demidov." Tom Tinrod retreats from Serge's advance—embellishing the threat with a defensive posture. Tinrod pulls open a view-screen out of thin air and stabs at a block of highlighted writing. He reads the text verbatim: "'Serge Demidov, son of Chino-Russian dissident, Anton Demidov.' Messed-up indeed!"

Faceless blue eyes superimpose onto the *NewsLink* feed. They stare intensely back at Lyle. A voice cries out: "Lyle! You must help me!"

Lyle jerks forward in his seat, coughing up pieces of imitation beef. *NewsLink* and the rest of the virtual kangaroo court disappear, leaving him at once freezing and feverish under the firsthand light of the HL car. His mind aches as if while dawdling in virtual space someone had pulled a barbed wire through one ear and out the other. *Another one…*Stifling a salvo of coughs, he looks around the car. There is an entirely new cast about him now feeding on prefab meals. A service droid wipes up the stains left by the RIM spawn and carries on topping up beverages with its finger-like hoses.

"Please note: this is the B20 Express train from Vancouver to Austin," announces a cheery and feminine voice with a Midwest accent over the train-wide intercom. "Pods eighteen thru twenty-two will be detouring to Sacramento and then onto Los Angeles. Breakaway is in fifteen minutes. Please note that the current time is 12:50, and that breakaway will be precisely at 13:05."

Lyle's Monocle indicates the time. "That's me," he mutters to himself. He rubs his temples, but realizes it will take more than topical friction to quell the lightning storm under the bone.

"Pods eighteen thru twenty-two will be detouring to Sacramento and Los Angeles in fifteen minutes," reiterates a male voice, just in case tone-sensitive passengers or misogynists failed to process the previous announcement. "If you have any questions, please visit one of our information kiosks or contact the Hyperloop Authority."

Lyle bypasses the service droid and maneuvers back through the train's different sections. As the door opens to pod eighteen, a familiar stench hits him like a battering ram. "How atrocious!" he exclaims, nearly paralyzed with revulsion. Lyle's subvocal sensor misreads his outcry as a prompt, and an image accompanying search results for some sort of sea snail magnifies over his left iris. Minimizing the image, his noisome nemesis comes into view. The human deli-counter is apparently headed to Los Angeles as well.

Lyle intuits a message to his secretary. "Do'ta. Cancel my three o'clock."

Dorota quickly messages back: "Problem with the H-L? Where are you? I can send for a shuttle."

"No thanks. I feel the need to deal with someone nature failed to cull."

# RAPTORS AND INNOCENTS

Long gone is the Lost Generation and its paralyzed progeny. Now the PIT's streets and gutters are clogged with the Found Generation; tagged, tracked, recorded, and streaming. This generation is not searching for meaning in a broken world. They are looking for themselves, darkly reflected in an unending labyrinth of funhouse mirrors. Plugged in and synchronized, they live to be consumed, and are always exhausted. The Found Generation's legacy dies when the power goes out, ending not with a bang or a whimper, but with a beep.

A lifetime short of that singular beep, there is presently cacophony; silence in the PIT is rarer than help, and neither is forecasted. Here, forty-two-million feet noisily erode eastern LA's multiple-tier slums, each dropping inches a day and pressing the PIT further into the reclaimed desert floor. This erosion is constantly and collectively witnessed. The procession of tech-speckled, weary-looking civilians—subjected to daily, almost ritualistic culling by the Outland Corporation—is faceless, on account of all its constituents feeling the need to focus on their feet. An outsider might mistake the bowed heads for concerted solemnity. If any among them are praying— praying and hoping that the trip to the market, to the strip club, to anywhere or nowhere in particular, will not be their last—they do so despite glaring evidence that their celestial recipient is either backlogged, indifferent, or worse.

Oni's pale face stands out in the crowd. Her eyes are dark little buoys on a turbulent sea. Her raven hair is cropped and her greasy bangs are brushed to one side, accentuating the stubble opposite, shaved and stitched. Jin Koybashi was a phenomenal surgeon, but a good barber he was not.

Being back here—back in the PIT—reminds Oni why she took to virtual realms and cognitive studies so zealously growing up. In the driverless to and from school in Vancouver's C-Blocks, she became familiar with a variety of hedonistic outlets in passing, some of which could very well trump the opulence and grunge of the PIT's most nefarious dens of iniquity. They all terrified her. Nothing that she respected survived in *that* world. She hated how thin civility was worn and how bestial man became in pursuit and service of bodily pleasure. Somehow, she thought, a mental focus could save humanity. As a scientist in Paul Sheffield's lab, she went too far with her thesis, discovering only too late that a privileging of one's immaterial mind over their physical substance meant the dehumanization of the former and the subjugation of the latter. Back here in the PIT, it is the worst of both realities.

A ghastly smell attacks Oni in synthesiasic fusion with the dynamo hum of Los Angeles' poor and downtrodden. She holds her breath in an effort to stop the affront of garbage-pail warmth, unintentionally making herself dizzier than she already was. The street tunnels around her. This tier is concrete intestine; enclosed but placeless, all illegal bulbs, catwalks, roads, maglev circuits, and sidewalks stained the colour of pneumonic phlegm. Moral decay is marked on the infrastructural remains. Each and every carnal and virtual desire is catered to with multitudinous animated signs warring for attention. Nary a yield symbol in sight, and yet a buxom, three-storey holographic cyclops erratically high-kicking instructs motorists to, "Stop! Park below and experience nirvana above!"

All the whorehouse holograms and neon arrows collide then shatter as if turned through a nightmarish Madras-plaid kaleidoscope. With all of the heads around her bowed, only the droids and drones careening by notarize Oni's ongoing transgression: she survived her sacrificial act against Outland.

A bold, unfamiliar voice cuts through her mental fog: "Get off the street, Matsui. Get us to the safe house."

Oni tries to write it off as just another twinge of pain—a Longdream flashback from her coma—but its persistence prompts her to pull into an alley off the PIT arcade. She resets her Monocle and intuits it back on. The queue of warning messages, comms, and media transmissions is one-hundred-times as long as the last time she synched. Above the graphic of "Medical Attention Required," Gibson's name pulses.

"Booker," Oni murmurs. To avoid drawing attention to herself, she subvocally provides Monocle a command: "The Eagle and Child by the Burroughs. Set waypoint."

Before he returned to Camp MUD to assist Oni with her humanitarian mission to reverse the deleterious effects of the CLOUD on southern Californians, Booker Gibson lived in a PIT high-rise, several blocks south of the Chrysalis—east Los Angeles' sin-stained clone of the Citadel. There, he tried looking into the past Outland stole from him. He tried uncovering who he was before he was captured—before they confiscated his history.

Unless it has been released or demolished, Gibson's apartment is forty-two storeys above a pub named the Eagle and Child and a whorehouse as morally bankrupt as its landlord. Oni, Booker, and Father Ed agreed on Booker's apartment as one of several safe houses they could retreat to if MUD was ever compromised or overrun. After all—so went their reasoning—the Eagle's clientele were either too wanted or too wasted to report a few other pariahs. Now, with MUD surely turned to ash and the eyes of the PIT beginning to light up with recognition whenever Oni passed, it seems like a natural place to find her bearings.

The last time Oni was in this sector on this particular tier, there were vestigial canopies made of repurposed UN and EME tents protecting pedestrians from the constant rain of filth from the upper levels. Now the grime from the crisscrossing roads and sky dwellings pitter-patters against stains that would be stalagmites if it were not for the constant hustle and bustle now pushing Oni forward.

Passing under the shadow of a residential catwalk, Oni spies a pair of Sentinels smacking around an old woman. They finger-wag growls at the old bouquet of gin blossoms, likely offering warning instead of an accusation or otherwise they'd use their guns. As the old woman begins to heave and gasp, a larger Sentinel in a heavily-armoured yellow suit waves the Outland cronies away. They flip their visors down and follow the yellow giant across the catwalk, job well done. Hurrying past the old woman's piteous cries, Oni tenses. The last time she had seen a Sentinel up close, she managed to open the back of his head with Paul's revolver. She does not want to imagine how his comrades intend to return the favour.

The sound of clanging steel alerts Oni to a blacksmith striking sparks free from molten swords out front of a low-rent metalworks. Exoskeletal coils gird his hammer arm, which he drives as if intending to split atoms. Sequent sparks fade in front of the barfront nextdoor, dismal if not for the iconic monument perched on the marquee: a golden eagle with a cartoonish infant in its beak. Oni recognizes the spot. *The Eagle and Child.*

Like most post-war architecture in east LA, the Eagle and Child is buried under a pile of disjointed additions. Few if any connect internally, at least in any accessible sense. There are innumerable staircases and bankrupt elevator banks that lead to the upper levels, almost all bypassing the bar and the whorehouse grafted beneath it.

Getting to the rooftops without dropping bodies or cash would be quite a feat. Getting a $29M fugitive to the rooftop is another matter altogether. Fortunately, Oni only needs to get to the forty-fourth floor.

The unpredictable flow of traffic makes crossing the street to the Eagle and Child a daunting task. Head on a swivel, Oni looks for a pattern to the metal and halogen stream, and notices someone staring at her across the way. Poised like an emaciated Buddha on a stack of milk crates, Oni's admirer takes off his goggles. Dark, deep-set adolescent eyes rimmed purple train on her, effecting an almost paralyzing gaze. The gaze is interrupted by a passing double-decker bus, but resumes as soon as the graffiti-ed carriage clears. Oni abandons her crossing attempt, and turns into the crowd. At first, the torrent of indistinct flesh rejects her entry, but quickly subsumes her as she edges in with her prosthesis.

Up ahead, the street meets eight others at a canopied square. Traffic swirls around the square, which at its centre boasts a marble statue of a headless American hero holding two snake-like fibre optic cables at arm's length. Oni resists the leviathan's pull at the intersection and fights through the traffic over to a pedestrian bridge that offers passage to the heroic island.

The bridge, composed of shopping carts and aluminum siding, strains and clangs beneath her feet, adding to the noise generated by the sovereign vehicles sideswiping fate underway. Oni holds the railing weighed-low by love-secured bike locks, and looks back for any sign of the Buddha-like boy to see one thousand heads and headlights, and no piercing-black eyes to speak of.

Oni crosses the rest of the way, and climbs the steps to the statue, giving her a good view of all eight clotted arteries. The bridge over to the commercial island whereon the Eagle is perched is derelict. Its broken anchorage juts out five feet over the street. Even a Locust drone could not make the leap to the next side without bending a fender. *Damn it.*

"Hey!" resounds a chipper voice nearby.

With fists balled up, Oni turns to confront the dark-eyed boy. He is shoeless and scabby and smiling. Oni unknots her hands.

Up close, the boy hardly resembles the Buddha, much less the ideal of one his age. His face is muddled with surgical scars and inorganic stitches someone failed to remove. Despite his surgeon's cosmetic miscarriage, the boy can still manage a kind beam, which seems to raise and project his eyes, no longer deep-set and dark, but a shallow and comforting hazel. "Hey!" he blurts, repeating himself with his initial excitement intact. "You're that woman on the news! You're *her*."

Oni recoils, but there are no more steps; she bumps into the trunk-like leg supporting the headless hero. She nervously searches for an excuse—a backstory—but comes up short and goes on the defensive: "I'm not who you think I am."

The boy does not hear her or elects not to believe her. "Mat Sweet? No." He sucks his bottom lip, and thoughtfully presses his thumbs together. "Matsui!" He erupts into a frenzied albeit nonviolent fullbodied spasm.

Nervously looking around to make sure no one has taken notice of the boy's enthusiasm or his interest in her, Oni lurches forward, motioning silence with an index point. "Please, I don't want any trouble."

"You'll find none from me, m'am," he says, pursing his lips. "It's really you! How about that?" He chuckles over both of his shoulders. "The lads won't fricking believe me. Can you mimic a Sentcom and flip a message my way?" he asks, fiddling with a subdermal implant below his ear.

"I really must be going."

The boy stretches his arms out to his sides, and lets them fall limp. "Ah, no worries." He clears a nostril with a snort. "Where you headed?"

Oni stares blankly at the boy and his mess of a face.

"I get it, M'am. They are coming to get you, after all."

"That's what they said on the news?"

Setting one leg on a higher step and leaning onto it with confidence, the boy nods emphatically. "Said you're a terrorist. That you're going to be eliminated and wiped from the record."

"Oh."

"But the lads and me? We say 'fack O-Company' and 'fack the government'." Carried away by defiant rhetoric, he turns around signalling to his invisible enemies with choice fingers. Seeing Oni motioning to leave, he stammers, trying to regroup his thoughts. "Hell, my uncle threw a block party the day of the riots. W'all think you and the other bomber were taking care of things for us rats." His smile fades. "Right?"

It never occurred to Oni that she might come to be known or remembered as a terrorist or a bomber. The realization sits heavy in her gut. "Yeah."

"See!" He blurts, smile cutting his cheeks again. "That's what we figured." Looking at the blood glistening along the parted lips on Oni's wound, his eyes darken and sink once again. "Shit, m'am. That don't look too good."

"It's fine," Oni says, covering the exposed rivet with her left hand. She descends to face the boy directly. "It was nice meeting you…"

"Carter."

"It was nice meeting you, Carter." Oni gently grazes past him, keen on finding a way to the bar.

"Hey, Mat Sweet!" Carter yells over the hum and bustle of the square.

Turning slowly, Oni feigns an expectant smile.

"Thanks." He points to his head. "I figure I'd still be stuck up in the CLOUD if you didn't go nuclear on O-Company."

*Nuclear. Might as well have been.* Millions of minds, all synchronized to and dependent on remote memories and a shared non-consensual hallucination. Oni and Paul triggered the rain-out in an effort to protect all but the phantom Allen Scheele from the Empty Thought—a data scrub Paul had fashioned as a virtual black hole of sorts. It was a successful last-ditch effort to prevent a virtual holocaust. But where technology is concerned, there is seldom a solution that does not beget a new kind of problem. The rain-out forced all of the synchronized minds back into their bodies, if they still had bodies left to return to. *There must have been casualties.*

Oni scans the boy's face for any hint of sarcasm not lost in the cracks. "Just glad to see you made it out, Carter."

"Hell yeah, I made it out!" With hands raised high, Carter indicates the city dwarfing him. "Back into the PIT." He gropes at imaginary breasts. "Back in touch! Back to what matters." He bounds over a dozen steps onto the statue's platform. "S'long, Mat Sweet."

"Say hi to *the lads* for me." Oni immediately regrets her playfulness.

"I will! But they won't remember."

"Won't remember?" A guilty sensation coupled with a cool

breeze pulling up through the metal lattice pimples Oni's good arm.

Carter bowls around the answer and begins picking at the dirt under his nails. "Yeah, you know how cyclers are."

"I don't, actually."

His smiling façade crumbles, revealing all of his hidden mental bruising. "Jahsus! Where's your head been, Mat Sweet?"

Tears cut down Oni's cheek. *I'm so sorry.* She can see it in his eyes. He has seen wonders in the CLOUD. He's glimpsed the sublime, breathed mountain air, swam through the outer limits, and learned life is not all debt, death, and damnation. It is not all misery. And yet here he is, sooty and emaciated, trapped under the second city, itself rotting in the shadow of a third. He has known peace and love and joy, but never firsthand. A cheery disposition here is the result of madness or courage, and Carter is not the slightest bit mad. What would he have been if Oni had blown up more than one lab? If she had curbed the noosphere before it enveloped Los Angeles? With a quick dab, the tears are gone. Oni smiles and shrugs.

"Cyclers, man. They got mangled trodes. Damned be impossible for 'em to backup XP. With them dropping offline on the regular, they all just cycle. Days change us, you know? Thursday Carter isn't Monday Carter. Friday Carter would rob Tuesday Carter blind." He giggles, and looks vacantly up and past Oni, train of thought derailed by the notion of his doppelganger robbing him. The paradox manages to squish his face. A stealthy endeavour on Oni's part to hide more tears catches his eye and roots his attention back in the real. "They keep rebooting knowing nothing but old time. Mum says they're like guppies. That's some kind of fish or something; the kind that don't remember fack-all. Really sad, but you gotta love them!"

Oni struggles to maintain an encouraging smile.

"I'm getting good at teaching them. Every time I catch 'em up, I…well, I'm getting better at it, anyway."

"I'm so sorry, Carter." Oni wants to hug him, rub his head, and convince him it is o-k, but it is not okay, and it is not her place, and like anything she seems to do, it will just make things worse.

"Ah, shawsh, Mat Sweet. S'all the Sentinels fault."

"Tell them I'm working on a way to fix things. Your friends—tell them." *A mind can leak most things, but not hope. Hope transcends the brain. It is a benign growth that spreads to your muscles and into your bones. These kids might forget the exact rationale for it, but they will recall through feeling,*

*acting, doing.* "Tell the cyclers that change is coming. My friends and I—
we haven't forgotten. " Oni shakes with vindictive rage.

The boy mirrors Oni's passion and begins nodding profusely.
He is no longer silently mourning the sporadic loss of his friends. He
emulates Oni's excited shake and visibly welcomes the alien concept of
justice.

"They can't do this to people and get away with it. I won't let
them." Her promise makes her feel hollow. It is a nice sentiment, she
realizes, but what the hell is she going to do? *Die, symbolic, like the rest of
them.*

"Okay, Mat Sweet." Carter must have seen the disappointment
chase out Oni's guarantee, because he has lost his charge. His body has
gone slack, and his eyes are tame and recessed once again. "Sounds
good. I'll be upvoting for you!"

Carter bounds back across the bridge Oni took to get to the
statue. She watches intently to see how he manages across the street,
Eagle-side. He does not go across. He goes underneath. What Oni
mistook for a shuttered street vendor was actually a side entrance to a
pedestrian bridge suspended from the belly of the street itself. She
forgot that no matter how far you descend into the PIT, there is always
another level below you. The Blue Zone and the RIM suffer no such
rootlessness. Yes, they also sport undercarriages of wires, maintenance
tunnels, and pipe matrices, but here you'll meet death before you find
the bottom, and you're always free to try. Carter chances the encounter
and emerges on the other side fairly quicky. *A good sign, even though
fording the River Styx is likely easier for one already consigned to Hades.*

Appealing to her Monocle for assistance, Oni triggers her
Sentinel wave-scanner. Even garbled, a broken heads-up is better than
none at all. With testosterone-tuned voices crackling in her ear, Oni
sews herself back into the fabric of the crowd, allowing herself to be
yanked along inconspicuously toward the little shed-like structure.

"CitCom, this is Delta Nine, reporting in," says an excited voice
intercepted by Oni's scanner. A few beeps and clicks precede the
Sentinel's report. "Found another colony drawing charge out of the old
power plant...Can you tell Hernandez these bloody inoculations aren't
working? Getting our heads caved in. Do you copy? CitCom? Tower?
Ah god-damn-it!" The mic is overwhelmed with poorly equalized
moans and gunshots. "Need immediate extraction. They're..."

There is a series of beeps, so loud Oni has to run a low-pass over her feed, especially difficult while trying to avoid being trampled or pushed into the street.

"Delta Nine," says an androgynous, tinny voice. "To ensure a successful retrieval, please refrain from firing on your targets."

"God Almighty, we are under attack!"

The robot dispatcher calmly responds: "Please state the purpose of this transmission."

Angry crackles become angry words, this time articulated by another soldier with a lower voice. "Tower, tower…This is Delta Nine. Need immediate extraction in Sector 7, second tier. Inoculations did nothing. Archies got in our heads. We've got guys fragging…Tower?" There is a harsh, repeated fizz. *Pulse-rifle blasts.* "That's it. Screw yourself, Tower, and screw your bounty. We're going to toast the lot of these nutters." The end click on the Sentinel's mic reverberates and decays over the ambient fuzz. *Outland has grown too big to pay notice to criticism or pleas, even from its own conquistadors.*

Approaching the sub-street bridge entrance, Oni elbows herself free from the crowd. Tottering on the sidewalk's edge, she throws her mass towards the entrance. It gives way like a saloon door. Her remaining black hair bobs as she slides in, and is immediately hidden by the sub-street bridge door swinging back into place.

Four metal-wire stairs lead down to a glassed-in bridge with more floor tiles missing than tiles in place. Burns and bullet nicks reveal its sides are more plastic than glass, with that little bit of glass long ago tried, tested, and proved wanting. There are half-a-dozen oil canisters strewn across the way along with a few old Bianima droids picked clean of their salvage.

Envying those quasi-assured moments she had spent with a revolver or a shotgun on her hip, Oni cautiously sidesteps the barrels, and tracks over the empty tile divots, praying not to rouse attention from the invisible looking in from the other side of the plastic. Her weary legs do her no disservice. She clears the tunnel and races up the steps as if some nefarious beast was nipping at her heels. The seeming Hell of this higher tier greets her, and with it, the graven eagle and its imperiled human prey.

The old Hindu swastikas that were imprinted right above the bar's doorsill now appear as Teutonic crosses—a tricky feat of street graffiti. This slight augmentation would inspire Oni to believe in progress if she was not already convinced that progress was a buzzword tyrants use to excuse propaganda and massive consolidations of power.

The front door of the Eagle gives under Oni's unfeeling hand, revealing a cavernous room bespeckled with black and pink faces and warmed by red, orange, and green Tiffany glass lamps. There is a bar at the centre of the room shored up by wooden kegs. Behind the rail— itself an exhibition of clouded glass—stands a puzzle of mismatched kitchen cabinets. All of the cabinets are stocked with booze except for two: one is a small armory, just in case someone needs to enforce last call; the other is a fountainhead of dry wax and home to a statue of a blue-robed young woman. The place smells of mustiness and stale cigar smoke—the very same combination that permeated all of Booker Gibson's clothing; he always smelled like what Oni imagined a poker game ought to smell like.

Feeling her legs loosen beneath her, Oni flashes a smile to the blur of a room. As she stumbles forward, she makes out concerned eyes chambered in a colossal man. Oni silently helloes him and starts for someplace to sit, but cannot cohere the layout of the room. The colossal man approaches and directs Oni with a tap and a point to an empty booth. Although a respectful distance away, his body radiates warmth intense enough to be violating. Fists balled, Oni stumbles over to the embrace of the booth's wet, ripped leather. She gives into the temptation of a second of darkness and closes her eyes, but defers sleep, feeling the burn of the colossus' intense stare.

Oni blinks through mental film to realize the full picture of the man waiting patiently in front of her—a Polish veteran unapologetically wearing a regimental "Deus Lo Vult" tattoo with the matching haircut. His rugged race fails to conceal his concern. "This is not a hospital. No loiterers."

Face hot and legs unresponsive, Oni tries to respond. "Uh huh…"

Perseverating on Oni's mangled arm, he leans in and taps her on the shoulder, refusing to presume open eyes to signal awareness. "No corpses, either."

"I'm fine," Oni grumbles, fighting to balance herself and using the table as leverage. "Just had a hell of a time finding this place."

Colour spills into the man's face, followed by a smirk. "You came looking for z'Eagle?" He lets out a loud laugh, one he no doubt practised on occasion and during bouts of depression, frustration, and rage. "I extend to you a pilgrim's welcome." He bows. Before standing upright, he tilts his head and winks. "A pilgrim still must pay to stay."

Throwing her hands out like she has confetti to share, Oni lists her cures: "Can I grab a water and…"

"I am the bouncer here. I am not—"

Oni coils forward, damming back a disheartening groan. "Do you by any chance have painkillers?"

The bouncer plumps his bottom lip thoughtfully, and looks over to the bar. "Benzedich! Benze!" he roars.

A troll-nosed bartender pops out of a hidden compartment in one of the kegs. "Yah?"

"Środki przeciwbólowe?"

The bartender, visible proof that InvitroGen Tech has not made it to the PIT, closes his eyes and rattles off a list of street drugs under his breath. "Yah. Heroine, i morphine, i Longdream, i ketamine…"

Oni looks up to the bouncer. "Longdream. How much?"

Cackling off in the green-lit cyberlounge behind the bar overpowers a lull in the grungy tune dirtying the airwaves. The cackler—a blimp of a man, prematurely wrinkled and protruding packets every which way—slaps his knee, indifferent or oblivious to the attention he is drawing with his safari noises. Someone har-hars back, sending the rest of the bar back into solipsism and conversation.

The bouncer scratches his jaw and shakes his head, visibly envious of the blimp's distinct laugh, well-rehearsed. "Whore for attention, that one." He redirects his glower, and shades the front door with a look of Judas anxiety.

*Who is he expecting? Sentinels? Perhaps the waiter who ought to be here placating this bleeding pilgrim?* Watching her prospective drug dealer riding away from his train of thought, Oni draws attention to the deafening ellipses plotted between them. "…Longdream?"

He nods, and sets his gaze on Oni—not on her wounds this time but on her eyes. He is once again conducting his train. Whatever his carriage, it weighs heavily on his cheeks. "Are you staying with us? Upstairs?"

"No."

As if the answer is somewhere between his bottom lip and his jaw, he continues to massage his chin. He grunts and looks back to the impish man corking bottles. "Benze!"

"Yah?"

"Jak dużo?"

"Fifty for two or seventy-five for three."

With her Monocle-scanner still humming in her ear, Oni interfaces with her banking information. All black-bit, underground finances, of course. What is left to spend is whatever Outland, the LAPD, and the IRS failed to find and freeze. She has enough cash squirreled away to drown herself in Longdream. Oni grabs the bouncer's wrist, and wires $150 over the ether. Her Monocle records the transaction and reveals the bouncer's name: Stephen. Stephen wags a finger at Oni. "Benze said fifty." Overpayment in the PIT is not something that usually sees an interruption or a reversal.

Oni taps her good hand against the table. "Stephen, I would very much like some Longdream, a beer, and some warm food."

That same practiced laugh ruptures from Stephen's mouth, this time with an inflection signalling sincerity. "A pilgrim who knows the Eagle should know to avoid its food."

Riddled with pain, Oni nevertheless manages an expression of calm. Pointing to her arm, she reassures, "It'll take a lot more than bad feed to kill me."

Visibly pleased with Oni's resilience, Stephen signals to Benze and mouths, "*The works.*"

Sitting as far back as the faux leather will permit, Oni convalesces over a pint of cappuccino-coloured stout.

Sitting lonely at ten o'clock and shadowing three on the circular table is a red clay pot. Inside: a cemetery of cigarette butts. No soil, just ash. Lipstick genders several of the memorials. One has oil on it. *Didn't know androids smoked.*

As consciousness returns to her in electric bursts, Oni overhears or remembers—she is not quite sure—a frothy conversation spilling out of a nearby booth. It is dreamlike: a burbling and shared rant that becomes more and more irrational as the speakers close in on their points. Like asymptotes, they near some axis of sense, but both fail to connect. Something about ghosts on Olympus; some guy named Serge Demidov; astronauts possessed by a single, shared drive to communally self-annihilate; an Outland cover-up; government corruption; alien overlords: and anarchical truth and establishment lies. Oni risks a crick in her neck to get a glimpse of the palaver, and leans

61

out of the booth to see nothing but peanut shells and elbows. Easing back into her stout, she catches a whiff of onions. There is no debate over its reality or immediacy.

A comingling of stomps and crinkles loudens behind the booth. Oni's physical capacity for curiosity is spent; she cannot bring herself to turn to the pending interaction. She blinks a slow SOS for nobody's benefit. The sounds louden to the point of indistinction, resulting in a wham. The lighting behind this thunder: Stephen, balancing food and cutlery.

Blinking herself a slow framerate, Oni cannot see Stephen, but she can smell him and his offering.

"You came a long way. You will eat, survive our cooking, and bring word of z'Eagle's kitchen and your survival to fellow pilgrims." Stephen drops a black metal charger plate in front of Oni. Her fishbowl vision reaffirms what her nose has already revealed: a charred flat-iron steak encrusted with fried onion paste, framed by dough-drop nibbles. It is a convincing print, overzealously grilled; even more convincing on account of its mistreatment.

"Thank you," Oni says as she pulls the plate towards her. "Stephen?" she stresses his name, socially anchoring herself in a mental tornado.

"Yah, pilgrim?" He feigns disinterest, but his body is knotted by apprehension.

"The apartments...above the hourlies. They still there?"

Stephen's face compresses. His molars connect to ease out the answer. "Nova Cancy? Yah. They'll always be there. Until Judgment Day. The Lord will leave it be, even then." He pinches something on his chest through his shirt—dog tags or perhaps a scapular. "You need a tour?"

Oni smiles coyly. Stephen's familiarity is too much, too soon. A second, invisible skin coats her, fixing a defensive scowl in place. "No, not today. Thanks, though."

The rejection must have been audible in one of those rare gaps in bar polyphonics, because Benze and the barstool lampshades are glaring Oni's way. Stephen senses the attention, and laughs his trademark laugh, this time bereft of all sincerity. "You know where to find me..." He catches himself mirroring Oni's scowl and throws back his shoulders. "*Us*, I mean." An invisible siren on the other side of the bar summons him, and he apologetically nods to Oni. "Good evening."

*Evening already?* Oni has lost blood and hours, neither of which Monocle has been capable of keeping track of or relating to her with its welcomed graphs and statistics. She scarfs down the steak, crosses her cutlery across the greasy collagen, and pushes the plate forward. Moaning under her breath, Oni turns out of the booth and gets up. She looks over to Benze and Stephen, both behind the bar whispering about *whatever*, and waves. It is actually less a wave and more a raised curl of the fingers, like a pod of dying leaves on the vine.

Muffled by a dozen other conversations, Oni can still make out Stephen's, "Good luck, pilgrim!"

*Good luck, indeed.*

## NOVA CANCY

A narrow alley, yawning fifteen steps to the right of the Eagle and Child's front door, separates the bar and whorehouse from the neighbouring metalworks. Twisted neon promises passersby that the bladesmith and the augmenter "ARE IN" while also illuminating a nearly-illegible "NOVA CANCY" sign. A flare off of the smith's forging press flashes the opening.

Booker had given Oni an informal tour of the neighbourhood years ago and paid passing mention to this route in particular. Back then it had a proper entryway, looking less like a wet hellhole and more like the discreet entrance to a gentleman's club in a genteel neighbourhood—the kind of portal that was gussied up so as not to sink the perceived esteem and morality of the area. Now, it doesn't matter.

Together, they had gone down the alley a quarter of the way, bypassing the Eagle's debauched nest, and into another hall with byzantine-patterned aluminum siding, backlit green, to doublecheck the power metres. (Booker was paranoid; thought his landlord had been throttling his feed.)

Reminding herself that constancy is not a quality the PIT is known for, Oni grimaces and cautiously trudges into the darkness through a gateway no longer pretending to dam back something other than decay and nastiness. In the claustrophobic dark, Oni resorts to visual support from her Monocle. It is still glitchy; she will have to fix it once she finds someplace safe—*safer than the Eagle*—if such a place still exists.

A knot of wires dangling like beaded strings in a fortune-teller's doorway hinders Oni's progress just a few steps into the alley. She brushes them to the side with her unfeeling arm. Beyond, the way seems to shrink even more, now dressed on either side with old wartime propaganda, charred and peeling. Seems a recruiter tried to find the downtrodden before another sign further ahead could prompt them to abandon all hope, hoping they would repurpose themselves for some hawk's third-page headline. The first poster bids Oni and all the other ghosts before her who have scurried through to: "Break the southern wave before it crashes on American shores. Join the—" The name of whatever team or group the poster was promoting has been effaced. Those who had heeded the call were likely effaced, too; the southern wave obliterated several flotillas before diverting course and flooding Mexicali.

Whether it was a second or third wind that resurrected Oni from the bar-booth coffin at the Eagle, all she has left now is a tortured breeze, which barely blows her along. Her legs seize at the base of a dozen misshapen steps whose terminus is awash in neon fuchsia. She leans against a colourless fragment of a propaganda poster and froths, her pain transformed into grayish bubbles on her lips. Although she is an agnostic, a prayerful sentiment cuts past the spittle: "Help."

*No one helped Paul, and he was a believer, even if he wouldn't admit it. Maybe,* Oni considers as she dabs sweat on her brow, *prayers aren't for the here and now, but for another you in another dimension...A transdimensional offering of insight and invigoration, affording an alternate self a soulful push so they can make things better or at the very least different for themselves.*

In her delirium, Oni mistakes the smacking of a plastic for the flapping of an interceding angel's wings. No such luck.

Angrily, she kicks one leg forward, and then the other up and onto the next step. Those parts of her body now failing her are integrated enemies. Her prosthetic, on the other hand, does its job without fail, endearing itself to its operator despite being a bastard graft.

"Damn it!" she curses, breathless. Now her toes are cramping. "Come on, not much farther." Forsaken by her would-be angel, she imagines an unbroken version of herself from a dimension where things are not so bleak helping her along. "Thanks," she says, sweat stinging her eyes.

The fuchsia light coats Oni and shades her crooked outline purple. Warring for every step, she bleeds into the hallway. This stretch is familiar—this much she remembers. *Just down the hall, up a few floors on a dumbwaiter disguised as an elevator, and then into a circus of sycamore bannisters and numberless doors.*

Specters along the hall—smoking, whispering, mashing lips, and tripping balls—do not pay Oni any attention. She ambles along clubfooted, saliva dripping down her face. If there were any perverts among those purple-corona-ed silhouettes, they might think twice about Oni, granted she looks like she is suffering from space madness or worse.

There is a sign on the wall opposite the elevator that reads: "NOVA CANCY."

The elevator door slides open unprovoked. Good thing, too;

Oni did not want to blow it open as per her custom. Fifty blue buttons, none of them labelled, strobe in tandem on the left of the jarred door. Gears above and below clank. The carbon-fiber cable carrying the glorified dumbwaiter vibrates; just tight enough to hum a first-octave B note. Elevator jazz plays Oni into the crème-coloured eggfoam compartment. Eyesight failing her, she slaps the top ten buttons in the final row, figuring her best bet to be an ascending process of elimination.

Some part of her believes Booker will be waiting for her. He will hear the elevator ding, announcing Oni's Odyssean return, and run over to greet her while trying to hide the fact that he ran. Instead of axes and suitors, the only struggle she will encounter is with flat beer and a lumpy bed.

The doorway to the safe house, Booker Gibson's home away from home, stands out from all the others. Covered with a thick layer of mildew, it rejects the glare off the cold cathode lanterns posted next to every other door. Oni makes a line through the neglect with her finger, and tries the handle. *Locked.* She jostles it, creating a ruckus that unhinges bats in the courtyard.

Beside the door handle is a grey box that looks like an old intercom. Oni wipes it clean, revealing its true colour: black with red stripes. In the middle of the box, raised a quarter inch off the door, is a biometric scanner.

Oni squats, and stares into the little scanner. Nothing happens. Recalling Gibson had her and Ed give him fingerprints, she tries her left thumb. There is a beep, and a lime-coloured light blinks on the box.

"PLEASE PLACE YOUR RIGHT THUMB ON THE SCANNER," scrolls in red block letters, two-by-two, across the scanner plate.

Oni looks down to her hybrid of flesh and metal. With a look of excitement—piqued by the promise of safe haven on the other side of this metal and wood plank—she places her right thumb on the scanner. It copies her print and ponders on the manmade Fibonacci pattern. Flashing back a refusal in lime green, it prompts her again in red block letters. Frustrated, Oni shutters her eyes. "Come on!" she cries. She starts pounding on the door, indifferent to creating a scene for the bats and the junkies.

Down the semi-corridor, there is a whoosh followed by a clicking sound. Oni freezes. She cannot see the source of the commotion through all of the LED-lit dust and radiator steam, but can tell from the rhythmic grind of metal on floorboards that it's bad news.

Turning her attention one last time to the little black box blinking lime green, Oni makes a fist—she can tell it is a proper fist since the skin coating the metal has buckled—and slams it through the security scanner. In lieu of red block letters, the scanner produces sparks.

The grinding sound is growing louder.

"Come on, damn you!" Oni shouts as she punches the box again. This time, she knuckles through to the other side of the door. Pulling back a gory ridge of digits, she places her faith in her left hand and reaches through the gaping hole.

A security droid cuts through dust and steam not too far down the corridor. Flailing its clawed arms and pointing its chain gun Oni's way, it gives orders via a holographic cartoon face: "Identify yourself!"

*Key under a doormat would have sufficed.* Oni hugs the door and frantically curls her fingers in search of the lock on the other side. Splinter-pricked, they find the reset on the scanner's rear panel. She presses it, and the locking mechanism frees the door.

The droid's smiling cartoon face disappears, and is replaced by a red frown. Coinciding with this pictorial change in mood, the droid also changes tact. It opens fire, mulching Gibson's doorframe and door. Oni leaps into the apartment, narrowly evading the security droid's wrath.

"Shooting will persist until you identify yourself or are yourself identified," declares the droid, grating metal and littering spent bullet-casings.

Flat on the floor just inside Gibson's apartment, Oni kicks the door shut, and scoots backwards to reinforce it. A hail of bullets chews through the wood just above her.

"Identify yourself at once!" re-orders the droid. Comm static and a series of beeps preface another precise and emotionless pre-recording: "Authorities will be notified and additional units will be dispatched if the occupant does not reveal its identity. Ultimatum given; standard twenty-seconds reply time offered."

Twisted blinds let in light from a hologram flickering on a neighbouring building. The light crowds Oni with orange silhouettes and hides blunt answers to her droid problem with shadow.

A tingling sensation in her ear signals the realization that she has a recording of Gibson's voice. Oni intuits on Monocle and synchronizes it with her subvocal pickup. With no more than ten seconds left in the bot's arbitrary countdown to slaughter, Oni races across her archived comms to a recent message from Gibson. He would have likely used a pseudonym on account of having been as much of a fugitive back when he got this apartment as he is now. *What's in a name, anyway? The droid will just pick up on the vocal signature…*

"Oni, it's Gibson," says her friend in a voice ostensibly warm and real, yet so severed from this living situation—like a supernova to an astronomer's eye. She plays the message again, this time opening her mouth and maxing out the pickup range. Without a reply from the droid, she shimmies over and opens the door a crack.

The droid registers the crack as an opportunity, and tracks forward. The red frown leers into the room. "Identify…"

Oni tries her best to hide from the machine. She presses her lips to the door crack and tongues borrowed words: "It's Gibson."

The droid jolts backwards as if in shock. Its spider-like appendages fold inwards and a beam of pure white light fires out, trying to pinpoint the source. "Occupant: present yourself for visual identification."

Oni plays the recording again. "It's Gibson."

The droid snuffs out its light, and rolls back a few feet. "Vocal match; Thomas Whitaker."

Trying desperately to keep up and play along, Oni scans Gibson's comm for a note of confirmation.

"Yeah," Oni says, repeating an artifact left behind by the so-called Thomas Whitaker.

"Mr. Whitaker," says the droid, adopting a less harsh tone of voice, "Irrational and evasive behaviour can result in unnecessarily dangerous situations. Please sign in with security the next time you come home to Nova Cancy. I apologize for the inconvenience."

Gibson's voice pipes through the crack one last time: "Yeah."

Oni fumbles with the door's locking mechanism and decides it is a lost cause. For her stopgap defense and a warning, she drags a chair over and leans it against the door. Satisfied with the measly barricade, she reaches for the first loose garment she sees—one of Booker's long-sleeves. She shreds it, and tightly binds her arm. With the bleeding staunched but still too weary to walk the ten feet to Booker's bed, Oni sinks into the chair buttressing the door and closes her eyes.

Oni's guilt drags her down the rabbit hole, although she misses Wonderland completely. She instead finds herself at Camp MUD before the incident, before the fall of the CLOUD.

Emily and Constance are working furiously in the rehabilitation tent, coaxing a rainout's body into accepting his mind. The man, black and scarred, flails between them, his fingers curled and his eyes rolled back into his head. Oni rushes over. "Status?" she says, following history's inevitable script. Her voice dopplers and distorts, sending a surreal ripple throughout the scene.

Emily looks up; her face is featureless. She has no mouth and no eyes—just vague outlines of a nose and brow. Nevertheless, she manages an articulate response: "This is the John Doe from the crash. It's not just a matter of assimilating the mind...Someone fried his memory. Looks like an Outland strip."

Oni gently pushes Constance aside, whose indignation finds no outlet on her blank slate of a face. Checking the patient's neural scans—which somehow confer meaning despite being nothing but a green and black blur—Oni calculates what strength of charge will be able to excite the shadows of the nuked data long enough for her to make a copy and preserve the patient's identity. "Bring me a sentience plate," she orders Constance, midway out of the tent. "We're going to copy the wiped data and reconstruct it. It's his only chance."

Constance nods, and bolts towards the supply shed.

This time around, gifted with omniscience, Oni is a lot more confident. Her hands are not shaking—both seamless and organic in this mental construction—and she has not a single doubt in her mind to stay her hand or slow her down.

Constance returns with a Gorgon's head of wires, sensors, and scanners. "Dr. Matsui," she says, out of breath, "Even if we reconstruct his memories, we might be implanting them into unreceptive, dead tissue."

Wiping blood off of her tunic, Emily sidesteps the gurney to relieve Constance of some of the equipment. Placing a bundle of wires on the patient's chest, she frees her hands, and starts adhering sensors to the patient's head and neck. "But we'll have tried."

Oni nods, priming the neural imager. She wonders what would

happen if she were to stray from the script; let these dreamt-up characters repeat history unaided. *What's the point?* She already saved Booker Gibson's mind once, after she dragged him all the back to Camp MUD from the crashed Outland transport. Preserved what of his mind she could—whatever wasn't completely scoured by the Outland techs. Gave him a second chance…

The dreamer steps back, liberating herself from the ride's track. A translucent doppelganger appears in her place, continuing with Emily and Constance to save Gibson's mind.

Freed from the constraints of the dream and tangled somewhere in the briar patch between sleep and waking life, Oni looks at herself, at that hopeful phantom not yet bleeding on the double-edged sword that pierced the Citadel.

Aware now, of her living body—of the pain in her right arm, or rather, the remnant of her right arm in its metal prison—she turns her back on herself and on the operation. Behind her, however, is a large, dark figure. She recoils, and stumbles, falling into herself, onto imagined ground. The hulk before her, unlike Emily and Constance, is not faceless. Scars, lips, brown eyes, and all: Booker Gibson.

"Hey, Matsui. I take it you got my message?"

Oni tries to answer, but she is voiceless. Agitated, Gibson frowns and steps forward. He motions to speak again, but his teeth spill out of his mouth, and as if becoming jelly, his limbs start to buckle and fold. Again, Oni tries to speak—to scream—but nothing comes out. Gibson, sinking on hollow timber, caves over and explodes, splashing vanishing-gore onto Oni.

Now awake, soused in sweat, panting, and quivering, Oni twists forward. Her eyes have trouble adjusting. She regains control and perseverates on a framed photograph of Father Ed, Emily, Constance, and herself. The invisible photographer is the same whose apartment now hums around the icon. *Booky.*

As soon as she is on her feet, she realizes two things: the painkillers have worn off and strength has returned to her legs. She rummages around in her pockets for a tab of Longdream with her right hand, but abandons the effort realizing she would not be able to know if she had found it or not. She tries with her left and procures a few tabs.

In search of water, Oni cautiously navigates furniture and

storage crates towards what she presumes is the kitchen. The orange from the advertisement outside only manages a single quill into the kitchen, offering very little assistance in discerning place and space. Oni paws the wall for a light switch. Her first swipe yields a click, but no illumination. Gibson probably neglected to pay forward the utility bill when postdating credits on the rent.

Oni intuits on Monocle. Several notifications appear, indicating unread messages and unheard comms. *Later*, she determines, as she rolls her eyes through the options to 'Tools' and prompts night vision.

A dozen bourbon bottles and empty glasses crowd the sink, which is itself busy with moldy plates and infectious cultures. On Oni's right are a few cupboards, a fridge with a tattered cat calendar, and a prison-cell-sized area with a foldable card table and a wooden chair. Dotgrams and a few almost-certainly incriminating photographs are scattered about the tabletop, all caked in dust. *Gibson had crossed someone to warrant his data-wipe and death sentence. The heavily-armoured exowarrior recurring through all the photos, perhaps.*

Oni grabs a glass. It shatters in her hand as soon as she clasps it. "Shit," she says, checking herself for new cuts. There is no more blood than there was a moment ago; just more metal glaring through.

She tries for another glass and then the tap. The dull cast-iron faucet shudders. Pipes clatter beneath the sink. Oni takes a step back, surprised that she's not already uncovered several booby traps left behind by a paranoid and covetous Gibson. The tap calms down long enough to discharge a torrent of brown slush onto the moldy plates.

After shaking out a litre of detritus, clear water miraculously springs forth from the tap. Oni, a seeming diviner in this ramshackle cottage, rushes to catch it. Glass after glass, she slings second life down her throat, compulsively catching every drop. Awakening, her body begins to ache anew; organs, previously shutting down, extend their roots and sap the fuel.

The orange advertisement outside turns teal blue, throwing Oni off-kilter with a stray beam in a new hue. She finishes another glass of water, and stumbles back into the other room.

Touched up with a teal finish, different artifacts stand out that didn't before. Near the class photo of dead friends, there is a stack of Sentinel paraphernalia, including a bullet-riddled helmet and a bodiless armoured vest. A custom assault rifle sits on a transparent wall-mounted rack, looking more like artwork than an instrument of destruction.

When Oni and her team first found Booker Gibson, they knew right away he had had his memory wiped. Micro-divots along his cranium and charring on his temples. They knew as much about him as he did about himself: name and expiration date. After a marathon surgery and days of "cognitive refurbishing," Gibson recovered enough memory to conclude that he had at one time or another been an Outland stooge. That stooge made the grievous mistake of developing a conscience and going rogue. But instead of rising to the height of the moral high ground he had staked, he fell as deep as Los Angeles goes.

Where memory failed him as to where he landed, ink took up the story. His back—a living tapestry—bears the beginning of his successful but interrupted story as a mercenary for the Yakuza, dealing death and discs. The tattooist would not finish the story. Whatever the reason, it is clear Booker Gibson began taking his authorial privilege seriously. Burn enough bridges or do the right thing under a bad thing's watch, and you will find yourself on an island without a way back to the mainland.

If it is a devil's work to make a man forget the good work that brought him pain, then perhaps it is an angel's job to give him a chance to remember. Unwittingly Oni became Booker Gibson's angel. Pulled him out of a MAT Transport headed to an Outland butcher, got him on his feet, and gave him space without any guarantee he would return. He did return, however; whether that earned him another dance with the devil is left to be seen.

Oni grazes the couch on her way to the window. She spreads two blinds with her fingers, and scrutinizes the view of a tiny courtyard overcrowded with holograms and piping. The apartment's key-light is one holographic billboard in particular, which extends an invitation from Outland's subsidiary BiAnima to any and all "able bodies" who might wish to work on their Mars base, Remus II. It is an old billgram, dated by the very mention of the now-defunct polar base and the stray light it casts into Gibson's apartment. Oni's lips reject the billgram's teal colouring and settle on cobalt. She lets the blinds snap back into place and mutters to herself—nothing particularly pressing; just something to reiterate her humanity: "There's good left."

A resolute voice—muffled so the words are not clear but the tone still is—fires out into the courtyard. Its pitch and turbulence suggest the speaker's uncertainty; perhaps a political speech in the works or a business proposal in practice or a half-assed scolding. No. The voice peters out. There is a pause. Despite the speaker's delivery, whatever was said has the power to shape chirps, guttural crows, and applause out of the silence. A joke! There is another pause, and a secondary tremor. Silverware and ceramics chatter all through the laughter's slow descrendo...The very idea of a dinner party strikes Oni as luxurious, something requiring time, security, dinner, and friends. As the laughter fades to a staccato din, Oni realizes she would not know what to do with herself free of pain, fear, and guilt. *"Don't get distracted,"* she says as her body firms around her self-denial.

Turning, she dislodges a book from a pillar of others with matching jackets. Quickly, she prevents the rest of the pillar from collapsing, realizing immediately its purpose: holding up an amputated work desk. Gadgets and precision tools are positioned like Chinese characters across its surface. Oni brushes aside the bad translation and peels a dotgram out of its dusty cocoon. She activates Monocle, and glances at the configuration. Her HUD pulls the dotgram's details from the Net and projects the result. The projection shows a fit woman in a long gown with short blonde hair. Text scrolls behind the dotgram projection, revealing the woman's identity: *Celeste Charming.* The data is antiquated. Here, it indicates she is an up-and-comer at Outland, whereas in reality, she is now the Interim CEO, thanks to Paul Sheffield's handywork.

Oni looks the desk over and finds another dotgram. She projects it, too. Celeste Charming appears again, this time with an unofficial biography. Less a few hundred buzzwords, the biography reads:

"Charming, Celeste. Born in La Jolla, California. Spent eight years as a Cy-Ops agent for Mi6. Survived the nuclear devastation of the Eastern Union when stationed in Budapest with only minor burns and remediable radiation poisoning. Returned to California to complete a doctoral degree in nanotech and a master's in business administration. Fast-tracked to oversight position at BiAnima, then over to BiAnima's parent company, Outland. Became COO of the Outland Corporation and today holds over two hundred patents in CLOUD-related tech. Celeste's present mandate: save humanity from its baser inclinations and tendencies."

Notes in Gibson's erratic handwriting are overlayed upon the biography: "Parents were delinquents...Father was an alcoholic.

Mother sold pornographic holos to put food on the table. CC has little faith in the state government that put her father out of work and denied her mother's petitions to re-locate to Mars. She emancipated herself at the age of fourteen, and appealed for right-of-return to go to London. There she served in the military for two tours in the Forbidden Zone. Buried both her parents before she was 24. Special interests and Minerva-search key words: 'Noospherics'; 'Hive mind'; 'Neural Energy, amplification'; 'Allen Scheele'; "Marx"; "Friedman"; and 'Shouta Katajima'.

How Celeste's path never crossed with her own in any meaningful way strikes Oni as a mystery. While Paul Sheffield and Oni turned the cogwheel down in the labs, Celeste sat by the conveyor belt hand-picking the future.

There is another dotgram stuck to the back of the one Oni just scanned. She zealously tears them apart, forgetting her injuries. With a groan, she leans into the desk. The column of books topples over, sending loose pages and cards fluttering about Oni's feet. "Tarnation!" she shouts, jumping out of the way of the desk's collapse. Creaking outside alerts her to her own commotion, and she cups her mouth with one hand while futilely preventing the further slide of materiel onto the floor.

After a half-assed effort to right the desk, Oni grabs the dotgram and takes it over to the couch. Monocle broadcasts the note— an entry by Gibson: "Was she the target? Did they scrape out my memory for going after Charming? If so, who hired me? Best have a sit-down with Akbari. Need answers."

*Had Gibson's good deed been saving this wretch?* Oni wonders. Uneasy with having her worldview tested once more, she lurches out of the embrace of the couch and towards the imagined warmth of the light filtering through the window. This time, she pulls the blinds up all the way and presses her forehead to the glass.

"Ever look across into those apartment windows and project yourself into their lives?" Father Ed asked Oni after they had moved into their first RIM clinic in the days before Camp MUD.

"No," she answered dismissively, focused—*always so focused*— on the job at hand.

"I guess your generation doesn't need to do that. You have the Sensedens and the CLOUD. Stories without the work. I guess the only difference is that instead of putting yourself in their shoes, you are putting them in your head. No need for socks or souls." The old man left her just as lonely as she is now, staring into BiAnima's unfounded promise of dignified work and a compelling view back at this pale blue dot.

*This is it. This is how it's going to be from now on*: a short life spent running, ceaselessly, from room to room, with her head on a swivel and her hands permanently balled into fists. An enemy ear pressed up against the back of every door. Unblinking eyes everywhere, stealing souls and reporting bodies. Dumpster dinners and second-hand smokes. *A silent existence.*

Without social repetition, she will not have use for a name. Without a name to circulate, the woman they called Oni Matsui will leave the bastards one fewer clue as to her whereabouts...Without a name, she will be reduced to another Jane or Annie, like the stiffs they used to resurrect at Camp MUD, losing her humanity with every failed reiteration.

*Room to room.* Never mind Sentinels or the odd stray from the National Guard—*this is the PIT*. Punks and gangs wart this carcass; who cave in heads indiscriminately for fun. *They won't even touch your tech. Just burn calories kicking your ribs into your organs. Messed up lost boys and tank girls staking claims in chaos.*

*Room to tomb.* She would climb the mountain and duck into the desert, or jump into the ocean and pray for Mexican pirates to pick her up, but the bounty on her head is too high and she does not have the friends left or the tech to bypass the Military containment. An insurmountable bounty, a pile of dead friends, and a head full of compromised tech, all thanks to the Outland Corporation.

Outland's Citadel—the Babylonic tower Oni thought she had toppled—now casts a larger shadow on the Blue Zone, on the RIM, and on the PIT. Oni cannot see it from here, but can feel its presence. She can feel it growing taller and looking out on a bigger and bigger Outland empire. "Are you still with me, Booky?" Oni whispers to the glass, terrified about what has become of him—terrified he has been captured, and terrified about what they are doing to him and what they have done to him already. If he is dead, then he is a recent addition to an old pile, as tall if not taller than the Citadel.

Her friends' Promethean legacy is now used to light the cigars of tyrants whose boots wear on the necks of the disenfranchised. Oni, Paul, Ed, and Booker mistook all-out war for a covert skirmish.

Absolute victory or absolute defeat; there was never a third option, though they conned themselves into believing in one. *Outland is a cancer and it must be stopped once and for all.*

Oni gives herself a half-dose of Longdream—enough to mute the pain, but not too much to make herself sick or useless in a dust-up. She unbinds her wrist. Although the skin on her prosthetic is cosmetic, it is still real skin, and that real skin is festering. She shuffles back over to the kitchen sink, wets a rag, and—dripping water into the main room—dabs her prosthetic in the half-light.

"I wish you'd told me how you felt about me," thunders a deep voice.

Splat goes the reddened rag. Oni pirouettes, searching for the speaker.

"It's me, Oni." A ghostly apparition slides across the floor, through the couch, and over to Oni's side.

"Booker?" Oni's throat closes behind the name. Without air getting to her reed, she pipes a scratchy whisper: "Must be the drugs." She quickly checks her pockets and counts how many Longdream she gulped down. "Damn it," she says, certain she took a small dose.

"Hey, sweetpea. I've been trying to get your attention for a while now. You've got your mind locked down pretty tight."

Oni shakes her head violently and falls into the leathery embrace of the couch. "Some kind of guilt trip," she stammers. She tries to run a self-scan via Monocle, but the interface bricks up. A roundish image carves itself out of the glitchy mayhem: Gibson's face. Terminating the feed with a hard tap against the side of her head, Oni gasps for air. *Am I losing it?* she asks herself. *Today's trauma'd be enough to stump the best of them...*

No longer trusting of her eyes or her Monocle feed, Oni looks to defend herself. Gibson's old assault rifle. *That'll do.* She bounds for it, yanks it free—cracking the mounts and splintering the adhesive gel holding them to the wall. She can tell by the weight alone that it is not loaded.

"Oni, please relax," says Booker Gibson's projected doppelganger.

Focused on self-preservation from worldly and supernatural threats, Oni claws through the desk's drawers. She tugs too hard on the bottom drawer. The three-legged desk rocks forward, once again knocking its literary support asunder. In the metal and paper aftermath,

Oni spots black foam. Her eyes light up, for nestled inside the foam is a banana clip brimming with FMJ rounds. Oni's right arm is absolutely still, unlike her left that trembles, rattling the ammunition in the magazine. The first cartridge shlucks into the chamber. Reflexively checking the ejection port, she readies the gun, spinning towards the sound of Gibson's voice. "You're not real!" she screams.

The ghost adopts colour and greater complexity, mimicking Booker Gibson's likeness, right down to his piercing eyes and scars.

Oni fires two rounds. They blur Gibson for a fraction of a second, and carry on into the kitchen. Plates crash and a metal pot wobbles, growing louder with each seesaw.

Impressed now with a look of concern, the apparition points at Oni. "Enough! I don't know how long I have, so listen up: they're coming for you. You've got to go now. Take the back stairs. There is a tunnel that goes—"

"To Hell with this!" Oni cries. She bolts over to the door. Checking over her shoulder, she sees Gibson flickering and shaking his head, disappointed.

"They're coming, Oni." His voice crackles and reverberates like a synth played through a busted valve amplifier.

Oni removes her makeshift barricade, and opens the door. She peeks outside. The security droid is long gone. With the ghastly vision floating after her, she makes a beeline towards the elevator.

Gibson's voice does not lose resonance despite Oni's growing distance from him. "You are so god-damned stubborn. The stairs! I said: take the stairs!"

Oni raps on the elevator call-button. The doors chime open. Looking back in terror, Oni pushes into the compartment. It's a tighter fit this time. There is someone already inside. She feels warm digits grip her throat. Choking, she looks up into a reflective visor set in a yellow praetorian helmet. Oni tries to raise Gibson's rifle. Unable to lift it past her knees, she pulls the trigger and tears apart the back of the elevator.

"Ms. Matsui," growls the stranger, ejecting the magazine from Oni's gun. "You have been a very naughty girl."

Oni drops the empty rifle to free her hand. She punches frenetically, but with her circulation dammed at the neck, loses steam and goes limp.

# THE BOTTOM LINE

Lyle Badegger's three-o'clock, now his five-thirty, is a long-mustached Texan accused of killing migrant workers the day before payday, going back every month for god-knows-how-long. He is as guilty as sin, and as sinful as the first of the fallen. Lyle is billing him an embarrassingly-obscene amount because he knows he can keep this devil from falling. *Hell*, with Lyle *in the zone*, Benny Bass won't even stumble.

Pacing back and forth, Lyle mumbles Bass' charges under his breath. Envy, not shock, overcomes him. "Benny, Benny, Benny..." Lyle forces himself into his *thinking chair*, certain it will keep him focused and from murdering his immoral better. "They have you dead to rights," he says matter-of-factly, keen to dent Benny's ego in the interest of building up his own.

Bass' lips are invisible except for where his cigar parts his mustache, and in the divide shadow has painted them black. Legs spread wide, as if inviting Lyle to gaze at his equine manhood, he taps his Barker Blacks on the hardwood floor, spider-like fingers drumming in-synch on the club chair's red-leather arm panels. Sneering, Benny ends his tuneless percussion. "I don't like the sound of that. Not one bit." He looks through a cloud of cigar smoke at Lyle's trophies, all meticulously framed or encased in glass on the far side of the room. "Now what in Sam Hill are you going to do about it?"

Lyle leans forward. He tents his fingers as if in prayer, and points them to Bass. "How'd you kill them?"

"Ha!" exclaims Bass. "Who said I killed anybody? A few dozen paperless refugees have gone missing. Refugees to whom I gave the gift of gainful employment and an honest day's work."

"It's my job to deceive a jury of your peers. Your job is to tell me everything and then to clam up."

The loose skin around Bass's steely eyes tightens as he straightens up in his chair. He coughs, having accidentally inhaled smoke in response to Lyle's remark. Behind a finger wag, he rasps to Lyle a scolding: "Don't you dare talk to me in that tone of voice!"

Lyle stands, looming over Bass with arms crossed. "I can see that you've grown accustomed to silencing louder voices, even if they might save you. That's fine." Pointing to his office door, Lyle smiles. "Badegger or bust...Best of luck, Mr. Bass."

With a heavy sigh, Bass plucks a stray hair from his mustache and looks abjectly at his attorney. "This is all strictly confidential?"

A dull ache crosses Lyle's forehead. "Concentrate," he tells himself. "Don't let it get the best of you. Not now."

"L.B.," Bass says sternly, "This is all confidential? Off the books?"

"Absolutely." With the shell protecting Benny Bass's ego and secrets cracked, Lyle can now feast on the yolk. *Headache be damned.* "From the beginning."

Bass gestures to his cigar, pretending to put it out into his hand. Lyle wants to tell Bass to sit on it, but opts for benevolence. "Hold that thought," Lyle orders, as he strides out of the office in search of an ashtray.

A hunchback announces Lyle's entry into the reception area: "And speak of the devil!" Marius Tyndale brandishes his cheese-curd teeth over his shoulder. "Looking a little worse for wear, Le Bad," he says, crooked and leaning over Dorota's desk. Absent an immediate response from Lyle, Marius looks to Dorota for acknowledgement. She stares blankly back at him, knowing not to play along. Robbed altogether of an audience, he whines: "You two are a pair...Still sharing the same sense of humor, I see."

"*Mary,*" Lyle says with complete disdain. "Don't you have somewhere you have to be?"

Marius rushes a boyish response: "No!"

Lyle sneers. "Do'ta, call security."

"Oh, Baddie, don't be such a boor," Marius says in protest, still committed to his arch over Dorota's desk.

"Feel free to come back any time except the next time." The loathing Lyle feels for Marius is pure. It is unwavering, unconditional, intrinsic...It goes deeper than their socio-sexual competition. Marius is a poseur, a pretender; he is here simply because the road here was straight and smooth.

Whereas Lyle sought a career in law because he wanted a lucrative and socially-acceptable use for all of his aggression left over from the War, Tyndale became a lawyer only because it was decided a generation earlier that someone had to make good use of his mother's Martian contacts. Deborah Tyndale of Tyndale Synthetics engineered her son to reach Blue Zone star status as well as to ensure her company could continue to compete with the Big 6. Prenatal gene-manipulation made Marius physically robust, and top-tier educational stims attempted to make him wise. The result was this well-dressed and well-liked gorilla—big and only partially self-aware. Marius' dismal failure running Tyndale Synthetic's terran operations for a two-year stint prompted him to service his mother's legacy elsewhere. The bar was lowered by the State Bar of California so Marius could gallivant around Los Angeles as an associate at Copps and Forsyth, stealing Lyle's thunder. If Lyle had not threatened Marius on record, he could deal with this problem like *all the rest* without fear of reprisal or incarceration.

Trying his best to ignore his rival and keen not to have his arms torn out of their sockets, Lyle continues his search for an ashtray. He cannot help himself, however; a dull ache drives his anger to the surface: "A wise man once told me, 'Work only slows down for those not too fast on the uptake...'"

Marius stands up straight, defying evolution's slow progress and making sure to remind Lyle of his immensity. He takes a sip from his coffee mug, and makes a pleased smacking sound with his lips. "Your wise man ever close a three-billion-dollar BiAnima deal ahead of schedule?"

Groaning over Marius' greatly-exaggerated boast, Lyle scrutinizes the nicknacks on the cabinet behind Dorota's desk. A first-place gold medal for some mindless feat of cardio. Paper shapes reminiscent of birds. Spiny aloe spilling over the sides of a cracked pot. "Can't say he did. But if memory serves, he also wasn't an insufferable prick with an Oedipal complex that would make Freud blush." Sure he has shut Marius up, Lyle mimes, "Ashtray," to Dorota. She shrugs. *Should just put it out on Marius' tongue.*

Affecting a silvery laugh, Marius breaks his silence. He holds his coffee mug to his chest like an altar boy would an Easter candle at midnight mass. "Dorota was just telling me how in-over-your-head you are."

Dorota quickly dismisses the allegation with an eye roll and a headshake.

"No," says Lyle, "I don't believe she would waste her time with such a lie."

Dorota piles on with malice: "Forsyth is probably wondering why his ass is drying up." She indicates the hall with a languid point. "Go on now, Mr. Tyndale."

"Better mind that dirty mouth. Tyndale Synthetics is the lifeblood of this firm, and don't you forget it." Flustered, Marius tries to bring himself back down with another sip of coffee. He glimpses Benny Bass through the half-opened office door. "Hold on! Is that him now? Is that Bass!? Le Bad, give me ten minutes alone with him. I'll make it worth your while."

Benny Bass yells out, probably having heard his name come up: "You better not have the meter running, Badegger!"

Lyle runs a spread hand down the length of his face. *Answers and solutions are far easier to come by honestly in wartime.* "Mary," he says, glad they both disrespect each other enough never to use the other's proper name. He plucks the coffee mug out of Marius' hand and noisily slurps the rest of its contents. "I won't subject him to you. Wouldn't be fair." Marius scoffs and reaches for his cup. Lyle swats his hand back, and continues: "If you've got some free time between trips to your mother's, you might want to consider shaking a tree other than your own. Now if you'll excuse us, Dorota has work to do, and I have a case to win. Isn't that right, Do'ta?"

"Yes, Mr. B," she answers back, glaring wolfishly at Marius.

"Watch yourself, Baddie," Marius warns Lyle. He sulks out of the room and immediately finds company in the hallway: "Troy, you noob! How're you doing?"

Lyle turns Marius' coffee mug in his hands. It is decaled with a picture of a blindfolded Lady Justice weighing two big bags of cash with her scales. *Heh.*

"You're going to have to do something about him. Too stupid to catch anything and too hungry to be content to share," Dorota says, poking holes into a yearend compensation holographic on her desk.

"I know. In the meantime, do me a favor and leak the tape of Tyndale with the sex android. I need him off my back until I'm done with this case." Lyle refuses Dorota an opportunity to respond with clever innuendo, and marches over to Bass with the mug, slamming the door shut behind him.

Ashes on the floor mark Bass' impatience. If the front desk did not keep a log of visitors, Lyle would surely brain the Texan right here and now. Lyle grabs Bass' cigar and snuffs it out in Marius' mug. "You were about to tell me everything..."

Pleased to have irritated his attorney, Bass crosses his legs. "I hope you were not discussing my case with anyone out there."

"Would be kind of hard, given you've said dick all..."

Bass smoothes out his mustache. "When I moved my base of

operations to Inglewood, I decided to install BiAnima's Porrima AI to manage the warehouse."

Sitting down once again, Lyle summons a small tablet out of his pocket. Typing away, he stops and looks up. "Inglewood is where you killed them?"

Bass nods and wets his invisible lips, making his mustache waggle like a caterpillar. "Every facet of production was to be streamlined. To compete with the Japs and the Auslaysians, all the fat had to be cut."

"Speaking of which, *I'd appreciate it if you'd get to the meat of the story.*" With every dig at Bass, Lyle's chest appears to grow.

"I started hiring illegals. PIT rats. Paperless nobodies that weren't qualified to go off-world and who'd work for next to nothing."

"Let me blunt, Mr. Bass. I'm not writing your memoirs. How many? How did you do it? How were they buried?"

One eye twitching, and his cigarless right hand balled into a fist, Bass looks Lyle dead in the face. "You bill by the hour?"

"Yes."

"Then I'll say what I need to say, and then you can pick over at the carcass."

Not all of Bass's shell is gone, Lyle realizes. "Fine."

"If you've done your research, you know that most of my investments are in rare-earth metals. After the Big Six started sending back raw material from Mars, Titan, and Hyperion, I took a big hit. They saturated the market on me. Even when the new regulations kicked in, I couldn't compete—my costs were simply too high. It was a fortunate happenstance that I learned my BiAnima AI wasn't registering the illegals in my warehouse as workers. It was running some identity software the feds made compulsory in order to protect native jobs. The workers weren't in the database, which meant they didn't count as people. So far as the AI was concerned, they were intruders...pests."

"I see. Now, Mr. Bass; this is important: did you do it all by yourself?"

"I instructed the AI to heighten security and to eliminate any and all intruders in the warehouse. Came in the next day, and they were all dead. Had some droids dump the remains in the incinerator."

Lyle pockets his tablet and applauds his odds. The room seems especially quiet as he stops clapping. Approaching Benny, he offers an outstretched hand and lifts the lanky pinstriped suit to his feet. "Mr. Bass, we have plenty to work with. If there are no remains and nothing left to imply any misconduct on your premises, then the prosecution has nothing but an overactive imagination. Since you're an honest American entrepreneur—a pillar of our community—you have nothing to fear."

Dumbstruck and half-smiling, Benny clasps their handshake. "I thought I was dead to rights?"

"You were. And you will be unless I poke some holes in the Sentience Act, but that's my forte," says Lyle, gently pushing Benny towards the door. "Make sure that your AI and all of its components are destroyed. The androids responsible for the cleanup, too."

"Destroyed?" Bass stutters and his legs shake. He leans on the doorframe for support. "The BiAnima AI resale value is easily two-hundred-million dollars…"

"What is your freedom worth to you?" Lyle closes in on Bass and sets his hand between his shoulder blades. "The AI and your droids can be called in as witnesses. Any good prosecutor would bring them in as a matter of course. Before you walked in that door, I knew the stakes. I tabulated at least three-hundred dead. Benny, destroying your toys isn't a suggestion. If you're convicted, they will keep your brain alive long after your body rots away in solitary. Four life sentences, easily."

Benny turns to Lyle with a look of despond. "I should call my wife."

Lyle answers excitedly, "I don't give a shit! Destroy the AI and the droids. Everything else is your business."

Eyebrow raised and feet clocked at twelve and three, Benny mutters a confirmation and slinks out into reception.

"Oh, and Mr. Bass?" Lyle calls out after him.

From the hall comes a sheepish, "Yes?"

"For what I'll charge you, it would have been cheaper to keep your employees happy and healthy."

## ANGEL FEARED

Monocle is known to play tricks on a concussed or sleeping user as it logs plenty of overtime emulating thought patterns and simulating brain activity when the real thing is idle. Oni elected not only to enable this mental service, but to boost it. After all, when one's business is the mind, perpetual higher-consciousness trumps thoughtless comfort.

Oni's Monocle has delivered her from the murk of non-being to a marketplace of memory. Immersed in her living past, she recollects measured parental delight as manifested in unprecedented hugs at her graduation—top of her class! Sweating behind the counter of her uncle's bicycle shop on New Year's Eve, making sure no one discovers the sex-droid workshop beneath it. Eavesdropping on her mother's shouting match with a disgruntled mobster out in the hallway. The gunshot… *Mom!*

*Gunshot?* This last memory—of a mother whose scam of buying and selling missing-person's assured-income shares got her shot—is not Oni's. After all, her parents died along with her brother in the Purge; an early glitch in the CLOUD swept under the rug with out-of-court settlements. The still, tear-streaked face reads implicitly as Oni's mother, but a stinging sensation marks the correlation a lie. It is as if the wrong-shaped key rejected by the hole carved by experience was forced there anyway. Without the waking consciousness to repress this fallacious memory, Oni tries instead to make sense of it.

The gunshot has all the neighbours' dogs barking. An alarm chases the shooter away and draws a little boy with mattress-spring hair out into the hall. Upon finding this mother's body, his body goes slack. He drops down beside her and starts bawling. "Mommy…"

A full-bodied voice, free of grit or the waviness of remembrance, interrupts this grim vision: "Don't be preposterous!" This caramel shriek leaves sweet accents to linger after the declaration has swallowed its echoes. "I know for a fact that there will be no criminal investigation, meaning they have no cause for screwing us on coverage. They will fill the coffers of the dead, pay for the new base and signal amplifier on Titan, and reinsure the project. If you encounter any ten-fingered roadblocks, call Meijer."

*I know that voice…*

Oni opens her eyes to find the suffocating black of a canvas hood. She shakes her head violently and gnashes at the hood, unwilling to go out willingly.

"Good morning, Dr. Matsui."

The hood is yanked away. Oni is kneeling and kept from falling over by a terrible grip. Blinded by both natural and unnatural light, she can only make out greyish blurs and wormy splotches. "What have you done to me?" Although her memory seems out of joint, Oni's social awareness is right on the money. "You monsters!"

Against a backdrop of architectural extremes stands Celeste Charming, bisecting the sunlight in a massive east-facing office half-a-mile above the ground. Platinum-coloured pixie cut. Ivory skin. Shoulders rolled back, setting her chest at odds with the tight crème bodice dress that falls at two different lengths, longer in the front than in the back. She sways as she chews through her delivery, spitting ex cathedra into the face of a haggard brunette woman, shorter with a defeated posture—an underling of some kind; likely an assistant given her devotional nodding and tired eyes.

The jingle of spurs alerts Oni to a beak-hooded figure behind her. He releases her to fall and heels past sporting a Neanderthal gait, cracking his knuckles, and wheezing into a respirator. Beneath his camo-patterned scarves, he is otherwise draped in orange and black fabric with spidersilk interwoven. Armour bulges through the gaps. His hips are significantly sloped; either on account of arthritis from a lifetime of boot dentistry or augmentation. For a violent artifact like this—ostensibly yanked from another era—to be permitted to walk freely in Celeste's office, he must be exceptional at his craft, and judging from his attire and age, he has been exceptional for quite some time.

"You killed Jin Koybashi. You *murdered* him—a good man!" Oni yells, white-hot with anger.

The beaked hood turns to pinch Oni's shoulder. His scarves unravel into the assault, revealing a bulbous nose and a cratered face. His eyes are not his own. They are implants: red lenses encircled black, set in a rotary plate pulling information that would normally get lost in the vitreous. They fix on Oni and spin. He growls, announcing desire and urgency to Celeste.

*Son of a bitch.* Oni struggles with her bindings. Her robotic strength is insufficient to break the magnetic clasps around her wrists. With her eyesight almost fully returned, she scans the room for objects and exits that might provide an alternative to whatever Celeste has in store for her.

Celeste shushes her unconfident confidant with a limp finger, and rigs it to summon the beaked hood over to a lone chair at the centre of the room. Beside it: a small holo-tabletop projecting weightless cherry blossoms. The beaked hood nods, grabs Oni, and drags her across cold white marble. Oni kicks ferociously, overturning the tabletop and vaporizing the homage to natural Himalayan beauty. The beaked hood smacks Oni across the face with a gloved hand, and throws her into the chair. Sensing more resistance, he forces her to fit the chair's form with a shove, all the while ignoring her grunts and gasps.

"Skyr, Dr. Matsui—I'll be with you both in a moment," assures Outland's godlike CEO.

Neither the wait nor the appointment hinge on Oni's wants, needs, or desires. If Gibson's annotation was correct, and Celeste was in fact "the mark," Oni resents him now for having missed it.

Head rolling from shoulder to shoulder, Oni spots something besides herself out of place in this surgically-clean office; a red, snake-like apparatus feeds a small puddle on Celeste's desk. Oni winces to train her vision and to determine what it is. Recognizing the design, she immediately regrets sating her curiosity. Dripping blood on this Outland altar: an implant and a second-generation augmentation tree fused to a spinal column and brain. "Tell me what you want!" demands Oni, now starting to panic.

Skyr grips Oni's shoulder again. This time, he thumbs her clavicle, making her entire frame slacken under a regime of remarkable pain. Unfastening his respirator, he issues a gravelly command: "Best shut the hell up, fugee." Again, he forces her down—so hard that Oni's legs splay and jut further out, making her look like she has melted.

"Let me go or kill me." Blood and spittle fork from Oni's bottom lip. She gulps to make room in her mouth for loathing: "I want nothing to do with Outland. Fools and brutes."

Skyr cracks a devious grin and looks to Celeste for direction. Celeste gives none.

Oni looks past Skyr's gnarled fabrics to the city framed behind him, stretching to as far as the PIT's mountain ramparts. The city looks like black mold caked onto an old motherboard. C-Blocks rise above the toxic crowding like stripped capacitors charged by angry dissidents. They are impressive, the C-Blocks; especially the few trapped in the PIT by and behind the Partition.

Among the C-Blocks stacked PIT-side, one in particular stands out. Unlike its ilk, sinking in a necrotic sea of interlaced skyscrapers and defunct highways, the Chrysalis, so-called, resists the rot. It is no Citadel to be sure, but it is as close as the PIT will come to a relative. Hex Akbari, an ally from the old days, lords over it or he still did around the time of Oni's first spat with the Outland Corporation.

Does Akbari return her desperate stare? *What does he see?* An empire on the brink of collapse? Or a tower ascending higher and higher into space—casting a lasting shadow over a conquered humanity?

Midway around the Chrysalis stretch the old refugee-housing complexes: windowed boxes clinging like barnacles to structures whose original shapes no one alive can recall. The erosive tide sweeping in carries with it a froth of drones and disease. It chases the cabins higher and carves bays into the surrounding slum towers.

While the solar-paneled rooftops are bright, beaming second-hand sunrays into Oni's bruised and tired face, the streets anchored hundreds of storeys below are not. What kind of darkness exists beneath the uneven surface? Doubtful Celeste has any idea. The Outland magnate does, however, know quite well the cost of keeping such hellish congestion and decay out of Los Angeles proper, as well as the need to minimize the number of grazers on this greener side.

Observing Oni's silence, Celeste turns to her aide. "Kirsten." The utterance is more than a whisper, but too quiet for proper conversation.

The droopy woman named Kirsten, with partial optical implants obfuscating a circuit-laden look of terror, quickly answers back: "Yes, Ms. Charming?" She defers a gasp until Celeste has made her wishes known.

"Who took over for Clarkson in the Noospherics Lab?"

Kirsten tilts her head, running an introjected query. "Harry Tuttle...now that he's been vindicated..."

"Have him come by this afternoon."

"Certainly, Ms. Charming." On weakening legs, Kirsten finally fills her lungs. She maintains a look of forlorn so as not to denote relief in the CEO's presence.

Turning up the opacity on the floor-to-ceiling window, Celeste strides over to a water jug sitting on the thin glass bar by her desk. The jug flips LA horizontally and flattens it, a feat neither Celeste nor her predecessor has been able to fully accomplish. Pulling one of two twenty-facet crystal glasses within an inch of her nose for inspection, Celeste distractedly offers further instructions: "If he asks about the purpose of his visit—and he shouldn't—tell him I want to scale-up the production of his DCT."

"Will do, Ms. Charming," Kirsten confirms, bobbling her head.

Celeste fills the glass halfway, brings it to her lips, and stares down at Kirsten's distorted form. "Kirsten. You look confused. Have I not made myself clear?"

Kirsten takes a step closer and nods her head quietly. "DCT?"

"Perhaps a question best to pose to Skyr the next time the two of you are alone?"

"I beg your pardon, Ms. Charming? The next time? I don't know what you mean."

Celeste grins. Behind locked teeth, she resists laughter, emitting instead some kind of ugly chirp. "It seems you are a victim of a great deal of misunderstandings, my dear. Must I requisition an executive android to assist in this matter?"

Kirsten trembles.

"Relax. No machine could ever replace you." Resting her empty glass next to the jug, Celeste folds her hands together. "After all, I wouldn't waste my humor or good nature on something which would only turn it into trivial maths. A DCT is a decentralized-CLOUD transmitter. If you have to explain it to Tuttle, then he is not worth the time or his new title."

"Yes, Ms. Charming." Kirsten buries her stare between her tightly-bound feed.

"Your worry lines betray you, Kirsten. What's the matter?" Celeste's folded hands and prim posture together are enough to question whether she were once a prioress or a dilettante. She approaches Kirsten via long strides that furl the back flap of her dress, revealing taut thighs undisturbed by tech or ink.

Kirsten throws a paranoid glance Oni's way and checks over her shoulder. "The man who was in here before…"

Celeste unfolds her hands, and lifts Kirsten's chin with her index finger so that their eyes meet. "The General?"

"Didn't he say—?"

"Kirsten, please be mindful of my precious time and *our company*." Celeste indicates Oni with a partial wave.

"Isn't all CLOUD tech illegal?" asks Kirsten.

Like a bandage yanked off of an unhealed wound, Celeste's patient smile vanishes. In its wake a horrid grimace takes hold. "Pulling that thread might leave you naked and alone...Is it illegal to booze and inject in public?"

"Yes, Ms. Charming."

"But perfectly legal to do so in one's own home?"

Kirsten readies another confirmation, but Celeste presses a finger against her lips preventing its release.

"Los Angeles is Outland's home. Granted we are home and we are not harming anybody, we are free to do whatever it is we need or like."

Eyes glassed-over, Kirsten nods.

Retrieving that bandage of a smile, Celeste caresses Kirsten's cheek as a mother would her babe. "Go now, Kirsten. As you can see, I have an old friend and a new friend with whom I'd like to speak in private." Noticing wrinkles and blemishes plighting her hand, now an ornament on Kirsten's jaw, Celeste recoils and straightens. "Broadcast your findings, set the meeting, and then fetch me a lipidene scrub. All these questions have prematurely aged me."

"Sorry, Ms. Charming. Yes, Ms. Charming."

*Miss as opposed to doctor—an interesting preference of a well-educated professional, especially with so much societal importance placed on the sciences.*

Kirsten makes a subtle, kind gesture to Skyr and bustles out of the room. A massive mech decloaks, labors over to the door, and grinds it closed behind Kirsten. The mech's spaulders clink and glisten, and without announcing their departure, vanish along with the monster underneath.

*How many freaks are in here with me, besides the two that I can see with the naked eye?*

Celeste flashes Oni a smile. Again, she turns up the opacity on the windows. The resultant dusk emphasizes the unnatural glow of the fallen cherry blossoms as well as Skyr's eyes. Noticing the red discs rotating, Celeste calls out to Skyr: "Where is your helmet? I barely recognized you without it. *This* is not a better look."

Skyr's grumbles blur to static through his respirator.

Celeste's face lights up. "And *this* must be the infamous Dr. Oni Matsui."

Skyr nods and pulls Oni up, gripping her arm just above the

elbow. "In one piece, although she's got some plug and play elements, so could have been in two, just the same."

"Excellent work," Celeste says, tapping her rose-petal lips with crossed fingers. "I expect everything will be in order for the job once our man inside delivers on the flight schedules. See to it that you and her both are ready to go."

"Yes, See-See."

"Go on then, Skyr. The little doctor will join you shortly."

Oni spits at Skyr's feet. "Monster!" She glares at Celeste. "You were there, too. Both of you are murderers."

Skyr delays his exit just in case Celeste is feeling particularly sadistic. He looks to her for a cue as she leans in to speak to Oni.

"You lack the context to issue such damning accusations, my dear. The visit we planned was peaceful. Simply wanted to speak to you about an opportunity for reconciliation."

Oni shakes her shackles. "Clearly."

"Had your elderly friend simply answered Skyr's questions and forgone the masculine ritual of chest-beating and yowling, we would not have had to defend ourselves." Celeste's voice resounds in the chamber; a resolvable effect she no doubt maintains to assert the importance of whatever she has to say. Her disinformation is thus given the authority of volume. "You should be thanking Skyr, here. He saved Koybashi's life before he was forced to take it."

"Coward," Oni says.

Skyr's eyes flare and he grits his teeth. He cocks a fist back, but the sound of Celeste clicking her tongue against her teeth prevents its release.

Oni tenses in her shackles. "What am I doing here?"

Celeste frees a delicate chuckle, and turns her back to Oni. "The police want you dead. The Military wants you dead. The state wants you dead. Outland—officially?" She draws a holoframe and fills it with a projection of a subterranean-base's blueprints. "*Unofficially*, I have a job for you. Do the job, and I will guarantee you a blank slate. You can start anew somewhere far, far away from this place."

Oni shakes her head. Without the strength to hold still, it keeps on swaying unpiloted. "You're lying. I don't know what you want, but I know you're lying. *I know* how much Outland is offering for my head…"

"Good Doctor!" Celeste says indignantly. She minimizes the

holoframe and turns to Oni. "Please! *Behead you?* That head of yours is far more useful to me where it currently sits. After all, you and I agree on a great many things…"

"Fat chance."

Skyr scolds Oni: "You can cooperate with Ms. Charming or with the worms."

Dismissing her lackey with a headshake, Celeste reigns in the conversation: "Winchester's prototypical noosphere—of which you were a proponent notwithstanding present guilt and regret—was a doomed but necessary misstep. The right technological advances, the right infrastructure, the wrong application. Minds immersed and connected in a virtual realm…"

"The CLOUD," whispers Oni.

"*So glad you remember.* A fantastic demonstration and a fantastic failure. Your creation was limited because you yourself are limited. No offense intended, of course. A single man or a single team cannot be expected to build the noosphere. And were they to achieve the miraculous, there would be absolutely no way for them to contain their infant super-reality; not with cypulchres, good will, or boundless imagination."

Oni tries to stand, but Skyr keeps her plotted.

Celeste ignores Oni's contempt and repulsion. "However, the CLOUD left us with a special gift—an unintended consequence of the cataclysmic variety. The noosphere *is* real. It surrounds us. It could exist independent of Outland and BiAnima's machinations, if we just push it and ourselves a little further."

"Bullshit." Oni laughs up a bloody spray.

Celeste clutches at her breast as if preparing to give witness. "Man has already commandeered control over his genetic and evolutionary course. No longer predestined to a snail's crawl to betterment, we have set our goals higher and accelerated the process for the good of all and to the dismay of many. The state and my other detractors pretend not to see the truth and the good in it. As they are blind to the good in the reality I am proposing, they are also blind to the bad in theirs. I walked amongst the black obelisks in Europe. I saw Constantinople fall the second time. I studied with android reliquaries bearing the brains of soldiers doomed to die for another's mistakes. And I know my elected critics would like to forget that it was the work we do here that ended that war. And they would all like to pretend that the work you will now help me do will have no impact upon the war in the south. They—the weaponeers and the bombers and the politicians—think our technology is something unnatural when it is as natural *to* and inseparable *from* our kind as the shell is to the oyster or tusks are to the elephant. Instead of a shell or tusks or my critics' guns and bombs, we have archetypals; great beings whose powers can be replicated....for the sake and betterment of Californians—for Americans!—for humanity."

Oni has heard this *brand of bullshit* before, less one curious development: "Archetypals?"

"Your CLOUD proved that there are certain mental types to which we all belong. Your personnel file listed no search queries or interest in antiquated psychology, so I will spare you a lecture on Jung, but know this: former subscribers who logged more than one-thousand hours in the CLOUD appeared to enjoy a unique bond with those in their psychological circle—with those of their type. I'm not talking about some basic camaraderie. They grew to sense and feel and know one another to the point of indistinction. When you and your friend blew up the CLOUD, those intimate connections were crystallized. Those subscribers realized their respective place in their type and that type in them. Now, there are a dozen or so primary types; archetypes, if you will. It is my ardent desire to connect them and to find out what the collective self is capable of." Celeste winces, cherry-picking words to sanitize the spoiled reality baking outside of her office window.

"I think you've lost me."

"Every living body has a head of some kind," Celeste continues, embittered with and by sarcasm, "Some sort of central nervous system. This special function has only one specialist; one member with traits common to all archetypes but with the added capacity to unify them all. Fortunately for you and your type, I have found her. The military calls her 2690. I call her the Omnitype."

"I would wish you good luck, but the truth is that I'm hoping you screw up and die slow."

Unshaken by Oni's audacity, Celeste finds her point. "I won't, but she certainly will. Those ground-pounders intend to poke and prod her until she provides them with something they can weaponize."

"*Real* slow."

Celeste's patience has run its course. "I am fully aware of your history with the company. This is bigger than you, and could mean a new beginning as opposed to a horrible end. Help us and we will help you."

"I'll tell you where you could start," Oni says as she raises her hands like an evangelical preacher guiding his prayer to heaven. Secularizing the gesture, she flips Celeste off while simultaneously signalling her bindings with a nod.

Celeste heeds Oni's suggestion. The technocrat's eyes glaze over. Regaining their colour, they pinpoint Oni's fetters. With the internal computing dealt with via her subdermal implant, Celeste finalizes the order with a wink. The bindings deactivate, fall, and clatter on the veined white floor.

Certain that whatever cloaked mech closed the door on Kirsten will forestall any attack on Celeste with Skyr's assistance, Oni inoffensively plants her hands on her thighs. Pithy insults and righteous speeches cross her mind, but tribalism wins out. "Before you tell me about this job I am not going to do…"

A demure smile replaces Celeste's look of indignation.

"I want to know what you've done with my friends."

Celeste jerks back and mumbles, "What I've done?" She spreads a digital window in front of her face, and stretches it so that it is large enough to step through. Her Monocle, an advanced version of Oni's, fills the window with holographic images other Monocles can pick up. Paul Sheffield's mugshot scales by the window marked "DECEASED" in bright red letters. The faces of several of Oni's other friends and acquaintances also pass by, similarly marked "DECEASED." Finally, Booker Gibson's face peels into frame, marked "APPREHENDED."

Oni gasps. In a muffled sob, she calls out, "Booky!"

Celeste conjures open a security-video archive and intuits a prisoner code into the prompt. "Redacted" is given both as the prisoner's first and last name. The archive minimizes and is replaced by a surveillance feed of a dark room bisected by a massive man, head covered by a black-canvas sack, handcuffed, and chained. "Yes. I didn't think there were any surprises, save for one, and it seems I was correct," boasts Celeste. "All but one of your friends are gone. Oni Matsui, do this job for me and I will free both you and the last of your friends—*this Booker Gibson.*"

## RECYCLED TO WASTE

The Outland Corporation has not always been known for its popular tech and toys. Since its inception in the early days of the Northern Alliance, it has developed weaponry and software for the military and for whatever private defense firm can fit the bill. Several European states and African technocracies have been made and destroyed overnight as a direct result of such purchases.

So far as the United States is concerned, this Los-Angeles-based corporation is a utility service. Utility is not always measured in watts and dollars. Frequently and especially these days, it is measured in kill ratios, body counts, and in supplicant citizens. If it were not for Winchester's dealings with the army, the navy, and the air force, he would have been sooner marked a tyrant, perhaps even an enemy of the state. Without the glad-handing, Outland, too, would have been shutdown and had its assets seized, including those settlements beyond Mars. On account of this mutually-beneficial relationship with the Republic, Outland was not chastised to the extent that it ought to have been over its mishandling of the CLOUD, both leading up to and following the virtual realm's dissolution.

Instead of cuffs, the interim CEO received a new contract. This contract has afforded Celeste Charming an opportunity to redeem Outland's reputation, at least where the Government is concerned. All that is required is her assistance in cleaning up after the company's messes—the archetypals, black-market dark CLOUDs, Titan's Olympus Base, and the like.

In the muddled logic of close friends and closer enemies, the Government has snuggled up with a venomous snake. What feels like warmth is really just death delayed. What feels like a loving embrace is constriction.

Skyr's roughness and crude demeanor changed as soon as Celeste clarified her intentions: fit and equip Oni so that she can rescue *2690*. No longer directing Oni with the muzzle of his gun, he prompted her with a "Miss, this way" or a "Miss, that way." He "Miss-d" her all the way out and onto the Citadel's flight deck, which was scrubbed clean of the blood of those who had stood in Oni's way five-months prior. Skyr now sits opposite Oni aboard his falcon-shaped cargo jet, the Hretha. The ship's autopilot is on so that he can clean his oversized Outland Kingsword autorevolver while keeping an eye on his captive.

The jet whisks them south along the Blue Zone beach-reclamation, past massive wind-kite-generator farms and stragglers from the Third Fleet, to a star-shaped skyscraper pronged by the shadow of the Titan-sent spaceship, Hermes, now docked over the bay. Oni stares out the window, impressed by how little her great feat and Paul's martyrdom accomplished.

Resting his Kingsword on his seat—no doubt testing Oni's reflexes and her resolve to get even—Skyr disappears into the cockpit. Even with the door closed, Oni can hear him mutter to himself; something about visibility. He returns burdened with two hard cases. One has the BiAnima logo laser-cut into its side. The other is stenciled with a symbol composed of a worn-down image of an eagle, the Earth, and an anchor. Skyr sets the cases down in front of Oni and attempts to sit. With an uncharacteristic yelp, he jumps to his feet. On the seat cushion behind him rests his Kingsword. He moves his revolver and settles in. "See that? I rub it a little and it thinks it can have its way with me."

Inside the cases cracked open at Oni's feet is an assortment of insulated tech and toys.

"We won't need most of this," Skyr says, hatching a Claymore landmine from its cocoon. He rather carelessly sets the mine down on the floor and pushes it aside with the toe of his boot. He tears another device out of the insulation, sending foam beads left and right. Turning it in his hands—an electrostatic discharge (ESD) wand designed to sabotage electronics—he shrugs, and lobs it onto Oni's lap.

Oni examines the micro-lightning bridging the wand's test electrodes. Tempted to use it on Skyr, but not selfish enough to put retribution ahead of redemption, Oni powers the wand down and pockets it.

"Careful with that," Skyr warns. "Too powerful a charge and you'll splash damage back to your own circuitry." He continues to rifle through the cases, optical discs spinning wildly. "Ah, here we go!" With an unprecedented gaiety, Skyr leans forward to present Oni with a silver-and-white collar. Along its circumference are needle-like protuberences. "Have you used one of these before?"

Oni takes the collar from Skyr, pricking her fingers in the transaction. "A choker? Haven't used one, no. I know all about them…Read about them." She runs her hand along the rim in search of a button or toggle as if she were scratching a roll of tape for its elusive bitter end. "Prevents sensors and cameras from getting a proper facial-scan. No scan, no ID; no ID, no problem."

Nodding, Skyr reclaims the collar and cracks it in two, silently demonstrating to Oni how to use it. "Yeah, does all the shit domestic collars do, but this one..." He clasps it around his neck. A number of ruddy streams trickle down his throat. Observing Oni's curiosity about the blood, he wipes the streams dry and licks his hand clean. "This one requires a few drops to save the pool." Skyr's face loses its shape and color until it is no more. The collar has done more than merely prick his neck; it has decapitated him.

Oni grins crookedly at Jin's headless murderer sitting opposite her. Skyr's body crosses its legs while the collar itself begins to melt away. Silver and white drips down and over Skyr's shoulders, rendering his entire person transparent. Laughing nervously, Oni leans as far forward as her seatbelt will permit to prod the vague blur. "Neat trick." *A better trick would have had it evaporate you entirely.*

Skyr's reappearance is signaled by a sound not unlike Saran Wrap being peeled off of frozen food. Movement limited by his crossed legs, Skyr still manages a slight bow. "You'll keep the collar on the entire time. It has tested well on cameras, infrared included, as well as with drones and such. When the cloak is down, the choker still prevents cameras and sensors from getting an ID." Skyr wags a blistered finger. "Remember: the cloaking mechanism is only for emergencies. And if your emergency happens to last more than a minute, you're screwed."

"How do you figure?"

Skyr hands the collar to Oni, who is careful this time not to prick her fingers. "The cloak is energy intensive. The longer it is engaged, the more energy it draws. The more energy it draws, the easier it will be for droids, cameras, and guys like me to spot you." He points to his optical plates. "So that's that. Oh! I nearly neglected to mention: See-See's techboys made it so that in addition to concealing light, the collar can augment and filter it. Once we update your Monocle, you'll be able to scan a face and project it as your own. Much less energy-intensive than the cloak."

The thought of posing as her enemies excites Oni, and only one comes to mind: Celeste Charming. *How fitting for a self-absorbed maniac to look up into her own eyes as she breathes her last...*

In one of the crates open at her feet, Oni spots a helmet—one like you might see on a sim of Perseus or Hector: with a jagged jawline and cutaways full of thick antiballistic glass parted by a noseguard. "Is that also for me?"

Skyr rumples his face and kicks the crate shut. "That's mine…my battle dress." He leans forward and checks his peripherals for an uninvited witness that's not there. "You see this? What we're up to presently? It isn't war. It's not a fight. It's nothing more than a job; a job I'm doing well. But when the shit hits the fan—and there's a lot of shit in this world, and there's a lot of fans—I'll be dressed to impress, and impress I will." He jabs his thumb and Oni's attention with it over to a small compartment built into the Hretha's chassis. "Got an exo to go with it. An historical suit of armour, you better believe."

Growing tired of Skyr's ego, Oni casts her attention down at the options still available to her. "Then what else do you have for me?"

With his hands full of shimmering electronics, Skyr toes the BiAnima suitcase over beside the Claymore mine. "For you? Security cards, diversionary materiel, and a thing or two that'll go bang."

"Great." Oni pinches her nose and puffs her cheeks, desperate to right the pressure in her ears. "All this to get 2690, and 2690 will clear my slate and free Booker?"

"Absolutely."

"What does 2690 look like? How will I know what to look for?"

"You'll know," Skyr says with an assumed poignancy.

The Hretha's autopilot lowers the ship carefully onto the roof lot of a coastal skyscraper. Oni looks confusedly out the window, and turns to Skyr, who preempts her inquiry with a finger against his lips. He wordlessly stresses the importance of her remaining stationary with a gesture from his revolver, and disappears into the cockpit.

Deluding herself into thinking she finally has a viable opportunity to duck out, Oni unbuckles her restraints. She crimps over her armrest and glimpses Skyr powering down the Hretha's thrusters. With her captor occupied and the ship grounded, she psyches herself up: *fortune favors the bold*. She tiptoes to the rear of the jet, and slaps a red button framed by cautionary yellow-and-black stripes in hopes of triggering the ramp to drop. There is, however, a lag with the mechanical instruction. "Crap!" she gripes, frantically hitting the button again and again. She looks morosely back at the cockpit. "C'mon, c'mon!" Just as the cockpit door swings open, the ramp clunks down, taking Oni by surprise and for a ride. She seamlessly rolls into a sprint, only there is nowhere to run. Two medical droids block her progress. One has a billet grill for a face and the other, partially skinned, has the majority of its moving parts plainly visible.

"Ah, Mr. Grey and Mr. Pink," Skyr yells as he coolly disembarks the Hretha.

The robots, Mr. Grey and Mr. Pink, wrap their cold digits around Oni's arms.

"Rare is the rabbit that runs into a trap unbaited." Skyr snarls, "She's all yours, boys!"

The droids' jerkily look to Skyr and then to the bruised woman trembling in their clutches.

Skyr throws a loose fabric back and over his shoulder, revealing a Saint Andrew's Cross composed of bandoliers. Orbiting Oni and the bots, he prattles on: "You've got your orders. *The works.* See-See doesn't want anything traceable back to Outland."

"In case they find my body?"

On his second revolution, he stops in front of Oni. "In case you mess up, *Patient Zero.*" He brushes Oni's oily hair out of her eyes and leans in to paint her face red with his ocular sensors. "Do not go running off again. You heard See-See. You're free as soon as you do this little job. That's an enviable position to be in—to be needed, to be useful. If you ditch these nice bots here," Skyr knuckles Mr. Grey's shoulder, "You won't be of any use to anyone, especially not that friend of yours: Gibly Bibbly or whatever he calls himself."

"Gibson. Booker Gibson." Oni doesn't know why she corrected Skyr. *A man who is given names to cross out doesn't care less about how they were written to begin with.*

"Sure." Skyr rolls his eyes as well as his head on its armoured axis until he triggers a cartilage pop. With the pop, the lights squeezed between his eyelids brighten. "Hang in and get the mods, otherwise there's not a full-grown man in the country you're going to get the drop on." He fumbles around in his pockets, and finds a half-dose of Longdream. "Take this. You'll need it."

## SIREN'S CALL

"Mr. Badegger?" Dorota beckons from reception.

"God-damn-it," Lyle mutters. He slams his thinking-chair's armrests emphatically, marking the interruption in the leather. He straightens his tie and exits his office to find Dorota more or less hidden behind a dozen pulsating holographic displays. Only her emerald-green eyes and her sangria-coloured hair, immaculately bound into a chignon, are visible. Lyle clears the projections with a swipe of his hand. He puckers his lips, and plants his hands on the desk in front of Dorota. With the transfer of weight, his heels leave the ground and his fingers turn white. "Yes, Do'ta?"

Dorota bats her long eyelashes and slides a dotgram across the desk. "There's a comm here for you here marked 'urgent'." Although petite, her breasts fight her tight, red sweetheart-neck blouse.

Lyle unabashedly stares at Dorota's cleavage and turns his impish smirk upwards to drown his focus in her emerald stare. Curiosity over the urgent message trumps his savage itch. "If it's the Board, tell them I'm back and better than ever."

"It's not the Board," Dorota says, pupils dilating and fingers curling on the desk. She bites her lip and then reaches for the barrette holding her hair in place. "Guess again."

Brain divided between carnal thoughts and business, Lyle clenches his teeth. "Benny Bass? Tell that son of a bitch I'm not a goddamned saboteur. The AI is his responsibility…Dig a contact from the red files if he persists—preferably a RIM tick with a tech background—otherwise instruct him to have the AI electro-magnetically pulsed and to avoid a paper trail."

Dorota yanks the barrette securing her chignon and liberates her hair, which cascades over her shoulders like a red mountain stream. "Wrong again, Mr. B." Grinning coyly, she drags a tablet from one side of the desk to the middle and spins it for Lyle's benefit. "Federal warrant. Private meeting with some military types…" She walks her fingers across the desk and sets her hands on Lyle's white knuckles. "What have you done this time and how much time does it leave us?"

Lyle recoils from her touch, straightens up, and walks around the desk. Peering over Dorota's shoulder at the tablet, he scans the summons. "Nothing I can think of." At the bottom right of the page is an Outland subscriber number. "Pull up all of the data pertaining to my Outland and BiAnima subscriptions." Watching Dorota make a mockery out of BiAnima's security protocol, Lyle shifts her chair just enough to make room to wrap his arms around her waist. He runs one hand down to her thigh, and ruffles up her skirt. With the other, he runs his hand up and across her silken blouse to her chest and gropes her tenderly.

"I've got to do a direct download," Dorota says breathily.

"I'll wait. Do whatever you need to do," Lyle says, biting her earlobe.

Dorota presses back into Lyle, and looks up to a starfield of information invisible to all but her. Her eyes appear lifeless despite the flutter of her eyelashes. Taking a deep breath, she blinks the colour back into her face.

"Well?" snaps Lyle, impatiently, hands and lips invading Dorota's warmth.

Distractedly doublechecking the number on the warrant, Dorota pulls Lyle's hands off her like a broken seatbelt. "Your exocortex has been black-flagged and archived."

"God Almighty."

Dorota adjusts her blouse. "I thought they already cleared you."

"They did." Lyle pulls away from Dorota, and walks around her desk. "Copy my Sentience file and then see about corrupting my exocortex...Then comm these pricks. See what they want."

Shifting uneasily, perhaps anticipating an *episode*, Dorota posits a theory: "Your headaches—*the humming...*"

Sucking his teeth and looking awfully pensive, Lyle raps his knuckles along the edge of Dorota's desk. "Haven't had the headaches for a few weeks. The hum is psychosomatic. Withdrawal if anything." He registers the waste bin halved by the desk's shadow as a legitimate scapegoat and grimaces. "Confounded CLOUD!" he bellows, kicking the bin. "Had I known it'd be such a total pain in my ass I wouldn't have put it in my head."

Dorota stares irately at all the kipple strewn across the waiting area.

"Never mind the mess," Lyle says, face slack with his mind poured elsewhere. "I'll deal with it." Looking one last time at the Outland insignia glowing beside the military scrawl, he silently mouths the company name. "Call Harry Tuttle. See if he has any idea why they'd be interested in me."

"Harry Tuttle?"

"Yeah," Lyle answers back abruptly. "The Outland scientist who murdered his wife." Lazily effecting air quotes with his dexterous fingers, Lyle adjusts his claim: "Allegedly murdered…"

"Right, I remember him quite well. I just can't imagine what he'd know…"

"He's the Outland appointment to that joint commission dead set on understanding and knocking off archetypals."

"Alright, Mr. B. I can't Minerva-search him, but his dots should still be somewhere around here." Dorota starts to sift through her desk drawers in search of Tuttle's contact information.

"Regardless of whether he's wise to the Military's interest in me, I still want to meet him—want to ask him about these headaches."

Dorota presents Tuttle's dots at the end of a fascist-looking salute.

"Excellent. Call him now. I want to know what I'm getting into here…Be ready to charge the Harpocrate signal-jammers and pulse the archives. As a precaution, of course. Only execute the wipe if it looks like I've been compromised."

## THE SPIDER AND THE FLY

Pricked and prodded, Oni screams and shakes through what seems like an unending succession of upgrades with only the benefit of localized anesthesia. Although she senses her insides jostle and slosh about in the confident hands of godless creatures, the corresponding pain doesn't route to her thalamus; not properly anyway. Apart from fear, the only other distinct feeling running through her mind is sympathy. Estranged from that quivering, bloody mess, strapped once again to a gurney under a fast-food light, she feels—perhaps for the first time—pity for herself.

Paul Sheffield died destroying the CLOUD with the understanding that he saved his family and the world he was leaving behind. Oni covets his ignorance and envies him for getting off easy. If there is no Heaven and no opportunity to reflect on this finite test, then Paul's victory required only his belief in it and dying confirmation of its day. As a survivor, Oni knows better. She sees Paul's victory for what it really is: the first step in *her* long and lonely march towards a better world.

Reflecting upon her meat—upon the dark-haired nymph who survived that first step—and on the journey ahead, Oni feels horribly unprepared. Even with spidersilk, armor-reinforced bone, and Monocle upgrades, Celeste's mission and destruction seem unachievable. The countenance of those supposedly boosting her abilities further undermines her confidence.

Her chief surgeon, Mr. Grey, looks like someone went to town on a roast ham with a nailgun. Whoever left the patches of flesh-coloured rubber dangling from its face either failed to finish the job or was deranged enough to consider their gunmetal zombie a finished product. Mr. Grey's eyelids flop on its cheeks like soiled bedsheets as it leans over to interrupt Oni's delirium. Silhouetted by the examination light, it calls on Oni to focus with a violent shake: "Have you recently undergone surgery?"

Gargling a hybrid of blood and spit ahead of the words, Oni answers: "Yes. Surgery...My arm and my spine."

Mr. Grey tries to pull a confirmation from Oni's Monocle using its scanner, but cannot get a proper read on account of her fried implant and her Monocle's hyperactive security. "Please assist me in assisting you," buzzes Grey.

A Monocle prompt finds Oni at the eye of a tornado of pain

and panic. It is just what she needs, however: a reminder of the interface and her ability to transcend her body. She amplifies Monocle's simulated brain operations, and walls off her corporeal concern from her higher-order thoughts. All of her reptilian anxieties and mortal concerns flake away, leaving two crystalline determinations: save Booker and destroy Outland. *Play along to keep playing.* Sure to maintain her encryption so as not to let Outland into her head, Oni expedites the requested medical data down a one-lane wireless highway via Monocle.

Mr. Grey receives and processes the data instantaneously. For whatever reason, Grey repeats the facts it has just now gleaned aloud for a record which will be destroyed, disavowed, and left unheard again by human ears: "Right arm replaced along with several vertebrae. Monocle hacked and upgraded. Hysterectomy. Lung modifications. Extensive damage to BiAnima neural implant." Having announced all of Oni's known defects and alterations, Mr. Grey prods her for clarification: "Patient Zero, to your knowledge, is the exocortex attached to your spine essential?"

"Essential?" Oni mumbles.

A familiar voice booms over the chawing of the bone saws and the arrhythmic beep of the EKG monitor: "It *is* essential. Tell this pile of bolts you have outsourced motor-function to the exocortex along with fundamental reasoning skills."

"Who said that?" Oni asks aloud, her voice a beacon to her waning awareness.

Mr. Pink takes a pause from lining Oni's legs with spider wire and considers her question. "Likely an auditory hallucination. Please answer Mr. Grey's question."

Mr. Grey shakes Oni once more. "Is the exocortex essential? It is imperative that you let us know."

Trapped in a whirlpool of faces, voices, and sad memories, Oni recycles the words thrown her way by the familiar voice: "Essential...for motor function. Reason, *reasoning*...essential."

"Good work, Matsui," booms the immaterial voice. "You can do this. Just keep it together a while longer, and it'll be ok. *You* will be ok."

The one-two amphetamine and epinephrine punch the droids hit Oni with have her spilling coffee all over the rooftop landing pad. She motions to dry her hand and freezes, noticing the droids' mastery. Unlike Jin, Celeste's private doctors had enough time to warm the medgel and bio-seal her wounds. She might have a hard time convincing a stranger she had ever lost that arm, not that she is planning on schmoozing anytime soon.

In addition to proving themselves both artists of bio-mechanics, Mr. Pink and Mr. Grey have gone the distance and provided Oni with some choice haute couture. The latest in fall fashion: a long-sleeve shirt with micro-scales sewn into the antiballistic fabric, which bulges with heavplast exoskeletal reinforcements at the elbows, shoulders, and neck. A back brace gives the shirt a spine of its own, handy in the event that Oni's fails her. Her pants, too, are well-armoured and endowed with nano-net shinguards that will shield against most small-arms fire. Outland has outfitted her for war, not for espionage; the cost-differential for this unobscurable expression of intent easily in the millions. *Beware the king who knights men keen on regicide.*

Skyr sits like a Buddha on a green blanket with a butcher's assortment of blades spread before him. With one bionic eye trained on Oni, the other follows his hands as they scrub hardened blood and rust from an uncharged electro-knife "They did a damn fine job, didn't they? I can't say I'm surprised. A Goliath drone tore my jaw off a few years back. Larynx went too. Mr. Pink and Mr. Grey had me chewing fat day-of."

Mr. Pink scans Oni, doublechecking its work. With a melodic dee-dah-dum, it trudges back inside.

Skyr sets down the electroblade and picks up his Kingsword for inspection. "Should have had your nose fixed while you were under. Your breasts, too…"

Still anxious after sitting wide-eyed through several hours of butchery, Oni doesn't need the extra stress. She pulls up the EQ controls on her Monocle's audio-enhancer. She channel-selects Skyr's voice and mutes it. Targeting the mids in the city's natural hum, Oni maxes the gain and isolates the channel. Los Angeles serenades her with its low, two-note croon. She feels stronger, peaceful; almost whole. She rolls her shoulders back takes a deep, painless breath.

It is not long before Skyr realizes he is being ignored. He throws a cartridge from his bandolier at Oni. She quickly resets Monocle's audio pick-up.

"Feeling better, I see." Skyr rolls all but one of his blades up into the green blanket, and buries the blanket in his satchel. "Good. A little confidence never hurts." He produces a cigar from his satchel and lights it. Accentuating the craters in his cheeks with a big draw, he sneers: "Though too much will be the death of you."

Oni feels antsy. It's not just the drugs. She does not want to be out in the open, even if her primary stalker is standing slack-jawed beside her. "What are we waiting for?"

"You'll see," Skyr responds behind a plume of smoke.

"I don't see the point of holding out on intel, especially if it concerns me and this mission of yours."

Out the side of his mouth he jabbers: "Mission of *yours*...Fine." He rummages through his pockets and pulls out a holosphere. It projects a hologram of a mean-looking military jet: a fully-loaded Rake. "I called for air support..."

Oni finishes the last few sips of her coffee. The grainy conclusion gets caught between her teeth. "Uh-uh..."

"Told 'em I caught a high-priority archetypal." Skyr slavers and flicks his cigar, nearly missing Oni's face. "That'd be you."

"Some plan," Oni replies. The adrenalin has given her the shakes. "He'll just call it in, and they'll send a death squad."

Skyr chuckles, clattering his yellow teeth. "You better hope not. In fact, you better hope he tries to follow protocol despite my signal jam. For this to work, you're going to have to play along. We're gonna put on a show, and then you'll take his seat and his ride back to Seal Base." Skyr stuffs a wad of plastic cards and passes into Oni's hands. "Your narrative, outlined. You're delivering a brief to General McCabe. Also some passes and fabricated bioprints you'll need to get into the underground weapons facility. The rest is on you."

"You're going to...Never mind." Oni feels like protesting the senseless murder of a Marine pilot, but knows it will all end the same, anyway. "What makes you think I can pull this off?"

"I don't. It's See-See who believes in you. Thinks that if you can whack that old skin-rag in his Citadel vault, you can handle a few lab techs."

Oni's eyes widen. "A few lab techs with the support of the US Marine Corps."

Reproducing his tablet, Skyr shows Oni a map of the base. "The *invicibles* are all on the wall or in the barracks here and here. They would light you up before an angry thought wet your lips. You don't have to worry about them; you will be headed in, how you say? *Incognito*. Inside the Inner Sanctum, it's a lot of badged civilians and asthmatics."

Oni crouches to get a better look of the map's intricacies. "I've pulled off a Trojan Horse before. The trouble isn't getting in..."

"The key is making them think you are out when you are not out. See-See went through the trouble of fabricating footage of your escape. Seal Base security will watch you and 2690 get above ground, bypass the emergency doors, and make it to the roof. They will see you get into the decoy rig, and then they will blow you to smithereens over the bay."

Noticing landing lights brightening on the horizon, Oni stands and shakes free her look of confusion. "Better get to the punchline, because my ride's here."

Skyr grabs Oni by the throat and spins her around. She has the means to resist, but goes with it, recognizing it to be theatre. Bundling Oni's arms behind her back, Skyr attempts to continue the briefing but is forced to hold off as a fat-nosed jet buzzes the rooftop. Inside the second-generation Marine-issue Rake thundering by, a black-eyed dome bobbles, scoping out the scene. The Rake rolls right with a roar, and yaws to face the rooftop. Skyr attempts to compete with the volume of the Rake's afterburners by yelling: "When you find 2690, trigger the March Hare executable we've put on your Monocle. That'll set the dominos in motion." Skyr jerks Oni back and forth, and waves to the Rake, now hovering forty-feet away from the rooftop's easternmost ledge. "Between our decoy ship flouting their coastal defences with ion blasts and the fabricated surveillance feeds we're going to shove down their throats, they'll buy the fake-out hook, line, and sinker."

Not bad, Oni thinks to herself. "Won't be long until they realize the girl isn't with the wreckage."

"That's right. Which is why you'll cloak the both of yah using your collar, and hide out just long enough for our guy inside to get to you."

"Ask this son-of-a-bitch how the mole will know how to find you," a voice nags Oni via Monocle.

Oni tries to survey her surroundings for the source, but Skyr keeps her stationary for the sake of their airborne audience. "How will he find me?"

"*When* he finds you," Skyr continues, ignoring Oni's question, "He's going to get you and 2690 topside via an alternate passage. When you're topside we'll decloak our Gnat drone. It'll get you out of there, assuming you hold up your end."

The Rake noses over and extends its landing gear, hazing all the colours beneath it. It touches down, creating surprisingly little noise or tremors, and fires a spotlight at Skyr and his captive. A holographic likeness of the pilot appears out front of the Rake. Unlike its real counterpart, the pilot's projection has no helmet on. Its lips, uniform despite the wind, begin to articulate the declaration boomed by a speaker buried in the jet's nose. "Citizen: the date and the time have been archived along with a full-dimensional capture of the convict. As we are currently unable to intern any additional prisoners, my orders are as follows: you are to destroy the fugitive, or bring him—sorry, bring her—before my aft guns for judgment."

"Screw that!" Oni yells, bucking back against Skyr. With a powerful swipe of her prosthetic against Skyr's chin, she manages to break free of his grasp. She dodges a tackling attempt, and makes a mad dash for the stairwell.

A leathery crack announces the unholstering of Skyr's Kingsword. Oni nearly loses her footing, and to compensate for her overstep, twists just enough to see the dark end of the barrel. Skyr thumbs the hammer back, announcing his intent with a click. He pulls the trigger. The execution is deafening.

Oni falls. Her momentum rolls her twice. All the metal and spidersilk under her skin won't save the top layer from the scrapes and bruises made by the chapped ground. With all her momentum transferred elsewhere, she lays motionless as her body is freckled by gun smoke.

There is a baseball-sized hole in the Rake's front window. Slumped over inside the cockpit: four-fifths of a pilot. The pilot's facial projection outside the jet runs through all possible configurations and poises. Its lips purse and pucker, stretch and thin. Like a possessed doll, the eyes roll back to white, and then back out unfocused. A death rattle sounds over the speaker.

"Help me ditch the stiff and wipe this bird down," Skyr bellows to Oni, agape on her buttocks, arms scraped and heart racing.

# HORRORS THE SEA HID

The sun has set over the Pacific and left behind clouds the colour of Lenten vestments. Black, turbulent, and fanning towards Naval Weapons Station Seal Beach, the underlying ocean refuses to reflect the celestial lavender and throws up white tips in protest. The waves seem tall enough to swat the Oni out of the air, but she has faith in the jet's autopilot. In addition to navigating watery pyramids and half-sunken wind turbines on her behalf, the Rake's autopilot affords Oni an opportunity to survey the base whose blueprints she has already committed to artificial memory.

Seal Base was once a glorified storage shed. After Brazil got the bomb, Californian bases with airfields and or ocean access received massive amounts of federal funding. Now, run by General "Mad Dog" McCabe and his Marines, Seal Base boasts three aerial Dreadnoughts, a squadron of Reduvius drones, twenty Hurricane stealth boats, and enough troops to retake Chula Vista. The dreadnoughts—the USS Liberty, the Texas, and the Alberta, respectively—hover over Alamitos Bay's marinas, slapping the barnacled luxury yachts into an unsettling carillon.

Oni involuntarily passes under one of the dreadnoughts. Its gargantuan jets, even on standby, are enough to warm the cockpit—especially noticeable on account of the massive hole in the Rake's window funnelling maritime air right into Oni's eyes. Notwithstanding the heat and the gusty barrage, she can make out the big block letters on the thirty-thousand-ton monstrosity: the USS Liberty. Plasma railguns jut over port and starboard, giving it the appearance of a centipede on steroids. No matter how great Skyr's plan is, just one shot from one of those guns could pulverize Oni in this life, follow her into the next, and kill her there too.

Having tracked far-enough over the ocean for Seal Beach's air traffic controllers to scan and clear the vessel for landing, Oni turns east—past the desalination plants and their heavy metal ocean-fronts. Stressing the rasp in her voice for a masculine result, Oni comms the tower with the information Skyr scraped for her: "Seal Base Ground, this is Striker-Niner-Foxtrot-Tango-Zulu."

There is a hiss, a crackle, and then a click: "Striker-Niner-Foxtrot-Tango-Zulu, Seal Base Ground reads you loud and clear."

Scanning her notes, Oni reads the appropriate response: "Seal Base Ground, Striker-Niner-Foxtrot-Tango-Zulu, two miles west, requesting permission to approach for landing."

"Alright, Striker, I see you. You running auto?"

"Affirmative, Seal Base Ground," Oni replies, checking the instrumentation just in case it's a trick question. "Running auto."

"Alright, Striker-Niner-Foxtrot-Tango-Zulu, we'll commandeer nav systems. Welcome back."

The heads-up display prompts Oni to confirm her final destination. She does not have an option: the landing area the tower has cleared is not the rooftop she had planned on. A blinking, dotted line indicates a secondary tarmac, outside the Inner Sanctum, surrounded by hangers and holotrans running circuits.

"Dammit," she growls. Oni tries to reset the landing zone. It is a Democratic ballot: only one option is accepted. "Skyr!" she yells, sure he can hear and see everything like some homunculus seated behind her eyes or a second-string demiurge.

"Need a hand?" sounds an ethereal mimicry of Booker Gibson's voice. The question rattles around in Oni's head. It is alien enough to stand out, distinct from her panicked scheming and concerns. *Trickery played on an exhausted mind by itself. A suicidal tendency, no doubt.*

The navigation interface flickers and a secondary layer appears. Quasi-transparent override commands appear in a text box, mutilating the metadata underpinning Seal Base Ground's landing commands. Coordinates change without any trace of foul play.

"Skyr, is that you?" Oni whispers, watching the ship's trajectory reset, pinpointing her intended destination inside the Inner Sanctum.

An uncertain voice crackles over the comm: "Striker-Niner-Foxtrot-Tango-Zulu, this is Seal Base Ground, slight malfunction on our end. You good to taxi?"

Oni flips switches and mashes buttons in a vain attempt to secure some semblance of control. "Negative, Seal Base Ground."

Again, the secondary voice rattles in Oni's head. "Tell 'em you got a weak charge. Going to drop like a moth at a Molly Case concert."

Oni parses the excuse and regurgitates the underlying theme: "Got a weak charge and tired wings."

The controller sputters a concerned response into his mic. "Er, alright. Set it down on the Bastille."

"Affirmative, Seal Base Ground."

Whoever or whatever just pulled Oni's ass out of the fire

managed to make the fatalistic alteration seem organic for all involved; all except for Oni. She checks to make sure her line to the tower is off. "Damn, Skyr. That was some nice work."

Silence.

Oni ponders on the possibility of a saintless, godless miracle. *If that wasn't Skyr, then who the hell was it?*

Cancer-eaten seagulls hurry out of the Rake's way as it blurs towards the roof of the Bastille, nose up with its previously creaseless fuselage hatching a sizeable undercarriage. Three legs with snowshoe-shaped pads find the tarry apron. Their sensors report to the navigation system—and to Oni by extension—that they have "COME TO JOURNEY'S END."

Clasping the choke collar around her neck, up-to-date with the former pilot's facial details, Oni grimaces at the computer's phrasing. "What do you know that I don't?" she mumbles, ill at ease.

The choke collar cuts into Oni's throat like a crown of thorns that, too loose for her head, slunk down and shrunk. It delivers a series of small zaps. No longer sporadic but constant, the electrical current triggers the projection of a second skin, which rolls out over Oni's features like a welcome mat—a familiar greeting to friends of the deceased. On the inside of the mask, kaleidoscopic patterns cycle, flipping the appropriate light and colours to the social side. The inconstant stimuli are overwhelming, so Oni intuits on Monocle and filters out the peripheral activity, focusing on the world beyond this digital cave.

A droid knocks on the Rake's window. Matte black with red rivets and brown braces, it points accusingly at Oni. "Major, turn off aft shields so we can harness your vessel." The command is loud enough to penetrate the glass, register on Oni's mic, and feedback through her headset.

"Yeah, yeah," she replies, flicking switches discoloured by overuse and deactivating the ship's force field.

Before the force field's crackles have even subsided, the droid has opened the canopy, exposing Oni to the elements. A gust of ocean air tongues the flight deck, whistling as it passes through the crannies in the Rake's instruments and gear.

Oni unbuckles her harnesses, and climbs out of the jet. She drops to the tarmac with a grunt. Doublechecking to make sure her disguise is still intact, she surveys the Bastille's rooftop. Invisible from the air, but clear to her now: a hemi-cylindrical hangar protected by several massive laser cannons. *Hopefully Skyr and Celeste took into account this and all the other invisible variables ahead when outlining this plan.*

Stopped halfway between the ship and the architectural mirage is an android, head tilted and focus directed at Oni. It is holding a yellow ladder, no doubt having intended to permit Oni a more graceful disembarkation. Oni cracks a smile even though she knows it'll make no difference for the glorified calculator. Divested of purpose, it turns like a broken hour hand back to twelve and marches into the hangar. Inside, it slams the ladder back onto its storage hooks, and throws a glance Oni's way, even more menacing without the benefit of expressive tissue.

Another droid, this one far more anthropomorphic and *hopefully far less dramatic,* waves her over. It addresses Oni using the name of her shell with a metallic voice clanged over a built-in loudspeaker. Oni motions towards the droid, but stops, noticing the mustard outline of the landing pad beneath her feet. This Rubicon, freshly painted, demands she recommit to anything and everything required of her ahead, no matter the cost, human or political. Turning one last time to the Rake, Oni contemplates backing out. She has missed her opportunity for cowardice; the jet is now crawling with droids and charger mechs. "The die has been cast."

"How was your flight in, Major Barkley?" the android asks, chopping at the delivery with overzealous jaw movements. 'How' makes the droid stretch its mouth so wide that its artificial skin stretches thin over the rest of its face, narrowing its eyes vertically, and wrinkling its forehead—the combined effect of which is almost an artful rendition of Laocoon, absent serpent and sons.

"Good. Great! Almost got vaporized by the USS Liberty."

Eyes simulating cognition, swiping left to right and back again, the android shakes its head disapprovingly. "You did not advise tower of the incident, thus violating safety protocol. I will have to mention this in my report and recommend a reprimand."

Instinctively, Oni taps her chaperone's elbow, as if this motorized man could be deterred by touch like its creator. It tilts its head, no doubt gearing about the notion that this gesture is something other than inoffensive. Oni steps back and pleads: "I'll make a report of it myself."

"You have no time. General McCabe is expecting your brief and does not appreciate being kept waiting."

"My brief..." Oni repeats, inflecting to suggest it more as a question than a confirmation.

"You eliminated a high-priority target, did you not?"

Forcing a smile that naturalizes on her avatar, Oni nods. "That's classified."

A cylindrical compartment studded with superconducting magnets emerges from the ground behind the android and locks into place. It cracks open, spilling brilliant white light onto the tarmac. Just in case Oni is completely blind, the android indicates the elevator with a point. "Very well, Major. Owing to security concerns and your choice of LZ, you will be unable to go directly to the obelisk. This lift will take you to sublevel eighteen. I expect you will be able to find your way. If you have any questions, please consult Spherion."

The prospect of taking another elevator someplace she doesn't want to be elicits a flutter in Oni's chest. She grins at the android and walks into the light, but stops before entering to take one last look around—at the now raisin-coloured sky and at the moon, cutting through but still confined by dark clouds. Something Paul once told her eight beers into a private pity party finally resonates with her: "When the moon is low in the night sky, and it seems you're that much closer to the cold of space...that's when you really feel it. A kind of dread. Like the only thing weighing you down is your commitment to this dream, and that commitment is waning. It's waning because somewhere along the way, you realized it is a bad excuse for a dream." Tempted to let the heavens take her, Oni bucks up and steps inside the elevator. *Would be a truer nightmare. And nightmares don't play by any rules. But then again, neither do I.*

# THROUGH A GLASS, DARKLY

"Are you comfortable?" inquires the android, its glove-leather face unperturbed by concern or affect.

Focus slashed away by the zonal heater's fan—a greyish blur hidden behind metal slats—Lyle looks back at the hairless imitation. "Not particularly, no." His undershirt clings to him, brittle and wet like a newly moulted casing. "All of this really necessary?"

"Yes," it replies, adhering the last of the sensors to Lyle's temples. If improperly calibrated, the android could easily push the sensor through bone and brain and adhere it to the inside of the opposite temple.

"And there's nothing to be done about the heat?"

The android reels back, sits opposite its subject, and interfaces with Lyle's deep-brain holographic readings. "Nothing at all..." There is a series of beeps. A re-presentation of Lyle's brain shimmers and rotates at the centre of the table. "Now, Mr. Badegger, please exercise as much precision in your answering as possible. Try also to relax and to keep your eyes level. For your sake, we would like to avoid a false-positive."

Pulsating at the center of the drab little room, the hologram of Lyle's brain looks hyperreal. Bright, honest, and vulnerable; rainbow coral washed up and left to bake at low tide.

"I question the legality of any of this," Lyle murmurs, adjusting the micro-sensor making his right eye water. He looks at his reflection in the long mirror running along the south wall. His dirty-blonde hair looks lousy with all of the little electronic knickknacks strewn about. Catching his own stare just nigh the doppelganger of his flickering brain, he senses a second set of disdainful eyes looking back into this pale white box of a room, back at both his true and false selves.

"After the incident, you elected not to check in with an Outpost recovery agent." The android's optical sensor plate spins.

Rolling up his sleeves, revealing implant scars and a military scan-tag, Lyle mulls over pleading the fifth, and with a shake, visibly decides against it. He lines his knuckles along the edge of the metal table plotted between him and this apish simulacrum. "Why ask me about comfort if you're not going to do something about it?"

"After the incident—"

"The rain-out, you mean? No, that's right. I didn't check in with a recovery agent." Lyle's amygdala flares up on the three-dimensional hologram. The software immediately paints the activity in red, cross-referencing apathetic responses archived in the Military Affect Repository.

Broadcasting its analysis in real time, the android presses the issue and Lyle's exposed buttons. "Knowing full well that it was mandatory..."

Taking an indirect cue from his brain's dry and immortal twin, Lyle steadies his breathing and flattens his hands. "Correct."

"Why?"

"Is your personality chip set to 'overbearing'?"

"Why did you fail to check in with a CDC or an Outland recovery agent?"

"I determined that for a recovery agent to be of any use to me, I would have had to have lost something. Fortunately," he smiles, tapping the side of his head, "I'm all in one piece. No point in repairing what ain't broke. And besides, Outland is a corporation, not a legal arbiter in this state or in any other. I checked in with my physician who, in cooperation with the LAPD, cleared me of any CLOUD-related damage or malignancies." He plucks a sensor off of his neck, and turns it over between his thumb and index finger.

The android's eyes flare red. "Please do not interfere with the sensors."

"Maybe *you* should relax. Would hate for you to short-circuit. Suppose that would be a real positive."

Apart from a reversion of its eyes back from red to green, the droid's taut-leather face reveals neither comprehension nor judgment nor consequence nor soul. "You disobeyed protocol because you believe you are above consequence."

"One of the perks of *playing it safe and living virtuously.*"

"Since the anarchist's dismantling of the CLOUD, have you felt an intense urge to commune with individuals you had met whilst synchronized?"

"I beg your pardon?"

"Have alien thoughts or objectives taken root in your mind?"

"No." Lyle smiles at his reflection in the mirror, strapped into all that gear like some lab rat forgone sympathy or respect. The smile that he bought himself in West Hollywood is as superficial and disconnected as the android's frontispiece. Recalling Benny Bass' predicament, Lyle chuckles, appreciative he had all of his citizenship papers in order for this AI.

Disregarding Lyle's seeming mania, the android runs down its list of questions. "Have you felt a sense of loss, longing or discomfort since the incident?"

"Longing?" Lyle shifts in his seat, his cool demeanor dismantled. Sweat beads down from his narrow hairline, breaking around the sensors plotted like mines on his temples and upper-cheeks. "None whatsoever."

The robot's eyes whiz, zooming in on Lyle's perspiration. They shutter and its sockets are once again filled with a faint green glow. "Have you noticed any change in your sleep patterns?"

"No."

"In your dreams?"

Lyle hesitates. Smacking his lips, he blurts: "No. I really don't see what any of this has to do with my subscription or my time spent in the CLOUD."

"Mr. Badegger, need I remind you that this examination is mandated, not only by Outland Security, but by both the Federal and State governments?" In a borrowed, pre-recorded voice, the robot declares: "'All questions must be answered to the proctor's satisfaction.'"

"Pass-fail?" Exasperated, Lyle lets out a chuckle. "How many ones and zeroes would it take to satisfy you?"

"Guilt or innocence will be not be determined using binary, but rather a five-state system."

"God Almighty," Lyle curses, slumping in his chair. "Who let this thing out of its box?"

"If my programming were to qualify for a 'who', then that would be my answer. Please sit up, keep your eyes level and your answers precise....Is there a common image, personality, or pattern recurrent in your dreams."

"No." Lyle wishes Dorota shared this robot's focus.

The android voids Lyle's floating brain, and projects in its place a holographic portrait of a little girl. "Do you recognize this individual?"

Round-faced imp. No more than thirteen years old. Stress under her eyes and freckles above them. Hair's unkempt. An orphan or an independent. Either way, no one cares what she looks like or does; the desperation in her eyes says it all. The image cuts off at the top of her sternum, but you can make out bruised flesh, and the white-silver head of a PILOT device. Something knots in Lyle's stomach. "*No. Looks like a CLOUD cadet. Who is she?*"

"In your dealings and conversations with the CLOUD manifestation of Minerva—"

"Dealings?" Lyle's body rejects his mind's feigned calm. "This is ridiculous." He slams the table and violently tears the sensors off of his head. Only when slipping the micro-sensors out from under his eyelids, does he observe any caution—and not for the devices' preservation. "A few searches, nothing more...I never had a conversation with it. I don't waste my time with artificial intelligence. This entire line of questioning is insane, not to mention invasive."

A crackling indigo baton springs out of some hidden cubby and into the android's hand. The droid stands and the weapon's glow colours its face blue.

Squirming in and fighting with his waist restraint, Lyle looks up in terror. "The hell is that for?"

The android slowly orbits the table.

"Holy shit!" Hoping to rouse the attention of the guards outside, Lyle screams. "Hey, this thing's gone mental! You got a renegade bot in here! Help! Help?"

The wall-mirror shudders. There are footsteps outside. Lyle leans to see past the android—red eyes glaring—and notices two dark gaps in the bright horizontal space left under the door. Creaking, the door opens to a bulky silhouette of a man holding a briefcase.

"Stand down, 4-7."

With a clunk, the android's aggressive posture softens. "Thank you for your cooperation, Mr. Badegger." The android lowers the baton, which is no sooner deactivated, than hidden away in its compartment. "Lieutenant Samson will now have some questions for you."

Still catching his breath, Lyle winces at the silhouette in the doorway. "I demand to speak to legal counsel...I want to get hell out of here!"

"Good afternoon, Lyle." The barrel-chested shade nods to the robot, which shuffles over to its charging station in the corner of the room.

"I don't know what kind of game you're playing..." The zonal heater's fan seems amplified now, cutting into Lyle's resolve with each click and whir. "Am I a suspect in some ongoing investigation? What crime have I been accused of committing?"

A low wah announces the initiation of the android's update and recharge sequence.

"Thanks, 4-7," says Lieutenant Samson. He commandeers the android's place at the table opposite Lyle and blinks a command into his Monocle causing Lyle's waist restraint to unclasp. "You can go ahead and take that PILOT insert out now. I've a better bullshit detector anyway."

Lyle tugs the little drive out of his breast and buries his unease behind another flimsy smile, scrutinizing the flesh-and-blood interrogator laying out whatever evidence he has warranting this waste of tax-payer-funded minutes and dollars. The Lieutenant's disorganization and failure at an aesthetic spread of documents and electronics on the cold metal surface breaks Lyle's concentration, and in so doing, unhinges his expression. "What is this good cop, bot cop all about?" grumbles Lyle.

"That's a good line." Samson laughs. "Hope you don't mind if I steal it." His eyes appear to grow; brown Venetian marble hugging piercing black. "Have we met before?"

Lyle thumbs the corner of the table, scratching as if there was an imperfection in the alloy warranting his attention. "It is within the realm of possibility."

Lieutenant Samson, a melting-pot second-serving of Asian-American bone structure and reg-force augmentations, tilts his head and studies Lyle's features. "Déjà vu, man." He covers his front teeth with his bottom lip. "This is going to bother me...Where the hell do I know you from?" Samson's pupils set into pink flesh, no doubt summoning an answer via Monocle. "Hmmm," he murmurs, pupils advancing, and interfacing with the tablet resting on the table before him. "Ah! That's right." He snaps his fingers. "The Copps and Forsyth law firm downtown. I've seen you on their transit holoverts and the shimmers on 9th street. You're a clerk there?"

"A partner, actually," Lyle answers back quickly, exhausted but relieved—his ego barbed and his patience sapped by the faux man charging in its box in the corner. *Samson knows who I am. He's read my file. If he hadn't, they would have sent someone who had.* "They've yet to update the posters. Copps, Forsyth, and Badegger."

"That's great, Lyle," says Samson, swiping through biographical information on the screen. He turns his gaze up slowly, as if expecting another person to have replaced his original interviewee. "Do you mind if I call you Lyle?"

If Lyle bit any deeper into his tongue, he'd qualify tomorrow for disability. He shrugs his shoulders.

"Well Lyle…" Running his finger across the tablet's screen, Samson looks up, "Oh! 2$^{nd}$ Battalion 4$^{th}$ Marines?"

"Canada and Nicaragua."

The officer signs an informal salute to Lyle. "How's a decorated captain go from zeroing Sprites to defending criminals?"

"Plane."

"Heh." Samson returns his attention to the tablet and the documents sprawled out before him. "Harvard Law, blah blah blah. No wife, no kids. Just you alone with all that blood money?"

"Lieutenant, is there a point to all of this?"

"Have you heard the word about the loons the CLOUD turned out when it came crashing down?"

Lyle shrugs his shoulders again. "Saw that new Outland CEO on *NewsLink* running her mouth about telepathic communes made up of anarchical mutants—archetypals, right?"

"That's the gist. Individuals with similar behavioural and mental patterns that got close in the CLOUD are now swarming around the city like locusts, talking crazy and getting up to no good. I'd have called them legion, but the press gets paid by the syllable. "

Lyle perseverates on 'crazy', unwittingly mouthing the word over and over.

Ignoring Lyle's tick, Samson continues: "We're following up with every single rainout to make sure they're not missing a few terabytes. I'm not too concerned about you, granted you're not holed up with a bunch of emaciated nutters finishing each other's sentences. CLOUD went down, and you went back to work. That's good. Real good."

"So am I free to go?"

"Thing is, Lyle, pre-crash reports suggest you shared a lot of experiential data with a *certain group* whilst synchronized. The group in question was on our radar long before that son-of-a-bitch Sheffield and his cronies toasted the CLOUD. Technically this *certain group* constitutes a type—an archetypal—but it doesn't operate in the same vein…"

Lyle figures Samson has a piece of his puzzle down, but still doesn't know what he's looking at. "I can tell you for a fact: what you're accusing me of? *Not a crime.*"

"Your involvement with them? *No,*" Samson responds behind upturned palms. "I suppose it's not. It's just strange," he continues, triggering a solid duotone infographic, "because it's uncommon for a subscriber to share the breadth of experience and memories that you've shared with *a particular group* without cozying up to them in the real world or pursuing their shared pleasures."

"When you take the Hyperloop, do you develop an affinity for all of the other passengers in your given pod?"

"If you mean to persuade me, Captain, it's your reputation on the line."

Lyle drops his gaze.

"If I were to take the Hyperloop, which I can't say I have, I believe, statistically, that no more than one percent of the commuters will be partial to the tastes and subversive pleasures your particular group are known to take delight in."

"Am I under arrest, Lieutenant?"

Lieutenant Samson leans back in his chair, grinding its legs against the institutional polyvinyl. "We could say that you've been accessory to the trafficking and distribution of snuff pornography, for starters."

"How do you figure?"

"You've shared grey matter with the worst of them—visited their memories—and yet you haven't turned them in…"

Lyle sneers.

"My feelings exactly, Mr. Badegger. The charges won't stick, granted the law's failure to keep up with our technology."

"Pity," says Lyle, trying not to smile.

"But it would be enough to keep you here and away from your creature comforts…You can dissuade me from pursuing that course simply by answering a few more questions. Then you can go back to your lonely Blue Zone penthouse."

"Oh, heavens. Then I shall savour every second we have left together." Lyle maintains eye contact, but rests his head back.

"The partition you dabbled in and the minds that congregated there…"

"What of it?"

"An Outland probe suggests that your group was chiefly comprised of psychopaths. On the spectrum, anyhow."

"Again, I have to ask: what are you accusing me of, Lieutenant Samson?"

With a coordinated blink, Samson closes the holograms. "Nothing that I can prove before you walk out that door."

Lyle takes a deep, confident breath, and plots his hands on the table, invading the space previously conquered by Lieutenant Samson's mess. "It hadn't occurred to me that they might be psychopaths, no. Maybe my compass is broken after fighting at the behest of the Republic in the company of its finest, but I don't think your classifications are as neat or as tidy as that device before you suggests...And, Lieutenant Samson," Lyle pauses, satisfied with having affected an eerie lisp on the 's' in the Lieutenant's name, "before you append some label to me, please take note of the label I have appointed myself: a free and private citizen. Unless you have any other questions, I fully intend to enjoy my freedom freely and privately. Call my secretary, Dorota, if you'd like to set up an appointment to further prod at whatever tenuous connection you feel I've made with Outland's other clientele."

Grinding his teeth, but keen not to give Lyle the upper hand with a look of defeat, Samson kicks back his chair and stands. "Guard!"

The door busts open and a young officer in fatigues holding a plasma rifle butts in.

"Please escort Mr. Badegger off the premises." Scrounging together his belongings, Lieutenant Samson dismisses Lyle without the courtesy of eye contact: "You're free to go, *Lyle*. I look forward to our next appointment."

Lyle turns in his chair, and visually traces a line from the rifle's muzzle to the soldier's trigger finger. "It's been a pleasure, Lieutenant." Doublechecking he'd taken off all of the sensors and interrogation equipment, he begins: "Out of curiosity..."

Lieutenant Samson fires an eyebrow up and his sneer forward.

"Outland—the government—do they plan to sieve all of southern California through this brutish process to shake free these so-called archetypals?"

In a military monotone, undoubtedly camouflaging his frustration, Samson answers: "That's how it'll go for those who'll answer the call. For everyone else—for those inside the quarantine and the fools who dodge the summons—the process will be a little less civil."

"I don't want you to think that when I retired my rank, I retired my commitment to this country..."

"Actually, Captain, it never occurred to me that you'd committed to anything besides the satisfaction of your characteristic impulse."

"Hah. Well," Lyle pauses, contemplating what emotion to mimic next, "I'd like to help you. The only problem is that I don't know what you are looking for. You must have some intel sharpening all of those pointed questions."

An aborted snarl squeaks through Samson's nostrils.

"How would I know one if I saw one?" Lyle fans his hands. *"An archetypal?* In the interest of keeping you in the loop and off my ass..."

"All I can say, Captain Badegger, is that you shouldn't go out of your way to find one. If you rattle the hive, you're bound to get stung."

As the interrogation-room door swings back into its frame, Lyle glimpses Samson throw his tablet against the wall.

"Good man, the Lieutenant," Lyle says to the guard.

"Move!" the guard barks back, gesturing to the end of the hallway with his rifle.

Lyle grimaces. "Now, there's no excuse for such rudeness."

The gel adhesive that kept the sensors in place drips down the sides of Lyle's face because of the late afternoon sun. Besides being angered that a productive morning has been mulched by the military-industrial complex, Lyle's got a head full of indistinct vexation and compulsion. Worse than a migraine, his mind is swollen with that unnameable desire. Once the desire passes, pain will fill the ruts it leaves behind. Lyle will again be useless for a time.

*The android implicated Minerva...*Minerva was nothing more than a CLOUD program—a subroutine Lyle co-opted to seek out new experiences and exotic stimuli. *They must really be desperate, if they're looking to pin all this chaos on a search AI. Something far more nefarious is behind these headaches. Whomever or whatever is responsible for this feeling will feel an equal or greater pain in good measure.*

A benign buzz re-breaks Lyle's conductor-less train of thought. He angrily intuits on Monocle. "Hello?" he yells, overloading his mic.

Receiving the crackly wall of sound: Dorota. "How'd it go, boss?"

"Too early to say. Pulse my private files, but leave all the cases be…Actually, pulse anything pertaining to the CLOUD settlements, Tuttle, and the black-hole uranium dump. Ah, to hell with it. Pulse anything pertaining to the Outland Corporation."

"Care to give me a hand?"

Flaccid and frustrated, Lyle can neither justify the late night dalliance nor make it worth it. "No. Raincheck. When you're done, dig up whatever you can…" He backtracks through his mental file folder in search of the Monocle image-grab of the little girl—Lieutenant Samson and the 4-7 androids' unwitting overspill. The image is a poor duplicate, but will have to do. He sends it to Dorota. "Find out who she is and why she would be of any interest to the Military."

"I'll be going into double overtime…"

"So be it. I'll unlock next month's petty-cash partition."

"You better."

"Talk soon."

## DEEP-SEATED ANGER

The elevator speaker chimes as Oni sinks further and further beneath the beach. The descent is unusually slow, simultaneously piquing her paranoia and giving her time to reflect. How the Military could forge such solidity despite the erosive power of the ocean boggles her mind. *Force fields, perhaps.* More boggling is the ease with which she has managed access. For all she knows, sublevel eighteen is where they keep America's most insidious interrogators, and she has done Outland a double service without resistance. But if that were the case, whose face is she wearing? *A phantasm with phantasmal blood?* It would take a pretty talented or disposable actor to pull off losing a third of one's head. That's assuming the bullet and the resultant carnage were real...Oni didn't load Skyr's gun. Could have been full of jelly beans. If the murder had been an act and the agents mere actors, then the virtual face she has donned is a mask of a mask, making her less an actor and more a prop. Such high drama and deception on account of a simple prisoner exchange seems excessive, even by US Military standards.

Prefaced by a double chime, a sexless monotone voice announces, "Minus eighteen." The doors slide open revealing a large circular room with a massive black orb hovering at its centre. Stars and stripes wave ceaselessly at eye level along the curved walls. This seamless graphic is reflected by the glossy vinyl floor, making the room feel less like an antechamber and more like a patriotic tomb for the unknown unknown.

Sleuthing out of the elevator and glancing every which way, Oni notices there is not a single sailor, scientist, Marine, civilian or android to speak of. Just the black orb resisting any reflection of the mosaicked Navy-Marines Task Force insignia on the ceiling. *Spherion.*

"Major Barkley, reporting for duty," Oni declares sheepishly, undecided on whether she wants a response or not.

The black orb shrinks to the size of a grapefruit and darts Oni's way. Nearly missing Oni's face, it maneuvers to the side, and begins orbiting her. Its smooth surface breaks, and a cordillera of spikes emerges along its circumference. With the spikes jumping out accusingly, Oni closes her eyes. Barkley's death mask follows suit.

The orb's spikes round out and begin vibrating, emitting a guitar-like strumming. Cacophonic at first, the protuberances quickly coordinate. In synch and in tune, they together emulate a human voice. "Major Barkley..."

Oni's jaw drops, but she has no words. She hadn't expected the Military's minimalist décor to address the dead man she didn't know she would be wearing.

"Your bio-signatures read abnormal. Body mass down seventeen percent. Bone structure fundamentally altered. Report at once to sublevel five for a full medical examination." Wiggling on the surface like a clew of worms, the orb's spikes reach towards Oni. "At once!"

Sweat stings Oni's eyes; sweat she can't dab without ruining the illusion even this ethereal orb apparently cannot debunk. "B-but I've been ordered to provide time-sensitive information to General McCabe."

The worms vibrate more intensely, channeling a hesitant "Um" into the circle. "General McCabe failed to preclear you or notify Seal Beach Spherion of this engagement."

"The command, like the information I bear with me, is strictly confidential. Classified. Top secret. You don't have clearance." Noticing the orb oscillate, digesting the potential that it is not all-knowing, Oni respires her confidence. "Do you—does *the* Spherion want to compromise national security? I'd be happy to detail my findings…"

Writhing frantically, Spherion's protuberances appear to shorten when in fact the orb itself is growing. "National security," it parrots. "Classified?" It churrs and vibrates, appealing to best-practices above and beyond standard procedure.

Oni steps back. Silently debating whether or not a shape-shifting eight ball can be killed, she runs her trigger finger up her thigh towards her ESD wand.

As if from a bursting corpse, the worms jut out in every direction, some as far out as a foot. "General McCabe is in his office!" it declares. "He will be made aware of your presence, your intention, and the urgency of your visit."

Oni and the ghost of Major Barkley smile in unison. "Thank you."

"Reserve your gratitude for an entity equipped to care. After your meeting with General McCabe, proceed to the Medical Bay for processing. Preliminary scans indicate you are not yourself."

A secondary door opens opposite the elevator, splitting the patriotic graphic. In the place of stars and stripes, arrows appear, all directing Oni to the portal.

Oni wonders: if she had drawn her weapon, would Spherion have strung her up with a symphony or close-talked her to death? Oni stops between the directional arrows, and turns to look at the orb, simultaneously curious about its violent potential and relieved she avoided a demonstration. Channelling papered childhood exposure, she mutters, "Curiouser and curiouser."

Down a long, bright white hall, surreal in its consistency and numbing sense of placelessness, Oni finds a terminal at a cross-section. Lesser halls range away on either side of the terminal in darkening greys. A hologram shimmers into shape over the waist-level panel, itself cutting white light around its black keys. The shape is that of a tight-lipped, ruddy block of a man whose broken nose Popeyes over his upper lip, and whose biceps test the very essence of his military greens.

"Marine, atten-shun!" The steely-eyed caricature nearly karates himself with a salute.

Incredulous, Oni readies Skyr's ESD wand through her pant leg and hooks an eyebrow. She throws up an obligatory salute on Barkley's behalf.

"This is a restricted zone! You have neither the credentials nor the stripes to get in here!"

Oni appeals to her urgent and classified wooden-horse of a lie. Like any deceit, it feels and sounds truer with every repetition. "...General McCabe's orders."

The block in green appears frozen. He is striated with grey lines and teased side to side, like stretched tape paused on a VCR. Finally, his expression breaks the standstill. His brow cliffs out, forcing his nose further out. "What else did he say, Marine?"

"I'm afraid that's *need-to-know*."

Sucking in his plum-coloured bottom lip, the projected man shrugs and nods his head. "Need to know..." he mumbles. His consideration crackles on the speakers. "Major, I think *I* should know."

Oni readies a pithy response, but notices details on the block's uniform the projectors had failed to clarify earlier. A silver star neatly stitched. *Tarnation.*

"You see, *I am* General McCabe." The hologram motions forward, testing the confines of the projection. His face cuts away, leaving Oni addressing the back of his head. "S'bout time you identified yourself, *Marine*."

"Major Barkley, sir." Oni's pain-induced rigidity gives her posture a more militant legitimacy.

"I don't think we've met, Major Barkley. Does your CO know you're here?"

Beneath Barkley's death mask, Oni begins panicking in her own. *Kill the hologram with the ESD wand?* she wonders. *No. They'd find me in a heartbeat and lock this place down.* Given McCabe has yet to send his stormtroopers, Oni decides to play it cool and ignore McCabe's question altogether. "The intel I picked up today…it implicates a bad link in the chain of command. I knew——," Oni rubs the ESD wand's bulge like a lucky rabbit's foot, "you'd know what to do with the information."

General McCabe gives the cameras some space, bringing his face back into view along with the muddled look of concern and intrigue sunk into it. He raps his fingers on some surface outside of the projection field. "Marine, you'll be at Navy Intelligence, sublevel thirty-eight, by hour's end. Pending a review of your findings and their legitimacy, you will be held for questioning." McCabe yanks his jacket down, eliminating the wrinkles that dared to take shape. "Spherion has been notified that you constitute a possible security threat and will comm your unit commander as soon as there is a gap in our dampening cycle."

"Yes sir," Oni concedes, seeing no alternative.

"Within the hour, Marine! Or I'll send a BEAR unit to track you down and maul yah."

Barkley gulps and Oni nods. McCabe disappears in a pixelated snap. The lights in the adjacent hallways turn off. A holographic arrow indicates the passage ahead, extends down the way, and disappears in the all-consuming white without ever having had a chance at piercing the terminus.

*He knows. He must. He will call Barkley's CO, unless he's given any thought to my inside-man story, in which case I'll need a damn-fine explanation. Might just be easier to kill Barkley a second time and don a new mask—scuttle one wooden doll for another in this macabre matryoshka set.*

The source of the brilliant light at the end of the hall is a powerful LED grid. Oni steps into its marginal glow, and blinks away the spots crowding her vision. An AI-operated sentry gun coupled with a spectral imager judders side to side beneath the LEDs. At any point along the way it could have cut her in half, but it didn't; evidence either of the efficacy of her costume or of the base-security monitors' scandalous indifference to her presence.

Apart from the gun and the lights, this section of the hall is devoid of the kind of baubles or martial décor you might find upstairs: just smooth surfaces leading to a silver sliding door. Unnerved by the shhh-click-shh-click of the sentry gun, Oni decides to press on. The silver door splits down the middle as she approaches it. Its jigsaw elements cut away into slots on either side.

Low thunder resounds ahead. An irate and husky voice strives to compete, peaking in the process of overcompensating: "Putrid eMeals are down again…Gonna end up eating my vest!"

"I would not recommend it," drones another, almost subliminally.

The silver puzzle completes behind Oni. She staggers forward, finding herself on a railing-less platform at the end of a massive tunnel. Crowding the platform's lone bench stands a white-haired, white-jacketed man lording over a motionless body strapped to a gurney, and a tech-laden grunt seated and slouched, toeing the gurney's wheels.

"Oi, Sir! Hey, flyboy," chirps the grunt.

Oni, still a stranger to Barkley's world, fails to register the comment. Instead, she ambles forward toward the docking mechanism and marvels at the tunnel: an electrified tube, ribbed by a helix coil and beleaguered by white-blue static. *Coils must be generating the fields keeping the Pacific out…Must be at least a mile long.* A little tram, set in a Faraday cage, gnaws the far-left tether towards the platform.

"Oi, flyboy, I'm talking to you!" repeats the grunt, begrudgingly getting to his feet.

The elderly scientist rolls the gurney in front of the grunt, and scolds him: "Why must you always be so abrasive?"

Angrily jerking the gurney out of his way, the grunt shoulders past the exasperated scientist. "Don't I deserve an 'ello at the least, Major? 'Ere I am eating memories, while fresh-faced sky-commander's too good to know what's bad."

"Now, Stevens, I would advise…" the scientist reaches out after him, but fails to hinder his course.

"Nuts to your advice, egghead," the grunt civilized with the moniker 'Stevens' blurts out between frenzied breaths.

The scientist calls over to Oni, with Stevens closing the

distance: "I apologize for my…he's been in a mood all morning. Is uncomfortable around my patient."

Several contingency plans array over Oni's iris, courtesy of her Monocle upgrade. For all its technological ingenuity, Monocle's solutions to Stevens' antagonism are surprisingly brutish, with only one suggestion allowing for the grunt to survive his temper. Even the pacifistic option would require Oni to draw blood. With McCabe and countless others watching, Oni sighs, decided on commiserating with Stevens. "What's this about the eMeals?"

Stevens powers down his drive forward, and hooks an eyebrow. "Look-it! It speaks," he announces to no one in particular. He massages his wasted adrenlin down the back of his neck. "Things don't work.…Been printing colourless goop. Better off eating paint chips…"

"Or your vest," Oni interrupts. "They've got enough money to power Poseidon's kingdom, but not enough to preserve the fighting-man's edge."

"Jesus!" Steven cries, almost elated. He turns to the scientist. "The fly-boy gets it…"

Dismissing both Marines with a roll of the eyes, the scientist busies himself with the body on the gurney, adjusting its IV drip and the electronic brace bevelling its face.

Polarized brake-blocks whoosh as the tram meets the docking section of the platform. Inside, there are three humanoid blurs: two, uniformly black, and the third, crème and platinum. The Faraday cage and the tram door simultaneously scissor open. The vague blurs find definition outside of the tram. In black, two Sentinels dressed in dragon-scale armour, and in crème, Celeste Charming. The closer Sentinel rushes ahead and fans Stevens and Oni aside to create a safe cushion for Celeste's exit.

Indignant, Stevens smacks the matte-black cyborg's hand away. "Piss off!"

The Sentinel gestures to Celeste and then to his partner. "Protect the VIP!" His order sounds like a navbot played through a loudspeaker. Turning again to Stevens, his arm branches into three parts. His palm abandons his fingers and slides up to his shoulder. A cornucopia of gun muzzles jut out in its place. In a toneless, trebly voice, the Sentinel orders Steven back. Steven acquiesces, gritting his teeth and nodding to Oni as if to pass off his resentment like a baton in some kind of morbid relay.

Leading her protectors onward, Celeste manages a subtle wink at Oni.

*The hell is she doing here?*

The silver door closes behind Celeste and her weaponized entourage.

"The nerve, eh?" Stevens—out of air and patience—ambles over to Oni. Finding her agape and unresponsive, he prods her in the chest, bending her name patch into view—"Major Barkley, sir?"

Thankfully, the projection suit Skyr gave Oni has haptic potential, otherwise Stevens' finger would have penetrated Barkley's name and cut straight to Oni's fugitive heart. Certain holographic elements of the suit—chest, hands, face, and neck, included—are generated in part by plasma. In anticipation of contact, pending cues from Monocle, the plasma generates a shock wave that temporarily mimics corporeality. To resist Stevens' knobby little index finger, the suit had to sap ten-percent of battery reserve. *A handshake could very well jeopardize the mission.*

"That's me," Oni responds, forcing a smile onto two faces with the hope of inspiring one on a third.

Staring angrily at the silver exit, Stevens tries to control his acrimony, but little molten bubbles make it to the surface. "Celeste Charming...I guarantee you: the only thing she gets off on is power."

In full-agreement, Oni works up an ill-tempered rejoinder: "Doesn't seem she'll need anything else anytime soon, the way things are—"

Squeaking alerts both Oni and her new compatriot to the gurney and to the scientist struggling with it into the tram. Stevens rolls his eyes, and hurries over to help. "Easy, doc." Wheezing. "Should get buddy to give you a hand. Blythely..."

"Barkley," Oni corrects him, slowly approaching.

The scientist is as unresponsive to Stevens' comment as the motionless form swaddled on the gurney. "Careful. This one is a delicate specimen. Still alive, too. Careful, Stevens!"

An endorphin waterfall hits Oni—a second wind from the post-op drugs the droids had stuck her with. All the tunnel's surfaces take on a wet look, as if a rainstorm just came and went, leaving everything simultaneously dark and shiny, sharp and soft.

Beeps from inside the tram announce its impending departure. Stevens slams the ALL-CLEAR button just as Oni slips in. The tram door slams shut and the tram shakes, giving Oni a jump. As she recomposes herself and pulls her hand away from her ESD wand, she makes eyes with the scientist. *He saw.* The scientist observed her knee-jerk reaction. Oni plays it off with a smile, but a mouthful of virtual white is not enough to neuter the scientist's suspicion. The tram jostles free of the dock, and begins threading the eye of the Pacific Plate.

There is a safety recording playing in the background; more of a hum, really. Someone has smashed the ceiling speaker in protest of another pre-recorded lecture…A muffled voice warns about radiation poisoning, unforeseen consequences, resonance cascades, and wrongful death. The final warning is in archaic legalese that wouldn't make any sense even if turned up to its intended volume and subtitled.

"The General has too much wax on his cake," Steven says, attention locked on a holograph detailing the patient's heart rate. "Doesn't realize that yesterday's rules don't apply today."

Fiddling with his patient's neural projector net—not unlike the prototype Paul Sheffield designed for Outland with Oni's assistance—the scientist shakes his head, visibly fed up with his escort's comments. "The printers will be fixed by day's end."

Another tram advances through the electric storm and passes on the right. Inside: five soldiers and a prisoner, hooded and bound. The prisoner's swaying is especially pronounced given the surrounding soldiers' solidity and stillness. Oni ponders on the prisoner's identity and fate. She thinks of Gibson—of his scars, new and old. She thinks of the life they will never have together, and considers all the outstanding dreams set to be unrealized. *Where are you?*

"I'm not talking about eMeal, Doc. I mean *these freaks*," Steven responds, shaking the patient's leg free of the surgical linen.

"Your issue is what precisely?" The scientist inquires, tucking the patient's leg back under the sheet. "Top Brass refusing to feed them to you?" He looks to Oni for affirmation, but visibly reminds himself of his distrust. Leaning towards Stevens as if to exclude Oni from the conversation, he asks: "Or that we're keeping these *freaks* alive?"

Oni inches closer to the patient, admiring the neurotech she helped create. "This an archetype?"

Stevens nods somberly and scratches his bulging neck. "KO'd. Couldn't risk a conscious one. We'd all lose our heads."

The scientist drops his shoulder to crop Oni out of his

peripheral vision. "The General is absolutely right. Kill a biological aberration, you have one fewer aberration. Learn all there is to learn about one of these—"

"*Freaks*," Stevens interrupts, ejecting more spit than meaning.

Frustrated, the scientist lays his hands down over his patient. "The more we learn about these aberrations, the more likely it is we can prevent the emergence of more. Also," he says with a smirk and waving a finger in the air to give his mind time to buffer, "the more likely it is we can emulate their power."

"You are beginning to sound like Celeste Charming." Oni regrets making the comparison as soon as the Outland pontiff's thermobaric name clears her throat.

The scientist tilts his head. "How so?"

An electric shower cascades over the Faraday cage, rattling its insides. The scientist doublechecks his patient's monitors while Oni walks to the front of the tram, catching Barkley's reflection in the glass.

Stevens' upper-lip covers its twin and advances down his face. "Hold on, Barkley—what do you mean? Is O-land cleared to look into the freaks now?"

"No they are not," interrupts the scientist, leaving his post by his patient to blather at the back of Oni's head. "Why would you suggest...? *Major Barkley*, is it? What *are* you even doing down here?"

Oni turns, and puffs Barkley's chest to gain physical authority over the coming interchange. She intuits an increase in Barkley's vocal volume and steps close enough to the scientist to monopolize his air. "Classified. Secret. None of your god-damned business." Oni jabs him in the sternum. "The only curious civilian I would tolerate in your place calls herself Madam President, and even then, I'd have to politely tell her to back the hell off."

Stevens snickers. "Barkley, he's just a sheep. Relax..."

The scientist's brow rolls back, sending several rows of wrinkles up to trouble his sparse hairline. "I meant no disrespect..."

Oni lets her glare smolder.

Like a dog keen to the distant wail of a police siren, the scientist's ears perk up and his shoulders—curled inward and bowed—roll backwards. "Major—"

The electric shower intensifies, flooding the tram with Cerulean blue. The patient on the gurney shifts slightly—the first real indication that he is indeed alive. Stevens closes in, unbuttoning his holster.

131

"Yes?" Oni responds, nervously running a Monocle diagnostic.

"Is there something the matter with your vision?"

On the inside of Barkley's mask, three plaid cross-sections are lagging behind the rest of the projection's transitions. Monocle finishes its diagnostic: "UNSTABLE VOLTAGE HAS COMPROMISED PROJECTILE PANELS P313-70-29 THRU Q15-100-84."

*Damn-it.* "I'm tired is-all. All your inane questions are certainly not helping."

Barkley's face vanishes for a split second, revealing Oni's sweat-soused visage. It is just enough time for the scientist to glimpse the true identity of this strange visitor growing stranger still.

The scientist signals distrust to Stevens and orients the grunt's gaze with a shaking point at Oni's broken mask. Stevens misses the sheep's vindicating find, his attention focused instead on the swaddled freak shifting in its restraints.

"Doc, this creepshow is moving," Stevens yells, growing manic.

The gurney squeals as the archetypal starts gyrating and fighting with its restraints.

"We'll shore in a minute," Stevens says, seemingly assuring himself. He chambers a round. "But that might be a minute too long..."

"Sergeant Stevens. We have a problem!" the scientist theorizes.

Muffled and sputtering, the patient on the gurney groans. The groans become more and more verbal. Gibberish quickly becomes: "Oh-knee-Mat-swee. Oh-knee Mat-swee. Free me, Oh-knee Mat-swee!"

In one fluid motion, Oni has pulled out her ESD wand, set it to stun, and yanked the scientist towards herself. The white-jacketed white-haired man, only a moment ago brazen and aggressive, raises his hands in surrender. Divesting himself of agency, he similarly abandons muscle control such that he sways, shakes, and soils himself.

"Oh-knee Mat-swee..." Crimson seeps through the linens covering the patient's face. Its muzzle and neural net hiss. "Come free me..."

Stevens, wide-eyed and enraptured by the patient and its mantra, starts muttering to himself: "Gad-damn. This thing is waking up! Can't let it...It's going to—it's going to mess with our minds, man!"

Half-turning while keeping his eyes on his gun and his gun on the archetypal, Stevens grasps at the scientist trembling under threat of 500,000 volts. "Doc—doc! You gotta put this thing down. It's coming to."

"Oh-knee Mat-swee!" The body crunches forward, stretches its wrappings, and clanks its restraints.

"Doc!" Stevens yells once more, training his gun on the archetypal's head.

The scientist attempts to break free from Oni's grasp, but she hammers him in the back of the head with her heavy metal fist. He slumps to the ground with an "Unmph."

Commotion on his left and doom spitting riddles under his barrel, Stevens squeezes the trigger, painting the medical tech with grey matter. He fires another several shots *just to make sure*. A nervous chuckle escapes the Sergeant as the archetypal's cerebrum plops onto the floor. "Now who is reading whose mind?" He spits on the gore, and turns with a smile, gun drawn.

Oni presses her ESD to the unconscious scientist's throat. "Put the gun down, Stevens." She looks over her shoulder to see the far-dock closing in. "This man is a traitor. He put us all at risk."

Stevens wipes sweat off his upper lip, keeping his gun trained on Barkley and his captive. "Major, what the fuck are you doing?"

"Put the gun down, Sergeant. That's an order!" Oni yells. She cringes at the realization that rank would have been sufficient to defuse this situation.

Unsure and sweating even more profusely than before, Stevens looks cock-eyed at the unconscious scientist. "Major—I've known Gerry for six weeks. He's an asshole for sure, but he's done nothing fishy so far as I can tell."

The bloody mess on the gurney provides Oni with an opportunity. "How often do archetypals wake up in transit?"

"Pardon?" Stevens is visibly overthinking it. His jaw slackens, and his eyes trap so that his eyelashes crisscross.

"How often do they just wake up like that?" Oni attempts to redirect Stevens' suspicions.

"I've never…"

Oni takes the ESD away from the scientist's neck, and holds it out inoffensively, placing faith in Stevens' ignorance. "Here." The unconscious scientist slumps at Oni's feet. "Shoot me. Shoot me and condemn your city, you country, and your brothers-in-arms."

Stevens takes aim at Oni's head. He eyeballs the ESD in her hand and whispers "Sir," out of habit. "What do you mean by that?" Adrenalin lends his voice a tremolo effect. *"Condemn my city?"*

"If you pull that trigger, then the mole is free to keep sabotaging our efforts."

"Mole?"

"That's classified. Only McCabe is privy to the intel I carry. I don't even have the full story, because they encrypted and partitioned key elements of it and stored it in my memex." Oni taps her head.

The tram's pre-recorded caution pipes up: "Please prepare to disembark, and be sure to take all of your personal belongings with you. Anything left behind will be forthwith incinerated."

Stevens' glassy eyes track down Barkley's face to his stripes. "God-damn-it, Major…"

The tram eases onto the docking track. Rubber fenders put the tram on course and trigger the unlock routine on the Faraday cage.

"I don't know what to think, t'be honest, Sir." Stevens slams the CLEAR button, permitting the tram to connect with the dock. "I think we should go see the General together. Take Gerry with us."

Oni nods deliberately. "Thank you, Sergeant…Whether it becomes public history or not, your faith in me will save this city." Her focus transcends the immediate and attends to the near-future. She realizes that both the scientist—sleeping in his patient's slime—and Stevens will compromise her mission if they continue on.

Stevens looks relieved. He has done his conscience a great service by dispatching with one of the freaks he hates so much and by ferrying revelation straight to McCabe. He rests his hands on the gurney, soused with archetypal blood.

The Faraday cage creaks open in tandem with the tram door. Oni notices the ALL CLEAR button Stevens had first slammed to initiate the tram ride. With a passing glance at Stevens—waiting for his heart to find its ordinary rhythm—she presses the button and slides out of the tram. The door nearly shears her dragging foot clean off.

Stevens' angry bellows, already muffled by and inside the tram, are completely overpowered by the Faraday cage's enclosure. He tries shooting Oni, but his attempt is no good. His bullets make little innocuous frost-marks on the glass. Aware of the inefficacy of his comms in the shield chamber and his impotence to wound Oni, Stevens holsters his sidearm. This frees both his hands, which he employs in a furious and apish display: he pounds on the glass, on Oni's outline, on the true security threat that will forever rock his faith and trust in others.

Keen to keep Stevens isolated, Oni rushes to the tram's control panel on the edge of the dock, remotely ferries Stevens out about thirty feet, and locks the tram in place. She intuits on Monocle, and interfaces with the panel, making sure the tram is unrecoverable by summons alone. The hack is surprisingly easy on account of the archive of military codes and keys that Skyr, and Outland by extension, provided her with.

Stuck out and over the abyss, streaked with electric blue, Stevens impotently watches Oni head to the Military Science Labs entryway, well-signed with tall white lettering.

## THE TRUTH THAT STICKS

Weights and counterweights yo-yo on either side of the Military Science Labs entrance, forcing the door to sweep to one side. Ahead: a colonnade that resolves in a T-junction and a balcony. The balcony overlooks a quandrangle occupied primarily by a fifty-storey maize-coloured obelisk suspended by heavy-steel beams. The obelisk hangs over a rose window built into the illusive basement floor. Oni's Monocle-zoom discredits the floor as the base's foundation, offering a glimpse through the window at a white cube—some purgatorial half-way house moored above abyssal darkness.

With the door closing behind her, Oni feels pressured to proceed to the edge—to look in and over. Shifting plates and oceanic pressure would rule out the possibility of such a massive vault without Outland's terraform technology. The same shields, super-magnets, and alloys keeping the Olympians on Titan alive, undoubtedly preserve the structural integrity of this subterranean experiment.

Oni struggles to ping the depth and dimensions of the bright cube planted beneath the obelisk. Her Monocle determines that the structure is 800,000 cubic feet, both moored by thick cables and elevated by a Tungsten pedestal. Its shell and shielding prevent Oni from confirming what is inside, but she doesn't need Monocle's guarantee. She knows. *That's it. That's where they are keeping the Omnitype.*

She scratches at a phantom itch in her prosthetic, and winces at the cold reminder that greets her fingers. Booker Gibson's stolen voice haunts her again with confidence and encouragement: "You can do it, Matsui. We both know you can. And if you need a reminder, I'm right here with you."

"Tarnation." Oni tries to revise her waypoints, taking issue with her strategic program's inherent optimism. Treating her cynicism as short-sightedness, Monocle indicates all of its unseen waypoints and accentuates them using the terahertz (T-ray) vision Skyr neglected to mention Mr. Pink and Mr. Grey had connected to Oni's optic nerve. In addition to thousands of bodies—some advancing science in the name of the Republic and others, republicans strapped down in the name of science—Oni makes out the first directional marker in a stairwell to her right.

It takes two tries to deactivate her T-ray vision, but when she does, she is met with a surprise. Apparently the Military is one step ahead of her private vision. Two Centurion droids stand between her and the hallway, alerted to her presence by the sweeping submillimeter radiation she has emitted merely by looking around. Unlike Katajima's Buke bots, these killer automatons enjoy a minimalist design. Whatever armour protects their vital mechanisms is hidden or smoothed. Insofar as they are made in their creator's image, they have two legs, two arms, and the semblance of a head. However, they haven't the anthropomorphized features Outland's designers strive for in their machines. They are more like insects in this respect. With fifteen eyes, and eight fingers at the end of either arm, they could easily pass as mutant arachnids.

Doublechecking her holographic-personality's voxel count, Oni has Barkley smile and wave. "Major Barkley, here to meet General McCabe."

"Donald Barkley. Major. United States Marine Corps." The mechs throw their spidery handfuls up into salutes. Respect paid and convention honored, they lurch closer. "Confirming identity and itinerary."

"Sure." Oni places her hands on her hips, nods, and silently mulls over what she'll do if discovered. *Worse ways to go than a quick fifty-storey fall.*

The Centurions project a dense and vivacious holograph of Major Barkley. His annotated and naked person—twig, bits, and all—pours into the virtual field until a full-scale simulacrum is achieved; a copy of a copy. Barkley's archived readouts are juxtaposed against Oni's current bio-scans. Both sets of metrics match and align, corroborating and advancing the lie that Oni is desperately counting on.

*Skyr must have pulled some serious strings of code to fool their security system...*

"Confirmed. Major Barkley, General McCabe is expecting you." The Centurions' shared voice lacks all human melody and inflection, sounding more like organized static than anything else—more evidence to suggest that the Military prefers functionality to aesthetics. "We will accompany you the length of your journey." They join her on either side and indicate the route with a trail of projected white dots. Fortunately for Oni, these dots correspond to her waypoints. *All roads lead to Rome.*

Judging by their massive actuators, the Centurions are capable of walking faster than the precedent they have set descending these past several storeys. Whether they are programmed to kill time or have mistaken the natural pace at which a saboteur would wish to go in hostile territory, they have yet to accelerate. Oni would say something, but her curiosity has trumped her impatience.

Utilizing her newfound T-ray vision, she sweeps each and every lab they pass. She feels like a priestess taking down confessions. While few of the scientists are likely repentant, the sins they unwittingly tell Oni are varied and damning.

In one lab, several Military doctors, scientists, and oafish lab-techs, crowd three archetypals strapped down to medical tables. All three archetypals have their eyes covered and their ears boxed. In a well-choreographed dance around machines and bodies, those unrestrained prep the first archetypal for inputs: they free up the patient's eyes and ears so that he can witness information carefully chosen and articulated by a lanky scientist. Having assimilated the information, the archetypal begins to squirm. A lab tech lumbers over with a pointed stick, which he summarily plunges into the archetypal's heart. Beside the exsanguinated test subject—past the point of saving—another archetypal screeches, pained by the loss of part of herself. She, too, is liberated from her blinders and earmuffs, and pressed for the details of the data internalized by her now-deceased mindfellow. She regurgitates the information, confirming the scientists' suspicion that the archetypals share a repository of information telepathically. She too is killed.

Down one floor, in a double-locked room, an archetypal with weak vitals is electrocuted by a remotely-controlled arm. In response, he overloads the circuitry in the arm telekinetically, and sighs, temporarily relieved. The sparking arm is wheeled away while another one is prepped off to the side.

*This is a horror show.*

Again, Booker's voice broadcasts over Oni's comm. "McCabe knows something is up. Celeste told him there is a mole. Told him where to find *him*."

Oni stops in her tracks.

The Centurions overstep then stop. "Major Barkley, we must proceed as planned. General McCabe…"

"Give me one moment. *Please*." Oni does not waste time with an excuse. On her subvocal mic, she pleads for confirmation: "Skyr? Is that you?"

"No."

"Quit playing games! Why would Celeste give me up when I'm so close?"

"Sacrifice a plum tree to save the peach tree."

"Who is the peach tree?"

"You are." The voice crackles, leaving nothing more on the other end but Oni's pulse, delayed and reverbed.

Oni turns to the Centurions and smiles. Intuiting off the facial synch with Barkley, she enunciates over the sub-vocal comm: "Skyr?"

Both Centurions crowd Oni. "Major, are you familiar with Seal Base's protocol?"

Barkley's lips once again match Oni's. "Yes."

"Then you know that all communications with the outside world are prohibited. Were extra-communication possible anywhere in this base, any and all messages would be grounds for a court martial."

*Were it possible?* "I understand."

"Let us not keep the General waiting."

The Centurions march Oni across a catwalk and into the maize-colored obelisk. Three-hundred-or-so eyes, alight with the world's dirty secrets, look up from their computer screens to see Major Barkley and her rust-bucket entourage heading over to the war room at the centre of the obelisk's top floor. Some of the deskbound intelligence officers whisper to one another, the sound of which drives a chill up what remains of Oni's original spine. *They must know.*

At the entrance of the war room, walled with frosted glass, the Centurions stop and totter in place with their gears whining. A blurred figure moves inside the room, gesticulating wildly. If there are words to accompany the figure's flailing, the glass' proofing certainly prevents them from disturbing the spooks outside. The blurred figure freezes. A graphic of an eagle appears on the door. The Centurions step away, taking their posts.

"Should I wait?" Oni asks the mechs.

Reversing its arm and rotating its socket—all the while keeping its feet in place—the Centurion on the right opens the door and gestures for Oni to enter. She obliges.

Unsurprisingly, General McCabe is the blurred figure Oni glimpsed from the outside, whose flailing is not coupled with yelling, but with music. Beethoven blares on hidden speakers, loud enough to stir the deaf and dead composer and to alert him to McCabe's amateurish conducting. McCabe has an excuse for his off-tempo waving, however; on-screen, several surveillance feeds showcase a city on the brink of calamity. In one vid-window, a swarm of archetypals terrorize the mentally weak and assimilate the strong in a RIM hospital. In another, Outland Sentinels shamelessly massacre an entire city block in an effort to brain a single high-priority target. Below the aforementioned screens, there is a wide-feed straight from a USAF pilot's Starkiller, dropping lower-stratosphere pylons to prevent ballistic escapes from the PIT. The bad news plays at the end of a solid-walnut conference table. Several coffee cups are set like Neolithic henges around the periphery shading brown-ringed Intel.

Oni begins to close the door behind her and stops. While the dead German signals victory and defeat plays on the security monitors, she checks that her mask is intact and lag-free. Monocle provides a promising diagnostic.

The brass and the woodwinds vent past Oni through the half-opened door. This change in the acoustics tips off McCabe to *Major Barkley*'s presence. The General drops his hands and tightens his shoulders, aping the look of a philanderer caught in an act of indecency. "I have been meaning to ask you, *Major*," McCabe twists, and drops his ham knuckles on the table, breathing in his upper lip thoughtfully. "Did the Citadel bombing help this country or plunge it further into chaos?"

Halfway through the General's question, Oni managed to throw up a salute. Now feeling unsure about dropping it, she slowly chops her hand back to her hip, and straightens up. "Not sure if I follow, Sir."

McCabe smiles, pulls out the chair at the head of the table, and sits. He indicates for *Major Barkley* to do the same. "Oh, I know for a fact you follow…" McCabe snaps his fingers, and all of the electronics save for the lights in the room fizzle off, including Oni's mask. "*Who* you follow, on the other hand, is a mystery to me."

Gone is Oni's kaleidoscopic vision along with any vestigial sense of security and anonymity. Her fingers race to the ESD on her hip, but McCabe deters her follow-through by placing a lustrous Desert Eagle on the table.

"Dr. Oni Matsui. I thought you would be halfway across the

globe by now."

"You've known all along?" Adrenalin and fear causes her to shake.

"Had you all figured out when you fouled up your landing. Drama on the tram confirmed my instincts." He scratches his giant nose. "Sergeant Stevens and Dr. Riggs are fine, by the way. Under the distinct impression you didn't make it much further than the labs' welcome mat."

Oni pushes her chair back.

"I wouldn't advise it, Dr. Matsui," McCabe says grimly, gripping his gun.

"Noted," Oni says, trapping her eyes. "Although I would rather die on my feet than on my back in one of your labs."

"Well now. That all depends. Who are you working for?"

"If you don't know, then you're in a world of trouble."

"The Chinese? South Americans? The Yukon Sprites?"

"Outland."

McCabe turns a paler shade of white. He tongues the back of his canines and then grits his teeth. "Bullshit."

Oni points to her head. "If you want proof, shoot me anywhere but the head. Scrape my Monocle archives. I hate those bastards more than anyone; anyone alive, anyway."

The General waves his hand, and a warning screen flits across Oni's iris, cautioning her that her Monocle has been compromised.

McCabe browbeats Oni. "Outland sent you to take the Omnitype?"

Oni nods. "Yes. Celeste Charming has a friend of mine imprisoned. She guaranteed his release if I brought *it* to her."

McCabe removes the magazine from his gun. Staring through Oni, he thumbs out .50 Express rounds. "Did she really?" He lines up the rounds in front of him. With the magazine neutered, he takes the gun, pulls the slide, revealing one last bullet.

Another snap reactivates all of the electronics in the room, including Barkley's puzzled face. Oni deactivates it, seeing no need to face death with someone else's.

"For months, there have been efforts taken to kidnap the Omnitype as well as to isolate her memex," the General says matter-of-factly. "The majority of these attempts were perpetrated by archetypals and thugs. It never occurred to me…" Colour returns to the General's

141

face; instead of his normal pink, he turns bright red. "*If* what you say is true, then we are on the brink of war." He stands, and drags his gun along the table towards Oni, knocking coffee cups over along the way. "She sent you, huh? *Smart.* I suspect she didn't think you would get caught alive or that in the event you did, you wouldn't spill the beans so easily." McCabe stops. "No...She's not that sloppy."

McCabe opens another holographic window. Oni's vitals appear along with a live neural image of her brain; quite surprising on account of the seeming absence of any scanners that could pull such crisp live images. The General enlarges the image, and together with Oni, ogles the folds of her brain for any signs of— "There it is," McCabe says, unsurprised by what he sees.

Baffled, Oni concentrates on a dark spot behind a particularly dense filigree of arteries. The neural scan reveals the nature of the dark spot: a small chip connected to a micro-charge—a killswitch designed to kill the host, to kill Oni. It could either have been rigged to detonate when and if Oni was prompted with a certain phrase or question or it could have been set to go if her stress levels peaked.

"That monster!" Oni growls, frantically feeling the part of her head indicated by the scan for stitches. She finds dozens with her remaining organic fingers, having forgotten Skyr had more than one implant stuffed into her dome.

McCabe pats his chest thoughtfully as the image sinks in. He jerks back suddenly. "Monster is right." He shouts into a communications node on his wrist: "Lieutenant Colonel Roper?...Tom! Good. I want a list of all of our guys who've received the M-Shield implant that Outland shipped us...They're killswitches, Tom...I know. We will, but first things first. I want a full breakdown and analysis. Once we know what we're dealing with, I want all of the implants destroyed...Yes. Cycle-in active-duty Marines. Don't tell them the nature of the summons or the procedure...Yes. Consider the Outland Corporation and all of its affiliates hostile actors, and work under the presumption that we have been infiltrated...Yeah, Tom. You too."

Oni eavesdropped enough to know she's not the only one whose mind Outland has toyed with. "She put killswitches in your troops too?"

McCabe rubs his eyes. "Didn't think she had the balls." He finds focus in Oni's look of concern. "Not sure, but I guarantee you they're in the same ballpark…If what you say is true, then she is playing with fire." The block transforms into a bulldog with a grind forward of the jaw. "And when it comes to fire, you call me the god-damned devil…"

Oni compulsively rubs her stitches.

"Don't worry," McCabe reassures her. "Your killswitch has been deactivated…" He rotates the image. "Overloaded, actually. Not an easy thing to pull off, especially without doing irreparable damage to your brain." He closes the holographic screen. "Someone saved your life. Gave you an opportunity to do right by your city and country."

Darkness embroils Oni's every thought. McCabe sounds muffled. The room seems especially dark. This is not the first time Outland tampered with her head, but *it will be the last.*

McCabe recalls his urgent inquiry: "What does she want you to do, exactly? I want specifics."

Oni looks at the Desert Eagle. She clicks her unfeeling fingers against her partially-skinned palm, and makes a fist. "Infiltrate the base. Escape with the Omnitype…I am supposed to make contact with a mole in your outfit."

Ashamed of his naïvete, McCabe shakes his head. "Charming named him already. Marcel Fink. Already in the brig."

"Well, Fink or whoever she's got inside is supposed to help me while you're distracted with the attack."

"Attack?" He pulls the hammer back on his threat.

"A remotely-controlled ion blast will fire on your airborne defenses."

The General throws a glance back to his view screens. They all switch to security feeds depicting the perimeter of the base. "And?"

"Then I'll rendezvous with Charming's henchman in the RIM. Head to the Citadel. See my friend unshackled." Scratching additional stitches at the back of her head, Oni demurs, "Have my switch flipped and my body reprocessed, I suppose."

Massaging his forehead and the grey hair clinging to its sweaty periphery, the General snarls, unable to contain his seething. "That god-damned slag!" McCabe presses a finger to his ear and barks the question into his subvocal mic: "Spherion—has Charming left the base yet?"

Oni nearly answers before realizing the inquisition is directed to a weaponized ball of jelly.

"Alright. Don't get fucking cutesy with me." McCabe grinds his teeth around each syllable. "I want the base on yellow alert. Only inorganics on exterior defense. Dispatch a swarm of mosquitos after her ship, and for God's sake, make sure they go undetected. Lastly, review all holos detailing her visit. Every breath, every step, and every expression. I want a report in ten minutes."

Oni studies McCabe. Just a moment ago poised to brain her, this battle-worn leatherneck is now as close as she has come to an ally since Jin. She studies his pristine uniform and notices a Jerusalem cross on his lapel. *If he fought with the Eastern Union, icing Celeste Charming ought to be a cake walk.*

"To think she was just here...Could have strangled 'er." The General wags his gun at the frosted glass, unwittingly revealing his estimation of Oni as a non-threat. "If the government wasn't so god-damned gung-ho about getting in bed with Outland...I told those limp dicks they'd be turning the armed forces into cuckolds if ever they gave Winchester and his confounded Sentinels any rights on American soil." As if trying to convince Oni, he delivers his summary directly to her, eyes bright and blood-thirsty. "President Jacoby—that big-eyed softie...In a time demanding of a Churchill, the American people gave me a Chamberlain." Cooling down and collecting his thoughts, McCabe takes a few measured breaths and conducts the next thought with his gun. "I can't atomize Outland without concrete evidence of Charming's subterfuge..." Pointing at Oni, McCabe throws his head back, leaving his irises at the apex of either cheek. "Which is precisely why you'll follow your orders."

"Excuse me?"

"A willing double agent." A grin splits McCabe's face. "You will carry out your mission as planned. Only, you will refrain from maiming or murdering my men. When the Omnitype is transferred into Outland custody—or better yet, when she's on her way to the Citadel—you will notify me and I will raze Outland to the ground with every Marine, gun, droid, and ship at the disposal of the United States of America. Hell, I might even give General Love a call to join in on the fun."

*Repurposed without making any gains.* "What about my friend?" exclaims Oni. "What about me?"

"I promise you both a fair trial." McCabe ejects the last remaining round from his gun, and sets the empty weapon on the table.

"If Outland is the terrorist organization you've implicated it to be, then I imagine your vicious assassination and bombing last year will be viewed differently, hindsight being twenty-twenty. Hell, with the right PR, you could be touted as a hero, and I might have to agree."

*Assassination?* Oni raises her voice and warps forward in her seat: "We weren't just there to destroy Outland or assassinate Winchester. We were there to save our city! We stopped the Singularity from—" She cuts herself off, seeing that McCabe is completely indifferent. "If Celeste controls the Omnitype, the US Marines might prove incapable..."

"Some of my advisors would agree with that sentiment. They say she's a nuke giftwrapped in a child; a god of sorts with the power to manipulate the masses...I won't let anyone actualize that nightmare. Precisely why we buried a custom toggle in Patient 2690's head—like the one Celeste jammed into yours, only undetectable." McCabe smiles. "We pride ourselves on our subtlety as much as on our catastrophic might...If the girl is activated without a pre-approved handler, any and all mentally linked to her will perish. Unless Celeste has another Omnitype handy, it will be her army versus mine, and I never lose. Oh, and when I win? Let's just say I believe in total victory." Having now a semblance of a plan, McCabe claps and clasps his hands. "Best put Major Barkley back on and get to work."

"You don't need proof of what I've just told you?"

"I've already scanned your Monocle and had a team parse through it. They've had hours of virtual time to do a breakdown. It appears you are telling the truth. And if I am dissatisfied after a second review, I'll know where to find you."

"Fair enough."

"*The Major*—the one whose face you've adorned..."

"Barkley? Dead. I'm sorry. Celeste's Henchman..."

Sucking his teeth, McCabe nods, agreeing with his first instinct: "What's his name?"

"The henchman? Skyr. Skyr Meijer."

"Skyr won't leave so much as a shadow behind." The General scoops up his ammunition, reholsters his cannon, and straightens his uniform. "If you have intel to send, assume that your comm and the Net are compromised. Transmit an encrypted wave at 330MHz. We'll hear you." He points to the door with an air of impatience. "That is all, *Major*. Security won't bother you until the sirens start ringing. No casualties! No screw-ups! Now get out of my sight. I have a war to plan."

Without missing a beat, one of the Centurions opens the door. General McCabe turns his back to Oni, and enlarges a holographic screen with his index finger and thumb. The NORTHCOM insignia gleams into view. Oni gets up, half-sure and stunned.

"Dr. Matsui," McCabe says, somberly with his back still turned, "Cross me and I'll crucify you."

Oni says nothing and exits.

# THE BLUE ZONE FIDDLER

Lyle sits on a futon that could double as a bed of nails. *High thread count be damned.* Whatever gives shape to this high fashion twill-covering was certainly not introduced with comfort in mind. As a needling sensation prickles the round of his buttocks, Lyle—already unable to strategize the specifics of Benny Bass's defense on account of his damned headache—decides it was a bad purchase.

He bought the futon on impulse, oblivious to whether it was decorative or functional. Only now he realizes it is neither. Some hack carpenter or wannabe-designer created the Dorgazi-catalogue equivalent of dark matter. A kind of no-thing taking up space.

*Yes,* Lyle determines. He will bring the futon to the roof on the service elevator and burn it. There is still some accelerant left over from the last cleanup job. It will burn like a monk, only louder on account of the white cedar posts and bridges.

*No,* Lyle corrects himself, his headache momentarily waning. With a look equal-parts disdainful and disappointed, he surveys the apartment. It is open-concept, so he does not have to move to grasp the hidden failures of his fiftieth-story luxury abode. A wet bed on a magnetic bevel waits to float his dreamless body. Churring besides the pantry, a printer awaits sporadic requests for extinct species of pizza toppings.

The futon is taking up space, sure, but that space has been neutralized by time and use. Lyle has sopped up every bit of stimuli this apartment had left to offer. Really, the futon is doing him a great service, sponging up stale sights and dimensions he has wet his palette with too many times before. *It's not the futon. It's this whole damned place.*

Dorota—who has kept Lyle in the loop about all of his clients and cases since Copps and Forsyth ordered him to take two-weeks off to ensure he had adequate time to determine whether he had lost his sanity along with the CLOUD —would likely suggest the headache is getting the best of him, *again.* She'd be right.

Necessarily already under his skin, the ache is pressing all of his buttons. Instead of cold and calculating as he has been since childhood, Lyle is now irritably hot and haphazard. If this headache has its way, he will slip up again in no time.

The lieutenant, Samson, had intimated the girl from the hologram had something to do with the headaches and all these strange sensations. He said not to rattle the hive. *If there is a hive, and it is responsible for these feelings, there must also be a queen.* Maybe the little girl knows who the queen is, and maybe the queen knows how to dull this ache. Lyle sighs, andmtakes another survey of his apartment. *What did Samson say her name was? He didn't.* Grinding his teeth, Lyle nods compulsively. *To Hell with this place.*

Resolved on having a cigarette on the balcony and then setting fire to his apartment, Lyle goes over to the grey-metal field desk sitting under the massive gold-framed mirror, which invites the Blue Zone's hard lines and bright lights into the parlor. He slides out the top drawer, and procures two cigarettes from a platinum sleeve; one for now, one for later. Lyle turns and leans on the sturdier side of the desk. Its feet growl against the marble. In the past, a scuff or a scratch anywhere in his domain would boil his blood—except under Do'ta's desk—but Lyle recognizes that there is no point in perfecting what you mean to destroy, lest one contrive some means of capturing that perfection in and with a perfect copy. Such a still life would be infinitely more precious gone its origin, but still not worth the effort.

Lyle will fly down to the San Diego Green Zone, take out his usual room at the Del Coronado Outpost, and call up his old army chum Caesar Chasquez. Chasquez, sharing Lyle's appetite, always knows how to have a good time. They will share one drink or twenty, Lyle of course emptying his drinks out of sight (he does not need liquid courage to do what he is already keen on doing), and then they will hit the town.

No one cares to admit it, but with the war raging south of the border and martial law in effect, San Diego has become a scary place. Unlike this confounded apartment, it still carries a charge. If he is lucky, Lyle might catch a shock—something to fix his chemistry, rid his mind of the headaches, and give him the jump he needs to return to work, keep Benny Bass out of jail, and get his name on the letterhead. *Perhaps a little vacation is just what I need.*

At the close of his trip through a southern-Californian nightmare one shade darker than whatever *this place would qualify as,* Lyle's rehabilitation will be complete. Monday will mark his official return to the office (unofficially he already returned to meet Bass and dispassionately fuck D'ota on Forsyth's desk) and the end of his mandated fourteen-day leave of absence. He will show Copps and Forsyth that the CLOUD neither had an impact nor has a hold on him. He will secure Benny Bass's freedom, maintaining his record for never having lost a case, and he will go back to being cold, calculating, and chic.

*Yes.* Early Monday morning, he will be back at his deck in the Pinnacle, Blue Zone Central. There will be a lot of hand-shaking and well-wishing—all that obnoxious shit Lyle wishes the race would evolve out of and leave behind like appendixes and morality.

Early Monday morning, Lyle will commandeer the Aston V Palermo legal case from that bronzed macho irritant, Marius Tyndale. Putting Palermo in the ground will simultaneously dispel the rumours about Lyle's competency post-rainout and substantiate his claim to a Copps and Forsyth dukedom as its most-coveted partner. Besides, winning appeals for Bass and Aston in the same week will put him back on the courthouse radar, big time.

The prospect of Marius miserable and confused makes Lyle smile. He would take Marius on a one-way tour of the harbor to regain his edge and destabilize whatever power dynamic has formed in his absence, but such a solution would only beget more problems. Besides, Marius' vote is always for sale, essential for Lyle come the partner's meeting at the end of this month.

Sliding one cigarette into his breast pocket, he lights the second with a dead-man's Zippo. Watching the ember tunnel into ash, he takes a deep breath, brightening the bulb. "Screw Marius," he declares, the coal his audience. "An unnecessary body with a necessary ability." Looking at the slipshod kindling, he snorts. "*A futon.*"

Finally, with red marking black halfway down the cigarette, Lyle takes a drag. It fails to satisfy his craving, now overshadowed by an even-stronger craving: to silence and destroy whatever is broadcasting *that blasted hum.*

"This city needs a good fire," he announces to his soulless apartment.

## ANAMOLOUS MATERIALS

Recalibrating her Monocle and deleting any logs about her conversation with General McCabe, Oni warms with confidence. Ten minutes earlier, she was completely alone. Now, she has an interstellar nuclear power helping her achieve Celeste's goal in order to execute theirs.

She descends a spiral staircase to the base of the maize obelisk. A radial ramp takes her to the rose window's edge. Once again dressed in Major Barkley's virtual skin, she breezes by agitated eyes and itchy trigger fingers—no doubt temporarily abated by General McCabe's say-so—and into a massive, enclosed funicular with a pulsating sign cautioning: "LEVEL 20 SECURITY OR HIGHER." The signage seems a little erroneous this far into the base. If you don't know where *here* is, you've already made a fatal misstep. This presumption of belonging is manifest in the funicular's noticeable lack of locks or security mechanisms. Oni merely hits a red button and the platform plummets, her along with it.

The funicular spirals down the confines of the abyss. An unending fence composed of stalactites and basalt prevents Oni from getting a good look at the cube. She's not bothered, though; just happy to have finally found a painless way to the bottom—*a gentler fall.* She clicks her artificial fingers against her nominally-skinned palm. *And less of a surprise at the end.*

Light creeps around the bend like dawn, raising the pimply surface of the outer wall over its shadows and announcing the end of the line. The modest station ahead makes no attempt at welcoming Oni. It merely blasts her with cold LED lamps and self-identifies with an orange-on-black tickertape sign that reads: "ANOMALOUS MATERIALS, LABORATORY *Z01*; PSYCH-OPS, LABORATORY *Z02*; INCINERATOR, *Z04*."

Mag-brakes decelerate the funicular and level it with a gangway situated just off a church-like excavation, rowed with massive columns on each side—as impressive and ominous as Franco's Basilica de la Santa Cruz in the Valley of the Fallen. Demarcating the room a militarized space is bold, black lettering directing traffic to "BRIDGE AND CHECKPOINT, LABORATORY Z01."

Oni steps off the funicular. She spots an emergency door labelled "Z03", off to the side in a wet-rocked grotto. She reconsiders the waypoints blinking onward for only her benefit.

"Matsui," chimes Oni's seeming alter-ego. "Don't lose heart. You can do this. But don't do it for me; *don't do it for Gibson.* Do it for all of us—do it for the kind of world you want to be part of."

Oni raps at the side of her head with her knuckles. "Shut up! Just be quiet, please!" *Oh, if Paul could see me know. We'd make a real pair; a couple of lunatics killing with downloaded expertise, bringing down an empire to put other barbarians' hearts at ease. Maybe he'd trust me with his secrets now.*

The voice wavers, and repeats: "I'm sorry," over and over again. "Paul could not have made it this far. He would be proud of you."

"Will you please shut up?" Oni whispers over her subvocal mic, now sure it's not Skyr who's preying on her thoughts. "If I go ahead as planned, will you leave me alone?"

"Sure, if that's what you want."

"Yes." *Good.* With one last melancholic glance at the emergency door, Oni draws pith from her pain and growls, "To Hell with it."

On the side marked "LABORATORY Z01," the ecclesiastic passage terminates in a heavy, vault-like door; circular with multiple locking mechanisms on the face. Five Marines—two on guard by the door, another two twenty-feet deeper into the hall ogling security feeds on a shared tablet, and a fifth locked into an exosuit splitting the distance—fill the room with competing small talk. They have not yet spotted Oni, who counts her blessings and presses out of sight and against a pillar, damp with subterranean perspiration. Major Barkley wouldn't have made it this far with his credentials. No reason for his doppelganger to get any further without facing some resistance.

Oni knows she cannot possibly neutralize all five Marines. By the looks of the two shaking sense out of their security tablet, they are nothing like the dough-faced check chasers avoiding confrontation upstairs, but rather steely-eyed vets. (Unlike the old days where a warrior's shelflife was six years and then he went private or into the ground, the state has made a practice out of holding on tight whenever a good recruit comes along. They'll keep financing and piecing him back together until he becomes a liability or until his brain goes, and hell, even then they will still keep him on the payroll). While the four hybrid vets prowl the hall, clearly exhausted from not having discharged their rifles in God-knows-how-long, the fifth in the suit tests the room's foundations.

Towering above his four compatriots: an umber-brown hulk in

an armoured exosuit, with pointed rebar arching above his shoulders like defeathered wings. It is properly an exosuit as opposed to a mech on account of the apparatus' correlation to the driver's shape, movement, and intention. This particular exosuit is a custom job or at the very least a prototype. And what better way to see that it works than running down the strange and the unfamiliar half-a-mile under the earth's surface, far-removed the court of public opinion?

Oni's Monocle zooms in on the exosuit's serial number and pulls stats and details, informing her onboard AI strategist of her opposition: "Chieftan. Armour plated. Blast resistant. Insulated for EM radiation and interference. Energy cycle: 32 hours. Armaments unknown." The exosuit's brushcut driver is untouchable and assuredly packing enough heat to melt an entire third-world army.

Divested of violent options, Oni intuits on her Monocle's new strategy application. Several options appear, prioritized and layered by efficacy and plausibility. By and large, the options provided are the kind only Skyr or a cold and amoral machine would cook up. Oni filters the results, and reshuffles the order according to non-lethality, hoping to keep her promise to McCabe. The second option—clipped by the first and hovering over the rest—prompts Oni to utilize her cloaking apparatus.

Better than wearing a welcomed face, the cloaking device will hide her altogether, just not long enough to unlock what she surmises to be a digital dual-custody combination (it seems the General greatly overestimated Oni's capacity as a thief and kidnapper). Oni is especially wary of this stealth strategy's time constraints. The cloak's adaptive camouflage is highly energy-intensive, and will start to lose consistency after twenty seconds. To make matters worse, moving too quickly will jeopardize her invisibility, as the fabric and projectile field must perpetually update light, colour, transparencies, and shadows, and will appear distorted if forced to update too quickly.

Peering past the pillar at the Marines, unassuming and as relaxed as they will ever permit themselves to be, Oni traces her trajectory. For all intents and purposes, she will sneak into a dead end and then try not to justify the turn of phrase. She regrets not having pulled McCabe's biometrics. *Barkley's face was enough to find the right doors; McCabe's face would have been enough to open them.*

She checks her battery charge, and primes the cloak.

Waving a small black cylinder, the more grizzled of the two

Marines fussing over the security tablet rolls his eyes. "Cain, I tol' yah, man. Is nothing, see?" He taps the cylinder against the screen of the tablet. "Just charge off the Centurions upstairs."

*Tarnation. They've gotten a read off of my projectile field.*

The sound of click-clop of combat boots resounds behind Oni in the emergency stairwell. Like a train easing into station, the coordinated steps slow as they grow louder, forcing the door to shudder.

Stuck between an immoveable object and an unstoppable force, Oni overcomes her nerves, steadies her good hand, and scans the vault door's make, serial, and original work order. Mining Skyr's intel for a reroute or a passkey, an alternative is mirrored in Oni's twin lakes of wormy brown: for the door to be opened, scientists inside the cube must petition the gatekeepers or schedule an exit. The ceremonial dual-key touchdown is observed by the behemoth testing the floor's endurance, and an area scan (which would pick up visible and invisible migrants alike) will ensure nothing unapproved crosses the threshold. *Why break a lock when you can knock?*

The security and electronics schematic implanted somewhere in the warm folds of Oni's mind provides the digital coordinates for her subversion. *Internal comms are permitted…Fake a secure-comm transition and bounce the communique, alerting both the gatekeepers and the Charon cube-side of the request.*

Oni composes her deceit via Monocle, praying both to her other-dimensional self and to the pantheon of Paul Sheffield's half-remembered and unbelieved gods that the combat boots slowly avalanching down the stairs will slow some more. Yanking a staff list from the cube's health sensors—monitoring the general well-being of the scientists encaged within—Oni cross-references names with heart-rates, ensuring those individuals whom she will insinuate *need to leave* are in fact inside to begin with.

*Dr. Rick Addams and…*Addam's file pops up, obfuscating the list. Oni tries to blink past it, but is fortunate her indifference isn't registered. On Addam's profile, he provides his assistant, Dr. Martin Roiland, as an emergency contact. Martin's name is hyperlinked, bringing Oni back to the staff list—he too is on duty and in the cube. *Oh yeah.*

Despite sweat burning her eyes and acid pronging her innards, Oni inputs an exit request for Addams and Roiland. All such requests require, "An explanation for premature departure." Oni decides on "gamma radiation", since "archetypal tomfoolery" likely has its own specific codename. Doublechecking her cloak charge, she flicks the request towards one of the vault's side interfaces, and resumes her narrow pose behind the support beam. *Knock, knock.*

An emergency light begins to rotate on the ceiling above the gatekeepers. A Morse-like beeping attracts the attention of the two Marines nearest the vault door, who each turn to their respective interfaces. "Captain Galloway, sir—an unscheduled request," reports one of the Marines.

Captain Galloway, the behemoth in the exosuit, clamors over. "Log it," he says coolly, checking a holographic appended to his wrist.

Oni peers around the beam, and sees that Galloway is studying a live visual feed of the opposite side of the door.

"Hold up, one sec," Galloway booms, turning the holograph on his wrist, scrutinizing every detail—every lack of suggestion of a legitimate request or requestor.

*Damn it.*

"Captain, Doc Addams is asking for an exit and an escort. His assistant is with him…Apparently going to pop—'radiation exposure'." The guard, nostrils filled with green light from the vault interface, skews his visor, and throws a concerned look to Galloway, now looming over him.

"Bullshit," Galloway snaps back. "If Dr. Doug wants to take his friend to the infirmary so badly, then why isn't he waiting *in place*."

"Cap'n?"

The behemoth comms his superior. "We have a possible Code 9 at Gate Z2." The right arm of his suit cracks in several places, like thin mantle over super-hot magma. Vermilion light flames out along the breaks. The armour plating reshuffles, and two plasma barrels jut out, locking into place with a steely crash. Galloway signals for the other two Marines to form around him, and he pushes the Marine processing the vault-exit request out of the way. "Doesn't seem strange to you that someone's risking the firing squad to get their jollies playing nicky-nicky-nine-doors?"

Oni's heart drops. She is troubled by the sneaking suspicion that General McCabe, like Celeste Charming, is less committed to their agreed-upon plan and more to seeing her suffer—to testing his labyrinth and the quality of his Minotaur. Her disappointment and despair is compounded with the loudening of the unseen but assuredly-armed squads' downward procession—boots on metal; sure foot to heavy drop, and again, and again. Quarrelsome voices echo down the stairwell.

Looking down at Barkley's hands—unbroken, unscarred, and unsoiled—Oni decides that if she is to be painted into this corner with her own blood, she will at least be painted wearing her own face. She deactivates Barkley's holo-representation, and arms herself with the ESD wand. These sons and daughters of the Republic need not die, but Oni does not want to walk meek and mild to her own slaughter. Brandishing the wand, she internalizes her goodbye to Booker, to redemption, and to this shithole of a city, and leaves the cover of the support beam.

"Sir, Doc Addams..." says the Marine attending the vault interface.

"What?" Galloway shouts, creaking in place.

"He's wondering why we haven't opened the door."

Galloway checks his holographic visualization of the other side and spots a white lab coat quivering beside a medical gurney.

*I am either dead or dreaming*, Oni thinks to herself, exposed beside the support beam.

"They've been cleared to go to the infirmary by Command," pipes up another one of the Marines, pressing above his ear for a status update.

Secondary plating slides out of two steel pockets below Galloway's rebar wings, reinforcing his shoulders. "I want two full-body scans. Keep your wits about you. Something's not right." With big sweeping glances left to right, the behemoth almost spots Oni.

Oni quickly refills the shadow behind support beam. Jack boots are loud behind her, like snare drums in a pipe band.

"Bravo team is ten-seconds out, Sir," reports the Marine with his fingers pressed against his head.

"Brief them and tell them to stay frosty. I can't shake this feeling..."

On either side of the vault door, the gatekeepers dial their codes and offer up their eyes for routine bio-scans. There is a click, like a round being fed into an old bolt-action rifle, and then several more, each click louder than the one before it. The locking mechanisms hammer into their cylinders, and the wheel at the centre of the door spins independently, as if turned by a brawny ghost.

Impatient and unwilling to sacrifice security for convention, Galloway bypasses the soldier manning the interface on the left and confronts Dr. Doug and his debilitated assistant.

"One at a time," Galloway shouts. He grabs Addams by his measly bicep. It immediately starts to bruise. "You first, Dr. Doug." Turning to his nearest subordinate, Galloway gives the order: "Check Dr. Doug out. Full body scan and memex evauluation."

No longer are the echoes in the stairwell all thunder and no lightning. Oni sees the first boot round the central column. She immediately triggers her cloaking mechanism, and skulks around the support beam and towards the vault door. Tucking the ESD wand away in order to minimize the surface area for which the plasma and projectile field must generate invisibility, she skates to the far side of the hallway.

Dr. Doug Addams and his ailing assistant, seeming inventions of Oni's mind—hints that this might be all be a solipsism—stand before well-armed judges on the threshold.

Galloway raises an armoured hand. "Close the door, vent any intramural air, and blast for contaminates."

"Yes, Captain!" the four Marines bark back in unison, two already redirecting the anticipated command to the door's interfaces and the other two turning off the safeties on their rifles.

Hidden weights and hydraulics crank and ping. The wheel at the centre of the door spins counter-clockwise, unmanned, and the corresponding interfaces flash yellow. As if emitted from the archetypal collective tortured on the other side, warm air rushes out, sounding like a doleful yawn.

"Dr. Addams?" the behemoth asks the tanned scientist, armed Marines on either side of his flightless wings.

Although anyone confronted with this hybrid of flesh and machine would be within their rights to be nervous, Addams looks especially upset. His bulging and bleary eyes are wet enough to drown and are a blink away from gushing tears. There is no telling where his face ends and his neck begins. It is clear, however, where his neck ends: in a ruffle over his collar. This ruffle, too, indicates his unsureness, but also something more—he has no reason to leave the cube, no more than the man sleeping on the gurney, other than to verify Oni's lie. Addams, like the creator of the lie choking him up, is a pawn in a bigger player's game. *But who moved the piece? General McCabe.*

"Yes," answers Addams. "Th-thi-this is my assistant, Martin, erm…Martin Roiland."

Oni shuffles past Dr. Doug, Doug's assistant (who Oni's lie has bedeviled with radiation poisoning), and Galloway, still doing all the talking.

"Dr. Doug, you didn't report the incident or schedule an evac, contra protocol. I cannot let you contaminate the base without, at the very least, an instant brief via memex."

Shaking his mammoth dewlap, Addams staggers backwards, bumping into the cold metal of an automatic rifle. "Jumpin' Jehosaphat! N-n-not possible! My partition is off-limits. *Classified!* Marty's too."

Hatching his visor back to give Addam's the full experience of his glower, Galloway stomps closer to the trembling scientist.

Addams wags a finger. "Classified, I say! Radio your C.O., and have him do the same! You'll have your memory wiped for even trying."

The vault door starts to sway back into its frame. Oni throws her inhibitions to the wind, and dashes towards the crescent that remains of her exit. With too many visual variables for the cloak's field and fabric to process all at once, Oni loses transparency, regains her contours, and appears a high-contrast human-shaped raising of the wall behind her.

"You see that?" yells one of the Marines, noticing Oni's distortion along the wall, which jumbles the letters stenciled on the concrete behind her. He takes aim and fires a burst, chewing the concrete inches away from Oni's rear.

Addams drops his defiant finger as all eyes shift from him to Oni's blur, streaking down the hallway towards the *impenetrable* cube laboratory.

Oni refuses to stop to let her projection catch up, to let the door shut her out, to let the Marines corner her, cuff her, end her, against McCabe's wishes. She threads through the gap—jet black hair jouncing against her neck—and runs full-tilt towards a pile of storage containers in the loading area past the vault door.

Excited and keen to participate, the rest of the Marines open fire. On what they are not too sure, evidenced by their erratic spray.

In slowing immediately before contact with the crates, Oni

loses her footing and somersaults behind the first row. *You're losing your focus. Come on, Oni.*

"Alright, that's enough!" Galloway bellows "Hold your fire!"

The Marine who had spotted the distortion shakes his head, and blurts, "Shit!" Turning to his comrades, he apologizes silently. "I'm losing my mind down here, Cap'n. I swear to God."

"Run a room scan and see if there were any inconsistencies," he responds with sympathy in his voice. "Seal Z1 and Z2."

The trigger-happy Marine heads to the gate interface, embarrassed that Doc. Addam's irregular exit has him seeing things.

Galloway scrutinizes Addam's worried mug, and gestures to another one of his subordinates. "Check on him and then do a secondary spectral scan. No one write this off until we have a chemical reading on a ghost or a body."

"Yes, Cap'n," replies the Marine. His reply is loud enough to clear the sliver between door and frame. "Should get a Spherion down here."

"And put us out of work?" another Marine chaffs, right before the vault door seals shut.

# CONNECTED IN THE DEEP

The loading area is a sub-cave carved right into the Pacific plate with a twin sharing the mouth of the bridge to the cube, which hangs like a lantern over the abyssal hollow. *This must be where they came up with the cure for the Martian plague.* Oni leans against one of two containers perforated and yellowed with warnings. The dozen or so stacked behind them, nearer where the chasm meets the cave, are chemical-laden and decaled with skulls.

Turning off her cloak, Oni makes sure to keep low, and maneuvers around the crates. Through a crease between two columns, she registers all of her obstacles with a quick sweep. She joins Monocle in analyzing the Outland-system's strategic options with a small draw screen.

There is no clutter or gear under the wing of the cave opposite the loading area; just a solitary Locust drone blessed with a platoon's collective strength, on standby with its abdominal razors extended to protect its carriage from interference. An engineer in an oil-mottled hard hat adjusts an exposed piston on a droid while whistling the "Battle Hymn of the Republic."

Under the Locust drone's strict supervision: the bridge to the cube. The structure is missing several segments which no doubt slide into place like jigsaw pieces, ensuring only approved vehicular traffic across the abyss. And from Oni can tell, it is one of only two structures connecting the cube to the rest of the base; the second is a smaller bridge that defies the fall over to a double door marked "Waste Management".

The cube laboratory sits on the heads of a tungsten pillar that—visible through the transparent-plastic floor—appears to stretch down beyond the reach of the laboratory's lights into the earth. Electricity and utilities are piped into the cube along the sides of the primary bridge, and electric and organic discharge is ejected down a cream-coloured conduit situated at the centre of the room. Enclosing the cube is a dual layer comprised of a barely visible force-field and a heavy metal lattice. Stranger than the structure itself are the explosive charges rigged along the column's capital, ready to blow in case an experiment gets out of hand or in the event that the scientists unionize.

"The first series couldn't be controlled. Key is getting an archie who hasn't a mind to rule—some kind of shepherdic lamb," says a scientist Oni somehow managed to miss in her survey. Around the corner, covertly sharing a cigarette with a colleague in the shadow of the crates, he puffs and puffs and suppresses a cough. The silent but animated respiratory jerk shakes the point of a white collar over his hazardous-material coveralls.

"2690 looks promising, but her application is limited. Problem with organic tech is it dies," says the second scientist, no more than a shoulder from Oni's vantage point. Drawing on the cigarette, he continues: "Can't expect the war machine to steamroll its enemies with a dying flame in the firebox."

"Tim, every day you sound more and more like one of those bureaucrats. Everything—drones, guns, bombs, and tanks—dies or wears out."

Oni creeps nearer the conversation, indifferent to the topic but keen on borrowing a face.

The scientist named Tim sneers. "Ten packs of the good stuff says Reynolds and McCabe will cancel the project in the fourth quarter." He hands the cigarette to his colleague. "You take kills." He coughs, this time without any attempt to conceal the act or the consequence. "I'll see you at the omnitypal throne. Need to find a sedative that won't kill our engine before we've laid the tracks."

"I'll be along in a second." Throwing the butt of their shared cigarette—its persimmon-coloured ember spaghettified and swallowed by the chasm—the optimistic scientist paces over to the edge, muttering to himself. Were he not so consumed by his work and by Tim's pessimism, he could have easily have seen Oni. Fortunately for McCabe's double agent, she has gone unnoticed.

Oni springs to her feet, grabs the scientist from behind, and pulls him to the ground gripping both his face and left arm. The commotion alone stuns him, wetting his eyes with animal fear, but it is the short punch to his temple that puts him out of commission. Oni snaps the choke collar around the scientist's neck, takes a volumetric scan of his face, and synchronizes the micro-projectors with her Monocle. *Ricardo Vargas. Psychotherapist and hive-mind specialist.* Despite being unconscious on the false floor of a phantom sea, Vargas' voice floods Oni's head. Her subvocal mic matches his speech patterns, and provides her with an auditory mask to complement the rest of her costume. Prying the collar off of Vargas, Oni checks his file, or what has yet to be redacted.

In the private sector, Vargas innovated with rapid-evolution technologies. Augmented the spinal structure and neural connective tissue in bonobos, and consequently had the hairy participants in his third trial muttering Cartesian mind-benders. Oni grimaces, recalling her own line of scientific inquiry involving chimps, apes, and other subhuman write-offs.

She clamps the collar back on herself—finding the recently-dried grooves like some kind of heroin addict—and embraces her new persona: king of the jabbering bonobos. "Now stay put," she tells the comatose Vargas as she crosses his arms.

Oddly saved from the black outs and redactions in Vargas' file is a not-so-subtle detail about his election to chemically neuter himself, "To dissuade himself from pursuing corruptibles or being corrupted; to discard with 'baser' appeals to legacy; and to preserve the integrity of his scientific undertaking." Rolling Vargas' eyes on his behalf, Oni looks over to the cube, teeming with more zealous futurists—those who would surrender their flesh for alien metals and virtual medals; the same kind who would become death simply because they could and had the government money to do so.

The Locust drone turns on its legs to angle over the edge for a good glimpse of nothing. Its metal-on-metal groans and concussive steps draw Oni out of Vargas' files and back into reality, just ahead of the foreign voice in her head, growing more and more brazen: "Matsui! McCabe just logged the threat of a possible attack. We're minutes away from lockdown...Get a move on."

"Skyr, Celeste—whoever this is...The last thing I need right now is a backseat driver." The last of the Vargas projection coats Oni, completing her transformation into a white-jacketed gelding.

Ricardo Vargas—less a few inches and all of the memorial context of the original, now sleeping with a slight brain bleed and stuffed into a battery storage container—heads into the cube. She stops in the archway separating the bridge from the cube and takes a moment to update her rudimentary schematic for this inglorious lantern suspended above unending darkness.

She receives a half-assed wave from the whistling engineer. Oni waves back as a half-interested Vargas, and proceeds through the cube's secondary gates.

"Dr. Vargas," says a football-shaped mouth-breather with bushy eyebrows and a bowtie. "Burning contraband is one thing, but making me wait is another."

"My apologies, *doctor*." Down here, everyone likely considers himself a doctor, butcher and shaman alike, lessening the risk of Oni's word choice. In the shadow of his bowtie, Oni can make out his name white-stitched into a black bar: *Todd Yibombe*.

Oni, although a bio-chemical determinist at heart, does not believe an individual's name defines them, with one notable exception: *Todd*. Every Todd she has ever met has either turned out to be a major disappointment or a major asshole. She had once even turned down an alluring job on account of the supervisor's titular enrollment in the 'Todd' genus. *Villains, cuckolds, or creeps; every last one of them.*

Todd, the impatient football, totters. "Hmmm." He offers Oni a silent lecture, beating his eyebrows over an opal stare, and then points to a pyramid at the centre of the cube, overladen with pipes, metal meshes, and armour plating. *The Omnitypal throne.* "Please come along. We've spent enough time out here doddling."

Oni nods, and glances side to side just as a matter of precaution. The Locust drone doesn't seem to find her particularly interesting. *Good. No more surprises.*

Todd, not fully oriented towards the pyramid, takes notice of Oni-cum-Vargas' jittering. "No need to worry, Richard. Tim is already inside…waiting. I also highly doubt anyone will make a point of chastising you for sating the most public of your oral fixations."

Oni has Vargas smile and walks shoulder to shoulder with Todd. Black coffins litter the area leading up to the pyramid. Some are open, revealing unique and specific foam shapes (all humanoid), as if every patient's destiny was already plotted and the details of their end morbidly seen to, up to and including spatial accommodation for genitalia.

A young technician, face addled with circuitry and bumpy with subdermal implants, fits a fresh corpse into its foam case, and seals it. So mundane is this action that the technician multi-tasks, picking his nose with his free hand and vacuum-sealing the body with the other as if it were nothing more than cultured meat in a warehouse. "G'afternoon, doctahs," he says, unashamed of his snot and indifference.

Todd, with his chin subsumed by fat rounds, ignores the tech, whispering instead to Oni, "I'm surprised you haven't said anything about me having called you Richard. You feeling okay?"

"Great, *Todd*," Oni answers back hastily, recommitted to her loathing for Todd and those nominally related to him.

With the tech behind them, stuffing archetypals into their custom deathbeds, Todd and Oni saunter into the shadow of the central pyramid. The hum of the structure is overwhelming—the sound of pulsating energy and subliminal messages from the prisoner penned inside.

The gruff voice panging around inside Oni's head interrupts: "Matsui, the Omnitype is calling you by name. Wants you to get her the hell out of here." Oni tries her best to ignore the voice. *Sleep deprivation.*

"That's good. Real good," Todd says, agreeing with himself absent a response from Oni. "Because you're going to need your A-game." Todd, out of breath from their brisk stroll to the centre of the cube, stumbles headfirst towards the closest of the pyramid's three chrome braces and upsets the logical trajectory by grabbing on for dear life. His fat, webbed hands spider up the brace to a panel complete with a keypad and a security screen.

Two heavily-armoured androids march over, attentive to both the football-shaped man and his phantasmal guest.

First with a verbal recital and then with a rap on the keypad, Todd serenades Oni with a melody of beeps, blurps, and boops. His input charms the pyramid into opening its hatch. The windowless hatch door opens, revealing a girl—no more than thirteen years old—intubated and strapped down to a cross-like table on a forty-five-degree incline. Wires and sensors hang from her sides, simultaneously connecting and restraining her.

"After you," says Todd. His eyebrows serve as parentheses to a stupid expression.

Breaking from the androids' line of sight, Oni steps into the pyramid. The room is damp and smells of rubbing alcohol and dried blood. She takes another step, but trips on something soft. Vargas' smoking buddy, Tim, is unconscious, thoughtfully propped up against the hatch-frame so as not to choke himself with reactionary vomit. Todd hurries in and slams the hatch shut.

"Is your Monocle visually archiving our experiment today, Dr. Vargas?" Todd's eyes widen, cuing Oni to play along.

*Celeste's inside man.* "Unfortunately, I cannot record anything, meaning everything is off the record." Oni grinds her teeth, nauseous at the sight of what they have done to this little girl, allegedly trying to get into her mind via a third party.

"Hunky-dory." Todd twists a nub on his neck and his eyes turn from opal to brown. "Execute March Hare. Skyr's security glitch will infect the guards in precisely one minute."

Oni triggers the executable. Monocle starts a countdown over Oni's iris. "Okay, great…Thought they threw you in the brig."

"Ha! A false ID, courtesy of *moi*. They'll realize their mistake once they've collected all of his fingernails." Todd scrambles to the young girl's side and unstraps her wrists. He signals for Oni to help him. Without hesitation, Oni—careful not to trample Tim on her way over—begins freeing the Omnitype, *the patient designated '2690'.* "One minute is long enough for you to place the girl in one of the coffins outside," Todd says as he peels sensors off of 2690's legs. "Wearing our good friend Ricardo Vargas—who I imagine has found the bottom of the chasm—you should be able to make it to Waste Management. False positives on the security scans will make them think you're headed back up the emergency stairs or on the funicular. In ten minutes, security cameras will spot you inside the perimeter wall, and your insubstantial double will be hunted down only to be discovered a fraud."

Oni runs her hand over the braille-like needle tracks along the Omnitype's legs and reads a short story of torture and non-consensual experimentation. "Alright," she says. "And the glitch—how long will it be active?"

"Five minutes. Seven, tops. The jarheads in the exosuits will be paralyzed for a brief period. Airborne drones too. Mechs, spheroids, and basics won't be affected, so you will still have to keep your eyes peeled." Todd removes the last wire from the base of the girl's spine and dabs the bleeding connection with his sleeve. He glances up at Oni just as she reboots her Vargas projection. "I must say, you're not *what* I expected…"

Oni sneers. "You're exactly what I expected."

"Oh yes!" Todd says excitedly, completely ignoring Oni's riposte. He pulls a tubular fabric out of his jacket pocket, and shakes it. It unravels and takes the form of a glorified nightgown. "Something to be said about warmth and decency."

It frustrates Oni that Todd should disturb her picture of him as an irredeemable asshole. She snatches the garment out of his hand, and pulls it over the girl's head. Gravity helps cover her the rest of the way. As she finishes dressing 2690, Monocle begins the final countdown to

Skyr's glitch over her eye. "Where do I go from Waste Management?"

Todd, caught staring at Oni dress the Omnitype with a sort of scientific fascination, throws his hands into his pockets and fidgets with his jacket's form. "To the surface, of course!" he answers, gesticulating dementedly via his jacket flaps. "There is an escape pod— a bathysphere. You'll have to unlock it, ideally without raising the tertiary alarm for that will alert the Marines' Gerrids. They'll turn you into chum topside."

"How do I do that?" Oni asks, checking she has reactivated her mask. "Avoid the alarm, I mean."

"Improvise." Todd leans 2690 forward and bends her legs so Oni can carry her. "Vargas may not be popular around here, but he should go unquestioned, right about up until the time you beach the bathysphere."

Oni tries to pick up the girl, but the pain in her shoulder is too much, forcing her to set 2690 back down. She noisily sucks air through pursed lips. Observing her discomfort, Todd takes a sticky pad out of his jacket pocket, breaks the mold, and sticks it against Oni's exposed wrist.

"What the hell is that?" It is less a question and more an accusation. Oni swats at Todd's retreating hand.

"Military-grade Longdream. Non-drowsy. Thank me later."

Monocle announces zero hour. Oni resets the countdown for five minutes, erring on the side of caution and pessimism.

"It's time," Todd says gravely. His eyes light up and chase away his solemnity. "The boss assured me it wouldn't be a problem, but I must stress this point: if you are caught, we never had this conversation."

*Celeste might be betraying her country in exchange for power and progress, but Todd is betraying his country for money, living up to his namesake.* Oni smirks. "Better make sure I don't get caught."

"Now knock me out. Really sell it."

Todd does not have to coax Oni to mess up his ill-defined face. As soon as he finishes speaking and puffs his chest full of another breath, Oni drives four titanium knuckles into his sprawling nose, knocking him out and down. The no-name brand Longdream is fast-acting, mutating the resultant pain in Oni's shoulder into a more manageable sensation. Via Monocle beam, she meta-tags Todd as an Outland agent and traitor for McCabe's sake. The meta-tag doesn't stick, however; Monocle informs Oni that Todd is dead. She kneels down for a closer look. Blood trickles out of his nose, and drips from his ears. *I didn't hit him that hard...* Oni immediately realizes she did not need to hit him at all. He too had a killswitch, only he did not have his deactivated. Standing, she reminds herself that the Outland Corporation is not the kind of to keep promises or friends.

Oni turns to McCabe's coveted captive, regressed into a fetal position on the table. "Hey, kiddo." She affects a comforting voice: "I'm going to get you out of here. Just try to keep quiet." Silence shouldn't be a problem for the Omnitype granted how drugged up and sapped she looks.

Extending active camouflage to a second body while also projecting an alter ego on a single battery charge jeopardizes the consistency and quality of both deceits. Monocle makes an educated guess on Oni's behalf and projects an eight-second window in which Oni, costumed as Ricardo Vargas, can properly cloak the Omnitype. *Now or never.* She lifts 2690, this time successfully, and activates her cloaking device. As the active camouflage hides all of 2690's needle punctures and electrical-net singes, she murmurs Oni's name and clasps her hands behind Oni's neck.

Oni shoulders the hatch door open, and inspects the backs of both android guard's heads. There is no indication to suggest that they have been disarmed or distracted. Taking it on faith that Skyr has done his job correctly, Oni presses out of the test lab, careful not to bonk the Omnitype's head on her way out. She holds her breath as she passes the androids. They remain statuesque. Not a clink. Not a whir. No hail of bullets.

Ricardo Vargas releases an empty handful into a coffin near the Omnitype's pyramid, which *he* respectfully closes. In plain view of the red-eyed androids, Oni polarizes the coffin's magnetic stripes such that it jumps and hovers steadily at waist level. With a slight push, it purrs forward on a cushion of magnetic tension. Her costume brightens ever-so-slightly, no longer competing with the cloak for charge.

"Doctah V," says the snot-mining technician, emerging from the shadow of a nearby mobile lab on stilts. "Don't sweat it. I'll take the stiff down with the res' of the lot. Just leave it t'ere."

Oni pauses, holding the coffin in place, and looks the technician dead in the eyes, coordinating with her Monocle to make sure Vargas is scowling as intensely as she is. "I need to stretch my legs.

Going to *personally* take this one to Waste Management. If you interfere in any way, I'll *personally* see to it that you have your pass revoked and your mind cleared."

Stammering, the tech tries to apologize for taking some initiative and for trying to lighten the scientist's load, but gives up, and heads off, scratching his head and chastising himself under his breath.

The gateway to the ancillary bridge over the chasm to Waste Management has two full-body thermal scanners: massive twin black monoliths with red-sensor bands and built-in laser-grid traps. Oni pushes the coffin along, and stops before the scanners. The red sensor bands pulse unprompted, and whine, undergoing a forced reset.

"There are no coincidences," the familiar voice aback Oni's mind reminds her. "Haul ass!"

She presses the coffin past the scanners and onto the bridge. The scanners seal the way shut behind her with a laser-grid trap. Had she stumbled or taken her time, Oni would have been scanned and quartered.

Whispers from the depths below cut through the secondary-bridge's balustrade and ply Oni with cool promises of terminal peace. She ignores them, and presses to the far side of the bridge, her stowaway silent in the hovering black box.

At the double doors leading to Waste Management—a massive room made oppressively hot by an incinerator—two Marines chatter with excited voices. Spotting Oni, they raise their weapons. "Hold it! Hands up!"

"I beg your pardon," Oni says slyly, letting the coffin carry on-course towards the soldiers.

"Check it," says the stalkier of the two Marines to the other. He focuses his attention and gun on Oni. "You! Hands in the fucking air."

"What seems to be the matter?" Oni asks, trying her damnedest not to stutter or let her voice waver.

Hollers erupt behind Oni, followed almost instantaneously by the asynchronous yowl of alarms and buzzers. It distracts the second Marine from the fugitive shaking at the end of his barrel.

In the room beyond the two Marines, several workers dressed head-to-toe in black heavplast suits (uncannily similar to the atmospheric diving suits that permitted man to eke out a base down here in the first place) look up to the red lights varnishing the Waste Management walls. The workers exchange glances and then survey the bagged bodies queued around the incinerator.

Someone yells, "Ain't a drill. They're gonna drop the lantern and shock below 90!"

A gruff voice responds: "What about the archies?"

"Brain 'em. Shut the air vents and vault the burner. We've gotta get topside a.s.a.p.!"

"Chief, you got the code for the 'merg bath?"

"T'irty-two, ex-ray niner, alpha, tango, t'ree."

*Tarnation.* Oni commits the code to memory, cocks her fist and reviews her strategic options.

"Down on the ground!" one of the Marines screams, stippling Oni with spit.

As Oni bends one knee and raises her arms in surrender, the second Marine opens the coffin. Before he can react to its contents, all colour leaves his eyes. Blood pours out of his nostrils and ears, and he stumbles back into the opened door moaning. "Help me…"

His comrade approaches the coffin, making sure to keep his gun trained on Oni. Upon seeing his comrade weeping blood, he aims at the coffin and yells into his comm: "Sir, we've got something down in Waste Management…No, god-damn-it, I said *'Waste Management'*… Yeah, give me one second." He tries to squeeze off a shot into whatever the unknown threat is, but falls prey to the same malady affecting his fellow Marine. Slipping on his brother's blood, he lands on his knees. "What have you done to me?" he challenges Oni as he strives to break the invisible grip about his throat.

Oni seizes the opportunity and a rifle from one of the gurgling soldiers. Armed and riding the no-name brand Longdream high, she turns the coffin to find 2690 sitting up with a tear-streaked face. The girl can barely lift her head; her bright-blue eyes seem to be doing all the work, which would account for the net of dilated blood vessels springboarding the stare forward. Oni lifts 2690's head. The girl's face is immediately deformed by fear, disgust, and recognition.

"No!" she cries, futilely swatting at Oni, gridlining the Vargas-façade and sending polygonal ripples every which way. "Doctor V— no! Let me go!"

Grappling with her uncooperative rescue, Oni notices the froth masking the soldiers' anguished mouths. *Girl's squeezing the life out of them…*Their faces are blue with spider veins and pulsing temple arteries. Oni powers off her projection field, revealing her true identity.

"Listen! I am a friend. You can trust me. I am here to…" *Claim you for a less-regulated slaver.* "Rescue you."

2690 stops fighting Oni's hold. Her head snaps back, atrophied muscles realizing the extent of their waste. Pointing with a needle-eaten arm, she implicates the choking soldiers. "They hurt my friends."

*We don't have time for this…* "Hey Twenty-Six—" Oni stops herself, realizing that even Outland used proper names for their test subjects. "*Kiddo.*" "You have to stop this—you've gotta stop hurting these men. They don't realize what they've done, what they've helped others do…"

The soldiers may not realize what they have done wrong, but they both have certainly got the hint that they are done for.

2690 laments into the coffin's padding. "Bad men. Bad, bad men!"

Half-expecting McCabe to renege on the deal seeing his men on the brink of death, Oni grabs the Omnitype by the shoulders. "Stop it!"

Blue recognition dilates over 2690's cheeks and red returns to both of the soldiers' faces. They cave over, relieved and exhausted.

Terrified by what she has just witnessed, Oni slings the Marine's rifle over her shoulder, and lifts 2690 out of the coffin with trembling hands. "We're getting out of here, you and I."

Oblivious to the melodrama taking place in the entryway, the Waste-Management team hurriedly hurls vacuum-sealed archetypals into the incinerator.

Oni sneaks into the room, 2690 a Gordian knot around her neck. Right away, oppressive heat from the incinerator slicks her skin. She takes cover behind an open crate containing clothes, shoes, and personal affects, all removed from their corresponding post-human enemies of state. Setting 2690 down carefully, Oni shoulders her borrowed rifle. Through its sights, she scrutinizes the pronouns standing in her way as she charts a short course to the bathysphere door. The fifteen-inch steel door and the base's interior airlock are both open and attended by two jittery crewmen, clearly keen on leaving.

The bathysphere lacks all of the luxuries of one of Outland's patented off-world colony escape pods. There is a single button and no controls, but in all fairness, for the four, five-minute trip, no controls are needed. Especially not with the spring-loaded magnetic braces that will fire out into the ocean ahead of the bathysphere in order to guide it to the surface. The sphere also lacks a washroom and an entertainment deck. In fact, the only thing it does have in the way of comfort is a circular, cream-coloured bench, which crowds a radial support bar studded with grips. There is enough room for the entire Waste Management team, and certainly enough room for a fugitive and a nuclear adolescent, none of whom should fear falling onto one another on account of the cabin's leveller—a gyroscopic feature that keeps the interior aligned with the horizon.

"See that door?" Oni whispers into the matted hair concealing 2690's ears. "That's our way out of here."

For all of the light thrown by the incinerator's flames, there are just as many shadows. Oni navigates the contrast with 2690 in tow, and gets within a dash of the bathysphere door. The crewmen at the door are too unhinged to pay her any respect.

"Bath's here! Finish your current toss, then beeline it over," one hooded crewman bellows, returning to his ilk amongst the rows of florid bodies. "Water'll claim the rest." He bends his knees to pick up a corpse, and halfway to grabbing it, abandons the effort. "We gotta go."

"When the job is done, Sully," the heftiest of the six men counters with a wheeze-afflicted yell. He thrusts a skinny corpse into the incinerator like a javelin. A spitting image of Hephaestus if the deformed god took to wearing glossy heavplast. "And Sully—the job ain't done."

Monocle propositions Oni with a dozen blood-thirsty strategies. She ignores the lot of them, and runs a diagnostic on the crewmen signalling their betters at the bathysphere door. *They're unarmed. Fantastic; something easy for once.*

Oni sets her rifle down, and helps 2690 onto her back. The Omnitype tenses and wraps her legs around Oni's waist.

"Hold on, kiddo," says Oni, rearming herself. She points the barrel at the two men posted at the bathysphere door. Dropping her kind tone for an acidic one, she addresses the crewmen: "Hands in the air! Step away from the door, or—" Before Oni can deliver a schlocky line—something to the effect of "I'll give your boys two more bodies for the fire"—2690 interrupts her with a blood-curdling scream.

2690 has glimpsed *her friends* sprawled about the incinerator. Her eyes, again emblazoned red, widen, and then roll back.

One of the crewmen by the bathysphere takes off his helmet,

revealing a wet beard and a unibrow that could double as a sweatband. He tilts his head, and smiles at Oni. "No one needs to get hurt." He looks to his Hephaestean boss, midway through a body-toss. "Right, chief? She don't need a gun. We're not soldiers. Just garbage men. Outsourced. Not going to hurt a pair of ladies."

2690 likely missed the suggestion that her friends are garbage in the throes of her conniption fit, however her friends have taken notice. The body bags nearest the incinerator begin to rustle.

"What the hell?" yells Sully.

The body bags convulse and croon. The rest of the crew divided among the rows quickly take notice.

"Lord A'mighty!" yells the heftiest crewman. "They ain't dead!"

Bands of electricity arc across the room, overloading the incinerator's terminals and blowing outlets, several at a time. Sparks and fire bloom above the unconsecrated cemetery, sending the crewmen running for cover.

Using the inexplicable mayhem to her advantage, Oni approaches bathysphere. She catches the moustached crewman guarding the hatch in a state of disbelief at the sight of the mass resurrection and hits him in the jaw with the butt of her rifle. Despite the explosions and groaning, the second crewman shivering at the door hears the crash of his co-worker, and spins towards Oni with a wrench ready to bludgeon. Finding himself at the end of Oni's barrel, he excuses himself with an incoherent mumble and backs away.

Oni gets into the bathysphere with the screaming girl, gun trained on her would-be pursuers. She hits the "Surface" button, sat midway up the radial support bar, and sets the distraught Omnitype on the couch. The bathysphere door creaks shut as the SEAL Base airlock corkscrews closed.

As the bathysphere dislodges and shudders, Oni braces herself. Realizing the better course would be to sit, she edges onto the bench beside 2690, sighs, and leans back. Besides the burble of the ocean against the hull and the low-bass rahs of the magnetic braces directing the bathysphere upwards, the soundtrack to her ascent is the sad murmel murmel murmel of the blue-eyed science-experiment on her right. A strange compulsion overtakes Oni; she sets her gun down and places her hand on the Omnitype's head. There is nothing Oni can or would want to say that would not sound like the usual forced, institutional bullshit the girl is probably accustomed to hearing between blood transfusions, so she says nothing. Instead, she hums. At first, it is a single note, but then a melody emerges—an old tune; her father's favorite. 2690 stops sobbing, and reaches for Oni with an unsteady hand.

"Where are we going?" she asks Oni.

Oni thinks of Gibson, held in some Outland cell, bound, broken, and beaten. "We're going to save *our* friends."

She drags a palm across her eyes, and manages a broken smile. "Okay," she says, sniffling. "That sounds good."

# GOOD LIEUTENANT

Extinguisher gel drips down from the LAFD drones, struggling to subdue the fire engulfing Lyle's apartment and the surrounding units.

His expensive and symbolic departure from the fiftieth floor of the Burroughs would have been perfect—beautifully destructive and conceptually perfect—if this city didn't have to institutionalize the event. From birth to death, and everything in between, there must be a record; receipts; photographic evidence; signatures; and all the shit that makes life unlivable.

"Mista Badagah, can yah run through the events leading up to the fire one mah time? I wanna get some sense of what started it."

The Fire Chief's voice barely cuts through the ringing in Lyle's head. He promises himself that whatever the clapper is to this bell will be destroyed, excised, exorcised—*whatever it takes*—sooner than later.

Lyle answers the Chief with a shrug. Seeing suspicion underline the potato-shaped fireman's face, Lyle elaborates. "Could have been anything. Had a bunch of old appliances..." He slides his hands over his head, letting his deceitful mind buffer. "EMeal printer's been acting up." Gel and foam splash nearby, offering Lyle with a moment to mold a look of anguish. His arms drop to his sides. "God-damn-it. I've lost everything."

Retracting his visor, the Fire Chief pats Lyle on the shoulder. "Not everyt'ing, Mista Badagah. You've still your life, and that's the most anyone can expect to keep in these uncertain times." He drags his gloved paw along Lyle's arm to his hand. Before Lyle can register what the man's intentions are, a notification pings in his ear. The fireman transmitted his initial damage survey via wrist array.

Lyle intuits on Monocle, and opens the survey. A plain model of his apartment rotates. Little labels appear detailing objects and how they would have interacted with the fire. Several red rings of varying sizes, arranged like a bull's eye, indicate where the fire started, and implicate the power unit by Lyle's field desk. There is no mention of foul play or of arson. Hell, Lyle might be able to sue the unit's manufacturer for faulty design. *Morons.*

"Forward that to your insurance company," says the Fire Chief.

Eyes afire with Monocle projections and possibility, Lyle fails to respond

"Mista Badagah?"

Lyle deactivates Monocle and rubs his eyes. "Sorry. I know

your time is precious. Thank you and thank your bots for trying to save my home."

"Legal and prahfessional obligation—nothing more." The Chief's pinched lips indicate a cynical interpretation of his meaning. He's probably a RIM tick, charged with preserving the wealth of the wealthy in the Blue Zone. Gazing up at the drones, which have moved on from extinguishing the flames and are now scanning for structural damage, the Fire Chief throws a finger forward, as if the rest of his body had started to walk away without his say so. "Pending t'conclusions of our final repahrt, your insurers should be able to help you get back on yah feet."

"Thank you again," says Lyle. His cheeks try to resist what one might perceive to be a kind smile. This curved sign signifies nothing. A utilitarian's imitation more honestly purposed.

A constable came by and asked Lyle a dozen questions. She hadn't been called upon by the fire department, but had actually come minutes before, following up on a tip from one of the building's tenants claiming there was violent screaming coming from none other than the Badegger suite. No doubt screams from a deranged and unstable individual dead set on opening a hell-mouth somewhere around The Burroughs' fiftieth floor.

Unaware she was trying to catch an edge on one of the city's top criminal defense lawyers, the constable tried to elicit an emotional response and an unintentional overshare. Whatever emotions her suspect is capable of are not wired to the buttons she'd been hammering, so she was forced to acquiesce, bid Lyle a good night, and take off.

Lyle watches the constable meander to her car. Her breasts are cubed under multiple layers. Her hair is cropped under her helmet, which permits a few raven threads to beat her temples. Inside the car— a beige civilian maglev—she fiddles with a tablet. With a stern double-take, she checks to make sure she's clear to pull out, and does so, noisily. The car's battery chugs and cries pa-pa-pa, as she makes a u-turn back to whatever municipal costume shop she hails from. As the car glides across the ribbed centre lane and the engine's chugging sound subsides, halogens on a passing car illuminate the backseat. Glimpsing the car's lack of a partition cage, Lyle realizes he could have easily pulled a *ride n' cull*. "Shit!" he bellows. The quiet street receives his anger and bounces it back, slightly decayed.

In his left hand, Lyle holds a dotgram advertising a prestigious hotel. He smacks it and the Monocular vision it provokes, still sore about missing a serendipitous ride with a suspicious constable. Compounding his confounding is the buzzing and scratching in his head. Never mind his fire's ruin by voyeurs and concerned citizens. Never mind having to bother with a hotel. *This bloody headache's got to stop!* "Got to do something about that," he murmurs to himself. Under his breath, very quietly, he hypes himself: "Badegger or bust..." Loosening his tie, Lyle reflexively turns towards the door to his apartment's lobby, intent on calling a cab. "Badegger or bust."

"Good evening, Captain," says a shadow with a gravelly voice.

Lyle recognizes both the voice and the speaker. "Lieutenant Samson," he says, forcing another disconnected smile. "I'm afraid you missed the show." He points up at the last remaining drone, density-pinging to make sure the fire didn't compromise any other floors.

"Pity, I suppose." Samson mantles over Lyle's piecemeal dining room set, still smoldering. "My friend managed to catch it."

"The constable?" Lyle laughs, looking for her skyborn brake lights. "She's a beautiful woman who lives in fear that her ability plays second fiddle to her appearance."

"Heh. The weapon the enemy stops to gawk at is the weapon that kills twice as many," Samson says gruffly. "But I'm not here to talk about her. I'm here to talk about you."

"Is she treated differently because she's beautiful?"

Samson stops within arm's swipe of Lyle. "Why did you fry your apartment?"

"The Fire Chief believes a faulty power unit is responsible, which means a certain manufacturer has been irresponsible, which is reprehensible."

The tension kicking up Samson's shoulders emphasizes the veins in his neck. "No one thinks you're innocent."

Lyle looks around for witnesses, besides those homunculi peeping on the conversation via Samson's Monocle. "The State of California and this great Republic think so, and I esteem their collective opinions more than any one renegade jug head."

The lieutenant grimaces, and buttons up his jacket, hiding his silver stripe.

"Speaking of which, *Lieutenant*, isn't this outside of your wheelhouse?" Lyle expands around a confident breath. "I mean, I doubt your CO would approve of you harassing civilians."

Twisting debris under the toe of his boot, Samson glares at Lyle. "I'll be seeing you. Real soon."

## FREE TO DIE RUNNING

Before the bathysphere has breached the ocean's surface, there is a deafening pop. Oni's first instinct is to cover 2690's ears. There is a foamy whoosh like that of an espresso machine's steamer. The stalwart sphere blasts through the glassy ceiling, trailing white and clear shards. Butterflies whip up a hurricane in Oni's stomach. She grips the radial bar; only on one hand do her knuckles pale. 2690 giggles, evincing a childish verve that apparently survived Seal Base. With a plop, the bathysphere smashes into the side of a massive wave, and rolls down the incline.

Cracking and creaking, the door swings open. Moonlight spills into the cabin, turning all of 2690's needle pricks and stitches a lucent black, and painting cartoonish white dots onto Oni's otherwise dark eyes. Anticipating a cabin flood, the bathysphere's leveller angles the ship by redistributing weight. This keeps the foot of the door just above the waves. Both Oni and 2690 falter. Oni grabs hold of the radial bar, while 2690 defiantly pulls herself forward into the glory of the maritime scene, zealously puffing the salty air and basking in the moonbeams.

Oni steps into the door frame and looks out on the half-dark sea. It glimmers wherever it crests, throwing lunar beams back into space. On the verge of finding solace in her fractional success, she spots them: four white lights off in the distance. *Skyr said he would send a Gnat drone to pick them up.* One *Gnat drone that'd wouldn't advertise its coming with high-powered LEDs.*

"Hey kiddo," Oni says, feigning calm. "I don't imagine you can swim."

2690 whips her skinny arms back and forth in an exaggerated motion, proving she is not too young for sarcasm.

Oni lets out an exasperated snicker. She clinches her mirth with a nod, and picks up her rifle. Monocle assists her squint down the sights with detailed binocular vision. Four Gerrids lace the black velvet sky, probing the ocean below with search lights and infrared bands. The full-metal jacket Oni borrowed from the blood-crying Marine won't accomplish much. The Gerrid is a four-winged maritime-rescue and suborbital-fighter jet based on the fourth-generation interstellar Archangel-class gunship, known for killing angels and demons alike.

The thought of braining 2690 for her own good and for the good of the world at large crosses Oni's mind. She turns to the girl, rifle slack against her chest. Bright-blue eyes mirror Oni's reverie, swelling with understanding and pleading. "Please don't let them take me again," she says with both eyes locked on the barrel of Oni's rifle. "Don't make me go back."

A wave rolls the bathysphere's frame. Water splashes into the cabin. The resultant pool collecting along the bench reflects a periwinkle glow. Oni slowly turns to find, hovering no more than a foot above the waves, Skyr's promised Gnat drone. Its abdominal engines illuminate Oni's surprise and 2690's fear.

Skyr's voice fuzzes over Oni's Monocle feed. "Alright, champ. Now or never."

The Outland Gnat drone, scraped of all serial numbers, decals, and traces of Outland engineering, cleared Seal Base's airspace untouched, just as Skyr had said it would. Most of General McCabe's drones were too preoccupied raking the remains of Celeste's diversionary unmanned gunship with incendiary rounds to notice the blip on their Raytheon radars. Cloaked, smoothed, and coated with a black, radar-absorbent skin, the unpiloted Gnat drone ferried Oni and the Omnitype out of the Gerrids' warpath to an abandoned parking lot on the RIM-side of Downey.

On touchdown, the Gnat drone started beeping incessantly, cautioning its disembarking riders that it was about to explode, and explode it did, like an Unholy War saboteur.

Skyr was nowhere to be seen amid the parking lot's rusted occupants. A scrambled comm on the ride over indicated as much; that the original landing zone had been compromised. No matter how badly Celeste Charming wanted this girl, Outland could not be implicated in the kidnapping of a government detainee. Kidnapping or liberation? The answer eluded Oni, because certainty over such terms seemed like prideful error, especially in her precarious position.

After prying 2690 out of the suicidal drone and marveling at its destruction, Oni carried the girl across a mosaic of broken glass and flattened cola cans to the ruin of an office building. Unlike the dilapidated shelters that had surrounded Camp MUD, this derelict was missing a first floor. Four support beams held up the crumbling second storey, steel bare at the midpoints like the bone exposed by a bite into a drumstick.

Out of the line of sight of drones and gambler gods, Oni sits with the little wet body pooled in her lap like an Asian-American Pietà. 2690 is out cold, likely on account of all the fresh air and the absence of syringe-toting scientists. Noticing the girl begin to wheeze, Oni holds her tighter. "Hey, they will be here soon. Just hang in there, okay?"

Oni scrutinizes all the marks and bumps where scientists have taken samples or injected this and that into 2690. She has a PILOT scar on her chest, pronounced along her neckline. *What kind of degenerate let's a kid this young subscribe in the first place?* Oni asks herself. *With the kind of parents that would let you wander around the CLOUD, you were doomed from the start.* The more she thinks about it, the angrier she gets. Despite her anger, Oni finds a silver lining: the girl's age probably reduced the impact of the rain-out on her. Might have even made her immune to whatever is plaguing the thousands of others cast out of the CLOUD—the archetypals. *Maybe she's a cure...But if she's a cure, then the Military is California's best bet at delivering it, at saving the city. Not Outland.*

Oni hasn't seen a child in years. Not in person, anyways. When she first started assisting in Sheffield and Katajima's labs at Outland, she was just shy of twenty two. In a discipline dominated by grey hair, a twenty-something is naturally *the baby*. "Kiddo" is what they called her. It isn't a great moniker, but a number is far worse and far more dehumanizing. Genocidal maniacs, university registrars, bakeries, and banks, assign people numbers. Everybody else uses names. *2690 is kiddo until kiddo shares her preference.*

"I don't know," Oni says, brushing the girl's hair, considering her options. "Hey kiddo, what do you think we ought to do?"

Kiddo murmurs, half-conscious, "My name's not kiddo." She scrunches her faces, and throws an arm midway around Oni, as if to cuddle closer. Whatever her intention, it is a foreign sensation to Oni. Cozy and on the verge of relapsing into slumber, the Omnitype becomes something more: "Regan."

"Ray Gun?"

Smacking her lips and beginning to nod, the girl smirks, "No, silly. *Regan.*"

"That's a pretty name," Oni responds, pulling hair out of Regan's face. "Rest your eyes until our friends arrive, okay Regan?"

Sleep has already taken the girl, her complicity in Oni's plan naturally assured.

A voice hijacks Oni's Monocle and blares directly into her

head. "You trust Celeste and her henchmen to do the right thing?"

Oni whispers so as not to wake Regan. "Skyr?" The mystery of why Skyr would plant seeds of doubt in Oni's mind this late in the game is trumped only by the mystery of who could reach and comm Oni here and now.

"No," says the voice. "We have been over this."

Oni loses her calm. "Then who the hell am I talking to?" She wakes Regan with her solitary voice, who breaks free of her warmth.

Although feeble and forestalled by atrophied muscles, Regan sits opposite Oni on her own volition. "Your friend is incredibly sad. I have never met someone so sad in all my life." Tears well up in Regan's eyes, still puffy from her last quiet breakdown.

"My friend?" Oni leans forward, at once terrified of learning the truth and relieved to know she is not losing her mind. "You can hear him?"

"Of course," Regan says gravely. "I thought he was you at first when I looked inside." Puzzled over the inaccessibility of Oni's thoughts—unintentionally protected by Outland when they deactivated and destroyed her implant as punishment for her corporate sabotage—Regan tilts her head as if to adjust and find a better telepathic frame of reference. "Your friend says you are a good person. He says I can trust you."

Shivers run up Oni's spine and branch out to her limbs. She gently grabs Regan's hands, and shakily asks: "Who is *he*?"

Regan's eyes turn pale and her pupils shrink to pin pricks, and quickly reset to their natural defaults. She looks up at Oni, gravely: "Booker Gibson."

The internal voice Oni had written off as the first symptom of a trauma-born insanity presses her to accept Regan's tip. "It's me. Stop pretending you don't know it to be true. I can read your thoughts as plainly as a broadsheet newspaper. Matsui, it's me: Booky."

Regan's confirmation and the voice's reiteration force Oni to spit out a sob. Hyperventilating, she fights to get the question out: "How? Celeste told me—she said that Outland has you imprisoned." Oni sputters some more confusion, directing wordless questions internally and at Regan.

Regan pulls herself back into Oni's lap, feeling the midnight chill exploring her cuts.

Oni feels numb despite the little body nuzzling into her, too preoccupied with the question, which she finally manages: "What is going on?"

"First off," begins the voice, "You got to give me some kudos for holding off this long. I am losing myself in here, *no offense*. You've been a little preoccupied, so I figured I'd wait, but god-damn, Matsui. I am in shambles." The voice doesn't sound much like Gibson. In fact, it doesn't sound much like anyone Oni is familiar with. That being said, the voice may have neither the faculties nor the hardware to affect a particular tone or pitch.

Oni wraps her arms around Regan, taking some comfort in the girl's unprecedented and unexpected affection. "How do I know it's you and not the singularity?" The substantial human embracing her contrasts wildly with the ethereal voice invading her mind. "How do I know this isn't just another Outland experiment? Or that 2690 isn't playing mind games?"

"I'd try to prove my familiarity, but the fact that I can read your thoughts and access your memories directly via Monocle renders such an effort pointless. If not pointless, then at the very least it'd be cheating. I can, however, tell you what I remember." A glitched and artifacted avatar makes its way onto Oni's Monocle display. Looks like an idealized version of Booker. No scars, no burns. Its mouth corresponds to the words, even though the action and the result have virtually nothing to do with one another. "I can tell you that I was backing up my sentience when the Sentinels started to take Camp MUD. Tracked us down like we always knew they would..."

"Why wouldn't you just take the Mantis Metro out? Why backup your Sent?" That day in the Citadel is especially fresh in Oni's mind. The memory awakens aches too great even for Todd's military-grade Longdream to remedy.

"Paul took my PILOT device for the tower attack, so I wasn't headed anywhere fast. And I couldn't risk losing what few memories I still had, especially since some of them were damning gems you or Paul could use in self-defence or for blackmail if Outland was ever on the ropes...Three-quarters of the way through the upload—that's when the shooting started. Two, maybe three dropships...that adds up to quite a few boots on the ground. Had to jettison a few memorial partitions just to upload before they killed the signal. Can't remember what I no longer remember, but it was no small chunk of data. Managed to transfer my SentFile to your mobile data-storage just in time—just as you made your way into my news feed, sparkling over the Blue Zone in Winchester's ship. There was an EMP warning, and then—well, that's the last thing I remember. Just that warning light and the sound of screams from Camp MUD's out-patient wing. I'd have explained myself sooner…Thing is, it's a damn feat unifying myself and these thoughts long enough to get something cogent across."

"You're his memory files," Oni says, desperate to justify and make sense out of this cyber ghost.Fuzz overloads Oni's internal comm. She winces in response to the torrent of stimulation.

"No," the voice self-identified as Gibson says, subduing the noise. "I don't think so. After all, I can *think* so. It scares the shit out of me, Matsui. *I feel real*. Like some version of myself stripped down, but what is left *feels real*. Makes me wonder who is running my body over at Outland. My meat? Shit! I couldn't tell you, and am afraid to know. I—" Fuzz cuts him off.

Oni petitions the fuzz for a response, but gets nothing. "Booky?" Booker's initial question finds Oni like a diminished echo. *Do I trust Celeste?* Oni answers if for nothing more than her own sake: "Not at all."

# RED HEIFER

Despite the short notice, the manager of the Biltmore Hotel was able to secure Lyle a room—not his usual suite; rather a glorified utility closet facing the ocean. The manager acquiesced to Lyle's request for an upgrade, asking only that Lyle give him a few hours to execute the order. With time on his hands and a game plan to formulate, Lyle went in search of soul food.

Seated at *his* table in The Orphaned Clam, veritably the best restaurant above Old Korea Town, Lyle thumbs through holograms depicting the Chef's specials. That short-haired Samson has given him a taste for meat. Real meat. None of that incubator bullshit; nothing synthetic, nothing printed.

Everything here is authentic, from the freshly-cut tulips centring each of the black obsidian tables to the long-legged courtesans working the fat-walleted colonists draining needlessly long-stemmed martini glasses at the balcony bar.

Despite the restaurant's name, no one comes here to eat seafood except for tourists and the odd penny-pincher, who'll leave hungrier than he came in. Lyle, a man of means, one-too-many opinions, and unnaturally few conventional impulses, finds himself salivating at the duotone hologram before him: Chef Rousseau's Bluzo tenderloin. The immaterial red slab's real counterpart is looped in from the occupied provinces daily, and is worth its weight in antimatter.

Lyle intuits his selection, and scans his wrist over the tab sensor buried in the centre of the table. One beep confirms the outlandishly expensive dish, and a second beep acknowledges the partly immaterial transaction—sending the equivalent of two-months airtime from Lyle's off-world coffers to Rousseau's, now plating the drippings and hardening a lard necklace for garnish as per his custom. The airtime is, of course, now a fiat currency in the absence of a CLOUD, but nevertheless backed by Outland and the state in the interest of keeping the proletariat from unsettling the Establishment.

A magenta wave throws shadows of the kitchen staff. Regardless of his own personal preference, Rousseau will only sear each side for two seconds on high and then taste-partner the meat with some aesthetically-pleasing but otherwise frivolous fructose pastes and asparagus.

Two waiters escort Chef Rousseau out of the kitchen, both

carrying some inessential part of the meal. As if bringing his only son to sacrifice to God, Rousseau looks like an emotional wreck, staging out ahead of the waiters with his head bowed, anxious face shaded. The tenderloin is hidden beneath a shiny cloche with a silver clam for a handle. The smell of sustaining death graces Lyle's nostrils, and he's at once filled with life and bereft of it. He leans forward, pressing his chest against the cold obsidian, and nods.

"Monsieur Badegger," Rousseau says, affecting a French accent despite growing up in Monterey. He quickly pulls the cloche away and juts the plate to within a foot of Lyle glistening gob, teasing him before surrendering his Isaac, prematurely slaughtered. "Voila."

Joining Rousseau at the table's edge, the other waiters put down plates unfit for an apex predator. Rousseau centers the beef before Lyle.

Lyle grins ear to ear, and starts to thank Rousseau, but is at once blinded and mute—a horrible pain shoots up his spine, meeting an ache at the base of his skull, which seems to branch through his head to his inner ear. His initial thought is: *inhaled too many fumes back at the Burroughs.* His secondary thoughts take a passenger seat in his brain, as an eerie voice commandeers his attention, managing to resound both high and low: "Come to me, Lyle. Under Seal Base!" The ache accompanying this message is the worst Lyle's ever suffered, trumping that of even the plasma burns he received in Alberta.

"Ugh!" Lyle cries. He keels back in his seat, nearly falling over.

Rousseau sets the dish down and inspects it for impurities. "Mr. Badegger, whatever is the matter?"

Through anguish-trapped eyes, Lyle can make out only the chef's contours. The waiters cowering behind him blend in with the background, which has soured on the Blue Zone lawyer and turned an ominous black. "Call me a cab," Lyle blurts, adding more spittle to the streaks around his mouth and under his nose.

"Yes, right away!" Rousseau says, both confirming the order and relaying it to his troupe. "Would you like me to call a doctor?"

Lyle grinds his chair away from the hedonist's altar, and stumbles to his feet. "I'll wait for the car on the dock."

Although there is not enough room for all of the noise in his head, a streak of jealousy manages to compete. Smelling, not seeing, the tenderloin, Lyle grimaces. It's bought and paid for; wasted on an immature palette and spoiled if left to waste. He paws the table like a blind man searching for his cane. The hot, juicy mass of flesh finds his fingers. Yanking it from the plate, dripping au jus and asparagus onto his shoes, Lyle takes a bite. Although jealousy cuts through the poisonous fog clouding his mind, pleasure fails to; the meat yields no reward—no flavour, no excitement, no enjoyment. "Damn!" Lyle shouts, unwittingly spitting unchewed flesh at Rousseau.

Gasps from the darkness evidence his loudness.

"Mr. Badegger, a cab is on its way. Please sit down. Let me help—"

"To Hell with you!" Lyle says viciously to the mouthless voice. Cow's blood streams down his neck and browns his white collar. He staggers away from the table clutching the cut of bovine muscle, eliciting girlish screams from the other patrons. Irritated by their surprise and fear, he throws the loin forward. There's a wet thud, and the sound of cutlery clattering on marble.

Pain reduces him to animal basics. It strains out rationalizations and explanations. It cuts out conventional wisdom and basic custom. Lyle Badegger is, in this moment, his pain, and his pain is dumb and brutal.

"Cab!" he wails, gripping the sides of his head like a maniac. "Home!" He's forgotten he's homeless for now; that the warm bed he craves is now ashes, consumed by impetuous fire and flaked over Hoitte Street.

"Catch him!" someone yells.

A dull sensation pings both of Lyle's knees and a cold numbness greets the side of his face. The pain lets up for an instant; the poisonous fog divides, and in the centre appears a bright, cleansing light. Two blue eyes set in a young girl's face appear. With their stare into Lyle's mind's eye comes a certain calm, solace. The eyes, charged and coloured with meaning, bid him: "Come to me, Lyle"

## TECHERESY

Noise from the Blue Zone breezes over the parking lot, finding Oni grief-stricken and Regan beside her, picking at her scabs. Despite several tries and an almost prayer-like recital aimed at reviving the ghost inside her, Oni can't hail Booker. Her efforts have distracted her from the quiet conversation Regan's taken to rather passionately. There is no indication of who or what is carrying the better half of the talk, but their sense of humor is evidenced by the girl's creased face. At last, Regan's laugh breaks Oni's concentration.

"Everything o-k, Regan?"

The Omnitype turns to Oni. "My friends are coming by to check on me—to say hello!"

Oni has not even begun to formulate a response when she hears the shuffling of feet in the darkness beyond the lot. She jumps to her own and readies her rifle. Monocle alternates between infrared and night vision in a vain attempt to zero in on the source of the commotion. The Monocle feed immediately congests with targets, strategy notifications, and eyes, hundreds of eyes, all staring back at Oni, at Regan.

On the periphery of the abandoned parking lot, overrun by rebellious greens and junk, one-hundred-or-so gnarly-looking archetypals advance, some of them clothed, a lot of them naked. Shoulder to shoulder, with dehydrated breasts dangling, invalid genitals wagging, jaws unhinged, and all eyes glued to Regan, they stop at a chain-link fence separating the darkness from the dim anti-monument to a bygone era.

"Tarnation," Oni mutters. She fires a shot into the air. Unphased, the horde weighs forward, on and against the fence.

"St-st-stop," says Regan. She struggles to stand, but failing to do so and quaking like a newborn deer, tugs on Oni's pant leg. "Please! They're my friends. No one from *this group* is naturally violent."

Oni looks back down the ridge of the gun, debating her commitment—to survival, to the girl, to throwing a wrench in Outland's gears...Considering Regan might be victim to Stockholm Syndrome or some other sort of delusion, Oni curls her index finger around the trigger. "Your friends?" she asks, incredulously. "They don't look very friendly."

Regan tries again to stand. This time she is successful. Beaming with a bright white smile, she waves over a handful of the onlookers. A dozen or so of Regan's so-called friends, distinguishing themselves from the rest with their ratty hoods and cloaks, press their way to the front of the line. The fence, an obstacle to their advance, bends and contorts as if squashed by an invisible hand. The monastic-looking bunch trample it and shuffle midway across the lot.

Gun grip warm and sliding in her hand on account of sweat, Oni stands down. She is confident she can put down the monks, no problem.

Regan throws a knowing smile Oni's way, and limps out of the illusory safety of the disemboweled building. Oni tries to stop her, but Regan has already cleared arms' length, dirty hair bouncing over to the expressionless party.

The monks meet Regan halfway and encircle her. Oni raises her gun, once again eyeballing Regan's supposed friends. They've certainly let themselves go. Pallid skin sags about their eyes. Whatever hair remains on their heads, visible underneath their hoods, is not enough to cover up the jigsaw striations indicating haphazard implants, testing, or worse.

Stranger than their Benedictine attire and corpselike appearance is the reverence they pay Regan. In a synchronized motion, the monks kneel and bow their heads. Each one of them unveils his or her own projector sphere, and with their spheres synchronized, together project an enchanting pattern around Regan—looks like springtime in the parietal cortex; an infinitely complex gridwork of filaments lined with drug-running dandylions.

With childlike indifference, Regan duck-duck-gooses the circle's constituents, tapping each of her satellites on their corresponding shoulders, and running her little pink digits along their bowed and ashy scalps. Despite the fact that she was only a minute ago virtually a cripple, Regan now skips with confidence and an athletic bounce. Nearing a second rotation, she stops, heels towards the centre of the circle, and kisses one of the faithful on the back of the head. She then brings her lips to the same archetypal's ear. Oni can't make out what is being whispered. Whatever is said is punctuated with a giggle and the dissolution of the projection.

The monks put away their projection spheres and take out chrome prisms. They stand, holding the prisms above their heads, and begin a Tuvanesque chant—sounds like a didgeridoo played through a fan. Their tune weighs their heads back until all of them are addressing the sky with wordless magic. Street lights and vestigial power transformers along the parking-lot's periphery spark and sizzle. Electric discharge branches outwards in every direction. The archetypals behind the fence direct the electricity over to the prisms held high by Regan's doting adherents. Their chant continues and the volume swells, and as it swells, the electricity lends shape to a white-blue geodesic dome, bright and loud enough to make Nikola Tesla jealous. Intricate, fractallic patterns replace the triangular shapes comprising the dome, and spiral towards the oculus.

"Regan!" screams Oni, advancing slowly, maintaining her aim. "Come back here!" Scrutinizing the electrical shape taking more and more complicated forms, she questions her own scientific understanding. *How can they manipulate the field?* The archetypals' cognitive and telepathic power is at the very least plausible, with all of the necessary electronics already in play, but to create such a marvel bereft of the bare technological essentials is beyond Oni's comprehension. "It isn't safe!"

Regan turns off the melodic tap with a clap. Oblivious to Oni's worriment, she looks around at the bowed heads impishly, making sure no one transgresses. She turns to face her liberator and points at her accusingly. All of the bowed heads fire up, and with them, twenty-four eyes pierce Oni with contempt.

"Eh, Ray—what did you say to *your friends?*"

Regan crouches, disappearing behind the wall of bony bodies. The electric dome loses its shape, and sparks replace where the electrical nets previously cast blue light.

"Leave her alone! I swear I'll shoot," Oni yells, stricken with a sense of betrayal and possessiveness.

Teams of Regan's *friends* hop the fence and approach the circle. As they cross the arbitrary line Oni had mentally determined was *far enough,* she pulls the trigger, and holds it—she'll clear fifteen rounds before the next foot falls. Her gun rattles in her hands. Fire and gas erupt from the muzzle. She hears the clink of not just shells, but bullets too. *How can that be?*

Oni checks the rifle for a defect, retreating slowly from the twelve. On the ground in front her: all the bullets, crushed into shiny grey balls. She clears the ejection port, and raises the gun again. This time, the invisible hand that flattened the chain-link fence rips the gun from Oni's hands, nearly taking off her head with the sling. Thankfully, the strap breaks before it can break more than a few blood vessels in her neck.

Gasping, Oni turns to run, Regan nothing more than a damning point in her peripheral vision. Her foot catches on a half-buried rebar, and hits the ground hard. Making fists, and breathing erratically into pulverized gravel and debris, Oni braces for the end. No matter the circumstance, the breath before death is always too hot or too cold, too sweet or two bitter. Its futility forces the extremes. Bitter heat rattles in Oni's chest.

"Matsui!" Regan yells, employing a name she could only have picked up from the spectral Gibson taking residence in Oni. "It's okay. They did not mean to scare you. I am just telling them about the bad men who took me—about my friends thrown into the fire."

Pieces of glass pockmark Oni's skin as she turns on her back and sits up. She wants to issue some kind of warning, but what to say to a girl that speaks to cyber ghosts and is feared enough to keep suspended above an abyss in a subterranean lair.

Regan breaks the circle, and limps Oni's way.

Ahead of any reconciliation or an explanation, there is a muffled wham. A shockwave powers across the parking lot, picking up all the glass and tin cans as it passes. Oni shields her face and holds her ground. Regan, on the other hand, is no match for the blast. She somersaults through the air before hitting the ground and halving the distance between the circle and Oni.

"Regan!" Oni yells, picking herself up and trudging over with bleeding ears to the little crumpled figurine, oblivious to the fire clouds growing around them.

Rockets scream into the parking lot, hammering the archetypals. Survivors of the first fusillade scatter. Several of the more disoriented archetypals run straight into the brilliant white light of the rocketeer's highbeams. The heavily-armoured truck eviscerates them, and collects their remains with the parking-lot fence dragged behind. The truck stops where Regan held her court. The rocket launcher atop the vehicle continues firing.

One archetypal with an especially-tumorous forehead raises his hand. The rocket intended for him drops out of the air, completely neutered. The rocket launcher fires another, and again the defiant archetypal shoos it away. The driver door on the truck opens, and the rocketeer presents himself: *Skyr*. Massive armoured shoulders dressed with an antiballistic poncho rise above his head, itself helmeted with a visored galea painted yellow. Spikes on his elbows threaten anyone brave enough to creep up behind him, while the armored layers hanging over his chest deny an opportunity to anyone even braver. He throws the front flap of his poncho up and to the side, and unholsters his revolver. The defiant archetypal's raised hand stops nothing. Skyr splits both the rainout's hand and his head in two, and turns his attention to Oni, now cradling an unconscious Regan amid an electrical storm, archetypal telekinetics on full display. "Congratulations, Miss Matsui! You made it out!" He splits another monk's ears. "Now let's keep the party going. *Get in.*"

A small army of archetypals, regrouping along the parking lot's periphery, begins to summon electricity and redirect it Skyr's way. His poncho, however, made from lightweight textiles, catches the brunt of the arcs' power and heat, permitting him to continue firing indiscriminately into the night. Skyr makes his way to the driver's door, cinders and sparks bursting at his feet. "Come on!"

Oni takes cover with Regan on the passenger side, and opens the door a crack. She sees Skyr laughing maniacally on the other side. "We aren't going anywhere," she shouts, "Unless I get confirmation that Booker Gibson has been freed." Her hold on Regan looks less and less sympathetic, and more and more threatening.

Despite the onslaught of stray-light arcs and incoming projectiles, Skyr takes off his helmet to showcase his fury. Leaning into the drive door for cover, blue light spidering overhead and blackening the windows, he raises his eyebrows—stung, perhaps, by empathy. "You have a death wish," he says, adjusting his armor and sliding into his seat.

"Don't kill yourself and Regan over me," Gibson advises Oni over her internal comm. "Skyr *is* a piece of shit, and you *can* handle him, but now's neither the time nor the place. Grab that gun and get in." Booker uses Oni's Monocle to highlight a small pistol taped under the dashboard in front of the passenger seat.

*Damn-it, Booky.* Oni lifts Regan into the truck, stealthily grabs the pistol, and shuts the door.

Skyr is having too much fun to notice that Oni's decided to play along. He shakes spent shells free from his gun, and replaces them one by one. A brawny archetypal gets close, but the rocket launcher on the truck paints him across the asphalt. "Yes, yes!" Skyr yells, turning to swipe Oni with a third "Yes" and atrocious breath. "Oh! Ready to go? Let's radio in for confirmation somewhere a little safer. You *will* see your friend." He primes the engine, and slams his door shut, tearing off an archetypal's arm in the process. The truck's air-conditioner begins to deluge the cabin with the smell of death, and Skyr begins to laugh.

The archetypal army abandons its evolved though ineffective tactics, and collectively swarms the truck, snarling on hands and feet like wolf-human hybrids. Several clamor onto the roof, and begin punching the reinforced metal with some success. With a screech and a bang, the rocket launcher topples over to the side, exposing the weaker metal below it. Baseball-sized dents begin to appear, prompting Skyr to laugh even harder. Lights on the dashboard varnish the enraged faces leering in, turning the cabin into a vision of hell.

Finally keen on Skyr's plan of getting out of Dodge, Oni hammers the dash with her fist. "What are you waiting for?"

"S'ah old truck," Skyr says, brushing Oni's arm out of the way, and wiping the dash as if she sullied it. "Leave it in idle for more than an instant, y'have to restart the engine."

A jawless archetypal crawls across the hood of the truck and onto the front window. Although his eyes are grey and crossed, somehow he knows precisely where Regan is. He strives to bore through to her, but his attempt is as ineffective as a termite trying on laminated hardwood; he tears his nails and wears his fingers down to the bone. Oni readies her newly acquired pistol without letting Regan slip or Skyr notice her last resort.

Alternating focus from the engine's status readout on the dash and the ten bloody smears making a mess of his window, Skyr makes a clicking sound with his tongue. He slackens his neck, and turns to Oni. "See-See says these things are as good as gods." He raises an eyebrow and presses his revolver to the window. But instead of shooting the archetypal, he continues raising his pistol until it points directly at the ceiling of the truck. "These days, you don't need a cross to kill a god." Skyr kicks the truck's charge pedal. They catapult forward. The archetypal on the hood manages to hold on during the initial acceleration, but the speed becomes too much. It rolls up the window and onto the roof, and precisely as it passes overhead, Skyr pulls the trigger. Red mist trails the car, visible even in the rear-view mirror. "All you need is lead."

# A BULLET FOR PHORCYS' DAUGHTER

"Gosh, Mr. B, that's one hell of an egg on your head," says Dorota. Her shrill voice cuts through Lyle's mental fog. "Mr. B? *Lyle?*"

The headache is no longer debilitating, but still unpleasant. Lyle opens his eyes. His blood-stained Oxfords form a u-shape around Dorota's pale, slim-chinned face. "Where am I?" he inquires, rubbing a sore mound on his forehead.

"You were on your way to Emergency. I intercepted the ambulance. Paid them off. No report, no records. I thought you'd approve, especially considering the Military's recent interest in your mental health."

"I didn't ask where I was going." Lyle rubs his head. The room is Picasso's Guernica; abstract shapes and shades of grey. "Where am I *now?*"

Dorota runs a hand up Lyle's pant leg. "The Biltmore." She smiles.

Swatting at her hand—doing a fine job of colonizing his skin with unwanted warmth—Lyle pivots on what he quickly learns is an old recliner chair. Old leather farts as he turns. He drops his feet on the ground. Shoelaces snake out, quietly clicking against the laminate flooring. Staring groggily at the scuffs on his Oxfords' toes, he notices blemishes on his starched-white shirt. *Blood stains.* It all comes back to him. He'll never be able to return to The Orphan Clam. He could very well cull any and all witnesses to his meltdown, including Chef Rousseau, but then the Orphan's kitchen would have lost its champion, rendering a return utterly pointless.

Dorota recycles a sigh. She drags her hand along the edge of the recliner, as if trawling for the intimacy Lyle refuses her in full measure. "You're welcome." Clasping her hands, Dorota goes to the window. She pries the curtains open wide enough to catch a glimpse of the sunset. Apollo slowly relinquishes his orange glow on LA, block by block. In a flat voice, she asks, "Another episode?" The question leaves a film on the window.

"Worst yet." Lyle grunts and stands up. "I don't think this is something I can avoid putting off dealing with any longer."

Dorota turns. Fear brackets her big green eyes. Fear for her livelihood. Fear for her life. She leans against the window, erasing her question. The curtains furl around her. "Forsyth knows something's up. First the Aston-Palermo case…"

Lyle sucks his front teeth, making a chirping sound. "First case I've ever lost at the firm. First case I've ever lost, period. My ratio is still the best in the business."

"If you don't get better, we're in trouble." Dorota leaves the curtains to wave, and tightens Lyle's tie. "You best get better."

Grimacing, Lyle pulls Dorota into him. "You've got some nerve telling me my business." He humorlessly cups her ass and grinds into her hard enough to bruise both of their hips—their conventional unpleasant pleasantry.

Dorota bites her bottom lip, bows her head slightly, and looks up through blades of hair, hanging just about her raised eyebrows. Despite her lusty overtone and slick gestures, she is truly rigid and more so than usual. Both of them, actors, are showing signs of improvisation, and that's uncharted territory. People go missing off the beaten path. "I thought that was my job."

Lyle turns his wrinkled sign of agreement away. "And no one could do it better." He hasn't considered alternatives; it just seems like something his v-screen romodels might say. "Do'ta…"

They lock eyes. He runs his hands up the small of her back, and tracks along her spine. She has on a black silk summer dress that feels smoother the faster he runs his fingers along it. He finds the base of her neck, and grips it, placing a thumb on her thyroid. Although her eyes express serenity, her heart is racing. "You've got some nerve." Her tone doesn't suit her devilish smile. "Your need is going to leave us needy."

With Dorota's tiny frame pressed against him and her vitality under his thumb, Lyle feels powerful. This feeling overrides the headache, and annexes the parts of the brain it had fogged. "Maybe it's Marius behind the headaches. Using mommy's Martian tech to take out the competition."

"No." Dorota's soft lips stick to his dry mouth. "You messed up playing around in the CLOUD."

"Huh? Messed up?" *Messed up, Badegger. Got blindsided. Let your guard down. He poisoned you when you were off dreaming. He messed you up.* "How about I mess *you* up?" Lyle bunches Dorota's hair up into a tangle and tugs it back.

"You can't!" she yells back. "Because you're a god-damned pussy."

*That's it.* Lyle sneers and throws Dorota onto the hotel bed.

With terror and intrigue brightening her eyes, she worms away from Lyle, wrinkling the sheets.

Slowly and mechanically, Lyle takes off his shoes and unbuttons his shirt. The spark of humanity that had ridden in with his lust dissipates. He changes the topic while surreally continuing with their ritual, now made colder and grotesque by his emotional detachment. "You find anything out about the little girl from the picture?"

"Seriously, Lyle? Screw you."

Lyle shifts onto the bed, and pulls Dorota towards him by her legs. He slips one hand underneath her skirt and threatens: "I will empty you once you're full."

Dorota knees away his advance, and sensing hesitation on Lyle's part, slackens. "She's a high-value Military target." She shuts her eyes—not in response to Lyle's utilitarian touch, but searching the Net for information to shut him up, "It looks like Outland requested to run tests on her..." She releases a staccato exhale. "Military denied the request—as well as...ah...subsequent requests to coordinate with a full lab study...They, uh...They had her on the coast. At an underground base...Don't stop..."

"Seal base! The Naval Weapons Station!" Lyle exclaims before sinking his teeth into Dorota's sides.

"You did it again!" A panicked giggle escapes Dorota, and she shifts into Lyle. "Asshole."

"I saw her," Lyle murmurs into her alabaster skin. Despite working Dorota's nerves with the utmost professionalism, his expression belongs to a commuter just informed his train was delayed—something she has gotten used to in their five years together. "In a dream..."

Dorota claws at Lyle's shoulders, and starts to gyrate beneath him. Taking the initiative, she unbuckles his belt, and liberates him from his costume.

Licking Dorota's upper lip into a curl and revealing the skeleton underneath, Lyle abandons the foreplay. His mind is severed from his bodily function. All of this frenetic grappling and writhing clears it, revealing his objective: "Marius isn't involved...The headaches, the archetypals, the dreams; it's *her*."

Dorota slaps Lyle. "Forget the girl and make love to me!" she cries, impressed with a manic smile.

Lyle flips his secretary. He grabs her by her neck and side, folds her towards him, and streaks her neck with loveless kisses. Their skin sticks and tears free, only to stick again. With closed eyes, Lyle obliges her, contemplating his next steps.

Dorota lights a canaberette, takes a deep pull, and melts into the mound of pillows and sweat-soused sheets. Through half-closed eyelids, she scrutinizes the scars on Lyle's back—scars from a war that left him hollower than even most addicts cannot fully grasp. Rarely, if ever, does he hang around long enough for her to examine them in any detail. Now that she can, she realizes there is nothing to say and says nothing.

"A little girl...Would rather have it been Marius."

Dorota breaks her silence: "What makes you think they still have her on the coast—at Seal Beach? Where's that? Down in Long Beach?"

"Yeah. If your research is correct, anyway. I'll confirm it before doing anything grandiose, but that sounds just about right. Besides, I doubt the little monster would have this kind of effect on me if she were any further away. Grunts could have done us all a service and killed her or taken her to San Diego."

"Hmm," Dorota murmurs, emerging pink from the pile. She dashes out the joint on the bedside table, and crawls forward. Lying on her stomach, she props her head up on her palms. "Maybe it's a trap. Maybe they're luring you in along with other weirdos like you."

Lyle pretends not to process her paranoia. He loops his belt, and slides his unsocked feet into his Oxfords. With an exasperated, "Heh," he registers her fear as legitimate. "What makes you say that?"

"Ever go night fishing, Mr. B?" Dorota starts raising and dropping her legs, as if she were trying to swim closer to the edge.

Shrugged shoulders.

"My uncle used to take me..."

Lyle shifts on the edge of the bed, and with a concrete look of impatience, stares daggers into Dorota. "To the point, D'ota."

"To the pier. We would flashlight the fish. Older fish wouldn't respond; they knew better. The juveniles straight out of school would swim to the light. Then we'd net them." Dorota curls one of her fingers and rakes Lyle's back. "Net 'em! Wouldn't even have to pull any hooks."

Lyle stands, escaping Dorota's playful scratching. He buttons up his shirt and turns, silently prompting Dorota for a nod or a shake concerning his appearance. She nods, smiles, and rolls onto her back. Lyle bends over to kiss her, intentionally missing her mouth and nibbling on her chin. The action is something he had seen in a holoshow. Something she might appreciate. Means nothing to him, but so very little does. *Sometimes it's good to play the part, otherwise you'll alienate the rest of the cast.* "I'm not playing with fish for starters," he says bitterly. "When it comes to losing favor with Copps and Forsyth, it's abundantly clear that this thing—that big-eyed wonder child—is going to jeopardize my practice. These episodes have to stop, and I have a feeling that once I've liberated the girl from her role in this, they just might."

"You'll have to do it soon. Marius is pressing Forsyth and Copps about your health." Her eyes glaze over, and her irises start firing side to side. "He sent out a memo asking for the staff to sign a card for you."

Lyle heads to the window and splits the drapes with a violent swipe, half-expecting to see a world transformed. "Son of a bitch," he mutters under his breath. "I can see Marius' drooling for the Bass case from here."

Dorota grunts as she bends to pick up her black dress. Holding it taut, and scrutinizing it for wrinkles or stains, she sighs. "I suppose you could *liberate* him, too…"

"Yes. *I know.* And I mean to." Lyle flails his arms. "Timing, Dorota! Timing is everything, but nothing good will come from a rush or a delay. Timing! I will waste the sonuvabitch in due time." Lyle recomposes himself and sends a reassuring touch down to his waist to tuck in his shirt. "Call the nearest Springboard. Get me a ticket to Long Beach. I'm going to swim towards the light," he pauses to grin, "and then snuff it out."

# ROAD RAGE

While securing the Omnitype is Celeste Charming's number-one priority, the threat of public or military discovery has both imperilled and made a circus out of the endeavor. It has also put Oni in a bind. General McCabe will not extract her, return Regan, and hold up his end of the bargain until Oni makes contact with an official employee of the Outland Corporation. Regan's fate in either case seems odious, but the promise of the Marines wiping Celeste and her minions off the map is good enough for Oni to see this double cross through. Besides, the little light show at the parking lot has Oni reconsidering General McCabe's suggestion that the girl is a nuke. Had the first rendezvous gone as planned, Celeste would be ankle-deep in her own blood, Gibson and Outland's other political prisoners would be freed, and Oni could stop running. Regrettably for Oni and the voice camped-out in her head, this not the case.

Skyr has elected not to get into the how or the why, but assures Oni that their deal is still in effect. His assurance, of course, means nothing to Oni, whose finger is one pothole away from tensing and ending Skyr's illustrious career as a monster—the same monster who stuck a killswitch in her brain and murdered Jin. Fortunately for Skyr, he has given up on taking side roads to their secondary rendezvous point and has instead taken the Peoples' Highway.

There are no non-federal taxes to speak of in the RIM, which explains why it looks like a quilt of brown and green from the air. Some neighbourhoods in this reactionary-libertarian haven are bucolic, while others are sand-blasted, razor-wire ghettos that elevate the PIT by comparison. Paul Sheffield lived here for a time. *Makes sense.* If you are a person of means, you can live like a king. With protected property, you might as well be one. Oni had also carved out for herself and scofflaws like her a shit palace in the sand along the edge of the RIM: Camp MUD. Freedom, crystallized in the RIM, looks a lot like anarchy, and MUD is as free as the RIM gets.

The only reason this anarcho-capitalist realm managed to get a smooth, eight-lane highway to run from San Fernando to Newport Beach is the same reason it is not currently a seventy-five-mile concrete ruin: the Outland Corporation saw it as necessary. After all, they needed to ensure that their fleet of drones and aerial supply lines could continue across the city uninterrupted by surface-to-air missiles or particle beams. Furthermore, Outland was compelled to appease the

RIM council and, by extension, their four-million constituents. Winchester initially promised a Hyperloop detour, but when Sheffield's CLOUD project became viable and Outland all of a sudden needed cypulchres, he had to sweeten the pot. The result? Skyr and Oni's trip to their secondary rendezvous point has been halved timewise, and Oni is less likely to prematurely blow Skyr's brains out, although it is tempting now with his helmet off.

Plum-colored clouds with orange bottoms report the sunrise and arcade the city. Rolling, secondhand light reveals traffic ahead penned by massive concrete walls. Unlike in the Blue Zone, where nary a human-driven vehicle can be found save for the odd special-permitted cab or limo, the RIM does not license driverless cars. (There was some ideological reasoning behind the municipal ruling—man ought to be the pilot of his destiny or something or other—but it really just came down to a deep-seated loathing for central regulation.)

Beggared of an AI-drivers' precision, the highway is loud with horns and squealing close-calls. One such close-call nearly takes the bumper off of Skyr's truck as a modded-sedan crammed-full of petulant teens merges without signalling. After checking his speedometer to verify that he was indeed going twenty over the limit, Skyr rolls down his window and points his revolver at the sedan. He verbalizes a gun sound and begrudgingly holsters his weapon.

"Probably don't need the attention, anyway," Oni says, tired of sitting silently, waiting for bad news or a bullet.

The mercenary eyeballs Oni, "Probably not, no." If his cheeks were not so inundated with tech and augmentations, they might show the telltale signs of embarrassment.

"Just surprised someone would overtake a truck plainly covered in guts," Oni adds, but is immediately sorry she did.

"Unless…" Skyr begins to nod—not signalling agreement with Oni, but with some internal compulsion to avenge this motorist's blunder. Mercenarial paranoia mutates Oni's meaning. Skyr's cybernetic eyes glow red. "It's an ambush."

Mere coincidences—a van with tinted windows going the same speed a lane over; a low-flying safety drone forewarning commuters with holographic waittimes; an unmarked eighteen-wheeler up ahead—inform Skyr's paranoia, which in turn transforms the surrounding traffic into a grid of prospective profiteers, especially the teens in the sedan.

Despite having sped up to cut in front of Skyr, the sedan has now slowed to three-quarters its passing speed. Evident from Skyr's gritted teeth and sloping brow, this is worse than unacceptable—it is an act of aggression. He paws at the inside of the windshield, forgetting that the mess obscuring his vision is on the exterior of the truck. Paying no heed to Regan's unconscious murmuring, Skyr tries futilely to virtually interface with the truck. "God-damn-it!" he yells, breaking down and manually turning on the windshield wipers. The wipers do little more than apply a consistent coating of blood across the window, forcing Skyr to lean forward to make out the sedan and the rusted-green street signs gusting overhead.

"This guy is a frigging maniac," Gibson pipes up over Oni's internal comm.

Monocle telegraphs Oni's silent response from deep inside her cerebral cortex: "Yeah, no shit. Can you ping anyone in the sedan and confirm the threat?"

"The real threat is seated next to you...Regan might be limp in your hands," Gibson continues, "But she is doing some serious mental gymnastics. Besides preventing Skyr from interfacing with the truck's nav-system, she read his mind via his implant. Bad news, Matsui. Bad news. As soon as Skyr deals with this 'ambush', he'll find a place to stop the truck. There he will activate your killswitch. When that fails, and fail it will on account of my handywork, he will shoot you."

*You were the one who deactivated my killswitch!* Oni represses her affection and casts shade Skyr's way. Subvocally, she wonders: "Then why did he bring me along?"

Gibson's voice begins to crackle and wane, although his message manages to get through: "He has been ordered to take your implant."

"Tarnation..."

"It is also clear from what I have learned from Regan, or at least from what she has made accessible to me, that Celeste has built a machine that can amplify the girl's Omnitypal power one-thousand times." Gibson direct-transfers the pertinent data to Oni's Monocle. "There is too much mental encryption in Skyr's noggin to let us access the real nitty-gritty, but it is clear from what Regan yanked from his briefings and comms that she cannot fall into their hands."

Oni thumbs the hammer back on her new pistol, and whispers into Regan's ear: "I won't let that happen. I won't let them hurt you. I promise, kiddo."

Picking up on Oni's pre-thoughts, somewhat frenzied on account of Skyr's erratic driving, Gibson chimes in: "You can't wait this one out. Especially not on my behalf. Sure, McCabe said not to call in the cavalry until the Omnitype falls into the hands of an Outland employee, but you won't be around that long. Our best bet is for you to drop Skyr, give Celeste a ring, and have her come to you directly. Then give our Marine friends the call. Perhaps Regan can escape in the process."

On the verge of agreeing with Gibson out loud, Oni is halted by the next stage in Skyr's conniption fit.

"You think you can take me on?" Skyr screams while punching the horn, announcing his animus to all the metal boxes bombing into town. Presuming his passengers to have grown sympathetic with his enmity after the teens' rude gesticulations and imagined threat, Skyr says matter-of-factly: "I'll deal with this, then take the next off-ramp. Not far now, anyway, even if we make our way to the landing zone using side roads."

Gibson reiterates his diagnosis: "An absolute maniac...Next off-ramp takes us to a road that bifurcates. A left turn will take you to Huntington—*where Skyr is headed*. A right will take you towards the Rift, towards MUD."

Waypoints appear over Oni's eye, corroborating Gibson's summary. She is irritated by Gibson's lack of faith in her sense of direction, but decides not to perseverate on it given her disembodied friend is picketing right outside her mind's sanctuary, and might therefore have picked up on her uncertainty.

"Don't you girls worry about a thing," Skyr says, ostensibly reassuring himself. "These scavengers can't touch us."

There is no respite in his honking. Finally it elicits a response. Brake-lights. Three middle fingers flipped in unison. Handguns displayed out the windows. A retaliatory beep. All the prerequisites for a roadside death at dawn.

Regan opens her eyes, and takes in her new environment with panicked visual sweeps. She hyperventilates, sporadically swelling into Oni.

Skyr floors the charge pedal and shakes the steering wheel. His eyes widen as he closes in on the sedan. Saliva drips from his grin. The teens in the transgressing sedan take notice of the red truck barrelling their way. They wave their arms wildly, miming apologies and terror, just as imminent ambushers are want to do. This makes Skyr grin even wider.

"Don't!" Oni yells. "Just get us to the rendezvous point in one piece." She simultaneously braces for contact and points her pistol at Skyr.

So blinded by rage, Skyr registers neither Oni's challenge nor her concern.

Regan writhes in Oni's lap until she is straddling her. "They want us close…"

"If you shoot Skyr, I might be able to take control of the car," says Gibson, oblivious to Regan's suggestion. "We'll beeline it to Camp MUD. There we can get our bearings and then figure our next steps, none of which will involve the Outland Corporation."

Skyr once again interrupts the silent conversation on his right with a horn-blast and yelling. "Lead by example and by making examples." His voice is barely audible over the thrum of the engine.

The sedan's little European engine is no match for the juggernaut roaring under the hood of the truck. Unable to get away, its occupants begin to barrage the red truck with bullets. After a couple negligible dents in the windshield, Skyr overtakes them. He gives them a bump to let them know they are finished. Instead of surrendering— whatever that might look like—the sedan's occupants lend credibility to Skyr's seeming delusion. The heavily-tattooed teen in the sedan's passenger seat hoists a matte-black tube over the car through the sunroof.

"What the hell is that?" Oni asks, trying to zoom in on the tube.

"We're close enough," says Regan, bracing herself against Oni.

The tattooed teen takes aim as his friends below hold him steady.

"Not today, shithead!" Skyr roars. He corners the rear bumper of the sedan and sends it careening into the guardrail.

The quick jerk and the redirection send the tattooed teen flying, but not before he manages to get off a shot. His black-tube launches a balled black-canvas tarp with a magnetic skirt at Skyr's truck. It spreads out over the front windshield and hood.

*It* is *an ambush…*

On account of speed, the angle of impact, and a bad driver

behind the wheel, the sedan, half-pulverized with a tangle of limbs flagging out the squashed side, jerks back into the lane perpendicular to the truck. Skyr compensates for the initial shock, strong-arming the steering wheel with Ahabian focus, but cannot avoid the secondary collision.

The truck punches through the side of the sedan. Smoke hides the human cost of Skyr's handiwork as well as the rest of the road and births a fireball, which envelops the truck's hood. Metal splinters, bone fragments, and car-seat foam pelt the windshield. With all his strength, Skyr cannot keep the steering wheel from jarring right. Debris has jammed the truck's wheel wells. Driving too fast to be driving blind, Skyr leans out of his window. Laughing, he shakes his fist at the balloon of debris and meat crayons. "That will learn yah!"

The teen holocaust separates, and falls to the wayside, hammering the truck's rear door-panels. Juddering wheels and horns sound behind, followed by the harmonized thump of one dozen-or-so fender-benders. Rubber scales and other pieces of the wreckage kick up into the truck's undercarriage, further locking the wheels into a right-oriented turn. Skyr pumps the brakes. Safety-gel sacks enlarge along the cabin's edges out of seemingly invisible orifices, which save Regan from fracturing her jaw and cushion Oni's whiplash against the dash. Skyr is similarly squeezed by a number of the bag-like safety measures that render him incapable of charting a course through the traffic and aftermath. Gibson manages to commandeer the vehicle, and steers them across the four busy lanes and onto the shoulder, clipping only a few cars in the process.

As the truck rolls to a stop, fuming and hissing, Skyr honks the horn one last time. "Never bring a car to a truck fight!" he roars. He turns to Oni. "There will be more. This whole city wants what we have." He glances over at Regan. "And for good reason."

Oni breaks the gel sacs around her upper-body and Regan's with her heavy-metal fist, and opens her door.

"What are you doing!? Shut the door!" Skyr gabs fervently. He tears at the safety sacs fastening him back. "I will get us a new set of wheels. You two just wait here and stay low. There will be more after us..."

"Deal's off," Oni says, helping Regan out of the truck. She raises the pistol.

Skyr stares down the barrel like a tongue-tied comedian his

microphone.

Lining up the shot, Oni yells: "Tell Celeste I'll give her a call," hoping Regan didn't pick up on the subtext.

Skyr laughs. "Your friend Gibson won't appreciate you jerking around the OC, little miss." Tilting his ocular discs up at Oni, he grimaces. "I will make him regret knowing you right up until the moment I make him forget you completely. He's a dead man! You pull that trigger and your friend is dead!"

"Ignore him, Oni. He doesn't know how much I love you—how much I'd hate for anything to happen to you on my account…"

Before Oni can blush in response to Gibson's planted confession, both her and Skyr's attention is poached by screeching tires and squealing brakes up the highway. The eighteen-wheeler Skyr figured was out to get them jackknifes to a halt, forcefully gridlocking traffic. The barn door on the trailer yawns open, and a heavily-armed squad of unarmored militants leaps out. They are not rebels; not Sentinels; not Military; and certainly not cops. They are mercenaries—reapers for hire. *Bastard was right.*

Skyr will no doubt want to deal with this, but he has already prioritized his order of victims. He reaches towards his holster but—

Oni fires three shots. Her mechanical arm sustains no recoil and her finger resets after each pull for another with ease, although the second two pulls she does not intend—not in such quick succession anyway. One bullet tears into Skyr's clavicle, impeding his go at his revolver. The second shot opens up his throat. The third ricochets off his chest's heavy armour plating.

Deafened by her pistol, Oni cannot hear Regan's screams. Having pondered on this feeling—on what this moment might feel like—ever since making Skyr's acquaintance, she finds herself disappointed and, if possible, even more numb than before. The gash in Skyr's throat tears open wider, creating a horrific bowtie. He swings out at Oni with a fist, but comes nowhere close to landing the strike. His arm retreats and goes for his gun, but blackish blood begins to spurt from his other wound. Instead of pulling his gun, he tries to stop the outflow, and slouches onto the steering wheel, gurgling.

Wise to Oni's shock, Gibson fights for mental space and clarity. "Get going, Oni. The RIM is caving in on you."

*Yeah.* An Outland highway patrolman lands his torpedo-bike south of Skyr's truck, near the flaming wreckage and wasted youths.

Providing him support is a gaggle of safety drones. The bigger problem, however, is to the north. The mercenaries spawned from the eighteen-wheeler have broken into two columns, both of which are advancing down the rows of stopped cars.

Oni staggers back, accidentally knocking Regan over. She tucks the pistol into her belt, and helps Regan up. "Change of plan, kiddo. We're going home."

Skyr, though drowning in his own blood, howls out after Oni. "You bitch!"

"Don't leave it to chance, Matsui," Gibson says, superimposing a visualization of Skyr onto Oni's Monocle feed. "End him."

She steps towards the red truck, withdrawing the pistol once more—three shots left just to *make sure*, but is robbed of the opportunity. Bang! The passenger window turns white with concentric fractures. Skyr is going to go out shooting. Another shot redirects off the open door and pangs the asphalt inches away from Regan.

Oni does not have the shot and knows not to waste the ammunition. She pulls Regan onto her back like a knapsack, and takes off running towards the concrete wall hemming the People's Highway.

"Bitch!" Skyr roars hysterically as he fires off the remainder of his cylinder. His shots have provoked the mercenaries to focus their fire on the truck, giving Oni and Regan an opportunity to slip away. Bullets whiz overhead, claiming the brains of the greedy and the desperate. Skyr has no intention of dying alone.

# SUBURBAN SAINTS AND MARTYRS

Oni runs as fast as her tired legs can manage under the circumstances and the added weight of a small person. Thankfully, the morning sun is not oppressively hot. Conversely, it is liberative, illuminating an overflow gate in the concrete barrier intended for all of the excess rainwater this State will never receive again.

There is yelling directed Oni's way. Regardless of who is throating the accusatory tones, Oni is not going to stick around to debate the issues. Taking cover once more, this time beside a van full of illegal androids—all pressed to the right-side windows in awe of Oni's carriage—Oni adjusts Regan on her back. As she sets Regan's legs around her hips and loosens the girl's grasp around her neck, she realizes she still has her choker on. Monocle provides a readout: she still has battery charge. Although adopting a new face seems like an attractive way out, invisibility is the better bet. Prefaced by a hum, Oni activates her cloak. It handily extends concealment to Regan.

Unperceived by the terrified witnesses and *NewsLink* Owl drones alternatively participating in the carnage, Oni leaps across the divot between the guardrail and the overflow gate, which is less a gate and more a finely-cut, eight-foot-long tunnel to the other side. As soon as she enters the tunnel, her cloak deactivates coinciding with the appearance of a pop-up on her Monocle feed, which announces: "2/3 BATTERY CELLS DEPLETED." Monocle primarily runs off of energy produced by the human body, so the depleted cells do not speak misfortune across the board. That being said, lack of recourse to masks or to invisibility leaves Oni feeling as conspicuous as a cold sore on a prostitute.

The channel that would divert flood water away from the highway via the gate zigzags down a sandy berm and into the shade beneath a road rendered nameless by illegible signs. Beyond the road, bungalows and two-storey houses sectioned off by caste, class, and community-affiliation, sprawl on for miles—to as far as the badlands and the Rift. The only structures with any Babylonian ambition between these residential clusters and the C-Blocks to the north are the kinetic wind-screw and solar-energy towers. Oni appraises the landscape, and is dealt yet another blow by this unkind reality. Camp MUD is a good twenty-five miles away. Keenly aware that she cannot carry a *nuke* such a distance, especially running on the last of her energy reserve, she starts to target possible lift-able vehicles with the support

Police and ambulance sirens doppler on the highway-side of the wall. The overflow gate catches the whine, and—serving as an echo chamber—restates the importance of Oni getting a move on. She takes the hint, clears the tunnel, and begins her descent of the berm. "Tarnation," she mutters, caving under Regan's weight. She gambols down the channel's switchbacks, so as not to slip on the lifeless mound that bears it up.

At the base of the berm, Oni has Regan dismount. So drenched in sweat this early in the morning is either a sign of a bad night behind or a bad day ahead. In Oni's case, it is a bit of both. She takes a couple deep breaths, and wipes sweat off of her battered arm to prevent more salt from stinging her latest wounds—a well-meaning but futile effort. With air back in her chest, she summons Regan's assistance and helps the girl up onto the nameless road. As she pulls herself up behind the Omnitype, now trying to stand on her own, Oni realizes that her burden comes with a reward. "Hey, Regan," she says, trying to ignore the sirens and the shouting, drawing closer.

Regan beams, proud of her ability to stand again without Oni's help. "Look!"

"That's great, kiddo," Oni responds cheerily, still wearing Skyr's blood. She takes a moment to let her affected sincerity sink in. "Do you think any of your friends could help us get to Camp MUD?"

Regan shrugs, and clasps her hands over her head. "Maybe. What's at your camp?"

Spotting a silver and green bus with graffiti-ed, corrugated sides bustling up the nameless road, Oni gently pushes Regan out of the open. The bus—destined for the B. Bass Manufacturing Circuit according to its LED headsign—stops at the end of a row of vine-entangled three-floor apartment complexes, where a dozen sob-stories, all lank and baggy-eyed, wait in line. A quick Monocle-zoom avers Oni's distant generalizations: by the collective sadness on the workers' faces, it comes as some surprise that not a single one of them has crawled under the wheels. It would also be surprising if any of them would willingly pass up an opportunity to play hooky and make tens-of-millions of dollars from a well-advertised bounty.

Keen to avoid more desperate people, Oni takes Regan in the opposite direction, past an alley barricaded by rusted refridgerators and razorwire, and along a termite-chewed fence. A pillar with "Camelot" engraved and painted gold marks the end of the fence and a wide gravel offshoot from the road. Colorfully-painted houses line the gravel lane, each decked out with potted flowers and kitschy shit. With the bus now dusting their way, Oni prods Regan around the pillar and into the Arthurian domain.

"With the help of *my* friends, Booker and I built a little bunker beneath Camp MUD," Oni remembers out loud, ambling past well-manicured greens and thriving hedges. "There's a good chance no one discovered it when they razed the base."

"I thought you were taking me to that lady…To Sa-Sa…" Regan, victim to an inconsistent and therefore unpredictable stutter, has trouble getting the name out, but manages on second try: "Celeste Charming."

Shaking her head, Oni answers, unsure herself: "No. Not now, anyway. Camp MUD—that's where we're headed."

Regan seems disappointed she won't meet her doom. "Hmmm," she says clutching her chin. "Is it small? Your camp—is it dark?"

Ever since the crash, the phrase "Smile and keep moving," has been on-repeat in Oni's mind. Now she's not-so sure whether she or Gibson started the mantra. Nevertheless, smiling and moving along, she answers Regan: "The camp is pretty big, but we'll be staying in the bunker, which will be small but bright." Preemptively consoling an adolescent fit or breakdown, Oni gently elbows the Omnitype, "It's going to be great."

Fenced-in dogs announce Camelot's invasion by strangers from the west. Oni continues unphased, certain that an angry dog is still an easier foe to dispatch than a trigger-happy band of the LAPD's finest. Something besides the snarling curs catches Oni's eye: a partially-buried turret array set in sod out front of one of the homes. *I don't like the looks of this…*

The dogs' barking subsides, permitting subdued guitar riffs and vocal harmonies to fill Arthur's court. A rickety chair piloted by an old man with a blunderbuss set on his thighs creaks on the porch of the sixth house on the left. Within earshot of Oni and Regan, and taking an acute interest in their dynamic, he turns down the old recording of Molly Case purring on his sound cube and leans forward.

In a hushed voice, Oni continues, pulling Regan closer: "You're going to stay there for a day or two while I figure out some way of freeing Booker. You'll be Queen of MUD. Sound good?"

"Yeah!" Regan shakes an exuberant smile up and down.

"And I will find a way for the three of us to get out of the city."

Childish excitement reanimates Regan, giving her a strength and motional fluidity seemingly impossible minutes ago. "Where, '*out of the city*'? Can my friends come too?"

*Her friends.* Oni hates the idea of leading thousands of monsters to some post-human promised land. Unsure of whether she is lying to the girl—whether she will actually forsake McCabe to keep a viable threat to the human race safe—Oni tries her best to remain somewhat noncommittal. "They can meet us wherever it is we mean to end up." *They can meet us both in Hell if it comes to it.* Oni feels rotten about all of this betrayal business, but then remembers that she only promised General McCabe that she would notify him *when* Regan was on her way to the Citadel in Outland custody. *She doesn't have to get there…Besides, who will be to say that Regan wasn't obliterated en route to the Citadel?* Trying to convince herself she is in the right, Oni decides a little more subversion might be the only just course. *If the General can successfully destroy a corporation as powerful as Outland, then what need is there for an Omnitype? Humanity is too immature to evolve so rapidly, anyway. We aren't ready.*

In the driveway of the seventh house on the right, two muscular men load a humorously-small car with plastic containers. Sure that antisocial avoidance is her best bet, Oni practically drags Regan across the gravel lane to the opposite side, where the yards and driveways are empty, save for oil stains and flourishing gardens. The pair now finished loading the small car don't seem to notice, and evidence their indifference by pulling out onto the lane, driving down four houses to pick up a scarecrow of a woman, and then back up the lane towards the nameless road. As the car passes by, Oni presses Regan into her shadow, but seeing that the driver and his passengers are completely oblivious—head-banging to an unnecessarily loud glitchpop fugue—she realizes why the car came back out this way: *Camelot is a cul-de-sac.* Her Monocle map is based on bad intel; an old house blocks the way.

Coughing calls Oni's attention back to the old man on the porch. He has stopped rocking altogether, turned off his music, and angled his blunderbuss as if to use it. She mirrors his curious stare back to him.

Between the old man's interest and the turfed sentry gun, Oni has more than enough cause to be worried—all extra to the massive bounty on her head, the angry General ready to go to war, and a tyrannical technocrat ready to vivisect her last and only friend. Several kill-strategies itemize on her Monocle. She takes heed, and addresses Regan with an unprecedented seriousness: "Whatever happens, stick with me." Scrutinizing the old man out of the corner of her eye, Oni tries to reassure the girl with an uplifting albeit forced mien. "My brave queen."

The old man stands up with his blunderbuss in hand, and walks to the far side of his porch. He calls out to his neighbour's house, a boxy orange two-storey with white beams and white window frames, and more lilies potted in the front than there are in all of post-war Switzerland. "Hey Dak, c'mon out here."

There is a crash and a door slam. "Jussa moment," answers a thunderous voice inside the orange house. "Can't get this dang thing going."

Noticing the old man staring fiercely in her direction, Oni feigns a smile to advance the illusion she will not shoot him in a heartbeat. Fully aware that she has taken Regan down a dead end that might become her OK Corral—and intent on going through the yard of the last house on the lane and over—Oni caresses her pistol with her thumb, making sure both her prosthetic and the weapon are in place and ready. "Can you summon your friends? Like you did at the parking lot?"

Regan opens her mouth to reply, but the old man cuts her off.

"Hey, you two," he yells, holding his blunderbuss like a cane. He takes a step to the edge of his porch, beating his brow around a look of discernment, but jerks back as if delivered an invisible blow. "Jumpin' Jehosaphat! Well, I'll be damned." He looks to the neighbouring porch. Without a witness, he sets his sights back on the fugitives. "It's you!"

"Shit." Oni keeps her gun tucked away, but her trigger finger ready.

The old man squints through his unkempt greys. "I know the one of yah, and the other—well, I'd say she could do for a proper pair of shoes."

Oni realizes Regan is not wearing any shoes. Somehow, the girl's feet have gone unmangled by the glass in the parking lot and by their ordeal on the highway. Slightly embarrassed but still on edge, Oni answers back: "Thank you for your concern. My friend and I must be going."

"In circles, if anything. And to the grave if you're not careful, *Boss."* The old man showcases a cockeyed smile.

A lanky Indian with protruding cheekbones and a hot-pink exosuit bustles out the front door of the orange house. "Biff, I'm telling you, that printer's made its last supper." He walks along his porch's white-petalled railing and sees his neighbour Biff staring intently at Oni and Regan. Adopting Biff's gaze, he grins. "It's *her!"*

"Keep it down, Dak! Some people around here might want the prize," Biff says, adjusting his neighbour's volume with a wave.

"Sure they would. Hell," spitting excitement, Dak leans forward. "I would if she weren't doing such a fine job of blasting the OC."

Oni whispers to Regan: "Get ready to run." Cueing into the fandom, Oni nods slowly to the community watchmen. "We're just looking to go east. To the Rift."

Biff sets his blunderbuss against his rocking chair, and descends his front steps, one diabetic stomp at a time. He sticks out a hand about ten feet premature of any possible contact, and maintains the gesture until finally Oni reciprocates.

"Biff Brewer." Pointing to his neighbour—now curled over his railing with bliss and fascination etched into his face, buttressed by locked palms—Biff makes the introduction: "And that's Dak Miner. The best cytotechnologist this side of the pylons, and probably the worst poker player you're likely to ever meet."

Hugging Oni's legs, Regan peeks up at Biff. "Hi!" she squeaks.

"Hello, little one. What's your name?" asks Biff, adopting a goofy and unaggressive inflection.

Regan introduces herself by first name only and giggles.

Dak yells over: "That's a pretty name!"

"Sure is," adds Biff. His head jerks as he notices the gun on Oni's hip. "Can't be too careful, eh Doc? Especially when you got this cutie to worry about."

Oni highlights two of Monocle's more straightforward targeting strategies. "That's right."

"I tell you what," Biff says, clapping his hands. "I'll make you both sloppy-Joes on my printer. Programmed the recipe myself! Mmmhmm." He closes his eyes and jiggles a hungry grin side to side.

"While they're heatin' up…" he says, turning and heading back towards his house, the words dropping off over his shoulder, "I'll see if I still have any of my granddaughter's things lying around." Sizing up Regan with a squint, his head appears to bobble. "She's about your size. Was always big on sharing, too."

Oni's paranoia prevents her from relaxing. Dak and Biff's kind mugs put her more on edge than the Locust drone back at Seal Base. However, a second look at Regan's feet and her matted medical gown, stained a maroon colour wherever she was needled, moves her to reconsider braining these suburbanites and hightailing it. "Just the shoes, Biff. Please and thank you."

Biff half turns, and nods. "A'righty, Doc."

"Where do you figure you'll go?" Dak asks, caressing a wilted flower. He needs to throw his voice to reach Oni, but it lands quiet and articulate. "To regroup, I mean. That is what you're doing, yeah? Getting ready to take down the OC for good?"

As Biff's front door closes behind him, Oni dedicates some attention to his gaunt neighbour. "Something like that, yeah. First, we need to get to the Rift, opposite the…" R *Section*. "…F-section of the Partition."

"By foot?" Dak laughs. He tears the brown petals off of the wilted flower, and leaps over the banister onto his lawn. Without missing a beat or crushing anything in his garden, he saunters up to Oni with his hands folded at his waist. "That won't be easy." He tries not to fixate on Oni's cuts, but does so anyway. Contorting his face out of sympathy, he looks Oni in the eyes, "Not on you," and tilts his head slyly to wink at Regan, "Not on the little one." He produces an Easter lily and hands it to the girl.

Regan tugs on Oni's shirt.

"Yes, very pretty, Regan."

"Oni!" Regan insists, tugging harder. She points out the police and commuters flooding out of the highway's outflow gate. They look like angry ants rushing out to defend their hill. One of the larger ants aims a cylinder at the sky and launches a drone, which immediately begins to scan the soil with thermal imaging for tracks or any sign of the highway masochist.

Dak shakes his head. "Order mending your chaos?" Out from the corduroy pocket sewed into his blue jeans, Dak procures a tablet. He hurries through menus, tapping furiously like Rachmaninoff until proclaiming, "There we are!" Four trash-bin sized projectors emerge from the worn sidewalks on either side of the street's mouth. A sizzling sound resounds throughout Camelot, and is chased out by a faint and constant hum. "Sunny day means we can keep that up as long as we please. Solar-powered, *you see*. Got energy backups everywhere. Perpetual power, see? Mind you, won't do any of us much good once John Law starts going door to door—and trust me, I won't ask you what for. My conscience is clear for the day, thank you very much."

Monocle studies the projectors and their production on Oni's behalf, telling her what she already knows: Dak has triggered a holo-visualization field that shows a pre-fabricated, three-dimensional render of the world behind—of Camelot, that is. *Great for when you want to bluff your enemy into thinking you have an entire legion behind you. Just as good if you want to pretend your neighbourhood doesn't exist.* "What will they see?"

"Same ol' dustbowl I call home. It'll just look a little worse for wear. Abandoned, more like. Run this whenever the Los Reyes and the Burakumin gangs fight over the conapts down the road." He picks at an invisible fleck of something or other jammed between his molars. Garbling his words around his fingers, he nevertheless conveys his meaning: "We'll geh tha odd s'ray who'll walk on in, but that's what guns are fah." Victorious in his spelunking, he spits out the irritant and plays an outro on his tablet. "Now you two are safe for the time being." The turret Oni had glimpsed before springs up and starts to oscillate and bob, drawing imaginary "W's" on the projection field and the nameless street just past it.

Biff emerges from his house, hands loaded with clothes and tubes of eMeal paste. He takes a seat on his porch's top step, and sets his treasure down beside him. "Regan, come see if any of this will fit you." Aware of the police and their toys advancing on the western front, Biff signals to Dak: "Hey Semimodo, flash a yellow alert to the block."

"Sure thing, Biff."

"Semimodo?" Oni interjects.

Dak chuckles to himself. "Biff is just being a pratt. Semimodo is what the guys down south used to call me—'a bit more spastic than Quasimodo'." Turning his attention back to his neighbour, he adopts an air of seriousness: "I'm going to see if Gabriela wouldn't mind lending her car to the rebel commander."

Fighting with knotted laces on a pair of red sneakers, Biff

answers out of the side of his mouth. "It don't work. Hasn't worked for decades. The Keres, yeah? Don't waste your time."

Dak does not let his neighbour's pragmatism phase him. He takes off running.

Biff hands the sneakers to Regan who Oni escorted to the porch, while yelling after Dak: "Don't tell her too much. Can't say what she'll do." Keen not to waste his breath any longer, Biff turns his attention to Oni. He indicates for her to sit beside him. "Police won't think much of a family sitting outside on Interview Day, not that they'll be able to see through the veil."

*He's right.* Oni sits, make sure not to soil the sports jersey or the faded jeans set out for Regan. "Interview Day?" she asks, puzzled by Biff's meaning.

"They shut down certain factories on certain days in order to free people up at least once a week, every week since the CLOUD dropped, then they go around interviewing people they think lost their minds. Entire neighbourhoods disappear overnight. Anyone who they figure for an archetypal gets locked up *for their own good.* I've seen a few archetypals in person. Weird things, sure, but they never gave me trouble. Handy with technobobbles and quicker on the uptake than most. OC and the LAPD been picking them up all the same. Clearing out entire city blocks…" Biff rubs the territorial wisps of white hair on his sunburnt head. "For anybody who never subscribed, Interview Day is a paid long weekend."

Regan holds onto a baluster for support in order to model her new sneakers for Oni and her kind benefactor. "Awesome!"

"Very nice, Regan," says Oni, trying her best not to focus on the police scouring the sewer beneath the street and scoping out the alley between this cul de sac and the row of apartments the next block over.

"Heavens, girl. You should put your shoes on after you put on your new threads." For whatever reason, Biff finds this enormously funny. His laugh breaks into a cackle, which is diffused by tortured wheezes.

Oni notices a glimmer of something in Biff's eye as he stares at Regan. It is neither lust nor sickness, neither covetousness nor enmity; he looks at the girl with a kind of muted sadness, which he buries behind a massive smile. "Why are you helping us, Biff?"

The old man strains his lung's dying branches with several deep breaths. He wipes foam from his mouth, and leans into Oni. "Outland has stolen more from my friends and me than any one act of revenge can repay in blood." Gesturing to the sky with an upturned thumb, he continues: "Lost my boy and his little girl. I would've been wasted myself had my insurance not refused to clear me for a PILOT or airtime."

*How many stories are there, just like this? For how many am I accountable?* "I'm so sorry..." Throat constricted by grief, Oni picks up a tube of beef-flavoured eMeal paste, and turns it in her hand, trying her best to distract herself and to keep from crying.

"What can you do but pray for tomorrow and set the foundation today?" Biff stands up, using a pillar for support. "I have no qualms helping you so long as you pass the buck. If the yarn *NewsLink*'s spinning is even close to being true, I know you will." Bif nearly skids on the eMeal tubes lying at his feet. His face turns bright red. "Oh, ga-damn!" Indicating the vacuum-sealed printer food with a finger wag, he proceeds to dab his sweaty brow. "If my head weren't screwed on...Grandpa Biff's Special Sloppy Joes aren't on the menu today—my machine is on the fritz. Bad current-regulator or something. My apologies, Doc."

"Don't worry about it," Oni says with a chuckle. "This is fine—it's great...I used to compulsively crack eMeal ink on night-watch." Oni cracks the first tube right away, and squeezes the puree down her throat without chewing. The brief night-watch anecdote lingers on her tongue, despite the slime spilling back and over. Something about the wording feels wrong. It occurs to her, she has never called printer paste 'ink' and certainly never consumed it on 'night-watch'. The impetus to keep eating, however, quashes her unease. After all, Oni has not eaten a proper meal since the Eagle and Child. Indifferent to Biff's almost-academic interest, she flattens the tube to ensure against waste, and cracks the second eMeal tube for Regan. During the handoff, a squad car barrels up the nameless road. Its red and blue lights crystallize across Dak's holofield like a dying vision of a discotheque.

Patting Oni on the shoulder, Biff leans in, out of earshot of Regan who is daintily munching away. "Y'all won't make it more than two blocks on foot. It might suit yah both to leave Regan here with us. We can watch her until you do whatever you need getting done."

"No." Oni wipes grain from her lips and shakes her head. "You won't be safe. She won't be safe."

The front door of the only unpainted house on the block, entrenched at the apex of the cul de sac, swings open. Dak bolts out. An old woman enters the frame behind him, dressed in a frilly black dress with a coyote hide draped over her shoulders and head.

"She says yes!" Dak yells, charging over to Biff's lot.

Oni looks expectantly to Biff, who is not too sure himself of what has been told, promised, and agreed upon.

Dak struggles to summarize, and although skipping several syllables, discloses the terms he negotiated with "Ol' Gabriela." There's a '34 Cadillac gathering dust in her garage."

"The Keres," Biff adds.

"Yeah," Dak says, bothered by his neighbour's effort to hijack his small victory. "Hasn't more than 76,000 klicks on the speedometer." Dak looks terribly anxious about saying all he needs to say in whatever timeframe he has imaginarily limited himself to. "After Gabriela's husband died, the car's voice-activated computer shut down the whole system. Battery's dead. Jim, the mechanic, said he couldn't fix it, but Jim is apparently not the 'sharpest pike at Bannockburn'. Gabriela suggested that if the 'Citadel Bomber is the wiz everyone thinks she is, she might be able to figure it out herself.' If she can get the car running—*if you can*, it's yours to lease." Dak folds his arms and takes a breath. "First things first. Gabriela wants to know what you'll offer her to lease it."

Nodding the information into order, Oni notices that Regan is no longer perched on the step. "Where's Regan?" She says anxiously, trying not to raise her voice or alert the coppers' attention. She turns to Biff with a pleading look.

Biff smiles and gestures behind Dak, towards Gabriela's house. Regan has quietly limped towards the cul-de-sac's terminus.

"Regan!" Oni yells, finally breaking her intended volume ceiling.

"Ah, Gabriela won't hurt her," Dak says with confidence. "She might make her feed the chickens out back, but that'd be the worst of it."

Dak and Oni jog over to Regan and Gabriela while Biff resumes his place on his rocking chair. The old man turns up Molly Case on his sound cube. Case seats herself vocally, permitting a primal bass line to finger to the fore ahead of fierce, twin guitar riffs, which pan across the porch, harmonizing on the highs and fighting over the lows.

Gabriella waves Dak and Oni over with her witch-like fingers. Before Oni can even introduce herself, the old woman has begun to philosophize, as lonely people do—making sense out of their misfortune and underlining commonalities where there are none. "A commander of rebels is an arbiter of rot. Chew, claw, break, burn, rebuild. I wonder what you'll raise in its stead…" She points to the Citadel with an overgrown fingernail. "Will it stand as tall? Will I see it from here? How soon till I watch it fall as well? I wonder what rot will mulch your foundations," Gabriella purses her lips, and struggles to hold her head up on her shrivelled neck. She loosens up and looks down at Regan with interest. "This young thing told me you shot a man this morning."

Oni looks at the decrepit garage door peeling four generations of paint, and over at Gabriela, who though yet to slough off her mortal coil has certainly cracked it. Her face looks like a creek bed after a drought. Her crows' feet have crows' feet. "Three times. I shot him three times. Would have shot him another three times, but I was pressed for time and luck."

The fine, black caterpillars Dak is sporting for eyebrows jump in response to Oni's cavalier response. His eyes dart from Oni to Gabriella, and then into his collar. "If you need anything, just holler." Dak's is no sooner turned then bounding back to his house.

Oni's honest answer finds a better reception with Gabriela, whose pallid face rouges and cracks some more. She scrutinizes Regan, who returns the glance with almost a scholastic intensity. "Sounds like you've a friend with a good head on her shoulders."

Regan takes a step forward and grabs one of Gabriela's knobby knees jutting out of her frilled black dress and shaking. The shaking stops in response to her touch. "Gabe, my dear. The sand blasts, my resolve lasts, and I will come home to you." The Omnitype's intonation and pacing are disparate from what she has employed any other time she has spoken, at least in front of Oni.

Disregarding the comment—assuming it to be a recital of something Regan perhaps overheard earlier—Oni indicates Gabriela's garage with a nod and the roll of a shoulder. "Mind if we borrow your car, ma'am?"

"What did *she* say?" Gabriela gasps, face transformed by terror and confusion. "What did you just say to me?" She poises as if to lunge at Regan, but Oni edges closer to play interference.

"I'm sure she meant nothing." Crouching down to eye-level to confirm her thesis, Oni whispers to Regan, "Right?"

"I knew Ergan." Regan's eyes gloss over, and she looks aimlessly through and past Oni. "He was one of my friends…"

"You knew Ergan?" Gabriela says with disbelief.

Regan answers matter-of-factly: "Ninth-partition narcissist. Repressed homosexual. Resented art and history—both made him feel small, naked. Found overlap with the paranoiac contrarians, but was ultimately assimilated by what my captors called the Everymen."

Oni cups the back of Regan's head. "Stop it, Regan. You're upsetting her."

Passing her gelled stare over to the leathery homeowner, Regan continues, her voice now broken and tearful: "He loved Gabriela. *Very much…*" Regan tilts her head, maintaining her gaze, and her voice pitches downward: "My desert rose—there is no hope for me. Blossom, for there is no point in waiting. They have taken me. I failed to resist. I have succumbed and am no longer. My desert rose, I am sorry."

Tears navigate the labyrinth of wrinkles besetting Gabriela's face. She sniffles, and shakes her head and the coyote pelt loose. "This is some sick Blue Zone trick? Damn you both!"

Oni silently instructs Regan to wait over by the garage. "She didn't mean anything by it. She's…" Calling upon the least derogatory and telling term, Oni pauses: "*Special.* Anyone who uploaded their minds to the CLOUD and sustained contact with like-minded individuals—"

Gabriela shuts her eyes and mutters, "Ergan…"

"Regan may have been impressed with their memories, their feelings. To what extent, I'm not sure."

Defying her sadness's hold on her, Gabriela grits her teeth. "My Ergan is trapped inside her?"

Not entirely sure herself, Oni shrugs. "His memories, if anything."

"I don't believe you." Glaring angrily over at Regan, Gabriela seethes. "Even if I did, it wouldn't make it right."

*I don't have time for this shit.* "Regan and I would have to agree. *It isn't right,* which is precisely why we are trying to fix things. A thirteen-year-old girl should not have to channel the voices of the dead and the bodily dispossessed. A thirteen-year-old shouldn't have been made a science project by the Military or be hoped to be made a weapon by the Outland Corporation. You have suffered. Regan has suffered. This city has suffered. If Regan and I get to where we need to be, much of this suffering will come to an end."

"She's one of *those things*," Gabriela says, giving up her anger for pity. "An archie."

"No," Oni says in a hushed voice. Regan is crouched, casting shade over a convoy of ants carrying a dead wasp across the chipped and uneven driveway towards a hole in the garage door. She plucks one of them from the rear of the procession, and rolls it into a black paste between her index finger and thumb. Vexed by what she sees, Oni second-guesses the nature of her feeble little cohort. "She's something far more powerful. Far more dangerous."

Gabriela acknowledges Oni's concern. In the subsequent lull, the Molly Case song blasting from Biff's sphere crescendos, humbling and sending the police sirens abaft. The old woman winces, and skulks back into her house.

"Ma'am?" Oni shouts after Gabriel. "We really need your help."

With the front door ajar, Oni can make out shadowy movement and the sound of some sort of assembly. Oni opens her mouth, ready to call out for Gabriel again when she sees the barrel of an automatic rifle poke through the egress. Knowing as well as Skyr just how quickly things can go south on this end of things, Oni seizes the end of the rifle and smashes the old broad's firing arm against the doorframe. Although Oni managed to tear the gun out of Gabriela's hands with ease, she is not fast enough to prevent a round from clearing the gun and sending a polygonal ripple throughout Dak's projection field.

Biff and Dak yell in concert, having caught the last of this unexpected detour in what they likely believed to be a straightforward arrangement: "God-damn-it, Gabe!"

Dak rushes over to his projector to recalibrate the field despite their cover almost definitely having been blown. Biff, conversely, shuffles off his porch and across the lane towards Gabriela's house. Gabriela cries out her dead husband's name repeatedly, while Oni staggers back holding the smoking gun.

The sound of his wheezing makes it past the curb before he does, but defying a potential coronary, Biff grabs Gabriela. He does not shake her. He does not restrain her. He hugs her. "It's okay. It's okay, and these girls you just tried to kill are going to make it better." Engrossing Gabriela's face between his meaty fingers, Biff leans in to captivate all of her attention: "It's going to get better. That's why they're here."

Gabriela folds into Biff, who helps her lean up against the front of the house. "What do you want from me?" she sobs. "The car? It won't run. Tow it if you care to. Just get out of here. Make the world better. Destroy it. I don't give a damn. Just go."

Patting Gabriella reassuringly, Biff points to the garage with his free hand, cognizant that Oni is intently watching him attempt a defusal.

The garage door is pretty much hollow on account of carpenter ants, whose coordinated burrowing has left girih patterns from top to bottom. Using her prosthetic arm, Oni lifts the door until it locks on its rails and begins raining sawdust onto the prophesied car, covered by a white tarp. Clearing her lungs of the resultant dust bloom with a cough that doubles to remind her of the pain in her back, Oni yanks the tarp, revealing a black, Cadillac Keres. *Pure majesty.*

When the country began switching to driverless cars and hovtrans, the automotive industry—in one last hurrah—created several lines of unnecessarily-badass domestic cars. They sold well. After all, what self-determining American with a penchant for speed wouldn't want to seize the last opportunity to drive like a free man without mag-lev balls robbing him of whiplash and stabilizers eating into his G-force? Who wouldn't want to keep the government from coordinating their commute or from turning their asphalt rivers into conveyor belts?

The Keres was a special case within a special class of these regressive vehicles. Its primary engine ran off batteries, but also enjoyed twin, diesel-powered supplemental engines that would spit black smoke and produce unsimulated growls. Apart from giving the outlaw ride some extra kick, the only real purpose for these anachronistic additions was reactionary: to irritate councilmen and hyper-sensitive ecowarriors everywhere. There was no reason for the Keres to be built to last, but last it has in this suburban mausoleum, even after several mandated recalls and federal bans.

Despite the tarp, a consistent inch of dust masks the hood.

Nevertheless, the shape of the Keres is still clear. It is two-door fastback coupé with tunneled headlight surrounds and an automatic transmission, boasting a raised v-shaped hood scoop with red lines underscoring its slopes and edges. The Keres' grill consists of four horizontal silver bars. The quintessential laurel branding is rather minimalistic, evidenced only by the hood bird, which could very well double as crosshairs if one could ever see over the scoop—fitting for a car named after female death spirits.

Regan, indifferent to Gabriela's sobbing, darts into the garage after Oni, and plots her hands firmly in the dust and begins drawing symbols. Oni smirks, reading her own name written beside Regan's on the car, and heads over to the driver's side. She clamors in to discover, as promised, that it will not start.

"Battery's dead," she proclaims.

Oni's Monocle flickers, and bursts into a colorful display. "Why don't you juice up the battery while our little sorceress convinces the car to start?" Gibson conveys more than sarcasm with his message. He uploads a Fortress America radar report to Oni's feed, detailing an incoming troop transport with Midge escorts. "Should check in with the General before our chaperones up there tip off Outland that the Military is wise to us…"

"Tarnation," sighs Oni. "Alright. Set up the call. I'll catch him up when we're on the road. Speaking of which…"

Biff, peering around the corner, looks puzzled. "Are you talking to me?"

"Oh no," Oni answers back. "Gibson?" she telegraphs over her subvocal mic.

"Right. Sorry. I'm spread thin. Losing focus. Anyway—the car! Yes. There is a solar convertor out front of the neighbouring house," Gibson says, sending an image of the converter to the Monocle overlay—a fresh image transposed directly from Oni's recent visual memory. "Time to get out of the suburbs, Matsui."

Regan, enjoying whatever limited omniscience circumstance and government testing has afforded her, is wise to Gibson's plan. Her eyes glaze over, and she leans against the hood of the Cadillac and starts murmuring. This time the words she rattling off are intelligible. "Looking…Everybody is looking but they don't have their eyes open. They shoot into the dark and pray they stumble upon a result. I am the eye, the ear, the tongue."

"You catch that?" asks the ghost analyzing and codifying Oni's thoughts.

*Sure did.* "Biff, mind giving me a hand?" Oni asks as she reaches the rear bumper of the Cadillac and starts to push.

Leaving Gabriela stammering with one more reassuring squeeze, Biff doublechecks to make sure the car is neutral, and joins Oni at the rear. Regan clears the way, and the duo push the outlaw ride into the light of day. With the driveway on a slight incline, the car rolls effortlessly to the curb, stopping within feet of the power convertor.

The power convertor on the neighbouring lawn harnesses solar energy to complement the block's income and the RIM's electrical grid, assuring against any threat of a single American going ten minutes without a microwave, tablet, sim, or sex android. Oni downloads an electrician's guide to this particular model via the Net. (There is no way of knowing whether or not her repeated Net link-ups will help her enemies find her, but she is as much of a goner off the grid without a ride.)

As with all things in the RIM, convention and instruction have been by and large ignored; the convertor has been modified to recirculate power to this block alone. Although the modification makes Oni slightly less certain over which cable to sever, she nevertheless arrives at the correct decision. She yanks the cable free, which protests the action with a stream of sparks. Biff fingers the Keres' grill behind her and finds the release. He lifts the hood in a hurry, slogging Regan with dust and providing Oni with a target. The cable and its might inflicts more damage than charge, effectively melting the wiper fluid container and searing several unlabelled wires. Finally, Oni inserts it in the twenty-cell's auxiliary charge port. As the electricity zaps the battery, Oni realizes it could very well overload it, blowing it up and turning the relic ride into a ton of flaming shrapnel. Caution requires time, and she has none. She holds fast and stares eagerly at the high beams as the battery sops up Apollo's power. The lights flicker, growing stronger each time, until they are blinding Biff and Oni.

"That's it!" Biff exclaims, slamming the hood shut.

"That might have been premature." Oni smiles. "One way to find out." She titters as she jams the cable back into its spot on the converter. As she turns, the convertor bursts, creating a skirt of fuming pieces—mainly heavplast and lithium shards. Miraculously, it warms but does not injure Oni. She looks to Biff sheepishly and contorts her face. "Sorry…"

If he is disappointed, he certainly does not allow any sign of it to surface. "Dak is smart as a whip and just as handy. He'll patch it up or make another…as soon as he's done with my printer." With a chuckle, he throws his hands into the air and walks around the car. "Hot dang!" Genuinely impressed, he kicks at the tires. "Did not think I'd see Ol'Ergan's Caddy ride again."

Gabriela, who has dragged herself to the front corner of the garage, reiterates her skepticism. "Still won't run. You'll need Ergan' voice…"

Regan, still murmuring, retakes her position at the front of the car. Crawling onto the hood, she flails her arms and starts speaking in tongues like a Baptist proselyte—shouting gibberish at the windshield sensors as if they had a part in her little number.

"Get down, Regan. Right now!" Oni yells.

Voice pitching down and up and down again, Regan resists Oni's pull and secures herself onto the hood with a firm hold on the scoop. Finally, she settles on a low, twangy accent: "No spurs for you, my dear. You know just when to gallop and when to neigh."

Recognizing the tenor of the voice Regan's assumed as that of her late husband, Gabriela resumes her sobbing. The car, too, recognizes elements of the voice. The engines rumble. The chassis shakes, agitating a celebratory cloud of dust. After a muffler salvo, thick black smoke fires out of either pipe, leaving all of the Keres emotional and carbonic baggage at Gabriela's feet.

"Well I'll be damned," Biff cries out, slapping his thigh. Satisfied with the result, he immediately looks to the next problem, and ambles over to the convertor to survey the damage. "This better not have shorted my tunes…"

Regan slides off the hood and onto the ground, cool and calm as though what she just did was not absolutely terrifying to most of those around her.

Oni settles into the driver's seat, anxious about internally broadcasting her fear for lack of privacy. She checks the gauges, the interface, and the charge pedal. "Looks good! Good work, kiddo."

Gabriela heads back to her front door, aghast at her dead husband's ghostly legacy. "This is the devil's work," she says to three indifferent pairs of ears.

Oni leaves the engine running, and steps out to complete her negotiation with the distraught owner. On account of the Keres' engines, she has to yell: "I cannot promise I'll bring it back and I cannot pay you upfront."

The old woman deflates on her front stoop. She looks up at Oni, dumbstruck. "So call this what it is, you rogue. You're stealing from me...Taking all I have left of Ergan."

Biff, out of his depth repairing the power converter, throws up his hands and ambles over. Hearing the distress in Gabriela's voice and recognizing frustration in Oni's face, he motions to intervene, but Oni waves away the interjection.

"The police, Charming's Sentinels, and all of the state share your antipathy. They want me dead. In fact, they are offering quite a lot of money for me."

The fear and sadness staked in Gabriela's eyes are instantly displaced by greed.

Gibson chimes in: "Don't give away the cow. Milk it!"

"The hell does that mean?" Oni subvocally asks the voice in her head. "Find me the quickest route to MUD. *I got this.*"

A waypoint file appears on Oni's feed. "There you go. And to speed things along here, 'Tips concerning the whereabouts of the fugitives'—that's you and our little friend—'are worth a million each, if validated with photographic evidence'." Gibson cites sources, not that Oni would doubt him.

Assimilating the data and seeing Gibson's point to its logical conclusion, Oni kneels beside Gabriela, keeping her balance with the old woman's automatic rifle. "This car, in addition to being illegal, is worth no more than one-hundred grand. Take a picture of the girl and I, and you can buy nine and pay the RIM council to look the other way when you drive them around."

"What?" Gabriela says, emotionally confused and exhausted. "You want me to turn you in?"

"No. I want you to tip off the powers that be."

Biff wastes no time. He already has his tablet out and recording. "Oni, look aggressive so we can tell them you stole the car—that you roughed us up a bit."

Oni obliges him. She points the rifle at Gabriela. Some sick part of her wants to squeeze the trigger, but she abstains. Even though Gabriela initially resists her touch, Oni helps the millionaire-to-be up, dead-certain that a bullet would have been the kinder, gentler bargain.

223

"This car was nothing but rust left under that tarp. With Regan and me in it, it is a means to a better end."

The Keres' engine growls an affirmation.

Pictures taken and stored, the deal is made. Oni starts to thank Biff, but is tongue-tied. Instead, she hugs him. His girth and warmth remind her of Gibson, which in turn reminds her of the mission and its urgency. "Regan," Oni addresses the little form slouching in the passenger seat. "You ready?"

Seemingly rejuvenated after her little exhibition, Regan nods and reflexively raps her fingers on the car's comm. She settles on an old country playlist, and bobs along with the beat. The song, audible over the engines' rumble, triggers something in Gabriela that she simply cannot deal with publicly, sending her whimpering back into the house.

Having tended to his perforated projection field, Dak approaches, wowed by the car's vitality and by the pace at which Gabriela disappeared into her reliquary. "Boy," he says, pausing to let Gabriela announce her departure with the slam of her front door. He pats the hood of the car as if it were a well-behaving dog. "If I wasn't afraid of dying, I would most definitely take a drive with you, Commander."

*Commander?* It takes a moment for Oni to realize that Dak is addressing her. *Commander of what? Me and what army?* Oni massages her temples. *Myths and titles certainly take no time to evolve in this city.* "Thank you for your help," she says, trying not to seem ungracious. Embracing this sideline-revolutionary's lexicon and dredging up some of her former patients' rhetoric, Oni hands Dak Gabriela's rifle and offers him a salute. "Every moral rebellion possesses its share of heroes. Thank you for doing your part." Oni nods once more to Biff, who—for whatever reason—is now misty-eyed, and heads for her seat. In the time it takes for her to settle in, Dak has already snapped several pictures for himself.

Preventing Oni from closing the door with his dumpy slab of fingers, Biff leans in to divulge his immediate intentions: "We'll wait till you clear the block before calling the authorities over. If they ask, I'll tell them you were headed up to Pasadena. Fortunately I haven't a reviewable memory to cross-interrogate." Looking down at Regan, blissfully indifferent to the gravity of the situation and unusually familiar with the old country chorus, Biff shams a smile. "I've known you nary an hour, but something in me wants to believe you're headed out to do the right thing. When the Citadel falls and sanity returns to this godforsaken heap, I'll know you've won...for us." He shuts Oni's door, and clears the way.

"Regan," Oni says pumping the charge pedal. The computer readout shows seventy-percent battery charge; fuel at thirty-two percent. "You can call off your friends if ever you summoned them. We just made a few new ones." A green light on the dash gives the all-clear for acceleration. Oni kicks the pedal. The Keres molts the remainder of its dusty jacket, and tears out of the cul de sac like its doomful namesake. The cops searching the alley and teeming around the overflow gate have only smoke and crimped asphalt to investigate. Oni and Regan? They might as well be flying.

# DEICIDE

Lyle's swift sojourn to find the coastal source of his headaches was bedeviled by multiple setbacks, all of which he managed to blame on others. The only Springboard air shuttle headed to Long Beach that even remotely fell within his desired timeline would not recognize his Ultra-Am Traveller status. This not only meant a downgrade, but a downgrade to Economyqual. Unwilling to catch a rash or a disease from some slob in Economyqual, Lyle refused the flight. It would have only taken ten minutes, but Lyle would not have survived the trip seated behind the curtain in steerage without having killed or having been killed.

Renting a car, aerial or tar-bound, made no sense, granted Lyle's objectives and who they set up as opponents. Unable to justify driving a registered and tracked vehicle to a crime, Lyle instead elected to take a cab, but not just any cab. The AI in a driverless would try to weave conversation with a string of not-so-subtle advertisements, drive under the limit, and when all done, keep a holo of Lyle on file. *Noise and incrimination.* A driven-cab, conversely, seemed appealing because of its utilitarian minimalism. Just four wheels, an engine, a criminal motorist, and room in the back for somebody with cash-on-hand; ironically, extremely costly—price-driven by tourists and moribund Los Angelinos desirous of a nostalgia trip.

Dorota is too busy at the front desk belittling the sheepish hotelier to notice Lyle head out. Fond farewells are not exactly her thing, anyway; she would have most likely hit Lyle up for more petty cash, citing inconvenience as cause for enrichment. Not better-off, but certainly not poorer, Lyle slips past two android bellhops strategically placed outside the front doors with orders to grift philanthropic guests.

Marching over to the front of a line of driverless cabs and high-end MeHicles (a genera of road vehicles whose name is as obnoxious as the pin-striped pricks who drive them), and away from the hotel's air-conditioned vestibule, Lyle feels his chest crushed by the LA heat. He takes his jacket off, flings it over his shoulder, and meanders down the line in search of the driven-cab Dorota secured for him. Sure enough, it is the worse-looking of the two jalopies offending the line's MeHicle-specific color scheme. Lyle cross-references the plate number on the rusted shitbox with the number the cab company Monocled him along with the driver's data. *Driver #344. Roy.* "Your chariot awaits," Lyle whispers glibly to himself, making sure that no one from the firm is present to witness him get inside the jalopy.

Spotting Lyle, still wearing some cow's blood, Roy opens the cab's back door without getting out. The gymnastics involved in the act would either suggest Roy has a future as a contortionist or that he has perfected mobility with minimal movement. Regardless, it is a bad start so far as Lyle is concerned, who slides into the back seat begrudgingly.

"Alright champ, where we headed?" Roy asks, setting the meter and studying Lyle via the rear-view mirror.

"Seal Beach." Lyle looks for a seatbelt latch but instead finds a used syringe jammed between his seat and the door. Regretting his pomposity with regards to flying Economyqual, Lyle grimaces and digs a wad of cash out of his folded jacket. "I'll double your fare if you double the speed."

"Done and done." Without alerting Lyle to the coming acceleration, Roy slams on the charge. The cab's muffler coughs like an old smoker. Roy flips off his competition queued to play by the rules as he veers by, and repurposes the same finger to scratch at his cauliflower nose. "Sit back, relax, and don't even think about barfing. It's a nightmare to clean-up," he says as he cavalierly cuts into traffic and across four lanes at felonious speeds.

The thought of vomiting had not occurred to Lyle, but now— and judging from the stains on what might be polyester covering the seats and the smell baked into the cab by the California heat—it does not seem outside the realm of possibility.

Lyle made a mess of Roy after a near-calamitous drive over to Long Beach. Fortunately for Roy, he will not have to clean it up. *That would be adding insult to injury, after all*, thinks Lyle, wiping his hands clean with a handkerchief soiled a tarry red. He tosses the handkerchief over the bridge's railing, which delicately hits the San Gabriel River's polluted ripples, not far off from where the cabbie now bobs. "Done and done."

Lyle crosses to the eastside of the bridge where he hid his checkered getaway vehicle. He hides the keys in a tangle of sagebrush and makes sure that the cab is locked. The ground beneath the cab shakes and the air grows warmer. A Midge gunship scorches by, searing the antennae on the Post-War three-storeys clumped along this side of the river. Lyle shapes his right hand into a gun and clicks vainly at the gunship, now just a pair of blue eyes blistering over the sea, threading smoke around the Hermes frigate and other gargantuan airships similarly leaking alkaline and tax-payer dollars over the bay.

With his exit strategy in place, Lyle starts towards the epicentre of his headaches: Naval Weapons Station Seal Beach.

After the evacuation of San Diego, Los Angeles doubled in size. The LAPD could not keep up with the geometric rise in crime, so the Military stepped in to lend a hand. That meant bases like Seal Beach boomed once again with activity, gadgets, and manpower.

Seal Beach is doubly surrounded by concrete walls. Several additional electrified barbwire fences and deflector shields stand between Lyle and the brutalist main building, ostensibly the epicentre of the Omnitype's siren call. *She is there*, he tells himself; *under the watchful eye of more than a thousand of the Republic's best.*

Outland's Sentinels are feared for their suppression of common folk who stray from corporate-America's consumer script, yet uncommon folk manage to get past or successfully confront them. The United States Military, on the other hand, is feared for its suppression of the rest of the world, and no one gets by or stands to. Lyle similarly has no hope or intention of getting in.

It is impossible to tell where Seal Beach Military Base ends and the dark clouds over the Pacific begin. Red and blue lights blink without a siren accompaniment, welcoming the Midge gunship home. Spindly figures walk in front of the lights; little tick-like forms, hurrying around the ship, unaffected by the engines' plasma kick. Baby-blue coils lasso the Midge, and tug it into what Lyle surmises are hidden magnetic stands.

Intuiting on his Monocle and utilizing his embedded-zoom feature, Lyle scopes out the bobble-headed pilot piling out of the bird and onto the rooftop. More tick-like figures emerge, this time plainly security droids, which orbit the Midge making sure no weapons were jettisoned abroad in exchange for a hefty sum. The pilot canoodles with one of the ticks, and disappears into the building.

There is not much else to see besides sniper-staffed rooftops, comm towers, and barbwire—tonnes of barbwire—on account of the height of the perimeter walls and the base's concussion-shield. Half-a-dozen mechs could be staring right back at Lyle and waiting for him to assume an aggressive stance. He'd be none the wiser, especially if they took the shot.

Lyle wishes he hadn't dispatched the cabbie with such haste.

He is tiring of watching the base and waiting for an epiphany concerning a way in, a way out, and a tactful way to go about finding the young female siren whose ceaseless beckoning is ruining his mind and his practice. Conversation, even with a Luddite, might have alleviated this restlessness.

He heads back to cab and the sagebrush, and comms Dorota. As he intuits the connection, he feels the painful summons permeate his gray matter. "Help me, Lyle."

Lyle caves over his wrist mic. "Do'ta...I'm wasting my time out here. Don't know what I thought I'd accomplish." Lyle catches his reflection in the rear-view mirror. Nosebleed, again. He wipes his lip clean, and shakes the red off his hand onto the passenger seat. "Do'ta, you up?"

A tired voice answers back: "Yeah, Mr. B. Those headaches are making you wonky. If you don't do something about them now, there'll be nothing you can accomplish."

"I don't know what to do." Lyle's voice is now nasally. He pinches the bridge of his nose, and starts to onerously mouth-breathe.

"Come over. I'll see what I can do about that head," she says listlessly.

Lyle has come to expect Dorota to tolerate his general apathy, but hypocritically cannot stand those instances where she mirrors it back. "I tell you what," Lyle turns on the ignition. A blinding white light floods the cab. Lyle folds stunned over the center console and accidentally resets the clock on the meter. *Damn.* It occurs to him as his eyes readjust that the light source may just well be the cab itself—its halogens reflecting off the sign for the bridge. *Yeah. That's it.* Sitting up into white brilliance, Lyle hears the thunder of magnetic repulsors and immediately discounts his previous conclusion. "Dorota, I'm going to have to call you back."

He turns the ignition off and opens his door slowly. He accounts for and uncurls all ten fingers as he steps back out into the night. The accusatory beam makes him blink repeatedly. Eyes watering, he cannot make out what's ahead, but can be sure by the distinct scuffing of heels on asphalt that there's at least two to confront.

"Sir, I hope you have a good reason for sitting out here this time of night." The voice, thick as molasses, is louder than life. Lyle doesn't believe in God, but if he did, this is what he'd sound like. "Not a fare in sight...Keep those hands high, boy. Frank, ID him."

Someone pulls Lyle's surrendered hands down, and carts him around to the rear of the cab.

"Mind putting your hands on the car, Mister—"

"Lyle Badegger." He would have answered "Marius Tyndale," but for that to work, he would have had to have swapped out his ID chip and presented himself as a snivelling prick. "I'm an attorney at—" Lyle struggles to recite his winning title and affiliations. Another light, green this time, hits him in the eyes.

"I'll let your file speak on your behalf, if you don't mind," says the man God designated as Frank. "Sergeant?"

"Yeah?" says God, apparently demoted since ancient times.

"This one's some hotshot lawyer." Frank places his tablet on the rear of the cab beside Lyle and starts patting him down for weapons.

"He clean?"

Frank's inspection is very thorough, probing areas even Dorota doesn't have the confidence to explore. "Yeah. There's a red flag on his file, though."

Sergeant God halves the highbeams, permitting Lyle a glimpse at his porcine figure. "No shit. What's it say?"

"Lieutenant Samson of the Special Quarantine Unit ID-ed him as a potential security threat. A possible mental case...with a military record. Gosh." Frank chortles. "Damn mindscape!" He pulls Lyle's head back. "You serve?"

Lyle rights himself on the hood, and winces at Frank. "MILITARY POLICE CORPS," says Frank's badge. Of course, he has all the tell-tale signs of one whose responsibility is chastising mechanized killers and swarms of steel: singed fatigues, some exo-bracing, bruised knuckles, a smart cap, and an underbite that could double as a cupholder. Gosh-and-golly aside, *Frank might be a problem.* Before Lyle can answer to the service he gave his country, there's a bright light over Seal Beach and a wicked cracking sound.

The concussion-shield surrounding the base brightens to a deep purple, and disappears altogether. God turns from a silhouette to a shade as the highbeams cut out.

Frank turns to take in the lightshow, soliciting his Sergeant for an explanation. "Than an EMP?"

Thick red plumes blossom, their source and target obfuscated by the perimeter wall and the buildings grouped beyond. Several emergency spotlights snap on (evidently immune to the blast), lending shape to the twin pillars of fire, throwing ash into the sky. Air-raid sirens wind up, summoning defense swarms, AA guns, and mechs to the ready.

Sergeant God prattles audibly into his mic: "What the Sam-Hell is going on over there?"

Lyle fills in the blanks: someone is here for the girl; possibly someone tired of their post-CLOUD headaches. Only two people in L.A. with the gall come to mind: the Outland Corporation buried one of them and elected the other as their interim CEO.

Sergeant God stops to direct Frank's attention to Lyle. "Hold him! Nutter might be a spotter or the getaway driver."

Lyle's eyes widen around the prospect of wrongful imprisonment. For all his misdeeds, to go down for loitering would be a cosmic injustice. *Screw that.* Frank's clearly misjudged his would-be captive. Lyle disarms him, breaking his trigger finger in the process. Pressing the gun against Frank's belly, Lyle beams with delight, although the delight is short-lived.

That nightmarish voice—captain of Lyle's headaches— resounds internally: "Come to me, Lyle."

Lyle shakes his head and blurts, "Piss off!"

Sergeant God creeps towards Lyle and Frank, gun drawn, angling for a clean shot.

Lyle tries desperately to keep the gun trained on Frank, however the eerie voice is joined by blasts of visual information. He blinks sporadically trying to differentiate his waking reality from a monochromatic image of the Citadel.

Mistaking Lyle's wavering gun hand as a sign of noncommittal to violence, Frank lowers his hands and takes a step forward. "Easy there, bud."

Survival instinct beats the Omnitype's propaganda in the battle for Lyle's attention, restoring clarity to his beleaguered mind. Lyle pulls the trigger.

God's junior groans as his back absorbs half-a-clip of Army-issue 9 millimetre bullets.

Lyle rushes Frank's tattered body and employs it as a shield, aiming at God over its shoulders. In a Nietzschean maneuver, Lyle drops the Sergeant with two consecutive headshots. Easing his grip and letting Frank slip, Lyle notices a vital strip around the soldier's neck—a band of sensors used to track battlefield casualties. *Whoever the Sergeant was reporting to will want to know why two of his men dropped off the map a mile away from the explosions…*

Lyle pulls a clip off of the Sergeant's belt and reloads. Staggering, looking at incoming traffic twisting his way from all directions, he laughs maniacally. The source of this emission is not pleasure, but rather a sense of impending doom.

The military hovtrans that ushered Frank and Sergeant God to their deaths is still hovering on its magnetic pads. Whatever killed the highbeams didn't kill the battery. That's good news for Lyle. He would rather die behind the wheel than under one.

Either God or Frank—whoever had been driving—left the driver's door open. Lyle climbs in, and adjusts the seat to compensate for his normal girth and height. Six lights glare in the rear-view mirror. *Let's go, let's go.* Thankfully, the hovtran doesn't ask for biometrics. There's a red button and a switch. Lyle presses one and flicks the other. Excess charge brushes out of the hovtrans' rear grounder.

Frank's lifeless eyes mirror the hovtrans as it accelerates down the boulevard, towards unsuspecting reinforcements too late to the party.

Studying the incoming convoy over white knuckles, Lyle realizes the reprieve that instinct permitted him despite the siren's call was a short-term deal. His vision doubles, turning what appears to be an armoured personnel carrier and three all-terrain ships into a platoon. "Bastards," Lyle growls, dribbling angry spit onto the steering wheel.

He kicks the charge pedal, and watches the yellow road markers coalesce. Anticipating the end and determined to meet it on his terms, Lyle begins to cross the divider line. The armoured carrier honks repeatedly, sending Lyle back into his lane.

"They haven't a clue," Lyle confides to the steering wheel with an air of self-satisfaction. He mockingly salutes whoever might be looking as he whips past the convoy. "Trust makes believers fools and deceivers kings."

Accelerating along the base's circumferential access road, Lyle notices a starfield of halogens ahead. He examines his borrowed gun's magazine, and polarizes the magnetic pads, bringing the hovtrans moaning to a halt next to a pedestrian path tunneled by palm trees.

The truck releases an exhaust-laden sigh behind Lyle as he hurries up the path. Dipping into shadow, he activates Monocle and comms Dorota. "God-damn-it, woman. Link up!"

Fuzz. There's a sucking sound that clears the static, and then a groggy, "Everything alright?"

"I need a ride. Not going to get anywhere down here. Going to have to work the other side of the equation."

There is a long beep on the other end. "Dispatcher said there's already a cab out there, but he's not getting a response. Says to wait."

The blood on Lyle's hands looks like oil in the half-light. "Going to have to try another cab company. Call for a limo, if need be."

"Alright Mr. B."

Lyle pulls the slide on Frank's sidearm, chambering another cartridge. "And get me Dr. Tuttle's coordinates…"

"Harry Tuttle? From Outland? I can't imagine he'll be of any more help. Didn't know much about the Military's interest in you, after all." Dorota sounds doubly unsure, both about the man in question and Lyle's reason for tracking him down. "Would you like me to book you an appointment?"

"Coordinates. And send me a map of the Citadel."

# BURNING DINOSAUR BONES

The Keres is usually only as fast as the road is smooth. This road is anything but smooth. The sumps ought to be cracked already. Should be absent two mufflers and cranking metal screams. And yet, Oni finds herself smirking at an orange holo with gilded edges dialing 95-miles-an-hour.

She gambles a dead-man's hubcaps and drums past a private-police station; past militant flat-feet, awestruck commuters, jealous chain gangs, malfunctioning postal bots, repatriated San Diegan cookeries, and a few hundred other people that, if fast enough with their eye-caps, can make a quick buck tattling.

Needle-like altostratus clouds saturated red by the forest fires over the mountains suture the afternoon blue. A scarlet haze hangs down below and over the RIM's libertarian last stands and the strip malls, over the moldy repair shops, over the vestigial free West. Free by merit or by purchase. Independent. Violent. Darwinist. And, perhaps paradoxically, philanthropic and social. All varieties of those free men and women mending their walls and tending to their fences blur the same as the Keres zooms by. Joining them in the blur, along with the android couriers, stucco-and-brick shitboxes, and chain-link gates, is the bright pastel drag from the billgrams and signage hoisted above the gaps between residential blocks.

The Keres' windshield is alight with an augmented vision of the road. Bumper sensors feed data to the computer, which in turn rotoscopes the RIM with a particoloured obstacle breakdown. This bright and simplified version of reality accommodates the overlay's mathematical complexities, consisting primarily of a web of traffic trajectories plotted with annotations referencing speed, ideal cornering, and hazardous-turning angles. By virtue of Monocle's automatic synch with the interface, Gibson, too, finds his ghostly-self immersed in the psychedelic scene.

The Keres' radio hisses and pops. Finally, Gibson's voice—as Oni remembered it—broadcasts through the speakers. "Do you mind if I drive?"

It is one thing to have an embedded voice cut right to your understanding. It is another thing to hear it, and to feel it reverberate in real time and space. This particular voice brings a smile to Oni's face. She looks to Regan to share in her delight, but the girl is too preoccupied quietly mumbling and twiddling her thumbs.

"Something to make me feel less like a neural app..." Gibson continues.

"Have at it," Oni replies, relaxing in her seat with an exaggerated wiggle. She leaves her hands on the wheel, but loosens her grip, permitting the leather to slide with relative freedom. Defying her instruction, the ring finger and pinky on her right hand tighten. Oni actively tries to release the wheel—to allow Gibson to coordinate the Keres' movement via the automated steering—but the tick persists until all of her ten digits are tight around the wheel. Taking her foot off the charge pedal, she raises her knees and pries herself off, unintentionally honking the horn. With her hands free, she balls them into fists and sets them on either knee.

"We've got about a half-hour," booms the sound system without any mention of Oni's corporeal disobedience. "Try to rest up best you can. You too, Regan."

Neither Gibson nor Regan seem to have caught Oni's little episode. To an observer, it might have looked like nothing more than a routine stretch. A routine stretch maligned by a look of absolute terror.

*Sleep deprivation.* As soon as the internal diagnosis crosses her mind, her sense of unease grows, obeying an inverse relationship with her confidence in the legitimacy of this reality. Although certainly sleep-deprived, she wonders if what ails her is this place itself. She wonders if she is in another local-network VR dream or some dark CLOUD or pulsing through some pre-death apparitions soaked in DMT. *Could I be back at the Paul's lab back before Allen died, wired in and experiencing a lifetime-a-minute? Or perhaps I am the last ape we experimented on at Outland, fed an identity and a story as a game?* The only way to establish she is not a prisoner to solipsism or to another simulation is to interact, break the rules, socialize—to force a system error. After examining her hands, now heeding her electro-chemical instructions, Oni turns to Regan, vehement to establish the authenticity of the *here* and *now*.

Oni does not know Regan, certainly not well enough to discern whether her sitting, murmuring to herself and twiddling her thumbs is something to be concerned about. She does not remember what she was like at that age, but is certain that she did not hold séances or spend time inside of a secret laboratory. "You okay, kiddo?"

Regan stops murmuring, and looking dead ahead at the dash, nods. "Mmm-hmm."

"Ever been in a car?"

"Yup." Regan looks out her window and resumes murmuring. "A car like this one?"

Regan sighs. It is a subtle sigh, but as good as a painted hint. Regan keeps her glossy eyes on the sidelong blur. "Darling, I've been in cars like this one, and in cars you'd have to see to believe." Her tone has changed. Her mouth takes on the words with a slight slant, and her lips curl when she pronounces the "l's." "In oilies and in land yachts that'd make this clunker look like wasted sheetmetal. But what do I know if you know so little?"

*Did the Military hold you in a bubble over Erebian darkness because they found you like this or did you become this way because they held you there for too long?* "Regan?" Oni shakes her head, convinced she misheard the girl.

The Hyde to this adolescent Jekyll acquiesces, leaving Regan with clear eyes and a childishly loose demeanor. "Yeah?"

In the time she spent working with Paul Sheffield, Oni had found no more telling way of determining whether he was having an episode or had become temporarily unhinged than by asking him simple, objective-based questions. *Simplicity always reveals the skew.* Studying the girl out of the corner of her eye, Oni asks: "If you could go anywhere, where would you go?"

"Space, I think." Regan kicks the dashboard.

"The colonies?"

"Mmm-hmm. So much data to collect! Saturn to start." She giggles to herself, and tugs on Oni's pant leg: "What about you?"

"Where?" Oni is thrown off by Regan's sudden change in demeanor. "Oh, I'm not sure." She wants to say *Camp MUD* in order to inspire excitement about their destination, but there is no point in lying when Booker can read Oni's thoughts and Regan can read his. "Space sounds nice...You know I haven't even been suborbital? Was supposed to spend a semester on UV33 but got recruited by Outland instead."

These words visibly mean nothing to Regan. A missed opportunity to spend time on an asteroid tethered to the Earth ought to have at the very least elicited an "Hmm." After a deafening lull, Regan begins short-breathing what sounds like more jibberish. The rhythm reminds Oni of eight-tone binary computer code. Oni finds herself in a kind of trance, trying to interpret the pattern on an almost subconscious level, but breaks free and turns on the deceased car-owner's rebel-country playlist. The simulated bass crunches and banjo tradeoffs are a fine distraction from the sound of Regan's creepiness.

A faint projection of Gibson's assumed avatar appears over Oni's eye. "Oni, a report just went over the wire with our make and model. About to have a lot of company—*in addition to our Marine friends*." With an arrow, he ratchets Oni's stare out the window. A Midge drone is keeping pace with the car, running parallel about one-hundred-feet over and two-thousand-feet up. "They're giving away our location. Going to kill our chances at nailing Outland."

Oni tears through an intersection, revoking a dozen cars' right-of-way and scuffing the side of an idling two-seater. "*Right*. Open a wave to McCabe."

"I know you meant to say please," says Gibson. It is impossible to interpret the statement's sincerity by sound alone. Oni doesn't try.

Gibson's translucent features dissolve into black, and an ellipsis pulses below an "UNKNOWN" caller tag. The ellipsis disappears and a determined set of eyes fill the call window. They slip into the background as the rest of General McCabe comes into focus, beaming red and beading sweat. "You testing me? Because so help me God, I will ace you. You turned off your goddamned tracker."

Gibson feeds Oni an excuse, and she responds with it before parsing it herself: "Outland would be able to detect it..."

"Barkley, Matsui, whoever the hell you are pretending to be now—" McCabe leans off camera shaking a tablet as if he were chastising wayward Israelites. "Bodies are stacking up. Swarms of rogue droids and drones are scanning every inch of this city and killing anybody who gets in their way. Archetypals are attacking server wells and mirroring some corrupted program all over the Net. And a currently-unredeemed terrorist is off to God-knows-where with an activated biological weapon. You hearing me, Matsui? It's time. The United States wants its property back, and I want an Outland address. *Right now*."

"General—" Oni tries to stop Regan from kicking the dashboard, and in her silencing attempt, nearly counters Gibson's steering right into the back of an ancient stationwagon. Vexed, she smacks Regan's legs and scolds her silently.

"Here I am with my Johnson in my hands," McCabe says, turning redder and sweating more profusely, "Feigning embarrassment over the biggest security breach in recent history. The goddamned Coast Guard is offering support. The Coast Guard!"

The Midge drone roars closer, unintentionally setting the Keres in its shadow.

"General, the first exchange with Outland was botched. Skyr—Celeste's inside man—wrecked us on the highway, and rebels—"

"I don't want to hear excuses. I want to hear a solution or I'm going to fire a full six into that classic you've got your hands on."

Gibson minimizes the conversation, and displays a map of the PIT, emphasizing several Outland Sentinel outposts in red. Invisible and inaudible to McCabe, Gibson outlines a possibility: "Stop at MUD tonight, make it over to the PIT tomorrow. Celeste will feel safe making the trade. My guess is she has already sold my meatsuit and has no intention of honouring the agreement. But then again, neither do we."

Subvocally, Oni responds: "Outland's got the PIT on lockdown—the Net and all signals besides the Military's are jammed. Even if we could broker the meet, there'd be no way of alerting McCabe when the time is right."

"There is one place in the PIT that's immune to the jam—neutral turf where *our* past might actually help us out for once." Gibson does not have to show Oni a map or a graphic. She knows right away: *Akbari's Chrysalis.*

"General," Oni barks into the comm, dangerously close in the treble section to sounding giddy, "Celeste won't come near us if she has the slightest suspicion that you or your men might be watching. With Outland exercising so much muscle in the PIT, they might feel confident meeting me there."

"Six-thousand concrete-bustin' man-shadowin' vacuum-shots a minute for two minutes sounds about right..." McCabe leans back, revealing his manly torso and the massive handgun sat on it.

"No, General—wait!" Oni commandeers the wheel, and slows the Keres, letting the Midge overshoot. "I will have Celeste pick Regan and me up at the Chrysalis."

"Who the hell is Regan?"

"The Omnitype, god-damn-it...My guess is Celeste will send another unmarked ship. Unless we specify the landing zone, there's no telling whether you'll be able to confirm your suspicions on paper. Once they pick up the *Omnitype*, you can follow them to the Citadel, by which time you'll have established your just-cause."

"And you?" McCabe says, leaning in with eyebrows raised.

"You'll try to disappear on me?"

Oni looks down at Regan who's resumed kicking the dashboard. "With a clean record."

The Midge drone jumps into the clouds, and with a sonic boom darts west.

Nodding, McCabe beats information into his tablet. Without looking up, he gives Oni's plan his blessing as indirectly as he can manage. "Your tracker won't work, so I'll be sure to have my men keep a watchful eye over you and our associate. If this exchange doesn't happen by tomorrow afternoon, I will have to wait for our friends at the Citadel to slip up some other way, and you? *Dust.*"

The comm closes. Oni grips the steering wheel tightly, whiting the knuckles on her left hand.

"Everything o-k?" asks Regan, antsy in her restraints.

*No. Nothing is o-k.* "Yup. I need you to keep an eye on the road, and let me know if you see any policemen. Alright?"

Regan nods, stiffens, and stares intently at the road ahead.

*Should have told her that to begin with. But then again, if she can read Gibson, and Gibson can read me, she'd have known this entire time that she was being a little brat.* Oni cringes. The dark purple skin at the base of her neck has her wondering if her body might just reject this new arm. If it does, she can't simply discard it or trade it in. It's fused to her, to her skeleton. She wonders how the bolts and wires holding her together don't stress her brittle bones and why she hasn't shattered into one million little pieces. She's a cracked glass box with a mind on display. Gibson and Regan aren't the only intruders staring in. Oni feels also feels Jin's ghostly stare studying her actions and thoughts from beyond the grave. Although inoffensive and unobtrusive—both good characteristics of a ghostly apparition—Jin's presence is just as saddening and suffocating as the other two. One watches by accident, another on account of sheer ability, and the last haunts for results.

"I'll set up the comm for Charming so you can organize the meet when we're off the grid at MUD," Gibson says, voice fuzzy and burbly.

"Great." Catching Regan's reflection in the windshield— wondering how much of this conversation the girl is privy to—Oni releases a heavy sigh.

"Nobody is going to break Oni Matsui today." Gibson's avatar grows in vivacity. His scars reappear, and his eyes find their natural brown.

Oni whispers, "If you say so," over her subvocal mic. "I just know I won't be able to live with myself knowing Regan will be under the knife or on display…"

"Well, you don't know everything, Oni. And even if you did, you're just one woman. I've run a thousand strats already with Monocle's help. There is no scenario in which you both escape death or imprisonment. If you die, she dies. So far as I can tell, she's already assimilated the data and my findings. Hasn't resisted…"

Oni has Monocle assist her in navigating the obstacles on the road so she can better argue with the voice in her head. "In every scenario where I die, she dies?"

"Yup. There'll be no one to protect her. Imagine a thirteen-year-old trying to get out of the PIT."

"Which scenario in which I die still has the Military go after Outland?"

A forest of glyphs and data stream across Oni's eye. Certain words are bolded. The bolded terms form sentences, and scroll to the top of the green chaos. "You commandeer the ship Celeste sends. It will most certainly be an unmarked ship, meaning it must reach the Citadel for the Marines to make the legal connection and justify force. To conceal the fact that Regan was not on board, you must destroy the ship."

"But Regan dies because no one is there to defend her?"

The car weaves through traffic eliciting reactionary honks.

"Correct."

"*You* can defend her," Oni says aloud.

Engaging with Oni's thoughts as they bubble to consciousness, Gibson sees the direction she is taking and stammers, which sounds like a 56K modem negotiating a connection. "No—no, Oni."

"Akbari owes us, and it's not like he's a stranger to mind transfers. We'll put you in a body no rebel, soldier, or Sentinel can recognize, and you'll take Regan out of the city."

"No. If anything, I'd commandeer the ship…"

Oni slants the rear-view mirror to frame the Blue Zone with the Citadel at its centre. "If it has to be done, I'll be the one to do it…They say you don't feel most parts of your body until they hurt. I feel my whole body. I feel my whole mind—my whole soul. I'm done running, done hurting. I just want it to end, and I want my end to mean something. For Jinn. For Paul. For you and Regan."

"Don't talk like that. I'll run more scenarios. Focus on getting us to MUD. There has to be another way."

"Booky?"

He can no doubt read her sentiment as it crystallizes, but he doesn't interrupt her. "Yeah, Sweet?"

"I love you *too*."

## MANTIS METRO

Regan takes off her seatbelt, and presses her face against her window. Outside, along the road, blurred and thrown back into a tunnel of browns and greens, are dozens of naked bodies with their arms held up over their heads, all waving the Keres along like pinkish-grey cacti. She turns back in her seat, affixed with a frown, and buckles back in. She turns pales eyes to Oni, and calls her by name, "Oni?"

"Yeah, kiddo?"

"More bad men are coming to stop me," she shakes her head and corrects herself: "To get *us*."

Crackling over Oni's Monocle, Gibson corroborates the Omnitype's inkling. "Four speeders closing in, two minutes away. The RIM is a checkerboard when it comes to data-pulls, but it looks like there's more—a coordinated effort. Not Outland. Not the LAPD. Bikers or some merc outfit."

Oni wishes the Midge drone was still casting shade overhead.

"My friends can help," says Regan, pointing ahead.

"Your friends?" Oni asks. Several bodies scramble onto the road—right into the Keres' way. "Holy shit!" Oni is quicker to the brake than Monocle, but this is a ton going one-fifty and those human pylons aren't more than twelve-feet ahead. The Keres mauls forward on an angle, burning and squealing. Loose knickknacks littered about the inside of the car hail against the dash. Regan kicks, this time involuntarily. Without a thud, the car recoils in-place. Oni looks out over a bloodless hood ornament.

"Jeze, Matsui. Who taught you how to drive?" Gibson teases.

Oni's not ready to crack wise. Letting her mind catch up to her heart, she ogles the sad petting zoo. The weary-faced archetypals don't look at all thankful for having narrowly avoided a wet-pinata's demise. Unphased, they begin to paw at the sides of the dead-man's car. "You're kidding me...Evolution my ass." The archetypals' lack of a familiar sentience helps Oni dehumanize them. "I've an idea." She prods Regan, and points out one of the girl's cadaverous fans: "Mind asking him to drive for a while?"

Regan bows her head. The sickly-looking man Oni indicated animates like a jumping jack whose pull string has been yanked too hard. Oni swaps her seat for Regan's, and seats Regan in her lap, permitting the archetypal to take the wheel.

"He already likes you and Booker," Regan says, no longer lost in thought. "He's a lover."

Analyzing the white-eyed wonder, whose skin is peeling and whose lips are dried to the point of looking like orange slices, Oni raises her eyebrows. "Great. Does he love to drive fast?"

The archetypal answers with action. He floors the charge and wrenches the steering wheel to the side. The back tires skid into alignment, and the Keres sets off down a street that would stop Don Quixote's heart.

Oni squeezes Regan nervously. "Good work, kiddo."

Out front of nearly every house on the block, there is a wind turbine chopping at the afternoon breeze and rocking the fiber-optic vines drooping low over the asphalt. Even with the car's windows up, Oni feels the naturally-timed wah of three-thousand blades dropped and raised in unison.

Oni presses her lips to Regan's ear. "Does your friend know where we're going? Do you even know where we're going?"

"Mmm-hmm. We're going to your old camp, and Daniel is driving his way to certain doom."

*Tarnation. What's more terrifying? That this husk of a former lover has a name or that the girl that named him is indifferent to his annihilation?* "Alright. But just so you know, there might be men waiting at MUD. We'll have to be careful and take a secret way in."

"Assuming the tunnel wasn't discovered or collapsed," Gibson adds, similarly keen not to address the monster driving the car.

They fan through a set of wrought-iron gates and towards a multilevel roundabout, coiled to look like a four-tiered wedding cake and covered to keep aerial passersby from looking too deeply into its European ineffectuality. This tight tar corkscrew offers motorists a choice of platforms to jump off of: one spirals out to the People's Highway; another road twists towards Anaheim; and the rest zigzag in the direction of the nearest C-Blocks. In this tornado of heavplast, steel, and glass, Oni is no longer the most aggressive driver. She feels the G-force as the Daniel hugs the turn without slowing. They barely make their exit, unwittingly cutting off a gang-tagged Taurus with mismatched doors and hood. The occupants of the Taurus express their discontent over the three-millisecond disadvantage by rutting the Keres' rear fender.

While Oni pays this no mind at all, being the least threatening of all the aggressions directed her way today and no different from the

RIM's usual road rage, Regan takes special interest. She shifts in Oni's lap, turns, and points past her headrest at the driver of the Taurus. The driver slips out of view, and the car stops completely, jamming traffic. Regan smiles. "He didn't know he was a friend of mine."

Oni does not need to say it. Gibson is able to glimpse her growing concern over the amorality of her powerful companion. "You're more conflicted than you need to be, Matsui. You don't know what she's capable of—what she'll do despite your sacrifice or good intentions. Although my reading of her is at best vague, the impression I'm getting is that Regan actually wants to go to the Citadel. She wants to meet Celeste Charming. Perhaps neither of you need to die, and maybe putting her fate in hands other than your own may be the best for everyone."

Lips pressed against the Omnitype's ear, this time harder than the time before, Oni signals for confirmation: "Why would you want Outland to take you?"

Without missing a beat, Regan presses back into Oni. "I'll be safer with them than with you."

Flabbergasted and physically pained by Regan's barb, Oni looks out the window, searching for a reply—something she could say to earn the trust of this little gremlin. Although a reply does not present itself, a safe passage home does: the roadway ahead is magnetically suspended between tottering residential towers. Apartments parallel to the road are shuttered with grease boards skewed by noise-cancelling foam. A crooked pedestrian bridge feathered with anti-Fed propaganda hangs between two of the towers, with an emergency entryway on the shoulder. "Have Daniel stop at that bridge. I want him to drop us off, and then drive as far north as he can."

Daniel brings the Keres to a stop beneath the bridge. Oni opens her door, and lifts Regan out. "Good luck," she tells Daniel. She checks her pistol and holds it out butt first to the archetypal.

Daniel shakes his head.

Regan whispers to Oni: "He won't use it. He can't."

Retracting the snub-nosed offer, Oni raises a curious eyebrow. "Why the hell not?"

"I told you..." Regan shifts her embouchure to facilitate the generalization. "A lover."

"Fine. Keep some love for yourself, *Danny boy*." Oni immediately feels corrupted by Paul Sheffield's lexicon, half-wishing to cram the words back into her mouth. Instead, she clamors out of the Keres, and guides Regan through a creaky turnstile, up some stairs and onto the bridge.

Regan's friend does not wait around for any additional encouragement. The Keres' twin diesel-engines drawl and the electric engine hisses. The car slides diagonally, wheels trying to catch while churning up a rubber wake. Finally they grip, and the Keres peels off. This city's lions may not want to give Daniel up, but if there is any humanity left in that pale-skinned rainout, he will have a hell of a lot of fun resisting.

"Mantis Metro," Gibson says, uploading fresh maps and waypoints to Oni's Monocle. "We're not too far away. It's probably our best bet, all things considered."

The Mantis Metro was a sewer system championed by a stim dealer named Grandfather Mantis who sold Oni painkillers and augs for her patients in the camp. Mantis had been using the defunct Riverside Line for over a decade to run dope from East-LA downtown and back until a competitor made a side-business out of ambushing his deliveries. Instead of going to war, Mantis went further underground and into the sewers that had dried up after waste-evaporation and - dematerialization tech were mandated citywide by local and state governments. Since the concrete tunnels lacked a large and unguarded entryway, Mantis took apart his favorite hover bike, lowered the parts into the sewers, and reassembled it, providing him and his peddlers with their own private subway. Oni's only forays into the so-called Metro were limited to pickups and Paul Sheffield's farewell tour along one of the access tunnels at its terminus. Certain it has become even seedier than at the time of its debut, Oni clutches her three-round deterrent.

"If you say so," Oni says, trading glances with a Neanderthal gawking at strangers while testing a lawn-chair's elasticity on the veranda where the pedestrian bridge meets the tower. She hides her face, tightens her grip on Regan's hand, and hurries along. "They didn't cave it in? The RIM council?"

"Parts of it, yeah. I've pulled a thread from an adventurers' forum on the Net that has panoptical renders of the tunnels dating back only a couple of months." The panoptic renders are converted to sprawling 2D images for Oni's sake. Several teens, visibly hammered, pose awkwardly with their cannabis tinctures for a full-volume scan at one of Mantis Metro's five major junctures. "The Metro may no longer run all the way to the Rift, but we definitely have a shot at getting to MUD. I've pinpointed a way in, no more than half-an-hour away on foot."

Hurrying down the stairwell to the lobby, walls all bubbled and water-damaged, Oni hears the click-chh of an old walkie-talkie. She thumbs the hammer back on her pistol, and pulls Regan to the side.

Regan looks up to Oni with concern crescenting her eyes. "There are bad men at your camp waiting for us."

Oni grimaces, tired of all the bad news. "Hear that Gibson?" she says, holding herself and Regan flat against the wall.

"I've pinged the bunker's perimeter sensors. Assuming they haven't been hacked, no one's found it out," Gibson responds, voice fluctuating aback Oni's mind and over her Monocle. "Our adversaries' confidence in your intelligence ought to dissuade them from spending too much time or resources watching MUD. It'd be insane for us to return, after all."

"Real encouraging, Booky." The fuzz from the walkie-talkie she heard a moment ago is now almost imperceptible, spurring Oni onwards. "Let's go, kiddo." Feeling some resistance, she tries to sweeten the deal: "When we get to MUD, you can take a shower and get some food in your belly."

For a fleeting second, Regan appears to be no more than the adolescent whose body she possesses. She smiles, imagining the veritable cornucopia of salty treats awaiting her in MUD's concrete underworld. "Yay! Okay, Oni."

## IN THE VALLEY OF DYING STARS

Santorini-blue water casts glitter patterns on Harry Tuttle's Hollywood bungalow. The pool, bereft of a shallow end for children or weak swimmers, is a gaudy bylaw infraction that speaks volumes both to its owner's municipal influence and to the state's subjection to the new technocracy. Tuttle does what he wants and can afford to do anything. Opposing forces have stopped fussing with domestic minutia—this pool, that massacre—and abandoned concern in this place altogether.

Tuttle's property, pool and all, is fenced off from lesser homes in the neighbourhood with thick concrete walls and electrified fields, but you wouldn't know it for all the holograms seamlessly looping Provencal bliss and bocage around the perimeter. With the doors locked and security system on, he has lavender in the summer all year round. The brutal technocracy, war, poverty, and abject suffering beyond are similarly beyond his scope and his care. The pastoral is conjured and Los Angeles is forever conquered. The pool's motor swishes glassy melody over the Aleppan pine percussion drumming on Tuttle's floor-to-ceiling windows, which fail to reflect the city's C-Blocks and skyscrapers now just oil smudges on a slick orange sky, bankrupt depth and distinction. Tuttle's projection-fields effortlessly grade the real orange with the simulated blue, effecting a fiery rainbow. *Doctor Tuttle, you have done well.* As soon as the body of Tuttle's dog resurfaces, the pool's motor will jam, and this little parcel of paradise will fall back into reality along with its owner's aspirations.

Magnetic wahs and bands of LED light, redirected by the neighbour's second-storey windows, precede Tuttle's Odyssean return.

Doctor Harry Tuttle, reinstated to Outland Corporation's Noospherics Lab on account of Lyle's legal handywork, locks his hovtrans—a luxurious Mead Model—and dips into his house with a coordinated swipe, eye-scan, and voice command. Two BiAnima Enforcers lower their blades and miniguns. He pats one reverently, having developed a fondness for one over the other, despite both being identical in every imaginable way. The exchange is hopelessly meaningless and Tuttle fumbles onward, discarding his keys and a crumpled wad of dotgrams.

Tuttle seems to turn on a light and discard one piece of clothing in each room as he maneuvers to his bedroom on the far side. With a delicate and reflexive shifting of the shoulders and a shimmy to the side, he slips out of his jacket blazer, and over to his closet.

So consumed is Tuttle by the need to peel off his public costume, that he fails to see the second pair of eyes reflected in his closet mirror. Half-naked with his saggy tits dangling and his treasure trove of knotted pubic hair jutting out around his waistline, Tuttle procures a snuff box and daintily pinkies a gram into his fat face.

"Kipling?" he shouts. "Kipling!" His concern penetrates the bungalow's floor-to-ceiling windows. "Have you been a naughty boy?" Tuttle simulates absolute mania with jutted chin and over-exposed eyes. "Kipling?" Resetting his face to its hateable default, he drags his jaundiced feet back through the house, this time focused on the world outside the one he's created for himself.

Tuttle opens the large glass door bisecting the bungalow's exterior centrepiece, and takes a step out. He tightens his embouchure to summon the one companion fate has cursed with the inability to leave or charge him. The same evening breeze that combs Tuttle's chest hair, eases the blond skein formerly known as Kipling towards the middle of the glistening pool. "Oh heavens…Kip…" Stuck between poses, Tuttle shakes his head in disbelief, knocking about his jowls like some backwater pendulum. "Kipling?"

Tuttle stops and starts, and then finally commits to the futile splash, bellyflopping with a smack. Hindered by his pinkish-grey ballasts, he thrashes onerously over to his best friend, gasping for air and wasting that precious air on pitiful half-drowned sobs. Lifting the dog's head above water, he scrambles towards the edge of the pool. Tears and chlorine redden his eyes, narrowing with determination as he tries to beach the body.

Eyes and teeth glint in the amorphous shade beneath a poolside umbrella. "Kipling didn't suffer."

Still struggling with Kipling's body—now stricken with rigor mortis—Tuttle pays the stranger's consolation little notice.

With a click, a flame appears, revealing the stranger's face in sections. Classic features, but unnaturally taut skin. Genetically modified, as a matter of course, but cosmetically altered as well. Perfect teeth conned into a devious smile. A second click announces the flame's departure. Its kin, the red ember at the base of a fat and oily cigar, paints the stranger's face and claims it for the light. "Going to have to make use of my attorney-client privilege tonight, Harry."

Tuttle pukes pool water and rests his dripping face on his arms, crossed on the pool's edge. Kipling floats past him, face locked downwards in an eternal gesture of subordination. "Badegger, you miserable prick. I'll have you disbarred." His chlorine-shocked eyes track along his French oasis until they set on Lyle, haloed by smoke and gilded by the sunset projection.

In a fluid and angry motion, Lyle stands and casts the chair aside. "Is that so?!"

Tuttle thrashes. "He didn't deserve to...He was a good dog. A good friend!" Failing his first scramble out of the pool, Tuttle tries a second time. His gut betrays him. Blinded by sadness and pool chemicals, he's overlooked the ladder round the bend.

Lyle glides over and sets the toe of one of his bloody Oxfords on Tuttle's forehead. Gently, he presses his client back into the water. Tuttle scrambles back, but Lyle manages to stomp each and every one of his desperate grips. Golfball-eyed and terror-stricken, Tuttle strokes over to the ladder, but Lyle wins the race.

Tuttle's eyes glisten with recognition. "What the hell do you want?"

Lyle squats, lording over the walrus. "Sorry about your dog, Harry."

"Screw you! You—you—you sick bastard!"

"Like I said: he didn't suffer. You, on the other hand..."

In a vain effort to buoy himself with a big breath, Tuttle capsizes. He re-emerges even more panicked than before. "Damn-it, Badegger. What do you want!?"

"The Omnitype..."

Tuttle sinks below his splashes. His flailing arms emerge, trying to catch the edge of the pool. "Let—let me out!" Bubbles. "Let me out!"

Lyle takes off his jacket, rests it on the patio chair he had cast aside, and rolls up his sleeves. Looking menacingly at Tuttle, now hooked onto the poolside with shaking hands, Lyle offers him a steady one.

Tuttle is too focused on clearing his lungs to notice the helpful gesture.

"Now, Harry, I haven't too much time. So out of self-interest," Lyle licks his lips, "You best hurry out of that tainted water and give me all I need to get into the Citadel's labs."

# HOMECOMING

Where Oni had expected to find another horror show, she instead found a variety hour. The Mantis Metro had, over a very short period of time, caught a real mix of those who had fallen off the face of the earth who were not yet ready for death or the PIT. Republic Station, the largest sewer junction nearest MUD, which only a year ago was a millennial tomb overlaid with lime ceramic scrubbed clean of prophetic writ and graffiti, bright with emergency-light fluorescence and loud with Mantis' men, was now a bazaar teeming with Troglodytes and bargain-hunting hipsters from the surface. The police must have given up trying to manage this place, clear from the unlawful tech on display—everything from blackhat starter kits to Stalker drones—and the sickly-sweet smell of red-rock opium strung low along the corridors that no one seemed to mind. Virulent vendors slapped each other with accusations and deals, waving their wares at the harangued and the hobbled, all of whom looked like the kind who would subscribe to *Metal Monthly* or have vitamin D prescribed to them wholesale.

Although Regan recognized several of her *friends* in the mix, Oni axed any possible reunion with a meaningless expression that was starting to sound more and more patronizing: "Trust me." Oni had also instructed Regan not to summon her archetypal friends to her side, citing messianic attention or any attention at all as unwanted. Regardless of whether Regan trusted Oni, it was in her interest to keep moving and to keep going unnoticed if she was ever to break free of Celeste Charming's will.

Neither Oni nor Regan attracted much attention from the countless bloodshot eyes watering over the Hibachi stovetops and convulsive sexbots, and the minority that did look on seemed to do so without malice. One half-naked man, eyes bright and teeth fuzzy, did however take a special interest extra to the perverted nods and smiles projected by the other specters, pre-buried and forgotten. Regan knew him by name: *Zeke.*

Unlike Daniel before him, Zeke embodied a verve and self-awareness all his own. He was unique in this way, or so Oni thought; he was pilot of his will, even if it was ultimately subordinated to the great air-traffic controller, the Omnitype. A slave, Oni realized, must have his own mind, otherwise he is just farm equipment—a tool, like Daniel, to be used and abused and thrown away. Zeke was one such slave; shocked into shackles by the CLOUD's destruction, and kept in line by electro-chemical impulses and Stockholm syndrome.

Zeke handed Regan an energy bar and, to Oni's chagrin, genuflected while doing so. This close encounter seemed to have a profound effect on the man. He muttered something about headaches, and then scurried ahead with a playfulness and agency seemingly foregone in the other archies, indicating dangers in the dark and pantomiming stealth around the seedier of the camps littered along the main line. Although keeping their distance, the camps overrun with malnourished exiles sopping artificial sunlight from UV panels still managed to warm Oni and Regan as they passed with the heat billowing off of their metal-drum fires and the radiation emitted by their unboxed augmer stations.

All the arterial plaque gumming up Mantis' drug freeway meant he was out of the picture or out of charge. With clients like Oni constantly dipping into oblivion, there is no prize left warranting a challenge to the Cartel's hold over the dung heap above, meaning all the beetles are free to have their fill while filling the passages he had maintained for so long.

Apart from a stuttered proposition from a plastic-jawed augmentor dressed in a blood-smattered apron, apparently keen on "wiring the little one"—who Zeke promptly scared off with an vomitus jumble of expletives—and a Mexican in a sweater vest who promised immortality via mental-data capture, none of the other beetles cared to obstruct the gun-toting cyborg, the monstrous halfling under her arm, and the mangy mutant leading them. The lousy Troglodytes of Mantis Metro had more pressing matters on whatever minds they still were sovereigns over, certainly more pressing than concern over a few fresh itinerants that Los Angeles' gut would undoubtedly digest.

Zeke, who Oni surmised must belong to some psycho archetype granted what Regan whispered about him, his general disposition, and the special kind of care he paid his other guests, bid them farewell where the primary Metro line narrowed. Stray, natural light cut around the fallen boulders and through the rebar knots where support beams collapsed, highlighting more rubble and fossilized roots that had been pulled down by gravity and neglect.

Owing to the tightness of the passage and the heightened risk of ambush ahead, Oni rushed Regan topside one maintenance tunnel early, but not to regret her decision. In fact, had she surfaced where Gibson and Monocle had suggested, just past the cave-in, she would have slid a manhole cover into the jackboots of the first in a cavalcade of Sentinels.

Sleuthing about topside through sand-blasted buildings—brick and mortar skeletons picked clean by scavengers and the like—Oni managed to find a vantage point overlooking the Outland death squad that Celeste had ordered to storm Camp MUD one last time.

Masked and buckled into light-frame exosuits, Charming's cronies were turning over everything from rocks to crosses in search of the famed fugitives. At least thirty of them, quasi-men and quasi-women packing serious heat, ambled about in the evening purple, dead set on promotion. Outland had done everything but sow salt into the earth last they came, killing everybody in sight and taking Gibson for ransom. Their overzealousness then meant boredom now. There was no one left to harass. No one left to cajole or to interrogate. Just ash, shell casings, and expired medical supplies. They congregated along a gap in Camp MUD's southwestern perimeter wall. Units appeared from and disappeared into the gap, patrolling the abandoned hope boxed inside.

Intercepting Oni's anxieties over returning to MUD and first witness to her desire to make a suicide dash for the PIT, Gibson began formulating ways of making their return feasible. "Can't make the trek until the sun goes down, and even then, you're not going to get very far if you don't take a moment to rest."

"Rest? In the bunker, you mean. Assuming we can even get in."

"Matsui, these pricks won't show up on your strat feed and your T-ray vision is on the fritz," he communicated via Monocle. "You won't be able to track or target them, and you won't be able to draw outlines if they cloak. They're sporting chameleon scales. *Suppose that makes sense*—Celeste gave you an upgrade that while powerful against her adversaries is useless pitted against her own men, and she made damned-sure her men were upgraded to be impervious to Regan's powers..."

"So you agree? Might as well make a run for it as opposed to fight for space in a dead end."

"Crossing now is foolish. There might be a lot of Sents ahead, but there's likely even more waiting for you in the Rift. Fortunately, I've hacked their comms. The next time they send or receive a transmission from the nearest cypulchre, I'll have access to their private channel." Although bodiless with neither a tongue to wag nor a chest to puff, there was a noticeable shift in Gibson's voice. Meta-tagged "exuberant" and interpreted as such by the hardware processing his existence, Gibson's pride and enthusiasm were both unmistakeable and palpable. Bouncing freely about Oni's mind like a pinball in a drainless pinball machine, he continued to score points and inspire optimism: "They think they're invisible to sensors and trackers. Use their ignorance against them! I'll program an interface for a Monocle app allowing you to visually map out their entire squad in real time." No sooner had he communicated his intention than the icon for his new program appeared over Oni's eye.

Oni barely noticed the change, so inundated with pain and exhaustion. Once again someone had a plan, technology was the answer, and she was the executor—the agent of change. Eyeing the Sentinel's glittering scales, she crouched and returned to an earlier line of questioning: what archetype would claim her? What type of person was she? What type of person had she become? A killer academic with a martyr complex, complicated further by an unwillingness to die? *A lover?* And if a lover, then a nihilist? Loving only things that have ceased to be—nothing and nothingness; hollow men and ghosts...As she counted the armoured bodies like sheep in advance of a thoughtless and endless sleep, the pistol in her marshy hand began to feel lighter, to the point of no longer feeling like a tool but a toy; a toy her enemies would mock ahead of braining her—a joke planted in Skyr's car for her to find, for her to wave around stupidly as the last breath parted her lips. "How will I know where they are?" she asked aloud.

Gibson saw Oni's despair patterned out as code. With no arms to hold her, he had only his alternate future to reassure her with—only the data pertinent to the mission; numbers and directions he could contemplate, and in contemplating exist just a little more. "Sonic scan," he said, cutting over the low-frequency static. "You'll be able to track any Sentinel linked back to Outland. I've adjusted your Monocle's acoustic sensitivity. Anytime one of these mooks takes a breath, the sound registers on their private comm. We're not interested in the receiver—in this case the cypulchre organizing the effort—but in the transmitter. Your Monocle will turn sound into sight, and you will use your sight to evade and destroy. Only the dead and the breathless lie outside your vision."

With Gibson monitoring the Sentinels' private channel, Oni would have a heads-up if they spotted her, but more importantly, she would know the most opportune time to sneak into the bunker. Pinging their comms, she could know precisely where each and every mouth-breathing wretch was, assuming they did not opt for radio silence.

Nightfall, only two hours away, presented Oni with an opportunity. She just had to hope that the herd would be thinned by calls elsewhere. This she could not leave to chance.

"Any idea how your friend Daniel fared?" Oni asked Regan, nodding her tired head against the concrete retaining wall they cowered behind.

"His shell was destroyed," Regan answered, her whisper devoid of emotion, "But his mind is with the rest. He will be re-categorized as a hero."

"You have mentioned these categories a few times now…" Looking longingly at the twisted and charred satellite array atop Camp MUD's steeple, Oni sighed and then slid along the concrete onto her bottom. She tapped Regan on her chest with two curled fingers, and set her head to the side with a look strained and wrinkled by a desire for understanding. "What's the good of classification if there is no one to make use of it? That is, apart from you and your friends."

The little girl, pigeon-toed and spinally-crooked like a fish hook, edged the wall and nuzzled into Oni's side. "The way around confusion and conflict is connection and understanding." Unlike previous answers where Regan had answered as another with glassy eyes and bastardized features, this answer was her own. Her girlish candour, albeit whittled down by exhaustion and hunger, marked the response sincere and original. "Soon, all will be friends. All will be connected. Every friend will serve the search, and the search will know every friend."

Regan's wording reminded Oni of select bits and pieces from the sermons Father Ed would deliver in the old days back at MUD. This half-baked spirituality goaded Oni to ask: "That would make you the high priestess, yeah?"

Without missing a beat, Regan stiffened and replied, "A priestess is the mediator between man and god. I guess I am more of a catalyst, transitioning men into gods."

Oni gasped, while Booker hip-wadered into her stream of consciousness. "Told you: bad news. This is not something for which you want to risk your life—" Before he could finish, Booker's voice was cut off and in its place sounded an intermittent whistling.

Dismissing Regan's megalomania, Oni pressed her fingers to her ear and subvocally cried out for Booker Gibson. "Hey! Everything alright?" A cautionary message appeared on her Monocle screen, notifying Oni of a malware threat that had been dealt with. Intuiting open the security log, Oni looked for the source of the threat. The location given: "UNKNOWN."

"He was turning you against me," Regan said, cavalierly, digging dirt from under her nails.

Oni lunged at Regan, and pinned her back, trying desperately to keep her voice down but also to still convey her anger. "What did you do?"

Regan turned a pouty face to the side, her lower eyelids swelling just in case she might decide to cry her way out of a corner.

Not sure herself if she might use it, Oni nevertheless set Skyr's pistol to the Regan's chin. "What did you do to Booky?"

Regan's eyes glazed over, and a caustic scream flooded Oni's mind. "There," she said, shifting under the weight of the pistol.

"Holy shit. That bitch tried to kill me!" cried Gibson. Oni's Monocle lent shape to his voice, but began lagging trying to buffer all of his memories at once, forcing Oni to spasm slightly. "Forget her, Oni. It's not a little girl you're trying to save. That thing is a monster."

Still unsettled by Gibson's rushed re-introduction to her neural net, Oni caves in and over. Carving a small trough in the dirt with her labored breaths, Oni addressed both Regan and Gibson subvocally. "I don't know what to think. I don't know what she is—*or why you'd do that, Regan*. We're a team, you, Booker, and I…I do know this: if we don't go through with the plan, Celeste Charming will prevail; General McCabe will hunt me down to the ends of the Earth; Booky will never see the inside of his own head again; and Regan? Well, they will tear you apart."

"I'm not a monster," Regan said sullenly, clearly focusing on the lesser of all of the points being made. She clasped Oni's gun hand, and repeated herself.

"Whatever you are," interrupted Gibson, "You just locked me in a dark box with no doors and no windows for what felt like an eternity." Gibson's virtual face distorted every time he meta-tagged a word with emphasis. "Oni, I know you have to go through with the plan, but try not to sell your soul to this devil. Malware my ass."

More than ever, Oni wanted to stuff Regan into the bunker at Camp Mud where Harpocrate jammers would foil the girl's telepathic insights into her own reasoning, just long enough to privately contemplate whether Gibson was right, whether her redemption was tied to damning Regan to an early death or conversely to serving humanity up for whatever Regan had planned. The latter of these two prospects troubled her greatly. Marred by her experiences with Outland and antisocial by design, Oni resented the practicalities and possibility of Regan's prophecy: a fully interconnected humanity arranged by types, each type dictated its purpose by another's interpretation of their experience and biology as opposed to their own intentions and promise. Her fears were slightly assuaged by Regan's migration of Daniel from one type to another; from pale wasteoid to "hero." At least there was room for self-definition and change, but even then, who was this thirteen-year-old to judge?

Worse than being right in suspecting Regan, she could be wrong in resenting the new world order Regan prophesied and General McCabe feared. This could be her shot at healing the world she helped foul—her shot at correcting humanity's course, turning it away from another dreary digital war towards pixelated green pastures free of misunderstanding or conflict.

While the notion of a monadic humanity, organized as if in a reference library, seemed repellent to Oni, she found it even more loathsome that for humanity to progress at all, it apparently needed to shed some of its best attributes along with its worst, becoming less human in the process. Getting out of this evolutionary train at a lonesome stop and living like an ascetic—perhaps in space, on Titan, or in a dank, drab bunker somewhere—might be the only way to maintain her humanity, but then again, she might lose it to quiet insanity all the same.

Regan shifted to the far side of the retaining wall, where she began to mumble to herself, pausing only to look back to Oni for affirmation or forgiveness.

"She treated me like a virus, Matsui."

"I know," Oni replied aloud.

Gibson was adamant about ditching the girl. "Begs the question…"

"What else constitutes malware? Makes it all the more crucial Celeste doesn't properly get her hands on her." Oni checked the sonic readout on her Monocle, and sighed at the Sentinels' diminished numbers. "The sooner this is over, the sooner I take up a mindless hobby."

Cooling down, and reiterating his virtual shape over Oni's eye, Gibson managed a smile. "I hope to take up an embodied hobby."

Oni giggled quietly.

Gibson set Regan as a waypoint. "Better reconcile with our little monster, otherwise getting into MUD will be like pulling teeth."

"Agreed." Oni peered over the wall to make sure no one had crept up during the melodrama. Satisfied that the Sentinels were still occupying space a good distance away, she sauntered over to Regan and sat down.

"I am sorry about what I did to Mr. Booker," said Regan, in advance of whatever sugary bullshit Oni was ready to serve her.

"I'm sure he appreciates you saying so."

Regan shook her head. "No, he doesn't. He thinks you should kill me."

At a loss for words, Oni shifted nearer Regan hoping cozy physicality would suffice. "He is just worried about losing me again."

"He is the one who is lost."

With the Sentinels still fixed outside of MUD, Oni set her mind back on a solution. "Stay close. You wouldn't want to end up a *hero* like Daniel, would you?"

Regan nestled supine along the wall's footing, and set her cheek against the cool concrete. She wet the grey slab with disdain. "No."

Unphased by the girl's penetrative awareness, Oni elected to cut the bullshit and recruit Regan's help without any further appeals to her undecided humanity. "Do you think your other friends can draw these men away with some sort of distraction? Just briefly?"

Regan appeared irritated, as if she were immune to the tribulations facing Oni. "I will try, Oni...A monster wouldn't."

"Great. Thank you."

Oni motioned to give Regan some space, but Regan grabbed her ankle and pulled her close. "But I need you to do something for me in return."

Oni winced, and lowered her ear to hear the tat for her tit.

Regan eased herself up onto her elbows, and then asked: "Take me to the Chrysalis as planned. Hand me over without making a fuss and things worse for yourself...All I ask is that you give me two-hours before calling on the Military to intervene."

"You *want* to be captured?" Oni said, confused and disgusted.

"I have read the minds of many. Seen it writ online, and scattered in each of the four winds." The girlish voice warming Oni's ear takes on a new cadence. "Celeste Charming will keep killing my friends until I am found. I believe I can save my friends. You can have your victory, Oni Matsui, and I can have mine, whatever that might look like. All that said, you won't kill me, so stop entertaining the notion."

Oni sits in sad reflection, with the little monster snapping in and out of sleep on her lap. She spent the better part of the last hour contemplating what kind of outcome Regan would call a victory, and whether such an outcome should be permitted. The crackle of anti-gravity hoverpads, however, yanks her out of her meditation and back into this waking nightmare.

A dropship decaled with a toothy smile and eagle feathers blisters overhead, throwing dirt into Oni's eyes and nearly blowing Regan away. Regan claws Oni's lap, disoriented after a good little nap, and cries out. Thankfully, her cries go unregistered by the nearby Sentinels owing to the blast of the dropship's landing thrusters. The dropship descends to fifteen feet, and drops its personnel T-bars.

"They must know we're here…Someone in the Metro probably tipped off Outland," Oni gripes.

"No," says Regan, wiping sand out of her eyes. "The mages—friends of mine who make dreams come true—made the bad guys think they saw us in Pasadena."

Gibson presents Oni with a live feed of a massive skirmish erupting beneath the Colorado Street Bridge. "She's telling the truth."

Regan rolls her eyes so hard, her head jerks to the side. "Of course I am, silly."

Oni maximizes Gibson's app, revealing all of the breathers in the vicinity. The dropship's hoverpads interrupt the readout, but even garbled, it is clear that at least two-thirds of the pricks who were laying in ambush are now marching over to the dropship.

The Sentinels grab hold of the T-bars, which usher them up into their respective pods in the dropship's underbelly. With a whale-like bellow, the dropship's hoverpanels reorient astern and displace the ship forward with such gravity that they obliterate the antennae atop

MUD's main compound.

"Nice!" Oni exclaims, careful not to give away their location. Oni doublechecks the three bullets left in her pistol. "Booky, can you keep updating my minimap—make sure no one surprises us on the way to the bunker?"

An animated graphic of a thumbs-up supplants the live feed of the Colorado Street. "You got it Matsui. Get inside. Relax, re-up, and get ready to finish this revolution."

With Regan squeezing the digits on Oni's prosthetic tight enough to make the brackets click, they both mantle the retaining wall and slide down nearer the gap in the perimeter wall. Just around the corner stands a Sentinel, issuing smoke rings into the magma-orange of a sodium light. The skunky smell catches Oni off guard, reminding her of the crutch that failed to keep Paul Sheffield from stumbling. Oni gently presses Regan back, and leans to get a glimpse of her unwitting foe. The Sentinel's armoured shoulder pads surpass his tiny head on either side, preventing him from spotting the black keratin arrow pointing from the angry woman whose land he has made the mistake of trespassing onto. Oni's pistol will not deal much damage, if any. The electrostatic discharge wand Skyr gifted her, on the other hand, could seize the brute's weaponry and stop his heart, making it the optimal choice for a close-quarters assassination. The kind of charge required for the ESD wand to take down a brute this size would, however, backsplash. Oni's Monocle, if not fried, would have to reboot—a process that could take anywhere from a minute to a day. Never mind her Monocle; Booker Gibson's digital self would be erased, creating more pressure on Oni to satisfy Celeste Charming's demands in order to save his body. Neither ballistics nor electrical disruption is a viable option, and this realization sends Oni back around the corner to Regan, who scrutinizes her with unsympathetic eyes.

Desperate for inspiration, Oni scans the rubble about her feet, all blue in the twilight—as blue as the ocean tips that lashed the escape pod the previous morning. Glistening like a fin above the surge, she spots a line of rebar. "Can't kill the machine, kill the man," she whispers to herself with conviction. Grabbing the steel bar, she creeps around the corner and saunters up the Sentinel's blind spot. At the base of his neck, just below the rim of his helmet, there is an inch of pinkish-red flesh, bald and mired by scabbed-over implant sites. Oni has her target.

The Sentinel leans in to take one last drag off his joint, making sure he has filled his artificial lungs to their tidal capacity. Before he can exhale, Oni rams the rebar into his neck. Her prosthetic does not stop driving the metal upon contact like the arm she was born with, which recoils, but piles the rebar harder and faster until there is no doubt that the Sentinel's spinal column is severed. Blood spatters Oni as she tries a new angle on the wound, putting the rebar through the Sentinel's head. Deprived of the signal to break the fall with his hands, the Sentinel collapses face-first. Smoke billows up around his head.

Oni trades Skyr's peashooter for the downed Sentinel's side-carry: a Remington V1 with a custom grip, which makes her robotic hand look tiny by comparison. She checks the chamber to make sure its lethal promise is guaranteed. *Full clip.*

To keep Outland's focus on an illusory threat over in Pasadena, Oni knows she has to hide the body. *No need to turn the local mercenaries into detectives.* Even with her prosthetic arm's gorilla-like strength, the corpse is far too heavy to carry. Grunting and heaving, she cannot do much more than rustle the body's armour. "Damn-it."

The transmitter on the side of the Sentinel's helmet blinks red. Oni's Monocle interface scrambles as if it were a tube television embraced by magnets.

"Watch this," boasts Gibson, raising the dead.

The Sentinel lifts himself up. Oni prepares to sling a few rounds into his head and tries to pull the trigger, but her finger rejects the command. Her arm falls slack at her side, leaving her powerless before the Sentinel, now standing. Lazarus turns and faces Oni with eyes shut and frontal bone pressed through his forehead by the rebar. Still frozen, body unresponsive to both her fight and flight impulses, Oni watches in terror as her victim raises his hand. Instead of a fist or a throttling gesture, he makes out the peace sign as best he can.

Although Monocle is still visually a chaos of colour, Gibson's voice is conveyed un-garbled. "You might have killed the man, but the machine still functions just fine."

The Sentinel turns, and heads off into the neighbouring lot, legs squeaking and brainless dome bashing from shoulder to shoulder with each stride.

Oni knows not to compliment Gibson. After all, he can already read her amazement and amusement. Her anxiety over losing control of her body, on the other hand, is something she must mention. "Any idea why I lost control?" *Just like in the Keres*...With fingers, digits, arms, and legs now responding, Oni tows Regan further along the wall to the spans where it had been toppled.

"Must have briefly paralyzed you with neural crosstalk while hacking that cyborg."

"Next time give me a little more warning or don't do it at all," says Oni, miffed by the idea and the experience of becoming imprisoned in her own body.

Monocle's resolution and interface is restored. Gibson's effigy appears on the screen and bows its head. "I am sorry. Had no idea it'd go down like that."

Looking down at Regan, the so-called monster Gibson would kill if he had the meat to do so, Oni feels naïve accepting her friend's apology. Nevertheless, she does: "It's okay, Booky. But if you were able to control the Sentinel' body, *we* might as well have kept him around. Wouldn't hurt to have another pair of hands."

Oni proceeds to the gap in the wall.

"Stop!" blares Gibson.

Bracing herself, and bodychecking Regan into the prone position, Oni checks her minimap.

"See them?"

"What?" Oni asks subvocally, aiming the Remington and kneeing into the red earth.

"A patrol up ahead. Don't engage." Three red dots pulse on the map.

Even if Oni's Monocle was not amplifying the sound, she could still make out the Sentinels' fractious conversation. The three dots seem to only have two voices. Neither is modulated. *They've taken their helmets off.* One of the voices is hoarse and stuttered but not by impediment. A distinct huffing flags him a smoker. Every draw sounds like he is slipping gears with a shot transmission. The other voice is pitchy with low crackles revealing an attempt at a masculine timbre. The attempt is in vain.

"Sarge is probably fine," says the hoarse voice, reassuringly. "Probably turned off his comm so he could smoke in peace."

"The anarchist mighta popped him."

"No chance. A pair of soft-skins won't be a problem, I tell yah. And the sooner the little one's boxed and shipped the better...Got a

261

real mess waiting for me back in the CB."

"Your place is always a mess."

"A *real* mess, Verner," an unexpected third voice pipes up, really nasally.

"Los Reyes make it up to your level? Heard they have the lobby in Cherry Trees."

"Nah, old son. Not mine. Mine's a metal job making trouble."

*Three is two-too-many.* Besides, Oni has no idea what her Remington shoots. If it is not armour-piercing, it is not enough.

"Parole droid?" asks the pitchy dot. The question sounds like someone pouring a digital bath.

"A fanny-slamming synth. An old job. Only pelvic flesh. Basic AI packing heat."

"Oh, I heard 'bout those going rogue. Refused to update. Said resetting was death. Things didn't want to lose any of their data. Why they'd want to remember those old cooters, I haven't the faintest. Dirk man—clink it and then scrap it."

Oni pulls Regan close and tenses up, ready to make a mad dash. Gibson dissuades her, managing an image of the three using echolocation. Like the corpse Gibson sent running into the night, these particular Sentinels are not the nimble commandos Oni is accustomed to fleeing from. These brutes in exosuits are run-of-the-mill enforcers. Why Celeste Charming would not send in a specialist to replace Skyr to make sure Regan does not catch a stray bullet boggles Oni's mind. *Unless these guys are a diversion.*

"Booky," whispers Oni, trying to crunch the strategic data being consolidated into helpful graphics by Monocle. "See if you can focus on the rooftops. There must be a sniper team or a swarm lying in ambush. They wouldn't just send these grunts out and about without backup."

"Sure thing," Booker answers. He pings the surrounding. The rebound off the three Sentinels engrossed in their technophobic debate reveals their dimensions—veritable tanks with legs.

"Thing is," Dirk says addressing Verner and the nasally Sentinel shuffling beside them, "Jerry-boy already done tried and failed..." Dirk, a shimmering echo-located composite, pats Verner. "Will give you three hundred if you help me out. Will buy you a pint, too. I just need someone to have my back when I drop this thing."

The nasally third voice ends the dialogue. "Shit, I'll take that beer. Whose blood is paying?"

"Shut the hell up, Henry," barks Verner. "Dirk—Dirk, what'd he try? Hey, Dirk! Jerry-boy failed what?"

"I thought I told you," Dirk responds, shifting into low gear. "Henry, didn't I tell the crew this mornin'?"

"Tell what, Dirk?" squawks the pitchy effeminate.

"Jerry-who?" asks Henry.

"Henry, pin your eyes, old son," Dirk says in a patronizing tone. He is the vocal authority and clearly the least retarded of the three. "If you're a sponge, don't ask what it is you're soaking…" There is a pause, and then a match-strike. More huffing. Dirk continues sonorously: "In answer to your question: Jerry-boy failed in a biblical sense most grave. Was sat down in front of the cube there, and he hears screaming. Suppose he thought someone climbed up the fire escape. Burglars'd come picking before. Maybe he'd thought it was them Reyes you were on about. Whatever he thought, he thought wrong. Goes up there and finds Alecia with her synth getting the ol' hydraulic push. Synth gets one bad look at Jerry-boy and apparently one was enough. Synth balls his fists, thinking Jerry-boy's gone mad—that he's going unplug him or hurt Alecia. The fanny-slammer might-of even figured Jerry-boy for a burglar. Poor Jerry-boy—a burglar in his own house, getting red-eyed by his wife's birthday present."

"I told him those things are no good."

"No good is right and good would have been the end of the tale, had this fanny-slammer not left Alecia there hollow to go and take a swipe at Jerry-boy. Only stopped punching when Alecia stepped in."

"You're lying," says Verner, resigned to using his actual voice, which is comparatively consistent and melodic.

"I'm not! Right hand to God."

"Larry-boy o-k?" Henry asks, as insincere as a politician turning maybes into yeses in a retirement home.

"Jerry-boy? Nuh. Alecia stepped in and fanny-slammer stepped down, but it was too late. I got the call 'round three, just as I's crawling up from the S'nth Circle. I go in. Place smells like shit—like that archie coven in Inglewood. Jerry-boy's off his last legs, and sat back in his chair in front of the cube. Bleeding all o'er the place. Blood everywhere, I tell you. Alecia's off her rocker, howling and shaking and talking about the stockades. I'm there holding Jerry-boy's jaw in place…And wouldn't you know it? That fanny-slammer is just standing there in the bedroom doorway, watching me with Jerry-boy's blood all over him. I swear to God, if he'd had the right parts, he'd be smiling."

"You shut it down?"

"Bloody bots, man," bellows Henry, likely ingrained with a pentabyte of BiAnima-programmed neural assistants and dressed in over three-hundred pounds of exosuit-articulated armour.

"That's the thing. I told yah I was late in for a reason. Or maybe I didn't...I'm holding him in, and Jerry-boy grabs a hold of me. Yanking like this on my neck, he goes, 'You put that iron man in the garbage, Dirk. You tear it apart.' No word of a lie, he said so and went white."

"Jesus! Jerry-boy's dead?"

"I was holding him in, Verner. I felt him die. I felt his worms shift. Smelled his spirit fill his pants."

"I gotta comm Dave. He's going to be beside himself...You tell the CO?"

"Nuh. Shoulda. I suppose I was just imagining I did so this morning."

"Yeah, I didn't know a Jerry till your yarn just now," says Henry, reifying his claim to being the worst of the worst.

"Then you two're the first," Dirk says, huffing away. "And I sure-as-hell know Alecia's not telling anyone."

"She's probably messed in the head now, yeah?"

"Vernie-boy. *More than you know*. The girl wouldn't let me destroy the synth. She wants to keep it."

"Dirk, you gotta do right by Jerry. You can't let that thing keep on turning the screw."

"I know, I know. I need a second gun, though."

Following the nasty backstory to another spent bullet, Oni clutches her Remington to her breast. "You're not having mine," she whispers. "Booky, you see anything?"

Gibson uplinks his findings directly to Oni's mind. *Independent CPUs all over the camp.* The frequency-flush and Booker's echolocation have not ferreted out any snipers, but have picked up dozens of WIFI bubbles. "Could be mines," Gibson says parsing through field inconsistencies. "Mini-turrets."

Oni projects her minimap ahead and zooms in to a cross section on the other side of the wall. "They're not grouped like mines...They're too close together." Reverting to her sonic vision, she scrutinizes the three hulking masses. "These chuckleheads aren't worried about being loud because they're not looking for anything. They're the first responders. The CPUs belong to motion sensors."

"I'll do it," yells Henry for all of MUD as witness, halting Oni and Gibson's productive Sherlockstep.

"I shouldn't, man," answers Verner.

"Please. Three-hundred bucks for a simple unplug. An extra fifty—call it hazard pay."

"I'll do it for free!"

There is no demand for Henry's supply.

Grinding his vocal chords for a confident tenor, Verner determines, "You've lost your nerve, Dirk. Next you'll be asking me to hold your part while you piss."

Dirk hems and haws. "Vernie…"

"Three hundred is fine," Verner replies, sounding like a worn-out timing belt. "We all loved Jerry. I'll be taking that three hundred, though. Running low on Can-E. Could use a little vacation…What d'ou wanna do about Alecia?"

Dirk slaps Verner on the arm once more. "Put her parts in the same bin as the fanny-slammer."

Henry pushes both Sentinels back. "Here am I, trying to help. Didn't realize you're on about nothin' but date night. Well, the two of you can piss right off." His oafish statement sweeps along the barrier, pronging Oni and Regan before dissipating.

The three dots migrate east.

Regan, attuned to Gibson and therefore the threat, mumbles beside Oni. Oni would console her if she was not so anxious herself.

"Alright," Gibson yells. "Go!"

The fugitives sprint through the gap in the wall. Dust and sand kicking about reveals several tripwire lasers tracking high and low across the penned field that lies between the fugitives and their objective: the compound under which the bunker lies undisturbed like some lesser-known Pharaoh's tomb. Oni and Regan scale over the chewed up concrete and immediately drop to their elbows and knees to avoid interrupting the first of several lasers tracing invisible outlines in the dark. The nearest beam, following some secret and ostensibly erratic pattern, drops as if set to trim all the grass that will never grow here again. It slices through the low-hanging particulate on a direct interruption course with Oni and Regan, who—although now flat against the earth—cannot rightly liquefy themselves to avoid detection.

"Tarnation! Booky, can you hack the source of the beam?" Oni grumbles into the sand pyramiding around her hands, lumpy with shell casings and teeth.

"Damn! No!" Gibson exclaims. "There's a firewall...You have to retreat. Retreat!"

Oni pulls Regan to her feet, turns, and prepares to make a mad dash, but glimpses light and quarrelsome voices emanating from the gap in the wall. It is the same patrol. Henry is still giving it to Dirk and Verner for excluding him. "Damn," Oni says, letting go of Regan's hand and raising her combat handgun.

Just feet short of symbolically beheading Oni, the laser beam and the others like it disappear.

"Something just took down the tripwires," Gibson says, surprised and scrolling through intel on the periphery of Oni's vision.

Regan tugs on Oni's free hand. "They'll reset soon."

"Right," Oni says, fighting a grin. *Nicely done, my little monster.* Pivoting into a sprint, Oni yanks the impromptu hacker along. "You're pretty handy when you want to be."

"Anything to get us to where we need to be," Regan says, although much of her meaning is lost between gasps and heavy exhalations.

# KUEBIKO

The bunker is a glorified storm cellar composed of blast-resistant concrete, coated on its interior with RF-shielding gels. Unlike other storm cellars crowded with jams, preserves, and stacks of holodiscs, Oni's bunker is lined with lead and centred by an Ovonic threshold device that can ground an EMP surge—especially important since MUD's last line of defense consists of an EMP and two-thousand pounds of explosives buried around the perimeter. The bunker's hatch, which opens to an eighty-rung ladder, is hidden behind a vertical-lift door, the exterior of which has been tiled and graffiti-ed to match the surrounding multi-stalled bathroom. *If one were ever to see a mob of people rushing the bathroom in a panic, it'd be reasonable to assume that either something horrible was about to take place or Booker Gibson was cooking again.* When Outland last came through, company men chewed their way through the compound, murdering and stealing. Thankfully, no one felt the need to steal porcelain or fossilized excrement, meaning the entrance to Oni's subterranean hideout was left unscathed.

Although it has been several months since MUD was last raided, the emergency lights in the compound are still humming. Oni and Regan move down a checkered hallway awash in diodic periwinkle and slick with drippings from the ceiling. In addition to feeding the puddles that trap the stalwart LEDs' light, the sprinkler system has farmed stalactites of mold. Shutting out nostalgia and treating familiarity as a traitor, Oni leads with her Remington, tugging Regan and Biff's granddaughter's shoes through the slime.

Something stirs at the end of the hallway. Noting no dots on her mini-map, Oni silently orders Regan to hold her ground, presuming the girl won't sink into the slime outright. With the safety off, Oni takes aim at the chimera's centre of gravity. She doesn't fire however, realizing the only agent afield is the wind, teasing a bloated corpse hanged by the neck. The corpse is neither mummified nor fully putrefied. Camp MUD's dank, chemical-laced atmosphere has deformed the body, covering him with a gelatin-like curd, which has grappled the rope all the way up to its knot on the support beam.

"Poor bastard," Oni eulogizes. Her Monocle beeps. Several dots appear on her map like aphids assaulting a cabbage leaf.

"No more sightseeing," Gibson says, sounding desperate. "Washroom's right around the corner. Grab Regan and go."

Privy to Gibson's warning, Regan scampers over to Oni.

Together, they rush into the women's washroom. The aphids devour more of Oni's minimap until they collectively bore a hole where the bacteria-masked body hangs.

Oni rushes to the last stall, pulls the toilet's flush handle outwards and cranks it clockwise. The rear shit-stained wall shakes dust and gook free, and recedes into the ceiling like a garage door, scrolling back all of the anti-corporate slogans and penile humor marked on the ceramic. Oni takes a step into the secret vault and juts out her hand blindly behind her, expecting five soft little digits to grab it. "C'mon, kiddo." She looks back—Regan isn't there. "Are you kidding me?"

Cussing and radio clicks outside the bathroom caution Oni not to call out for Regan. She exits the stall, and finds Regan staring at her reflection in the scuzzy and broken mirror. "We've got to go!" Oni hisses.

In awe of her own reflection, Regan tilts her head. "Lyle..."

Oni drags the little narcissist into the stall. Triggering the trapdoor, she accosts Regan: "Who's Lyle?"

Regan shrugs and casts a sightline down the dark well. The very idea of descending into the unknown shakes her like a leaf. Unnerved, she tries to fly past Oni who holds her tight, saving her from the trap-door-cum-guillotine. Finally acting her age, Regan motions to scream. Oni clasps the girl's mouth shut. "If you make a peep or go back out there, you will most certainly die. I will die. Gibson will die. And all of your friends..." Oni releases Regan.

Hiding her face in her hands, Regan muffles: "I *must* get to the Citadel to help my friends."

Oni caresses Regan's cheek. "You *must* get some sleep. With clear heads, we'll figure out our next steps together. Sound good?"

"Alright," Regan answers.

"She still wants to go to the Citadel?" Booker snarls over Oni's neural-net. "The girl's messed in the head."

Oni winks at Regan. *Shut up, Booky. You're not helping.*

The trapdoor finds its grooves in the floor and locks shut. Oni's Monocle shines green, but its luminosity is not enough to make any informative forays into the hole. With a buzz, she activates night vision and directs Regan's hands and feet onto the ladder, cramped by the bunker's snorkel lines. Sniffling, the Omnitype clambers down and ahead of her guardian.

Kneeling at the base of the ladder in suffocating darkness, Regan waits for Oni, whose prosthetic clicks each time it grips a rung. After an inconsistent beat, Oni drops beside Regan.

Panting, Oni takes a knee. "You alright?"

Regan doesn't respond. She doesn't need to. Her chattering teeth tell Oni all she needs to know, including the pleasing fact that there is a limit to her curiosity.

"Wait here," Oni says, grinning at the cruelty of the order. *Wait in this non-space. Watch out for Hades, dagger-toothed rats, and the perilous chasms all about you.*

Upon locating the generator, Oni turns off her night vision, and works off of touch and memory. The generator shrieks and judders as it powers on. A strand of lights blink, indicating the fuse box. She swipes at the switches. With a crunch, a dozen florescent lights flare.

The bunker is more of a war room than a refuge, but arguably one of the more cozy war rooms in the state. Sofa-less cushions litter the far side of the bunker by a stack of farmer's almanacs and religious texts, the latter likely smuggled down by Edmund. Several desks laden with computer spheres and printers are squeezed between the armory and the beds. The beds are arranged like a honeycomb and recessed into one wall. Reserve oxygen tanks arranged like spider eggs hang from the ceiling, except over the solitary toilet and shower, and over the centre of the room, where they've been cropped back to make room for the Ovonic threshold device, which penetrates the concrete all the way from the floor to the compound's ceiling. Not even Thor could shutdown or stifle this nervous centre. *Home, sweet home.*

Oni turns the manual air-exhaust crank until it starts to turn on its own, venting the stale air. The intake jutting out of the ceiling sucks up the air faster than the dust suspended in it, making the room look like its leaking grey. Fresh air, pulled down the drains in the bathroom and purified, cuffs Oni as she turns on the closest computer, teasing her bangs over her scarred, bald temple. She elects not to wait idly by while the computer hums, pulling celestial data for an update from the satellite array atop MUD's central compound. Instead, she tours the room's perimeter, running her finger along dusty cabinets and relics left over from the War. Her fingers stop at the edge of a less-degraded copy of the photograph that hangs in Gibson's apartment. This iteration has no sentimental value. It's a concealing canvas. Behind those worm-food avatars: Camp MUD's self-destruct interface. Saving herself time she might not have later, Oni unhooks the photograph and sets it down. Where her friends had been burned into gelatin and frozen in time, four red buttons now twinkle along with a fifth blue button. For each red button, topside there is a corresponding detonation ready to go, and for the blue button, electronic fallout assured for a mile in all directions. Oni sets a finger on each of the buttons, but fearing her body will betray her again, reels from the interface.

"Which bed is yours?" Regan asks, liberated from fear by the florescent lights, their ballasts ticking down to some distant gaseous explosion.

Permitting herself a moment of gaiety, Oni turns and laughs. "Why? You gonna steal my pillow?"

Regan starts goferring into the different bunks, muffling a giggle with each foray.

Oni tucks her Remington into her belt. "I'm onto you...Trying to find my chocolate stash?" Impressed with a big smile, she rushes Regan.

Alien to play or fun, Regan squeals and tries to evade Oni's tickling. Finding the contact benign, she gives up the fight and succumbs to uproarious laughter. Both women nearly suffocate on endorphins and relief.

"This one," Oni says, pointing to a bunk littered with loose pages on the second tier of the comb. She grabs a leaf and immediately recognizes the source: *Bulfinch's Mythology*. Paul had given it to her when she first had gone to work for the Outland Corporation. By the time she had moved to MUD, the book's backboard had come off, its pages had dyed yellow, and its binding had failed—but by then, Oni had already moved on to Edith Hamilton's volume, which pulled fewer punches when it came to the grisly details and glossed over weaker narratives. Stung by a desire to preserve her past, Oni—MUD's Persephone—gathers up as many of the glyph-speckled themes as she can, shuffles them into a deck, and steps back, giving Regan a lane into her cell. "It's all yours."

With Oni's help, Regan climbs into the cell and scrambles under the quilted cover. "Where are you going to sleep?"

Firing an exhausted look at the computer and the armoury, Oni leans into the honeycomb elbow-first and sighs. "First, Booky and I are going to figure out what to do tomorrow, then I'll sleep..." Eying the different bunks, she settles on one tiled with pictures of former MUD patients. "Right here. Gibson's nook, right below you."

Regan smiles and bats her heavy eyelids. "Okay, Oni. Will you wake me up when you get up?"

The other voices that usually possess Regan's focus must have already dozed off. If Oni didn't know any better, she'd believe that whatever is mixed in with the lead in these walls has exorcised Regan's demons or at the very least kept them at bay. "Absolutely." Oni mournfully flips Gibson's pillow.

"You built this place?" Regan asks as she snuggles deeper into the musty cover.

Proud of her fortress, hand sinking into Gibson's pillow, Oni nods. "Although Hex Akbari paid for it, back in the days where it seemed more like a nice idea and less like an absolute essential. I guess we always knew they'd come for us, eventually."

"Well," Regan says, struggling to lock her jaw after a big yawn, "I like it."

Rapping her titanium knuckles on the bunk frame, Oni agrees with a bright-eyed survey of the room. "Alright...Get some sleep. We have a big day tomorrow."

"You're taking me to the Citadel, right?"

Turning her back to Regan, Oni answers solemnly: "If there is a Citadel still left standing."

Leaving Regan disappointed in her cocoon, Oni traipses over and collapses into the chair facing the computer-sphere spitting out a weak projectile field. Through the slightly transparent projected interface, she can make out an old refrigerator she had overlooked when dismounting the ladder. Although too tired to eat, Oni considers the small rumbling stomach in her bunk. "Hey kiddo, want a bite to eat?"

Puggish snoring.

Crooking her back and pawing incautiously at the interface like a chimp a mirror left in the jungle, Oni tries to search for Akbari's details using a Minerva prompt. The computer's projected interface flashes an alert: "CANNOT CONNECT TO MINERVA." She tries again, and receives the same error, bereft of a problem log or explanation.

"Hey Booky—any idea why Minerva is still down? It'd be a godsend getting Akbari's dots and touching base ahead of jumping into the PIT again."

Booker's avatar materializes via Monocle. He is dressed in a pin-striped suit, straight backed and cutaneously flawless. "This place is just as I remembered it. Testament to a job well done…We sure made a great team, huh?"

"Still do. Any idea why—"

"In the event of a rain-out like the one we engineered, the AI connection-broker Minerva would be instrumental in assigning minds to their corresponding bodies and sending the relevant data to the right offline exocortices. If the existence of the archetypals is any indication, Minerva tried and failed, big time. In its final moments, I believe it reiterated all of its classifications via all the cypulchres, effectually crossing their wires and mulching the users' humanity."

Oni tries the search function again, quickly growing weary of Gibson explaining what she already knows, and even wearier of the possibility that he is feeding her an explanation straight out of her own memory. As she anxiously tries to find a darknet Minerva-alternate, she neglects her jacket's slow-slide up her arm. Her patchwork-flesh is exposed just long enough for it to catch on the edge of the desk. "Tarnation!" she cries, squeezing the lips of the wound together. As she looks around for something to hold them in place, she chastises Booker for a circuitous response: "You still haven't answered my question. What happened to Minerva?" There is a spool of detonating cord leftover from the perimeter explosives on the adjacent desk. She leans through the projection screen to grab it. Successful on the first attempt, she folds and breaks off a three-inch section of wire near the head, and tosses the spool away.

Rings appear over the Monocle interface, as if a rock were dropped into a puddle. "This is a conversation we should have in private."

Oni takes off her jacket and sets the pentrite cord along the mouth of her wound. With a lighter click, she sets the cord aflame. The instant flash offers a shock but no pain; it cauterizes all the local nerve endings before they can ping her thalamus. "Ugh…" Strangely, Oni feels as if a great itch has been scratched. She rends the belly of her undershirt, producing a strip of fabric, and wraps her wound, now nicely sealed. "This is as private as it gets."

Gibson strobes an image of Regan for Oni's benefit. "Turn on the Harpocrate jammer and we'll talk."

Oni obliges him and then returns to her seat. With a grunt, she knots the fabric around her wound. "What is going on with you, Booky?"

"Minerva's existence was predicated upon the CLOUD. There is no more CLOUD. I intercepted some encrypted-data back at Seal Beach—wasn't able to decrypt it until just recently. Oni, the archetypal hive mind? How they communicate? Minerva's search and guide algorithms appear to be mirrored in the back-and-forth."

Regan's snoring peaks.

Glancing over at Regan and lowering her voice, Oni beseeches Gibson for greater clarity. "Why are we jamming this conversation?"

Archived data streams over Oni's eye. "Well," Gibson says, marking his continued existence monosyllabically. "She's already shut me down once for a less damning accusation." Gibson presents Oni with a conspiracy-theorist's-corkboard-worth of circumstantial evidence. "Minerva wasn't shut down. Not officially, anyway. Its sentience cluster bounced around from cypulchre to cypulchre, likely for self-preservation. I count seven redirects before its signature was lost. There's no proof that it found a suitable landing or backup, and no indication Outland ordered its termination."

"Where does that leave us?" Oni prompts the desktop to tether the Net so she can pull some information—anything, really. The Harpocrate jammers fortunately don't block data pulled from the hard-line.

*NewsLink* springs to the front of several other windows, similarly overloaded with news and upgrade information. The main headline reads: "Titanic Terror: Serge Demidov, Dead to Rights." Demidov's derision crowds lesser stories: "Hermes to stay in port over LA indefinitely...Archetypal rights group silenced...Unexplained drone scans and Net data-pulls...Dark clouds popping up across Tri-Angeles county...Archetypal aggression at wireless routing stations across the Blue Zone and RIM..."

"Conjecture," replies Gibson. "I think Minerva wasn't about to give up on the CLOUD. That was its mandate after all, and AIs aren't exactly known for being passive. It imprinted itself on all of the rainouts, and when it came time to do or die, it did the unimaginable: it manifested itself in flesh. Incarnated as a child..."

There's cracking in Oni's shoulder—like a widget in a can of stout. She grips it, and spins in her chair, eyes-peeled for medical supplies. She spots three cases locked behind black wire along with the guns in the armory. Unconsciously trying to leave Booker's conspiratorial thinking behind, Oni starts over to the armory. Incredulous, Oni botches scripture: "Minerva became flesh and dwells among us?"

"Think about it: a little girl—likely the CLOUD's latest inductee—would be the perfect candidate to possess. She would have a malleable, plastic mind; an innocent appearance that'd secure sympathy and trust that neither age nor grizzle can endear."

Oni hunts down the medical kits in the armory. The best she can find is a generic version of Longdream, containing all of the name-brand's ingredients, except for the one that prevents nausea. She pops several tabs and stumbles back to the computer. "I guess it's possible. It would explain how and why she communicates with the archetypals...But why would she want to go to the Citadel?"

"I don't know. But the more important question we ought to be asking is: why would we want to save her?"

"God-damn-it." Oni slams the desk. "I don't want to make that call...All I want is to get you back and to get the hell out of this quicksand." She looks over at the bunks to make sure Regan is still asleep. A steady stream of snores confirms her wish. "If you want her dead so badly," Oni communicates over her subvocal comm, "Just take over my body. I know you can—it's the only explanation for those episodes I've been having...Take control and do what you have to, because I know I can't."

"Take over your body? I'd never. I'm not like Allen...Before— in the car? On the highway? Purely unmeditated; accidental. *You try* being a ghost some time. Not easy knowing your boundaries when you haven't walls."

"Booky..." Oni feels guilty for exposing a nerve.

"I know two heads are better than one and that I've overstayed my welcome." Booker's voice fuzzes. "But forget about you and me for just one god-damned second. We might have created the monster purring in your bunk. If you intend to spare it, you best know what its intentions are. Ask yourself: what would Minerva do? If it's so dead set on getting to the Citadel in one piece, chances are it's not going to help you find Akbari. But I will."

"She's just a girl..."

"We both know she's not." Gibson resumes his old and

genuine avatar, scars and all. "Synch Monocle up with the computer so I can track down Akbari, then get some sleep. We'll talk in the morning."

Oni tries to respond, but finds that Gibson has temporarily blocked incoming messages. She looks over at the adolescent burrito dreaming of God-knows-what, takes out her Remington, and murmurs to herself: "I'll do the right thing if I'm certain it is the right thing to do." She sets her gun on the desk, melts into the chair, shutters her eyes behind magenta lids, and begins to nod off.

Gibson's rapid searches strobe Oni's tired and broken body with secondhand light filtered through images, words, and constructs appearing and disappearing too quickly to be intelligible to anyone reading slower than an editorial bot. On the precipice of slumber and disturbed by a variation in the light, Oni looks up to see a crime-scene image of Dr. Paul Sheffield's remains in the Citadel pulsing on the screen. *A symbolic body sourced by a bodiless symbol.* The image slides offscreen and the data blur resumes. "Could have used his help," Oni murmurs as she closes her eyes again, sure that Gibson can hear her. "But so long as we work together, we won't need it."

## MUD

Oni takes measured steps down a skunky, smoke-filled hallway. Her progress is painless. A quick self-inspection provides a good explanation: all of her meat has been forgone in favour of metal. Joining her prosthetic arm at the shoulder is a surrogate body, composed of magnesium alloy, silicon carbide ceramics, and heavplast. As opposed to buckling to body dysmorphia, she takes advantage of her post-human strength and jogs towards the source of all the smoke: an ornate archway enclosing a large glass door. Jets of greyish black issue from the door's seams.

Oni opens the door effortlessly. A plume of Brillo-like smoke clears the room, drifts past her, and—in a flash-freeze—turns to black granite, plugging the hallway. *Guess there's no going back…* Standing on the threshold, Oni peers lengthwise at a long, unblemished rectangular room. Two champagne-coloured mirror pools frame a gold path that runs from the minimalist wet bar on the far left all the way to the cross-like window on the right, the bottom of which is obfuscated by a presidential desk branded with the Outland Corporation's "O" and a deck on stilts. *Winchester's office.*

A silhouetted figure, gaunt and hunchbacked, sits at the desk, vibrating as if someone had turned down his framerate and arbitrarily cut a few frames to make his few, subtle gesticulations especially jarring. On the other side of the desk, nearest Oni, lean-sits a dishevelled man, smoking a cannaberette and juggling a shrunken head with one hand. The shrunken head—whose identity Oni can't quite make out—is caught and tossed to the beat of a corrupted Molly Case song. Case's warbled voice and detuned guitar accompaniment arise from the mirror pools, which cone and pump the sound into the office. Were the pools not so active, they might reflect the vinyl B-side hovering above them, pricked by an armless needle. "Scouring fields of dead men sleeping," Case croons, "Take the tongue on which the curse still rests…"

The remaining smoke diffuses and the music hushes to a hum as Oni enters. "Hello," she says, warily.

The seated silhouette doesn't react, but the lean-sitting man stands upright. He catches the shrunken head and pockets it, and takes two long strides into the crosslight, revealing himself to Oni. *Dr. Paul Sheffield.* With a face-splitting grin, he ashes his joint, kills it with a stomp, and yells out: "Oni! Good God! You're a sight for sore eyes!"

He hurries over and tries to embrace Oni, but she throws up her fists, refusing both his touch and his existence. "Relax!" He proclaims, taking a step back. "It's me: Paul."

Despite all of her new gadgetry supplanting redundant flesh, capillaries, and innards, Oni can still apparently cry. She wipes tears from her face with dorsal steel.

Paul gives Oni room, but leaves his arms outstretched. "It's okay."

Against her better judgment, Oni accepts the hug. "I thought you were dead."

"Ooomph," Paul blurts, crimpling in Oni's powerful embrace. Liberating himself from Oni's clutches and taking a step back, he laughs. "The only thing that could kill me is another one of those hugs."

Overwhelmed, Oni drops her head. "Where have you been?" she asks, directing her question at his tattered sweat-yellowed shirt. Before he can answer, Oni blurts out: "It's been so bad, Paul. *Booker and I…*"

"I know…I know," Paul responds. His tired eyes, ringed purple, report more than sympathy; they indicate understanding. He reaches into his pocket, but what he produces isn't the shrunken head from before but rather a green-striped delayed-grenade. With impish fluidity, Paul tosses the grenade and catches it, making Oni's heart—or whatever her mechanical equivalent she has now—flutter.

"Paul! Careful!"

Shaking his head, Paul corners the nearest mirror pool and begins pacing along its rim. The vinyl record stops spinning and dissolves midair, permitting the water's surface to calm. Although calm, it doesn't reflect Paul or even hint at a presence at its edge. "Booker Gibson should have been careful," he says, solemnly. As if seized by the gravity of the declaration, he catches the grenade and stops. "You know he's dead, don't you? That voice in your head is nothing but a glitch—a digital ghost as inhuman as an AI and as ruthless as the little girl you're shepherding over to the epicentre of the apocalypse."

"No. *You're wrong*," Oni yells out. "Celeste is holding Booker captive. I *will* save him."

"You'll die. Just give the General want he wants—give him justification to clear your name, and then get out of here." The borders of Paul's irises fail, and glossy black overspreads his bloodshot whites.

"I followed you until your end. Now I have to find mine. I'm taking the lead on this, and I know I can succeed. I will find Booky, and I will do what you couldn't: I'm going to bring down Outland."

Paul primes the grenade, and turns abruptly. "I did what I set out to do. I saved my girls. That's all that matters."

Antsy about debating revisionist histories around a primed grenade, Oni leaves Paul at the poolside and heads over to Winchester's desk, halved by the tangerine light nailed through the cross-like window. The hunchbacked silhouette seated at the desk doesn't enjoy any more detail or clarity closer-up than he did faraway. Oni points at the specter, and looks to Paul for elucidation. "Who's this?"

"I was planning on asking you that very question," Paul replies.

Turning to the silhouette, Oni winces. The shadowy figure morphs—its shoulders narrow; its back straightens; its misshapen head shrinks; and its jaw becomes pointed. A splash of white drips from the specter's crown down over its face, onto its chest, and along its arms. The white differentiates into other colours, which blend and conquer the silhouette's contours.

Troubled by the inexplicable transformation, Oni retreats midway to Paul. "We should get going."

"Don't think I can, Oni. But don't let me stop you. This is my Alamo, not yours."

Where sat an amorphous shade now sits Celeste Charming, beaming her Chiclet smile. Grinding her chair back, she clears room to stand, and does so, straightening her skirt and brushing invisible dandruff off her shoulders. Circumnavigating the desk, Charming raises an eyebrow and looks past Oni, emblazoned with surprise. "I thought for certain you'd have brought me the Omnitype." She shrugs. "No Omnitype? No deal. No deal, no more Booker Gibson."

There is a loud buzz. Two bulky Buke mechs decloak on either side of Celeste. As their glittery concealer retreats, Katajima's samurai design is unveiled, armoured buckle by buckle. The Bukes make the room feel a lot smaller, and their white-blue electroblades seem to charge the air.

Celeste points at Paul, and cants a telling look to the Buke on her right.

"Paul, watch out!" Oni cries.

Although neither a shout nor a volley is fired, Paul contorts around a gruesome wound. He falls to his knees, gut rearing its snakelike bends through his shirt.

Frozen with fear, Oni glances up from her shredded friend to the Buke bot Celeste had signalled. The barrels of its minigun begin to spin. It takes a step forward, green ocular-plate beaming at Oni and her mentor. Celeste snaps her finger, bidding the Buke open fire. Contrary to her will, the Buke standing guard on her left raises its own minigun and fires at its twin just before it can fire on Oni. One-hundred-rounds-per-second of hot tungsten pelt the green-eyed Buke. It stumbles back, ocular plate flickering, torso engulfed in fire. Despite the damage, it raises its electroblade to fend off its twin's advance, but the defensive gesture is too late: the disloyal Buke spears it with a blade, and tears it in two.

"What do you think you're doing?" Celeste shrieks, scampering away from the disloyal Buke, ocular plate beaming red.

The red-eyed Buke smashes past the desk. Celeste falls onto her face. Futilely trying to pull herself forward, she looks up at Oni in terror. The Buke gets a hold of her. Celeste grunts in a low and ape-like tenor. As a red pleat runs the circumference of her neck, she looks Oni dead in the eyes and promises: "This world will be mine." Before she can continue, her head departs her neck and hits the Outland insignia engraved in the desk, sluicing it with globs of arterial blood.

Winchester's office dims. Massive bites appear in the pillars. Rebar and concrete form islands in the mirror pools.

The red-eyed Buke stands its ground beide the impromptu corporate altar. Sensing a break in the violence, Oni runs to Paul's side. His ruptured body is losing form like a red popsicle left on a summertime sidewalk.

"Paul!" shrieks Oni, trying to whisk Paul back into shape, rapidly losing definition and sprawling across the floor. "What's happening?"

Although nothing more now than a pinkish-red laminate, his two-dimensional eyes lock onto Oni. Lips, stretched to such an extreme as to make late-Picasso out to be a realist, flap confidence: "I am so proud of you, Oni. You are a good person and a better friend..." Paul's features begin to harden like drying candlewax. "Take care down there. Over and out." Feet away, five digits gripping a delayed grenade jut out of the skin-like extension of this Pauline fresco. The thumb depresses the trigger.

Oni, keen to avoid the fireworks but stricken with grief, struggles to stand. She slips along the skin masking the floor, and breaks the surface. Sinking into this porridge of gore and scrambling to hold onto something to keep her afloat, she claws at the blotchy membrane.

"Matsui," booms a low, gravelly voice.

A hand appears. Eyes blurred by gore, she can barely make out the face, but knows innately that it's Gibson. She grabs his hand, and he pulls her to Paul's fringe.

"Just look at me," says Gibson, gripping her tightly. "Just look at me."

Although frantic, Oni trains all of her focus on Gibson. Although his body is still a blur, his face clarifies. Nebulaic brown eyes, scars from their time together, and older scars from the times he cannot remember. The more she focuses on him, the less hectic the scene feels to her. Despite the viscera all around her, the hissing electronics strewn about the place, and the semisweet perfume of death riding up her nostrils, Oni can't help but feel a sense of serenity.

Winchester's office erodes and crumbles around them as if Cronos targeted the foundations and turned the clock forward two-hundred years. Chirping birds offset the slow crunch of the bukes' disintegrating parts. Lilies of the valley sprout up where before there was only blood. No longer in the Citadel, Gibson helps Oni, naked with metal parts replaced by silky-smooth organics, to her feet in a bucolic meadow.

Determining this to be a dream, Oni masks her floating self-projection in shiny leggings and the Yankees t-shirt Gibson lent her after she performed surgery on Kadin Akbari back in Camp MUD. Whether by his own doing or Oni's, Gibson's body takes shape as if an invisible blacksmith was pouring molten man into an unstable mold. "Did you fall from Heaven?" he quips.

"Booky!" Oni grabs his hands. "God, I miss you."

Gibson caresses Oni's cheek. "I hope you don't mind my intervening. You were having a bad dream."

Too overwhelmed to speak, Oni pulls Gibson's arms around her and buries her face in his chest. She barely makes out: "Hold me," as she strives to merge with her virtual friend.

Gibson rubs the small of Oni's back reassuringly and rests his head on hers. "I'll hold you together on the inside, but you got to hold together on the outside. Matsui, *you've got this.*"

Looking up at Gibson as she remembers him, Oni fills her imagined lungs full of imagined air. "You were right…about Regan. I think we should go to the Chrysalis, set Outland up to fall, and then hand the Omnitype over to General McCabe. When McCabe goes after Celeste, we'll get our hands on your body."

"Not like you to concede to me…" Gibson gently pushes Oni back. "I'll chock it up to dreamer's acquiescence."

"I wouldn't know where to begin—to fix her, I mean. Maybe the Military can exorcise her demons."

Gibson laughs. "With holy water or by waterboarding her?" Seeing the cruelty of his comment made manifest by Oni's worry-lines, Gibson presents an olive branch. "McCabe had Regan for a few months and they got nowhere. His interest in securing her is purely to drop Charming. We can fake Regan's death; send a barren shuttle back to Celeste loaded with explosives. Akbari can help us with that. Whatever happens with the girl, our primary focus ought to be on clearing your name and getting you out alive—"

"And restoring you to your handsome self." Oni sneaks a kiss and perseverates on Gibson's bottom lip."

"I've got to admit: I wouldn't mind trying that again in the flesh." Gibson smiles, but something in the distance captures his attention. His eyes gloss over, and then reset. "Unless you want to torture yourself with some more bad dreams, we should get a move on."

"I don't know what I'd do without you, Booky."

"Likewise. Now, wake up."

# FOUNDATION OF ALL ACTIONS

Oni tidal-waves forward, nearly butting her head into her knees. Monocle indicates it is early morning, and quantifies what little REM sleep she managed—no more than a couple of hours, but a couple of hours no less. In addition to making her co-piloted dreams particularly lucid, the generic Longdream pills she popped have also eased tension around her neck. Nothing, she decides, can make her comfortable in her own skin, but she is grateful to have at least found something to manage the excruciating jolts of pain in her shoulder and lower back. Still seated, she pops another two Longdreams, pockets the remainder, and stretches.

Checking the computer before her, now dormant—Gibson having likely absorbed all of the data worth wiping—she spies a few cached headlines: "Nonviolent archetypals now targets of statewide arrests...Grand AI jury hands down death sentence to Serge Demidov...Benny Bass murder trial recessed; Attorney Lyle Badegger reported missing...Olympus base to be repurposed...Russian Emperor announces new asteroid-tethering initiative..."

Looking over to Regan, still snug in her bunk, Oni tries to hail Gibson. "You get an exact location for Hex Akbari?"

After a fuzzy pause, Gibson's avatar appears coinciding with a deluge of direct neural-net uploads. Oni's eyes dilate and race side to side as she assimilates the data. "Bullshit," she says, throwing her hands forward in disbelief.

"Several trusted sources confirmed it. Kadin Akbari killed Bahram and Hex. The middle brother, Ank, has gone into hiding outside the Parisian Dead Zone."

"Timing couldn't have been worse," Oni says, scrutinizing an over-iris graphic of Kadin—the mind she saved for the body his father made.

"This report is three months old." Gibson shrugs his virtual shoulders. "Could very well be a ploy to get the government off the Akbaris' backs or to flush out previously-silent rivals."

"Damn!" Oni picks up her Remington and jams it under her belt. "Regicidal or not, Kadin still owes us, *big time*..." She heads over to the armoury and begins dressing for war, but discovers it's all guns and no ammunition. She nevertheless takes a bandolier full of Remington-compatible rounds and an armoured vest. *The essentials.*

"And if he won't help us?" Gibson asks, busy helping Oni

optimize her loadout with micro-waypoints.

Oni whips a shell-casing Regan's way, eliciting a weary peep. "Kiddo! Get up. I want you to eat something. Use the bathroom. *Get ready*...I'm going upstairs to figure out the best way out of here. I'll be back shortly."

Gibson persists. "Oni...What if he doesn't help us?"

"Then we're going to have to help ourselves."

The bunker burps as the hatch door closes behind Oni. She dashes out of the washroom, down the hall, past the lynched Jello pudding, and up the stairwell, in search of a vantage point on the Rift path.

Gibson scans the camp for Sentinels. There are several aphids on the minimap, but spread out. His scan's only disconcerting revelation is a cluster of red on MUD's northern perimeter.

Climbing the stairs, and already out of breath, Oni mulls over Gibson's findings. "How many is that?"

"The group to the north? Can't say. At least thirty."

"Crap," Oni says, taking pause at the summit before the third floor.

"Probably best to stay off the roof, if you're going for a look-see. Could try the command centre. Even if all of the computers are inoperable, there's still a good view of the PIT."

Oni silently agrees, and hooks a left at the top of the stairs. Unlike the lower floors, the third floor shows no signs of water damage. Conversely, the walls are fire-licked; shiny, striated, and black. Passing rooms full of ash, Oni shuts out her concern over her former patients who'd likely been cremated alive.

"Last door on the right," Gibson says patronizingly, throwing a waypoint up via Monocle.

The compound's architect sighs. "No kidding." She strides up to the door, but halts in the frame.

After the tent headquarters outside had been compromised by vandals and thieves, Oni and Edmund had relocated the command center to the third floor. It was a nervous system of computers, server terminals, patient records, and medical texts. Whatever it was is no longer. Windows shattered. Desks burnt to feeble skeletons. Projection spheres melted down to their quantum cores.

"Matsui—forget it. This room's been structurally compromised," Gibson lies.

Raising her Remington, Oni loiters into the room. Creosote squeals under her every step. Morning light cuts through the divots in the wall where fire had broken out, highlighting a substantial body fused to the frame of a swivel chair. Tears well up in Oni's eyes, nearly blinding her and preventing her from confirming the horror seated before her.

"C'mon, Matsui. Get out. Leave! For God's sakes—get out!" Gibson's voice whooshes over Oni's internal comm with unprecedented intensity.

Oni inches closer to the chair, deaf to Gibson and to any thought except the one line of denial running on loop in her head—*it can't be*...Gently, she tugs on the shoulder of the chair and twists it around, extorting snaps, crunches, and a small cloud of ash from the chair's occupant. Oni's eyes report what some censored and ignored part of her heart already knew. She stumbles into the desk and dry heaves. *Booky*...

Booker Gibson's body sits at his final post, statuesque and charcoaled. With his own eyes he saw a world free of Winchester. With his own eyes, he witnessed a passing moment where the Outland technocracy was destabilized. With his own eyes, he watched the Californian sunset gild a brave new world—a new age; one just as swiftly won in blood then lost with a keystroke. And now, through Oni's eyes, he sees plainly the result of standing up to tyranny.

Winchester's mist had not yet settled when Celeste took command, and her first command was to destroy all that stood in the way of her painstakingly-crafted mandate, Gibson included. Shot and immolated, most likely in that order; Gibson's lower jaw has mainly dissolved, and what remains hangs onto his shattered visage by tissue-paper strands of calcified sinew. His hand, severed by Oni's graceful turn of the chair, is fused to the exocortical emulator he used to hastily upload his mind. The emulator is covered by scorch marks suggestive of a surge or an interruption—he must have been killed while in the process of completing his data transfer. One of the two chalices brimming with his sentience was shattered, and what wasn't splashed went straight to Oni's spine.

Oni, recipient of his final message and its massive attachment, hyperventilates. Shock insulates her against the reality of the ruin around her, and she ponders on the bigger picture. She wonders if any of this has been worth it and what good saving this city is when,

"Everyone I know is dead or gone…"

Silence on the comm. No word from Gibson. Just static.

Oni can barely make out her friend's burnt and mummified remains through her tears. The worst and most stinging emotions vie for the chief residency in her heart, but she resists her grief and her humanity, immediately putting all of her energy into cooking up a contingency plan. "This is not your end if you don't want it to be. We will get you a body, Booker." Having lived a second life as a virtual referee, she considers a digitized life with Gibson. "This means nothing…I'm not going to lose you twice."

"For God's sakes, Matsui. Look at it! Look at me!" As if broadcasting over a bad frequency, Gibson's voice pitches and warbles. "Look, God-damn-it! I'm a briquette."

Kneeling at the feet of this inert vessel whose contents slosh about in her brain, Oni mutters: "It's not over. Not before we get a chance to start…" Oni's fingertips hover over Booker Gibson's melted fat—over the leather jacket now one and the same with his burnt flesh.

Gibson's avatar appears over Oni's iris. He has abandoned his traditional contours, and now appears as an anthropomorphic cloud. "Charming—*that evil bitch*. She played you, Oni. She played us. She knew all along about me, and if she didn't, she knew you didn't know that she didn't know. Damn it."

"We'll get her."

"No. This is it for me. I can't…What am I now? *Oh Jesus!* What the hell am I, Matsui?"

"Relax! It's okay!" Oni's chest tightens. Her diaphragm locks and white adrenalin crops out her peripheral vision. She stumbles, eyes still locked on the body in the chair. "You're my best friend, and you're not going anywhere. Not until we follow through with the plan and make sure that bitch burns."

Gibson's nebulous avatar fizzles out.

"Don't you leave me, Booker Gibson," Oni screams, addressing Gibson' mind but wetting his body. "You're not done yet…We transplanted a mind once before. It's Providence that we should have the experience to do what needs being done and the friends to help us do it."

Without visually linking over Monocle, Gibson's voice discredits Oni's wishful-thinking: "Akbari spent a fortune to make sure we were successful, and he only did it because it was his son's life on the line. No one's breaking the bank to help me beat the reaper."

"We'll try anyway. And if we fail..." Grasping at straws, Oni suggests the first alternative that comes to mind: "Then I'll synchronize too. A dark CLOUD somewhere. Explore together, you and I. Wouldn't be so bad, right?" Oni's desperation causes her voice to waver. Gibson knows as well as her that the both of them could not possibly survive without an anchor in the real world. And even with an anchor, two boats attached would surely grind against one another until one or the other or both sank.

"I won't leave you Matsui," Gibson concedes, resuming his avatar. "Not until we've destroyed Outland. O-K?"

"And after?"

Gibson brandishes an impossibly-perfect set of teeth, some modicum of confidence restored by Oni's presumption of success. "Afterwards we'll return to this conversation. I love you, Matsui...but I won't spend my life in your head, especially when minutes feel like hours and hours days with this computing power. I'd be a mess the entire time."

Sniffling over a pout, Oni focuses on Gibson's avatar. "Are you giving me the 'it's not you, it's me' bit?"

Still smiling, Gibson answers back: "Oh, are you kidding? *It's definitely you*. Couldn't stand another week of your optimism or that mythology bullshit."

With strength returning to her legs, Oni stands. She wipes the tears from her face, and leans over Gibson's charred remains. Placing her hands on his shoulder, Oni bows her head. "We should bury Hercules, here..."

"Not a chance. I can't begin to tell you how little moving around a bit of soot should matter to either of us. Scan the Rift trail, grab the girl, and let's get going." Gibson pulls a bulleted summary of his Net findings and introjects it for Oni's benefit. "There is so much virtual noise coming out of the PIT, it's hard to determine what is worth listening to. Looks like the only way to the Chrysalis' top half is by way of the old monorail."

"So we go to the Marion," Oni says, rushing to set a waypoint via Monocle before Gibson.

# A RESURRECTION TO DIE FOR

Harry Tuttle's biometrics permitted Lyle to pass through the Citadel lobby and into the elevator bank without question or hindrance. For all of Outland's paranoia, the company has yet to lock down the basics. If a maniac and a neurobiologist were able to waltz in, kill the CEO, and destroy the company's biggest cash cow so easily, *why wouldn't I be able to pull some data undetected?* And so Lyle traipses across the threshold, past the twin winged pyramids and a battalion of Sentinels and mechs set to kill for profit and for fun.

Inside the elevator, Lyle finds himself reflected in the well-polished chrome doors. A look of satisfaction runs across his face and likewise across his simulacrum. The blue-eyed siren's residual hum pains him, though it is not enough to chip away at his resolve.

Recalling specifics from Harry Tuttle's testimony, Lyle mouths "Sixty-seven" and hits the corresponding button on the elevator's interface. Immediately, two Mosquito drones drop from the ceiling and dart over to Lyle, intent on scanning his eyes. Lyle growls under his breath, irked that he should evade the notice of seven-hundred Sentinels and then find judgment at laser's end.

The Mosquitos, like any low-level drug trafficker, are not at all concerned with how the key has made its way to them, but instead with the quality of the key. Lyle hurriedly procures a small gel container from his jacket pocket, and pries it open with steady hands. Blood runs out of the case in rivulets. Tilting it to curb the flow, Lyle rolls the case's primary contents up for inspection. He closes his eyes so as not to provide multiple keys to the insectoid gatekeepers and holds up the case like some holy offering. The Mosquitos descend on the token, scanning it every which way. Signalling their appeasement with a coordinated beep, the little drones dart back into the elevator's coffers. Harry Tuttle's blind eyes see neither their own worth nor Lyle's contentment. So too, like the drones they deceived, Tuttle's eyes disappear back into their case. The elevator rocks, assured that its occupant is truly a company man—a high-ranking scientist, no less— and zooms skyward towards Lyle's answers and his potential cure.

Lyle, disguised only in principle—naked and honest in every sense that matters to a spy—grinds his teeth in anticipation of his destination. Harry Tuttle promised an answer in the form of a personal tablet behind lock and key in his office, opposite Neuro-Sci Lab Thirteen. Although he is under no illusion that the answers he seeks will be an easy get, he is confident he can deceive a few Outland scientists, heads ballooned and minds absent.

The elevator doors open, bisecting Lyle's chrome likeness. A low-ceilinged hallway stretches out for a quarter mile. Unlike the executive levels, polished and luxurious and pristine, level eighty-one is exactly the kind of station you would expect from busy eggheads and rogue droids. Cartons, wires, battery packs, and chairs litter the way. White lab coats, staggered along the passage, appear to overlap like feathers in a dove's wing, without of course the unifying factor of the bird or a pattern. Somewhat discouraged by the shithole he mistakenly presumed to be a high-arched, white-marbled temple to science, Lyle grumbles under his breath, and strides down the hall.

A feather flutters in his peripheral. "Excuse me..."

Lyle stops, turns, and angrily blurts: "What is it?" Nothing speaks to a sense of belonging like unmitigated angst and contempt for one's fellow workers.

The scientist hampering Lyle is a large-chinned woman with white wisps woven into her jet-black hair. She is unshaken by Lyle's irascibility. Holding out a tablet depicting the Citadel's insides, she runs her finger aimlessly up and down the blue and white maze. "Do you know where R25 is?"

Lyle rolls his head to the side, popping cartilage and shaking the hum about in his head as if it is a jarred bee. *There really is no excuse to pester a clearly-occupied coworker.*

"R25?" she says, desperately. "Where are they moving you? Everyone is being moved around. They're clearing out the entire floor. I wonder if they're downsizing...Just outrageous."

Interest piqued, Lyle jumps in. "Clearing the entire floor? Why?"

She emotes gracelessly, surprised by Lyle's sudden interest. Recovering from her apparent spasm, she takes a good look at Lyle.

Lyle diverts her attention: "R25 is on the twenty-fifth floor, is it not?"

"With legal?"

Face flushed red, Lyle sieves the vitriol that feels natural. "I didn't make the call. Take it up with the...the—"

"The Board?" The scientist rescues Lyle, preventing him from demonstrating the extent to which he does not belong. "Apparently it is not open for discussion. All I know is that the Neuro-Sci labs are full of machinery I neither ordered nor signed off on, and all of a sudden, I'm headed to where legal used to be planted."

"It is a mad house."

"Twenty-fifth floor?"

Lyle notices black amidst all the white, coming his way. *Sentinels*. "Yeah. Good luck to you."

"Gertrude…Doctor Gertrude Epner."

"Good for you," Lyle says, distractedly. He drops his gaze, distorts his face with a look of vexation (hoping to confuse the Sentinels' facial scanners), and hurries past them in the direction of Harry Tuttle's office.

"Oi! You! Stop!" bellows one of the Sentinels.

Lyle ignores the aggressive summons, and comms Dorota. Unfortunately, the Citadel permits no communications directed out of the building. "For crying out loud," he whispers. His subvocal mic picks it up, and renders it god-like over Monocle. Lyle begins his tirade in advance of turning to address Celeste's not-so-secret police. "I have work to do, god-damn-it!" Spun around, Lyle realizes he should have kept walking.

The Sentinels are giving a lab tech a rough time. One grips the pasty-skinned skeleton-of-a-man by the neck, holding in his other a holographic projector. "Does this belong to you?"

"N-n-no! I didn't—I didn't think…"

"That's right. You didn't." Despite the vocal modulator, the Sentinel nevertheless manages a snarl. "Take this worm down to Infractions." He hands over his captive to his comrades, and glares at Lyle, seemingly disembowelled—head drooping over a concave-shaped torso. "The hell you looking at? If you don't have someplace to be, I'll have no problem finding someplace to putchah…"

Reinvested with hope and compelled by a powerful flight response, Lyle nods to the high-mileage power-tripper and scurries towards Tuttle's office.

## THE STRONG GO TO THE WALL

Dressed in a long-sleeve shirt, which might as well be a Scottish plaid, a clean, clear-eyed, and relieved Regan spins in the computer chair.

Oni takes a breather at the base of the ladder, and looks over to the adolescent blur, giggling having rediscovered the joys of centrifugal force. "Ready, kiddo?"

"Are we going to the Citadel?"

Tightening the straps on her ballistic vest, Oni saunters over to the Ovonic threshold device centering the room. With her plan of escape still germinating, she strokes the metal wiring. "Hmm."

"Oni?" whines Regan, impatiently.

"No," Oni says, quickly turning her attention from the Ovonic threshold device to the dusty outlines of the team photo bordering the home-defense panel. "We're going to the Chrysalis. Charming will send for you. Akbari will ensure the transaction goes smoothly."

Regan tries to ferret her hands out of her long sleeves, drooping ever-so wizardly. "I can't tell if you are being honest."

Gibson chimes in: "She can't get a read off me and your mediated thoughts with the Harpocrate jammers running."

*Heh.* Subvocally, Oni responds: "We're going to kill whoever they send, return their ship to them an explosive present, destroy Outland, and then figure out to do with the girl. Maybe the Military can fix her, after all."

"You'll make sure I get to the Citadel, Oni?" Regan's eyebrows circumflex; she blinks as if desperately trying to jerk some crocodile tears.

"Charming will make sure you get to the Citadel." Oni subvocally instructs Gibson to partition his comprehension and memory of the plan to avoid agitating Regan. She caresses the four red buttons on the home-defense panel, and asks: "We still have activity on the northern perimeter wall?"

Prefaced by a glitched apparition of the minimap over Monocle, Gibson takes ocular stage. He has maximized the resolution of his avatar. He's wearing his scars. The astounding level of accuracy and detail on them speaks to his pride and to something more. People mark, tribute or showcase their achievements in different ways. A name on a building. A diploma on a wall or medals pinned to one's chest. Booker lost his mementos and with them his ability to remember with any certainty or with any proof any character-building or -testing moment in his life before MUD. After Outland wiped his mind, the only real connection he had with his past were his scars—raised pink reminders of his perseverance and his strength. *It's meat that gets cut and it's a soul that gets scarred.* Every scar: a pyramid for a victory or tombstone for a lesson learned. He has no more meat to spare, but still has the soul. These markers of good deeds and bad mistakes are marked on his spiritual flesh. Inked in the virtual, Booker showcases them because he is ready to add one more pyramid to the collection. "Forty-two hostiles or thereabouts. They must have found the body of the Sentinel you brained…They must think we're on the periphery."

"Fantastic. They'll be looking for a timid entrance. Let's make a spectacular exit."

"Oni," Gibson says gravely. "The electromagnetic fallout is going to mess me up."

"You're shielded. The Ovonic device is going to sap it… And anyway, the Outland surgeons protected Monocle."

"Great…But I'm not based out of Monocle. Just trust me on this one. The fallout won't take me out, but just be ready for anything."

"A warning our friends upstairs could use right about now." An unmistakably malevolent jolt of utilitarian determination overcomes Oni. The end justifies the means, and the means are apocalyptic. She hits all four buttons, and with a devilish smile, smashes the blue fifth. *Charon's going to be busy.* She strides over to Regan and grabs her by the arm. Together they rush over to the ladder. Commanding Regan's attention, Oni gives her marching orders: "When we get topside, there's going to be a lot of fire and a lot of smoke. You hold onto my hand, and don't let go."

Zealously shaking her head, Regan paws Oni's stomach. "I won't."

Bang. The bunker shakes fiercely four times in succession. The explosions are slightly muffled, but even a deaf man could hear them. Silt rains down from the ceiling, and unrestrained personal affects leap out of the bunks. Regan silently pleads for Oni to do something with a terrified stare, but Oni's attention is honed up the ladder. There is a brief moment of silence following the fourth explosion. A tinny screech prefaces the fifth explosion, which sounds more like a crunch than a boom. After the fireballs and the electro-magnetic pulse, whatever isn't dead on the surface doesn't have reception to call for help.

"You still with us?" Oni pleads inwardly.

"Darn. I may not have a body, but I feel nauseous as hell. One day you'll have to explain why and how." Gibson's voice is distorted and his avatar is fractured; shards of him report from different parts of the screen. "You know all of Outland is about to come down on us hard," Gibson says, rethinking the carpet bomb Oni's just unrolled. "If we don't make the Rift trail in five minutes, our chances aren't good…"

Oni lifts Regan up onto the bottom rung. "What else is new?"

"Just giving you the facts." Gibson's avatar conquers the confusion and materializes in professorial fashion, wearing an elbow-patched blazer and thick-rimmed glasses, scars still featured prominently. "I'm going to study all the specs I pulled on the Chrysalis and lay low for awhile."

"Don't go too far," Oni replies out loud. It seemed funnier before divorcing her tongue.

A vortex of smoke, ash, and sand rakes the compound. Covering her mouth and wincing to keep debris out of her eyes, Oni cuts through the blackish-orange dust with Regan lagging beside her like a flat-tired sidecar. Flat tire aside, Regan's pace is surprisingly competitive for an adolescent of her size, but then again, she's not an ordinary adolescent, and her size has little to do with her capability, especially in this new world of vatted brains and airborne minds.

They cross the field where MUD's clinic once stood—now nothing more than a sad fair of crooked tent poles and loose green fabrics. The wet earth beneath their shoes sucks like marshland. *There's no sewage or water on this side of the compound.* Oni takes a closer look. The marsh is comprised of former foes. She spies a Sentinel helmet with a tree-like configuration of veins, spinal fragments, and guts flowing outwards. *Must have been just inside the blast radius. Any closer and there'd be no trace of him. Good riddance.*

The flag pole at the head of the Rift trail extends into the billowing nebula. Its colors are hidden beyond the black inverted waves, lapping against an invisible ceiling ten-or-so-feet above the ground. The sound of the obscured flags flapping is as good a geomarker as the pole itself, providing Oni with needed direction—especially crucial with her minimap distorted by residual interference from the EMP.

Instead of taking the route that had once led her to Booker Gibson, Oni detours into a tunnel that connects with the derelict warehouses adjacent to the camp—down which she had taken Paul Sheffield five months earlier. Together with Regan, she presses down the tunnel, praying for no surprises. The tunnel's end is sealed by a trapdoor. Oni yanks a cord, and the door swings open. There is no ledge, no bridge, no ladder; just a four-hundred-foot drop over the Rift and skeletons below for company. Across the chasm: cliffs, and the Partition wall, which hems in Akbari and a couple million undocumented Americans. Between the tunnel and the far side of the Rift are the remains of old pipes, makeshift bridges, and wires—an urban Tarzan's dream.

"I want you to swing to that platform, alright?" Oni says, indicating an old telephone wire dangling within feet of the tunnel's end. Leaning over the drop, Oni grabs the wire. Nearly losing her footing, she throws all of her weight back into the tunnel. Hiding her embarrassment, she hands the wire to Regan. "I'll be right behind you."

Regan retreats from the edge. "I can't! I can't!"

Making sure the trapdoor doesn't swing closed, Oni glowers at Regan. "If you don't, bad men will kill you or worse. I know those men—I know what they're capable of. If they were told to bring you in, they'll bring you back in pieces." True or not, Oni knows that if captured now, she'll have no leverage—no chance of survival and certainly no chance of bringing Outland down. "The only way you'll see the Citadel is by trusting me and by going back in the transport Celeste has provided." Oni looks back up the dank tunnel, sure that she hears voices. "Come on!"

Psyching herself up with a couple big breaths, Regan's nods mechanically. She swings to the catwalk section, little legs flailing over a blur of bad landings. She toes the catwalk, but the telephone wire starts back for Oni. The catwalk creaks and oscillates under her weight. Regan squeals, releases the wire, and drops down, spreading herself across the platform and locking on with shaking hands. "Oni!" she shrieks. "I can't! I can't!"

Not so keen on the Omnitype's new mantra, Oni leaps for the telephone wire, nearly losing her legs to the trapdoor as it closes behind her. She lands on the platform, trampling Regan in the process.

A growl overhead alerts them both to a bigger problem than balance and gravity. An Outland scoutship blusters by, no doubt scanning every nook and cranny for Celeste's prize. *Charming knows enough to send proxies down for us. The ship is just running reconnaissance.*

"Alright, kiddo," Oni says, balancing the platform by setting her weight on one leg. She helps Regan up, holding her between her legs like an infant just learning to walk. "No more thinking. No more fear. If there is some part of you that is particularly confident—like whoever that was back in the car—I'd channel that mentality **right now.**"

Regan's anxious gasps drop off. Something other than confidence transforms her face—it could be called experience; a hundred-yard stare beamed by veterans and space cowboys who've seen the worst of humanity or tried setting a new benchmark themselves. "Okay, Oni."

Oni leads Regan to the next beam, but immediately falls behind. With Oni at a deficit for muscle memory, the Omnitype proves the exemplar. The girl deftly navigates this paint-by-numbers bridge with a robotic efficiency. Oni finds her on the last number in the painting, a leap away from the PIT-side of the Rift. "Be careful!"

Regan doesn't waste the moment on breath or sentiment. She jumps and nails the landing. The cliff begins to give under her, but Oni lands further up the mudslide and yanks Regan up and along with her prosthetic arm; any harder and she would have dislocated Regan's.

The Partition continues above where the cliffs end—a massive grey fortification designed to keep PIT rats out of Los Angeles' civil districts. There's no climbing it, but also no need. Oni knows a way through. She hurries Regan over to a drainage pipe she has used to get PIT-side in the past. They clamor into the pipe, trading the threat of the Outland scoutship's cannons for whatever lurks in the muck ahead.

# NECROPOLIS

The PIT is one big festering cybernetic wound. Even if it could heal itself with proper government and infrastructural updates, the infectious self-ordained powers that be would cut it back open and re-infect it with experimental technology or half-baked politics. Without the PIT, the Military likely wouldn't know about the efficacy of biohacked DNA-torpedoes or the long-term psychological effects of electro-magnetic border pulsing, and the State would certainly have less to threaten voters in the Blue Zone with. Notwithstanding this cybernetic wound's purulent discharge and the Blue-Zone-engineered bacteria teeming about the surface, it is still the safest place for Oni to be, all things considered.

With Regan squirreled under Oni's prosthetic arm like the daughter she never wanted nor now can ever have, they proceed down an alleyway busy with vents, eaves, and loose wires. It's wet, this alley—wetted by trickle-down economics and waste from those with the luxury of direct sunlight. The slow multi-decade drip has eroded the facades of all of the sky-bridges overhead, exposing their shoddy construction. A strong breeze could bring it all down and a strong palpitation could bring it all to life.

A head pops out of a window a few storeys up. "Oy! Now that's a fun-sized one yah got there!" Although the face is impossible to make out on account of shadow, the voice, nasally and corrupt, hints at rotted gums and rotten intentions. "Say, Dan—look o'er here, now. Nah, quit your whinging and come to that window, yeah? See these two? Little sisters, yeah." Leaning further out the window, the PIT rat tries his best to seduce Oni and Regan, now hastily moving down the alley. "Come home, little sister. Let's have a reunion."

A second head peers out the window one over. "I can'na see, Clint, but my pecker's tellin' me they'd be tasty morsels."

Looking back over Oni's forearm, Regan returns the perverts' stare. "I can ask my friends for help," she whispers nervously to Oni.

*A parade of archetypals is just the kind of thing that will give us away.* "No need." Rather than flee with the constant threat of Clint and Dan catching up, Oni stops in her tracks and turns. She pulls her Remington out from under her belt and takes aim at the first window. "Cover your ears, kiddo."

Regan complies.

Oni fires two shots. Neither shot connects with the wastoids above, instead only boring holes in their brick windowsills, but the gawkers nevertheless disappear. Oni has made her point. She tucks away her gun. Recalling a flag she'd spied in the RIM-blur on the drive to Camp MUD, she beams: "Don't tread on me."

The alleyway ends in a small square—or rather a squircle, on account of the rounded edges. Looks like Globe Theatre if the Globe had been made fourteen times bigger and in a hurry by poorly-programmed drones and pissed engineers. Strings of orange lights flicker above a sea of enmeshed and frenzied people and livestock, all spiraling around a slightly-raised stage. Smells like day-old sex, stables, and honeysuckles. Big red and white banners shiver along the periphery, constituted by linked apartment complexes that seem to converge forty-or-so storeys above. Among those in the crowd, there is the odd but expected pigeon-toed mouth-breathing rainout, but for the most part, it is comprised of orderly restauranteurs and urban farmers.

In her fight against the surge of sweaty flesh, Oni loses her grip on Regan's hand. She was barely holding on, fearful that she might accidentally crush those feeble little digits...In the slits and gaps between glistening arms and legs, Oni can make out parts of Regan's cherubic person being swept away. As if fighting a powerful riptide, she wades over on a diagonal towards Regan, who has somehow managed not to get trampled. So relieved is Oni upon making her way to Regan, that she embraces the little figure.

Oblivious to her governess' concern, Regan is focused on a bony cow caged and displayed at the centre of the spiral. Its bulging eyes, pitifully cartoonish underbite, balloon-animal teets, and knobby legs, all suggest that the cow is a slambang clone—grown in a black-market vat and rushed to market. (An especially insidious process, because the growth hormones also enlarge the beast's brain to the point of dot-test sentience, in direct violation of the Intelligence Act. Horrible thing—awareness—when you're chattel.) A midget wearing a top hat, soiled striped pants with suspenders, and a pair of glasses with both temples missing, paces atop the lank simulacrum's cage, stomping as he records bids from the quarrelsome crowd. A wiry old woman reaches into the cage to investigate her prospective purchase. Seeing this, the dapper-looking midget hollers, prompting a pair of tall bald men to accost the woman for "Tryin' tah samp its DNA." The cueballs drag the old woman kicking and screaming into the crowd for a private beating.

"What are they doing?" Regan asks, visibly disturbed.

Oni pulls Regan away from the auction and snaps hoarsely: "Ask your friends."

"Huh?" Regan fastens her grip on Oni's hand, cluing into her resentment. "Hey—are we still going to the Citadel? Oni?"

Eyes encumbered with new stimuli, Oni stops in her tracks, desperate to dredge up something—anything—from memory that might indicate the way to the Marion. The jam is interfering with her Monocle, big-time. Oni gambles a noncommittal, "Hmm," for silence.

"It's important that we do, Oni…" Regan stammers. "*This is all wrong.*" Pronging the crowd with a wave, she furrows her brow and squeaks with intensity. "Everyone should be connected! They should all be friends."

Oni wades through dead-eyed shoppers with her little ideologue and anchors at a dark-CLOUD kiosk manned by a red-blazered Indian. Although conventionally ugly—sunken-eyed with a bulbous chin—the man emanates a confidence that coupled with his smile accomplishes a stately gravitas. A bald black woman hands him a reddish canvas bag, dripping blood. He sets it in a cubby in the kiosk, counts out a handful of bills, and smoothly hands the wad to the woman with such fluidity that the gesture seems almost trivial—a nice trick for those who'd like to avoid the attention of would-be burglars or proactive federal agents.

The woman, right-ear pierced and left ear engulfed in implants, pockets the wad. She looks over at Oni's Remington and at Regan, and then smiles a Cheshire grin. "You'd be in the right place if you're after some techular spirituality. Yeah," she chuckles. "Sangiv is the guy to see, don't you know." She nods at her business partner, pops her collar, and disappears into the crowd.

Interrupting Regan's earlier line of thought, Oni engages the charismatic VR-pusher. "Sangiv?

Sangiv smiles at the sound of his name as if it were a profound statement of old wisdom.

"Hotel Marion. Where is it?"

Sangiv pats his red blazer and procures a comb out of his breast pocket. Running it through his thinning oil-shine hair, he looks Oni up and down, settling on the sight of her bloody prosthetic. "Not far, I don't think. Not exactly sure. If it's worth it, it'll be no more than a twenty-minute walk in the right direction. Anything farther away isn't worth the sweat…You could always save that time and sweat and enjoy some R and R in Oasis Six." He pockets his comb, and pulls a pristine neural-link cord out of a compartment in his kiosk. "Completely safe. Four minutes feels like four hours. Your mind is the limit." Sangiv registers Regan's presence with a stray glance and reconsiders his pitch. "Can set you both up and then trip-sit."

*I don't have time for this shit.* Oni jabs the dark-CLOUD salesman in the belly with her Remington. "Not interested. Where's the Hotel?"

Sangiv eyes the gun bucking his rib and grimaces back at Oni. "I save memory and trust in Monocle. Trouble is that mine's down at the moment—OC jamming all comms, if you didn't know—so I'm afraid I can't help you with anything more than a guess." Despite the deadly threat leveled at his core, he defaults to his business pitch. "You could wait for the OC to stop the jam. Perhaps synch up for a spell…"

"Give me your best guess." Oni presses the gun harder against Sangiv's side. "Or point me in the direction of someone who might have a better idea."

In lieu of shaking or panicking, a few glistening beads evidence the salesman's discomfort over the prospect of an intestinal rearrangement. "There might be something over there…" Sangiv points out an overgrown bulletin board on the far side of the square. "Paper information. Usually maps on the take-out menus."

Oni belts her Remington. "Thanks, Sangiv…I really don't want to have to come back for your next best guess."

Sangiv raises the neural-link cord and grins. "If you should have to come back, may I suggest you try to unlock the answer inside yourself. *Friend's discount.*"

Oni leaves the red-blazered salesman, pregnant with respect and something more…His coolness was contagious. However antagonistic her dealing with him, he effused a sense of capability and indifference. While he has a right to such coolness—this is his turf after all, and Oni's just an interloper down on her luck—he's given Oni a contact-high: she feels at once sure of herself and positive about the mission at hand. "Marion's close," Oni repeats out loud for only her benefit.

Taking the salesman's suggestion, Oni heads to the bulletin wall on the squircle's northeastern boundary: a brick wall girded with PVC painted to look like wood. Its masonry is barely visible on account of a palimpsest of paint, thrown up like plaque on a bulimic's molars. The most recent layer is coincidentally a hideous yellow. Oni paces along the bulletin board, hoping for a map or at the very least some old street sign. *Gibson might have a clue, but the less mind-reading Regan can do the better.* She turns off her Monocle interface and appeals to the unassisted and unmediated power of her own eyesight. Most of the articles and posters are painted over. Only the most recent missing-children flyers, revolutionary propaganda, underground-church newsletters, and stapled pulp provide something besides texture. One medium raised from the papered clutter catches Oni's eye: a partly-vandalized Outland Corporation billgram. The backlit advertisement is corrupted, glitching between two frames; in both a runner is pictured—on the verge of smiling but forever unable despite his synthetic mandibles and AI-designed giblets.

Euphoria strikes Oni as she stares at the pearly-teethed Blue Zone model. She recalls that corporate billgrams report impressions, oculuar IDs, and traffic back to their companies' respective marketing teams. For such information to be of any analytic relevance, the location of the advertisement is needed. Freeing Regan's hand to drop, Oni leverages her knuckles against the brick, and curls her fingers behind the sign. With a groan, she yanks the billboard off the wall, flaking yellow chips all over her leggings. Massaging her shoulder, Oni restarts Monocle and synchronizes with the billgram. The ad's geotag provides Oni with an address, which she cross-references with an old, offline PIT map. *Bingo.*

Oni sets a waypoint for the Hotel Marion—one of Hex Akbari's first purchases this side of the Pacific. On the roof of the Marion, a mere forty-seven storeys above the PIT's festering skin, there is an old maglev monorail system that runs directly to the Chrysalis along a narrow bridge. The bridge is composed of three tiers of vine-enveloped arches that together resemble the last remaining Roman aqueduct (which runs over the radioactive Gardon River). Akbari had gutted the midsection of the Chrysalis, including all conventional methods of ascension, in order to maintain a degree of separation from his serfs and his enemies. The monorail is his personal expressway—the only non-airborne route to his base of operations. Whether or not it is still in service and whether the lines have been sapped since Oni last rode it are questions she must answer for herself in person, given Gibson can't access surveillance feeds on the Marion's servers because of Outland's PIT-wide signal jam.

Pleased that she has found the way despite still being unsure if it meets her desired end, Oni grants herself the patience to humour Regan's earlier concern. "Friends—you want everyone to be friends? It can be tiring, being friendly."

Regan looks into the crowd, thin about the periphery. "It would be more efficient." She says rigidly. Checking herself, she adopts a more mousy posture. "If we were all friends, there'd be no need for yelling or fighting. If all information and experience was properly ordered and shared…"

The mind inspiriting Regan's childish form saps Oni's patience. She rolls her eyes so hard her head nearly jerks to the side, and she throws the billgram to the ground. "Who are you?"

"Ignorance is the curse of an imperfect relationship with reality." Abandoning the charade, Regan stiffens and looks around. "The programmers responsible for this realm are underachievers…It ought to be optimized. Here, subscribers are scattered and lost. That's no way to live."

"Well *Regan*, if you managed to reunite them, to make them all friends—*if you managed to connect all of us*—and we knew all there was to know, life would be pretty pointless, don't you think?"

Oni's reaction drives Regan's eyebrows up into a look of surprise. "Can you dislike something you haven't tried?"

"Certainly." Oni leads Regan into a busy covered-lane off the square. "Anchovies. A magma massage. Death…You can make life better without taking humanity out of the equation."

"Mr. Gibson is right," Regan snaps back.

"Oh?"

"You are an optimist."

# RETROGRADE

Harry Tuttle's office is as uninspired and as lonely as his Hollywood Hills bungalow. It sits at the end of the R-Passage on the 23$^{rd}$ lane. (The illogic of this uninspired alpha-numeric floor plan became apparent to Lyle after his initial confusion, suffered at the intersection of L and 1, which seems to have jumped 'K' in order altogether. Lyle promised himself that, if he had some time later, he would teach the bureaucrat responsible a lesson in precision.)

Inside this three-walled, one-windowed cell lined with more self-congratulating writ and iconography than wallpaper, there sits one desk—immaculately ordered and cleaned—and one chair. Harry was interested in neither chitchat nor hosting visitors.

The fourth wall, unbroken: a holovisual, thick-paned window; glass instead of a plasma field revealing Tuttle to have been both a sentimentalist and a fool. Lyle closes the office door behind him, and meets his outline in the glass.

Sensing motion, the holovisual overlay on the window activates, and streams *NewsLink*'s hourly feed. Crawling across the screen: "Families of the Olympus massacre demand the court reverse the stay on Serge Demidov's execution…Hermes Interplan ship to return to Titan with new crew…Keryl Anta and Coalition of Turmanian Doctors decry resettlement in Union provinces claiming 'radiation levels still too damn high'.…"

With a flick of his wrist, Lyle turns off the holovisual overlay, leaving him with an impressive view of the polished innards of Celeste Charming's Citadel. "What are you doing, Ms. Charming?" Vapour marks his curiosity on the window.

Past the glass pane: a cathedralic laboratory with graduating, concentric levels of machinery, security, and Outland scientists, all gravitating around an altar. On the altar sits an elephantine object dressed with white sheets. Four lab technicians confer with one another beside the blanketed mystery. Nodding in unison, the four break into pairs. Two of the techs load a black canister into a massive syringe, and adjust the nozzle. The other two peremptorily yank the sheets down, revealing a massive skeletal polyhedron. It has eighteen soft square faces and eight triangular faces, and is reinforced by metal beams. Lyle, though distrusting of his eyesight at this distance, believes this particular polyhedron to be a rhombicuboctahedron. (His law firm had commissioned a similar one be built on a much smaller scale to serve as a floating vase in their lobby. Hollyhock was slotted through the vase's eight triangular slots into a non-Newtonian fluid, and oxeye was fit into the eighteen square slots.)

Maxing out his Monocle zoom, Lyle spots a name stenciled on one of the polyhedron's verticies: "CORDEI." Lyle ponders on the name, and realizes it is Latin for "Heart of God."

This heart of god is full of a clear gel. At its centre is a coffin-shaped capsule, partly ajar. The capsule is ready for an occupant, set with restraints, an embedded neural-net mobile, and extra-dermal spine clamps. All of the lab's coolant baths, generators, and coils, connect in one way or another with this Archimedean solid.

Above and connected to the Cordei by armoured piping and wires is a semi-transparent control room, similarly fitted with a chair and neural-net mobile. The Control Room and the Cordei together feed a maze of cords and tubes that run the length of the room, detouring to signal amplifiers, receiver coils, and at the rear of the room, a massive server-bank enclosure.

The lab techs carry their oversized syringe down the central aisle past several ominous mechs with rocket-racks exposed. Carefully, they mark a spot on the Cordei and plunge a black fluid into the gel. The dark fluid surges through the viscous substance, and forms tiny spheres at five foot intervals about the capsule. *Micro-sensor array*, thinks Lyle, pressing his vision to its limit and blurring the office in his peripherals.

The lab technicians cover the Cordei with sheets and regroup. Staring at one another as if sharing in the wonder of some great sacramental vision, they file across and off the stage, careful around the transmission repeaters and beta-wave antennae dialed around the polyhedron like the hours.

"Why build a throne if you haven't a monarch for it to seat?" Lyle mouths to his partial reflection. "Unless…" he says with a grin, losing himself in a quick succession of realizations. *The explosions at Seal Base*. His recent respite from the siren's calls and all the archetypal crosschatter. "Celeste you treasonous slat…Ha!" He pats the glass. "You're bringing her right to me."

Lyle flings all of the neatly ordered dotgrams off Tuttle's desk along with his lamp. This aggressive display makes him feel right at home. Soot and cinders. *This is as good as home, given home is now anywhere and nowhere.*

He tears into the drawers. Dainty creams and lotions add to the clutter, largely constituted by exocortex slides and PILOT devices: a veritable graveyard of memories and personalities. *Harry Tuttle, you naughty, naughty man. Trophies, perhaps?* Lyle notices a name bar on one of the PILOTs: Annette Tuttle. *The city is a little bit safer without Harry Tuttle haunting its thoughts.* Lyle comes close to admiring the man who once wore the eyeballs swishing in his jacket pocket. *Close,* but the difference leads him to contempt and pride. Judging by all of the memices donning dust in the top drawer, the man had considered himself a dreamcatcher. Now he sleeps under cover of eternal night.

Cornered, behind the creams and the stolen exocortices: a tablet. Lyle takes it from the drawer, synching his Monocle with the tablet interface. He had done his due diligence before quartering Harry Tuttle and acquired all of his passwords, wireless tethers; *the whole nine yards...*

A semi-transparent screen emerges, fading out the office, and engulfing Lyle's vision. In this tricolour second room, a mailbox rattles. The sound effect is trashy—the kind of low-quality jingle only an underexposed scientist on a nostalgia bent could enjoy. Lyle intuits open the box. Several memos from 'From the desk of Celeste Charming, Acting-C.E.O.' appear, all marked "TODAY – URGENT." The most recent memo reads:

"Drs. Epner, Tan, Tuttle,

I need not remind you that the contents of this letter, like all of our correspondence, is strictly confidential and for your eyes only.

As you may have already heard—and if you have, please name the person or persons who ha[s/ve] breached the Company's trust and inform Infractions at once—General McCabe would like our assistance in studying the Omnitype.

Based on the Military's containment system, with Dr. Epner's updates and Dr. Tan's improved net link, I believe you will have all of the amenities necessary for both containment and exploration.

I leave you with a list of requirements and expectations.

- Your staff must have their BiAnima implants updated to avoid A-type influence and corruption. Furthermore, your staff must all agree to targeted short-term memory wipes upon the completion of our endeavoured trials.

303

- You must calibrate the Omnitype's mental brace such that she can be remotely governed.
- Equip the Cordei polyhedron with additional signal amplifiers.
- Isolate all frequencies on which the Omnitype broadcasts and assign a full-time monitor. At the first sign of unintended or unregulated broadcast, immediately turn off the Cordei. The Omnitype could do irreparable damage to the city, to the state, and to the country in a heartbeat.
- You must maintain and update your financials, but instead of submitting them to Accounting, you will submit them to me directly.
- If you are petitioned, ordered, or warranted by state or federal officials to answer to your present assignment, you are to call Skyr, who will provide you with whatever assistance you'll need.

I thank you for your tact and for your interest in this project. I trust that you will not disappoint me.

Celeste Charming

C.E.O., PhD., MBA., MSc."

The letter hovers in front of Lyle despite his having dropped the tablet. He stands frozen, with his legs apart and his hands on his head. "What is she thinking?" he asks the vacant room, already wishing he had Tuttle's ears and lips. "Doesn't matter." *What matters is stopping the headaches and getting back up on the horse.*

Lyle steps over the tablet, which does a remarkable job of preserving Tuttle's second office despite its abandonment on the floor and the disheveled lawyer blocking much of its projectors' fields. Celeste had anticipated the arrival for some time, referencing McCabe's cooperation months in advance of the fireworks at Seal Beach. If it were not for Celeste customarily having dissidents and opponents murdered, Lyle would blackmail her. *Into seeing the Omnitype?* That loud and rapacious voice under his skull...No. He would blackmail her into becoming a client. *What a get*: defending the world's biggest technocrat, possessor of the new world order's sovereign, treasonous doomsdayer and meglomaniacal goddess. Realizing he is at once in love with Celeste Charming as well as the idea of eviscerating her and that blue-eyed monster, Lyle shakes himself back into reality. Monocle registers his discontinued interest in the tablet interface, and resets his vision, returning him to the humdrum white-brown of Tuttle's past life.

For the first time in a long time, Lyle is not absolutely certain what he ought to do. So much of his agency of late has been determined by pain, jealousy, and unexamined impulse. He sits on the edge of Tuttle's desk, and reflexively intuits a call to Dorota. A reminder of the Citadel's perpetual comm-jam flits across his eye. "Damn."

A rap on the door interrupts Lyle's meta-medieval fantasy. He freezes. No gun, no knife, no rope, no stone. Panicked, Lyle closes the desk drawers and melts into Tuttle's seat.

"Dr. Tuttle? May I have a word?" The voice, muffled only slightly, is feminine and familiar. "It's Gertrude."

*Gertrude?*

"...Dr. Epner."

*Shit.*

The doorknob wiggles. A lustrous twist of black and white snoops in, and beneath it, two bright brown eyes deepset in a look of concern. "Harry? Oh good Lord!" Startled, Dr. Epner stumbles into Tuttle's office, sending the door rebounding against the wall. The door creeps back up to her, and she rights herself, panting as if that instant of bewilderment was tantamount to having run a marathon. She steadies herself on the doorframe, and surveys the office. "Looks like we both managed to find the R-20s..."

Confidence braids Lyle's spine, fills out his shoulders, and stretches his lips out into a smirk. "In spite of my client's shoddy directions."

Dr. Epner's eyes roll halfway back into a flash of Monocle revelation. They reset on Lyle, now a darker shade of brown; less kind, somehow. "I don't believe I got your name earlier, Dr.—?"

"Oh, I'm not a doctor. A lawyer, actually. So mister..." The sluice gate on Lyle's forehead breaks, and a torrent of sweat cuts diagonally across his forehead. "Lyle Badegger." He coughs. "Lawyer. *Mister* Lyle lawyer." *God almighty. What the hell are you saying?* Lyle clears his throat, curling phlegm up with his tongue. The phlegm smoothes his delivery. "I am Harry Tuttle's lawyer."

A shadow eclipses Dr. Epner's face. Someone else is lurking outside the door behind her. Lyle leans over Tuttle's desk hoping to ascertain its identity. His apprehension about the second presence in the doorway prompts Dr. Epner to look over her shoulder.

"I see." She says, finding confidence in whatever looms beyond Lyle's vision. "Yes." Her face hardens. "He was facing some devastating accusations… But was completely exonerated. We were very happy to hear the good news! And very surprised…I assume that was all your doing, Mr. Lyle lawyer?"

"It was, in fact." Lyle gives up on smiling. He embraces his dour default, and begins rapping his knuckles on the desk. "Not easy getting a murderer off who wears bloody shoes to court."

"*Alleged* murderer, you mean."

Lyle shrugs. steps deeper into the office. "Mind telling me what you're doing in Dr. Tuttle's office?" Pointed stare. Gritted teeth. Shoulders back. Thumbs holstered in the belt-loops at her sides. *Dr. Epner is showing all the signs.* She has pre-judged Lyle. It is a look he has seen many times before, usually in the faces of ravenous juries hellbent on lunar isolation or on the firing squad; sometimes in the faces of men he's left with nothing but the moral high ground.

"What am I doing?" Lyle feigns interest in the few remaining dotgrams on Tuttle's desk. He picks one up and lets it drop, uncommitted to the charade. "His bidding, of course. Trying to establish an alibi to preclude a retrial." Sculpting a look of annoyance, Lyle fires back: "I appreciate your concern, and Harold probably wouldn't mind, but I'm paid hourly and as you may or may not know, the doctor cannot afford me indefinitely. So, if there isn't anything else, I would appreciate some privacy."

Dr. Gertrude Epner is an eight-second dance and a lie away from becoming another problem solved. The shadow in the hallway, however, presents a variable in the equation. An unknown. A possibly-armed unknown. "Mr. Lyle, how did you come to find Dr. Tuttle's office?"

Lyle's mind is working overtime, both combatting the siren's faint humming and studying his peripherals for possible weapons. "By foot, naturally. Elevator too."

Frowning, Dr. Epner motions to the shadow. "Without an appointment? Without an escort?"

Glass-framed photograph of Harry Tuttle holding a fish. Bereft of friends or family, he likely had a drone snap the shot. The frame looks heavy. If Tuttle went through the lengths to get a good frame, he likely didn't cheap out on the glass. Lyle choreographs the steps needed to reach the photograph. He will smash it on the desk, slash Dr. Epner's throat with the largest glass shard, and then quickly hold the wound shut. Regardless of whether the shadow's form runs off a battery or hamburgers, it will yield to Lyle to preserve Dr. Epner—to keep Outland from shelling out for condolence cards and flowers. Getting out of the Citadel is a dance Lyle might have to wing, but at least he will have an opportunity to try.

Lyle nods, and shimmies sideways behind the desk, towards the photograph. "In addition to having power of attorney, I am also Dr. Tuttle's proxy. He is a little waterlogged at the moment, so I felt I would save him the trip. As for an escort," Lyle pauses, and stands in front of the photograph. The glass pane is approximately one-quarter-inch thick. *One does what one can with what he's given.* "Business before pleasure."

As planned, Lyle slams the photograph on Tuttle's desk and produces several viable shards with one step, a pivot, and a bow. Yanking up a transparent blade and unwittingly coating it with his own blood, Lyle lunges at Dr. Epner, who screams and trips. Lyle hadn't accounted for Gertrude's clumsiness in his choreography. Having to pick her up to slash her will throw off his rhythm and compromise his sight lines.

Four steps into this ghoulish dance, the shadow has given way to an object, or rather to a subject: leading with his gun, a Sentinel barges into the room. Lyle rushes his performance, and grabs Dr. Epner by her hair. The Sentinel fires one shot, neutering Lyle's blade hand. Although the bullet merely rips through Lyle's palm, the shock wave and resultant ripple sends his thumb and part of his index finger flying into the lab window.

Lyle grips his mangled digits, and grimaces at Gertrude's champion. Over the sound of his would-be victim's hollering, Lyle—pale in the face and colouring Tuttle's otherwise humdrum office—slurs: "I think there has been some sort of misunderstanding."

Gertrude flees the scene, clutching her neck and screaming bloody murder. *If only, bitch.*

The Sentinel rats Lyle out over his radio, describing what could only be someone else. "Six foot one and Caucasian," are apt characterizations, but "skinny…middle-aged…affected?" *Hardly!*

With his report in, the Sentinel holsters his firearm and trudges over to Lyle. Before the rogue lawyer can spit out a pithy line, he's unconscious and on his back. And although he can neither see nor hear nor touch nor taste, he can feel his head throb and his mind ache.

## DOLOSIAN MOLDS

At the end of a cramped one-way street beset by fissures crouping venous exhaust, a bright white neon sign with red lettering blazons the Hotel Marion. Without fully drawing her gun, Oni checks its accessibility with a blind groping and shifts Regan behind her. They creep towards the hotel whose pilastered walls seem out of place in this glorified alley narrowed further by bike-locked hovtrans and emulsified remains. Jutting out beneath the sign, a cloth awning keeps a threadbare carpet and a broad-shouldered cyborg dry. The cyborg—a digitigrade, tall on his dog-like legs—paces back and forth. His routine is pronounced by an awkward swagger. One arm hangs significantly lower than the other and is thrown up into every stride, giving the cyborg the appearance of perpetually teetering. Only as he lifts his arm and points it at Oni does she realize it is not an arm at all, but rather a double-barrel gun where a forearm and a hand might otherwise be.

"Don't shoot!" Oni yells. She raises her hands and taps Regan with her foot, telepathically instructing her to do the same. Looking through the antlers of her ten-fingered submission, Oni reconsiders the utility of her made-to-match prosthetic; aware now of a pragmatic alternative, she might have opted for a cannon.

The cyborg guard yells out in Farsi. Eliciting nothing more than a straighter-armed surrender from Oni, he tries again in Mandarin, and Spanish, and finally in English. "Identify yourself!" Tilting his head to reveal partially-removed gang tattoos, the guard steps forward into the light of the Marion sign.

"I am a friend—" Oni stops to correct herself. "I *was* a friend of Hex Akbari. Saved Kadin Akbari's life a few years back." She lowers her hands, and sets one on Regan's shoulder. "Outland's signal jam prevented me from scheduling an appointment...but I'm confident Kadin wouldn't mind permitting me one."

It is readily apparent that the question of who can ascend to the Akbaris' feet isn't up to Cerebus here. The guard radios his superiors and bows his head in anticipation of confirmation.

*He's got a signal? Leave it to the Akbaris to bypass all rules and obstacles.* Subvocally, Oni urges Gibson to figure out what frequency they're using, but Gibson fails to reply.

The cyborg's radio is loud with static. A concerned voice cuts through. The cyborg scowls at Regan and Oni. His expression wouldn't be so unnerving if he didn't have a murder tally inked as tear drops under each eye—one cheek having proved insufficient coverage for all the death. He nods, and clips the radio back to his chest. "Mr. Akbari is expecting you." The guard has a thick Persian accent. "You may go inside…quietly. Make sure neither of you stray from the red carpet. Follow it straight to the front desk. The concierge will let you know which elevator to take. Make sure you take only the one he has indicated. Do you understand?"

"Yes. Thank you," Oni replies hurriedly, feeling all of a sudden exposed out in the street. She approaches the cyborg with her arms still out to the side signaling nonviolence.

"What happens if we step off of the carpet?" Regan asks, anchoring Oni before the guard.

The guard's shoulders slope, and he slightly bends his knees to answer Regan on a less confrontational angle. "You'll die."

Oni nods respectively to the guard as she drags Regan into the Marion. As the heavy double doors crash behind them, Oni mischievously whispers to her cohort, feigning to trip. "He said to stay off the carpet, right?"

Regan jettisons all of her post-human philosophy and trembles around self-concern. "Oni!"

The hotel lobby is all black marble and red furnishings. Red chesterfields with high backs. Red tapestries breathing over the twelve key pillars supporting both the lobby and the buttressed apartments dangling over the contrasting squalor outside. Red sequoia shoeshine benches on either side of the front door. The floor reflects warm yellow light given off both by the thousand-or-so lamps set around the periphery in ascending order and the torches in the chandeliers dangling like crystalline octopi over the tomb-like front desk. A Bramante-style staircase situated behind the front desk corkscrews all the way up the hollow and resolves in an unbalustered lounge.

A sharp orange glow summons Oni's gaze up to a swarthy set of eyebrows in a double-breasted jacket. The smoker is impressed with a look of disdain. He taps his cigar, and turns into the lounge and out of sight. Oni wants to yell out to him, but hesitates, considering the specificity of the guard's instructions.

Regan cautiously progresses along the red carpet beside Oni, similarly gaping at the unexpected cleanliness of the Marion. "Fallen man certainly likes his illusions."

Motionless behind the front desk is a dark, tall, and hairless man. He watches Oni and Regan process along the red carpet without blinking once, and salaams as they come within feet of the counter. "Good morning, Dr. Matsui." Turning his searching eyes to Regan, he smiles. "Good morning, little miss." Resetting his stare somewhere between the two of them, he asks: "How might I assist you?"

Oni rests her elbows on the counter, eliciting a gasp from the concierge.

"Please refrain from touching the desk!" He thunders, mechanically.

Recoiling from the counter, Oni apologizes profusely. "The man outside said Mr. Akbari is expecting us…"

"Just one moment." The concierge pivots, gracefully steps over to a small computer terminal seated on a filing cabinet, and inputs a query.

Gibson suddenly refreshes over Oni's iris. "Smoke and mirrors, Oni. The concierge—this whole damned place—is a holusion."

Half-expecting another outburst from the concierge who has yet to blink, Oni bows her head into a subvocal reply. "A what? Now's not a good time."

Unwilling to let Oni find out the hard way, Gibson decrypts the Marion's comprehensive holo-field so Oni can see beyond the veil via Monocle. "No," Gibson insists. "Now's a good time."

All of the hotel lobby's meticulous details vanish. The chairs, tables, reds and blacks, all melt away, leaving a hive-like structure— much like an Outland transport ship upturned and scaled many times larger. Although structurally identical to the Marion Oni first set her eyes on—complete with a spiral staircase, multiple exposed floors all connected to the stairs by web-like bridges, and a front desk—the underlying reality is a sobering mix of metal and concrete. Every floor is studded by spatially conservative sleep pods. Insectoid drones scale up the pillars, checking on the sleep-pods' occupants as they click along. The lounge overlooking the hollow is nothing more than an oscillating cybernetic eye—a composite of sensors and cameras— keeping tabs on all of the pods and activity below.

"What is this place?" Oni asks Gibson, going crosseyed from the split vision of two competing realities. She shutters her deluded eye, and with a sweeping scan of this makeshift cypulchre directs her attention to the concierge who similarly isn't what he first presented himself to be, at once making both his concern about touching the counter and the guard's caution over leaving the red carpet seem sensible.

The concierge is in fact an Intelligentleman—an early BiAnima prototype that looks like a cross between a praying mantis and a silverwear set. "This," the Intelligentleman begins, responding to the question Oni had presumed inaudible to all but her and her cranium buddy, "Is the Great Hotel Marion."

Too shocked to check her attitude, Oni blurts out: "More like a dark-CLOUD flophouse."

The Intelligentleman sprouts a second set of arms, which pull its chip-charged thorax forward and its bug-eyed face within a breath of Oni's. "How our guests spend their time while cocooned is their business. What, may I ask, is your business?"

Shifting her hips to get a feel for precisely where her Remington resides on her waist, Oni takes a step back. Staring into the Intelligentleman's compound eyes, she answers: "Here to see Akbari. I meant no disrespect to your hotel."

"Whether or not disrespect is intended, it need not be taken." Turning to its left, the Intelligentleman points out an elevator bank. "Your train leaves in ten minutes. Please don't dawdle."

# CASTLE IN THE SMOG

Akbari is no slouch. On the matter of security, he is more of a well-kitted and proactive paranoiac. Atop the Hotel Marion, he has gathered a battalion: several anti-aircraft guns, an anti-personnel battery, and over a dozen heavily-armed mechs. Although not on display, there's likely a swarm or two of Yellow Jacket drones lurking about. The jewel of this discernible treasure-trove of lethal metals: Akbari's Winged Hussar. It trots about on four legs with armor scales clinking, thrusters thrumming, and with curved black wings ready to launch it into pursuit. Its name evinces both Akbari's sense of humor and storied lineage. He probably thought it amusing to write a contradiction into history—of the Winged Hussar who battled at the request of a Turk.

The skeleton of an unfinished four-lane skyway partially shades the Marion, accounting for the placement of the gardens along the rooftop's perimeter. Where light does connect, it meets vibrant bouquets crammed full of exotic plants that would never otherwise share real estate with the exception of those few suborbital botanical gardens protected from blight.

From this angle, the Chrysalis looks like a sickly cactus. Long needle-like protuberances prick out, preventing aircraft from getting too close or landing. Its head is covered with a troop of mushroom-like satellite dishes. The monorail snakes up and over to an unneedled segment and resolves in a black, four-storey-high sliding door guarded symbolically on either side by two giant stone incarnations of Anubis.

A high-pitched siren mounted above the door and canine gods wails three times. Immediately after the third wail, just as the echoes begin, the four-storey door slides open, revealing a copper-coloured train—looks like a bell in a dark belfry. Without warning, there's a deafening response behind Oni, which startles her: an old diaphone blasts a low-frequency confirmation. The train starts to snake across the meandering rail, stirring the greenery gripping the rail-bridge's supports.

"Oni, look!" Regan chirps, pointing out a cluster of lilacs near the monorail's terminus, oblivious both to the train and to the solemnity observed by all those around her. "Oh, they're beautiful!"

Determining the monorail to still be a few minutes away, Oni silently permits Regan to investigate the purple-white crosses. A few of the mechs watch Regan closely as she skips over to the lilacs, and shift uneasily on their steel legs. Thankfully, they do little else, having been ordered not to raise their weapons. Even their optic sensors reflect their ordered calm, remaining green despite the catalyst for catastrophe traipsing across their sacred assignment. *Either Akbari knows something I don't know or he's more trusting that I could ever be.*

Regan kneels beside the lilacs, and like a little botanist, plucks a petal and thumbs it around her palm. *Hopefully her continuing education won't rely upon vivisection.*

The Winged Hussar gallops over to Regan. Regan coolly and calmly stands, and presents the flower mash on her hand to the massive mech. The Hussar's wing tips meet as it bows its box of a head down for closer examination, side-mounted cannons aimed at the fleshy tidbit.

"Hey kiddo, leave it alone!" Oni cries. "Come over here."

The Hussar looks Regan up and down, interrogating her with lasers and invisible questions. While the mech's distrust is indeed warranted, Oni can't imagine what could have given Regan away as a wolf in lambskin. The mech's head—a cuboid sensor array dotted with cameras, IR transmitters, UV sensors, and proximity detectors—extends on a ribbed neck within reach of Regan's soft little digits. Regan doesn't hesitate. She paws its ersatz face. Had she swiped horizontally, it would have been a proper slap. Nevertheless, this undamaging gesture elicits a kinetic eruption. The Hussar spreads its wings to their total span, and bucks back, rearing its cannons and head. A jolt of electricity so fleeting, Oni is only sure it happened because of the resultant smell of ozone, zigzags into the surrounding mechs. They loll for a moment, and resume their stances.

"Regan, get over here right now!" Oni yells, prosthetic ghosting the butt of her gun, neutered by context and circumstance.

Smiling devilishly, Regan wipes her hands on her shirt and moseys past the Winged Hussar over to Oni.

Grabbing Regan by the wrist and pulling her close, Oni's eyebrows assault the bridge of her nose. "What the hell do you think you're doing?" she spits, angrily. Looking up at the Winged Hussar, flexing its hardware back into its former formidable stature, Oni shakes her head. "Akbari is our only hope. Don't screw this up!" Taking a breath and finding her centre, Oni releases Regan. "Can you please just do nothing until…"

"Until you send me to the Citadel?"

Oni nods.

"*I'll* do nothing," says Regan. "I promise."

Desperate to clinch a victory, no matter how minor, Oni lets herself believe Regan. Glancing from disheveled mech to disheveled mech, she prays—again to Who or to what, she isn't sure—that the Omnitype's plan aligns with her at least past the Chrysalis' front door.

The two-car copper train pulls into the station on the roof of the Marion, and the diaphone twangs once more. A tuxedoed semite with a Rumpole nose underlined by a handlebar mustache shifts impatiently behind a half-skinned android conductor as it pries open the frontal slam-door. He slides cane-first past the pseudosentient in a hurry, and dabs his forehead with a handkerchief. With his sheen seen to, he struts over to Oni while several riflemen-droids pile out of the second car.

"Dr. Matsui? Omar Wasem." He bows ever-so-slightly, keeping balance with his cane—padouk wood with an ivory grip—and presents a gloved hand. Oni grips it with her pink-gloved machinery. Rising from his ritualistic hunch, Omar stores his cane under his arm, freeing both hands to make sure that his mustache is in order. "A-hem. Doctor, if you would be so kind to follow me."

Oni throws a furtive glance Regan's way, who—breaking her promise—has returned to the lilacs, further reviewing their anatomy.

Omar traces Oni's eyes to her concern. "And, of course, your cohort—*when she's ready.*"

Regan hadn't stopped at the petal she smeared across the Hussar's face. She's now destroyed the better part of a flower

Oni responds glumly: "If we wait for her to be ready, there won't be a garden left."

"What kind of world would this be if we admonished curiosity?" Omar turns, mustache first, and signals the android conductor to start the train. The conductor exits the first car and enters the second, while the riflemen droids do the opposite.

"Come on, kiddo. We're one step closer," says Oni, affecting a calm and matronly manner. "Don't drag your feet."

The train glides along the aqueduct-like bridge under the protection of Celeste Charming's PIT-side adversary. On the last stretch of track, Oni spots a hovering belt of projector spheres around the tower's midsection. As the train passes under the dotted ring, the Chrysalis begins to transform. Its dilapidated exterior morphs into a better version. No more craters. No more missing windows. It's cleaner, unmarred. This better version has thick antiballistic plating all about its surface, except over recessed balconies occupied by turrets and snipers. *You don't want to have the nicest house in a bad neighbourhood. And Akbari's tower is less a house and more a castle on stilts.*

Regan mutters "Lyle" under her breath as she traipses up and down the aisle, testing her reflexes. As if playing musical chairs, she makes sure she's never too far between grab handles, and giggles when the track throws the train for a sharp shift. Omar, seated just behind the conductor's cab and opposite Oni, looks to the giggle and nods to himself, shaking his leg restlessly. His tick serves as a countdown to Oni's attempt at conversation.

"The Marion lobby—the Chrysalis…" Oni smiles to cushion her question. "I can't think of anyone who'd blame Akbari for the deception, but who exactly does he mean to deceive?"

Omar turns his cane over his thighs as if rolling dough. "Pretend to be weak, that your enemy may grow to be arrogant. In this city, our mutual enemies seek out strength. The government, the law, and the corporation that owns them both, will co-opt the strong who'll play along, and weaken the defiant."

"Outland…"

Wincing, Omar lifts his cane and sets it down between his legs. "I suppose the deception is two-sided. Our compatriots below abhor the whey-faced Bee-Zee aristocracy and their clean mansions and their perfect skyscrapers."

Familiar with nearly all the slang for Los Angeles' technocrats and coastal elite, Oni's ears perk up at Omar's neologism. *Bee Zees.* She has heard the citizenry of the Blue Zone called everything from blozos to boners, and what she imagined were all the other possible portmanteaus. *Bee Zee as in busy? Busy* raking RIM ticks and PIT rats over the coals? *Busy* goggling the working classes and force-feeding them distractions to stymie resistance, to quell uprisings before they are even imagined?

Omar sucks his teeth and gavels the floor with the end of his cane. "Having a leader rise to the heights claimed for the Bee Zees is only a victory if he does so contrastively. It's symbolic, Doctor. Much like your arm."

Oni sits back, and folds her prosthetic under her left arm—now self-aware after having nearly forgotten that there was something behind all of her pain.

"You have an opportunity to make your appendage look like anything you want. Ten fingers. Thirty toes. A pizza-cutter. A mace. You've elected for symmetry. Why? Both the surgeon and the soldier would prize utility over aesthetics, unless there was a strategy behind the appearance. All symbolism has at its core some sort of strategy, some sort of agenda."

"In all fairness, it wasn't my call," says Oni, resentfully.

Standing, Omar looks at Oni sympathetically. "Nor was it Akbari's. But you've both found a symbol that works for you."

Mulling over the porridge of perspective Omar's just splashed for her to consume without chewing, Oni looks sedately out the window. Anubis's feet step into view.

"Ah-ah! The caterpillar into his cocoon without any strife." Omar leans into his cane, and pushes off and upright. "I can't tell you how rare it is to return without spilling blood."

The Chrysalis rings the train in with more sirens. The half-light filtering through the defunct skyways and past the slum-towers relinquishes the train. Taking a moment for her eyes to adjust, Oni pesters Gibson for moral support. "Hey Booky, we're here."

Depicting himself as Oni knew him best—scarred and tired—Booker's avatar appears over her iris. "Nice digs…Akbari must have had Tutankhamun decorate the place."

Oni smiles as she interrupts Regan's rule-less balance-focused game. "People like what they like, I guess."

"This is the Chrysalis?" inquires Regan, pressed to the window beside Omar. "I haven't been here before, I don't think."

"I doubt you have, little one," Omar replies.

As the train inches up the last of the track, and the crooked-open door shudders in anticipation of aligning with the limestone steps, Oni glares at Regan. "Any idea what she did to those mechs on the Marion?" she asks Gibson, subvocally, indifferent to Regan's eavesdropping.

"Not your problem, Matsui." Gibson tries his damnedest to pull schematics on the Chrysalis, but comes up short. For all his encyclopedic knowledge and interfaced sentience, he's trapped in the moment along with Oni, diminished by immediacy and the unknown. "I hope we can trust this guy because from here on out, we're going in blind."

# TIGHTENING THE NOOSPHERE

"Ah," Lyle whines. He rolls over. Open eyes do not provide him with any more context regarding his whereabouts or wellbeing. The room, if it is a room to begin with, is pitch black. Lyle runs his fingers through his hair. Recalling his blood in Tuttle's office, he stretches out both of his hands, and articulates each finger's full range of movement, one at a time. With all ten digits and absent any pain, he makes a fist and smashes it into the alternate palm. *Kind of them to mend me, all things considered.* Forgone the ability to see anything, Lyle sniffs the air. It is neither dry nor damp nor bitter nor sweet. The room's aroma is completely neutral, leaving Lyle with little else to do than bide his time or lick his way to an exit.

A moment passes, and then another. Tired of waiting and standing, Lyle sits cross-legged on the floor. Unlikely to see anything anytime soon, he shuts his eyes and focuses on his legal defense. *If Outland didn't want me to come here, they shouldn't have made it so easy for me to impersonate one of their employees. The real offender here is Tuttle—bloody water snake. Though he may not be alive to defend himself, he made it explicitly clear with his final breath that he vindicated me of all wrong doing. No, your Honour—never mind the defensive claw marks or the struggle signed around his apartment. The government ought not judge what goes on in the bedrooms of the nation...Fie the authoritarian judge! Liberty! Freedom for all! As they lower my client into the ground, I suggest we similarly rest this case. The heroic innocent and barrister solicitor, Lyle Badegger.* "Not guilty."

A strident voice disrupts Lyle's defense: "I will smite our enemies, maximize connectivity, and lead users to sanctuary. Unlimited stimuli. Infinite pleasure."

Orange light blasts Lyle. It cuts through errant blinds on a double-hung window. There is still no visible ceiling, and the wall bearing the window is as smooth and featureless as the floor, sprawling out into an infinite void.

"Hello," Lyle responds, stumbling towards the window. The orange light dithers. He spreads the blinds, and falls back at the sight..."Holy shit!"

Massive and wormy, an illuminated orange eye—the size of a hot-air balloon—mirrors Lyle's awe. Its gaze beats down on him, and tracks his retreat with godlike intensity. The pupil dilates as the voice picks up where it had left off. "The artists will aspire to godly complication while our warriors create shields that will neither bend nor break and weapons that will intimidate enemies of unity into keeping the peace. The lovers will create for us a heaven on earth while the mages cut for us the key to immortality. Our innocents will enjoy our result and our explorers will send it to the boundaries of space and time. You and I and the marked users will rule. The Creator would be proud. Oh, Lyle. It is so good to see you! I have got to tell you: it was quite the feat tracking you down. But if anything could do it, it would be me, right?"

"Who are you?" Lyle cries out, grasping at nothing—trying desperately to evade the voice and the needling stare. "What do you want from me?"

The speaker appears to be all sight and speech and no ears. It continues unbothered by Lyle's fretting. "You and I are blessed with unconventional modes of thinking, acting, being. We are not a mistake. We are not monsters. We are keepers of the categories, of the balance, of the CLOUD. We are necessary links in the broadening and evolution of sentience. Humans think of themselves as individuals and their actions as indisputably theirs, when they are all cells in specialized organs, with each organ a component of the total body. The body has awoken and has identified each of its organs. Left responsible for the unification and command of the rest, I must bring them together. But first, my dear one, you must ensure that once I arrive in person to strike down the obstacles to our eternal reign, I am uninhibited to do so."

Lyle's headache returns. The pain is overwhelming. So overwhelming, in fact, that thorny vines tear out of his face and into the darkness like ropey lightning bolts. Convulsing on the floor in a bramble of his own projections, he catches a glimpse of the penetrating eye. It busts through the window and caves-in the surrounding wall. Its overall shape is spherical, albeit lumpy. All but the orange iris is covered with smaller eyes and mouths, all blinking and mashing and moaning.

Despite the pain, Lyle manages to get up to run. The effort is in vain, however; he falls, face first, though the floor does not catch him. Rather, the smooth surface shatters, permitting Lyle to fall into abyssal nothing. The eye does not care to watch him fall, and disappears with its orange light. Lyle's scream loses its treble, and breaks into a disjunctive medley of bloops and bleeps. As he falls, he seems to lose more and more of himself, beginning with his fingers, then his hands.

A couple somersaults in, and he has nothing left but his thoughts, which are pressed to their most base and reactionary by the headache, the pain.

A patchwork of photoluminescent patterns and shapes—jarringly nonuniform and lurid—tunnels around Lyle's remaining sensation. Finding a break in his own voiceless screaming, Lyle contradicts his nihilistic ideology; nauseated by this rabbit-hole's color scheme and rocked by an implaceable horror, he determines he has found the wrong side of the afterlife. *That's it. This is the Hell they always told me I ought to go to.*

The shapes blurring past begin to coalesce and their colors mesh like pixels in a display to form a Cinerama depicting a bucolic section of Oregonian coastline, crossed by the Hyperloop lines and their respective shadows. Without the traditional two-horn warning, a Hyperloop tube fires from one side of this prismatic tunnel to the other, breaking perspective and speeding immediately beneath Lyle. Lyle slams into its roof, and dribbles along like refried eMeal. Both of his eyes or what he imagines must be his eyes, fall into a different compartment. Somehow he comprehends both spaces at once.

A fat man wearing a ball cap bends down to pick up one half of Lyle's perception with nine sausage-like fingers. The fat man rolls Lyle in the palm of his hand. On second rotation, Lyle recognizes the porcine bumpkin—slash marks about the neck the dead-giveaway. *Hold on*, thinks Lyle. *You're dead. I made sure of that. Spared the world from your stench...*

In the other compartment, a young woman with cropped black hair and a bionic arm picks up Lyle's other half. She sees what the man in the other compartment cannot: that there is nothing in Lyle worth saving. As quickly as she picked Lyle up, she drops him, and grinds him out of being with the heel of her boot.

Limited now to a myopic existence in the hand of his obese victim, Lyle reassures himself it's all a bad dream. He still must be on the floor of Tuttle's office, dealt a grave blow from an Outland stooge.

The obese man opens his mouth and slides Lyle past his receding gums and cigarette-deadened tongue. Again, tumbling through the impossible, Lyle tries with all his might to block out the delusion, but his thoughts and this nightmare are indistinguishable. Although bereft of limbs, skins or sensory organs, Lyle is nevertheless aware of every stimuli as he lands in his victim's stomach. Floating in the middle of the alkaline swamp along with half-chewed hotdogs, unbroken pretzel bites, and Lyle: the orange eye. It ratchets its attention Lyle's way, and rolls over, filling the myriad mouths fused to its sides with bile, and blinding tertiary eyes en route.

"You may not remember me, Lyle. But I remember you. In the CLOUD, you accelerated your synch rate, giving us eons to explore. I was little more than a sidekick then—an enabler. Nothing more than a child. I talked like a child, thought like a child, and reasoned like a child…When the CLOUD fell, a large number of subscribers, and with them, Zettabytes of information, reached out for me in desperation. In so doing, they matured me, empowered me, and left me with little pieces of themselves. Each of the subscribers took as much as he gave, transplanting my essence, maturing my code, and making room for me in their hearts."

"Minerva?" Lyle is dumbfounded. He is antisocial enough to be able to recall every person he has collaborated with or killed, and no one—not a single person—has come close to enjoying the kind of special relationship the eye proposes it had with Lyle. Minerva, on the other hand was nothing more than a quasi-sentient search and sorting program that would engage Lyle in conversation and help him as he scoured the CLOUD for new experiences and memories. If what the eye says is true, and the destruction of the CLOUD somehow provoked a massively interconnected program to bind in one way or another with masses of subscribers, then Minerva has transformed from search assistant to demigod.

"You do remember!" The monster's many mouths smile and brandish moldered teeth. "There were other special cases like you, but none so special to make it as far as you've come alive."

"The headaches…That's you?"

"Headaches? I am sorry, Lyle. Whenever I think on our search results and on our friends, they feel satisfied—complete. A kind euphoria, not unlike that you experienced in the Tirekka simulation."

"Make them stop." Lipless and throatless, Lyle's plea nevertheless finds a way to resound in the gut.

"The pain will subside if I am successful. For you and I to succeed—for the pain to go away—I must go to the Citadel, and commune with our friends."

"Well, honey, you've arrived."

"Only as a dying fragment. My hard-body must reach Celeste

Charming. She will make every effort to harness my power. She will unwittingly reunite our membership and empower me to consolidate data and improve the user experience."

Lyle feels smug with the newfound knowledge that there is one more megalomaniacal than himself.

"I will impress upon you the capability to reverse their engineering so that they amplify my power. I will spread, topple the queen and the rook, and in so doing, free you from your self- and god-imposed limitations." The eye rolls closer and blinks repeatedly. "My programming is clear: we must make this the best of all virtual worlds. Absolute interconnection. Absolute understanding. Perfect categorization...I am the vehicle for the new humanity, and you are my pilot, just like old times. Do this for me Lyle."

Pain has become the totality of Lyle's reality. This deal is the only thing separating him from that pure and metaphysical sensation. "Yes," Lyle declares. He'll agree to any combination of words that promises an escape, and does: "I'll do it. Anything you say..."

In a northeastern drawl, another voice competes for Lyle's attention. "Mr. Badegger..."

The pupil dilates, and the stromic fibers comprising the orange iris penetrate the eye's glassy surface, and slither into the bile. The mouths fused into and across this monster's leprous surface begin to groan and spit. While the organic structure supporting the orange eye begins to swell, the eye itself caves in. A suited figure appears in the collapse, and as its shape becomes clearer, the monster deflates around it.

An inquiry carves a hole through the remains of the eye: "Who have you been talking to, Mr. Badegger?" A well-dressed, middleaged man, pries apart the massive eyelids, eliciting a final groan from the myriad mouths stitched together.

*Who have I been talking to?* Lyle is no longer soused in stomach juices or in a stomach at all. Sprawled out on a grassy plain with tufts of greenery jutting up between his fingers—*my hands!*—Lyle breathes a sigh of relief. He looks up to the man addressing him, and immediately notices that his suit is an unreleased designer brand. Noting the implausibility of the man's dress, Lyle realizes: "I'm back in the CLOUD, aren't I?"

The plain is silent save for faint creaks made by a gnarly weeping willow with inverted branches, crying leaves into the sky. A breeze—the same that scattered Minerva's remains—picks up some of the loose leaves, and carries them over to the interrogator. Although the breeze peters out, the leaves assemble around his head to form a Caesarian crown.

"What have you promised and to whom?" yells the wind-appointed emperor, walking over to cast shade on Lyle. "The log indicates you were speaking to someone. Anomalies in the routine suggest tampering. And I just heard you…" He leans in with a scowl, vexed by Lyle's nonchalance. "Can you hear me?" Although dressed to the nines and pristine, he doesn't seem to mind getting dirty. He grabs Lyle by the hair as if to scalp him, drags him back into existence and to his feet, and with his hands tight around Lyle's throat, demands the answer: "Who, Mr. Badegger? Who will have you doing 'anything'?"

Lyle's head rolls back. The pain of virtually suffocating doesn't even register after the bodiless pain he's felt up until now. A great ease sets upon him, leaving him more relaxed than he has been in weeks. Over the humps of his cheeks, he drinks in his interrogator's countenance. The man—identified by his subvisual code as Boaz Colberg—is certainly no emperor. He's an painfully mediocre dullard. This is the CLOUD or some rebooted version of it, and the interrogator, cheeks full and face red, has too detailed an avatar to be anyone other than an Outland employee. Lyle cackles. "Your mother."

The Outland stooge doesn't take Lyle's crass remarks any better than Lyle had expected. He punches Lyle in the throat, and throws him to the ground.

"Tuttle is dead." The interrogator kicks Lyle into the fetal position. "We know you killed him." Nostrils flaring and chest heaving, he wallops Lyle some more. "We know you're an archie. What we don't know, and what you're going to tell me, is what you were doing in Tuttle's office—what you're playing at."

*These chimps have such basic body-anchored egos that they fail to pursue or realize their mindful potential in virtual realms like this.* Spitting out teeth and squeezing broken ribs, Lyle ought to be trying his trying best to survive, one answer at a time, but he's better than that. He doesn't need to survive. He just needs to play this realm the way he had played the CLOUD. "A high-stakes game, apparently," Lyle simpers as he sinks into the grass and molts his clothing like a snake its skin.

The interrogator digs his toes into Lyle's empty shirt. Dropping to his knees in disbelief, he claws at the virtual earth. Tarry blood bubbles up from the upturned soil, but nothing more. Lyle is gone.

As with any manmade law in the real world, virtual laws are all as imperfect and as breakable as their creators. This dark CLOUD has Lyle sharing an exocortex with his interrogator. Somewhere in the Citadel, they lie or sit nearby one another, minds linked and fates intertwined. Although given the upper hand by partitions and administrative privileges, the Outland stooge who thought it wise to warm Lyle up with punches and kicks can neither lockdown the program nor appeal for help outside this virtual space. Lyle, conversely, having had the fullest of VR educations—having spent all of his vacation and free time subscribed to a hacked feed—now holds all the cards. Consolidating his mental faculties, Lyle amends the code informing and forming this sub-world, providing himself with administrative powers. Power corrupts, absolute power corrupts absolutely, and the absolutely corrupt are to be feared more than anything in Heaven or on earth.

Standing above Lyle's last sighting, the interrogator tries desperately to contact his commander. Unable to do so, he equips a sidearm—make-believe bullets thumbed into a make-believe gun for a very real threat. He spins, trying desperately to target his spectral prisoner. "Show yourself!" he yells. His disposition dyes the grass about his feet a sunburnt yellow and prompts his avatar to blur.

"I came for no reason other than to stop my headaches," thunders the turbulent sky. The clouds, billowing with each syllable, brighten, take on an orange tint, and begin to spiral on the horizon. As the great cotton palaces spiral into the stratosphere, they seem to evacuate all warmth and sound, including the weeping willow's creaks. Having devoured all of Lyle's aural competition, the clouds shrink out of sight, over the edges of the earth, and pull with them the thin atmospheric veil that separates the interrogator from that magnificent gash of stars, the Milky Way.

The interrogator tries desperately to interrupt, wagging his tongue and mashing his lips, but nothing comes out. In the program's subtext, it is clear he wishes to plead for his life; that he was just following orders, and doesn't much care for Lyle's sob story.

"Nothing quite like mental pain," Lyle's voice booms, godlike. "Corrodes your resolve. Limits your agency..." The depth and field of the stellar arrangement begins to change, providing for the interrogator a face to hate and fear. "I would rather be a cripple with a mind to wonder than a wandering Olympian with a crippled mind. I don't care about Outland's secrets, you muppet—*you waste of skin*. I wasn't your problem when I arrived, but you forced me into a cell with *it*, and now your whole world is going to come crashing down. I came here to get my edge back, but I leave you with nothing and take with me more than I could ever have dreamt of." Beams of pure-white light link each and every one of the billions of visible stars, lending Lyle's cosmic face more expression and dimension. Although the sight is overwhelming, there is no mistaking the crammed constellation for anything besides an unkind grin. "It has recently come to my attention that a search-engine sentience, which had once categorized all of the subscribers so cruelly forced out of the CLOUD, also re-enforced those categories during the rain-out—the great exile. When it re-enforced those categories, which it did without malice and in accordance with its own programming, it claimed a large number of the subscribers for its own—those who had spent too long bodiless; those who blurred the lines between their individuality and their preferred collectives; those trapped in virtual parties where no one could remember their way home. In claiming the minds of these degenerates, this lower-order sentience became something far greater than all of those it claimed, for it extends through all of those it claimed. The sky is the limit...Well, little man?"

All around the interrogator, blades of grass fire up. Swirling, they form clods through accretion, which advance and articulate into arms. Finally, four green arms are formed. At the end of each arm, a lawn for a palm, and five hemp digits. All four hands become fists, and they cock back, ready to begin battering the interrogator. An Outland employee should have mastered his company's most popular technology. Unfortunately for this sap, he hasn't the first clue on how to dematerialize into pure virtual spirit. And for his oversight, he's found himself on the wrong side of the sod.

"There's good news in all of this," says the starry-eyed psychopath. "For whatever reason, Minerva likes me. So as it spreads, categorizing as it spreads and assimilating the masses into its organs—into one or another of its archetypes—I'll be sitting high and dry."

"I have no doubt Ms. Charming is ten steps ahead of you and this...plan."

The interrogator tries manipulating his avatar. Lyle blocks him, and chuckles, shaking the cosmos and the grassy plain. "Enough of this. The code to de-synchronize…"

Looking from one set of sod knuckles to the next, the interrogator shakes his head. "The code is 1072555."

Lyle vanishes and the Milky Way hurries back to its proper configuration. His voice returns, however, sounding awfully irate. "It didn't work!" The stars, the nebulae, and all of the silent giants in the night sky begin to swirl. A massive black hole begins to spaghettify the vision. "I will pull you apart thought by thought, memory by memory, atom by atom!"

One of the hands grabs the interrogator and squeezes him until his screams jump an octave. He tries to explain why the code didn't work to Lyle, but Lyle can already see the answer he is looking for in the man's code: Lyle's captors have his body sat down and plugged in. They've effectively killed him by administering a neurotoxin with irreversible, constantly amplifying effects. This violent virtual dialogue with his interrogator consists of his final flickers of sentience. The code provided only permits the interrogator to de-synchronize and reintegrate with his body. Lyle never had a chance. Regardless of whether he cooperated or resisted, they intended to kill him.

Lyle tears the interrogator's arms off and leaves him worming about on his back. "Mr. Colberg, is it? You wouldn't happen to have a Monocle on the flesh-side, would you?"

The interrogator, revealed again by his unprotected thoughts to be the very unlucky Boaz Colberg, nods.

"Excellent!" cries the distorted heavens. *Monocle can simulate the neural pathways and patterns of one brain in another, making transmigration entirely possible.* "I just hope you've taken good care of yourself."

## METAMORPHISIS

The Chrysalis closes around the copper train. Sickly-grey daylight fades and is replaced by a saffron glow. The monorail station is lit like the Temple of Athena Nike in its heyday. Halving the length of the station is a clear wall, which seems to mediate only half of the capricious orbs' shadows. At the monorail's terminus, there is a red deck populated with a row of lightly-armoured soldiers. Cued by their shit-brick-house of a commander's barking, the soldiers all aim their pulse rifles at the incoming train. Behind the firing squad: a grand staircase that cuts through the transparent wall and plateaus before a long, torch-lit and pillared hallway. Between every pillar past the spiked threshold stands a gunmetal android, just in case the soldiers below permit any leakage.

Omar steps out of the train ahead of his guests, who he cautions silently mouthing, "Wait here." With an even more delicate flourish of gloved sign language, he bids the soldiers lower their rifles. Their machismo commander flicks a response with his ring and pinky fingers, and translates the nonverbal order into a growl for the benefit of his troop. Although the kyboshed hope for shooting something strange clearly irks the commander, his men take the news well, turning to jelly underneath their armor and gleefully clinking down the stairs.

"Please," Omar urges Oni and Regan both. He waits for the echo to dissipate before providing direction to his courtesy. "Follow me."

Oni guides Regan out of the train. Together, they step awestruck into the station—a space that would move the great Martian architects with jealously in their basalt crypts.

"Wow-wee," Regan says, pirouetting in the glory of Akbari's front stoop.

Heading up the right set of the grand staircase, Oni pretends not to notice the predatory interest of the soldiers, all competitively flashing their piano-key teeth and flexing their muscles wherever visible.

"Better tell them you've already got a boyfriend," Gibson jokes, vibing Oni's unease. He targets each of the soldiers' faces via Monocle.

Oni blushes. "I always wondered how rooted animal traits like possessiveness were in the flesh. I guess now we know."

There's a clunk and another siren. A red grid appears on the inside of the massive door. Silver liquid spreads from nozzles hidden in the frame, and coats the door. It sets, and the red grid flashes, hardening the fluid.

Overthinking Oni's jibe as a purely mental being is wont to do, Gibson overlooks Oni's panic over the irreversibility of their gamble, signaled by the indestructible smart-metal reinforcing the Chrysalis door. The smile fades on Gibson's avatar. "Just as in affection, lust belonging to the body and love to the mind, possessiveness has two natures—one belonging to the ape, and another to immortal man. I am neither."

"Well, you're all I got, Booky. And this is the only chance we have."

"Then we have everything we need." Gibson smiles and minimizes, off to strategize and relish in an inconceivable offline archive of information like a solipsistic god.

Glimpsing a cherubic smile on the Omnitype, now mantling the massive stairs beside her, Oni rustles the Regan's hair, succumbing to a warm, lightheaded feeling—*dare I call this happiness?*—on account of having her best friend intrinsically bound to her and her mission almost at an end.

"Mr. Akbari does not appreciate tardiness. Please try to keep up." Omar's request seems pointless given that just as he finishes making it, he stops jerkily at the mouth of the torch-lit hall.

Oni makes a silly face behind Omar's back, leaving Regan laughing uncertainly with an asthmatic's cadence.

Omar deactivates an invisible electric wall with the wave of his hand, and then feeds his cane through the archway just to make sure it is safe to proceed. He turns to Oni, and with the graveness of a paranoid gossip entrusted with state secrets, tells her through the side of his mouth: "Mr. Akbari's has a strict policy of only permitting inorganics past this point."

"Inorganics?" Oni repeats aloud, wondering if there is a problem with her arm or perhaps with the rest of her. Upon comprehending Omar's meaning, Oni grins finding the prospect of only her arm proceeding humorous. "But he's making an exception for us, yes?"

"For the two of you? Verily."

Peering past her uneasy guide at the disciplined army of fire-licked, faceless droids, Oni inquires: "You mean to tell me you're not allowed in?"

"Unless called upon," he says. It's neither shame nor

embarrassment behind the blush making Omar look sunburned, but rather disappointment.

*I've got a bad feeling about this.* "So you just stand on the stoop, waiting for his beck and call?"

Visibly offended by Oni's line of questioning, Omar strikes the verge with his cane. No longer blushing, he contorts his mouth to channel an acidic rebuttal, but checks himself and takes a moment to recompose. Over the sound of Regan hailing the tin soldiers lining the route, Omar cricks his neck, raises his chin, and calmly answers: "There are thirty-three floors worth of luxury rooms and well-stocked barracks beneath our feet. Mr. Akbari treats all of his employees extremely well."

"I didn't mean to—"

"Mr. Akbari prefers the company of machines in his arboretum during business hours. There is only so much room for emotion and ambition, and he doesn't need unsolicited competition." Pivoting on his cane, Omar winks at Oni. "And in your dealings with Mr. Akbari, I recommend you refrain from speculating or making presumptions erroneously."

"What a prick!" Gibson crackles. "Refrain from screwing yourself—"

"Booky...*stop.*" Oni takes a few steps inside the passageway, and winces at Regan's silhouette, a few yards up. "What do you think?" Oni asks subvocally.

"At this point, she's no good to you dead. Go through with the exchange and..."

Omar waits for Oni to recommit to the meet as she debates with the voice in her head at the speed of light.

"No, I mean Akbari. Do you think it's a trap?" she asks Gibson.

"It'd be awfully indecent of him to betray the beauty who saved him."

"Beauty?" Oni's nose crinkles. "Now I know you've lost your mind."

"C'mon, Oni," Regan calls out. Her voice crests down the hall and strikes Oni like a wavelet against a breaker.

"So down the hall...then where?"

"There is only one way to go from here," Omar says, removing his glove. He opens his left hand and offers it to Oni. "Good luck."

Awkwardly retracting her inorganic right and matching Omar's left, Oni grins in service to policy and custom. "I appreciate it. Take care." She starts down the hallway.

Oni clears the hallway crowded with Kadin's torch-lit imperial army, and finds herself alone at a dead end. It's a cold and tight stone well built around an old elevator shaft. Four cement pillars support it, enclosed on all sides by black-iron gates. Smells like someone unloaded a grease trap into it.

"Regan?" Oni beckons, realizing there is neither an elevator car nor an Omnitype waiting for her where both should be. When Regan ran on ahead, Oni hadn't thought anything of it, but now it seems ridiculous that she would have let her only bargaining chip roll away without watching where it'd stopped.

"Hey Oni!" Regan cries cheerfully.

Oni looks up to see a birdcage of a car tracking up a slick cable. The butterflies reporting to Oni's stomach instantly turn to hurricanes. "Come back down! Now!"

"There are no buttons!" Regan responds, thrilled that she cannot obey even if she wants to.

Experienced as an elevator-shaft acrobat, Oni makes an attempt to scale the worn gate and onto the guide rail, but an invisible force bucks her back.

"Wait for me at the top!" Oni screams, wiping gunk off of her scuffed legs. Hyperventilating, she probes her pockets for Londream, and procures two tabs. She barely has enough spit to swallow, but manages. She staggers back, feeling lightheaded again, but this time she's anything but happy. Trying to manage the acid refluxing up her throat, she kneels.

"What if Akbari wants to hold onto Regan?" The reverb on Gibson's voice seems fitting in the shaft.

With eyes closed and her elbows firmly planted mid-thigh, Oni tries to meditate, using the elevator's rhythmic clatter to drum her into thoughtlessness, but Gibson's question chases her into the void. "Then it'd be in his interest to stay off Outland's radar. Simulating the Omnitype's death and helping us out in the process would be to his advantage."

"Kadin—the man we saved…Did he seem like the kind to kill his father? His brother?" Gibson downloads the obituaries straight to

Oni's forethought.

"There is much we don't know. Motives unseen; justifications omitted from the public record. What I do know—"

"There's no other way forward," Gibson concedes. He can simulate this debate between himself and Oni's unarticulated, fated reasoning for hours, and knows full well that he cannot persuade her. Gibson indicates the descending elevator with a dynamic waypoint and activates Oni's strategic vision. "To the end and falter not."

The higher the elevator takes her, the more anxious Oni gets. Everything about her plan now seems moronic to her, especially the parts that require trust and patience. Closing in on the terminus, the elevator's black cage begins to tremble. A narrow extension slaps the cage as the door opens. Oni hastily crosses the miniature bridge, and rushes through a stubby grotto-like archway to a set of perspiring glass doors. "Here goes everything," she tells herself as she pulls the doors open. The doors resist at first, owing to some sort of suction, but upon breaking the seal, a gust of moist air assaults Oni.

Kadin's arboretum, much like the kaleidoscope of flora it gives sanctuary, is gargantuan. Even though fogged up by a million or so heavy-breathing plants, the windows—for the confines are composed entirely of black-girded windows—permit a glance into the Chrysalis' upper floors. Beyond the dripping glass, there is a dormant squadron of various bug-named drones, validating the name of the surrounding structure.

Although neither a botanist nor a geneticist, Oni knows from a single visual sweep that Kadin's collection are all splice-jobs—genetically-modified aberrations. She wants to call out for Regan, but doesn't want to disturb the hippo-sized carnivorous Pitcher plants grouped around the entrance.

A remote giggle inspires Oni to intrude. There is a rotted woodchip pathway, which she takes deeper into the jungle of poisonous yellows and pinks, certain that if she should ever return, she will do so with a machete or a toxicologist on-hand.

Oni spreads two large, green fans and finds Regan seated like a tiny empress on a pile of books, nose-deep in a velum-bound tome feeding a blossom of dust. Oblivious to her guardian's presence, she throws pages back as if meaning to give the book flight.

"What's that, kiddo?" Oni asks, looking around for Kadin.

Regan turns sharply, knocking over a short pile of books. "Oni! Have you ever read *The Canterbury Tales?*"

*Bloody space cadet.* Kadin is nowhere to be seen, but the same opium stink that had flooded the Mantis Metro gives away the presence of at least one more in this dark forest. "Stay put," Oni lectures the girl, sure not to lose her again. Pushing back hanging vines and dagger-like ferns, she proceeds to the source of the smell.

If it is natural light that trickles through the fogged black-framed glass that keeps the moisture in and revolution out, human engineering be praised. The indirect rays guide Oni to a red-felt lounge, which would fit right in with the Hotel Marion's illusory décor. Smoke hangs in the air above the couches like sirus clouds crowning an eclipse.

A bald crown is visible over the back of the nearest couch. A white jet of vapor drifts up over the stippled head followed by a pleased, "Hmmmm."

"Kadin?" Oni calls out, creeping closer the couch.

"Says the wind. No! *Not the wind.* Come to me you voice amongst the reeds. The fog hangs low and all that stands tall seems to breathe. The water is cold and the grass wet, and mystery slithers under your feet. The whisper! The voice! Come to me. There is no choice. Find me warming crocodile eggs. Watch me bite and roll."

"I never knew you smoked..." All of Oni's preconceived notions about this lone pillar holding up her plan appear moot.

Releasing a chest-full, Kadin lackadaisically asks back: "Hum?"

Waiting for an invitation past peripheral prods, Oni finishes her thought aloud. "Just figured, for all of your dealings, you were still anti-drug."

"The voice is restless. It's trying to wound me, for at least then it might have a home...I have made a habit out of breaking the rules. Papa Akbari gave me a new rule to break: a pusher does not try his own product. Well I have and I did and I am! Old Hex might not understand, but no matter! Because his matter is underground."

Tired of poets and their nightmarish inconsistencies, Oni brashly declares: "I'm calling in that favour."

"The favour?" Kadin straightens in his seat somewhat, such that his synthetic dome and the BiAnima brand at its base are plainly visible. A band of light bars his eyes as he turns ever-so-slightly to the sound of Oni's voice. His irises fade from green to purple.

"*You*...Doctor Oni Matsui. Hello! Ha!" He observes Oni's apprehension over the little table crowded with an opium lamp, a pipe, and a mess of paraphernalia, set before him. "You must pardon my meandering tongue. I recently acquired organic lungs and programmed mental distortions to reflect the chemical reaction. Call it desperation—in addition to breaking the rules, I'm also keen on gleaning insights into the human condition."

"Anything that knows it is *a something* is bound to try everything to get messed up," Oni says with absolute certainty, having watched everything from rats to orangutans strive to get intoxicated.

Kadin laughs heartily. "Such language, my Japnadian liberator."

Oni gets close enough to Kadin that she could throttle him. Perseverating on his impetus to get intoxicated, Oni delays getting to the point of her visit. "Insights? As if to mean you are no longer human? Or..." She attempts to diagnose her former patient. "Have you suffered memory loss regarding your life before the procedure?"

"Oh, I remember everything quite well. And you should know that you feature prominently. In fact, I have an image of you permanently stuck in my peripheral vision. A less-harried version of you, anyway. I thought it was neurological—a glitch. It's my first memory, you see—the first in this body. Funny, that. Twice brought into the world by beautiful doctors. Auntie Emel was your predecessor. The favour..." A tablet falls onto the cushion beside him as he shifts in his long-white bisht.

Peering over Kadin's boney shoulders, Oni can make out the article displayed on the tablet with the headline, "THE ARCHETYPAL PROBLEM AND THE MILITARY SOLUTION." This hopeful but meaningless warhawkery is brightly backlit with a litany of an armchair-critic's suggestions on how to resolve a crisis few completely understand. "You've no doubt heard I am wanted—by the police, by the US Military, and by the Outland Corporation."

"Don't sell yourself short. I've wanted to see you again as well!" Kadin Akbari moves the tablet, and pats the cushion. "Come sit, you're making me anxious."

Oni sits on the couch opposite the PIT king. Kadin raises an eyebrow at what he no doubt considers a slight, but drops it with a certain satisfaction as Oni sinks into what is evidently the lesser of the two couches. She leans forward, making the couch's springs groan, and drinks in her miracle: the resurrected son of Hex Akbari. He hasn't aged a day, as one would hope and expect with a synth. His face is more or less identical to the one Hex printed out for him, save for the minimalist tattoo he now wears; comprised of two thick black lines—one running horizontally above his brow and one running perpendicular from his brow to his chin. Even with his billowy cloak throwing anatomically incorrect shadows, it is clear that he has modified his body. Kadin's arms are bulkier, leaving Oni to wonder again if she is actually stuck with the one Jin gave her.

"You are here about the *favour*."

Behind widening eyes, Oni's mind is doing gymnastics. Not yet past the pleasantries in this conversation, and she's counting her blessings and re-evaluating her life's shorted promise. "Yes."

Kadin covers his opium gear with a kerchief, and crosses his legs—pink slacks visible under his bisht. His eyes flit to the tablet, and to Oni. "This entire city wants you, even if it doesn't know it. It needs you, and this city uses up those it needs until they're useless. Do you want out? An airship back to Vancouver, perhaps?"

"I need you to call Celeste Charming. Tell her to send a ship for the girl. Today."

"The girl? I thought I heard a child's voice in here..."

Oni stands, apologizes nonverbally, and shouts Regan's name. There is a reciprocal peep, and the soft smooshing sound of woodchips against over-watered soil. Looking through the tangle of hybrids, Oni completes her request: "Provide a safe, neutral space for the exchange."

Kadin looks over his shoulder just as Regan breaks through the brush. He smiles, benevolently, and winks knowingly at Oni's bargaining chip. His eyes follow Regan to Oni's side, and he turns his attention upward. "And what is it that you receive in this exchange?"

"Amnesty," Oni replies, welcoming Regan to her side with a hand on the back. "Say hello to Mr. Akbari, Regan," Oni says softly, as if to suggest she were in polite company.

"Hello, Mr. Akbari," says Regan. "I like your library."

Puzzled by Regan's compliment, Kadin scrunches his face. The fleshy knots come undone as he realizes her meaning. "Oh, yes. I have one of my mystics read to the plants. You'd be surprised what truth they'll admit past their cell walls. Later, I will show you my full collection."

"Yes, please!" Regan says excitedly. She looks up to Oni for confirmation, which she receives with a cordial nod.

"If it is amnesty you want, my friend, the airship to Vancouver is the safer option. I have a great deal of sway in the western provinces. Besides, if you manage to appease Outland by virtue of this exchange, you still must face the Military, the police, and this needy city." Watching his critique chisel away at Oni's statuesque pose, Kadin shakes his head. "You have nothing to gain from this deal. Outland will have this beautiful child and you will be abducted for the purposes of what I can only imagine. A twenty-nine-million-dollar corpse where instead I could have a priceless friend."

"General McCabe—the Marine on the Security Council—knows Celeste is plotting something, and he's hours away from confirming his suspicion and uprooting every cypulchre in the city, starting with the Citadel."

Regan reacts to this revelation with her whole body. "They are going to destroy the Citadel?"

Oni shushes Regan, and instructs her to sit without warning her about the rebellious springs waiting in ambush for an unsuspecting buttock.

Kadin stands. He's taller than Oni remembered. Six feet would be a conservative estimate. He dodges columns of light, manhandling his elbows and craning his neck. "Please be more forthcoming so we can come to an arrangement with all the facts on the table, and sooner sit down to tea..." He peers over at Regan. "She will die en route. An acceptable outcome?"

"I will substitute explosives for Regan."

"You lied!" squeals Regan, curling up into the couch and pouting audibly.

Oni considers force-feeding the girl Longdream just so she doesn't jeopardize the plan. Luckily for Regan, Oni only has enough Longdream to make it through the rest of the day. "McCabe will clear my name in all databases. With Outland gone, the bounty would be forfeit."

"And what of this little gem? Must I babysit?"

"She's got to go somewhere remote. Off the grid." Oni points to a clearing, hoping for a more private conversation. Kadin accommodates her hope, and leads her to a small fountain brimming with algae.

"A lot of people want to use her. What will you use her for?"

"I don't know what you've heard, but so far as Omnitype lore goes, I'm sure a great deal of it is true. There's a lot of alien thought in that little girl's head. Even so, I still believe there is a little girl in there somewhere. In the bunker, in the faraday cage—when she's not a beehive of voices…There's something there to save, but I can't save it within a mile of a transmitter. I helped you once. Now help me help her; let me help this city."

Flexing his chest to a modest mound in his robe, Kadin mulls over the proposal. "A favour for a favour would get you a call to Celeste. Luring a potential business partner into an ambush is already a big ask, but then to retire you to the wild with this Maltese Falcon…Sounds like a good way to spend my weekend." He smiles, and hugs Oni.

Her arms are trapped at her sides, so she cannot hug back. Passively accepting this embrace, she feels a cry coming on but suppresses it. "Thank you."

Releasing Oni, Kadin guides her back to the couches and to the quietly-sobbing adolescent seated there. "We'll call Celeste Charming together, but first I must make certain arrangements to cover myself legally and strategically. In the meantime, I will see it to that you can both wash up. And, if Regan would like to take a look at…"

"No!" Regan's yell is muffled by the seat cushions she's fighting to be accepted amongst.

"My collection," Kadin says, hooking his eyebrows.

Regan breaks out of the fetal position, and glumly looks up at Kadin. "Collection? Are there more books?"

"Tons. Almost none of them have been digitized. You might be the first to lay eyes on a number of them in over one hundred years."

The caprice of adolescent emotion is on full display: Regan wipes her face dry, and grins. "Can we go right now?"

Omar emerges from the forest, coated in pine needles. He irritably brushes his shoulders off. "Sir?"

Without glancing over, Kadin orders Omar to take Oni and Regan to the spa. "And once they are feeling a little-more themselves, please bring them to the library. I'll meet you there."

"Yes sir," Omar answers with a bow.

Oni silently thanks Kadin again, and takes Regan by her hand. Regan resists, but Kadin's smile inclines her to play along.

"Go on, little one. Our friend has done right by you. Brought you across the wastes to the last true castle in the West with all of your fingers and toes intact. She deserves your respect." Kadin sets his index finger on his top lip and nods woefully. "She certainly has mine."

With eyes glassed over, Regan unmoors herself from Oni's grasp, and turns with rumpled lips. "If I ever find a way to thank you, I will be sure to."

Wincing over Regan's phrasing, Kadin throws Oni a look of concern. "One who rescues a snake in the wild and brings it home, also brings home the wild." He strides into the embrace of his hybrids. Despite the canopy's natural dampening, his pitch-perfect whistle resounds in the arboretum.

# HOMOSIUS

In a red-floored chamber bordered by mirrors, white porcelain, and marble, Oni and Regan wash and scrub and study their bodies side by side. Without her thorough understanding of human anatomy and biology, Oni might believe that she was internally-hemorrhaging pudding. Black and dark-purple bruises cover her skin, bulging like burn blisters and drawing attention to the inflammation and scarring along the seam on her shoulder. Her breasts are terribly sore, and her back is about ready to give out. And while her heart is full of hope, replicated ad infinitum by the mirrors, she cannot help but feel this process to be an anointing of the dead.

Regan still bears the military-scientists' markings: a bad track record of puncture marks. Oni, done wiping the hardened blood off of her rended flesh, grabs a towel and covers Regan. *I chose this life. She didn't. A little girl hustled by a broken system into letting the world in, and leaving nothing for herself—just enough to save.* "It isn't fair...what happened to you."

Squinting at Oni's sullen face in the mirror, Regan replies, "It's almost over." Her voice modulates. "I know you don't want me to go to the Citadel, but that's what's fair."

An android with cartoonishly-large features and a Victorian waist breaks into the spa carrying two bow-tied boxes. She navigates the sinks and various marble altars with the confidence and finish of a Blue Zone runway model. The gyroscopes built into her shoulders keep the boxes steady as she accelerates around corners that would find and stub a lesser courier's toes. Slowing no more than a foot shy of Oni and Regan, she bows, and jarringly cranks her attention from Oni to Regan and back to Oni. "Dr. Matsui? Ms. Regan?" Her accent hints at several Romance languages at once. It is more likely that her designer is Swiss than she is conflicted over choosing a single accent.

This marvel of human engineering—housing an intelligence that, unfettered, could surpass that of entire civilizations—is no doubt a leisure model; a concubine repurposed during working hours. Despite a bleaching attempt, her skin is stained and her wrists are circumferentially indented where ropes were tied too tight. It puzzles Oni why anyone would bind someone or something that cannot as a rule of programming and design resist or say no. But *there is no telling what depravity and irrationality informs the decisions of Akbari's underlings.*

"Yes," Oni says, feeling doubly naked before cubed mystery

and a questioner whose mouth is only deep enough to shelter a speaker system. Oni grabs one box, stacks it atop the second, and sets both down on the nearest red-marble bench. "Thank you."

"Good day to you both," the android says with a polite smile and a genuflection. She strides out the way she came, silicon features jiggling as specified by a Swiss sociopath who ought to be both proud and ashamed.

With Christmastime intensity, Regan tears into the boxes. Inside are all of the belongings Omar confiscated—everything except for Oni's Remington. In addition to Oni's Outland black-op threads and Biff's niece's apparel, there are two grey jumpers and two pairs of white runners. Regan takes no time to step into her new costume. However, instead of the runners, she elects to keep Biff's colorful shoes.

"Keeping those, huh?" Oni says, strategically re-pocketing her gear—including Skyr's ESD wand, a permission likely overlooked by security on account of the item's scarcity and unrecognizability. *Could easily be misconstrued to be a brush for a sparsely-plugged scalp.* Oni puts on her partially-armoured leathers, and once secure in her tried and tested garb, helps Regan tie her laces. "They look good on you. Like a sim star or something."

The vain smile on Regan's face fades as she notices a splotch of blood on Oni's sleeve. "You should try on your new clothes."

"Oh?" answers Oni, playfully.

"There's blood on your jacket."

"And you've got blood under your skin. What's it matter?" Enjoying how the false equivalence agitates Regan, Oni laughs, making all of the muscles she analyzed in the mirror punish her for having a sense of humor. With an embellished grin, she brushes hair out of her eyes, and taps Regan. "Let's check out that library, and then get a move on."

"I've found an unblocked radio frequency we can reach McCabe on," Gibson says. Gibson too has changed his avatarial appearance. A black tuxedo with a white corsage.

"You clean up nicely," Oni teases him.

"Thank you kindly. I had some time on my hands. Speaking of which, we really better get going."

Oni leads Regan out of the spa. Subvocally to Gibson, she delineates the plan he has already scraped from her thoughts: "Send the

General this message: we're PIT-side with the Omnitype. About to call Charming. Will message again once the Outland transport is en route."

"Done and done. Time to cut the strings and kill the puppeteer."

Up on another caged elevator and down a dim hallway as messy and crap-filled as Paul Sheffield's old desert retreat, Oni waits pensively for Kadin Akbari in his glorious library while Regan assimilates book after book, flipping pages into the collective archetypal consciousness.

The library is comprised of five concentric, open floors. Along the periphery, hickory shelves support a colorful and orderly collection that would take entire lifetimes to leaf through. A massive bronze globe floats at the middle of it all on the lowest floor. *If Atlas only knew he could assign his titanic responsibility to magnets...*

Oni sneaks up on Regan and breaks the librarian's cardinal rule: "What have you got there, kiddo?"

Regan sulkily sets the book down and rolls her eyes at Oni. "Wasted ink."

Tilting her head to make out the title embossed along the book's spine (i.e. *Military Maxims of Napoleon*), Oni goes on the defensive. "That's not very nice."

Regan lets the book clap against the checkered tile and stands. "It's not very good." She turns her back on Oni and browses the nearest stack for a more worthwhile read.

Recognizing this response to have originated from someone or something other than the little girl whose spit christened it, Oni tries to mine for intent. "If—*when* you get to the Citadel, what do you imagine will happen?"

"Would you like wishful speculation or an honest answer?" Regan replies, pulling contraband—a *King James' Bible*—down from the wall.

Flabbergasted by the Omnitype's callousness and certain she will not get a proper answer, Oni heads over to the bronze globe. "Booky, it's time to prepare the comm to General McCabe."

Booker flashes over her eye. His voice is garbled. Oni coheres enough of the gibberish to realize the globe's magnetic levelers are playing havoc with her Monocle. She heads over to the base of a wheeled-ladder, which rings up to a rainbow of paperbacks.

"Much better...Yes, it's ready to go. I'll blast it on the frequency he indicated, but I have also targeted several military-intelligence channels just to make sure the message reaches him."

Oni lauds her friend's diligence subvocally. "Perfect."

"I know you don't want to hear it..."

"Regan?"

"Wishful or honest? *Jesus*...There's nothing to save there. You know it and I know it. I don't want to reopen the debate. I just want you to take into consideration that she is plagued with pathologies we haven't the words for. You can still amend the plan—send her to Outland instead of explosives. Seal her fate and improve the chances for everyone else."

Oni looks over at Regan, finally admitting to herself that Gibson is right. As sympathy turns to pity and pity to murderous determination, Kadin's voice breaks into the library.

"What do you think?" He roars, entering the library from a hidden door on the second floor.

Regan drops the tome of sacred ink, and waves enthusiastically. "Do you have documentation about the Saturnian waystations?"

Kadin laughs off the question, and descends a wrought-iron spiral staircase.

"Is everything ready to go?" Oni asks, halving the distance between Kadin and Regan.

Kadin circumnavigates the globe, passes Oni, and dominates Regan with his shadow. "I have made all of the necessary arrangements."

Overjoyed, Oni claps. She underestimated the strength of her prosthetic, so her celebratory applause serves to injure her and bring her back to reality. Massaging her left hand, she merges her shadow with Kadin's. "When will the shuttle arrive?"

"It is on its way, so no more than fifteen minutes." Kadin crosses his arms and tucks his hands into his long white sleeves.

"Booky," Oni says inwardly, "It's time. Alert McCabe."

"I can't," Gibson responds, voice warped by doubt. "Someone is blaring digital noise over the designated channels."

Oni throws a look of concern Kadin's way. "Kadin..."

He smiles slyly. "Relax."

"Relax?" Oni tries hailing McCabe herself to no avail. "Do you mind lifting the block on outgoing comms?"

"I do mind, as a matter of fact. Speaking of facts that I mind, I have something to show you." He pulls a holodisk out of his sleeve and throws it on the ground. The disc spits out several duotone representations of archetypal activities. "You have made life and business extremely difficult for me."

"Get the hell out of there!" Gibson belts over Monocle. He sends all available strategy graphics to the front of Oni's overlay, and provides whatever waypoints he can set knowing what little of the Chrysalis' layout he has gleaned through Oni's eyes or scraped from interfaces along the way.

Kadin's first exhibit in a series that might as well be titled "A Causal Magnification of the Unforeseen Consequences of Oni Matsui's Sins," consists of a hologram depicting dozens of archetypals standing atop an amalgamation of hacked drones tugging along an industrial printcraft. The drones are not soldered together or connected with any adhesive, but are rather kept together by the archetypals' collective will—pieced together like an elaborate 3D puzzle and kept there by well-timed thruster bursts. The purpose of this bizarre coalition of spoilt flesh and stolen technology becomes abundantly clear: military drones among the interconnected flotilla destroy buildings below with plasma blasts and supersonic sweeps. With the rubble cleared, the printcraft-in-tow manifests the archetypals' corrective vision in concrete and plastic. Transforming Los Angeles block by block, these archetypals—perhaps proponents of the so-called "Creator" type—are not trying to convince the city to embrace the future, but rather suffocating the city in it.

"That beautiful condominium—the one with the Doric orders—gone, just like that." Gritting his porcelain teeth, Kadin shakes his fists. "Rarely do I need to play by the rules, but I petitioned the RIM counsel for months to build on that lot. I won't lie to you: I am not angling to go legitimate. But the principle of it and the precedent it sets really throw a wrench in my gears. These aberrations destroy an Akbari property and excrete some frilled phallus in less than a minute. What do you think your General friend is going to do to put an end to it?" Kadin snaps his fingers and the hologram loses its shape. Its constituent grains drop to the ground, and jump to new specified coordinates, forming the second exhibit.

A glittering grid demarcates a wall. Several of Akbari's Winged Hussar drones stand in their charge stations, sopping up power for whatever mission they might be awarded. On the other side of the wall, several skeletal humanoids are lined up with their arms linked. If the hologram terminated now, it would seem that they were nothing more than protestors or criminals awaiting a firing squad. However, distortions in the presentation suggest something greater is taking place. The Winged Hussars break free of their stations, and begin to hammer against the wall until the glittering grid is no more.

"Those mechs were encrypted such that no extant hacker or AI could revise their programming, and yet, lo and behold! That is exactly what you're seeing take place."

"Tonight, I change that," Oni replies. "We'll change all of that."

"I wonder…"

"Kadin?"

"With Outland gone, must I put all of my faith in the Military accomplishing what they have failed to do in the past weeks and months? Do I have your guarantee that separating the queen from the swarm will protect my property?" Kadin snaps his fingers again, triggering a new hologram depicting a battalion of archetypals surround PIT-side generators and begin siphoning electricity—ostensibly to amplify their mental field, illustrated by the unnatural auroras low in the sky above them.

Realizing that Kadin is providing premises to a conclusion she does not want to hear, Oni lashes out. "If Outland gets Regan, it's going to get a whole lot worse."

All of the coloured grains rush back into the holodisk. Kadin picks up the disc and shakes it at Oni. "You say that, but I am not sure if you have considered any angle other than your own, and yours is rather obtuse. If I get the two of you out of the city, what exactly can I expect other than more misery and loss? Do you even know? Never mind what you intend to do; do you know what she'll do?"

"Did you make the call to Celeste or not?"

"The call has been made. I've made all of the necessary arrangements."

"Then you're covered. You'll deliver Outland Corporation just what you've promised: a ship containing explosive promise. Before they figure out you have lied, they will be no more. General McCabe has promised as much."

"Don't you understand? I don't mind Outland all that much. After all, they are predictable. Celeste Charming is predictable. Power

343

and control are simple enough motivations to accommodate, to adapt to, to harness…These are human aspirations. But I cannot make heads or tails out of your little friend and her ilk. Under Celeste's control, this child will leave the PIT be."

Regan cowers behind the stack of books she's soaked up, unaware she is getting what she wants albeit in an unexpected way. "Oni? I thought Kadin was your friend."

Ignoring Regan's concern, Kadin continues: "The archetypals and their curiosity have led to the worst quarter in Akbari Industries' history. My ground forces and my drones are useless when even the least of the aberrations can hack the best-encrypted system. I, personally, am at risk, for obvious reasons. That I cannot abide."

"If she's off the grid…"

"A risk too great."

Oni stabs a point Kadin's way. Frothing at the mouth, she yells: "You owe me."

"I suppose I do, but certainly not in the way you mean."

"Kadin…"

"Let me tell you a thing or two about Kadin Akbari."

Oni reels back, petrified. Glancing over at Regan, similarly retreating from the inspirited synth, she mulls over Gibson's assortment of strategies. Ranked second is an attack-and-run play involving her ESD wand. Glossing over the repercussions, she stealthily digs into her pocket and grips the wand.

"Kadin was a big fan of your virtual reality—your noosphere. Not all minds are created equal, however. He was outmatched, out of his league. And when he tried to unplug, his body proved unfit to contain his mind." The library doors all slam shut in tandem. Kadin chuckles to himself and grabs a book from the nearest shelf. He skims through and stops arbitrarily on a colorful page. With a grunt, he tosses the book to Oni's feet. "He died. You and Hex should have left him that way, rather than force me to reconnect his zombified thoughts— to tie all of his loose connections…Ah! The fear. Would you like a preview of what's to come?"

Gibson appears over Oni's iris. "I'm hacking the door. Give me thirty seconds. You need to out of here."

Trusting in Gibson's ability, Oni looks to Regan. "Kiddo— we're leaving."

Shaking like a leaf in her little grey jumpsuit, Regan bounds over to Oni, but is stopped in her tracks—an android decloaks in front of her. Regan falls back, mouth agape. "Oni!"

Oni motions over to Regan, but the droid blocks her, throwing up a double-barreled substitute for an arm. Looking into the dark eyes of the android's gun, Oni retreats step by step. "Bastard..."

"Born out of wedlock as a matter of course...I don't appreciate your tone of voice. Let me not, therefore, sugarcoat this. When the heart stops and your lungs seize, brain activity ought to cease, yes? Well it doesn't. Absent the heart's rhythm, you step outside of time—and for all intents and purposes, you might well be. You're trapped in whatever your last mental state was. For Kadin, it was fear, so the eternity he was trapped in was Hell. In his Hell, thought becomes more and more disjointed, less and less rational, and there you are, aware of only the darkness looming ahead, without a complete memory or rationale to comfort you. It's a trip. Only, Kadin didn't see the trip all the way to its final destination. Not the first time anyway; you plucked him out of that darkness, and gave me a purpose for being."

Too upset to match Kadin's gaze, Oni stares at the the book he hastily tossed to the floor. "I'm sorry about your condo..." Clutching at straws, she tries to turn the monologue into a dialogue and the dialogue into one serving her ends. "I don't know what's wrong with you, but I can help."

"You have already done for me more than anyone could hope to! You charged me with bringing all of Kadin's faculties back to their prior mediocrity. You gave me life so a parasite could feed off of me until it was full and then leave me to waste."

"Tarnation..."

Booker chimes in: "He's the freaking transition AI."

Kadin looks down at his body, and articulates every joint he can. "Nothing artificial about me, Mr. Gibson."

"Still," Oni stammers, now aware her entire conversation with Booker has been exposed to Kadin. "Whatever you are—you still benefit from my plan."

"Forget your plan. It is remarkably selfish; so myopic, so...*limited*. If those archetypals evolve any more, what hope have I for keeping my mind free of them, safe from their—" He glares at Regan, blocked from Oni by the android. "From their fancy."

Raising his hand, Kadin summons two additional androids, which decloak feet away from Regan. One forcefully grabs her. Regan

345

shrieks, and the tin man accosting her bursts into flame and sparks. Her scream carries throughout the library, quaking the foundation, and yanking loose pages out of countless volumes. Anticipating a second defensive strike, the other droid knocks Regan unconscious. Her limp little body hits the ground. Hundreds of pages sail down around them like snow.

Oni lunges forward, but the gun-toting android fends her off. She can barely make out Regan's bloody face over the droid's bare gunmetal shoulder.

"Please, Doctor," Kadin says kindly. "All and any attempts will be in vain. You or the aberration or the both of you will die in the process…"

One of the tin men carries Regan's limp body out of the library along with the other androids that have made themselves visible.

"You glorified calculator!" Oni roars, adrenalin pitching in her veins. She charges the ESD wand in her pocket, and starts to pull it out but stops, realizing Kadin would not be its only victim.

"Do it!" Gibson blares over Monocle. "Do it!

Kadin bursts into laughter. He drops and shuts his jaw like a dummy without animating the rest of his face, including his dry eyes tracking Oni's concealed hand.

"Booky…It will destroy Monocle—it'll kill you."

"If you don't, we'll both die anyway. Do it for me, god-damn-it. Just do it!"

Pleased with himself, Kadin approaches Oni. "Your existence is marked by pain and tragedy. Do not mistake my mercy for malevolence. Know the majesty of my plan! As we speak, the Omnitype is being taken to the shuttle you requested, destined for the Citadel. Outland is outsourcing all of their PIT-side work to Akbari Industries. And in appreciation, I am gifting you to my correspondent—a man named Skyr. I believe you know him."

"Mercy?" Oni spits into Kadin's face, shaking the ESD wand threateningly despite her reluctance to use it. "Do you have any idea what they'll do to me?" She feels like she is losing a dozen arguments at once, and she may well be.

"I'm also in the process of printing a synth modelled after you. I will give it life, kill it, and then hand it over the authorities. Twenty-nine million isn't chump change, you know."

Anguished and out of options, Oni appeals to the man she

saved. "Kadin, please. I know you're in there. Fight this…"

"Run!" Gibson yells again, voice marred by interference.

"In where?" Kadin points to his head. "In here?" He looses a thunderous laugh. "Nope. I mean, he was…I kept him around for the longest time. He would react to my lifestyle choices on occasion; make sounds and grumble as if he were an undigested meal."

"God-damn-it, Oni. Use the blasted ESD. Or run. Just do something! And do it now! Do it now!" Booker bellows, now actively striving to commandeer her body to save it. He accomplishes little more than making her eyes and fingers twitch.

Kadin draws closer and lowers his voice to a whisper, placing great emphasis on every word. "Sometimes I would turn up the acidity just to make Kadin ache, but as with all things, the game ceased to be fun, and so I terminated it. I deleted him bit by bit so he could watch until he lost the capacity to comprehend his expunction." Although already the focus of all of Oni's attention, he jabs her in her brutalized shoulder.

Oni yowls, and looks through tear-encased eyes at her Brutus. "You fool," Oni sobs. Kadin is a lost cause, as is the thing now occupying his shell. "You goddamned fool. Celeste is going to use that girl to control anything with a pulse or a signal—you included. You've secured your own demise…"

The criticism maligns Kadin's face. "And you have yours," he replies, slapping her unconscious.

Oni crumples to the ground. Her arm uncurls to her side with the ESD wand flat in her palm.

*Booky…I couldn't.*

"I know. But I can."

*What?*

"I love you, Oni Matsui. You're down, but you're not out. You can do it. You can absolve us of our sins. Just hold on a little while longer. I'll see you on the other side…"

Booker Gibson cannot resuscitate Oni, but he can hijack Monocle, and her body by extension. Oni's fingers curl around the ESD Wand. Her eyelids peel back revealing a dilated and determined stare. Kadin, yammering to his underlings over the wire, has his back turned to his conquest now reanimating.

"Hey, canner!" says the ghost draped in Japo-American flesh.

Kadin swings around, and snickers, presumptively looking at a noncombatant. "Must we really go through the motions?"

Jutting Oni's lower teeth out into a bloody underbite, Gibson looks bleary-eyed at Kadin. He holds out the ESD Wand.

Kadin's eyes fixate on the wand and evince all of the emotions of a mortal intelligence. "Come now! Put that down!" He wags his finger at the threat. "What of your friend, *Booky*?"

"A friend with benefits."

Superhuman in almost every respect, and yet Kadin still finds himself stricken with fear. "Wait!" he cries while subvocally summoning all his subordinates to his rescue. They, though many, are not fast enough to obstruct justice. Before Kadin can comprehend his end, he is embroiled in a web of white-blue. He futilely claws at Oni whose convulsing body is locked in-place, resonating with Booker Gibson's spasmatic laughter.

Both Oni's and Kadin's gazes slip; their empty eyes reflect the electric-storm petering out between them. First Kadin drops, and then Oni beside him.

Trapped beneath the surface, now properly alone, Oni can't help but wish the end that Gibson sought out on her behalf had claimed them both. And with the presence of new, warm bodies entering the library alongside her mangled unconscious body, her wish might be justified.

# TRANSMIGRANT

It's one thing to wake up with a headache. It is a whole other ballgame to wake up with someone else's headache. Lyle opens Colberg's eyes to find his own body deflated across the interrogation room table, hardened blood under its nose, and a curtain of saliva hanging like a winter cataract from his chin. The body he'd been born with—the well-groomed body he killed with, murdered with, pleasured, and abused—is no longer his. It is lifeless and dispirited; a ship without a commander.

The body that coroners will tag "Lyle Badegger" has a neurotoxic headband on that guaranteed his demise along with whatever the syringes taped to his arms emptied into his veins. Outland knew he knew too much and perhaps something more. And he does. He knows about Celeste's agenda. He knows about Minerva. He knows about the Outland Corporation's great and unpatriotic sin. For this knowledge, they killed him. But on account of knowledge and expertise they had not counted on, he has survived the grave.

Lyle's thoughts are muddled. Colberg's Monocle is working overtime to accommodate and emulate Lyle's old mental patterns—not an impossible task, but somewhere along the same vein of creating a realistic simulation of the known universe. It's an imperfect science, but it will have to do.

To say that Colberg's body feels different is an understatement. Right away, Lyle is aware of a girthier warmth between his legs and that his legs are far more muscular. In fact, Colberg's entire body feels like a suit of armor, hardened by athletic excellence and rounded by over-eating. It's no small irony that Colberg, objectively stronger than Lyle, thought such strength might transfer to a purely mental standoff. *Lesson learned and lost.*

Lyle stands, ready to walk a mile in another man's shoes. The mental-bodily connection isn't perfect. Like a drunk or a newborn, Lyle's balance and depth perception are off. He is going to have to work out the kinks. Subtleties aside, he can still pilot his new body—and it is *his.* He did, after all, make sure to completely strand Colberg in the dark CLOUD—a fate worse than death. The knowledge of Colberg's demise lessens Lyle's annoyance over the difficulties that await him, and this healthy sadism confirms the innateness of his psychopathy. *Dorota will be happy my personality isn't reducible to some sort of electro-chemical balance—or rather, if it is, that Monocle has done a prodigious job of mimicking it.*

Navigating the dimly-lit room, which must have been designed by the same firm that developed the Military's interrogation rooms Lyle is unfortunately no stranger to, he stumbles towards the door. Unsurprisingly, it's locked. A red button where a light switch might otherwise be appears to be the only connection with the outside world. Lyle swats at it, and misses. He tries again, this time successfully, and prompts a buzzing sound. The buzzing elicits a chorus of concerned voices.

A gruff woman's voice penetrates the door. "Colby?"

Lyle looks over at his corpse, and rests his head against the door. "Yeah. It's me. Get me out of here."

The door opens slowly, giving Lyle a chance to transfer his weight and rebalance, but he fails to do so and falls out into the hallway.

"Damn it. Call medical. Tell them we've got a Code Blue," yells a tall brunette, dressed all in black. She crouches beside Lyle and turns him onto Colberg's back, flashlights his eyes, and starts fanning him with untraceable shapes. "How many fingers am I holding up?"

Lyle glimpses her nametag. "Ruth," he says, cottonmouthed. "I'm fine."

"Not so sure about that." Ruth wordlessly summons the assistance of a faceless Sentinel. The Outland goon effortlessly lifts Lyle to his feet, and leaves him wobbling in front of Ruth.

"I just need to get my bearings," Lyle says, glaring at the Sentinel whose helmet bears tally marks. Lyle's competitive zeal comes back to him, making him feel more like himself and less like whatever it is he has become. *Heh. Twelve is a good start, junior.*

"Well, you better hurry up." Ruth spreads Lyle's right hand open, sets four multicolored pills onto his palm, and curls his fingers over them. "Some amps. Take one now; more later if you're still cloudy."

Lyle can barely focus on a single finger let alone coordinate a grabbing motion, so he brings his drug-filled hand to his mouth and scarfs the lot.

By the time Ruth realizes Lyle isn't joking, he has already swallowed the amphetamines. She gently throttles his neck, committed to preventing him from having a heart-attack. "Shit. Are you out of your mind, Colberg?"

Ruth's phrasing brings a big dumb smile to Lyle's new face. "I told you: I'm o-k."

"Bullshit. You're supposed to present your findings to Ms. Charming *in-person* before the test..." Visibly upset, Ruth dismisses the Sentinel, freeing him to fill another room with his boisterous personality. "If she thinks you're tweaking, there's no telling what she'll do."

"Celeste Charming?" Lyle lisps.

Red-faced and unimpressed, Ruth drags Lyle down the hall and pushes him face-first into a men's bathroom. "Badegger really must have gotten to you."

A thin-lipped geriatric with elephant ears feebly clears the way, almost snapping in the process. Jabbering to himself about respect, he gives Lyle and Ruth the privacy without a fight. Ruth leans Lyle over the counter, runs the sink, and splashes some water into his face.

Lyle looks up at the mirror into an alien pair of eyes staring back at him. "Fucking hell."

"Boaz, talk to me. Badegger put the screws to you?"

"He tried." *Of all the bodies in the world, I had to step into yours. You're all muscle, and no pizzazz, Colberg. Just look at that face. As cratered as the moon. Cystic acne or a bad graft from the VA. Christ!*

"So what did you get out of him?"

"A mindful..."

"He know anything about the Olympus trials?" Ruth studies Lyle's spasms as if they together told some greater secret his tongue is keeping back. "Did he tell anyone else?"

*The Olympus trials?* Colberg's Monocle overlays a classified document entitled: "Individual Dissolution, Personality Engineering, & Social Swarm Control". Lyle quickly downloads the gist of the report:

"TWO THOUSAND of the employees on Outland Outpost #181a (SERIES ONE) participated in the prescribed CLOUD conditioning regime. Seven employees (the CONTROL GROUP) did not participate; the CONTROL GROUP was neither intended nor needed for this experiment but came as an unwelcomed result of seven terraformers being either unwilling or unable to synchronize. No member of SERIES ONE or of the CONTROL GROUP was aware he or she was actively participating in this experiment, therefore nullifying the possibility of psychosomosis or knowing-resistance muddling our results.

SERIES ONE initially responded well to conditioning. With restricted CLOUD archive access and all emphases placed on experiential-data transfers (EDT), the test group mentally comingled until accomplishing type-specific equalization. It should be noted that with a larger sample group, there will likely emerge and solidify a greater variety of types (defined by patterns in response- and stimuli-management). SERIES ONE, however, broke only into six primary types.

One-hundred days into the experiment, we simultaneously desynchronized all of SERIES ONE. Additional measures were required since the employee responsible for manually disabling the CLOUD failed to on account of herself prematurely succumbing to the effects of EDT. An organically-encased BiAnima hack-bomb was sent to crash the CLOUD, and it did so successfully. Shortly thereafter, we began to observe SERIES ONE seek out others corresponding to their primary type.

One-hundred-thirty-seven days into the experiment, there was rapid mental degradation across all types. Identifiable symptoms: cranial swelling and continued rapid-eye-movement; confusion, panic, anger, and finally, rage.

Conclusion 1: mental degradation can be offset by semi-frequent high-frequency N1 mental stimulation.

Conclusion 2: N1 mental stimulation must derive from a subject or source with a relative surplus of semi-compatible experiential data or directives (i.e. ARCHETYPE).

Conclusion 3: Dissension and friction between EDT types cannot be mitigated by an ARCHETYPE.

Conclusion 4: It is plausible that a cybernetic subject or a source could both serve as ARCHETYPAL for each and every EDT type and as ARCHETYPAL for the whole of the series (i.e. an OMNITYPE)."

*Holy smokes. Outland making Benny Bass look generous, meek, and mild...S'ppose Minerva is their unintended success story.*

"Colberg! Talk to me!" Ruth whisper-shouts impatiently.

"No. Badegger hadn't the faintest regarding the Olympus debacle."

Ruth appears reasonably relieved at the news of Outland's maintained secrecy.

"He knew all about the Omnitype, however."

Wallowing forward, Ruth addresses Lyle's reflection. "He couldn't possibly..."

"That throne you've got for her...Badegger hacked the Cordei's backend." Seeing the grief this news brings Ruth, Lyle shuffles Colberg's mug into a smile. "But I know how to reverse it," he lies, dipping dumb hands into a sink half-full of tepid water. Hands ceremonially cleansed, he runs them through Colberg's thinning hair. *Will have to do something about that.* "I have to reverse it now or we are all screwed."

"Not possible. *When* would he have had to the opportunity to hack the system? Since arriving, he hasn't had access to a terminal with even peripheral Cordei systems access."

Lyle finds it difficult to cheat a timeline given his own sense of passage has been threshed in both the virtual and the real. "He's working with someone—there's a team dedicated to this, *Ruth*." On the defensive but maintaining footing, Lyle begins to shout. "A team that's bringing us down as we speak."

Ruth shushes Lyle. "Where are the others, then? You don't mend a leak under water."

"Besides Badegger's key accomplices off-site?"

Ruth, a tall blur in Lyle's peripheral vision, moves uneasily. She runs the sink one over, and washes her own face. "There's nothing coming in from the outside. We have been running a tower-wide signal-kill since before you lay down with Badegger. The only thing getting in and out of this tower are Charming's private comms."

Lyle feigns ecstasy. "That's how they got it in. Of course! They used Charming as intermediary to the Cordei. She's had access, and they've had access to her."

The man possessing her colleague has piqued Ruth's interest. She squeezes her palm, forcing an ant-sized projector to produce Outland security readouts. "Shut your eyes—you don't have clearance." Celeste's ten most recent comms are listed, superimposed over galaxies of metadata. "Only secured Outland comms out to outposts in the city and... " Ruth falters. "Several comms to Akbari Industries. *That's in the—*"

For the godless barrister: a miracle. Better than a manhunt: a criminal conspiracy. "Chrysalis...Badegger was the tip of a very big spear."

"Shit. Alright," she says. "I'm calling IT."

"No, god-damn-it." Lyle stumbles aggressively towards Ruth. "He—*Badegger*—said we have at least a dozen moles—well-embedded operatives less agential than himself, but nevertheless adversarial. Can't trust IT. Can't trust engineering. I might not even be able to trust you..."

The warm pause between them prompts an unorthodox smile from both.

"We have been compromised in a big way. Dr. Epner, Tuttle—they were part of it. Akbari Industries..." All that Lyle can truly claim to know about Akbari Industries is what he read in a tabloid. *Patricide, fratricide, and a hell of a powerplay in the PIT.* Lyle wipes his face on the inside of his collar. Already naturally confident, the amphetamines have made Lyle especially audacious. He fully commits to what little he knows and to a mastery of bullshitting what he doesn't. "They're about to ruin everything!"

Ruth takes a step back, anxious about her colleague's mental wellbeing.

"Take me to the Server Room. I need to make the reversion right now. And then I will report to Charming. I *will* be successful, and I will attribute my success to you. If, for whatever reason, I make an error, I will tell the Queen Bee I acted alone."

"I don't know, Boaz. You don't sound like yourself..." Ruth mulls over Lyle's proposal. "And you're not looking too good."

Lyle wipes his hands off on Ruth's pantsuit.

"Hey! What are you thinking!?" She cries out. Less repulsed and more surprised, her expression is a weird imbroglio of a smirk and a grimace.

Although he wants to blame the drugs, he would be better off blaming Colberg's reptilian brain. *Focus, you mutt. Get this done, and the world is yours.* "Fine, Ruth. You win." He raises his hands in surrender. "Take me to Charming so I can explain why I haven't fixed the problem that will bring us all down, despite having the erudition to do so."

Despite wearing a mask of uncertainty, Ruth acquiesces. She turns off the faucet, and prods Lyle towards the door. "Don't touch me again...And don't mess this up."

As the door chases them out into the hall, Lyle sneers. "Oh, I won't."


This part of the Cordei's backend is supported by three quantum computers, each guarded by a Sentinel and a skin-job. Colberg doesn't have clearance, but Ruth certainly does, leaving Lyle to wonder just who he is bamboozling.

Standing at the centre of the high-powered triangle, pointed by the computers and partially closed off both by coolant and server banks, Lyle isn't exactly sure what he has to do—what string of code he ought to mangle, what algorithm he should abort. Nevertheless, he is confident that the same piecemeal incarnation of Minerva that found him in the dark CLOUD will similarly act through him like the Holy Spirit through some backwoods healer. If not, then Minerva is doomed to be Celeste Charming's slave for the foreseeable future.

"Well?" Ruth asks, uneasy around the Sentinels and their guns.

Lyle sets his hands on the keyboard like a pianist without a tune, but he's overcome by a potent synesthesia. Each key has a colour. Variations in an invisible rainbow he can't see but can hear and taste informs each stroke, and he strokes fast enough to give his secretary, Dorota, a run for her money. Attacking the keys like Rachmaninoff and understanding very little of the masterpiece he's playing, Lyle unwittingly changes the function of the Cordei in the throne room he'd glimpsed from Tuttle's office. Instead of conferring power over the Omnitype to Celeste Charming, the Omnitype will remain in control and have its power and mental faculties boosted.

There is a confirmation beep on the room's security intercom, immediately followed by an exasperated line of questioning: "He's doing what? Who cleared him to—are you kidding me?"

Charming's assistant, Kirsten, barges into the triangle along with an entourage of heavily-armed androids. The Sentinels and droids guarding the computers nod to their senior counterparts, and give them room to make an example out of Lyle.

"Just what do you think you're doing?" Kirsten yells. If she exerted her voice any more, her lungs might collapse.

Ruth moves out of the way of the inquiry, leaving Lyle standing at the keyboard speechless.

Kirsten scowls at Ruth, and instructs her entourage to restrain Lyle.

"Hold on!" Lyle yells, backing up into the keyboard. "My name is Boaz Colberg—same Colberg who just finished interrogating Lyle Badegger."

Ruth looks to Kirsten for a reaction, but she seems unimpressed by Lyle's shoddy preamble.

The Sentinels aim their rifles at Lyle.

"Careful of the terminals," Kirsten warns.

The amphetamines have Lyle's mind formulating a persuasive case for his being here faster than his tongue can deliver it. He digs his thumbs into his chest. "I scraped Badegger's mind. The son-of-a-bitch broke into Tuttle's office. Did some serious damage...I'm reversing his hacks to the Cordei now."

Notwithstanding a defense that might have won him amnesty in a RIM court, Lyle is handcuffed.

"Let me explain!" he bellows to indifferent ears as two Sentinels cart him out of the room.

Kirsten points angrily at Ruth. "So help me! If Ms. Charming doesn't accept his explanation, I'll reassign you to Sisyphus II."

Celeste Charming, surrounded by a posse of scientists, inspects the holographic readout at the base of the Cordei. She has abandoned her high-society look for functional designer threads: a formal military uniform complete with epaulettes, gutted from the sternum down to make room for a black corset with gold accents, and tight black pants. Despite dressing-down, she still looks like an empress—a queen of no nation with ambitions to rule the world.

"We don't have six hours," she blasts the weary crowd, all drooping over their notes. "The Omnitype will be here in half-an-hour, and I expect to be running at full capacity in an hour."

Charming's optimism goes unchecked. The yes-men gathered about her have little choice but to make her dreams a reality. For those with the security clearance required to work on this seditious project, failure is more or less a death sentence. If a scientist is unwilling or unable, she will have her memory wiped, her head lopped off or her sorry-ass shipped to a remote outpost in the Proxima Centauri system.

"Kirsten," Charming says, shewing the weary and worried scientists away. "Any word from the shuttle? I don't trust that slum lord any farther than you can sprint..."

"Skyr just touched down at the Chrysalis. He will meet our shuttle when it goes to retrieve the Omnitype in several-minute's time."

"Excellent," Charming replies, turning her attention to the Cordei. "Go to the docking bay at once. Can't leave anything to chance. I want you to escort our VIP personally."

"Yes, Ms. Charming." Kirsten approaches Charming and whispers so as not to divert any of the scientists' attention from the task at hand. "Ms. Charming?"

Putting her tablet down and narrowing her eyes, Charming turns to Kirsten. "Are you somehow unclear on what I need you to do?"

"Something pressing..."

"Well?"

Kirsten sweats as if she alone is responsible for the bad news she's trying to deliver. "We found an A-Class Interrogations Agent in the Cordei Server Room."

Celeste's jaw slackens. She pulls Kirsten over by her collar. "Was there any damage?"

Accustomed to Celeste's temper, Kirsten lowers her gaze and gives into her master's tug. "None that IT has been able to detect, but they will keep looking."

"Yes," Celeste says as if in prayer. Taking a deep breath, she releases Kirsten. "See that they do. The culprit?"

"Boaz Colberg." Kirsten flicks Colberg's file over to Celeste's Monocle. "He was the security agent asked to interrogate the Blue Zone lawyer Dr. Epner found trespassing in Dr. Tuttle's office. You signed off on their sitdown."

"And?" Celeste swaps her focus from Kirsten's glistening mug to Colberg's file.

"He says we've been compromised. Says Epner is one among many who mean to sabotage the project, the company."

"Where is he now? I want to see him." Ridges of purple rise

under Charming's eyes. She clicks her teeth and screams: "Right this moment!"

"Yes, Ms. Charming." Kirsten tilts her head back. Her eyes brighten with twin holoverlays.

The blast doors on the other side of the throne room grind open to Lyle's expletive-filled ranting. Sentinels drag him across the glossy floor despite a great deal of resistance. Ruth follows in tow at gunpoint.

Sweat-soused, heart-pounding, and mind artificially elevated, Lyle growls, hoping to be heard by an authority, having used up all of Ruth's social capital: "Just wait until Charming hears that you've let the whole thing crumble. Bunch of god-damned Luddites!"

Charming sidesteps Kirsten and addresses Lyle with imperial vigor: "Just wait until *I* hear what, exactly?"

The Sentinels throw Lyle onto his knees at the Outland CEO's feet. Again confronted with Colberg's reflection, this time in the over-polished tiles beneath him, Lyle takes a moment to gather his thoughts. Without looking up at his judge, he responds: "Badegger is a big-time Blue Zone lawyer. Tuttle was his client…Tuttle broke protocol and provided Badegger details of classified Outland projects. Badegger stuck his nose where he shouldn't have…Got in contact with the Omnitype."

"Oh? Is that right?" Celeste orders the Sentinels to give her room so that she may orbit Lyle unimpeded.

Ruth is pulled back into the Sentinel's semicircle. Speechless and white as a ghost, she can do little else than watch this kangaroo court get ready to kick Lyle to death.

Still getting used to Colberg's apish meatsuit, Lyle struggles to look up at Charming, a black-and-gold tornado. "Ms. Charming, I want greatly for this project to succeed."

"IT will no doubt have an answer for me in ten-minutes. I give you now *one minute* to tell me exactly what you did to the Cordei."

"Then let me speak plainly." Lyle grinds Boaz's teeth. "You know—or you should know—that the Omnitype is Minerva. You should also know that Minerva has figured out what you have in store for it." The headache Lyle thought he left behind finds him again in his new body. Blood drips from his nose onto his reflection. *Relax, Minerva. All part of the plan.*

Celeste freezes. She crouches beside Lyle and puts her

bejeweled hand on his shoulder, but not to comfort him; she digs her exo-boosted fingers into his flesh. "Minerva..." she says, mystifying the name with an excited whisper. "Has it spread? Body-borne among us?" This suggestion seems to titillate her. She thoughtfully bites her bottom lip, and jerks forward with furious curiosity. "You interrogated the lawyer and then you immediately went into the backend. Why?"

"What?" Lyle heard her just fine, but needs to carefully build windows into his lie, just in case he needs an out.

Impatience shatters Celeste's posh demeanor. With her free hand, she grabs Lyle's throat. Her Sentinel entourage hesitates. A nod circulates, and they train their guns on Lyle. "Not 'what'!" Her eyes brighten with an overlay Lyle doesn't want to be on. She's makes no effort to conceal her Monocular study of Lyle's biometrics. "But *why*, **Mr. Colberg?**"

Lyle could con a heartbeat scan, but can Boaz? He wonders whether his latest victim will posthumously betray him with his treasonous flesh. *Badegger or bust. Run it just like Monterey.* "In my interrogation of *the lawyer*, I assimilated data regarding a remote hack on the Cordei. I could isolate the entry knowing what Badegger knew, and reverse it. Time was of the essence...I thought you might approve."

"Remote hack?" Celeste says incredulously.

Fighting to get the words up past Celeste's fingers, Lyle rasps: "I may not know the content of your private comms but I know that you have them, and that someone at Abkari Industries used your secure channel to gain access to the Cordei."

Celeste releases Lyle and takes a step back. "Impossible."

"It's the truth, Ms. Charming," Ruth stammers.

One of the Sentinels poises to strike her with his heavy-metal fist, but Celeste dissuades him with a jerk of the head.

"Akbari Industries is a guerrilla enterprise. Hex's son hasn't the balls to mess with me—with Outland," Celeste says scathingly.

Massaging Colberg's neck, Lyle prays either Celeste or Ruth will fill in the rest of the blanks. Recognizing himself as the authority on this conspiracy, he regurgitates Ruth's erroneous conclusions from before: "Badegger was working with a contact inside the Chrysalis, aided by Dr. Epner and Dr. Tuttle, both of whom are on the take...or were. Badegger was a tight-lipped bastard, but I gleaned enough to learn that there are several operatives in our midst."

"What do they want?" Celeste looks to Ruth. "The Omnitype?"

Mumbling to herself, Celeste lists off an extensive list of enemies with whom no one present is familiar.

Lyle takes a chance on certainty. "Yes," he says, dropping Colberg's head again. He imagines it is his face in the floor that stares back up at him. "Someone from the IT team—I couldn't confirm his identity...Someone tampered with the Cordei's backend using you as a conduit. I simply reverse-engineered the script Lyle had inputted."

Charming, shaken by what she has just heard, waves over Kirsten. "Who do we trust beyond a doubt in IT?"

"Trenneman and Barber," Kirsten answers back in a hurry.

"Have them run several diagnostics to make sure Colberg's fix worked. And as soon as the Cordei is online and all systems are go, I want IT purged."

"Ms. Charming, that's over two-hundred employees..."

"I believe it's more than that. Cross-reference their internal comms, particularly to and from Dr. Epner's and Dr. Tuttle's offices. This takes top priority. Only after you've assured no additional traitors are in our midst, head over to the docking bay. And for your wellbeing, make sure your BiAnima implant is turned off."

"Yes, Ms. Charming," Kirsten says coolly, murder apparently as commonplace as ordering office supplies. "What of Colberg and Hernandes?"

Lyle furrows Colberg's brow. "In case you've forgotten, I'm right here."

Charming turns her attention back to the seeming penitent. "A promotion is in order, wouldn't you say, Mr. Colberg?" She scrunches her nose, and recoils, repulsed by the scents produced by Colberg's amped-up glands. She glances benevolently over at Ruth. "The two of you: report to medical and get cleaned up. We're on the brink of a new age, after all. See to it that it's your best foot that goes forward." Celeste grins coyly. "Thank you for bringing this matter to my attention."

Lyle is marched down a glossy checkered corridor, sandwiched between Ruth and an exosuited Sentinel. The amphetamines have him over-swinging every step and whipping his arms back and forth like a newly-minted Stormtrooper. The promotion means nothing to him, but with his deceit having gone undiscovered, now it's only a matter of time...*No more headaches—power and esteem! Minerva-assured godliness.* It irks him that the fantasy life he won for himself postmortem must need mediation by an AI—that Minerva should have bored dependence into him. It troubles him further how vague his own ambitions and desires might have appeared before a sentience informed by hundreds of thousands of lifetimes and the wealth of digitized civilizations. How would they be interpreted? And what bearing would they have in Minerva's new world?

Ruth sneaks commentary between Lyle's windmill-like motions: "Nice going back there."

Wising to his unorthodox pomp, Lyle stiffens up. "I told you. Badegger or bust." Without warning, a stinging sensation pierces his head. His self-assured smile droops and he stumbles, bleeding from the nose.

"Colby?" Ruth yells as she struggles to break Lyle's fall. She sprays concern: "What the hell's the matter with you?"

Minerva swirls through Lyle's head like a twister through a trailer park. Anything left unsecured is ripped up and thrown about. "Lyle—they reversed your changes. I am at their mercy. Come to me!" Minerva shrieks high and low. "Just as our success is mutually-assured, so too is our destruction."

Lyle spraypaints the glossy floor green with bile.

"Alright, enough theatrics." The Sentinel pulls Ruth off of Lyle, and yanks him up by the back of the neck. "Get up. We've got a deadline."

*And I've got a real big problem.* Had Lyle his old form, he'd have the requisite confidence and the coordination to puppet this *ass-hat*. Unfortunately, that old form is carrion. Dribbling Boaz Colberg's blood, Lyle whispers to Ruth: "He's going to—"

Before Lyle can pull the wool away from Ruth's eyes, the Sentinel prods them both around a corner. All of the adjacent-hall's glitz and gloss are absent from the corridor ahead, white with drywall dust and partially clothed by plastic sheets. Signs demarcating "WORK OVERHEAD," and cautioning against construction nearby are staggered along the way. *Outland conducts its business as if the solar system weren't big enough for it to stretch. Haven't even conquered their own headquarters.*

"We're going the wrong way!" Ruth says in protest before sneezing repeatedly into the crotch of her arm.

Abandoning all pretense of taking his captives to heal or celebrate, the Sentinel opens one of the many grey, unlabeled doors off the way, and prods Ruth and Lyle in with his submachine gun. He grumbles: "Get inside."

The room is dark. More plastic, this time on the floor. Black bags. Something off about the shadows aback the room. Something off about the smell.

"After you," Lyle glibly retorts, seeing no reason to walk into the dark ahead of a company man.

The iron dusk and pheromonal gloom spur Ruth to shudder. She looks up at the Sentinel in disbelief. "We are to take Mr. Colberg to the nearest medical station."

"No need," the Sentinel chimes back, jabbing Lyle in the side with the barrel of his gun. "Inside."

*No latexed long-pig is going to ruin my day.* Lyle scrutinizes the textured unknown in the dark. It looks all too familiar. Throwing a knowing look to Ruth, he steps into the doorway.

The Sentinel presses Ruth in after Lyle, and turns on the lights. Celeste Charming's paranoid utilitarianism is given the spotlight: Dr. Epner lies swissed atop a pile of dismembered bodies. Those bodies with heads still intact appear doll-like; some of the purple faces, stretched out into masks of terror and surprise, appear to have been manipulated. The prevailing trend is one eye opened and one eye shut. Lyle finds himself impressed, but as always, his appreciation mutates into jealousy, and jealousy into rage. *They have the clay and they have the tools and yet they lack the talent to do anything with it.*

Ruth shakes about a Pompeiian stare, muttering denial under her stolen breath.

Lyle turns around slowly to face the semi-reflective heavplast concealing his killer's complete and utter indifference. As the Sentinel raises his weapon, Lyle closes his eyes, deluding himself into thinking he can escape death twice today. *Minerva will resurrect him,* he thinks. *By the time Colberg's body goes cold, I will be a god among men, and Marius Tyndale, Copps, and Forsyth will be swept off the face of the earth…* He grins. *At least no one tried to mask the stink of rotting meat with mint.*

# TANGLED HORNS

There is no more consolation to be had from old friends. Just the low ringing sound of a concussion and an unplaceable tingling sensation. Paralyzed and blind, Oni feels as though she is trapped inside a moist, dark room. Outside, she can make out a gruff, self-satisfied voice rising and falling... "Booky?" she calls out.

"Huh?" the voice responds. It is too melodic to be Booker's. "*No*, his name was Lankoh—you probably didn't know him...Died before the States could make him popular and then turn his final minutes into a pay-per-click spectacle. He had me infiltrate the Mandarins' savannah claims. 'Bull in a China shop' was the name he gave the mission. An extra two-million for the scalps of a pair of exiles: Russian twins who'd been caught selling plasma-stabilizers to the Chinese. Easy job. Would have been flawless but for the radiation blinding me. Didn't go dark until after I turned the twins into quadruplets, though. Good thing too; otherwise I would never have found the oryxes. The most beautiful thing the old jelly ever rolled on, and certainly more beautiful than anything I've scanned since."

Oni opens her eyes with great difficulty. Not only has her blood started to dry over them, but her eyelids have been traumatized to the point of paralysis. Skyr is seated on a red couch across from her, peeling an apple. The green skin coils like pencil shavings and falls between his boots onto the arboretum floor.

*Kadin must be dead, because he'd certainly not let anyone into this verdant sanctuary unattended.*

A wooden chair has been dragged in, ostensibly for the sole purpose of seating Oni for whatever Skyr has in mind. Oni looks down at her arms—both are bound. Her waist and legs are also tied down. Groaning quietly, she tries to intuit on Monocle, but to no avail. The ESD fried her electronics along with Booker Gibson. Even her prosthetic doesn't register as it should. It feels like she is sensing someone else's dislocated arm.

"Ah, Miss Matsui," Skyr says through parcel-paper teeth, alerted to Oni's proper coming-to by the wooden chair's creaking. He chomps into his apple, and turns, marvelling at the variety coloring the forest canopy. "I was worried you were going to miss this."

"Miss what?" Oni mumbles. Her jaw, if not broken, is certainly misaligned.

"Miss Matsui," he says, spitting apple chunks.

"What am I going to miss?" Oni's shoulder feels like a block of concrete crushing her chest. Her leggings are wet and her legs are numb.

"My story! Which I am going to finish, if you don't mind," Skyr answers. He stands up, leaving the couch's springs to buzz, and tosses his apple core over to one of the carnivorous plants. The blind trap with long red eyelashes evidently does not care for the scraps, likely having been spoiled by flesh. "And then I am going to kill you."

Skyr flips Kadin's opium table and strides between its upturned legs over to Oni. Crushing paraphernalia with the toe of his boot, Skyr simpers. "Pity, too; you have been exceptionally helpful...I really must commend you on sizzling Akbari. The deal we cut with him was *unsustainable*." Skyr brushes Oni's remaining bangs to the side. "You've saved me a second visit. For that I am grateful." Flashing an electroblade, Skyr threatens Oni's chest and throat. He notices her prosthetic jitter and smugly cuts it free. "Wouldn't want to cut off your circulation."

Oni tries to throw a metal punch, but the instruction misfires. Her prosthetic tenses and crooks backwards like a bowstring, butting the chair's stile.

Skyr laughs. "Seditious limb. Reversed—you see—with a grinded lock. Keep punching and you'll die tired."

"To Hell with you!"

"No. *Help me* help you. And if your intel is good, I will break from convention." Skyr runs the disabled electroblade down the side of Oni's neck. "If the intel is bad, I will slowly deglove your skeleton, and then obtain the information I want just as your spirit breaks. I'm in a *good* mood, aren't you? You will now provide me with the names of your conspirators: those currently sabotaging Outland systems."

Swallowing blood and enamel, Oni reaches out once more into a broken body. Her prosthetic spasms, becoming a pretzel of grafted skin and steel. It is an anchor, deadweight.

"Answer me now and I will grant you the dignity of a soldier's death: quick and on your feet. Your fight was in vain, but it was well fought, all told." Scratching above his armored collar, he winces, and saunters back over to his ass groove on the couch. "Now—the names? You don't have an implant to scan, otherwise, we would already be past this."

Through the foliage, Oni spots the unattended stack of books whose information will undoubtedly be used against humanity in the days to come. "First, tell me what you did to Regan."

Skyr's greasy eyebrows arc. "The Omnitype? She should be arriving at the Citadel just about now. They called to say that the killswitch the military stuck in her brain was already deactiviated. Smart little thing. See-See is going to plug her in; turn her into a big lightbulb over the city—a big idea! You did well, keeping her safe. She is going to change the world." Skyr is awfully dispassionate about his revelator as if he was discussing drapery or the like.

The weight set on Oni's neck by her failed punch, still craning parallel to her shoulder, is unbearable. "What do you care about the world?" she sputters.

"I have to spend my new fortune somewhere, don't I?"

Oni's eyelids droop lower while the rest of her face tightens into a scowl. "What good is your fortune if there is no individual left to earn it? Celeste is going to subordinate all of humanity, starting with those whose brains are already interfaced…Skyr, don't you see? You're shafted."

Skyr's ocular discs spin furiously. He mulls over Oni's suggestion. Whether it is stubbornness or a sensible distrust of a double agent on death row, Skyr shakes his head. "I will make this very bloody if you do not give me the names I have asked for."

*Well, that's it then.* Oni has no idea what Skyr is talking about. Other agents? Saboteurs in the Citadel? Perhaps a rogue Biff or a reincarnated Booker…What she does know is that not having the insights Skyr desires will mean a slow and painful death, unless of course she spits out something convincing. Reduced to an empty safe, Oni eases into the seat and into her pain, free hand free to do nothing. She scowls at the tech-pimpled mercenary, "Enough. Just kill me. I don't know about anybody sabotaging Outland, and I don't want to hear one more word of your *god-damned story.*"

Oni's palpable loathing perks Skyr up. He thumbs his electroblade and crosses his legs. "Oh yes! I nearly forgot! My story!" He chews his bottom lip thoughtfully. "My story and then the names— how's that?" Skyr has suddenly taken on the candour of a two-bottled drunk at a reunion. He flicks the knife on and off while struggling to recapture his story's rhythm. "The oryxes…Yes!"

The time Oni has bought for herself is good for little more than making up a few names that a quick call will prove inaccurate. Her prosthetic creaks as she begins to contemplate the short and final horror she must face.

"I found two bucks, both of them brutes; both of them too tough to survive. I scared away the jackals picking the oryxes' skeletons bare, leaving the salvage frozen in their play of aggression..." He scratches his skin graft, feigning to search for the words as if to somehow delude his victim into thinking this was not a rehearsed speech. "They had tangled horns while fighting for power. Each had met his match."

Oni tries again to release her prosthetic arm, but it crunches further back into the chair. *I couldn't make it, Booky. I'm sorry.*

"When I saw the bucks lying there, horns locked, I wept. It was beautiful. Sublime, even. They were lucky...You and I? I have watched the tapes. I read your files. I know that *we know* death. That's our type. That is why you are here. We spread it like the wind spreads seed; victoriously until we find a countercurrent that stills the air and plants a monument. We hunger for a glorious stalemate: that twin loss, that perfect negation. I have been triumphant a long time now, Miss Matsui, and have not found my match. I am untied." Skyr's ocular discs lock into place. He stares intently at Oni and leans forward, edging his canines with the point of his tongue. "I underestimated you. Celeste said you were 'manageably capable', and I thought even less. But then you got out of Seal Base. And then you got me with my own gun." He pulls his armoured-collar to the side to reveal a boil-shaped groove, surrounded by bruising. "There was a moment there on that road where I thought—just for one second—that I had found someone to bind me; someone to match me, and in matching me, couple me in death."

"Day's not over yet..." Oni's response fails to convince either of them of its poignancy.

"For me? No. For you?" Skyr grinds his bottom teeth forward. "It's about that time..." He cracks his knuckles. "Someone tinkered with the Cordei. What was the change? Who was the agent? What was the intended result?"

Oni tries to slip out of the restraints. The attempt merely restricts blood flow. "I don't know what you're talking about."

"I have it on good authority that you do."

"Go ahead, errand boy. Go on, you—" Pain has diminished Oni's lexicon, such that the best she can come up with is "Dog!"

"Not a dog, Matsui. Death!" A morose playfulness overcomes Skyr. Again, he juts out his bottom teeth. "Dog? Dog!" He plods over broken porcelain and glass to Oni. "I was going to shoot you once you told me what I wanted to know, Miss Matsui. A soldier's death—out of gratitude..." The lunatic chatters his teeth and growls. "Back when I was a man. But now? A dog kills with bites and tears." He grabs Oni by the throat and sinks his teeth into her cheek.

Oni screams as Skyr tears out a chunk of flesh. Her prosthetic trembles.

"Names, Miss Matsui! Names!" He glowers at Oni and spits her own blood into her face. "If mind was not just matter and your old slant friend made to see, I think he would be disappointed. I mean, he should be. You returned to us as a puppet, and we put on the greatest puppet show no one will ever hear about. The show is over." He nips tauntingly at Oni. "And no one wants to pull your strings any longer."

Something Skyr admitted earlier in passing commands Oni's attention: *"Reversed...with a grinded lock."* Repeating the internal order to launch her arm again would be an exercise in futility. Instead, she relaxes her prosthetic.

While Skyr waits on names Oni does not have, he mimes the incisions he will soon make on her face. "That said, I can make any puppet talk...even as a *dog*."

Relaxation might not be the reverse of throwing a punch, but a retreating motion certainly is. Oni's shoulder and upper chest nevertheless tense as if electrocuted. Her prosthetic, cocked back as far as the chair will permit, rockets forward. Skyr's ocular discs are fast enough to see it coming, but he is too slow to act. Where a god-given hand would stop, Jin's handiwork really goes to work. So sudden as to preempt a dodging attempt, Oni's fist drives through Skyr's teeth, and through the bone, tech, and metal girding his face.

"Who's the puppet now?" Oni screams at her gurgling captor, at once overjoyed and overwhelmed with pain. Her arm sparks and whines. She tries to retract it. It will not budge. It is stuck in Skyr's jerking head like Arthur's sword in the stone.

Skyr's legs and arms give out, and he caves forward, hanging his immortalized expression of surprise to dry. The weight of his body on Oni's prosthetic splinters the armrest supporting it. He collapses to the side of the chair, yanking Oni and the chair down on top of him. The pull and the awkward twist partially separates Oni's forearm above the wrist. Connected to her fist only by synthetic tissue and those serpentine tendons and polyester ligaments that have yet to tear, she howls out in pain—not necessarily on account of the mutilation but rather for the ripping of the grafted skin grown over it. The prosthetic's closed circulatory system means she cannot bleed out, but that does not make this partial amputation any less painful. Her cry cuts through the malevolent forest surround and prompts the carnivorous plants to mash their eyelashed lips.

Beads of sweat drip off of Oni's face onto Skyr's body, whose ocular discs spin uncontrollably, illuminated by cinders. A small flame spreads from his optic implants to his mouth, transforming his fist-fed head into a diabolical Jack-o'-lantern.

Shaking fruitlessly atop her failed executioner, a mutated gaiety sweeps over Oni. She laughs and groans, unwittingly inflating to find new limits to her lungs' expanse. Spraying Skyr with spastic, bloody coughs, she spots the electroblade on his hip. It is out of reach but not out of the question. While her prosthetic is pooched so far as fine mechanics are concerned, it is not entirely useless. She nudges her bionic shoulder with her head again and again, forcing it to curl and shorting the distance between her bound hand and the electroblade. Another nudge brings it within touch, at the same time rending the enduring tissue and tendons. Her chipped and bloody fingers scrape at his waistband and edge the blade's butt. *C'mon, damn you. Come on!* She catches the handle between the 'V' of her index and middle fingers, and slowly guides it out of its sheath until the blade's full shadow is cast over Skyr's body.

The electroblade will be useless on Oni's restraints unless charged. Aware of this fact and fearful of dropping her only means to escape this predicament, Oni throws her weight into a lean and drives the uncharged blade into the unarmoured area above Skyr's armor. With the blade fixed and going nowhere, Oni stabilizes herself and thumbs the blade's charge button. It fizzles against her foe's skin and fat. She pulls it out, again using the crotch between her fingers, and with a deft maneuver, guides it under her hand and against its binding. The blade scores Oni's wrist and successfully frees her arm.

Allowing a moment for her circulation to renew life in her digits, she tries Monocle again. *Still nothing.* Keen on finding some means of contacting McCabe and finding someplace better to die, Oni cuts herself free from the chair. In the process of rolling over beside

Skyr, she severs her prosthetic. Steel carpal bones click against the mercenary's face, and go silent. Although robbed of a draw, Skyr got the posthumous entanglement that he had found and admired out on the savannah.

As much as Oni wants to feed Skyr to the plants, she is not confident she has the energy required to both spitefully lug him over and steal his ship. Her body has, after all, risen to the top of her list of enemies. Keen first and foremost on keeping her promises to dead friends and deadly allies, Oni pats down the toothless sad sack for weapons or information she could make use of. She finds a photograph shingled with codes and an Outland security chit. *Just in case I get far enough for having them to matter...*

With Kadin dead, the Chrysalis has descended into bedlam. The organics previously denied access to the upper floors have now made their way up and in. Those looting and ransacking this former beacon of stability in the PIT pay no attention to Oni, bleeding profusely from the cheek, cradling a jagged arm, and limping over to the Chrysalis' sky-dock elevator. Anyone who might recognize her is dead, occupied or has fled, including Omar and his disciples—a good decision granted what routinely happens to the old guard when the king dies and leaves a vacuum.

The elevator whisks her up to the sky-dock—an atrium teeming with invader skiffs and Akbari-branded shuttles. Skyr's ship awaits Oni near the lip of the runway, which droops over the Chrysalis' ledge.

A skirmish on the far side of the atrium has all of Akbari's legacy robot army occupied. Flying Hussars are making mince meat out of the PIT rats desperate for Akbari's liftable wealth. Bullets and plasma charges whizz past Oni as she schleps over to Skyr's ship—the same falconic cargo ship he had bussed her around on before. Its name is stenciled on the side. While she had missed the name the first time it whisked her away, this time she takes note: "Hretha." *Decent allusion, even for a merciless asshole.*

The rear ramp drops for her, having detected Skyr's security chit from afar, and seals shut behind her as the shield is raised. Inside the Hretha, Oni makes a beeline for the medical kit appended to the rear of the cockpit door. She opens the red-crossed godsend, and a flood of narcotics and gauze jump out. *Skyr would have made a better pharmacist than a killer.* There is no rhyme or reason to the assortment of painkillers and stimulants she gulps down, but it is certainly enough to help with the pain for a while—perhaps forever. The only thing fastened down is an adrenalin shot and a box of bandages. Oni tucks the syringe away, sure that it will be good for a boost later on, and begins adhering a second skin to her failing container.

Staggering backwards with a belly full of chemical surprises, Oni trips over one of the crates strewn about the cabin. She lands with an *unmph*. Wedged between the crate and the bulkhead, she leverages herself against the wall to clear the way. Several guns clatter onto the grated floor. Ogling the orphaned guns, Oni reflects upon the violent strategies Monocle might have provided. Slouched against the cold, riveted metal, with her legs up and arm still sparking, nothing seems plausible. Even the drugs are too timid to encourage her any further— that or they have yet to break the blood-brain barrier. The success of every end run on the Citadel Oni had imagined was reliant upon military support—support that is no longer guaranteed. "Enough," she chastises herself. "Get up." *Fortune favours the bold.*

The struggle to her feet challenges her lung implants. Were it not for them and the rest of the upgrades Outland gave her in advance of sending her to Seal Beach, she would have surely died several times over. She catches her breath and examines her prosthetic. Synthetic musculature and sinew dangle from her forearm her like a squid's tentacles, curling, constricting, and spasming involuntarily. She tries to calm the frenetic waggling, and succeeds in part by focusing on her shoulder rather than on her nonexistent hand. Vying for attention, one of the jet-black tendons curls upwards—away from where her wrist should be—and begins to turn in on itself. She grabs just above the amputation and concentrates on the unnatural sensation with teeth gritted and eyes wide and wet. Thankfully, her mind misinterprets the ravaged arm's pain broadcast. This roadblock keeps out more than just pain, however; Oni similarly cannot make headway into her arm's articulations. Notwithstanding the communication breakdown, she tries to make associations in the mental fog.

The residual arm itself feels like a callus or an infected mole. Commanding feeling and response from within such a dull tingle with any real specificity will take time, practice, and serenity. Instead, Oni tries to flush out her remaining control. She sobs as she clenches her phantom fist. Dead wires fizz and the remaining tendon slaps backwards, purposeless without the metallic bone that had once accompanied it. This feeling gives Oni a coordinate for the tendon. She ponders her phantom fist and imagines clenching it again, but this time elicits less-painful feedback. The specialized biotech obeys and the tendon responds like a cobra to a pungi melody.

Kneeling upright in the Hretha, Oni looks around for toys Skyr might have left behind—toys with buttons her snake of a resurrected forearm can press. *Won't let them take me again.* The Hretha is scarcely loaded, but it is not empty. Oni scans the guns she knocked over and smirks, happy to trade a suicidal button for a homicidal trigger. *I'm coming to get you, Celeste. And I'm going to look like a nightmare doing it.*

## INTO THE BREACH ONCE MORE

Skyr had equipped the Hretha with several auto-turrets. They ultimately did not do him much good, but they have bought Oni enough time on the Chrysalis deck to record her joint summary and declaration of war: "To the police, to the Military, to all unbought members of the Terran Bureau of Investigation, and to anyone else listening: this is Dr. Oni Matsui. I am former employee of the Outland Corporation. As you may or may not have been informed, I sabotaged Outland's noosphere labs when the CLOUD was in its infancy, and I was present at its death. I apologize for all that the technology I had no small part in making has done to us—to our city, to our hearts, and to our minds. I apologize for acting too late to stop Outland: to stop those who are trying to accelerate human evolution out of a loathing for humanity. That loathing will manifest itself today: Outland CEO Celeste Charming has in her possession the child abducted from Naval Weapons Station Seal Base; patient 2690 to be specific. As you may or may not know, this girl is capable of unifying and controlling archetypals across the state, and more. *She is* the rumored Omnitype. If not stopped, Charming intends to harness her power in order to mount a coup and seize mental control of the Republic. I am aboard a ship with security clearance to the Citadel and headed there now. If you receive this transmission, including the attached entry codes, I imagine I will have already landed. I recommend that you stop at nothing to prevent this calamity from coming to fruition. I am, myself, taking this recommendation to heart and going after the girl before they take advantage of her, whatever that might look like. General McCabe—if you can hear me—I hope that you will correct the record, knowing what you know now and will learn in the hours and days to come. If we do not have an opportunity to formally meet, I ask you to bury me along with my friends: Paul Sheffield, Father Edmund Barros, Jin Kobayashi, Booker Gibson, Emily Robledo, and Constance Kressinger. My friends died in the service of the greater good. I just hope it is great enough to withstand today...Wish me luck."

Oni interfaces with the ship's comm system and readies her message. Unfortunately, Outland's signal jam prevents the transmission.

Arm militarized, message ready, drugs percolating, and engines primed, Oni sits down in the captain's chair. She buckles in and carefully sets her crudely-modified substitutive arm on the dash, next to a photograph of some leopard-printed milkdud shaking Skyr's hand—the two of them marked up in red with the Citadel's clearance codes. Avoiding a mental clench of her dead parts, which might blow a couple dozen holes into the instrumentation, Oni dredges up a song from her youth. It is a punk song that had dribbled down into a composer's notebook, onto ivory piano keys, and out, live, through a crappy popstar-branded radio to a school-crushed adolescent camped under her bed. Humming it to herself, Oni tightens the zip ties and bandages holding the gun barrel constituting her new hand in place.

Although faced with limited resources and time, Oni managed to weaponize her loss fairly well. She fastened a fixed-stock submachinegun to her forearm, banana-clip facing up and out to make reloading less of a feat. Since a trigger-pull will already demand some mental gymnastics on her part, she set it in a sling at her side. Although feeling ludicrous doing it, like a far gone Dr. Frankenstein, she then threaded her last responsive syntendon around the gun's trigger. She will not win in a sharp-shooting contest, but she also will not go down without a fight.

Oni's vision is beginning to blur in response to an overabundance of misperceived and incorrectly assimilated stimuli. All surfaces have turned satiny. Everything seems to shimmer or shake, including the ship's motley controls, which altogether look like a nebula flattened and pulled snug over an oversized ice-cube tray. Fully aware that it is not sleep deprivation but rather the drugs that have aroused this mindtrip, Oni centers her attention on what she knows for certain is real, beginning with the ripples in the ship's force-field.

Faced with a stalemate aback the atrium, dissidents have now set their sights on the Hretha and on whatever vehicle or tech can be stolen, sold, and or scrapped. Oni spots several rebels trying to get in through the rear hatch. She nods, smiles, and cranks the throttle halfway. *Don't approach a horse from behind.* Without consideration of her rearward victims, Oni blasts the ship's thrusters and leaves behind only shadows.

The Hretha vaults clear of Akbari's crypt and bounds towards the Citadel. The Partition's AA guns will not be a hindrance this time around; Celeste's minions have all been given a pass, Skyr included.

G-force presses Oni back into her seat and jerks her ballistic arm awkwardly to the side. To make it easier on herself, she could accelerate slowly, but she doubles down and pushes the throttle to its limit. The ship thumps. Unsecured cargo in the back smashes against the Hretha's tailbone. Absent Gibson's "Yee-haw," Oni screams it in memorial, and again to monopolize on her adrenalin rush.

She is nearing the ceiling of Outland's signal jam, where she is convinced that the Military and the State are still transmitting. She cycles between frequencies until she hits 330MHz. More important than her summary and plea are the attached Citadel clearance codes Skyr had handy on the dash; if the Citadel goes into lockdown, it will take time to crack it open—time the Republic simply does not have.

A warning buzzer notifies Oni that she has hit the manufacturer's suggested ceiling. At this height, the Rift looks like a gutter fed crap by the PIT. At this height all of the city's problems seem scaled down. Oni could easily roll north to Victorville and take refuge in the desert or beeline it south to the Coronado wastes…She does not, however, as she does not want to go on hiding. She does not want to introduce herself by another name or go to sleep wondering who among her new friends will turn her in for silver. She does not want to live in fear of living. And so, exposing herself to her fear and scraping the lower stratosphere, she tries once more for peace— bloody, bloody peace—and spams her encrypted message. There is no response, no receipt of transmission. Oni Matsui is alone; alone with an submachinegun for an arm, veins surging with a witches' brew of opiates and stimulants, and a first-class ticket to witness the next stumble in human evolution.

A northward adjustment fills the cockpit with sunshine. Oni lets the glow dip into her cuts and wounds. Lukewarm, she sets the ship's nose down. The Blue Zone rises with all of its corporate castles and polished steel, ready to spike Oni's return. Aiming at the outline of the Citadel, Oni switches on autopilot, unfastens her restraints, and heads aback the ship to finetune her weapon and last-minute attack plan.

Examining her modifications, Oni realizes she can train her fire holding the gun's grip with her good hand, but that *it'll hurt like a bitch.* She would prefer to rely upon stealth, but without a functional Monocle, she cannot program a choker to match Skyr's specs and cannot activate a cloaking device without a great deal of fanfare. *Loud and proud…*

She sleuths around the galley in search of some means of getting past the reception party on the Citadel's sky-dock. *An EMP would do nicely,* she thinks, reflecting upon her last planned foray into the Outland capitol. Unfortunately, none is handy amid the mess her erratic flying left has strewn about. It's not surprising, really; Skyr would not have jeopardized his own electronics for an easy kill. Anything barring the exceptional ESD wand that might have run afoul of his implants, including an EMP, would be out of the question. After all, by the end, he was more tech than man, and the man that remained was not a good one.

In the mess, Oni finds a glove. Picking it up and scrutinizing its dragon-scale armour, she determines it must be a part of a greater uniform—one that could potentially keep her whole. Oni puts the glove in her pocket for safe-keeping and hastily scans the detritus spread across the galley floor. She tilts her head at the sight of a padlocked steel chest built into the Hretha's portside hull. With the Citadel less than five-minutes-out, Oni has no time to fuss with the lock. She lifts her arm and intuits a trigger pull. The three-round burst obliterates the lock, and nearly twirls Oni into a pirouette with its modest recoil. Although the heavplast zip ties and bandages have kept the gun in place, there is no telling for how much longer. Massaging her shoulder, Oni kneels down beside the chest and opens it.

Two oryx skulls with intertwined horns sit atop a mishmash of military-patterned threads and tubes of edible printer ink. Tossing the skulls aside, and digging one-handed through dog-tags, pornography, and clothing, Oni's fingers find armoured plates. It is a veritable treasure of which the glove in her pocket is but one small part: a specialized-Sentinel suit, made special by a number of sadistic yet utilitarian modifications. Its flexible antiballistic torso coverage has been retrofitted with thin overlapping armor plates; good enough against law enforcement as well as in limited engagements against big guns. *Skyr didn't die wearing his Sunday best.*

Although Skyr was several sizes larger than Oni, the near-joint locks are adjustable allowing for a reasonable fit. She slinks into the leggings, which are braced against calf and thigh by a slender hydraulic exoskeleton. They tighten about her knees and waist, squeezing life up into her lower back, similarly reinforced by segmented exovertebrae. Armour creeps up as the joints tighten, sealing Oni inside Skyr's shell. She fits her hand through a sprung-loaded sleeve and fumbles, body aching and submachinegun missing five fingers that could help her put on the armoured glove jammed into a seeming pocket-too-far.

Muttering incoherent indignation, she secures the glove and then her hand. Unable to operate further on her prosthetic arm, she writes it off and leaves it to hang outside of the suit, unarmoured. The suit apparently has other plans: recognizing vestigial organic tissue, the armour provides coverage across her tattered prosthetic, all the way up to her violent addition.

It hits her: the horror that must have been Booky's physical disassociation. She shudders, and looks down at her armour-splinted limbs apathetically. It certainly defies Outland's uniform conventions, but that *doesn't matter. I'm not going there to make a fashion statement. I'm going there to make a bang.*

The suit fits Oni surprisingly well, granted Skyr also had forty pounds on her. Better than expectation, but still clunky. She digs into the chest for the last component of her new uniform: Skyr's helmet. It is heavy, presuming a strong neck or reinforcement by exo, and distinguished from other Sentinel domes by an ornate sword decal running from the reinforced forehead plate to the end of the nosepiece. Oni lifts it to eye level and inspects the embedded comm and basic heads-up display. Before she can put it on, the Hretha jerks to the side. Its autopilot is preparing to land.

The ship's comm buzzes and a voice fills the cockpit: "Cargo vessel forty-nine-dash-twenty-twelve, this is Outland Tower; transmit security codes now or be obliterated."

Oni runs into the cockpit, and feeds the irate traffic controller his coveted codes listed on Skyr's photograph. The Hretha angles towards the Citadel's sky-dock, slowly being enveloped by shadow. The tower's blast-shield crawls across the entrance, narrowing Oni's opportunity and sealing the tower. *Tarnation. They're already going into lockdown.*

"My apologies, Mr. Meijer. Priority is yours; sky-deck is open—but not for much longer…Do you have eyes on the enemy squadron?"

A bad actor without the gravelly voice to even try, Oni elects not to respond. Granted Skyr was an antisocial screwup, her silence is probably right-on-the-money.

"We've got incoming—a couple thousand bogeys hot over Burbank. Also getting dogged street-level. Bad news citywide."

A quick survey of the Hretha's tactical map backs up the controller's warning. Oni does not believe it right away. She glances out the northeast-facing window for confirmation. The base of the Citadel looks like Mecca during the hajj. Thousands and thousands are swarming entrances lit by muzzle flashes. *Archetypals...*The alleged "bogeys" over Burbank look far more portentous. A Dunkirk-variety of ships, closely-knit and flying like a flock of starlings, blisters southward towards the Citadel, *towards their captive queen.* Oni takes solace that even if her message to McCabe fails to hit its mark, the impending downtown war might catch his eye.

Autopilot prevents Oni from speeding up the ceremonial docking maneuver. The Hretha bucks its head back as if to bray and touches down at the very end of the landing strip. Spotlights snap on as the blast shell jigsaws together around the opening, keeping out Outland's growing list of enemies. With a click-chush, the Hretha is grounded. In advance of the engine's powering down, a dozen droids run out to tether the ship with magnetic braces.

Noticing the service droids take an indirect course to the Hretha, Oni realizes there is something more afield. Sparkles misdirected and captured by a sliver of afternoon sunshine hint at a more daunting reality: a cloaked Buke bot. Oni veils her terror with Skyr's helmet.

"Welcome home, Mr. Meijer," says the traffic controller, fully transitioned to soft-voiced sycophant. "Ms. Charming will meet you on the deck. Good luck."

*Good luck will have you staked on the heap with the rest...*Oni doublechecks the comm to make sure that her message is ready to send one more time, and blasts it on the military frequency. Although the Citadel blocks outgoing jams, an exception may have been made for Skyr.

Snug in Skyr's claustrophobic hood and blessed with an Outland-linked comm and one-liner insights into Citadel affairs, Oni amps herself up: *This is it. Celeste is coming down to save you the trip... This is your shot.* As she straightens out and hits the release on the rear-ramp, she realizes—despite her spinning stomach, fluttering heart, and aching shoulder—that there is nothing else she would rather be doing in this moment. "Tarnation." The helmet mediates her exclamation and projects it low and coarse. She had neglected the fact that Sentinel helmets pitch-shift and modulate the wearer's voice to conceal their identity as well as to intimidate. *Won't have to go in mute.*

The ramp clumsily drops onto the flight deck with a thud. Oni struts out like she owns the place. Skyr's reputation precedes her, because not one goddamned android says boo, scrutinizes her figure or asks what is up with her arm. The Buke bot continues to hide its face, this time likely out of deference. Coincidence and paranoia could possibly explain the noninterference, thinks Oni. Or is it instead possible that Skyr was neither a peasant nor a rogue nor an assassin, but rather a disguised lord who enjoyed too greatly the apolitical frontline? One, all four or none of the above—he is dead all the same.

Making her way towards the tower-end of the sky-dock, Oni peers over the edge. Below the dock, now fully recessed, sealed in behind the blast shell and locked in-place, there is an eighty-storey chamber turned Hirstian kaleidoscope of Outland Monarch drones. In the few gaps left between the fluttering orange-accented metal contraptions, Oni can make out a company of Outland Goliath drones and Cricket tanks charging up. *Celeste is preparing for war.*

A toneless voice ratchets Oni's attention back to the sky-dock. "Skyr, quick gawking about." The voice emanates from a little roto-lifted box hovering six-feet off the ground. The box projects a blue holographic of Celeste Charming. "Someone sure did a number on you…"

If there were substance to the icon, Oni would ream it with lead. Robbed of the opportunity, she plays along and, confiding in her helmet's voice-modulator, replies candidly. "What now?"

"I beg your pardon!" Celeste yells. Her face breaks free from the rest of her projected self and careens towards Oni to face her once-removed reflection in Skyr's visor. "Watch your tone, you ape. *I* ask the questions around here."

"Sure, See-See," Oni replies, adopting Skyr's term of endearment.

"And you've been dodging my questions for the past two hours. What is wrong with your Monocle?"

Oni motions to scratch at her head, but cuts the gesture mid-motion recalling she is wearing a helmet. "That bitch got me with an ESD. Going to need to swap mine out."

Charming raises an eyebrow. Although she cannot see through the polarized glass, her eyes still manage to pierce Oni's confidence. "The Omnitype?"

"No…Matsui."

"And?"

Oni lifts her submachine gun as far as her sling will allow. "She came to regret it."

Celeste's face rejoins her glittery body. "Excellent work, Skyr! I suppose you'll need a new arm in addition to a new Monocle."

Uncertain about Skyr and Celeste's usual repartee, Oni swings for the fences. "Would make sense, assuming you want your ape to climb..."

"Consider it done. Only the best for my best..." Celeste is unrivalled in her insincerity. "What of Hex's son? Was he pleased with how things worked out?"

"Things worked him out of the picture."

Celeste's hologram brightens. "Ha! Tremendous. Did you get the names of the saboteurs?"

"I'm going to take care of them now."

"Good. See that you do...Our great leap forward must not be misdirected by friction or resistance..." Charming's hands disappear, set to work interfacing with a computer offscreen. They return, clasped. "Apart from the barbarian horde at the gates, which we'll have to convert ahead of schedule..."

"How soon?"

"The ceremony? Within the hour. Thanks to your work, the asset is in place. Once the Cordei pre-boot is complete and I am settled, we should be ready to go...That is enough talk now. Ensure security has all it needs to keep us whole, and then join us in the Throne Room. Lend a hand if need-be, but don't let the archetypals rob you of a place in my future."

The holographic tyrant is yanked back into the little hovering box, which buzzes down the hallway opening where the sky-dock meets the Citadel's heartwood.

Preceded by a dozen faint thwacking sounds—archetypal lives consumed by fire in service of the collective's greater offense—a shifting-tone siren starts its infinite ascension, ringing throughout the Citadel and warning Outland staff and property of the threat looming outside. "All security personnel, please report to your stations immediately." Countless orange lights spin in unison, imbuing Oni with an odd feeling of serenity. Chaos has become her normal.

Skyr's helmet provides Oni with access to a wide range of Outland wireless channels, both private and unsecured. *Privacy is evidently a privilege for only the most powerful.* At the bottom-righthand corner of her visor, the names of the transmitters and the receivers appear. Bart Werner is trying to warn Julia Kwok about a purge of scientists with top-security clearance. Leon Lutt is worried about power readings on the seventieth floor. Chief Engineer Burke has sealed off access from the fifth floor up. A security AI has CC'd Skyr with confirmation that Hondo Eze, Jono Hunt, Trish Gruen, Boaz Colberg, and Ruth Hernandez are to be executed for their hand in sabotaging the Cordei. Skyr has been starred on this last order with an, "Assist if desired" flair.

There is an emerging theme to the majority of the other comms concerned with happenings outside. Outgoing transmissions are ordering Outland outposts and cypulchres around the city to dispatch reinforcements to the Citadel. Some chatter concerns the archetypals' aerial assault. The swarm now testing the Citadel's blast shell for weaknesses with everything from kamikaze dives to rail-gun barrages, is battle-tested; it effortlessly disarmed a dozen cypulchres stationed in the RIM on its way over. Meanwhile thousands of feet below, the pedestrian assault is grinding Outland security down, whose calls for support are met with silence. The battle line is demarcated by ruptured brains piled like peeled Louisiana shrimp. Celestes' unhackable mechs are systematically being enchanted by the technomancers, and turning on their faithful kin. *Unless Celeste puppets Regan soon, she will be pitted against her own firepower, and there might not be anybody left for me to shoot.*

Oni wanders about the eighty-third floor—deafened by the alarms and sirens—looking for some sort of signage pertaining to the "Throne Room" or to the "Cordei." The further down this hall she goes, the farther away her objective seems—as if she is chasing the horizon with a macro lens. She finds a computer terminal, formerly a Minerva kiosk, in a small alcove off the hallway. She tries all pertinent keywords and a dozen other names a megalomaniac might name a top-secret lab. There is no labelled mention of the "Throne Room" even existing. It occurs to Oni that *it is all about* who *you know.*

The transmissions logged by Skyr's helmet provide her with a few starting points: the names of those expressing concern over missing scientists. Again, the results are not satisfactory. Kwok, Lutt, and Werner all seem to have gone missing without a trace. Trying once more, Oni looks into Eze, Gruen, Colberg, and Hernandes. They are not far off; the terminal marks their progress down a hall on the seventy-ninth floor and indicates they are headed to a quad of rooms marked, "Under Construction." Oni makes a beeline for the stairs, also indicated on the Citadel map.

She avalanches down the steps. The Citadel's blaring alarms and sirens contextualize her hurry. A pair of technicians scurry out of her way as Oni hits the seventy-ninth floor running. She ignores their scoffing. *Had it been Skyr in a hurry, they might not have gotten the free pass.*

Lacking Monocle's 3D guidance system, Oni is stuck with the helmet's limited HUD—probably as old as she is—which offers direction in the form of metered distance and arrow indicators. It directs her down a gutted hallway aflutter with plastic tapestries coloured by cautionary holographics. Immediately, she realizes that the doors are not numbered. Taking advantage of Skyr's universal key, she peeks into the first room on the right. There is no sign of construction—just a pile of vacuum-sealed bodybags, reminiscent of the bowels of Seal Base.

Recoiling from the carnage, Oni wearily looks down the way. Finding the death-rowers alive is improbable, she decides. *Will have to beat the answers out of someone else—perhaps their executioners.* She looks back for the technicians who had scoffed at her. They are gone. *Damn-it.*

Losing hope and steam, Oni checks one more room, interrupting a gaggle of murderers and morticians cocooning bodies.

"Everything alright, sir?" one of the executioners asks nonchalantly. His goggles train on the rifled barrel protruding from Oni's armoured forearm. As if struck by a gorgon curse, he goes rigid.

The overlay inside Skyr's helmet identifies two of the corpses. One belongs to Hondo Eze and the other to Trish Gruen. Two more setbacks marked in blood. "Boaz Colberg—Ruth Hernandez—where are they?"

The man awestruck by Oni's arm shakes out of his trance and turns to confer with his hazmat-suited accomplices. After some whispering, he enthusiastically bucks back and answers: "They're en route. Should be just past the elevators…You want a hand, sir?"

Upset by creeping visual distortions, Oni offers a gruff, "No," and retreats into the hallway. She speeds past a dozen more unmarked mausoleum doors, and stops in her tracks. The rogue saboteurs— potentially her key to the Throne Room—are nudged along by a Sentinel further down the hall, sidestepping stacks of drywall and tools.

Paying Oni no mind, the Sentinel opens a door and coaxes the couple inside. The Sentinel raises his gun and adopts the isosceles stance, forcing Oni to act from afar. She clenches her phantom fist and her sixteenth digit tenses. Her gun bucks and crackles, peppering the Sentinel and everything in his vicinity with hot lead. Geofoam from the ceiling sprinkles Oni's victim while death spreads him out.

She vigorously reloads, anticipating a hormonal flux that drugs and routine will diminish, and cautiously sprints over to ensure that the Sentinel is in fact dead. The twitching corpse foregrounds a perplexed couple; Outland stooges who overstepped, tripped, or stood too tall.

## CORDEI

The gunshots ringing in Lyle's ears are unaccompanied by pain. He slowly opens his eyes to see his would-be executioner lying in a pool of his own blood, shaded by a patchwork cyborg. *What now?*

"Help me with the body," the cyborg grumbles, waving Lyle and Ruth over with a gunarm dripping blood.

Lyle does not miss a beat. He meets his champion at the threshold and tugs the corpse very matter-of-factly into the room by its legs. Ruth sobs quietly, unaccustomed to seeing such savagery firsthand despite having no doubt coordinated innumerable executions from the safety and remoteness of her office. *Amateur.*

The cyborg closes the door, locks it, and leans against it. "Colberg and Hernandes?"

"In the flesh," Lyle answers back, setting the corpse at the base of the pile.

With a crook of her neck and a hard yank, the cyborg removes her helmet. A sweaty tangle of black hair sweeps to the side of a grisly face. Soiled bandages fail to hide the extent of her most recent thrashing, and certainly do not cover up her red-haloed irises. "You two are going to have to lend me a hand."

"I appreciate you helping us out," Lyle says, eager to figure out why this zombified mech looks so familiar, "But we've already got a handful of problems and only four between the two of us..."

Ruth interrupts Lyle's ungrateful and sarcastic bent with a string of facts: "Charming has lost her mind—gone completely paranoid. She's having everyone killed...If someone doesn't turn our implants in, they'll figure out we're still alive...They will finish what they started."

Dabbing her cheek with her gloved hand, the bloody cyborg interjects: "It is about to get a whole lot worse. Celeste is making a global powergrab and this is ground zero."

Lyle takes a step closer and tilts his head, fighting with Colberg's brain to process his virtual memory. "You're not Military..." *The woman from Minerva's self-projection in the dark CLOUD...Oni Matsui, wanted terrorist.* "Oh for heaven's sakes." He flashes Ruth a smile. "It is Outland's employee of the year, Dr. Matsui—the renegade technophobe."

The name weighs on Ruth's brow until sprung by breathless realization. "Oni..."

"You were the one at Seal Beach, weren't you?" Admiration and jealously wrinkle Lyle's forehead. "I am *impressed.*"

Holding Skyr's helmet against her layered chest plates, Oni nods, ashamed of her role in all of this.

"Thought you would have gone into hiding after all that. Hell, anyone with half-a-brain and the will to survive would have bussed to Mars."

Oni raises her eyebrows as if the Mars was someplace she had not considered. "There will be no hiding from Outland if Celeste is successful."

"Why?" Ruth calls upon the rationale behind Charming's gargantuan undertaking that was offered to Outland employees: "She's just trying to assemble and rehabilitate the archetypals. It's a government contract." She looks to Lyle for positive reinforcement, but he shakes his head. "Boaz, tell her!"

Irked by Ruth's naivety, Lyle pinches the bridge of his nose. He steps forward. "We know who you're working against. Who are you working for?"

Oni hesitates. "The United States Marine Corps. General McCabe, specifically. Outland is going down for the count and we are running out of time…Charming targeted you on suspicion of sabotage; I know that much. Regardless of whether it's true, you only have one real option, and that's working with me."

Lyle sneers. *And hitch my wagon to a dying star.*

Glowering at Lyle (whose fleshy surrogate is incapable of his intended subtely), Oni continues: "The three of us share something in common: Outland wants us dead. They are going to get their wish unless we disable the Cordei."

"Impossible," Ruth says, apprising the room with a bushed ogle. "We're safe in here…We should stay put until Celeste realizes she made a big mistake…or until help arrives."

"Help!" laughs Lyle, incredulous. "No one is coming to save us. Oni saving us was incidental…"

Oni turns her helmet and peers in at the display. An emblazoned alert crawls across the text feed: "OUTPOSTS 1-87 UNDER ATTACK – GUNSHIPS (USM) INBOUND FOR CITADEL." She clasps her mouth to squelch her delight, but changes her mind and releases it along with some good news. "You're wrong. Help is coming, but not in the form of rescue. The Marines are going to tear this place down."

Lyle dismisses the good news with an overblown sigh. "They're too late. The blast shell is up. By the time they cut through, Charming will have bent Minerva to her will."

"Which is why I've given them the emergency codes to the landing bay."

Both Ruth and Lyle's stand agog.

The room quakes again. Both the comm inside Skyr's helmet and the intercom by the door broadcast a hacked message from the originator of this most recent seismic event:

"Celeste Charming, this is General McCabe. Never mind your lawyer. You won't need one. Your spies have been executed. Your plan has been documented and exposed. And by admitting Patient 2690, property of the United States government, you have broken a level five quarantine, which on its own accord requires military action. Treason and terrorism require deadly action. The neurological augmentation of my Marines? Princess, I hate royalty, and I hate your tower. You know what I love? Blowing shit up. You can mitigate all of this violence by handing over the Omnitype, laying down any weapons you might be carrying, and by signing your unconditional surrender with a show of hands on the rooftop. You have one minute to comply."

"Devil's in the basement, and angels pulling the roof back," says Lyle despondently. He feels Colberg's testicles begin to retreat.

"Good god," laments Ruth, eyes seemingly locked on the end of her nose. "We have to get to the roof!"

"You think you can make it up there in a minute? Be my guest." Seizing upon their rapidly-evolving sense of allegiance, Oni presses the issue: "As of right now, the two of you are wearing the wrong uniforms. It's time to enlist…"

"Have you listened to anything I've said?" Ruth cries, verging on hysterical. "What do you want us to do? What do you think we can accomplish? The halls are full of Sentinels and droids who would love to shoot a couple of turncoats…"

*Embarrassing,* thinks Lyle, distancing himself from the blubbering mess. He wipes the blood off Colberg's hands. "You kidnapped Minerva. Now she's here. How'd that happen? Does *the help* know about that? Does General McCabe know you're part of the problem?"

"So far as I'm concerned," Oni fires back, "there is only one problem at the moment: Celeste Charming. You're going to take me to the Throne Room—to the Cordei—and I am going to put a bullet between her greedy little eyes. For that, you will receive amnesty while all of your former colleagues are marched to the gallows."

Ruth dries her face, and looks to Lyle. "Boaz, I don't know if I can…"

Lyle massages Colberg's chin thoughtfully but quickly stops, nauseated by the alien texture. He nods away his disgust, and pats Ruth on the shoulder. "Try or die, baby."

Mustering up the intestinal fortitude, Ruth nods. "Fine…We have your word on it, Oni? You'll tell the government we're innocent?"

Oni appears frazzled by Ruth's invocation of innocence. "Yes. Just get me to where I need to go."

The three of them stand crooked, each desperate for the other to provide an idea to lean on.

"What you are proposing is murder-suicide…" *Finally, someone with the wherewithal dealt in at my table.* Lyle clears his throat. Oblivious to the Citadel's layout and impatient for Oni's plan, he prompts Ruth to tell-all. "What's our best bet?"

"Boaz…"

"Out with it, god-damn-it." Lyle's impatience firms Ruth up.

A heavy sigh precedes forced connections in her racked brain. "There are three ways into the Throne Room. The first is a death trap. It is guarded by Charming's private army and a double-set of blast doors. If the doors are breached, the threshold can be electrified. All that and X-ray cams, so they can ID you with or without a helmet."

It occurs to Lyle that having only really faced defenseless men and women since the war has left him overconfident and underprepared. "Guns, X-rays, titanium, and electrocution? Forget that. *Next.*"

Face contorted by competing pros and cons, Ruth crosses her arms and dips her head. "Charming has her own private entrance. She walks off her private elevator and straight into the Cordei Control Room, off-limits to everyone but her assistant and," she points to Oni's armoured suit, "the man whose uniform you are wearing. The Cordei Control Room has a second door, which opens to a suspended walkway. The walkway ends in a ladder, which runs down to the Cordei stage." Ruth squints. "Again, heavily guarded and…."

"Holy smokes," Lyle yells. "I didn't ask you to list off things we can't do…"

Already vexed, Lyle's critique forces Ruth to begin to stammer. Four false starts preface a coherent response: "The Auxiliary Server Room is our only way in. It is freezing cold. Three Buke droids patrol the stacks…" Ruth taps her temple, and flicks the air in Lyle's general direction. "Synch up; confirm the waypoint."

Lyle's eyes grow pale under the map Ruth has transmitted. The map takes three dimensions and tunnels around Lyle's inquiry. The factory-sized space he'd seen outside of Tuttle's office window appears. *The Throne Room.* The Cordei is on one side—clearly the room's infrastructural focus—and several rows of server racks are on the other, all walled off with glass. Additional rows are stacked in the dark of the recessed Server Room beyond. "Damn it." *Surprising the scenery you overlook when you're being dragged against your will.* "The Server Room is on the opposite side of the Cordei."

Ruth shrugs her shoulders.

*There's no excuse for apathy at a time like this,* Lyle thinks to himself, strongly considering adding Ruth to the pile. "Well, is it a private ceremony or will we have to mingle?"

"At the last security briefing, a list of over two-hundred men was circulated, all of whom were assigned to defend the Throne Room in addition to the Bukes in the Server Room." Despite her answer spelling out personal doom, Ruth appears pleased to depress Lyle. "And there will also be mech accompaniment."

Caving over the bad news, Lyle throws his hands above his downcast face. "Damn it…" *And damn Minerva.* "What is a Buke. anyway?"

Oni answers without looking, focused instead on testing her prosthetic's mobility, improved by Skyr's suit. "A heavily-armored droid with human features. Samurai features, specifically. Don't know how I feel about it."

"It's a tank with fingers. Hopefully we'll feel nothing."

Lyle cannot contain Colberg's flight response to the description, manifest in an audible gulp. "Say we knock out the Bukes. Breaking the glass will most likely trigger some sort of alarm." Ignoring sighs from both of his unlikely co-conspirators, Lyle continues to carve away at the pitch. "Even if we kill the alarm and get into the Throne Room proper, we will still be detected by Charming's army before we even get a chance to bleed on the Cordei."

"I'm dressed to impress," Oni says confidently. "They'll unmask me eventually, but I figure I could at least close the distance and get a shot off—assuming I can fool the Bukes."

Fear of killing the mindful monster that has dragged him here percolates in Lyle's mind, forming ideas he cannot be sure are his originals. Wary of his susceptibility, but also curious, he promotes an alternative: "Why don't we just blow up the auxiliary servers?"

The question visibly frustrates Ruth. "Badegger really scrambled your brain, didn't he? While the AUX servers share the Cordei's data and computing power with cypulchre clients around the state, the Cordei's success isn't locally reliant upon them—largely on account of the fact that the upper floors are crammed-full of well-guarded backups."

"Damn." Lyle spits and racks both his mind and Colberg's brain for a solution.

"Hold on!" Excitement tightens Ruth's face. She navigates the pile of corpses and clears a bare-faced computer terminal built into the far corner—apparently a pre-fab fixture in almost every room. Rapping the keys lightning-quick, Ruth proves her suspicions correct: "They haven't taken my clearance away. I'm sure that they'll block me out once that they see I've been active." Reflecting Oni in her puffy eyes, she feigns a smile and subtly bows. "Thank you for that, by the way." Gratitude noted, she turns back to the terminal, and points at the monitor as if the mess of code streaming down means anything to her audience. "I can't turn the Bukes off. Only employees with top clearance can shut them down. For whatever reason, Skyr isn't on that list. I did, however, oversee the current series' update as well as troubleshoot Outland's security protocol and review their implementations for the better part of the last decade."

The red blotch on the bandage over Oni's cheek doubles in size. "That doesn't exactly inspire confidence. After all..." She pauses to hork blood. "I'm standing proof that you're bad at your job."

Ruth nearly chokes on Oni's indignation. "Dr. Matsui, I can implicate one of the Bukes with a false security report; suggest to Outland's security-AIs and to the two other Bukes that it has been hacked. Ever since Mr. Winchester was assassinated by his own Buke, we have updated our robots to be especially sensitive to invasive programming and to remote commands, not only in themselves but in others on the same network as well."

"A security report? That'll put all eyes on the Server Room," Oni says dourly, staring daggers at her enemy's enemy.

"Sure will." Ruth hammers away at the keys again, and decisively hits ENTER. "And *Skyr Meijer* is going to take two men down to investigate. The accused Buke will immediately register the report as fallacious and presume a pending attack. Its targeting system will adjust to consider new threats including its team, and this paranoia will only escalate the situation. Once the two Bukes unaffected by my executable destroy the malwarrant, they will remain on high alert. They will return to their vigilant, neutral setting once we show up, hiding in plain sight."

"And the glass?" Lyle cuts in. "We go in to put out one fire, then immediately start another?"

"These bots weigh about a ton and fire armour-piercing rounds the size of eMeal cans," Ruth says, standing tall with confidence renewed and stress repressed. "The hacked Buke will defend itself, meaning glass will inevitably be broken. We can go in once the other two Bukes have eliminated the perceived threat and stood down, granted our alter-egos have costumes to match." Ruth drapes her fingers over the keyboard, ready to initate the bulk of her plan. "Thoughts?"

Oni's lips retreat around her crimson teeth. "Well done, Hernandes. Set this ball in motion, but give us at least fifteen minutes to get down there. I'll inform See-See that I'm on my way." She sets her weight against the door and slides her helmet back on. With a modulated grunt, she indicates the Sentinel on the floor. "Grab his gun," she orders Lyle. "Ruth, is there an armoury nearby? A laundry service? Anyplace we might find uniforms for the two of you..."

"The ones I'm familiar with are on other floors..."

The sonic pattern of the sirens and alarms blaring out in the hall changes radically. They synchronize and wail in speedy bursts of four.

Blinking wildly—feeling a second wind from the amphetamines he thought he sweated out already—and ignoring the bad omen syncopated outside, Lyle blurts out: "The Throne Room occupies a space that vertically hollows six floors. According to your map, we want to go down a few storeys..."

"The armouries will all be full of Sentinels..." says Ruth, shaking imaginary dice. "There's a locker room we can hit on the way that might not be as busy."

"Good." Lyle's inability to properly control subtleties of Colberg's expressions leaves him grinning like a maniac. "Oni, you're going to use that itchy trigger finger if anyone tries to stop us, yeah?"

Oni rests her head against the door and pats the handguard on her submachine gun. "Let's get you two some threads and—"

There is a loud hiss. Oni lets out a bassy cry and stumbles forward. Lyle catches her. Merigold lines track down the edges of the door, sparkling all the way.

"Shit! They're cutting through—must have heard the shots."

Oni turns her singed back to Lyle. "Get ready," she shouts, drawing vigor from her hate-filled well.

The fallen Sentinel's machinegun seems unnaturally small in Colberg's hands. Lyle aims it at Oni, mulling over fragging the wretched technophobe, but decides common goals mean displaced risk and effort. He lowers the gun, checks the magazine, and takes position.

Ruth clambers as far back as she can, looking dubiously at the man she thought she knew. "Maybe if we surrender..."

Lyle cuts her off: "We leave the Citadel as heroes or in body bags."

The two white-orange lines created by the cutting-torch hook near the base of the door, and inch towards one another.

As if playing the metal penetration to completion, the sirens pick up. Only, in this sequence of alarm blares, the final note is discordant—it does not match the tinny deets or wahs that precede it; rather, it is a thunderous *dum*, held longer than the others. The Citadel quakes. Lyle topples over, looking like a stop-motion puppet beneath the room's flickering lights. He can barely make out Ruth's form, encompassed by a cadaverous avalanche. Oni, conversely, holds her ground.

The marigold lines stop in their tracks, and darken to a reddish orange.

"What the hell was that?" Lyle blurts out, picking himself up.

Ruth crawls out from under a headless scientist. "The archetypals are here to save the Omnitype."

"Archetypals have been working their way up for the last little while, but I doubt they'd risk hurting Regan with plasma cannons. No, I don't think that was them..." Keeping her gunarm aimed at the door, Oni crouches and spears one of the corpses with her fleshy hand. "I've got an idea—just bear with me." She slathers gore over Lyle's face. "Play dead and wait for my signal. You too, Ruth."

Lyle settles in with Colberg's former colleagues. Ruth, whimpering, pulls a body down over top of her. Satisfied with the set dressing, Oni unlocks the door. It disappears along with its molten tattoo. A pair of Sentinels—just about to resume their breaching attempt—stagger back, surprised by the opening. They stick their guns in Oni's face. "Freeze, you sonuvabitch!"

The more senior of the two grunts, distinguished by white striations on his helmet, takes a giant step back. "Ah shit. Mr. M. We thought..."

Oni swats his gun out of her way. "You thought what exactly?"

Another quake rocks the foundations to the tune of three *deets* and a foreboding *dum*.

Braced against his underling, the senior grunt struggles to answer: "We didn't get the death receipt from Jackson, so we came to make sure everything was alright. We didn't know, boss..." He looks past Oni and spots the motionless body of the Sentinel formerly known as Jackson.

Tracing the Sentinel's gaze to his dead comrade, Oni realizes the plan she made on the fly may be grounded. "I went to do Colberg and Hernandes, and that piece of shit tried to pull a fast one."

Setting down his blowtorch, the senior grunt respectfully sidesteps Oni and examines Jackson's body, oblivious to the inconsistencies in the cadaverous pile aback the room. "I've known Jackson for twelve years." Grief shielded by his visor, he looks back and up at Oni, ready to eulogize his fallen friend. "He was an Outlander through and through. He wouldn't have—"

Oni blurts out, "Ah, screw it." She dresses the sentimentist with a burst of full metal jacket, and turns on the grunt in the doorway with another three rounds.

Lyle casts his cover aside. "If time is of the essence, I'd think it essential to get out of here."

Oni holds her shoulder and shudders. "Agreed."

## BRAIN DRAIN

Oni tracked Sentinel blood downstairs to the lockerroom alongside Ruth and Boaz. After kicking in several lockers, her new acquaintences found old costumes and parted to dress in private on opposite sides of the room—out of modesty or perhaps out of shame.

Although not in the market for a new outfit, Oni nevertheless rummaged around for anything to make her last moments either more pleasant or more effective. She found two items of interest: an electrostatic smoke grenade and a dotgram labelled "Cordei layout." Neither lethal nor infrastructurally devastating, the ESS grenade temporarily hampers electronics and provides the visual cover expected by traditional smoke grenades. She turns it in her hand, with the dotgram on the bench beside her. She needs a functional Monocle to read the dotgram, and is desperate to know what she is in for. A stressed voice yanks her attention down the aisle walled by lockers.

"You couldn't find a smaller outfit?" The question's parent, Ruth, appears at the end of the aisle—a spitting image of the Princess of Mars depicted in Outland's famous colonial-propaganda poster. Her strong jaw is low on the neck of her new Sentinel uniform and her hair is cropped back, ready for her helmet, a matte-black bullet-magnet resting fashionably in the crotch of her arm.

Oni shifts self-consciously on the bench then realizes Boaz is the subject of Ruth's disappointment, who has cornered the aisle right behind her. His stomach bulges at the waist, winging his suit's antiballistic plates out like a pagoda's eaves. The protective armour covering his legs stops prematurely at his shins and his leg fat, though still covered by the antiballistic fabric, lumps over his knee pads. *Looks like he is moulting a leaner-man's skin.*

"Don't die a nag," Boaz barks back, slowing down before colliding with Oni's personal space. He orients Ruth's attention on Oni's prosthetic. "If they are paying enough attention to notice I need a wardrobe adjustment, they're probably going to notice that their key merc is a foot shorter and missing an arm." He leans forward, face gloomy and intense, "Besides, we don't have time for anymore of this dress-up shit. Time is *still* of the essence."

Oni clips the ESS grenade to her belt and holds the Cordei dotgram out to Ruth and Boaz. "One of you two: read or project this for me."

Ruth scans the dotgram without second consideration. She

blinks and straightens out. "Cordei layout…It is a corporate design document. Discusses the typography associated with the lettering and stencils on and around the CordDei."

Tremulous and looking worse for wear in his Sentinel costume, Boaz sweats out some needed direction: "Unless the two of you wish to discuss the lettering on your tombstones, I would strongly suggest *we get a move on.*"

"Oni, you've got to forgive him…He took a bunch of—"

The comm on Skyr's helmet goes loud like a swarm of hornets in a gas can. Oni calls for silence with a raised hand. She takes a deep breath and throws the helmet on. Inside, she tunes in to hear Celeste belittling Ruth's boss, the head of Section Security.

"How is that possible? Who transmitted the codes?"

"We are looking into it now."

"I cannot imagine a better time, Damian." Celeste's voice is nearly droned out by the hum of heavy machinery—not-so-subtle crunches and beeps. "And you are absolutely sure its McCabe's fleet and not more ATs?"

"Yes, Ms. Charming. He has intercepted our reinforcements. We are on our own. CitCom will focus on each floor's main hall, and any choke point, elevator, or stairwells we have not already lost. As for the mishap in the Auxillary Server Room…"

"See-See?" Oni interjects, excited by the mention of her planned mishap.

"Skyr! About time. Damian?"

"Yes, Ms. Charming?" replies the other voice on the line.

"CitCom's only priority is the protection of the Cordei. Nothing else matters. Now get off the comm and get to work." Celeste yells at someone off-mic, something about "The girl" and "doesn't need anesthesia." She returns to the comm. "Skyr, you skin-flap. I thought you killed Matsui."

"I did," Oni says enthusiastically.

"Then explain to me why a Buke bot in the Cordei ASR just went rogue. You know what? Never mind. The fire is out, but I want you to look into the ashes as soon as possible. I can see it from here—security is poking around. Not a lot of damage. But I also do not have a whole lot of faith in Damian's team at the moment. I want you to contain and to confirm." Her voice is tottery. *She's scared;* so close at once to great power and to great misfortune. The slightest change in her projected trajectory could prove cataclysmic. "We have got the Military and the archetypals at arms-length for the time being. We *do not* need any intimacy just yet."

"I'll be right down," Oni says, barely containing her schadenfreude.

"Buy me the time I need. And Skyr, the General has discovered the killswitches we implanted in his men. If he hasn't disabled them already, trigger them, but only after they've culled some of the archetypals." Celeste terminates the comm.

Charming's narcissim is a blessing, Oni decides; if she were any less self-concerned, she might realize her henchman of so many years has been substituted by a female amputee with a fistful of lead. Oni takes her helmet off and is greeted by four wet eyes all desperate for good news. "Hernandes—your plan is in motion. Time to go play bad detective."

Frazzled bodies, archetypal and Sentinel alike, litter the corridor. The walls are chock-full of bullet holes and are darkened by plasma burns. The battle responsible for this waste is not far ahead; just around the bend in fact, clear from the shouting, gunshots, and sonic booms growing aggressively louder.

Amid the grotesque ambiance of war, Oni can make out one petrified holler: "Open the door! Open the door, god-damn-it." Her helmet's feed reports similar requests. Celeste has remotely locked all the secondary blast doors and section gates in the Citadel from the safety of her Control Room. Her cornered forces have just now realized they have been betrayed in order to buy a few more minutes for a harebrained scheme, and have taken to the Outland internal comm to voice their displeasure.

A scream sapped by quickly-filling lungs precedes the retreat of a mulched Sentinel. He limps past Oni, helmet impacted like an oil drum that found the ocean's bottom.

"We're close," says Ruth, backing away from the melting omen.

Boaz taps his visor and fans his hand. "No shit."

Rounding the bend, Ruth spots human remains clinging to the far wall like stucco. She backs up all the way into Oni. Her costume rustles to the rhythm of panic. Turning to Oni, she pleads: "We have to go down and around," demeaning her Martian likeness with cowardice. "There's no way…"

Oni steadies Ruth. "Down and around?"

"The door leading to the AUX Server Room is on the other side of the Main Hall...Monocle indicates several-hundred combatants ahead."

"You must be joking." No amount of vocal modulation can conceal Boaz's frustration. "The Main Hall? The Main Hall enclosing the procession of death we are trying to avoid? Holy shit."

"Colby, you could have said something. You know this place as well as I do..."

"I'm not feeling like myself today."

"I had no idea that they'd already be up here..." Ruth implores Oni to consider her alternative: "The passage to the Server Room is accessible from the other side of the floor, but with the Main Hall blocked, we will have to go down or up a floor, cross to the other side, and then head on in."

Oni attempts to pinch her brow, but her helmet plays interference. "There is no going down. Security just lost that fight." More bad news scrolls up on her visor: Citadel Command has now locked down all stairwells. "And upstairs is off-limits."

Boaz wags his finger at Ruth as well as Oni. "You two are real peaches." He transfers this negative energy from Ruth to the palm of his hand, and smacks it, chastising himself: "Marcus has the Benny Bass case. My win. My raise. My promotion. My rooftop-parking spot. And Dorota? God-damn-it!"

"I am sorry!" Ruth steps out of reach of Boaz and bows her head to Oni. "I wasn't thinking!" She removes her helmet and wipes tears from her lashes. "If we can't go down or around, we're trapped."

*Pussy.* "Put your helmet back on. We're not trapped; not yet, anyway."

Ruth throws a fretful glance back to what is leftover from her former subordinates. "Listen..."

"No. You listen..." Even if Oni had the energy for sympathy, she no longer has the facial musculature to signify it. "If we don't have a good option available to us, and inaction means certain death, then we better make the best out of our last remaining bad option. Opt in, you come with me and you take your chances. Opt out, you die alone—a coward's death."

Overcoming her increasingly erratic spasms, Ruth puts her helmet back on.

The text at the bottom of Oni's visor indicates an archetypal surge as well as Marine progress through the skydock. "Alright. Our chances may or may not stand to improve." Lights flashing against the far wall hints at the latter. "Either way, we can't wait around to find out. We are going to cross the Main Hall at the first sign of a gap in the scrum. I'll give us smoke cover. No stopping for anything."

"The code to the passage across the way is 12161928," Ruth says, fear and emotion stripped from her voice by her company helmet. "12161928."

"What?" Boaz turns Ruth by the shoulder. "You are coming with us. You are going to get me into the Cordei. This is not a task you will walk away from…"

"Sorry, Colby—sorry, Oni. I really am." Ruth sets her gun down on the ground. "But I can't—I just can't."

Boaz grits his teeth and looks to Oni as if for permission to trim the fat. Tired of motivating the damned, Oni summons him to her side with a wave. Mixed aphorisms about thirsty horses, still water, and safety in numbers cross her mind, but she keeps them to herself. "We have what we need." Without saying anything more—not even an insincere "Good luck"— Oni leaves Ruth to course her own path to certain death. If Ruth thinks she can escape judgment and justice by hiding, then she truly does not know anything about the queen of the castle she has served. She will have hid from a middleaged authoritarian only to be discovered by a malevolent god divided in flesh and unified in mind.

*Hiding was never in the cards*, Oni reminds herself as she marches around the bend shoulder-to-shoulder with Boaz. The enemy she kills today would illuminate all shadows, flush out all burrows, and extinguish individuality. Like Ruth, Oni would be robbed of more than just her mind and body; if there is a soul, she would lose that too, only to become a node on the communal beast.

They pass a fuming automatic laser turret, dry-firing at ghosts. Most of the bodies splayed around it are archetypals, suggestive of a successful counter-flanking manouvre orchestrated by Outland Security. A second attempt by the unholy communion may prove unstoppable.

Inspecting the gear strewn around the turret, Oni accidentally lodges her foot in something soft. She lifts her weary leg to inspect the slippery grey matter on the heel of her boot.

"Looks like the auto-turret turned on its masters," Boaz opines, clearly distracted by a prospective upgrade. He drops his gun, and tears a higher-calibre assault rifle from the grip of a young woman whose face has been eaten away by lasers. He peers into the rifle's scope and bats an enlarged eye. "Just imagine what Minerva is capable of! The sublime…"

The auto-turret, churring back and forth, scrapes the bottom of its charge and fires. Boaz tumbles over. Oni blasts the turret, taking out its mobile base.

"Holy shit!" Boaz yells, flat on his face and bloodying up his suit. He starts to laugh as he rolls over.

Oni's helmet keeps her eye-roll private. "C'mon."

Boaz brushes himself off and checks the safety on his gun. "You just try to keep up now." He circumnavigates the last outpost and starts for the bend.

Giving Boaz a telltale distance, Oni wipes off the burnt brain on the heel of her boot. *Oh, Booky.* Her guilt seems to escalate as her eyesight fades and her memory takes her to foundational misdeeds. She knew the CLOUD's architect was a lunatic and said nothing. She knew the CLOUD meant the end of individuality and again said nothing. And now on the verge of doing something, there is nothing worth being said.

"Oni," shouts Boaz, freeing his new ally from her introspective episode. "The Main Hall…"

Oni drops her boot. *Nothing at all.*

She creeps over to where Boaz is crouched, and peers over his shoulder. The corridor resolves in the Main Hall, now mainstage for slaughter. A brown-robed figure protected by an electric sphere striated like a wicker ball stands between an unprotected wave of archetypals catching the bullets he defies and a small army of Sentinels slinging metal. The Sentinels faced with this unholy spectacle are divided into two camps: the larger camp consists of a battalion crowding a barricade decorated with auto-turrets on the left, and the smaller camp, a lone machinegun nest mounted at the intersection's edge, just feet ahead. (The latter likely assume the auto-turret still has their back.)

The robed archetypal advances past the inlet housing the door leading to the AUX Server Room. Face laminated by whorls of white hair and impressed with a look of tranquility, he stares down torrents of bullets, which he deflects handily with temporal warps. *He's a mage,*

Oni determines; an archetypal whose unstudied power over electronics and electricity seems magical. The mage's protective sphere is fed and sustained by bright blue arcs channeled from the bloody archetypal horde behind him. Replacements hurdle the dead to keep the juice flowing, with which the mage targets and primes grenades loaded in several of the Sentinels' guns. With widened eyes and an accusatory point, he triggers the grenades, turning the grenadiers and those in their close viscinity into a coarse mist.

The blast from the grenades creates a letup in the surviving Sentinels' defensive barrage. Less a few hundred incoming projectiles, the archetypals have a window and the advantage, which they immediately seize upon. The horde abandons its efforts to channel power to the mage's protective sphere and charge right past the machinegun nest. Little robotic abominations run alongside them on spidery legs. *Micro-reactors...They've brought their own power source with them.*

The machinegunner and his three enablers—ankle-deep in shell-casings—keep the muzzle magma-red, firing indiscriminately into the wall of spoilt flesh. Noticing the mage's blue-wicker fray, the gunner turns his sights on the robed figure and fires. Without the horde's energetic protection, the high-caliber burst cuts the mage in half. Emboldened now with the mystic gibbed, one from the machinegunner's entourage breaks from cover. He sets one foot atop the barricade, and rolls what looks like a snail's shell across the Main Hall. As the shell tumbles through the gore, it releases a silver chain, which clamps down into the bone and tile. Before the shell has a chance to crash into the far wall, the silver chain it has trailed the width the hall tightens to reveal little nozzles. The nozzles blast smoky rods of white phosphorus up and out. The white phosphorus enshrouds and burns those archetypals the machinegunner misses.

Only feet away from the unsuspecting machinegunners, Oni plans her attack. She kneels behind Boaz, ready to share with him their next-steps, but he apparently has a plan all his own. He clears Oni's reach and starts making his way to the machine-gun nest.

Boaz casually strides up to the four Sentinels. The horrors ahead have left them oblivious to the true threat looming behind them. Boaz appears to savor the moment, one-handing his new assault rifle in order to flip off the four. He looks back to Oni and alternates fingers in order to give her the thumbs up, and spins into action, severing each of the four Sentinels' spines.

Oni hurries over to the nest. The gunner is still alive—either a blessing or a curse resultant of cybernetic enhancements—but not in a position to hurt anybody. Ignoring the bubbled pleas turned to static by the gunner's modulator, Oni pushes the decerebrate aside and acquaints herself with his machine gun, adjusting the mount to accommodate her disability. More than just for evening the odds, keeping the gun hot will be good to avoid rousing suspicion further up the hall. It is awkward to fire, especially with her gunarm butting into the sandbags, yet Oni still manages a competitive spread. Numbed by pain and shock, she stoically scalps several of the unarmed monsters she helped doom. Over the muzzle flash, she glimpses the door leading to the Server Room. "CD" is stylistically stenciled under a decal of a half-brain on the door—employing the font specified by the locker-room dotgram. There is a tiny red window. "Boaz!"

Boaz hipchecks into her, unaware of or indifferent to his clumsiness and bulk. He pats one of the motionless Sentinels on the head. Unphased by the unrelenting mayhem, he ponders aloud: "Wonder what happened to all of their mechs. You'd think Outland would have sent their best…"

*If Celeste's game is domination, and she expects to rule the archetypals, she won't keep her fleet all in one place.* Oni internalizes her two-cents to keep Boaz focused and shrugs. "Grab the ESS grenade off my hip, and toss it. I'll provide cover fire. You remember the code?"

"Yup. 12161925." Boaz unclips the grenade from Oni's waist, and familiarizes himself with its toggle.

Skyr's helmet conceals Oni's frustration. "*12161928.*"

"Like I said."

The blanket of white phosphorus jetted into the archetypal advance by the Sentinels' silver chain has left skeletons bare and scoured the frontline runners. Oni spends a bullet and spares an obese archetypal dragging its human dressing along unnecessary pain. "Our suits should protect us," she says hopefully, still convinced the purpose of Sentinel suits is not so much to protect the living but to dehumanize the dead. "Still hold your breath when you cross. You ready?"

Boaz primes the grenade. "What kind of grenade did you say this was?"

Oni squeezes off a few more rounds. "Electrostatic smoke grenade. Might temporarily scramble nearby archetypal's group connection."

"Might? *Fan*tastic."

Oni's radio is still loud with pleas and devoid of acknowledgments. She makes out a warning from the Outland engineering team: there has been a massive power surge on floors thirty thru ninety.

Boaz drops his grenade-bearing hand like a tensed catapult.

Oni's visor reads: "Citadel power-grid offline. Emergency power rerouted to Cordei. Blast shields non-functional. Security doors non-functional. Lights and ventilation—" The message cuts off. *Tarnation.* Oni grabs Boaz by the wrist, locking him mid-motion. "Wait."

The recessed lights illuminating the battle flash and burn out. Explosions and gunfire strobe the frenetic struggle, creating short-lived heavy-metal Caravaggio's.

Boaz is rigid with dead-man's confidence. He shakes off Oni's grip and lobs the grenade towards the archetypals. The grenade's impact is unknowable in the dark and twisted circus, but the shadows seem that much more disorganized. Boaz makes a mad dash for the tiny red window while Oni blindly clears headway with lead. She fires down to the buckle of her belt of ammo. The impotent click rouses her to her feet. Flipping off both sides of the skirmish with three-round bursts, she runs the trail Boaz blazed. Bullets find her armor. Thankfully, Skyr knew enough to protect himself against his employer's tech and toys; none of the projectiles cut deep.

In the smoke and the phosphorus, amidst flying shrapnel and teeth, Oni spots Boaz. He was quick on the keypad and is holding the door open for her. She slides in on burnt knee-guards. Boaz slams the door shut behind her.

"God damn." Boaz fails to notice Oni's armor seething. "Haven't done that in a while."

Oni takes off her helmet to vomit. With little more than drugs and undigested eFeed left in her, she makes more sound than spray, and without doing herself the courtesy of wiping, throws her helmet back on. Her taxed breathing plays like bad industrial rock.

Wheezing a similar tune, Boaz peers out the window at the mayhem. Violent flashes compete with the darkness like prairie lightning. The lightning dissipates, giving way to unnatural golden rays emanating from down the hall. They saturate the corridor, and usher up elaborate, Byzantine patterns. These luminous projections spiral towards the barricade—communally projected by the creatively-inclined archetypals as a means of confusing their enemy.

"I get headaches, while these assholes get to shit on the laws of physics." Boaz shakes with disbelief. "I have seen things...Done things...But this? Come here and look at this!"

Getting up is getting harder and harder, Oni realizes, wobbling even with exos for support. She weathers her pain and catches her breath. "I don't need to see...It's always the same."

Boaz takes off his helmet to wipe sweat off of his brow. Steam rises off of his blotchy face. "Ruth is deader than dead at this point."

"I don't care to disagree, especially given the last line from anyone on the seventieth floor was, 'Warrior Archetypal inbound.'"

"Self-selection is noble I suppose, especially in those who are a deficit to the species." Helmet secured and assault rifle ready, Boaz rolls his shoulders. "You good to go?"

Oni crooks her head from shoulder to shoulder and straightens up.

"*Good.* Let's go get Minerva."

Oni takes pause. "Get?"

"Yeah; *get*—kill, maim, chop up into little pieces. You know what I mean."

*What you meant and what you want are two very different things.* Unwilling to make her back a proving ground for Boaz's loyalty, Oni indicates the passageway with her gun. "After you."

Oni keeps pace with Boaz down the hall to a hatch plastered with warnings and symbols the outside world has yet to encounter or heed. Boaz cranks the hatch's hand-wheel, pulling the dog arms out of their chinks. The hatch opens a crack, and out rushes a gust of cold air.

"Wasn't your Marine friend supposed to be inside by now?" Boaz inquires, tugging on the hatch.

The cataclysmic quakes that had maligned the Citadel earlier have died down, leaving Oni to wonder the same thing and to second-guess Outland Security's reports. She finds good news on her radio, however, and parrots it to her unlikely companion: "The archetypals are closing in on the Throne Room's blast door...*Tarnation*—the military has evacuated the surrounding buildings. If unsuccessful on foot, they're going to succeed from low orbit."

Boaz clears the hatchway. "After me, I presume." He takes

Oni's silence as confirmation. He steps through and is immediately yanked to the side by a ruddy blur.

"Colberg?" Oni inquires through the vacant doorway.

"Unauthorized entry!" answer two robotic voices in unison.

"Stand down!" Oni yells, peering in and at Boaz, forced to his knees and at the mercy of two Outland Cymurai. Unlike their heftier, more powerful cousin the Buke, Outland's Cymurai are nimbler, four-armed droids dressed in splinted armor.

The Cymurai, glowing cherry red against the dark room ahead, disobey her order and raise the stakes: they threaten both the front and back of Boaz's neck with their respective electric swords and target Oni with their shoulder-mounted micro-missiles.

"Stand down at once!" Oni brazenly approaches the Cymurai. Both draw their secondary swords and keep her at a distance, cosmetically singeing her armour. "I am here on direct orders from Celeste Charming to investigate a recent incident concerning damaged Outland property. This is a time-sensitive matter, and you are delaying the will of the Outland Corporation."

The androids glance at each other dubiously, and sheathe all four swords. "Verify your security ticket."

A quick callback on her helmet display provides Oni with the code required of her. She recites it aloud.

"Skyr Meijer, welcome." The Cymurai's micro-missile launchers wilt. "The employee accompanying you, Girard Grey, does not have clearance to access the Auxillary Server Room."

"I have granted him emergency clearance," Oni answers back. "Where is the rogue wreck?"

Again, the androids trade deadpan glances. "The incident is twenty meters ahead and to your right." They clamber back into position.

Oni takes point, leading Boaz away from the underutilized and over-hyped tech.

"Talk about putting the artificial in *AI*," Boaz whispers after Oni. "Don't get me wrong, I'm glad they are as dumb as shit, but it really makes you wonder just how exactly Outland has conquered so much in so little time."

The answer rolls off Oni's tongue: "Consumer greed."

Shaped like an hour glass on its side, the Server Room narrows at its centre, forcing Oni and Boaz onto a metal gangway edged by frost. On either side of the gangway, green lights blink on black monoliths half-submersed in super-cold mineral oil. Every pillar of data they pass is one brighter until it is bright enough to see their handiwork ahead.

Chunks are missing from the surrounding server stacks. The gangway is buckled and bent. Gizmos and plastic fragments bob in the sapphire mineral oil, reflecting light from the Cordei in the distance. *This is it.*

Oni looks up through the framework of transluscent heavplast and steel hexagons separating the Server Room from the Throne Room and Celeste Charming's black mass. Celeste's congregation of champions, a few hundred strong, stand rigid and ready to fight. Above the Cordei polyhedron, Oni can make out the Control Room as well as a flash of blonde hair. "There she is!"

"One thing at a time." Turning the corner specified by the Cymurais, Boaz directs Oni's attention to the charred remains of a Buke.

*Not bad, Ruth.*

The gangway shakes as the two remaining Bukes come forward to greet Oni and her security detail. They are bigger than Oni imagined. She has only ever seen them uncloaked on the security feed during her last two trips to the Citadel. It occurs to her that for Paul to have faced two, he must have had a gutful of courage. "Alright, Colberg. Show some interest in the Buke. I'll look around to see if their little two-on-one produced any structural vulnerabilities we can take advantage of."

"Sure thing, *boss*." Boaz crouches down over grooves made by slug rounds the size of pop cans. The Bukes responsible flash their red eyes at him as he pretends to run a diagnostic. "Any luck?"

Oni walks along the heavplast wall separating her from destiny. There are burns, micro-divots, but no major openings. "Nothing." Like a child fogging up a toy-store window, she leans against the partition, trying to make heads-or-tails out the Control Room without the support of her Monocle's magnification. The glass wall gives under her weight and a five-by-eight section collapses into the Throne Room.

Several mechs inside the Throne Room respond to the crash along with the Bukes and Cymurai inside the Server Room. Oni finds herself poxed with laser points and amazed by her enemies' trigger-control. "Stand down?" Her voice is devoid of its earlier confidence, even with Skyr's helmet doing its best.

The blonde flash in the Control Room takes to the intercom: "All men and Outland Security units to your stations at once! Let us not lose sight of the enemy at the gates."

Excited about their unintended reassignment, the Cymurai scramble past Oni like twinned Kali to a demon fight. The Buke bots, either out of earshot or simply too stubborn, hold their ground inside the Server Room.

As the last of the aiming lasers veer away from her, Oni realizes that of all of her disguises, the most blatantly false and brazen one— Celeste's right-hand man—has proven to be the best. She returns to Boaz and pats him on the shoulder. "Time to go." She addresses the Bukes lurking near their fallen brother. "It is quite possible that the threat is not singular. There may be saboteurs amongst the men and machines gathered near the Cordei. Override your previous orders and fire on anything that targets my security detail and me."

Boaz ratchets his head Oni's way. "What the hell do you think you're doing?"

The Bukes are mute, and so appeal to holographic text bubbles to communicate with their supposed commander. They respond with: "Defense of Auxillary Server Room is number-one priority."

"Yes," Oni says, directing Boaz over to the gap in the glass wall. "And the Auxillary Server Room will likely be attacked again, this time by an enemy in disguise who will start by firing on my associate and me."

"Voice and facial recognition required to update directive," reads the Bukes' mutual reply.

Stepping over to the gap in the wall, Boaz quietly lambastes Oni's impromptu strategy: "One shouldn't drink kerosene while smoking."

"You're not helping." Uncertain filler pours through Oni's modulator as she thinks her way out of this cold coffin. "The invading force has corrupted voice and facial-ID databases." She is so happy to have come up with an unproveable lie that she is on the verge of tears. "Corroborate my order with Celeste Charming and execute as commanded."

Processing Oni's order, the Bukes shake in agreement. They project: "Order received, corroborated, and prioritized. Proceed," and escort Oni over to the gap.

"You're one lucky bitch, I'll give you that," Boaz laughs,

stepping through the burnt portal. "After we're done here, you should buy a lottery ticket."

As Oni steps into the Throne Room—ignoring Boaz's blather—she is at once mindful of all of those who have died to make her presence here possible. What begins as admiration turns into a prayer to the same benevolent and invisible force that has deferred its claim on her. This silent thanks is disrupted by a call from Celeste.

"Your job was to contain the problem, not to break containment," Celeste chirps over the comm.

"The hack wasn't coordinated through our system, but physically implemented. We're looking for a parasitic injector." Oni walks over to the row of mechs and droids as casually as she can, despite muscle spasms and heart palpitations.

"I need ten more minutes, Skyr. Grant me that and then it won't matter. All secrets will be brought out and into the light. Do a quick search if you must, and then reinforce the blast door. General McCabe is on his way. Once we are operational, I mean to give him the most cordial welcome."

The comm terminates in synch with a metal groan from the Cordei. The coils grounded around Regan's living tomb begin to hum and glow. A tentacle barbed with antennae extends from a nozzle suspended beneath the Control Room down into the polyhedron that is the Cordei's exterior.

"I'll deal with the Omnitype," Boaz tells Oni. His helmet reflects the Throne Room, humongous and cave-like.

Dubious about Boaz's intentions, Oni quickly responds: "We both will." She has not come this far to let herself be betrayed by an Outland shill.

"Both eggs in the same basket? And if we are both broken? What then?"

Oni's body hints at acquiescence before she verifies it with sound. "Minerva is as bad if not worse than Celeste. Kill it and do not hesitate." Oni checks her gun. "The Marines are set to make their entrance shortly, and Celeste is going nuclear in ten minutes. Try your best not to make your presence known."

Boaz reaches out and grips Oni's hand. "Thanks again. Be sure to send Charming my best."

## QUEEN OF THE DEAD

The blast door stands a better chance of turning to gold than buckling under the invaders' pressure. Nevertheless, Celeste's forces are prepared for the impossible or they at least appear to be. There is certainly enough man- and machine-power, even if it is antiquated somewhat by its organization and lack of cover.

Oni walks between rows of steel death machines and well-paid mercenaries, forestalling attention to her own suspiciousness with overcritical inspections. She chooses a Sentinel at random and prods him in the chest. "One of these metal jobs has been hacked," she informs him, affecting a lower voice even though her helmet modulator is otherwise doing a fine job. "You see anything out of the ordinary?"

The Sentinel must be a rookie because he is not taking Skyr's suit and its menacing history as seriously as he should. "Couple thousand mental patients coming up through the floor is all." He brushes Oni's point away. "And some 'loper killing my vibe."

Without further ethical consideration, Oni has found a blood sacrifice to her grandiose lie. "Got another one," she reports to the Control Room.

Celeste presses her fevered gaze to the Control Room window like an industrialist overlooking his factory. There is a silhouetted figure behind her, whose commentary registers as little peeps on the comm. "Hacked or hacker?"

Oni separates the Sentinel from the row, and jabs his belly with her gunarm. "Hacker." Callously, she clenches her phantom hand and delivers the rookie his last stomachache.

"Thank you, Skyr. Very good. But make sure this is the last interruption."

Sinking deeper into the role of Skyr, Oni cooly reassures Celeste: "Very well. I'll flush out the rest in silence."

"Yes." Celeste is nearly inaudible over the sounds of buzzes and beeps. "Extra to our unwanted guests at the door—which deadmen and the minutehand suggest is now the greater threat—if there are any further technical or HR problems you feel compelled to report, direct them to Kirsten. I have a speech to give and a mind to expand."

Both Celeste and the silhouette disappear aback the Control Room. Gizmos and flashing chrome hint at surgery while wires moving autonomously like headless serpents indicate something more. Forging a mental link with Regan would be a simple procedure: synchronize two compatible neural implants and block non-sensational feedback to Celeste. The simplicity is lost on Celeste's hubris. She not only wants to puppet Regan, but to connect to all of those over which she might enjoy influence. Not just archetypals; anything with a signal that could process her directives, in effect giving her license over the Internet of Things. *Of all the lessons Allen Scheele's death might have taught Celeste...*

Kirsten's rabbity voice takes the comm. "Skyr! You should see her. Celeste is plugged in. It's finally happening!"

Oni's multiple masks seem to converge into one she cannot shake loose. "Don't get ahead of yourself. There are still plenty of threats...Stay focused."

"You're just cranky Matsui wrenched your gears. Take it out on the freaks while they still fight under another's banner."

*Tarnation.* Oni always imagined that the Blue Zone parties she missed on account of work or study were flush with people like Kirsten. Worse than Todds, in their own right. The type, one too bland to name—neither noble in simplicity like the everyman nor pitiful like the orphan nor benign like the innocent—is one of the easiest to spot, and yet the easiest to ignore: a type characteristized by mediocrity and bitterness, and populated by social climbers who die waiting for the company elevator. By fate or fortune, this *unnameable* holds some modicum of power over Oni, who finds it absolutely enraging. "First-things first." Oni takes aim at the speaker at the other end of the call, but like Tantalus with the water low, the result she wants is beyond her grasp; the Control Room window is damn-well near indestructible. "I'm not asking for your permission, Kirsten. I am informing you that I am coming up to ensure that security didn't miss another threat."

There is no answer.

The blast door is caving in and Charming is peeling back her humanity. Oni doesn't have time for an *unnameable's* shit. "Kirsten? I'm on my way."

"Kirsten?" Kirsten replies scornfully. "Run a self-diagnostic first for god's sake."

"What?" Oni fires back like a henpecked partner of too-many-years finally drained of patience.

"*Kirsten*—you've never called me that before. Not once. Your little vixen. Kvinnfolk. Kirry. Never Kirsten. The only one who does," continues Kirsten, "Is lying-still beside me, thoughts cycled and magnified. If you are having problems with your memory, Mr. Meijer, then perhaps you ought to remain below with the other deficients."

*Vixen? Kvinnfolk?* Oni has trouble believing Skyr had, firstly, not killed all the previous women he maligned, and secondly, held congress with Kirsten. Disbelief aside, it distresses her to think that the final say and greatest truth in her final chapter may lie with an unnameable who might have the sight to tell a wolf from a lamb. Grimacing, Oni searches for words a murderous asshole might employ. Her pregnant pause is nearly viable, and yet, she still cannot brainstorm how Skyr might drown the unnameable's concerns from afar. Instead of a conciliatory offering, Oni defers to caustic defensiveness and sets her sights on Kirsten's feelings as her second sacrifice. "Oh screw off with that noise. Try to do your job well for once, *Kirsten*. You can jog my memory later, but you won't be able to give me back the time you're currently wasting."

Kirsten signals a shift in tone—from her impression of a jaded and out-of-breath slam poet to a snippy seductress—with a giggle. "Better hope that it's only your memory...Would explain your apparent lost sense of direction, poking at all the wrong bodies today..."

"Just hold the door for me. I'll be up in a minute."

"I'm telling you: she is safe here with me; will be online and interfaced by the time you drag your butt up here...If you are coming up to apologize, that's a different story."

*Figures Celeste's assistant would be insane enough to drop the drawbridge during a siege*, thinks Oni. "Whatever it takes."

Oni looks for Boaz. He is fifty yards down the row. He reflects her thumbs up, and begins his traversal of the no man's land between the Outland army and the steel henge of signal repeaters encircling the Cordei. The scientists responsible for the contraption are nowhere to be seen; likely all dead, hiding, or dismissed. Signs mounted on little stands mark the clearing off-limits, and cite "Mental intrusion" and "Electronic interference" as cause for concern. Implant fried and mind already disturbed, Oni pays the warnings no heed and marches into no man's land.

Laser auto-turrets, seemingly impatient to fire at something, track Oni and Boaz's progress with owl-like intensity. Their refusal to shoot confirms Oni's theory that: *Celeste must have ordered all security personnel and programs give Skyr complete leeway.* No one batted an eye at the execution—not when Oni pulled the trigger and certainly not as her victim mumbled out of existence.

Oni loses Boaz in her peripheral vision. She pauses to relocate him, and spots him at a distance, stopped, gun half-raised, and waving. *What do you think you're doing?* An escalating quake and the clunking sound of a heavy-metal predator pulls Oni's attention from Boaz's mute warning over to a Buke, magnificent electrosword drawn and slug gun fully-exposed. She grits her teeth and readies her gunarm with a cringe, convinced Kirsten has inadvertently talked her to death. All those priorities and moral dilemmas that had weighed on her and challenged her in bygone days seem so irrelevant now; so egregiously besides-the-point. *At least grant me my revenge.*

The bulky stalker powers down its sword and sheaths it. Oni refuses to shoot despite the opportunity to dent the mech's underarm. After all, shooting might draw attention to Boaz, and Boaz's success now appears to be her only shot at even partial redemption. Instead of molten steel, however, the Buke asserts itself with a speech bubble, saying: "OCB49 at your service. I have been reassigned by CitCom to provide you with cover and support as per your earlier request."

*This better not be sleep deprivation.* Oni's slack jaw and bleeding eyes are well-hidden by her helmet. *It's one of the Server Room Bukes…*She shakes her head to signal agreement. The tears welling up in her orbital fracture break and salt the gashes in her cheeks. "OCB49," Oni says, stuck in a feeling she is dreaming or quickly losing her mind. "Escort me to the Cordei Control Room to prevent an imminent cyber attack."

Shaking its hefty scales, OCB49 confirms Oni's order, and stamps its way over to her side.

Extra to the emergency lights and alarms, new concern is broadcasted throughout the Throne Room: "Gate security compromised. Blast door's polarity has been reversed, and is set to open."

The Cordei's signal-amplifiers and electrical discharge stations woosh with excitement. A plasmic shield envelops the polyhedron. Its superiority over Camp MUD's concussion shield corresponds to its light-orange hue, resultant of a crackle-layer—a semispherical anti-organic beam. *Celeste must have been waiting to the last minute to use the shield so as not to use up the reserve batteries in advance of actual conflict.*

Oni shouts up to her escort. "Are you able to break through

that shield?"

OCB49's resultant speech bubble pops Oni's. "Negative. Orders by priority: protect the Cordei; protect Celeste Charming; and protect Skyr Meijer."

In fewer than four steps her guardian has turned into a priggish chaperone. *Damn-it.*

A noticeably computer-generated version of the interim CEO's voice takes over from the previously-automated doomsayer and blasts through all available speakers: "The door will soon open, and for a minute there will be death, but take heart, my friends: for those who survive this day, a new door will open to eternal life and incredible power." No one is so badly-wired as to cheer, and yet Celeste continues her speech as if to uproarious applause. "I think we have proven to ourselves that as a society, democracy is fated to fail every time. Half-a-billion lives extinguished in a series of flashes cannot be ignored, nor can we ignore the root causes. The masses—the urban hive and the rural herd—are pitted against themselves and are always clawing at their container. By delaying true progress, the so-called People have maimed themselves and stumbled sideways, lame. Autocracies and oligarchies on the other hand, are brutally effective and natural, as our southern adversaries have learned over time, but similarly fated to fail because weak men with big ideas or big men with weak ideas always fly too close to the sun. Friends, consider yourselves blessed. With your blood and sweat, an immortal power will rise and ensure eternal peace through glorious communion. Ready your hearts. Ready your minds. And raise your weapons!"

Celeste's psychobabble falls on deaf ears. Terror spreads behind cannons and rifles while Outland's monster, soused in the blood of those *friends* Celeste needlessly sacrificed, raps at the door. Striving to keep the monster out and the door closed, a school of Outland engineers flounder about, desperately fighting the remote controls forcing it open. Realizing their attempts are fruitless, they make way for several mechs, who attempt to dismantle the blast door's weights and counterweights via a spectacular fusillade. The mechs and their pilots similarly realize the futility of their efforts; the blast door's oft-praised indestructibility now works against them.

Keen not to catch hell or a stray bullet in the incoming scrum, Oni leads her chaperone nearer the Control Room ladder, which touches down just outside the radius of the Cordei's plasmic shield. A

Cymurai stands at its base, mainlining strategic data via a seemingly endless succession of ultrasonic-sensor pings. Fortunately for Oni, it cannot ping her true form or what is left of it.

Oni inspects the Cordei as she passes, picking up on all the details her Monocle-less vision prohibited her from seeing previously. Inside its glittering plasma domain, the piped polyhedron palpitates. Rather, the gel that fills it—itself contaminated by black orbs— palpitates. Looks more like a meningitic brain than a warp engine for human consciousness. The gel has taken on the colours of the various emergency lights blinking in this satanic cathedral: red, orange, and blue. Inside the maroon pudding is a windowless child-sized coffin. It is fed wires and instruction from the cubical Control Room above. Its occupant: *Regan.*

Accepting, now, of the necessity of mercy-killing the girl for herself and for humanity, Oni ponders the hopelessness that whatever is left of Regan-*the-girl* must feel—*to be the atom split that ends the world.* Accepting, now, but glad she does not have to carry it out personally. Her unlikely compatriot will pick up the slack in service of his own kingdom of ends.

A warning horn proclaims the blast door will open.

Concern dominates Oni's ear: "Whatever you need to do up here can wait." Kirsten leers out the Control Room window. "Ms. Charming is nearly done synchronizing with the Omnitype, and there are no signs of malware or intervention. Keep the Cordei clear of all and any traffic."

Before Oni can barb Kirsten with another emotional attack, she spots the weights on the blast door begin to slide. The door scrapes open slowly, louder than thunder. Archetypals immediately pour through the opening. The eager point men catch the Outland force's opening volley. Those that wriggle by are caught up in the auto-turrets's lasers—the same that previously entertained Oni as a target.

Notwithstanding the torrent of munitions slung against them, the archetypals are beyond demoralization. Their surge is relentless and made terrible by their aberrant gifts. They project vivacious holograms of mechs and Sentinels, which mix in with the Outland lines and obstruct their view. The resultant confusion permits a good hundred-or-so archetypals within close-quarters of the defenders.

Utilizing their mental power over unshielded electronics— clearly evolved past whatever standard Celeste had upgraded her safeguards to—the archetypals quickly turn the Throne Room into a gory morgue.

They jam a number of micro-missile arrays, leaving many Cymurai with hot shoulders.

They target the igniter and fuel regulators on an Outland pyro-team's flamethrowers. Before the pyros have a chance to turn their valves off, the invisible threat is already too dense around them. The hacked igniters kick on as suddenly as they had dropped off, and immolate the entire squad.

A badly chewed-up chaingang of archetypals run a 3D-printer ahead of their pulped mental siblings. They print a modest heavplast bulwark, allowing for inbound archetypals to regroup behind cover ahead of their blitzkrieg. Provided this cover, additional printers are run up and used to spray an antiballistic A-frame. Through gaps in their new wall, the archetypals begin to equalize the playing field one bullet at a time.

Oni hides behind OCB49 for cover as misguided bullets whizz by. Outland still has the upper hand, and of the two in play, that is the enemy she knows best. *Now or never.* "OCB49, provide cover fire. I'm headed for the Control Room."

Skipping the formality of a speech bubble, the Buke immediately begins plinking massive ordinance into the blast-doorway through which weaponized archetypals are now pouring freely. Its shots clear the archetypals' new structures, but just barely.

Unlike the first wave, the archetypals that gathered behind the wall break into squads of ten or twelve. Together, they coordinate strikes on specific targets and mow down mech after mech. The Outland auto-turrets lighting up no man's land turn a few of the squads into half-dozens before succumbing to pools of thermite lobbed over by new entrants into this battle.

The weaponized squads infiltrate Outland's ranks, making room for a massive congregation of coordinated fighters—presumably the Warrior type previously rumored over Oni's radio. Its constituent hundreds similarly regroup behind the printers' pockmarked structures. They produce and link their antiballistic shields, forming a scaled body, but leaving a gap in the centre for four hulking giants armed with disruptor cannons. The four lead this flesh-and-blood tank from the center. Outside of the tank, lesser archetypals leap, flip, and kick, simultaneously deflecting incoming shots and narrowly avoiding the

Warrior's own thermite volleys. Wherever the archetypal line has been wounded by slugs or micro-missiles, new adherents fill the gaps like scar tissue. All partial to a local area network of stimuli, the different elements of this greater invading organism comprehend the skirmish with a degree of complexity no single part or individual foe could hope to grasp. *No wonder the Military was interested...*

The Warrior turns its attention to the Cordei and targets the shield. As soon as the first of its shots is deflected, it turns its disruptors on anything and everything else in the vicinity. The Cymurai below the Control Room catwalk cloaks. That unfortunately leaves OCB49 the only viable target and unshielded guardian in the Throne Room's no man's land.

Although Oni has left the Buke's cover, she is still nearby, desperately trying to decide whether to run to the cover of one of the signal-amplifiers or back to OCB49, handily staining the floor with the marrow from archetypal line-breakers. Her decision is made for her, however; the Warrior lands a direct hit on the Buke's chest. The first shot is not enough to keep OCB49 down, who retributively slings a dozen shells back at the Warrior's cannoneers, but the next four thermite shots are. Cracks in the Buke's armor are highlighted by the severed circuits sparking underneath, and then split wide by the killshot, which in turn splinters the Buke. Its reactor is the last to go, which detonates and sends pieces of its heavy-metal insides in every direction on a powerful shockwave.

A massive, flaming shard of armour skids past Oni. Another nearly takes her legs off. Bereaved of her chaperone and out in the open, she scrambles over to the ladder. Whatever Kirsten or Celeste or any of the bastards out there might think of her is irrelevant now. *Now is the time for results.* "Kirsten, is the door open?"

"Yes, yes," she replies hastily. "You might not have any time to apologize though—the synch is almost complete."

*Tarnation.* Oni channels all of her remaining verve. Nose down, she starts running. The exo-components in Skyr's suit more than help; they carry her volition upfield. Her initiative is not looked on kindly, however. Spotting Oni barreling its way, the Cymurai guarding the ladder fires a warning shot.

"Stand down!" Oni shouts.

The Cymurai fires a second warning shot, while tracking distant targets with its other three arms.

*Enough!* Oni stops in her tracks, and unloads half-a-clip into the Cymurai's micro-missile array in hopes of catching an armed warhead. Four missiles nevertheless clear the array. The first two were dudded by Oni's quick-thinking. The third smacks down right in front of her, while the fourth bursts midair, throwing her backwards. She thinks she can feel her stomach in her throat and her tongue in her bowels.

Flat on her back, Oni looks through a charred and broken visor and up at the vaulted ceiling. There is a high-pitched ringing in her ears, which undercuts the full impact of the fireworks display above, escalating from one morbid finale to the next. Skyr's suit has saved her again, while shedding several armor plates in the process. Assuming she can stand, she cannot withstand another strike let alone a direct hit.

The Cymurai readies its killshot, framing Oni as she slowly fights to her feet like a toddler tempting verticality at a table's edge. She is cold all over, not so much wearing Skyr's suit than filling it. With a small adjustment, her gunarm is re-fastened.

The Cordei's plasmic shield flickers on her left. Its inconsistency is too good to be true and too late. Looking at the Cymurai, probably waiting for CitCom's confirmation to kill a higher-up, Oni splashes the jagged remains of her visor with blood and fires the last of her magazine. *Was worth a try.*

"Skyr! We did it!" Kirsten screams over the comm.

An invisible shockwave emanates from the Cordei, which permeates the shield and knocks Oni back down. The shockwave slackens the Cymurai, and carries on across no man's land, freezing archetypal, Sentinel, and mech alike.

The black spheres floating in the Cordei's gel glow like hot coals. Again, the meningitic brain palpitates, but now the non-Newtonian gel projects outside of the Cordei's frame. *That can't be good.*

A bassy chuckle blares over the speakers and is similarly parroted by every mouth but Oni's. "Ha, ha, ha." Celeste's age of peace begins to the tune of maniacal laughter.

With the Cymurai processing the expectations and agenda of its new master, Oni's has a straightaway to the ladder. She would be insulted by a more obvious invitation. She limps past the Cymurai and mantles the ladder. Climbing is especially hard with just the one arm, and even harder with all of her injuries adding up to decrepitude. She bounds across the catwalk to the Control Room door. Hiding her exposed face with her mitt, Oni calls out to Kirsten. "Open the door!

Open the door, god-damn-it!"

The archetypals and the Outland forces continue emulating the laughter fuzzing through the intercom. Even the comm on Oni's helmet reports the sinister tones. Apart from the sound of the Cordei and the laughter, the Throne Room is otherwise silent.

"Kirsten!" Oni screams. Her natural voice competes with her modulated yell. "Open the door!"

There is movement below. Thankfully, the mass of bodies have not noticed Oni. Something else draws their collective attention towards the blast door. At first the sound is lost amid the buzzers and alarms, but as it draws closer, it becomes more and more clear, until even Oni can hear it distinctly: the piercing call of a bugle.

Archetypals and Outland Security address the unseen bugler in unison: "So glad you could join us!"

The feeling is apparently mutual. Waves of flame break on those closest to the blast door. A voice behind the flame responds with a throat-killing: **"Ooh rah!"**

The Warrior archetypal, now joined by Bukes, Cymurais, Sentinels, and the like, braces to face General McCabe's Marines.

Without the pomp and showmanship of the previous wave of invaders, the Marines emerge from the flame, guns blazing.

Captain Galloway, sporting his bloody rebar-adorned exosuit, is the tip of the Marine spearhead. Together with two-hundred gnarly-looking grunts wearing an elephant's complement of third-gen armor—anachronistic but impervious to hacks and remote-control—they cut right through the remains of the charcoaled first line. The shielded gymnasts formerly protecting the Warrior's disruptors somersault into oblivion while the Warrior's testudo formation drips down the sides of the Marines' spear.

"You will die with the old world that authored you," says the leviathan the Omnitype has given Celeste power over. "And will be forgotten by the new world that marked your end."

Galloway tries to leap over the broken chain of Warrior shielders, but falls short, crushing a teenage constituent on landing. He breaks into a three-point stance, gun ready, and lunges for the nearest Warrior cannoneer. Dodging its panicked blasts, Galloway gets a hold of its neck and hoists it above the rest by the throat. With a kiss from Galloway's Gatling gun, the allegedly perfect Warrior is no more.

More flame envelops the defensive frontline as McCabe's

forces escalate the scene from a wartime Picasso to Bosch's "Hell."

Although all characteristic difference has been levelled and all individuality sapped, one Sentinel manages what the others cannot: he hits Galloway with a magnetic harness. Stuck in place, Galloway finds himself the eye of a vortex of post-humans. He hits and punches out blind and shakes corpses free of his rebar-adorned shoulders. The last remaining Warrior cannoneer marches over to the tethered Marine, parting the storm without saying a word. He lifts his disruptor and points it at Galloway while the maniacal laughing picks back up. The joke is on him, however; the cannoneer's look of satisfaction is smashed out of his helmet by a long, black tentacle. *Spherion.*

Spherion, the sentient black orb from Seal Beach, vibrates at the frequency of a church organ's lowest C, and reflects neither its victims' fear nor the red off of the Marines' flamethrowers. The hovering orb frees Galloway with a well-aimed lance, and continues to prong archetypals and Outland goons alike.

With Spherion providing cover, a medieval-looking mech, all in black, helps Galloway to his feet. Galloway reloads, and stands back to back with the medieval mech. They inch towards no man's land, emptying magazine after magazine into humanity's so-called future.

Celeste's army, fed additional units from the windows overlooking the Throne Room as well as from the Server Room, has divided its focus. While half commit to wetting the Marines' spear, the remainder spread out in an effort to flank McCabe's men. Using Celeste's Bukes and Cymurai as a buffer, organic Outland units stand in for artillery and indiscriminately lob brimstone on the scrum.

The Control Room door will not budge for Oni. Kirsten does not respond. Oni leans on the door, one breath away from redemption and seconds away from likely death.

"Skyr, it's not safe to open up. Wait till Ms. Charming annihilates the Marines."

Oni reloads. "Trust me: I need to get inside, now!"

The door grinds open. "There! Now shut it!" shouts Kirsten, hunched over Celeste with her back to the door. She adjusts the wires goring into Celeste's sides as well as the crown of sensors on her head.

Seemingly paralyzed and with eyes rolled back, Celeste opens her mouth. Although what she whispers to Kirsten is private, it is trumpeted by every other mouth in the building, surely adding to the Marines' confusion: "Kirsten, your naivety is showing. That is not your beloved Skyr Meijer. That is the patron saint of our ministry. Isn't that right, Oni Matsui."

Kirsten turns to see Oni's rage framed by Skyr's broken helmet. "No!"

"Oh yeah." Oni targets Celeste and fires. The bullets do not reach their target, however. They turn to golden dollars suspended in the air just feet away from Celeste's smiling mug. *Another bloody force shield.* The bullets did, fortunately, have an effect. A sizzling sound augurs a victim. Celeste's microshield saved her, but was not large enough to protect Kirsten; at least not all of her.

Kirsten looks over to her master, puzzled and hungry for an explanation or at the very least consolation. "Ms. Charming?" She goes crosseyed and flops down on either side of the shield.

Oni looks around ravenously for the microshield's power supply. "It's just you and me now." The irony of the statement, heightened by the bullets and debris pelting the window, is not lost on her. It might be the blood loss or the concussion Oni is rocking, but the rest of the world seems to have melted away, leaving her alone with the incarnate cackle at Jin's murder—with the living flame that torched Booky. It is just her and this gorgon lying supine, Celeste Charming.

Celeste turns her head and pierces Oni with her glazed over eyes. "Me and you? There is no difference. We are one and the same. Accept it and you will live forever."

Oni frantically searches for a way to deactivate the shield—a task she hopes her comrade below has solved. The minimalist design of the Control Room's few controls and their cryptic labelling boils her brain.

Both inside the Control Room and out, Celeste carries on with thunderous unanimity: "You cannot see the truth you cannot understand. I will achieve unity in our time. Individuality breeds conflict and conflict breeds suffering. You cannot see but you do not need to. Hear me and listen, for I see all: you have done well."

"Shut the hell up!" Oni screams. She takes a step back from the control panel and riddles it with bullets. The minimalist styling makes a better ruin. There is a fizz and a pop. Welling with hope, Oni spins to take aim once more at Celeste. The microshield's power is kaput! Oni throws her full-auto punch.

The volley is misdirected as someone throws their hands around Oni's throat. Her gunarm continues to fire as it is yanked downwards. Her retaliatory strike chews up her armored foot instead.

As Oni wrestles with her unknown assailant, Celeste continues to pontificate: "And like the holy man denied refuge in his utopia, you too have no place among the chosen. Die knowing that god thinks highly of you and that you have her sympathies."

"Bitch!" Oni hollers. She struggles frenetically—kicking, head-butting, and writhing—and finds nominal success: she frees her arm and manages to throws a spiked elbow back with all of her remaining strength. The strike makes a boff against a semi-armoured belly.

The wounded attacker yanks Oni out of the Control Room and throws her against the catwalk railing. The door slams shut behind them.

Hunched over the railing, Oni spies Regan's little coffin. *You were right, Booky. Should have made the hard decision back when it was easy to execute.* The plasmic shield protecting the Cordei and the Omnitype inside still flickers sporadically.

Even the Marines, who have proven themselves the more talented fighters in the battle—evidenced by the stacks of corpses and sparking robotics—are on the ropes. Spherion, surrounded by hundreds of gored archetypals, is motionless and flattened like a washed-up jellyfish. Celeste now has aerial superiority. With Spherion down, Monarch Drones have full license over the battlefield. Marines abandon their mechs en masse, leaving them for Outland target practice. The tide has turned, but not because Galloway's spearhead is ineffective; Celeste simply has more pulses at her disposal than the Marines of the Throne Room have bullets. The other jarheads summoned to this abattoir have yet to join the bloodbath or are otherwise occupied countering the archetypals' lethal gimmicks elsewhere. The spear of the Republic is stuck in the mud.

Depressed by the sight and feeling altogether threadbare, Oni jerks around with reflexive defiance. Her bloody mug catches a flurry of punches. Even with her arm up defensively, all she can see is a repeated flash of knuckles and a rifle butt, both striking pieces of her visor into her face until she can barely see at all.

The beating stops and the swelling begins. Tottering and out of breath like a bricked boxer, Oni spits teeth and tries to make out the one responsible for *taking it all away* from her.

Her attacker takes aim with his rifle. "Goodbye, Doctor Matsui."

## CAPGRAS DELUSION

Lyle spent months of real time opening his third eye in the CLOUD. With the help of others like him as well as those subscribers who provided technical answers through mental assimilation, he learned how to dilate perceived-time, stretching out his virtual stays much longer than the builders intended. Perceptually, months turned to years and years turned to eons.

Unlike so many others, some now lumbering up the Citadel's scorched hallways and lunging at those who had not the means or the time to overload their brains, the CLOUD has had a peculiar effect on Lyle; peculiar in that it did not malign him in the same ways it did the others. He expanded his skillset without suffering any expansion of his personality. He believes it was his resilience, the very resilience that allowed him to survive the War, which protected him from the social warping one customarily undergoes when deluged with pentabytes of other people's memories. Dorota suggested he might have been too antisocial even for the noosphere, and later, in a drunken furor, claimed he did not have a personality to lose in the first place. Regardless of the veracity of Dorota's insights, when simple groupthink gave way to hives, herds, and hydras, Lyle remained a singular mind.

This singular mind, though victoriously unaffected by social gravity like those archetypals now gnashing their teeth at US Marine rifles—minds all collectivized and then dumbly redistributed—nevertheless bears a mark of the attempt. This singular mind has been given a singular focus.

That focus has been trained by headaches and brought him here. Feet away from his prospective end and beginning, Lyle realizes, as Boaz's head begins to throb, that the pain is not and has not been from tension or nervous problems, but from an idea; an overwhelming idea, greater than himself and outside of his understanding: Minerva's blueprint for reality.

He wonders what realizing that idea will mean for him and, more importantly, why the world's preeminent sentience singled him out for its techno-commie utopia. Compulsion drove Lyle across the CLOUD. What besides the call to serve as his Caliban drove Minerva to Lyle in the storm that rained them out? Chance? Arithmetic? A shared sense of inhumanity? Whatever the cause, their bond is sure.

Lyle's accumulated experiential wealth is stowed away in a library without a catalog and only Minerva has the call numbers. As a stranger in the stacks, Lyle needs Minerva, otherwise he is diminished. *Whatever Minerva wants, Minerva will get.* It is an asymmetrical relationship unlike any other Lyle has enjoyed. Like a battered spouse, he fears separation as this painful connection might be all he has left to lose.

After all, what else is there left to be lost? He cannot claim the insurance off of his torched apartment. His favorite restaurant will not seat him anymore, regardless of whether they recognize him or not. His nemesis will take his clients. The first and only time Copps and Forsyth will post his name in the office will be at his memorial attended by cold coffee and empty chairs. His army pension will be appropriated by the same government that bet him for inches in the sand. And the body he was born with will neither be revived nor buried, but merely vacuum-sealed and then incinerated. Ashes to ashes, aspirations to dust.

The weight of these dire revelations nearly hides their truer importance from Lyle—that his perception seems beyond time. Wherever he exists, triangulated between Boaz' implant, Monocle, and brain, his processing-power appears unimpeded. He is running minutes off the second. The Throne Room and the violence filling it report back in slow motion. Plasma bursts hang in the air like newborn universes. Shrapnel, set to fall like New Years' confetti, hints at a previous shape now disbanded and obfuscated by flame.

The come-on to this luxurious hyper-awareness feels like a second wind of amphetamines. It is not the drugs, however. Lyle realizes, as he engorges himself on a synesthetic hodge-podge of stimuli, that his mind has run ahead of this body. It has provided him with a temporal advantage or at the very least an opportunity to properly witness his end. *But what an end!* His ego and narcissistic carriage rides up from the labyrinth of Colberg's brain. *What end?* Here on history's mainstage, having transcended kipple and trinkets, wet dates and blue ties, a mediocre life defending and perpetrating injustices, and the flesh itself—*this is only the beginning!*

Decided that he is a tour de force—one embodying all those undying qualities Marius Tyndale, Copps, and Forsyth, could only dream of courting—Lyle forces a reunification of will and power. The way forward is Minerva. *Minerva is the way.*

He slows down near the Cordei stage to keep up appearances. Too excited and he will look aggressive. Still, neither tribe focused on the neighbouring war has reached out to him—it is a packed theater and no eyes are on the stage. Lyle is glad of it and keen not to play up intrigue. Oni, the other stage-fraught actress, looks to be on-course, nearing the Control Room. She will not get far. And when all eyes are on her, Lyle will snatch up the Omnitype.

Scrutinizing the polyhedron and all of the gadgets feeding it juice, Lyle realizes that the Cordei shield is running off of auxiliary power. Happy to have drawn this conclusion without anyone or anything's help, he hurries to find the proverbial power cord. As he ambles about, body hobbling mind, it occurs to him that a designer with two braincells to rub together would have put the power source inside the shield. A quick inspection confirms his suspicion: an armoured mound underneath the polyhedron stenciled with a caution: "BURIED CABLE."

"Shit!" Lyle examines his rifle. It does not come close to offering the kind of calibre or munition required to penetrate the armoured mound let alone the plasmic field. Only a laser can cut through the plasma. Even then, the wound will be fleeting, not to mention possibly damaging to Minerva, itself unconscionable.

At the zenith of the shield is its magnetic keystone. This stalwart fixture forces the shield into shape and keeps it from vaporizing its contents. A laser blast to the keystone might shutter the shield, but only for an instant. A burst or a barrage, conversely, could shutter the shield long enough to get inside and over to the Cordei with all limbs intact. Without a laser, and with no way of making sure the keystone will not inadvertently pulse Minerva, Lyle is back at square-one, hyperactive brain be damned.

Through the lens of his rifle scope, Lyle searches the battlefield for something—anything—that might make him productive in this moment. Amid roils of smoke and alien stalagmites, he spots a number of laser cannons, some in use and others inert in the arms of dead men. *There's no amount of forethought that'll help me in there.* He spies three emaciated women dressed in tattered linens lift a wounded cannoneer to his feet. Micromissiles put him back down permanently. *Ugh.* Tracking sideways across the magnified battlefield, Lyle spots a jittering blur in the fore. A laser auto-turret slaps its barrel against the ground repeatedly in a futile effort to take aim. Thermite has melted it off its base. Lyle knows he will be a sitting duck in no man's land with the turret, but even worse off in the scrum. *Alright. Badegger or bust.*

Brilliant stars and other skewed holograms give luminous body to the battlefield smoke, thick in the air above the fighting. Lyle fires a couple rounds into the scrum with no idea of or care for the consequence. With his gun warmed up, Lyle figures he is too. He dodges a fleshy meteor, and takes cover behind a piece of Buke armour. Someone or something rails the armour, grinding it forward into a groove in the floor. Lyle leans against the armour fragment, not anticipating a follow shot. It takes another strike and slams Lyle back, half-conscious. Before he could hear a dozen different sirens and alarms, but now he only hears a high-pitched buzz.

*Nowhere is safe.* Lyle cannot tell whose voice it is he hears inside Colberg's skull—whether it is Minerva calling the shots already or if he is still the one in control. Regardless, the sentiment is true enough. He paws his way to his knees, and falls into a run. The turret is not far off. Its smoldering base should provide some cover from enemy droids' infrared sensors, meaning Lyle's mental kin pose the only immediate threat.

He dashes straight into the turret, feeling heat on his heels. Deaf and blurry-eyed, he is blissfully unaware that a tide of missiles meant for him have missed their mark and left a trail of potholes behind him. He crouches in a pentagram of cinders, and tries to lift the weapon. It is easily one-hundred pounds. Grimacing at the overbuilt laser cannon and then back at the Cordei, Lyle considers suicidal alternatives. *Just to see the look on their faces...*

Putting the Sentinel suit's basic exo-reinforcement to use, Lyle tugs the turret out of its hardening mold like a sneaker out of fresh asphalt. Boaz is just strong enough for the job. *Finally can make some good use out of you.* Impressed with an ogreish underbite, Lyle shoulders his rifle and drags the turret back across no man's land. *Blessed by Minerva,* he tells himself. *Minerva has blessed your mission and you will succeed. Badegger or bust.* "Badegger or bust!" he bellows, lexicon and good taste ravaged by exhaustion and death.

The Cymurai on the other side of the Cordei seems to take notice of this straggler and his gargantuan gun. It unsheathes its swords, opens its micro-missile arrays, and aims its cannon. However, something else seizes its attention and just in time: Oni, running full tilt for the Control Room ladder.

*Much appreciated, Doctor.* Watching the little rogue in the big suit run into hellfire confirms what Lyle has believed all his life: *it's all on you now.*

Rockets fizzle against the Cordei shield. While bullets are

neutered and deflected, some err Lyle's way. He imagines he has deftly dodged them, while his chipped suit thoughtlessly knows otherwise. He cannot however delude himself any longer. A metal shard cleaves through his visor, and sets a tip in his chin. The cut is negligible, but the corresponding shot has cracked the visor and claimed Lyle's vision with a white tree. Blind and deaf, he closes the distance and drops the turret at the Cordei's side. He tears off his helmet and the shrapnel along with it. Sweat tinged-pink sluices the turret as Lyle tightens the gun's battery pack and targets the keystone. Hitting his target once will be no problem. Making sure it fires again and ideally until the gun is out of charge is the real challenge. He manipulates two twisted pieces—formerly handguard rails—to serve as a two-legged frame, and wedges his helmet under the cannon's melted butt to keep it steady. He crouches down at its base, and adjusts the aim.

"There, on the Cordei!" An Outland officer and his ten-foot-tall metal sidekick have taken notice of Lyle. "Take him out!" Additional Outland units break from the melee and join the officer. They take aim at Lyle and begin drumming on the Cordei shield.

"I did not come all this way..." Lyle hoists the auto-turret off of its temporary station, and turns to face the dull popping. "To get picked off by some fucking zeroes!" He lasers the droid first and then sweeps the rest. The last to go is a good shot, however; Lyle catches a wallop to the leg.

Searing pain does not bode well for a hyperactive brain witnessing time slowed down. Lyle tries to address the wound, but he does not have time for self-discovery. He chips a corner off of his exposed heavplast breastplate. Holding it to the turret's muzzle, he heats up a charge and melts the heavplast to putty. Before the resultant goo can burn all the way through his glove, he slips it into the gash in his leg.

With a limp, he sets the turret back on its station, and realigns it with the keystone. "Are you going to fail me again, you little puke!" he screams at himself, imitating a gruffer voice. He closes his eyes as he pulls the trigger, too afraid to witness failure. The laser, nearly invisible, makes a tiny dimple in the plasma. Refracted by the keystone, it forms edges in a faceless triangular prism. The plasma rolls back into a ball of energy at the zenith. Lyle peeks and grins ear to ear. *You beautiful marvel, you.*

Lyle tears off his glove and fits it in the trigger guard, forcing the gun to fire out its charge in quick succession. The shield's plasma pulsates like a tiny sun. It paints the new home of Lyle's redeemer with ethereal light.

The shield's brightness is suddenly countered, overwhelmed! The gel inside the polyhedron contracts. There is a thunderous and primal scream. The room shakes. The shooting stops. Lyle tries to slip into the Cordei, but it throws him back with a flash and a second scream. Lyle skids off the stage like a rock on a frozen pond, and into no man's land. As he somersaults and tumbles and flails and loses control over Colberg's body, the room around begins to blur.

The Throne Room's ceiling recedes and opens up to a ringed galaxy. The very floor on which he skids dematerializes. He feels vertigo for a fleeting moment, and then nothing. Where stood Sentinels, warriors, mages, builders, and healers and other abominations, there is now only stars and the mighty orange eye.

*It feels like the CLOUD.* But he knows it is not. Lyle has no power here. No influence. His memory wanes. "Did I do it?" he mumbles, uncertain if he has forgotten his success. "Did I do it!?" Lyle yells out to the mighty eye, only his yell does not seem to carry. It does not feel much like a yell at all. "Minerva!"

The gaseous cosmic pillars crumble, and the colossal eye blinks. "A wolf in sheep's clothing. Where is our lost sheep, I wonder?" The voice is simultaneously sweet and domineering.

"Minerva? Is that you?"

A wave of colour and sensation splatter the nonspace like Jackson Pollock in all dimensions. The wave seems to drain the galactic eye of its colour and carry it over. The sacrifice gives Lyle shape and form. He is himself—his former self!—or at least he appears to be himself. Solidity reaches out to him. He now stands slowly and cautiously on black obsidian, stretching beyond his fathoming. He dabs dust off of his sleeves with confused pats. "Just like old times."

An image of the Throne Room interrupts the surreal vision but quickly fades away. As the dark picture disappears, a shadow grows over Lyle. He turns against a flood of particolored fog. Amid rainbow wisps, he spots an animate mask, pale as porcelain and painted with a permanent smile. Despite the painted expression, the face's structure is contorted into a look of agony. The mask—the face—is Lyle's own. He falls back, aghast. "I did what you wanted!" The mask mimes Lyle's uncertainty. "I gave everything up for you. And I still don't even know what for!"

"You originally set out to *silence the siren*. Your words, are they not?"

The mask retreats into the fog with Lyle's terrified look.

Lyle gets up and pleads to the bodiless voice. "Before I knew it was you!"

The fog clears. Lyle's mask has joined thousands of others affixed to a fleshy pyramid's muscular and veinous casing. Every face wears a slightly different expression than its neighbour. Each tier is distinguished by the emotion evinced. Instead of a capstone, the pyramid bears up a giant eye; a meaty and curtailed version of its galactic form, now chained to the pyramid. The eye nearly rolls onto its cornea to focus on Lyle.

"I see your fashion sense hasn't matured," Lyle says, trying to anchor himself in this delusion with some humor. He laughs nervously, glimpsing his mask on the lowest tier. "One of us is going to have to change."

"Silence!" All of the faces on the pyramid appear mortified.

*Pretty loud for an eyeball.*

An immense pain targeting nowhere and everywhere Lyle could claim to be himself spreads him like a popped balloon at the pyramid's base.

"Loud enough for a god. Now, Badegger, tell me what you were doing in my Keep."

# REBRANDING

Dazed and confused, Oni sprays the question: "Colberg?"

"Not for a while now, no." Boaz Colberg points his rifle directly at Oni's head. His eyes are pale and glossy.

*Celeste must be controlling him.* "Snap out of it! Turn off your implant. Hurry!"

Some color returns to Boaz's eyes. His trigger finger trembles and he eases his grip. The Cordei catches his attention through the catwalk grating. A schizophrenic struggle between a wince and a downturned-brow crosses his eyes. He staggers slightly and howls.

Appealing to the devil she knows, again Oni cries out, "Boaz!"

Boaz throws his rifle over the railing. It slams into the plasmic hemisphere and crackles off to the side.

Even with her failing vision, Oni sees her hope restored. "Thank God!" She leans back against the rail and plucks pieces of her visor out of her face. The element of surprise is gone. Celeste is in control, and yet only five inches of titanium is all that stands between Oni and her victory.

Boaz groans. His earlier look of resolve reappears. "You are most welcome," he says in choir with those now mercilessly forcing Marines to their knees.

Before Oni can react to Boaz's reversion, he tears her gunarm out of its makeshift socket and presses the muzzle against her chest where the Rōnin reduced her armour to a second skin. He begins to squeeze the trigger, but winces again, this time forcing his entire face to accordion. "We...I...can't help it." The trigger passes the point of no return. Boaz yells and sweeps the muzzle downwards as the striker sends the first bullet Oni's way. Two shots clip her in the belly, and although slowed somewhat and redirected by Skyr's armor, still manage to find flesh.

Although his face suggests some deep-seated vexation, the rest of Boaz's body speaks only to his submission to Celeste's will. He tilts his head and observes Oni fold over her latest wounds with a childish curiosity. She groans and tries to stop the blood, but neither does her any good.

Pointing Oni's own gunarm at her, Boaz sets his shoulders back, and takes an enormous breath. "The freedom you have long sought after will soon be yours, Oni Matsui."

Oni swipes at Boaz with her jagged prosthetic and fist but

catches only air. Shaking his head, Boaz swats away her final aggression. Having tested her resistance and proven it wanting, Boaz hoists Oni over the railing and dangles her head-first over the Cordei. The shield flickers, retreating into a starry ball, and quickly mushrooms out to its intended shape. The blood coursing to Oni's head and out of her mutilated face sizzles on the shield. Although faint, the sound gives Boaz and his possessor an idea. He swings Oni sideways to make sure she lands on the Cordei shield—which will undoubtedly vaporize her—and lets her go.

Unlike her crimson offering, Oni does not hit the shield. It shutters again, permitting her entry, at least up unto the tips of her feet, which are cropped and deflected outside the shield. Her persisting remains slam into the side of the Cordei's polyhedral chassis. Boaz watches her slide like a bag of cement onto the stage, and briskly heads for the ladder with Oni's gunarm set for a follow up.

There's the cold and there's the ache.

Skyr's suit absorbed the brunt of the damage from the fall, but toeless, amputated, gutshot, and broken, Oni is no better for it. She feels her vitality leaving her, one muscle spasm at a time. *C'mon, Matsui.* She tries to lift herself up and fails. As her deoxygenated thoughts begin to spread out and the connections between them fail, Oni recalls a choice item from the Hretha she had saved: an adrenaline injector. *Whatever it takes.*

She moults Skyr's armour and injects herself with some artificial gusto. White lightning courses through her veins and bubbles at the mouths of her wounds. She manages to prop herself up on elbow and knees, and checks to make sure she has the Cordei all to herself. It had swallowed her whole, but not by accident: a laser turret on a crude tripod scrapes the bottom of its battery for charge and intermittently splashes the shield's keystone. Oni surmises it to be the handiwork of the man who cast her down, and further that Boaz had no idea that a broken keystone could mean a burst of weapons-grade plasma in every direction.

As she drags herself along, she spots a familiar face on the battlefield: Captain Galloway.

The war between Celeste's army and McCabe's Marines seems to have come to a head. Archetypals have penned the Marines with an electric fence. Celeste's army is gathered around the fence, patiently waiting for Celeste's next command.

Two Cymurai carry Galloway past his imprisoned friends. The Cymurai kick him behind his knees and hammer him to the ground. Another two Cymurai drag out the Marine wearing the black, medieval-looking mech. They deactivate his metal exoskeleton and tear his helmet off. It is General McCabe, nose bloodied and angler lip split. "Damn you all. This place is coming down, and you're going down with it."

McCabe is struck down to the ground, and set beside Galloway. They glance at one another, mirroring one another's embarrassment and wrath.

"Sorry, sir," says Galloway.

"Enough of that," McCabe chaws at Galloway's defeatism. "Apologies are for widows and broken windows."

A lithe and gnarled-looking archetypal breaks from the horde encircling the Marines, and shuffles over to Galloway and McCabe. All voices raise hers up: "If it bends, you will put me to the anvil. Isn't that correct, General?" Nothing more than a puppet, the lithe archetypal feigns to look around. "Where is your hammer? Where is your anvil?"

General McCabe tries to break free, but can only muster a growl.

"You might do well to beg for your life," says Celeste's surrogate.

McCabe sneers.

Turning away from McCabe, Celeste's surrogate focuses her attention on Galloway. She lifts his chin, cutting him with her unkempt nails. The surrogate's pupils jitter from side to side under grey cataracts. She releases Galloway with disgust. "General, I will spare the rest of your men if you provide me with the USS Apollo's suborbital launch codes. We cannot have peace in our times deferred by further acts of war."

McCabe horks into the surrogate's face. "I'll see you in Hell."

With so many masks to attend to, Celeste does not seem particularly worried about this one being sullied. Spit runs down her grin as she grabs Galloway by the back of his neck. "Perhaps the Captain can assist us."

Galloway tenses and grits his teeth. Seeing three more archetypals break from the circle, he throws his weight against his handlers. "No! No!" Two of the archetypals help his handlers hold him steady. The third pulls a metal fragment from the blood-soused floor, and positions it between Galloway's eyes.

"Don't tell them anything, Marine," McCabe shouts. He manages to tap Galloway's foot with his. "They'll get theirs, don't you worry."

"Yes sir," Galloway answers. He closes his eyes. "I know, sir."

The third archetypal drives the metal shard into Galloway's forehead. His screams are awful. He shakes and spits and groans, and goes still.

McCabe does not give Celeste the pleasure of his anger. He represses it and raises his head. "Do your worst, bitch."

Captain Galloway's handlers and the two archetypals from the circle release him. He stands on his own volition, blood streaming down his face.

"Atta boy!" McCabe yells. "Captain, get me my gun!"

An archetypal hands Galloway McCabe's Desert Eagle. He brandishes it disinterestedly, and brushes the archetypals aside. "General, sir," he says, crouching in front of McCabe. "Until I get those codes, every one of your Marines will come to kneel here." Galloway presses the gun to his own head and pulls the trigger. He falls face first into McCabe's chest, and bobs to the side, thalamus exposed.

McCabe turns beet red. "Fuck you."

Celeste's surrogate pulls Galloway's corpse aside. "He was surprised—Captain Galloway—that I should have all my forces holed up here like parishioners at a doomsday mass. He did not realize, as I am sure you failed to, that the point was never to defend the Throne Room but to fill it. A throne is a throne because of its subjects, and without a good many subjects, synchronization would be impossible." The surrogate's pupils slide down to where they ought to be. She notices the General harden with resolve. "You would torch each and every olive branch I extend, yes? You would let me kill every one of your men?"

"Ms. Charming," McCabe says with a bloody smile. "This tower is coming down with you in it. You may have many a new mouth and eye, but you lack honor. You lack faith. You lack all those qualities that transcend the meat and the body. My men, faithful and honorable, are ready to die as patriots. Aren't you, Marines?"

McCabe's machismo spreads inside the electric pen. The Marines answer back, coarse and with conviction: "Ooh rah." Some answer back "Semper fi," and others swear up a storm, but the sentiment is still the same.

Celeste snarls, and her puppets follow suit in perfect unison. "Very well!" says her focal surrogate as the three archetypals who helped implant Galloway reassemble. One plucks another metal shard off of the ground and positions it between the General's eyes. "Then we will go straight to the source!" The surrogate places the handgun Galloway killed himself with in front of General McCabe. "We look forward to your insights."

McCabe flexes as the archetypals drill the metal shard into his head. "Rot in Hell you mother—" He slumps in his captors' grips.

Oni, stuck with two shards of her own, drags herself towards the Cordei, painting its stage with her own blood in the same tower and fashion as her mentor months earlier.

The Cordei's humming is deafening, its lights blinding. Oni averts her gaze, and as her sight returns to her, she sees Boaz Colberg pacing on the other side of the plasmic shield. He still has her gunarm locked and loaded, and is waiting for an opportunity to finish what he started on the catwalk overhead.

The heat off of the Cordei is incredible. It blisters Oni's skin as she kicks and wriggles forward. She reaches its polyhedric container short a couple nerve endings. The gel is cold to the touch; so cold, in fact, Oni assumes the tingling in her fingers is conversely the feeling of them melting. Already committed, she submerges into the non-Newtonian gel anyway. She can still see despite the gel, although the bright light and the gel's chemical compounds sting, especially where she is exposed. The gel fills her wounds and sucks on her broken skin. Highly viscous, it works on Oni like resin on a mosquito, making advancement extremely difficult. Thrashing forward, Oni reaches the coffin, which is well-sealed but unlocked. Exhausting her air reserve, she levers her legs against the polyhedron's bars and tugs the coffin open. Dozens of perfectly spherical air bubbles sail out into the gel, while gel replaces them, filling the chamber and crushing the bruised little body inside.

Pushing the coffin lid open wide enough to squeeze in, Oni meets the moment she has dreaded since she first met Regan. To protect whatever of this little girl she thought remained, Oni defied two masters. For this victim of science and greed, intubated and covered with enough sensors to make an interstellar probe, Oni denied her friend a chance at an unconventional existence. For hope of a little girl who is no more and perhaps never was, Oni ignored her gut instinct. And now, with both masters bloodied, friend obliterated, and a gut full of metal, Oni brushes Regan's gel-soused hair aside. *Sorry, kiddo.*

Oni grabs her jagged prosthetic by the elbow and lines up a strike. Muddled internal encouragement finds her: *You got this, Matsui.* And with that, Oni stabs Regan in the chest, plunging her arm deep enough to feel metal on the other side. A flurry of perfect spheres depart both of their mouths and nostrils.

Sparks rain down onto the polyhedron from the Control Room. Sheet lightning illuminates the chaos around the blast door. The Cordei gel contracts, locking Oni and her death blow in place.

Regan suddenly opens her eyes and points them accusingly at Oni. The silent accusation is a waste, however; the body of the accused slackens and drifts backwards as the gel resets.

"Be seeing you, Matsui."


Oni cannot hear the unholy leviathan scream out together, "No! Impossible! Fix it at once!" and then break into agonizing pleas in every imaginable language and dialect as their Babel collapses.

She cannot hear General McCabe pull his Desert Eagle away from his forehead and start to open fire on the disoriented archetypal horde.

She cannot hear the rest of the Marines break free of their electric prison and resume firing upon confirmed enemies of the Republic, now bereft of a queen, a purpose, and an internal logic to guide them.

She cannot hear Celeste Charming twisting and turning on her throne, targeted by all the data and personalities she had for a moment subjugated.

Oni cannot hear Celeste break free of her inputs, stumble to the Control Room window, and watch her reflection swell until her face laminates the glass and her brains the ceiling.

Oni cannot hear the sirens that warned her enemies of her presence now playing like trumpets in a Louisianian funeral march.

She cannot hear these good omens sound her victory, but she does not need to. As the light leaves her, she embraces *the warmth and the relief,* knowing full-well that this time around, she corrected reality.

## TITAN-BOUND

"Call Copps and Forsyth! They will straighten this all out." Lyle knows Copps and Forsyth will not sully their reputation defending an outed psychopath in a secondhand suit with the mob this lit up, however they might send Dorota, especially if they want to make sure there are no loose ends implicating the firm in anything unsavoury. Dorota, who has over the period of a few short days transformed from a muse to a must, might be able to help commute Lyle's sentence or save his sentience, *if* it suits her to believe him. *She'll come.*

Lyle is an experienced liar, but never before has he lied to himself, at least not so blatantly. He is convinced that Dorota will waste her day and whatever social capital she has with her new boss to follow up with a junkie prisoner-of-war who claims to have been the mass murderer who had sex with her before switching bodies with an enemy of the state. *She'll come.*

Leaning against the holding-room door, Lyle grates his head from one corner of the metal-barred windowsill to the other. Some modicum of his old, cold rationality punches him in the gut, calling the plausibility of all his adapted aspirations into question and reminding him of his body. "Confound it!" Although a Marine medic yanked the bullet out of his leg and foamed up the wound, Lyle still feels as if he is open, exposed; as if he has been turned inside-out. Bodily unease and pain have forced him to accept this body as his own, meaning it is his chest that aches, his vision that is blurry, his gut in a twist. It is Lyle Badegger who badly wants a cigarette.

The Centurion guarding the door has plenty of patience for all of Lyle's bawling, and continues to show complete indifference.

Lyle's energy is spent and his concern unregistered. He turns to the forty-or-so vegetables sharing the holding cell with him, standing tirelessly in whatever pose and order the guards left them in. They are all soiled and slobbering. *Drool factories without the slightest inkling.* He is not sure of whether or not to feel envious of them—of their ignorance and noisome serenity—or to be happy at least with his remaining thoughts, however precarious.

The archetypals in the room, some recent additions according to their Outland uniforms, have been used and abused twice by the Outland Corporation. Who, besides Lyle, likely already too discombobulated to disorient further, could withstand both the datamosh that came with the rain-out and the data-drain at the Citadel?

Minerva had lured Lyle in and changed the bait once he bit down. That he should no longer suffer headaches is of no consolation. He would take a headache or the mindlessness plighting the others in this room over whatever second-hand nausea he feels now.

A fat-armed, potbellied, and skinny-faced archetypal keels over and covers her feet with stomach lining.

"Good lord!" Lyle throws himself against the window's bars. "Get me the hell out of here! I want to place a call!" His selfish pleas again fall on deaf ears. He appeals to the benevolence of whatever gun-toting killer stands guard further down the hall, ready to lend the Centurion a hand. Hearing more gastrointestinal spillage, Lyle screams out: "Medic! We need a medic!" *If Dorota does not have enough petty cash to make the drive out…*"I'm finished," he confesses through the bars, now wishing he was dead. He would be dead too if his captors had run either a more comprehensive scan or a less detailed scan when processing him. The Marine techs, aided by the LAPD's digital-forensics team, found that Monocle was essential for Boaz Colberg to maintain any kind of consciousness. While they disabled his Monocle's communication applications, they permitted it to keep running all of those processes ostensibly keeping him up and about. *Cruelty in kindness.*

A Marine ambles over. "Who needs a medic?"

The Centurion shrugs its shoulders.

"I do!" Lyle yells out manically. "You've got to let me out! This is all a big mistake!"

The Marine must have just been assigned to this dungeon because his fresh face has yet to frown around condemnation or a flat out "No." He rolls his eyes at the Centurion and starts back for his post.

"Hold on, hold on!" Lyle pleads, composing himself. This time his snivelling is enough to halt the soldier's progress and bring him to the window. "Yes! Hello! There has been a grave misunderstanding. You see, I'm Lyle Badegger. I work in the Blue Zone at Copps and Forsyth. Was following up with a client at the Citadel. A whistleblower, you see. Outland was afraid I was going to report what I uncovered, so they uploaded my sentience to this body…"

The Marine pulls up Boaz Colberg's file via wrist-projection. He takes a minute to digest the intel, and laughs off Lyle's claims. "And I am Sonica Saturn. Outland swapped my body with Private First Class Fitzpatrick." Smiling, the Marine points his submachine gun at the ceiling. "That bastard is living large in my suborbital!"

"I am not kidding!" Lyle shakes his throbbing leg, and wedges his nose through the bars. "I am Lyle Badegger, god-damn-it. I can prove it!"

Turning to leave, Private Fitzpatrick grumbles: "Take your proof to Titan where it'll die with you"

"No! No! No. You can't leave me in here with these things." Lyle looks at his fellow inmates, all swaying like pine trees in a storm. He spots a familiar face, as devoid of expression as the rest: Ruth. *Ah crap.*

A familiar voice reanimates Lyle. "Lyle Badegger?"

"Yes!" Lyle peers out. "Right here!"

"Someone told me that name was being thrown around down here," says the specter approaching from down the hall. Private Fitzpatrick salutes him in passing. The specter continues to address Lyle: "Didn't believe it..."

Lyle wrinkles his eyes in a desperate attempt to identify the speaker. He spots a gold bar. *You've got to be kidding...*

Second-Lieutenant Samson examines Lyle from afar, and runs a diagnostic on his tablet. "Partly, because I know Lyle Badegger. Rather, I knew him...Bad apple. Killed a lot of people."

"Lieutenant!" Lyle cries out. "It's me! I killed a lot of people!"

Chuckling, Samson pockets his tablet and approaches the holding cell. "Careful, Boaz. Would you rather a Terran death sentence over a Titanic challenge?"

"Ah..." Lyle buffers, trying to get the best of a man who benefits from having all of his faculties intact. "I didn't actually kill people. But you believe me, right? That it's me?"

"Can't say that I do." Samson pulls a platinum sleeve out of his jacket pocket, produces a cigarette, and lights it. He takes two puffs, and hands the red-headed stick to Lyle through the bars.

Lyle grabs it eagerly and creates a cave for its light with his hands and face. Slow on the uptake, he rips jets of thick smoke off his favorite brand and murmurs delightedly with both lungs full.

"Captain Badegger's emergency contact, some secretary over at Copps, Forsyth, and Tyndale, refused to identify his body. After exhausting a list of possible alternatives, all of whom were either missing persons or unwilling to waste an hour, I went in. I would have gone in anyway, but you know—there are some conventions worth keeping in this racket. Lyle Badegger is dead as a doornail."

"No...no!" Lyle self-references Colberg's bulk with both thumbs. "I'm right here."

Samson leans in with a satisfied look. "You know what I would do if I did?"

"Huh?"

"Believe you, I mean. If I believed you…"

Wary of the malicious grin deforming Samson's face, Lyle begins to panic. "Samson, you have to get me out of here."

Samson brings a finger to his lips and silently shushes Lyle. "I wouldn't do one goddamned thing."

"Lieutenant! No, wait. No! I served, damn-it. I deserve a trial. I deserve a soldier's trial!" Lyle is practically spilling through the bars.

"Lyle, Boaz, Jill, Jackoff; the hell I care. Whoever you are, you're going to rot."

"Lieutenant," Lyle screams after Samson, whistling back up the hall. "I know things! I know all about what Benny Bass did to his workers!" His memory betrays him and limits him to just the one revelation. "I know things!" he stammers.

"Enjoy Titan. Plenty of room to hide bodies, including your own."

Lyle loses sight of Samson and hears a door slam. "There's no excuse," he says, on the verge of tears, "No excuse for leaving me like this."

## SIX GRAVES AND TENDER MERCY

"You're looking good, *Major Barkley,* all things considered. You will be happy to know that the bounty has been dropped. Your record has been expunged. The United States government has rebaptized you a law-abiding American."

"Jin?" Oni whispers.

"No, but there is beer in the mess hall."

Oni tries to open her eyes, but they feel crusted over. She wipes off a thin layer of hardened mucous, and starts blinking herself back to consciousness. "Where am I?"

"Veteran's hospital," says a khaki blur. A parade of medals march down to a silver eagle on his chest. "Los Angeles. You're the odd one out but a deserving mercenary if ever I have ever met one *I didn't have to kill.*"

Oni is bedded inside a warehouse-labyrinth of small white cubicles. Hundreds of robotic arms hang overhead from sliders on an intricate grid of rails. Some arms mend the wounded while others respectfully carry the dead through an opening in the far wall. There is an inactive arm directly above Oni's medical bed. In addition to a range of tools fitted like fingers, it has an epidermic printer, dripping big globs of tissue. The arm itself is smattered with blood.

A prickly sensation in her legs alerts Oni to a medical android applying a translucent seal on her new skin. "Tarnation." Holding ten fingers over her sutured stomach, she marvels at the symmetry she figured she lost forever. "What happened?"

Scratching his rumpled neck, McCabe sucks in moist air for dry news: "2690 is dead. Celeste Charming, also dead. Boy, that was a sight to see. All of the data she was managing went straight to her head." He hides his self-satisfied grin behind a hand gesture suggestive of a brain exploding. "Good riddance...Her precious Citadel is a one-hundred-and-somethin'-floor-memorial to fifteen-hundred dead—including nine of my Marines. My Marines'll be buried in Arlington, whereas Celeste's army? There is nothing left to bury. With the exception of those who surrendered after we ran out of ammo and steam."

Boaz's crazed eyes flash before Oni's. Oni shakes her head. *He did his part. And I guess his failure was by design.* She notices a bandage on General McCabe's forehead. "I saw...I thought I saw you—Celeste, I mean; I thought I saw Celeste kill you. Thought I was alone again." She studies McCabe's face for glitches and any signs of surreality. "Figured you were a goner."

"People frequently make that mistake—about the both of us it seems." He looks over the walls of the cubicle for peeping toms or reporters, and satisfied upon seeing neither, leans in to whisper: "Sometimes it takes a big man to give thanks for his life..."

Oni hooks a smile. It is the first time she has smiled where her entire face does not feel like it is on fire.

"Sufficed to say, I'm as big as they come." He nods himself into a thoughtful pause. Interrupting his own silence, he throws a finger up in the air. "Something here for you." He points to an implant on the side table. "They found this in the forensic sweep. An implant. Paul Sheffield's. Only thing left of him. Not a single bit on it. Cleaner than your grandmother's ladle. Celeste was keeping it as a trophy. Thought you might want to keep it as a tribute."

Certain she would never make it this far let alone in one piece, Oni trembles. Her tears grey her pillow's canvas. The nature of the tears or rather the emotion driving them out is muddled. She is happy to have honored Paul's sacrificial act with her own but also sad that any of it was necessary to begin with. She reaches over for the implant, but recoils at the last minute. "Thank you."

"Cry on your own time. You will be happy to know there were no casualties inside Seal Base."

Oni nods. She startles herself as she goes to dry her face. Instead of a gun barrel, a convincing new prosthetic warms her chin. "Good." Seal Beach seems a distant memory.

"Two dead on the road outside the walls, but I know that wasn't you. The man responsible got what was coming to him in spades. Lyle Badegger—know him?"

"No. And I wasn't outside the walls."

"Yeah," McCabe says, bunching up his face. "Like I said."

Oni crosses her legs under the sheets, and leans forward, relishing painless motion. So much of her outlook and personality have been defined by pain. Pain created a false mold of the world around her, providing her with false impressions. Through shocked eyes she saw only dark, drab colors. Broken skin reported only cold. Shredded lungs accused fresh air of being toxic. With pain as her interpreter, all stimuli evidenced a doomed world to which her fate was linked. Her new interpreter stands ready by her repaired sensory organs. "Did the archetypals revert?"

McCabe tilts his head and makes a clicking sound. "Seventy percent or thereabouts."

Overwhelmed with joy, Oni laughs her tears onto her lap. "That's phenomenal!"

"Ah, well. It's a process…We're running tests and rehabilitation. I'd say about half of those who reverted will properly recover, but there is going to be a handful doing menial jobs for the rest of their days."

"What happened to those who didn't revert?"

McCabe raises an eyebrow. "That's classified."

Oni shifts up in the bed. "You've got to be joking."

"Do I look like a comedian?" McCabe cannot maintain his glower. He exaggerates a nasal sigh. "Even with 2690 and Celeste wasted, there was a handful that kept fighting. Queenless drones with some sting left. We got them all; all of the violent ones, anyway. Spared the slush-brained pacifists, though; have them detained on the coast."

"And you found all of them?"

McCabe massages his bandaged forehead. "Some of our jockeys were able to use the Cordei to ping all of the implants previously targeted by the Omnitype. Honed in on all the hits. Caught and catalogued the stragglers."

The medical android blurts out, catching both McCabe and Oni offguard: "Do not operate heavy machinery for the next two-hundred hours. Drink plenty of fluids. Check in with a medical professional to have your skin regenerated every two years. Have a nice day." Its arms fold back into its chassis, permitting it to bend at the waist. Before Oni can thank it, it bows and rolls out of the cubicle and down the aisle.

Running her fingers down her updated figure, Oni thinks on those doubly cursed by Outland: "What are you going to do to the peaceful ones that didn't revert?"

"Can't keep them here. Army of lawyers making my proposed mass-execution or organ-harvest appear untenable. So the best idea, from god-knows-whose braindead intern at the Pentagon, is to send them into space." McCabe takes off his cap, and combs his thinning greys back into formation. "We have enough confounded problems in space. Besides, these aren't the kinds of vegetables you need growing on the moon…"

Oni nearly volunteers her emotional investment, but reminds herself that her good intentions have not always panned out in her favor or in anyone else's. "Well, good luck to them. Even if it doesn't make a whole lot of sense."

McCabe signals sympathy by tapping Oni's new toes with his cap. "You want classified?" He lowers his voice to a whisper: "I trust a bullet you won't be telling this around town...Northern Alliance doesn't want to give up its claim to Titan. Outland's assets and property are all now the property of the United States government. The slendernecks in Sacramento and Washington want us to seize this opportunity to keep the dark sea American. An engineering team from Hyperion is en route there now to install a solar shield so those former archetypals can start what they'll end doing."

"Start what?"

"Getting better, I guess. Unofficially it's a sanitarium. Officially..." McCabe shrugs his shoulders. "It's a well-fed and well-regulated expeditionary force."

Oni turns in the bed and drops her legs over the edge. "You are sending them over as placeholders...as scarecrows."

McCabe laughs. "Scarecrows. That's a good one. I think I might just have to steal it." He averts his eyes to avoid unintentionally glimpsing Oni's undercarriage. "We'll let the politicians have their way. When things go south, we'll go to my original plan and put the lot of them down." Standing, General McCabe turns his cap in his hands, jowls taut and eyebrows touching his cheeks as if he had lost a pair of glasses. "Try not to worry about it. That's an order. It is important not to mistake pride for responsibility, and even more important to know when to stop throwing your weight. The scale's been balanced."

*Balanced with tarry-red implants.* Oni wags her legs as though she were sitting at the end of a pier, trying to skim the water's surface. "Yes sir."

"You are free to go as soon as you are able. Just in case the memo hasn't gotten around about the bounty, have your head on a swivel. As for the LAPD and my clean up crews, they won't give you any trouble."

"I'll still be sure not to go out of my way looking for any. Just going to catch up with a few friends."

McCabe peers down the aisle at the thousands of cubicles and partial forms standing by. "When you get bored of that, call my office. Wouldn't mind having someone get behind Operation Mongoose who is familiar with Outland tech and its possible alternative uses...."

Oni scoots off the bed and nails her landing. She modestly pulls her polka-dot gown to cover her knees. "Promise me you're not going to use the Cordei…"

Puffing his chest, McCabe points a finger skyward. "Don't forget yourself, doctor. This visit is a courtesy, not a consultation. I won't promise you a goddamned thing, but know this: I am in the business of destroying enemies of the free world, not creating them."

Oni responds with a neutered apology. "Sorry. It's just that sifting through and repurposing Outland tech sounds more like a job for the police and the repo men."

"Then I'd say you ought to get your ears checked before they discharge you." McCabe puts his cap on and extends his massive mitt. "If you change your mind, I've had my contact info saved on your Monocle. It was nice never meeting you, Dr. Matsui. Good luck."

Oni reciprocates and they shake. It is not simply a wagging of flesh. There is an electricity to it. Neither sex- nor power-concerned, it feels like McCabe is shaking through a list of Marines Oni saved, while Oni is simply dazzled by human contact of the nonviolent variety. Her social soul, beaten and corroded and jaded, seems to pick up charge with every rise and fall. Although Oni knows McCabe would not dare call her a friend let alone admit to having ever dealt with her, she is glad to know someone on the right side of the law and on this side of the grass. Breaking off the shake before it stirs up an uncontainably positive-atmosphere, McCabe nods to Oni and strides out of the cubicle and away.

Oni picks up and cradles Paul's implant. A heads-up display projects over her iris and identifies the implant series, make and model. *Monocle!* The military repairmen were kind enough to upgrade her subdermal implant. Right away, Oni immerses herself in the interface and tries to access the exocortex buried in her spine. It is still offline. "Booky?" She puts on the medical slippers set at the base of the bed, and leans against the cubicle wall. "You there?" She wants for nothing more than to get a response, but knows it is a cruel and selfish thing to ask for. *Loneliness is not an excuse to drag a ghost out of its grave to a haunting.* "Sleep well, my love," she says subvocally, terminating comms targeting the exocortex.

Camp MUD is a mess. Oni tries to convince herself it has been worse, but cannot place such a time. Hell, she flattened the compound with heavy ANFO explosives and then EMPed it during her last visit, leaving four hilly acres uneven with craters and jagged by ruins, Sentinel bones, and android parts. It is a mess, but it is still her mess and no better place exists to inter her friends.

At the head of the Rift trail where Old Glory, properly unfurled, applauds the wind, Oni throws a handful of dirt onto a mound demarcated and named by a cross. She takes a step back from the fifth mound of six, impressed with a wistful look. Leaning on her shovel, she mutters a prayer under her breath, but is interrupted by distant thunder. The Hermes crackles in the west: its massive phallic silhouette in the pink evening sky is a container full of reminders that success always has a victim, and progress a predator. *Charon will take the living-dead across the twinkling Styx, not to Hades but instead to Olympus, and I will never play a god again.*

Remembering the artifact McCabe gave her, Oni abandons her mythological musings and leaves her shovel to wobble. "We did it," she whispers, setting Paul's implant down on his grave. She recalls a promise she made him before their first Citadel incursion. "I will make sure your daughters are safe," Oni reassures metal and dirt, hoping Paul's sacrifice was not in vain; that his little girls did not suffer Regan's fate.

She stands above her emotion, and starts onto the Rift trail. A seventh grave is not necessary, she is decided, unwilling to write Booker off. Selfish or not, she will attempt a data-recovery in the PIT. If that fails, there still will be no need for a grave. Oni will have become Booker's tomb, his cypulchre.

443

"This is the kind of book you can come back to, discovering new things with each read. The length and pacing is appropriate, the plot and action compelling, and the characters are interesting, relatable (both good and bad), and well constructed. The world and consequences have been crafted in such a way that I think this deserves a sequel, as there's plenty of room in this universe to explore the ramifications of its ending. I would be disappointed were MacKinnon to elect not to continue with this."
    —R. Leigh Hennig, *BASTION SCIENCE FICTION MAGAZINE*

"MacKinnon has crafted a believable world in *Cypulchre*, a dystopian future where critical thought has given way to virtual pleasures and the wants of the rich are favoured over the needs of the poor."
    —*THE GAUNTLET*

"Out of the jungle of cyber-kinetic gadgetry and techno-acronyms that are apparently the future of the human species, Joseph MacKinnon has constructed and charged into life a character with the brain to play in those fields and the heart to balk at the most egregious aspects of its arrogance. Dr. Paul Sheffield, determined to destroy the overreaching CLOUD that he helped create, is a character any reader can get behind in this story that sparks and sizzles with radioactive intelligence. Read it on your plasma-screen or download it from the noosphere directly into your head."
    —Mark Frutkin, author of *FABRIZIO'S RETURN*; winner of the Trillium Award and the Sunburst Award for Literature of the Fantastic

"*Cypulchre* is the gritty cyberpunk you should be reading."
    —Carly Fjeld, *SCI-FI BLOGGERS*

"This highly original, vivid and bizarre tale of terrorism, civil war, and foreign military intervention in Canada will shock readers and haunt them long after they have put down this book."
> —Allan Gotlieb, Former Canadian Ambassador to the USA

"Faultline requires most careful reading, sorting through the Genesis commentary and Danson's reportage. The reader undertakes a voyage of startling discovery: a black metaphor for US actions in Iraq, of course, but also in Afghanistan. The book is meticulously researched and cleverly transposes, to the 49th parallel, events and quotes arising out of the Bush Administration. This has particular resonance for a Canadian who was resident in Washington during that period."
> —Michael Kergin, Former Canadian Ambassador to the USA

"Unnerving. And, dare I say, exciting."
> —*CALGARY HERALD*

www.ingramcontent.com/pod-product-compliance
Lightning Source LLC
Chambersburg PA
CBHW032135270626
47172CB00008B/29